The Paying Guests

SARAH WATERS

The Paying Guests

virago

VIRAGO

First published in Great Britain in 2014 by Virago Press

Copyright © Sarah Waters 2014

The moral right of the author has been asserted.

A CIP catalogue record for this book
is available from the British Library.

Hardback ISBN 978-0-349-00436-5
C format ISBN 978-0-349-00458-7
Deluxe edition ISBN 978-0-349-00547-8

Typeset in Spectrum by M Rules
Printed and bound in Great Britain by
Clays Ltd, St Ives plc

Papers used by Virago are from well-managed forests
and other responsible sources.

MIX
Paper from
responsible sources
FSC
www.fsc.org   FSC® C104740

Virago Press
An imprint of
Little, Brown Book Group
100 Victoria Embankment
London EC4Y 0DY

An Hachette UK Company
www.hachette.co.uk

www.virago.co.uk

To Judith Murray,
with thanks and with love

Part One

1

The Barbers had said they would arrive by three. It was like waiting to begin a journey, Frances thought. She and her mother had spent the morning watching the clock, unable to relax. At half-past two she had gone wistfully over the rooms for what she'd supposed was the final time; after that there had been a nerving-up, giving way to a steady deflation, and now, at almost five, here she was again, listening to the echo of her own footsteps, feeling no sort of fondness for the sparsely furnished spaces, impatient simply for the couple to arrive, move in, get it over with.

She stood at a window in the largest of the rooms—the room which, until recently, had been her mother's bedroom, but was now to be the Barbers' sitting-room—and stared out at the street. The afternoon was bright but powdery. Flurries of wind sent up puffs of dust from the pavement and the road. The grand houses opposite had a Sunday blankness to them—but then, they had that every day of the week. Around the corner there was a large hotel, and motor-cars and taxi-cabs occasionally came this way to and from it; sometimes people strolled up here as if to take the air. But Champion Hill, on the whole, kept itself to itself. The gardens were large, the trees leafy. You would never know, she thought, that grubby Camberwell was just down there. You'd never guess that a mile or two further north lay London, life, glamour, all that.

The sound of a vehicle made her turn her head. A tradesman's van was approaching the house. This couldn't be them, could it? She'd expected a carrier's cart, or even for the couple to arrive on foot—but, yes, the van was pulling up at the kerb, with a terrific creak of its brake, and now she could see the faces in its cabin, dipped and gazing up at hers: the driver's and Mr Barber's, with Mrs Barber's in between. Feeling trapped and on display in the frame of the window, she lifted her hand, and smiled.

This is it, then, she said to herself, with the smile still in place.

It wasn't like beginning a journey, after all; it was like ending one and not wanting to get out of the train. She pushed away from the window and went downstairs, calling as brightly as she could from the hall into the drawing-room, 'They've arrived, Mother!'

By the time she had opened the front door and stepped into the porch the Barbers had left the van and were already at the back of it, already unloading their things. The driver was helping them, a young man dressed almost identically to Mr Barber in a blazer and a striped neck-tie, and with a similarly narrow face and ungreased, week-endy hair, so that for a moment Frances was uncertain which of the two *was* Mr Barber. She had met the couple only once, nearly a fortnight ago. It had been a wet April evening and the husband had come straight from his office, in a mackintosh and bowler hat.

But now she recalled his gingery moustache, the reddish gold of his hair. The other man was fairer. The wife, whose outfit before had been sober and rather anonymous, was wearing a skirt with a fringe to it and a crimson jersey. The skirt ended a good six inches above her ankles. The jersey was long and not at all clinging, yet somehow revealed the curves of her figure. Like the men, she was hatless. Her dark hair was short, curling forward over her cheeks but shingled at the nape of her neck, like a clever black cap.

4

How young they looked! The men seemed no more than boys, though Frances had guessed, on his other visit, that Mr Barber must be twenty-six or -seven, about the same age as herself. Mrs Barber she'd put at twenty-three. Now she wasn't so sure. Crossing the flagged front garden she heard their excited, unguarded voices. They had drawn a trunk from the van and set it unsteadily down; Mr Barber had apparently caught his fingers underneath it. 'Don't laugh!' she heard him cry to his wife, in mock-complaint. She remembered, then, their 'refined' elocution-class accents.

Mrs Barber was reaching for his hand. 'Let me see. Oh, there's nothing.'

He snatched the hand back. 'There's nothing now. You just wait a bit. Christ, that hurts!'

The other man rubbed his nose. 'Look out.' He had seen Frances at the garden gate. The Barbers turned, and greeted her through the tail of their laughter—so that the laughter, not very comfortably, somehow attached itself to her.

'Here you are, then,' she said, joining the three of them on the pavement.

Mr Barber, still almost laughing, said, 'Yes, here we are! Bringing down the character of the street already, you see.'

'Oh, my mother and I do that.'

Mrs Barber spoke more sincerely. 'We're sorry we're late, Miss Wray. The time just flew! You haven't been waiting? You'd think we'd come from John o' Groats or somewhere, wouldn't you?'

They had come from Peckham Rye, about two miles away. Frances said, 'Sometimes the shortest journeys take longest, don't they?'

'They do,' said Mr Barber, 'if Lilian's involved in them. Mr Wismuth and I were ready at one.—This is my friend Charles Wismuth, who's kindly lent us the use of his father's van for the day.'

'You weren't ready at all!' cried Mrs Barber, as a grinning

Mr Wismuth moved forward to shake Frances's hand. 'Miss Wray, they weren't, honestly!'

'We were ready and waiting, while you were still sorting through your hats!'

'At any rate,' said Frances, 'you are here now.'

Perhaps her tone was rather a cool one. The three young people looked faintly chastened, and with a glance at his injured knuckles Mr Barber returned to the back of the van. Over his shoulder Frances caught a glimpse of what was inside it: a mess of bursting suitcases, a tangle of chair and table legs, bundle after bundle of bedding and rugs, a portable gramophone, a wicker birdcage, a bronze-effect ashtray on a marbled stand . . . The thought that all these items were about to be brought into her home—and that this couple, who were not quite the couple she remembered, who were younger, and brasher, were going to bring them, and set them out, and make their own home, brashly, among them—the thought brought on a flutter of panic. What on earth had she done? She felt as though she was opening up the house to thieves and invaders.

But there was nothing else for it, if the house were to be kept going at all. With a determined smile she went closer to the van, wanting to help.

The men wouldn't let her. 'You mustn't think of it, Miss Wray.'

'No, honestly, you mustn't,' said Mrs Barber. 'Len and Charlie will do it. There's hardly anything, really.' And she gazed down at the objects that were accumulating around her, tapping at her mouth with her fingers.

Frances remembered that mouth now: it was a mouth, as she'd put it to herself, that seemed to have more on the outside than on the in. It was touched with colour today, as it hadn't been last time, and Mrs Barber's eyebrows, she noticed, were thinned and shaped. The stylish details made her uneasy along with everything else, made her feel old-maidish, with her pinned-up hair and her angles, and her blouse tucked into her high-waisted skirt, after the fashion of the War, which was already four years over. Seeing Mrs Barber, a tray of houseplants in her arms, awkwardly hooking her wrist through the handle of a raffia hold-all, she said, 'Let me take that bag for you, at least.'

'Oh, I can do it!'

'Well, I really must take something.'

Finally, noticing Mr Wismuth just handing it out of the van, she took the hideous stand-ashtray, and went across the front garden with it to hold open the door of the house. Mrs Barber came after her, stepping carefully up into the porch.

At the threshold itself, however, she hesitated, leaning over the ferns in her arms to look into the hall, and to smile.

'It's just as nice as I remembered.'

Frances turned. 'It is?' She could see only the dishonesty of it all: the scuffs and tears she had patched and disguised; the gap where the long-case clock had stood, which had had to be sold six months before; the dinner-gong, bright with polish, that hadn't been rung in years and years. Turning back to Mrs Barber, she found her still waiting at the step. 'Well,' she said, 'you'd better come in. It's your house too, now.'

Mrs Barber's shoulders rose; she bit her lip and raised her eyebrows in a pantomime of excitement. She stepped cautiously into the hall, where the heel of one of her shoes at once found an unsteady tile on the black-and-white floor and set it rocking. She tittered in embarrassment: 'Oh, dear!'

Frances's mother appeared at the drawing-room door. Perhaps she had been standing just inside it, getting up the enthusiasm to come out.

'Welcome, Mrs Barber.' Smiling, she came forward. 'What pretty plants. Rabbit's foot, aren't they?'

Mrs Barber manoeuvred her tray and her hold-all so as to be able to offer her hand. 'I'm afraid I don't know.'

'I believe they are. Rabbit's foot—so pretty. You found your way to us all right?'

'Yes, but I'm sorry we're so late!'

'Well, it doesn't matter to us. The rooms weren't going to run away. We must give you some tea.'

'Oh, you mustn't trouble.'

'But you must have tea. One always wants tea when one moves house; and one can never find the teapot. I'll see to it, while my daughter takes you upstairs.' She gazed dubiously at the ashtray. 'You're helping too, are you, Frances?'

'It seemed only fair to, with Mrs Barber so laden.'

'Oh, no, you mustn't help at all,' said Mrs Barber—adding, with another titter, 'We don't expect that!'

Frances, going ahead of her up the staircase, thought: How she laughs!

Up on the wide landing they had to pause again. The door on their left was closed—that was the door to Frances's bedroom, the only room up here which was to stay in her and her mother's possession—but the other doors all stood open, and the late-afternoon sunlight, richly yellow now as the yolk of an egg, was streaming in through the two front rooms as far almost as the staircase. It showed up the tears in the rugs, but also the polish on the Regency floorboards, which Frances had spent several back-breaking mornings that week bringing to the shine of dark toffee; and Mrs Barber didn't like to cross the polish in her heels. 'It doesn't matter,' Frances told her. 'The surface will dull soon enough, I'm afraid.' But she answered firmly, 'No, I don't want to spoil it'—putting down her bag and her tray of plants and slipping off her shoes.

She left small damp prints on the wax. Her stockings were black ones, blackest at the toe and at the heel, where the reinforcing of the silk had been done in fancy stepped panels. While Frances hung back and watched she went into the largest of the rooms, looking around it in the same noticing, appreciative manner in which she had looked around the hall; smiling at every antique detail.

'What a lovely room this is. It feels even bigger than it did last time. Len and I will be lost in it. We've only had our bedroom really, you see, at his parents'. And their house is—well, not like this one.' She crossed to the left-hand window—the window at which Frances had been standing a few minutes before—and put up a hand to shade her eyes. 'And look at the sun! It was cloudy when we came before.'

Frances joined her at last. 'Yes, you get the best of the sun in this room. I'm afraid there isn't much in the way of a view, even though we're so high.'

'Oh, but you can see a little, between the houses.'

'Between the houses, yes. And if you peer south—that way'— she pointed—'you can make out the towers of the Crystal Palace. You have to go nearer to the glass . . . You see them?'

They stood close together for a moment, Mrs Barber with her face an inch from the window, her breath misting the glass. Her dark-lashed eyes searched, then fixed. 'Oh, yes!' She sounded delighted.

But then she moved back, and drew in her gaze; and her voice changed, became indulgent. 'Oh, look at Len. Look at him complaining. Isn't he puny!' She tapped at the window, and called and gestured. 'Let Charlie take that! Come and see the sun! The *sun*. Can you see? *The sun!*' She dropped her hand. 'He can't understand me. Never mind. How funny it is, seeing our things set out like that. How poor it all looks! Like a penny bazaar. What must your neighbours be thinking, Miss Wray?'

What indeed? Already Frances could see sharp-eyed Mrs Dawson over the way, pretending to be fiddling with the bolt of her drawing-room window. And now here was Mr Lamb from High Croft further down the hill, pausing as he passed to blink at the stuffed suitcases, the blistered tin trunks, the bags, the baskets and the rugs that Mr Barber and Mr Wismuth, for convenience, were piling on the low brick garden wall.

She saw the two men give him a nod, and heard their voices: 'How do you do?' He hesitated, unable to place them—perhaps thrown by the stripes on their 'club' ties.

'We ought to go and help,' she said.

Mrs Barber answered, 'Oh, I will.'

But when she left the room it was to wander into the bedroom beside it. And she went from there to the last of the rooms, the small back room facing Frances's bedroom across the return of the landing and the stairs—the room which Frances and her mother still called Nelly and Mabel's room, even though they hadn't had Nelly, Mabel, or any other live-in servant since the munitions factories had finally lured them away in 1916. This was done up now as a kitchen, with a dresser and a sink, with gaslight and a gas stove and a shilling-in-the-slot meter. Frances herself had varnished the wallpaper; she had stained the floor here, rather than waxing it. The cupboard and the aluminium-topped table she had hauled up from the scullery, one day when her mother wasn't at home to have to watch her do it.

She had done her best to get it all right. But seeing Mrs Barber going about, taking possession, determining which of her things would go here, which there, she felt oddly redundant—as if she had become her own ghost. She said awkwardly, 'Well, if you've everything you need, I'll see how your tea's coming along. I shall be just downstairs if there's any sort of problem. Best to come to me rather than to my mother, and—Oh.' She stopped, and reached into her pocket. 'I'd better give you these, hadn't I, before I forget.'

She drew out keys to the house: two sets, on separate ribbons. It took an effort to hand them over, actually to put them into the palm of this woman, this girl—this more or less perfect stranger, who had been summoned into life by the placing of an advertisement in the

10

South London Press. But Mrs Barber received the keys with a gesture, a dip of her head, to show that she appreciated the significance of the moment. And with unexpected delicacy she said, 'Thank you, Miss Wray. Thank you for making everything so nice. I'm sure Leonard and I will be happy here. Yes, I'm certain we will. I have something for you too, of course,' she added, as she took the keys to her hold-all to stow them away. She brought back a creased brown envelope.

It was two weeks' rent. Fifty-eight shillings: Frances could already hear the rustle of the pound notes and the slide and chink of the coins. She tried to arrange her features into a businesslike expression as she took the envelope from Mrs Barber's hand, and she tucked it in her pocket in a negligent sort of way—as if anyone, she thought, could possibly be deceived into thinking that the money was a mere formality, and not the essence, the shabby heart and kernel, of the whole affair.

Downstairs, while the men went puffing past with a treadle sewing-machine, she slipped into the drawing-room, just to give herself a quick peek at the cash. She parted the gum of the envelope and—oh, there it all was, so real, so present, so *hers*, she felt she could dip her mouth to it and kiss it. She folded it back into her pocket, then almost skipped across the hall and along the passage to the kitchen.

Her mother was at the stove, lifting the kettle from the hot-plate with the faintly harried air she always had when left alone in the kitchen; she might have been a passenger on a stricken liner who'd just been bundled into the engine room and told to man the gauges. She gave the kettle up to Frances's steadier hand, and went about gathering the tea-things, the milk-jug, the bowl of sugar. She put three cups and saucers on a tray for the Barbers and Mr Wismuth; and then she hesitated with two more saucers raised. She spoke to Frances in a whisper. 'Ought we to drink with them, do you think?'

Frances hesitated too. What were the rules?

Oh, who cared! They had got the money now. She plucked the saucers from her mother's fingers. 'No, let's not start that sort of thing off. There'll be no end to it if we do. We can keep to the drawing-room; they can have their tea up there. I'll give them a plate of biscuits to go with it.' She drew the lid from the tin and dipped in her hand.

Once again, however, she dithered. Were biscuits absolutely necessary? She put three on a plate, set the plate beside the tea-pot—then changed her mind and took it off again.

But then she thought of nice Mrs Barber, going carefully over the polish; she thought of the fancy heels on her stockings; and returned the plate to the tray.

The men went up and down the stairs for another thirty minutes, and for some time after that boxes and cases could be heard being shifted about, furniture was dragged and wheeled, the Barbers called from room to room; once there came a blast of music from their portable gramophone, that made Frances and her mother look at one another, aghast. But Mr Wismuth left at six, tapping at the drawing-room door as he went, wanting to say a polite good-bye; and with his departure the house grew calmer.

It was inescapably not, however, the house that it had been two hours before. Frances and her mother sat with books at the French windows, ready to eke out the last of the daylight—having got used, in the past few years, to making little economies like that. But the room—a long, handsome room, running the depth of the house, divided by double doors which, in spring and summer, they left open—had two of the Barbers' rooms above it, their bedroom and their kitchen, and Frances, turning pages, found herself aware of the couple overhead, as conscious of their foreign presence as she might have been of a speck in the corner of her eye. For a while they moved about in the bedroom; she could hear drawers being opened and closed. But then one of them entered their kitchen and, after a purposeful pause, there came a curious harsh dropping sound, like the clockwork gulp of a metal monster. One gulp, two gulps, three gulps, four: she stared at the ceiling, baffled, until she realised that they were simply putting shillings in the meter. Water was run after that, and then another odd noise started, a sort of pulse or quick pant—the meter again, presumably, as the gas ran through it. Mrs Barber must be boiling a kettle. Now her husband had joined her. There was conversation, laughter ... Frances caught herself thinking, as she might have done of guests, Well, they're certainly making themselves at home.

Then she took in the implication of the words, and her heart, very slightly, sank.

While she was out in the kitchen assembling a cold Sunday supper, the couple came down, and tapped at the door, first the wife and then the husband: the WC was an outside one, across the yard from the back door, and they had to pass through the kitchen to get to it. They came grimacing with apology; Frances apologised, too. She supposed that the arrangement was as inconvenient to them as it was to her. But with each encounter, her confidence wobbled a little more. Even the fifty-eight shillings in her pocket began to lose their magic power; it was dawning on her just how thoroughly she would have to earn them. She simply hadn't prepared herself for the oddness of the sound and the sight of the couple going about from room to room as if the rooms belonged to them. When Mr Barber, for example, headed back upstairs after his visit to the yard, she heard him pause in the hall. Wondering what could be delaying him, she ventured a look along the passage, and saw him gazing at the pictures on the walls like a man in a gallery. Leaning in for a better look at a steel engraving of Ripon Cathedral he put his fingers to his pocket and brought out a matchstick, with which he began idly picking his teeth.

She didn't mention any of this to her mother. The two of them kept brightly to their evening routine, playing a couple of games of backgammon once supper had been eaten, taking a cup of watery cocoa at a quarter to ten, then starting on the round of chores—the gatherings, the turnings-down, the cushion-plumpings and the lockings-up—with which they eased their way to bed.

Frances's mother said good night first. Frances herself spent some time in the kitchen, tidying, seeing to the stove. She visited the WC, she laid the table for breakfast; she took the milk-can out to the front garden, put it to hang beside the gate. But when she had returned to the house and was lowering the gas in the hall she noticed a light still shining under her mother's door. And though she wasn't in the habit of calling in on her mother after she had gone to bed, somehow, tonight, that bar of light beckoned. She went across to it, and tapped.

'May I come in?'

Her mother was sitting up in bed, her hair unpinned and put into plaits. The plaits hung down like fraying ropes: until the War her hair had been brown, as pure a brown as Frances's, but it had faded in the past few years, growing coarser in the process, and now, at fifty-five, she had the white head of an old lady; only her brows remained dark and decided above her handsome hazel eyes. She had a book in her lap, a little railway thing called *Puzzles and Conundrums*: she had been trying out answers to an acrostic.

She let the book sink when Frances appeared, and gazed at her over the lenses of her reading-glasses.

'Everything all right, Frances?'

'Yes. Just thought I'd look in. Go on with your puzzle, though.'

'Oh, it's only a nonsense to help me off to sleep.'

But she peered at the page again, and an answer must have come to her: she tried out the word, her lips moving along with her pencil. The unoccupied half of bed beside her was flat as an ironing-board. Frances kicked off her slippers, climbed on to it, and lay back with her hands behind her head.

This room had still been the dining-room, a month before. Frances had painted over the old red paper and rearranged the pictures, but, as with the new kitchen upstairs, the result was not quite convincing. Her mother's bits of bedroom furniture seemed to her to be sitting as tensely as unhappy visitors: she could feel them pining for their grooves and smooches in the floor of the room above. Some of the old dining-room furniture had had to stay in here too, for want of anywhere else to put it, and the effect was an overcrowded one, with a suggestion of elderliness and a touch—just a touch—of the sick chamber. It was the sort of room she could remember from childhood visits to ailing great-aunts. All it really lacked, she thought, was the whiff of a commode, and the little bell for summoning the whiskery spinster daughter.

She quickly turned her back on that image. Upstairs, one of the Barbers could be heard crossing their sitting-room floor—Mr Barber, she guessed it was, from the bounce and briskness of the tread; Mrs Barber's was more sedate. Looking up at the ceiling, she followed the steps with her eyes.

Beside her, her mother also gazed upward. 'A day of great changes,' she said with a sigh. 'Are they still unpacking their things? They're excited, I suppose. I remember when your father and I first came here, we were just the same. They seem pleased with the house, don't you think?' She had lowered her voice. 'That's something, isn't it?'

Frances answered in the same almost furtive tone. '*She* does, at any rate. She looks like she can't believe her luck. I'm not so sure about him.'

'Well, it's a fine old house. And a home of their own: that means a great deal when one is first married.'

'Oh, but they're hardly newly-weds, are they? Didn't they tell us that they'd been married for three years? Straight out of the War, I suppose. No children, though.'

Her mother's tone changed slightly. 'No.' And after a second, the one thought plainly having led to the next, she added, 'Such a pity that the young women today all feel they must make up.'

Frances reached for the book and studied the acrostic. 'Isn't it? And on a Sunday, too.'

She felt her mother's level gaze. 'Don't imagine that I can't tell when you are making fun of me, Frances.'

Upstairs, Mrs Barber laughed. Something light was dropped or thrown and went skittering across the boards. Frances gave up on the puzzle. 'What do you think her background can be?'

Her mother had closed the book and was putting it aside. 'Whose?'

She gave a jerk of her chin. 'Mrs B's. I should say her father's some sort of branch manager, shouldn't you? A mother who's rather "nice". "Indian Love Lyrics" on the gramophone, perhaps a brother doing well for himself in the Merchant Navy. Piano lessons for the girls. An outing to the Royal Academy once a year . . . ' She began to yawn. Covering her mouth with the back of her wrist, she went on, through the yawn, 'One good thing, I suppose, about their being so young: they've only his parents to compare us with. They won't know that we really haven't a clue what we're doing. So long as we act the part of landladies with enough gusto, then landladies is what we will be.'

Her mother looked pained. 'How baldly you put it! You might be Mrs Seaview, of Worthing.'

'Well, there's no shame in being a landlady; not these days. I for one aim to enjoy landladying.'

'If you would only stop saying the word!'

Frances smiled. But her mother was plucking at the silk binding of a blanket, a look of real distress beginning to creep into her expression; she was an inch, Frances knew, from saying, 'Oh, it would break your dear father's heart!' And since even now, nearly four years after his death, Frances couldn't think of her father without wanting to grind her teeth, or swear, or leap up and smash something, she hastily turned the conversation. Her mother was involved in the running of two or three local charities: she asked after those. They spoke for a time about a forthcoming bazaar.

Once she saw her mother's face clear, become simply tired and elderly, she got to her feet.

'Now, have you everything you need? You don't want a biscuit, in case you wake?'

Her mother began to arrange herself for sleep. 'No, I don't want a biscuit. But you may put out the light for me, Frances.'

She lifted the plaits away from her shoulders and settled her head on her pillow. Her glasses had left little bruise-like dints on the bridge of her nose. As Frances reached to the lamp there were more footsteps in the room above; and then her hazel eyes returned to the ceiling.

'It might be Noel or John Arthur up there,' she murmured, as the light went down.

And, yes, thought Frances a moment later, lingering in the shadowy hall, it might be; for she could smell tobacco smoke now, and hear some sort of masculine muttering up on the landing, along with the tap of a slippered male foot . . . And just like that, like a knee or an elbow receiving a blow on the wrong spot, her heart was jangling. How grief could catch one out, still! She had to stand at the foot of the stairs while the fit of sorrow ran through her. But if only, she thought, as she began to climb—she hadn't thought it in ages—if only, if only she might turn the stair and find one of her brothers at the top—John Arthur, say, looking lean, looking bookish, looking like a whimsical monk in his brown Jaeger dressing-gown and Garden City sandals.

There was no one save Mr Barber, a cigarette in the corner of his mouth, his jacket off, his cuffs rolled back; he was fiddling with a nasty thing he had evidently just hung on the landing wall, a combination barometer-and-clothes-brush set with a lurid orangey varnish. But lurid touches were everywhere, she saw with dismay. It was as if a giant mouth had sucked a bag of boiled sweets and then given the house a lick. The faded carpet in her mother's old bedroom was lost beneath pseudo-Persian rugs. The lovely pier-glass had been draped slant-wise with a fringed Indian shawl. A print on one of the walls appeared to be a Classical nude in the Lord Leighton manner. The wicker birdcage twirled slowly on a ribbon from a hook that had been screwed into the ceiling; inside it was a silk-and-feather parrot on a papier-mâché perch.

The landing light was turned up high, hissing away as if furious. Frances wondered if the couple had remembered that she and her mother were paying for that. Catching Mr Barber's eye, she said, in a voice to match the dreadful brightness all around them, 'Got everything straight, have you?'

He took the cigarette out of his mouth, stifling a yawn. 'Oh, I've had enough of it for one day, Miss Wray. I did my bit, bringing up those blessed boxes. I leave the titivating to Lilian. She loves all that sort of thing. She can titivate for England, she can.'

Frances hadn't really looked at him properly before. She'd absorbed his manner, his 'theme'—that facetious grumbling—rather than anything more tangible, more physical. Now, in the flat landing light, she took in the clerkly neatness of him. Without his shoes he was only an inch or two taller than she. 'Puny,' his wife had called him; but there was too much life in him for that. His face was textured with gingery stubble and with little pimple scars, his jaw was narrow, his teeth slightly crowded, his eyes had sandy, near-invisible lashes. But the eyes themselves were very blue, and they somehow made him handsome, or almost-handsome—more handsome, anyhow, than she had realised so far.

She looked away from him. 'Well, I'm off to bed.'

He fought down another yawn. 'Lucky you! I think Lily's still decorating ours.'

'I've put out the lights downstairs. The mantle in the hall has a bit of a trick to it, so I thought I'd better do it. I ought to have shown you, I suppose.'

He said helpfully, 'Show me now, if you like.'

'Well, my mother's trying to sleep. Her room, you know, is just at the bottom of the stairs—'

'Ah. Show me tomorrow, then.'

'I will. I'm afraid it'll be dark, though, if you or Mrs Barber need to go down again tonight.'

'Oh, we'll find our way.'

'Take a lamp, perhaps.'

'That's an idea, isn't it? Or, I tell you what.' He smiled. 'I'll send Lil down first, on a rope. Any trouble and she can . . . give me a tug.'

He kept his gaze on hers as he spoke, in a playful sort of way. But there was something to his manner, something vaguely unsettling. She hesitated about replying and he raised his cigarette, turning his head to take a puff of it, twisting his mouth out of its smile to direct away the smoke; but still holding her gaze with those lively blue eyes of his.

Then, with a blink, his manner changed. The door to his bedroom was drawn open and his wife appeared. She had a picture in her hands—another Lord Leighton nude, Frances feared it was—and the sight of it brought on one of his mock-complaints.

'Are you still at it, woman? Blimey O'Reilly!'

She gave Frances a smile. 'I'm only making things look nice.'

'Well, poor Miss Wray wants to go to bed. She's come to complain about the noise.'

Her face fell. 'Oh, Miss Wray, I'm so sorry!'

Frances said quickly, 'You haven't been noisy at all. Mr Barber is teasing.'

'I meant to save it all for tomorrow. But now I've started, I can't stop.'

The landing felt impossibly crowded to Frances with them all standing there like that. Would the three of them have to meet, exchange pleasantries, every night? 'You must take as long as you need,' she said in her false, bright way. 'At least—' She'd begun to move towards her door, but paused. 'You will remember, won't you, about my mother, in the room downstairs?'

'Oh, yes, of course,' said Mrs Barber. And, 'Of course we will,' echoed her husband, in apparent earnestness.

Frances wished she'd said nothing. With an awkward 'Well, good night,' she let herself into her room. She left the door ajar for a moment while she lit her bedroom candle, and as she closed it she saw Mr Barber, puffing on his cigarette, looking across the landing at her; he smiled and moved away.

Once the door was shut and the key turned softly in the lock, she began to feel better. She kicked off her slippers, took off her blouse, her skirt, her underthings and stockings . . . and at last, like a portly matron letting out the laces of her stays, she was herself again. Raising her arms in a stretch, she looked around the shadowy room. How beautifully calm and uncluttered it was! The mantelpiece had two silver candlesticks on it and nothing else. The bookcase was packed but tidy, the floor dark with a single rug; the walls were pale—she'd removed the paper and used a white distemper instead. Even the framed prints were unbusy: a Japanese interior, a Friedrich landscape, the latter just visible in the candle-light, a series of snowy peaks dissolving into a violet horizon.

With a yawn, she felt for the pins in her hair and pulled them free. She filled her bowl with water, ran a flannel over her face, around her neck and under her arms; she cleaned her teeth, rubbed Vaseline into her cheeks and ruined hands. And then, because all this time she'd been able to smell Mr Barber's cigarette and the scent was making her restless, she opened the drawer of her nightstand and brought out a packet of papers and a tin of tobacco. She rolled a neat little fag, lit it by the flame of her candle, climbed into bed with it, then blew the candle out. She liked to smoke like this, naked in the cool sheets, with only the hot red tip of a cigarette to light her fingers in the dark.

Tonight, of course, the room was not quite dark: light was leaking in from the landing, a thin bright pool of it beneath her door. What were they doing out there now? She could hear the murmur of their voices. They were debating where to hang the wretched picture—were they? If they started banging in a nail she would have to go and say something. If they left the landing light burning so furiously she'd have to say something, too. She began trying out phrases in her head.

I'm sorry to have to raise this matter—

Do you remember we discussed—?

Perhaps we might—

It might be best if—

I'm afraid I made a mistake.

No, she wouldn't think that! It was too late for that. It was—oh, years and years too late for that.

She slept well, in the end. She awoke at six the next morning, when the first distant factory whistle went off. She dozed for an hour, and was finally jolted out of a complicated dream by a hectic drill-like noise she couldn't at first identify; it was the ring, she realised blearily, of the Barbers' alarm clock. It seemed no time at all since she had lain there listening to the couple make their murmuring way to bed. Now she got the reverse of it, as they emerged to mutter and yawn, to creep downstairs and out to the yard, to clatter about in their kitchen, brewing tea, frying a breakfast. She made herself pay attention to it all, every hiss and splutter of the bacon, every tap of the razor against the sink. She had to accommodate it, fit herself around it: the new start to her day.

She'd remembered the fifty-eight shillings. While Mr Barber was gathering his outdoor things she rose and quietly dressed. He left the house at just before eight, by which time his wife had returned to their bedroom; Frances gave it a couple of minutes, so as not to be too obvious about it, then unlocked her door and went downstairs. She raked out the ashes of the stove and got a new fire going. She crossed the yard, returned to the house to greet her mother, make tea, boil eggs. But all the time she worked, her mind was busy with calculations. Once she and her mother had had their breakfast and the dining-table had been cleared she settled herself down with her book of accounts and ran through the bundle of bills that, over the last half-year, had been steadily accumulating at the back of it.

The butcher and the fishmonger, she thought, ought to be given large sums at once. The laundryman, the baker and the coal-merchants could be kept at bay with smaller amounts. The house-rates would be due in a few weeks' time, along with the quarterly gas bill; the bill would be higher than usual, because it would contain the charge for the cooker and the meter and the pipes and connections that had been installed upstairs. There was still money to be paid, too, for some of the other preparations that had had to be made for the Barbers—for things like varnish and distemper. It would be three or four months—August or September at the earliest, she reckoned—before their rent would show itself in the family bank account as clear profit.

Still, August or September was a great deal better than never, and she put her account book away with her spirits lifting. The baker's man came, shortly followed by the butcher's boy: for once she was able to take the bread and the meat as if really entitled to them and not somehow involved in the shady reception of stolen goods. The meat was neck of lamb; that could go into a hot-pot later. She had no real interest in food, neither in preparing nor in eating it, but she had developed a grudging aptitude for cookery during the War; she enjoyed, anyhow, the practical challenge of making one cheap cut of meat do for several different dishes. She felt similarly about housework, liking best those rather out-of-the-way tasks—stripping the stove, cleaning stair-rods—that needed planning, strategy, chemicals, special tools.

Most of her chores, inevitably, were more mundane. The house was full of inconveniences, bristling with picture rails and plaster-work and elaborate skirting-boards that had to be dusted more or less daily. The furniture was all of dark woods that had to be dusted regularly, too. Her father had had a passion for 'Olde England', not at all in keeping with the Regency whimsies of the villa itself, and there was a Jacobean chair or chest in every odd corner. 'Father's collection', the pieces had been known as, while her father was alive; a year after his death Frances had had them valued and had discovered them all to be Victorian fakes. The dealer who'd bought the long-case clock had offered her three pounds for the lot. She would have been glad to pocket the money and have the damn things carted away, but her mother had grown upset at the prospect. 'Whether they're genuine or not,' she'd said, 'they have your father's heart in them.' 'They have his stupidity, more like,' Frances had answered, though not aloud. So the furniture remained, which meant that several times a week she had to go scuttling around like a crab, rubbing her duster over the barley-twist curves of wonky table legs and the scrolls and lozenges of rough-hewn chairs.

The very heaviest of the housework she saved for those morn-ings and afternoons when she could rely on her mother being safely out of the way. Since today was a Monday, she had ambitious plans. Her mother spent Monday mornings seeing to bits of parish business with the local vicar, and Frances could 'do' the entire ground floor in her absence.

She began the moment the front door closed, rolling up her sleeves, tying on an apron, covering her hair. She saw to her mother's bedroom first, then moved to the drawing-room for sweeping, dusting—endless dusting, it felt like. Where on earth did the dust come from? It seemed to her that the house must produce

23

it, as flesh oozes sweat. She could beat and beat a rug or a cushion, and still it would come. The drawing-room had a china cabinet in it, with glass doors, tightly closed, but even the things inside grew dusty and had to be wiped. Just occasionally she longed to take each fiddly porcelain cup and saucer and break it in two. Once, in sheer frustration, she had snapped off the head of one of the apple-cheeked Staffordshire figures: it still sat a little crookedly, from where she had hurriedly glued it back on.

She didn't feel like that today. She worked briskly and efficiently, taking her brush and pan from the drawing-room to the top of the stairs and making her way back down, a step at a time; after that she filled a bucket with water, fetched her kneeling-mat, and began to wash the hall floor. Vinegar was all she used. Soap left streaks on the black tiles. The first, wet rub was important for loosening the dirt, but it was the second bit that really counted, passing the wrung cloth over the floor in one supple, unbroken movement . . . There! How pleasing each glossy tile was. The gloss would fade in about five minutes as the surface dried; but everything faded. The vital thing was to make the most of the moments of brightness. There was no point dwelling on the scuffs. She was young, fit, healthy. She had—what did she have? Little pleasures like this. Little successes in the kitchen. The cigarette at the end of the day. Cinema with her mother on a Wednesday. Regular trips into Town. There were spells of restlessness now and again; but any life had those. There were longings, there were desires . . . But they were physical matters mostly, and she had no last-century inhibitions about dealing with that sort of thing. It was amazing, in fact, she reflected, as she repositioned her mat and bucket and started on a new stretch of tile, it was astonishing how satisfactorily the business could be taken care of, even in the middle of the day, even with her mother in the house, simply by slipping up to her bedroom for an odd few minutes, perhaps as a break between peeling parsnips or while waiting for dough to rise—

A movement at the turn of the staircase made her start. She had forgotten all about her lodgers. Now she looked up through the banisters to see Mrs Barber just coming uncertainly down.

She felt herself blush, as if caught out. But Mrs Barber was also blushing. Though it was well after ten, she was dressed in her nightgown still; she had some sort of satiny Japanese wrapper on top—a *kimono*, Frances supposed the thing was called—and her feet were bare inside Turkish slippers. She was carrying a towel and a sponge-bag. As she greeted Frances she tucked back a sleep-flattened curl of hair and said shyly, 'I wondered if I might have a bath.'

'Oh,' said Frances. 'Yes.'

'But not if it's a trouble. I fell back asleep after Len went to work, and—'

Frances began to get to her feet. 'It's no trouble. I shall have to light the geyser for you, that's all. My mother and I don't usually light it during the day. I should have said last night. Can you come across? You'll have to hop.' She moved her bucket. 'Here's a dry bit, look.'

Mrs Barber, however, had come further down the stairs, and her colour was deepening: she was gazing in a mortified way at the duster on Frances's head, at her rolled-up sleeves and flaming hands, at the housemaid's mat at her feet, still with the dents of her knees in it. Frances knew the look very well—she was bored to death with it, in fact—because she had seen it many times before: on the faces of neighbours, of tradesmen, and of her mother's friends, all of whom had got themselves through the worst war in human history yet seemed unable for some reason to cope with the sight of a well-bred woman doing the work of a char. She said breezily, 'You remember my saying about us not having help? I really meant it, you see. The only thing I draw the line at is laundry; most of that still gets sent out. But everything else, I take care of. The "brights", the "roughs"—yes, I've all the lingo!'

Mrs Barber had begun to smile at last. But as she looked at the stretch of floor that was still to be washed, she grew embarrassed in a different sort of way.

'I'm afraid Len and I must have made an awful mess yesterday. I wasn't thinking.'

'Oh,' said Frances, 'these tiles get dirty all by themselves. Everything in this house does.'

'Once I've dressed, I'll finish it for you.'

'You'll do nothing of the sort. You've your own rooms to care for. If you can manage without a maid, why shouldn't I? Besides, you'd be amazed what a whiz I can be with a mop.—Here, let me help.'

Mrs Barber was on the bottom stair now and clearly doubtful about where to step to. After the slightest of hesitations, she took the hand that Frances offered, braced herself against her grip, then made the small spring forward to the unwashed side of the floor. Her kimono parted as she landed, exposing more of her nightdress, and giving an alarming suggestion of the rounded, mobile, unsupported flesh inside.

They went together through the kitchen and into the scullery. The bath was in there, beside the sink. It had a bleached wooden cover, used by Frances as a draining-board; with a practised movement she lifted this free and set it against the wall. The tub was an ancient one that had been several times re-enamelled, most recently by Frances herself, who was not quite sure of the result; the iron struck her, today especially, as having a faintly leprous appearance. The Vulcan geyser was also rather frightful, a greenish riveted cylinder on three bowed legs. It must have been the top of its manufacturer's range in about 1870, but now looked like the sort of vessel in which someone in a Jules Verne novel might make a trip to the moon.

'It has a bit of a temperament, I'm afraid,' she told Mrs Barber as she explained the mechanism. 'You have to turn this tap, but *not* this one; you might blow us sky-high if you do. The flame goes here.' She struck a match. 'Best to look the other way at this point. My father lost both his eyebrows doing this once.—There.'

The flame, with a whoosh, had found the gas. The cylinder began to tick and rattle. She frowned at it, her hands at her hips. 'What a beast it is. I am sorry, Mrs Barber.' She gazed right round the room, at the stone sink, the copper in the corner, the mortuary tiles on the wall. 'I do wish this house was more up-to-date for you.'

But Mrs Barber shook her head. 'Oh, please don't wish that.' She tucked back another curl of hair; Frances noticed the piercing for her earring, a little dimple in the lobe. 'I like the house just as it is. It's a house with a history, isn't it? Things—well, they oughtn't always to be modern. There'd be no character if they were.'

And there it was again, thought Frances: that niceness, that kindness, that touch of delicacy. She answered with a laugh. 'Well, as far as character goes, I fear this house might be rather too much of a good thing. But—' She spoke less flippantly. 'I'm glad you like it. I'm very glad. I like it too, though I'm apt to forget that.—Now, we oughtn't to let this geyser get hot without running some water, or there'll be no house left to like, and no us to do the liking! Do you think you can manage? If the flame goes out—it sometimes does, I'm sorry to say—give me a call.'

Mrs Barber smiled, showing neat white teeth. 'I will. Thank you, Miss Wray.'

Frances left her to it and returned to her wet floor. The scullery door was closed behind her, and quietly bolted.

But the door between the kitchen and the passage was propped open, and as Frances retrieved her cloth she could hear, very clearly, Mrs Barber's preparations for her bath, the rattle of the chain against the tub, followed by the splutter and gush of the water. The gushing, it seemed to her, went on for a long time. She had told a fib about her and her mother's use of the geyser: it was too expensive to light often; they drew their hot water from the boiler in the old-fashioned stove. They bathed, at most, once a week, frequently taking turns with the same bathwater. If Mrs Barber were to want baths like this on a daily basis, their gas bill might double.

But at last the flow was cut off. There came the splash of water and the rub of heels as Mrs Barber stepped into the tub, followed by a more substantial liquid thwack as she lowered herself down. After that there was a silence, broken only by the occasional echoey plink of drips from the tap.

Like the parted kimono, the sounds were unsettling; the silence was most unsettling of all. Sitting at her bureau a short time before, Frances had been picturing her lodgers in purely mercenary terms—as something like two great waddling shillings. But this, she thought, shuffling backward over the tiles, this was what it really meant to have lodgers: this odd, unintimate proximity, this rather peeled-back moment, where the only thing between herself and a naked Mrs Barber was a few feet of kitchen and a thin scullery door. An image sprang into her head: that round flesh, crimsoning in the heat.

She adjusted her pose on the mat, took hold of her cloth, and rubbed hard at the floor.

The steam was still beading the scullery walls when her mother returned at lunch-time. Frances told her about Mrs Barber's bath, and she looked startled.

'At ten o'clock? In her dressing-gown? You're sure?'

'Quite sure. A satin one, too. What a good job, wasn't it, that you were visiting the vicar, and not the other way round?'

Her mother paled, but didn't answer.

They ate their lunch—a cauliflower cheese—then settled down together in the drawing-room. Mrs Wray made notes for a parish newsletter. Frances worked her way through a basket of mending with *The Times* on the arm of her chair. What was the latest?

Awkwardly, she turned the inky pages. But it was the usual dismal stuff. Horatio Bottomley was off to the Old Bailey for swindling the public out of a quarter of a million. An MP was asking that cocaine traffickers be flogged. The French were shooting Syrians, the Chinese were shooting each other, a peace conference in Dublin had come to nothing, there'd been new murders in Belfast . . . But the Prince of Wales looked jolly on a fishing trip in Japan, and the Marchioness of Carisbrooke was about to host a ball 'in aid of the Friends of the Poor'.—So that was all right, then, thought Frances. She disliked *The Times*. But there wasn't the money for a second, less conservative paper. And, in any case, reading the news these days depressed her. In the quaintness of her wartime youth it would have fired her into activity: writing letters, attending meetings. Now the world seemed to her to have become so complex that its problems defied solution. There was only a chaos of conflicts of interest; the whole thing filled her with a sense of futility. She put the paper aside. She would tear it up tomorrow, for scraps and kindling.

At least the house was silent; very nearly its old self. There had been bumps and creaks earlier, as Mrs Barber had shifted more furniture about, but now she must be in her sitting-room—doing what? Was she still in her kimono? Somehow, Frances hoped she was.

Whatever she was doing, her silence lasted right through tea-time. She didn't come to life again until just before six, when she went charging around as if in a burst of desperate tidying, then began clattering pans and dishes in her little kitchen. Half an hour later, preparing dinner in her own kitchen, Frances was startled to hear the rattle of the front-door latch as someone let themself into the house. It was Mr Barber, of course, coming home from work. This time he sounded like her father, scuffing his feet across the mat.

He went tiredly up the stairs and gave a yodelling yawn at the top, but five minutes later, as she was gathering potato peelings from the counter, she heard him come back down. There was the squeak of his slippers in the passage and then, 'Knock, knock, Miss Wray!' His face appeared around the door. 'Mind if I pass through?'

He looked older than he had the day before, with his hair greased flat for the office. A crimson stripe across his forehead must have been the mark of his bowler hat. Once he had visited the WC he lingered for a moment in the yard: she could see him through the kitchen window, wondering whether or not to go and speak to her mother, who was further down the garden, cutting asparagus. He decided against it and returned to the house, pausing to peer up at the brickwork or the window-frames as he came, and then to examine some crack or chip in the door-step.

'Well, and how are you, Miss Wray?' he asked, when he was back in the kitchen. She saw that there was no way out of a chat. But perhaps she ought to get to know him.

'I'm very well, Mr Barber. And you? How was your day?'

He pulled at his stiff City collar. 'Oh, the usual fun and games.'

'Difficult, you mean?'

'Well, every day's difficult with a chief like mine. I'm sure you know the type: the sort of fellow who gives you a column of numbers to add and, when they don't come out the way that suits him, blames you!' He raised his chin to scratch at his throat, keeping his eyes on hers. 'A public-school chap he's meant to be, too. I thought those fellows knew better, didn't you?'

Now, why would he say that? He might have guessed that her brothers—But, of course, he knew nothing about her brothers, she reminded herself, even though he and his wife were sleeping in their old room. She said, in an attempt to match his tone, 'Oh, I hear those fellows are over-rated. You work in assurance, I think you told us?'

'That's right. For my sins!'

'What is it you do, exactly?'

'Me? I'm an assessor of lives. Our agents send in applications for policies. I pass them on to our medical man and, depending on his report, I say whether the life to be assured counts as good, bad or indifferent.'

'Good, bad or indifferent,' she repeated, struck by the idea. 'You sound like St Peter.'

'St Peter!' He laughed. 'I like that! That's clever, Miss Wray. Yes, I shall try that out on the fellows at the Pearl.'

Once his laughter had faded she assumed that he would move on. But the little exchange had only made him chummier: he sidled into the scullery doorway and settled himself against the post of it. He seemed to enjoy watching her work. His blue gaze travelled over her and she felt him taking her all in: her apron, her steam-frizzed hair, her rolled-up sleeves, her scarlet knuckles.

She began to chop some mint for a sauce. He asked if the mint had come from the garden. Yes, she said, and he jerked his head towards the window. 'I was just having a look at it out there. Quite a size, isn't it? You and your mother don't take care of it all by yourselves, do you?'

'Oh,' she said, 'we call in a man for the heavier jobs when—' When we can run to it, she thought. 'When they need doing. The vicar's son comes and mows the lawn for us. We manage the rest between us all right.'

That wasn't quite true. Her mother did her genteel best with the weeding and the pruning. As far as Frances was concerned, gardening was simply open-air housework; she had enough of that already. As a consequence, the garden—a fine one, in her father's day—was growing more shapeless by the season, more depressed and unkempt. Mr Barber said, 'Well, I'd be glad to give you a hand with it—you just say the word. I generally help with my father's at home. His isn't half the size of yours, mind. Not a quarter, even. Still, the guvnor's made the most of it. He even has cucumbers in

31

a frame. Beauties, they are—this long!' He held his hands apart, to show her. 'Ever thought of cucumbers, Miss Wray?'

'Well—'

'Growing them, I mean?'

Was there some sort of innuendo there? She could hardly believe that there was. But his gaze was lively, as it had been the night before, and, just as something about his manner then had discomposed her, so, now, she had the feeling that he was poking fun at her, perhaps attempting to make her blush.

Without replying, she turned to fetch vinegar and sugar for the mint, and when the sauce was mixed and in its bowl she removed her hot-pot from the oven, put in a knife to test the meat; she stood so long with her back to him that he took the hint at last and pushed away from the door-post. It seemed to her that, as he left the kitchen, he was smiling. And once he'd started along the passage she heard him begin to whistle, at a rather piercing pitch. The tune was a jaunty, music-hall one—it took her a moment to recognise it—it was 'Hold Your Hand Out, Naughty Boy'. The whistle faded as he climbed the stairs, but a few minutes later she found that she was whistling the tune herself. She quickly cut the whistle off, but it was as though he'd left a stubborn odour behind him: do what she could, the wretched song kept floating back into her head all evening long.

2

There was more jaunty whistling, in the days that followed. There were more yodelling yawns at the top of the stairs. There were sneezes, too—those loud masculine sneezes, like shouts into the hand, that Frances could remember from the days of her brothers; sneezes that for some reason never came singly, but arrived as a volley and led inevitably to a last-trump blowing of the nose. Then there was the lavatory seat forever left in the upright position; there were the vivid yellow splashes and kinked wet gingerish hairs that appeared on the rim of the pan itself. Finally, on the dot of half-past ten each night, there was the clatter of a spoon in a glass as Mr Barber mixed himself an indigestion powder, followed a few seconds later by the little report of his belch.

None of it was so very irksome. It was certainly not a lot to put up with for the sake of twenty-nine shillings a week. Frances supposed that she would grow used to it, that the Barbers would grow used to her, that the house would settle down into grooves and routines, that they'd all start rubbing along together—as Mr Barber himself, she reflected, might say. She found it hard to imagine herself ever rubbing along with him, it was true, and she had several despondent moments, lying in bed with her cigarette, wondering again what she had done, what she had let the house in for;

trying to remember why she had ever thought that the arrangement would work.

Still, at least Mrs Barber was easy to have about the place. That mid-morning bath, it seemed, had been a freak. She kept herself very much to herself as time went on, doing more of that 'titivating' her husband had pretended to grumble about, adding lengths of beading and swaths of macramé and lace to picture-rails and mantelpieces, arranging ostrich feathers in jars: Frances caught glimpses of it all as she went back and forth to her own room. Once, crossing the landing, she heard a sound like jingling bells, and glanced in through the open doorway of the couple's sitting-room to see Mrs Barber with a tambourine in her hand. The tambourine had trailing ribbons and a gipsy look about it. Gipsyish, too, was Mrs Barber's costume, the fringed skirt, the Turkish slippers; her hair was done up in a red silk scarf. Frances paused, not wanting to disturb her—then called lightly into the room.

'Are you about to dance the tarantella, Mrs Barber?'

Mrs Barber came to the doorway, smiling. 'I'm still deciding what goes where.'

Frances nodded to the tambourine. 'May I see it?' And then, when the thing was in her hand, 'It's pretty.'

Mrs Barber wrinkled her nose. 'It's only from a junk shop. It's really Italian, though.'

'You have exotic tastes, I think.'

'Len says I'm like a savage. That I ought to live in the jungle. I just like things that have come from other places.'

And after all, thought Frances, what was wrong with that? She gave the tambourine a shake, tapped her fingers across its drumskin. She might have lingered and said more; the moment, somehow, seemed to invite it. But it was Wednesday afternoon, and she and her mother were off to the cinema. With a touch of reluctance, she handed the tambourine back. 'I hope you find the right spot for it.'

When, a little later, she and her mother left the house, she said, 'I suppose we might have asked Mrs Barber to come along with us today.'

Her mother looked doubtful. 'Mrs Barber? To the picture-house?'

'You'd rather we didn't?'

'Well, perhaps once we know her better. But mightn't it become awkward? Shouldn't we have to ask her every time?'

Frances thought about it. 'Yes, I suppose so.'

In any case, the programme that week was disappointing. The first few films were all right, but the drama was a dud, an American thriller with a plot full of holes. She and her mother slipped away before the final act, hoping not to draw the notice of the small orchestra—Mrs Wray saying, as she often did, what a pity it was that the pictures nowadays had so much unpleasant-ness in them.

They met a neighbour, Mrs Hillyard, in the foyer. She was leav-ing early too, but from the dearer seats upstairs. They walked back up the road together, and, 'How are your paying guests?' she asked. She was too polite to call them lodgers. 'Are they settling in? I see the husband in the mornings on his way to the City. He seems a very well-turned-out chap. I must say I rather envy you, having a young man in the house again. And you'll enjoy having some young people about to argue with, Frances, I expect?'

Frances smiled. 'Oh, my arguing days are all behind me.'

'Of course they are. Your mother's grateful for your company, I'm sure.'

That night there was skirt of beef for dinner: Frances worked up a sweat beating it tender with a rolling-pin. The next day, with an hour to herself, she cleared soot from the kitchen flue. The muck got under her fingernails and into the creases of her palms, and had to be scrubbed off with lemon juice and salt.

The day after that, feeling rather as though she'd earned a Friday treat, she left her mother a cold lunch and bread already buttered for tea, and went into Town.

She liked to go in when she could, sometimes as a shopping expedition, sometimes to call on a friend. Depending on the weather, she had various ways of making the journey; the days had kept fine since the Barbers' arrival so she was able, this time, to make the best of it on foot. She caught a bus as far as Vauxhall, and from there she crossed the river and wandered north, taking any street that caught her eye.

She loved these walks through London. She seemed, as she made them, to become porous, to soak in detail after detail; or else, like a battery, to become charged. Yes, that was it, she thought, as she turned a corner: it wasn't a liquid creeping, it was a tingle, something electric, something produced as if by the friction of her shoes against the streets. She was at her truest, it seemed to her, in these tingling moments—these moments when, paradoxically, she was also at her most anonymous. But it was the anonymity that did it. She never felt the electric charge when she walked through London with someone at her side. She never felt the excitement that she felt now, seeing the fall of the shadow of a railing across a set of worn steps. Was it foolish, to feel like that about the shadow of a railing? Was it whimsy? She hated whimsy. But it only became whimsy when she tried to put it into words. If she allowed herself simply to feel it . . . There. It was like being a string, and being plucked, giving out the single, pure note that one was made for. How odd, that no one else could hear it! If I were to die today, she thought, and someone were to think over my life, they'd never know that moments like this, here on the Horseferry Road, between a Baptist chapel and a tobacconist's, were the truest things in it.

She crossed the street, swinging her bag, and a couple of gulls wheeled overhead, letting out those seaside cries that could be heard sometimes right in the middle of London, that always made her think that just around the next corner she would find the pier.

She did her shopping at the market stalls of Strutton Ground, going from one stall to another before committing herself, wanting to be sure that she was ferreting out the bargains; she ended up with three reels of sewing thread, half a dozen pairs of flawed silk stockings and a box of nibs. The walk from Vauxhall had made her hungry, and with her purchases stowed away she began to think about her lunch. Often on these trips she ate at the National Gallery, the Tate—somewhere like that, where the refreshment rooms were so bustling that it was possible to order a pot of tea, then sneak out a home-made bun to have with it. That was a spinsterish thing to do, however; she wouldn't be a spinster today. Good grief, she was only twenty-six! She found a 'cosy corner' café and bought herself a hot lunch: egg, chips and bread and butter, all for a shilling and sixpence, including a penny tip for the waitress. She resisted the temptation to mop the plate with the bread and butter, but felt quite vulgar enough to roll herself a cigarette. She smoked it to the satisfying chink and splash of crockery and water that floated up from the basement kitchen: the sound of someone else washing up.

She walked to Buckingham Palace after that, not from any sentimental feeling about the King and Queen—whom, on the whole, she considered to be a pair of inbred leeches—but simply for the pleasure of being there, at the grand centre of things. For the same reason, after she had wandered about in St James's Park she crossed the Mall and climbed the steps and went up to Piccadilly. She strolled a little way along Regent Street simply for the sake of its curve, pausing to goggle at the prices on the cards in the smart shop windows. Three-guinea shoes, four-guinea hats . . . A place on a corner was selling Persian antiques. A decorated jar was so tall and so round that a thief might hide in it. She thought, with a smile: Mrs Barber would like that.

There were no smart shops once she had crossed Oxford Circus. London made one of its costume changes, like whipping off a cloak;

it became a shabby muddle of pianola sellers, Italian grocers, boarding-houses, pubs. But she liked the names of the streets: Great Castle, Great Titchfield, Riding House, Ogle, Clipstone—her friend, Christina, lived on this last one, in two rooms on the top floor of an ugly, newish building. Frances went in by a brown-tiled passage, greeted the porter in his booth, passed on to the open courtyard and began the long climb up the stairs. As she approached Christina's landing she could hear the sound of her typewriter, a fluid, hectic *tap-tap-tap*. She paused to catch her breath, put her finger to the push of the doorbell, and the typewriting ceased. A moment later Christina opened the door, tilting up her small, pale, pointed face for Frances's kiss, but narrowing her eyes and blinking.

'I can't see you! I can only see letters, hopping about like fleas. Oh, I shall go blind, I know I shall. Just a minute, while I bathe my brow.'

She slipped past Frances to wash her hands at the sink on the landing, and then to hold the hands to her forehead. She came back rubbing at an eye with a wet knuckle.

The building was run by a society offering flats to working women. Christina's neighbours were school-mistresses, stenographers, lady clerks; she herself made her living by typing up manuscripts and dissertations for authors and students, and by odd bits of secretarial and book-keeping work. Just now, she told Frances as she led her into the flat, she was helping out on a new little paper, a little political thing; she had been typing up statistics on the Russian Famine, and the constant fiddling about with the margins had given her a headache. Then, of course, there were the figures themselves, so many hundreds of thousands dead, so many hundreds of thousands still starving. It was miserable work.

'And the worst of it is,' she said guiltily, 'it's made me so hungry! And there isn't a bit of food in the flat.'

Frances opened her bag. 'Hey presto—there is, now. I've made you a cake.'

'Oh, Frances, you haven't.'

'Well, a currant loaf. I've been carrying it about with me, and it weighs a ton. Here you are.'

She brought the loaf out, undid its string, parted its paper. Christina saw the glossy brown crust of it and her blue eyes widened like a child's. There was only one thing to do with a cake like that, she said, and that was to toast it. She set a kettle on the gas-ring for tea, then rummaged about in a cupboard for an electric fire.

'Sit down while this warms up,' she said, as the fire began to tick and hum. 'Oh, but let some air in, would you, so we don't swelter.'

Frances had to move a colander from the window-sill in order to raise the sash. The room was large and light, decorated in fashionable Bohemian colours, but there were untidy piles of books and papers on the floor, and nothing was where it ought to be. The armchairs were comedy-Victorian, one of scuffed red leather, the other of balding velveteen. The velveteen one had a tray balanced on it, bearing the remains of two breakfasts: sticky egg cups and dirty mugs. She passed the tray to Christina, who cleared it, gave it a wipe, set it with cups, saucers, plates and a smeary bottle of milk, and handed it back. The mugs, the egg cups, the cups and saucers, were all of pottery, heavily glazed, thickly made—all of it with a rather 'primitive' finish. Christina shared this flat with another woman, Stevie. Stevie was a teacher in the art department of a girls' school in Camden Town, but was trying to make a name for herself as a maker of ceramics.

Frances did not dislike Stevie exactly, but she generally timed her visits so that they fell inside school hours; it was Chrissy she came to see. The two of them had known each other since the mid-point of the War. With the coming of Peace, perversely, they had parted on bad terms, but fate had brought them back together—fate, or chance, or whatever it was that, one day last September, had sent Frances into the National Gallery to escape a torrent of rain, had nudged her out of the Flemish rooms and into the Italian, where she had come upon Christina, as sodden as herself, gazing with a mixed expression at *Venus, Cupid, Folly and Time*. There had been no chance of a retreat. While Frances had stood there, disconcerted, Christina had turned, and their eyes had met; after the first awkwardness, the more-than-coincidence of it had been impossible to resist, and now they saw each other two or three times a month. Their friendship sometimes struck Frances as being like a piece of soap—like a piece of ancient kitchen soap that had got worn to the shape of her hand, but which had been dropped to the floor so many times it was never quite free of its bits of cinder.

Today, for example, she saw that Christina had re-styled her hair. The hair had been short at their last meeting, a fortnight before; now it was even more severely shingled at the back, with a straight fringe halfway up Christina's forehead and two flat, pointed curls in front of her ears. Rather wilfully eccentric, Frances thought the style. She thought the same of Christina's frock, which was a swirl of muddy pinks and greys, and matched the Bloomsbury walls. She thought it of the walls, for that matter; of the whole untidy flat. She never came here without looking at the disorder of it all in a mixture of envy and despair, imagining the cool, calm, ordered place the rooms would be if they were hers.

She didn't mention the haircut. She closed her eyes to the mess. The kettle came to the boil and Christina filled the teapot, cut the cake into slices, produced butter, knives and two brass toasting-forks. 'Let's sit on the floor and do it properly,' she said, so they pushed back the armchairs and made themselves comfortable on the rug. Frances's fork had Mother Shipton for its handle. Christina's had a cat that was playing a fiddle. The bars of the fire had turned from grey to pink to glowing orange, and smelt powerfully of scorching dust.

The cake toasted quickly. With careful fingers they turned their slices, then loaded on the butter, holding plates beneath their chins as they ate, to catch the greasy drips. 'Only think of the poor Russians!' said Christina, gathering crumbs. But that reminded her of the little paper she was working for, and she began to tell Frances all about it. It had its office, she said, in a Clerkenwell basement, in a terrace that looked as though it ought to be condemned. She had spent two days there this week, and had passed the whole time in fear of her life. 'You can hear the house creaking and groaning, like the one in *Little Dorrit*!' The pay was wretched, of course, but the work was interesting. The paper had its own printing press; she was to learn how to set type. Everyone did a bit of everything—that was how the place was run. And she was already 'Christina' to the two young editors, and they were 'David' and 'Philip' to her ...

What fun it sounded, Frances thought. She herself had only one piece of news to share, and that was the arrival of Mr and Mrs Barber. For days she had been imagining how she'd describe the couple to Chrissy; the two of them had had long, sparkling conversations about them, in her head. But what with the new haircut, and the Russian Famine, and David and Philip—She finished her cake, saying nothing. In the end it was Christina herself who, yawning, extending her legs, pointing her neat slipperless feet like a ballerina, said, 'You've let me run on like anything! What are the excitements in Camberwell? There must be something, surely?' She patted her mouth, then stopped her hand. 'Wait a bit. Weren't your lodgers due, when I saw you last?'

Frances said, 'We call them paying guests, on Champion Hill.'

'They've arrived? Why didn't you say? How deep you are! Well? How do you like them?'

'Oh—' Frances's smart comments had shrunk away. All she could picture was nice Mrs Barber, the tambourine in her hand.

She said at last, 'They're all right. It's odd having people in the house again, that's all.'

'Do you put a tumbler to the wall?'

'Of course I don't.'

'I would. I'm glued to the floor every time the girl downstairs sneaks in her gentleman friend. It's as good as a Marie Stopes lecture. If I had your Mr and Mrs—What are their names?'

'Barber. Leonard and Lilian. Len and Lil, they call each other.'

'Len and Lil, from Peckham Rye!'

'They have to be from somewhere, you know.'

'If I had them in the next room I wouldn't get an ounce of work done.'

'The novelty soon wears off, I assure you.'

'Well, you don't paint much of a picture . . . How's the husband?'

Frances recalled his unsettling blue gaze. 'I'm not sure. I haven't quite got his measure. Pleased with himself. A cock among hens.'

'And the wife?'

'Oh, much better than him. Good-looking, in the fleshy sort of way that men admire. A bit romantic. Really, I can't say. We pass each other on the stairs. We meet on the landing. Everything happens on the landing. I had no idea that landings could be so thrilling. Ours has become the equivalent of Clapham Railway Junction. One of us is always going across it, or backing out of it— or lurking in a siding until the line is clear.'

'And how's your mother taken to it all?'

'Yes, Mother's keeping her end up.'

'She doesn't mind sleeping on the dining-table, or whatever it is she's doing? Rum to picture her as a landlady, I must say! Has she steamed open any post yet?'

Frances made no answer to that. But Christina didn't seem to expect one. She was yawning again, and stretching, making those Lopokova points with her toes. They oughtn't to leave the fire burning, she said, without toasting more cake. Had they room for a second helping? They decided that they had, and speared another two slices.

And they had eaten the cake, and drunk their tea, when they heard the sound of a barrel organ starting up, out on the street. They tilted their heads to listen. The melody was a jumble of notes to begin with; then their ears got the thread of it. It was 'Roses of Picardy', the most banal tune imaginable, but one of the songs of their youth. They looked at each other. Frances, embarrassed, said, 'This old thing.'

But Christina scrambled to her feet. 'Oh, let's go and see.'

The organist was on the pavement directly below them. He was an ex-service man in a trench-coat and Tommy's cap, with a couple of campaign medals just visible at his breast. He had the organ on a set of pram wheels; it appeared to be held together with string. Its sound was so raw and almost discordant that the music seemed not so much to be rising from the box as tumbling out of it, as if the notes were physical things of glass or metal, landing clanging at the man's feet.

After a minute he looked up, saw the two of them watching, and lifted his cap to them. Frances went to her bag for money. She dithered, for a moment, when she found nothing smaller than a sixpence, but she returned to the open window and carefully threw the coin down. The man caught it in his cap, very neatly, tucked it away, and waved the cap again, keeping the organ going as he did it, without the slightest interruption.

The sun had warmed the window-sill with real, summerish heat. Christina settled herself more comfortably, shutting her eyes, turning up her face. There were crumbs of cake at the corner of her mouth still, and butter on her lips: Frances smiled to see the shine of it, then let her own eyes close, giving herself over to the sunlight, to the niceness of the moment, and to the tune, that was so piercingly reminiscent of a particular phase of wartime.

The note of the music wobbled. The man was moving on, still

paying out the melody. As he turned to leave the pavement a board was revealed on the back of his trench-coat, on which he had painted the words:

WILLING TO
GRIND!

WILL YOU
EMPLOY ME?

Frances and Christina watched him cross the road. 'What's to be done for them?' asked Chrissy.

'I don't know.'

'There's to be a meeting at the Conway Hall next week, "Charity versus Challenge". Sidney Webb is to speak—for what that's worth. You ought to come.'

Frances nodded. 'I might.'

'Only, you won't.'

'I'm not sure I believe it'll help, that's all.'

'You'd rather stay at home, scrub a lavatory pan or two.'

'Well, lavatory pans must be scrubbed. Even the Webbs', I expect.'

She didn't want to talk about it. What was the good? In any case, she couldn't quite tug her mind free from the music. The tune came more faintly as the man turned a corner, the last few strands of it like the fine but clinging threads at the edge of a piece of unhemmed linen. *Roses are shining in Picardy, in the hush of the silver dew. Roses are flow'ring in Picardy, but—*

'There's Stevie,' said Christina.

'Stevie? Where?'

'Down there. Just coming.'

Frances leaned, peered over the sill, and spotted the tall, rather handsome figure making for the entrance of the building. 'Oh,' she said, without excitement. 'No school for her today?'

'The school's shut for three days. Some naughty boys broke in and flooded it. She's been at her studio instead. She has a new one, in Pimlico.'

They remained at the window for another few moments, then returned, in silence, to their places on the floor. The electric fire was grey now, ticking again as it cooled. Soon there were footsteps out on the landing, followed by the rattle of a latch-key being put into the lock of the door.

The door opened almost directly on to the room. 'Hullo Stinker,' said Christina, as Stevie appeared.

'Hullo you,' Stevie answered. And then: 'Frances! Good to see you. Your day up in Town, is it?'

She was hatless and coatless and smoking a cigarette. Her short dark hair was brushed back from her forehead, completely against the fashion; her outfit was plain as a canvas overall, the sleeves rolled up to her elbows, showing off her knobbly hands and wrists. But Frances was struck, as she always was, by the dash of her, the queer panache, the air she had of not caring if the world admired her or thought her an oddity. She had a hefty satchel over her shoulder, which she let fall with a thud as she approached the arm-chairs. She looked at the fire and the toasting-forks, smiling but wary.

'What's the idea? A nursery tea?'

'Isn't it shaming?' said Christina. Her manner had changed with Stevie's arrival, had become arch and brittle in a way Frances knew and disliked. 'When poor Frances comes to see us she has to bring her own tuck. Aren't we lucky she's so clever! Swap you a slice for a couple of cigarettes?'

Stevie fished in a pocket for her case and lighter. 'Done.'

She helped herself to a piece of the loaf, then sat down in the velveteen armchair, her knee just touching Christina's shoulder. Her fingernails were dark with clay, Frances could see now, and there was a dirty thumb-print like a bruise at her left temple.

Christina noticed the thumb-print too, and reached up to rub it away.

'You look like a chimney-sweep, Stevie.'

'And you,' said Stevie, surveying with satisfaction Christina's unpressed clothes, 'look like a chimney-sweep's trollop.' She took a large bite of cake. 'Aside from your hair, that is. What do you think of it, Frances?'

Frances was lighting a cigarette. Christina answered for her. 'She hates it, of course.'

Frances said, 'I don't hate it at all. It'd cause a stir on Champion Hill, though.'

Christina snorted. 'Well, that's a point in its favour, in my book. Stevie and I were in Hammersmith last week. The stares I got were out of this world! No one said a word, of course.'

'No one would, to your face,' said Stevie, 'in a place like that.' She polished off her slice of cake and licked her dirty thumb and fingers. 'I lived on the Brompton Road once, you know, Frances. The gentility—my God! My neighbour was a man who worked for one of the big shipping firms. His wife kept a Bible in the window. Church three times on a Sunday, all that. But at night, I'd hear them through the walls, practically hurling the fire irons at each other! That's the clerk class for you. They look tame. They sound tame. But under those doilies and antimacassars they're still rough as all hell. No, give me good honest slum people over people like that, any day. At least they have their brawls in the open.'

Christina put out a foot and nudged Frances with her toes. 'You taking note?' To Stevie she explained, 'Frances has her own little clerk now, and her own little clerk's wife . . .'

Stevie listened to the story of the coming of the Barbers with the sort of wincing expression with which she might have heard out the symptoms of some embarrassing disease. As soon as she could, Frances turned the conversation. How were things, she asked, in the giddy world of ceramics? Stevie answered at length, telling her about a couple of new designs she was trying out. They were nothing avant-garde, unfortunately. No one wanted experiment any more; the art-buying public had become frightfully conservative since the War. But she was doing what she could to push the figurative into the abstract ... She leaned over the side of the armchair to fetch a book from her satchel, found pictures and passages to illustrate what she meant, even made a couple of quick sketches for Frances's benefit.

Frances nodded and murmured, glancing now and then at Christina; she was looking on, saying little, fiddling with the lace of one of Stevie's polished flat brown shoes. With her head tilted forward, the line of her fringe seemed blunter than ever, and the curls in front of her ears looked so flat and so pointed they might have been the blades of can-openers. In the old days, her hair had been long; she had worn it puffed around her head in a way that had always made Frances think, fondly, of a marigold. She'd had that marigold hairstyle the very first time Frances had caught sight of her, on a drizzly day in Hyde Park. She had been nineteen, Frances twenty. God, how distant that seemed! Or, no, not distant, but a different life, a different age, as unlike this one as pepper was salt. There had been a pearl brooch on her lapel, and one of her gloves had had a rip in it, showing the pink palm underneath. *My heart fell out of me and into that rip*, Frances had used to tell her, later.

Stevie ran out of steam at last. Frances seized the opportunity to rise and gather together the tea-things, visit the landing, wash her hands. 'Thanks for the smoke,' she said, as she pinned on her hat.

Stevie offered her case. 'Why not take one or two with you? They must make a change from those gaspers of yours.'

'Oh, I'm happy with the gaspers.'

'You are?'

Christina said, in her Bloomsbury voice, 'Let her be a martyr, Stevie. She likes it.'

They parted without a farewell kiss. Down in the lobby, Frances

47

caught sight of the porter's clock and saw with dismay that it was well past five. She had stayed longer than she'd meant to. She would have enjoyed the walk back to Vauxhall, or at least to Westminster, but there was dinner to be started at home. Rather regretting, now, having given that sixpence to the organ-grinder, and feeling guilty about her cosy-corner lunch, she decided to save a penny by taking a tram instead of a bus. She walked to Holborn for the tram she needed, had to wait an age before it came; then was rattled queasily across the river into the low, close streets of the south.

Almost the moment she left the tram she was approached by another ex-soldier, this one more ragged than the last. He limped along beside her, holding out a canvas bag, telling her the details of his military record: he'd served with the Worcesters in France and Palestine, been wounded in this and that campaign . . . When she shook her head at him he stopped, let her go on a couple of paces, and then called hoarsely after her:

'I hope you're never broke!'

She turned around, embarrassed, and tried to speak lightly. 'What makes you think I'm not broke already?'

He looked disgusted, raising his hand and then bringing it down, turning away. 'You've done all right, you bloody women,' she heard him say.

She had seen the same opinion, scarcely less bald, in the daily papers. But she arrived home more disgruntled than ever. She found her mother in the kitchen and told her all about it.

Her mother said, 'Poor fellow. He oughtn't to have spoken so roughly to you; that was certainly wrong. But one does have sympathy for all these fighting men whose jobs have been lost.'

'I have sympathy for them, too!' cried Frances. 'I was against their going to war in the first place! But to blame women—it's absurd. What have we gained, aside from a vote that half of us can't even use?'

Her mother looked patient. She had heard all this before. 'Well, no one is hurt. No one is injured.' She was watching Frances unpack her shopping. 'I don't suppose you found a match for my sewing silks?'

'Yes, I did. Here they are.'

Her mother took the reels and held them to the light. 'Oh, clever girl, these are—Oh, but you didn't buy Sylko?'

'These are just as good, Mother.'

'I do find Sylko the best.'

'Well, unfortunately it's also the most expensive.'

'But, surely, now that Mr and Mrs Barber have come—'

'We still need to be careful,' said Frances. 'We still need to be very careful.' She checked that the door was closed; they had already lowered their voices. 'Don't you remember, when I showed you the accounts?'

'Yes, but, well, it did cross my mind—I did just wonder, Frances, whether we mightn't be able to afford a servant again.'

'A servant?' Frances couldn't keep the impatience out of her tone. 'Well, yes, we might. But you know how much a decent cook-general costs nowadays. It would be half the Barbers' rent gone, just like that. And meanwhile our boots are falling in pieces, we dread ever having to send for the doctor, our winter coats look like things from the Dark Ages. And then, another stranger in the house, someone to have to get to know—'

'Yes, all right,' said her mother, hastily. 'I dare say you know best.'

'When I can take care of things perfectly well—'

'Yes, yes, Frances. I do see how impossible it is. Truly I do. Don't let's talk about it any more. Tell me about your day in Town. You made sure to have luncheon, I hope?'

Frances, with an effort, made herself sound less shrewish. 'Yes, I did. At a café.'

'And after that? Where did you go? How did you spend your afternoon?'

'Oh—' Turning away, she answered at random. 'I walked about a bit, that's all. I finished up at the British Museum. I had my tea there.'

'The British Museum? I haven't been there in years. What did you look at?'

'Oh, the usual galleries. Marbles, mummies, that sort of thing.—Look, how hungry are you?' She had opened the meat-safe door. 'We've skirt, again. I might run it through the mincer.' I shall enjoy doing that, she thought.

She did not enjoy it as much as she had hoped to. The beef was poor and kept clogging. She'd meant the meal to be an easy one, but, perhaps because she was discontented, the food seemed to turn against her, the potatoes boiling dry in their pan, the gravy refusing to thicken. Her mother, as sometimes happened, disappeared at the critical moment: she still liked to change her gown and re-pin her hair for dinner, and she tended to misjudge the minutes as she was doing it. By the time she had re-emerged, the food was cooling in its dishes. Frances almost ran with the plates to the drawing-room table. Another delay, then, while her mother said Grace . . .

She swallowed the food without enjoying it. They discussed the various appointments of the days ahead. Tomorrow they were off to the cemetery: it was her father's birthday; they were taking flowers to his grave. On Monday they must remember to change their library books. On Wednesday—

'Oh, now, on Wednesday,' said Frances's mother apologetically, 'I've promised to see Mrs Playfair. I really must see her next week, to discuss the bazaar, and Wednesday afternoon is the only time she can manage. We shall have to miss our trip to the cinema, I'm afraid. Unless we go another day?'

Frances felt absurdly disappointed. Could they make it Monday, instead? But, no, Monday wasn't possible, and neither was

Thursday. She could always go alone, of course. She could always invite a friend. She did have friends—not just Christina. She had friends right here in Camberwell. There was Margaret Lamb, a few houses down. There was Stella Noakes, from school—Stella Noakes, with whom she'd once, in a chemistry lesson, laughed so painfully hard that the two of them had wet their flannel drawers.

But Margaret was always so awfully earnest. And Stella Noakes was Stella Rifkind now, with two small children. She might bring the children along. Would that be fun? It hadn't been, last time. No, she'd rather go alone.

But how dismal, at her age, to be so disappointed over something like this! She pushed the food around on her plate, enjoying it less than ever—and picturing Christina and Stevie, who would almost certainly at that moment be eating some jolly scratch supper of macaroni, or bread and cheese, or fried fish and chips, and who might be heading off shortly to the sort of brainy West End entertainment—a lecture or a concert, cheap seats at the Wigmore Hall—to which Frances and Christina had used to like to go together.

Her spirits lifted slightly when, at half-past seven, Mr and Mrs Barber left the house, giving the distinct impression that they would be out until late. The moment they had gone she threw open the drawing-room door. She walked in and out of the kitchen and up and down the stairs, purely for the sake of being able to do so without fear of meeting anyone on the way. She lit the temperamental geyser and ran herself a bath, and as she lay in the water she summoned up a sense of possession and allowed it to expand across the house: she felt it as a physical sensation, a letting-out of breath, a loosening of nerves, through every blissfully untenanted room.

But by twenty to ten the Barbers were back. She heard the front door open and close and couldn't believe it. Mr Barber came straight out to visit the WC and caught her in the kitchen, in her dressing-gown and bedroom slippers, making cocoa. Oh, no, he said blandly, when she expressed surprise at seeing him, no, he wasn't home earlier than planned. He and Lilian had been for an early evening drink with a friend of his. The friend was an old army chum, and they'd gone to meet his fiancée . . . Not noticing, or not minding, that she gave him no encouragement, he settled himself in what was becoming his 'spot' in the scullery doorway, and told her all about it.

'The girl's a saint,' he said. 'Or else, I dunno, she's after his money! The poor devil lost both his arms, you see, Miss Wray, from here down.' He made a cutting gesture at his elbow. 'She'll have to feed him his dinners, shave him, comb his hair—do everything for him.' His blue eyes held hers. 'The mind fairly boggles, doesn't it?'

There it was, she thought, the little innuendo, as reliable as a cuckoo coming open-mouthed out of a clock. She wished he didn't feel it necessary to go on like this. She wished he'd leave her to herself in her kitchen. She was conscious of her dressing-gown, of the strands of damp hair at her neck, of her slightly downy ankles. She went rigidly back and forth between the counter and the stove, willing him to go; but, just as he had that other time, he seemed to like to watch her working. His colour was high, she noticed. He smelt, distinctly, of beer and cigarettes. She had the sense, perhaps unfair, that he was enjoying having her at a disadvantage.

He headed out to the yard at last. She washed up the milk pan, carried the cocoa through to the drawing-room, and as she handed the cup to her mother she said, 'I've just been collared by Mr Barber. What an annoying man he is. I've made every effort to like him, but—'

'Mr Barber?' Her mother had been dozing in her chair, and pushed herself up to sit more tidily. 'I am growing quite fond of him.'

Frances sat. 'You can't be serious. When do you see him, even?'

'Oh, we've had our chats. He's always very civil. I find him cheery.'

'He's a menace! How his wife ended up with him, I can't imagine. She seems such a pleasant woman. Not at all his type.'

They were speaking in their special furtive 'Barber' voice. But her mother blew on her cocoa and didn't reply. Frances looked at her. 'Don't you think?'

'Well,' she answered at last, 'Mrs Barber doesn't strike me as the most doting of wives. She might take a little more care, for instance, over her household duties.'

'Doting?' said Frances. 'Duties? How mid-Victorian you sound!'

'It seems to me that "Victorian" is a word that's used nowadays to dismiss all sorts of virtues over which people no longer wish to take the trouble. I always saw to it that the house was nicely kept for your father.'

'What you saw, in fact, was Nelly and Mabel keeping it nice for you.'

'Well, servants don't manage themselves—as you would know, if we still had any. They take a great deal of thought and care. And I always sat down to breakfast alongside your father looking cheerful and nicely dressed. That sort of thing means a great deal to a man. Mrs Barber—well, I am surprised that she returns to bed once her husband has gone to work. And when she does attend to her chores, she seems to do them at a gallop, in order to spend the rest of the day at her leisure.'

Frances had thought the same thing, with envy. She opened her mouth to say as much—then closed it again, and said nothing. She had noticed, perhaps belatedly, how weary her mother was looking tonight. Her cheeks seemed as slack and as dry as overwashed linen. It took her an age to drink her cocoa, and when she had put the cup aside she sat with her hands in her lap, the fingers moving restlessly together with a paper-like sound, her gaze unfixed, on nothing.

In another ten minutes they rose to go to bed. Frances lingered in the drawing-room to put things tidy and to turn down the lights, then headed across the hall, yawning as she went. But as she entered the kitchen passage she heard a cry of alarm or upset; she went running, and found her mother in the scullery, shrinking back in distress from the sight of something that was wriggling in the shadow of the sink.

They had been bothered by mice for a week or two, and Frances had put down traps. Now, at last, a mouse had been caught—but caught badly, pinned by its mangled back legs. It was making frantic efforts to escape.

She moved forward. 'All right.' She spoke calmly. 'I'll see to it.'

'Oh, dear!'

'Now, don't look.'

'Shall we call Mr Barber?'

'Mr Barber? Whatever for? I can do it.'

The mouse grew even more panicked at Frances's approach, its little front paws scrabbling uselessly at the wire that held it. There was no point in attempting to release it; it was too injured for that. But Frances didn't want to leave it to die. After a moment of indecision she ran water into a bucket and dropped the wriggling creature into it, trap and all. A single silvery bubble rose to the surface of the water, along with a line of blood, fine as dark red cotton.

'Those beastly traps!' said her mother, still upset.

'Yes, he was unlucky.'

'What will you do with him?'

She rolled up a sleeve, drew the trap from the bucket and shook off the drips. 'I'll take him outside, down to the ash-heap. You go on to bed.'

The water had made greasy-looking spikes of the mouse's fur, but in death the creature appeared oddly human, with pained, closed eyes and a slack lower jaw. She carefully released the little body, catching hold of it by its gristly tail. On a rack beside the back

54

door were various old coats and shoes. She thought she would do without a coat, but the grass might be damp; she stepped into a pair of galoshes that had once belonged to her brother Noel, and let herself out into the yard. With the mouse dangling from her fingers she clumped across to the lawn, then began to pick her way along the flagstone path that led down the garden.

Lights showed at one or two of her neighbours' windows, but the garden had high walls, a towering linden tree, shaggy laurels and hydrangeas, and was almost completely dark. She went by sense rather than by sight, having made the journey so many times before. Arriving at the low wooden fence that formed a screen around the ash-heap, she tossed the tiny corpse over. There was a percussive little rustle as it landed.

And after that there was a silence, one of those deep, deep hushes that sometimes fell or gathered up here on Champion Hill, even by daylight. They gave the place a lonely air, made it impossible to believe that just a stone's throw in any direction were houses with families and servants in them, that beyond the far garden wall was a cinder lane that led in a trice to a road, an ordinary road with rattling trams and buses on it. Frances thought of her walk through Westminster earlier that day; but she couldn't recapture it now. All that sort of thing had fallen away. Bricks, pavements, people: all melted away. There were only the trees, the plants, the invisible flowers, a sense of stealthy vegetable activity just below the surface of sound.

It was rather creepy, suddenly. She drew closed the lapels of her dressing-gown and turned to head back to the house.

But as she did it, something caught her eye: a point of light bobbing about on the darkness. A second later, smelling tobacco, she realised that the light was the burning tip of a cigarette. Her eyes changed their focus, and she made out a figure.

Someone was there, in the garden with her.

She let out a yelp of fear and surprise. But it was Mr Barber, that was all. He came forward, laughing, apologising for having given her a fright. The night was such a nice one, he said, that he'd stayed out to make the most of it. He hadn't liked to speak, before; it had seemed a pity to disturb her. He hoped she didn't mind, that he'd wandered down the garden?

For a moment she wanted to hit him. The blood was roaring through her ears; she felt herself quivering like a bell. She'd supposed that he'd gone up to bed ages ago. He must have been out here for—well, close on half an hour. She didn't like to think that he had been near by while she'd been standing at the ash-heap so unguardedly. She wished she hadn't let out that yelp. She was glad, at any rate, that he couldn't see her in Noel's galoshes.

And, after all, he had only done what she herself had done, been tempted to linger out here by the balminess of the night. Her quivering began to subside. She explained stiffly about the mouse, and he chuckled. 'Poor blighter! He just wanted his bit of cheese, didn't he?' He lifted his cigarette to his mouth, so that the blazing point of it reappeared, briefly illuminating his slender hand, his moustache, his foxy jaw.

But when the cigarette had faded he spoke again, and she could tell by the sound of his voice that he had tilted back his head.

'A grand night for star-gazing tonight, Miss Wray! I used to know all about the stars when I was a boy; it was a regular hobby of mine. I used to sneak out my bedroom window after the family were asleep and sit for hours on the scullery roof, with a library book and a bicycle lamp—matching the sky, you know, with the pictures. My brother Dougie caught me at it once, and locked the window on me, so that I had to stay out all night in the rain. He was always pulling stunts like that, my brother. But it was worth it. I had all the names: Arcturus, Regulus, Vega, Capella . . . '

He was murmuring now, and the words had a charm, spoken softly in the darkness. It was odd to be standing there with him, in her night-clothes, in that lonely spot—but then, she thought, it's only the garden. Looking back at the house she saw the lights: the kitchen door standing open, the window with its blind half lowered, the window above it, at the turn of the stairs, with the old Morris curtains not quite meeting in the middle.

And he had been right about the night. The moon was slim, the merest paring; against the deep blue-black of the sky the stars stood out, precise, electric. So she put back her head, and, 'Which one is Capella?' she asked, after a pause. She had been attracted by the name.

He gestured with the hand that held the cigarette. 'The bright little chap above your neighbour's chimney. That's Vega, over there. And up there—' He shifted about, and she turned to follow the glow of the cigarette. 'That's Polaris, the North Star.'

She nodded. 'I know the North Star.'

'You do?'

'I know the Plough, and Orion.'

'You're as good as a Girl Guide. How about Cassiopeia?'

'The ones shaped like an M? Yes, I know them.'

'They're a W tonight. You see them? That's Perseus beside them.'

'No, I don't see that.'

'It's a matter of joining the dots. You have to use your imagination. The fellows who did the naming—well, they were short on entertainments back then. How about Gemini, the twins?' He moved closer, and sketched an outline. 'You see the two of them? Holding hands? And just across from them there's the Lion . . . To the right of him there's the Crab. And there's the Whiting.'

She peered. 'The Whiting?'

'Just over there, beside the Whelk.'

She realised two things at the same moment: one, of course, that he was teasing her; the other that, in order to steer her gaze, he had moved very close to her and raised his free hand to the small of her back. The unexpectedness of the contact gave her a jolt: it made her start away from him, her shoulder clipping his as she did so, her galoshes noisy on the path. He seemed to step back too, to put up his hands in an exaggerated way, like a man caught out at something, playfully pretending innocence.

Or perhaps he really was innocent. She was suddenly uncertain. It was too dark to make out his expression; she could see only faint gleams of starlight at his eyes, his teeth. Was he smiling? Was he laughing at her? She had the tricked, trapped feeling she'd some-times had with men in the past, the sense that, through no act of her own, she had become a figure of fun, and that whatever she did or said now would only make her more of one.

And she felt the loneliness of the spot again, the moist and crafty garden. It seemed to be on Mr Barber's side, in a way it hadn't been before. She tightened the belt of her dressing-gown, straightened her back, and spoke coldly.

'You oughtn't to linger out here, Mr Barber. Your wife must be wondering where you are.'

As she expected, he laughed, though with a sort of wryness that she didn't understand.

'Oh, I dare say Lily can live without me for another minute or two. I'll just have my smoke out, Miss Wray, and then I'll wend my way to bed.'

She left him without a farewell, stumping back to the house, feeling just as much of a fool as she'd known she would. Once she had kicked off the galoshes she saw to the stove and the breakfast things at top speed, not wanting to have to encounter him for a third time that night. But in any case, he didn't appear. She was up in her room, groping for the pins in her hair, before she heard the back door closed and bolted.

She listened to his step on the stairs with a lingering crossness—but found herself curious, too, as to how he would greet his wife. She thought of Christina asking her if she had put a tumbler to the wall. But it wasn't eavesdropping, was it, if one simply stole closer to the door and tilted one's head?

She heard Mrs Barber's voice first. 'There you are! I thought you'd got lost. What have you been doing?'

He answered with a yawn. 'Nothing.'

'You must have been doing something.'

'Having a smoke, out the back. Looking at the stars.'

'The stars? Did you see your future in them?'

'Oh, I know that already, don't I?'

That was all they said. But the *way* in which they said it—the absolute deadness of their tones, the absence of anything like affection—took Frances aback. It had never occurred to her that their marriage might be anything other than happy. Now, astonished, she thought, Why, they might almost hate each other!

Well, their feelings were their own affair, she supposed. So long as they paid their rent . . . But that was thinking like a landlady; that was a horrible way to think. She didn't want them to be miserable. But she felt unnerved, too. She was reminded of how little she knew them. And here they were, at the heart of her house! Her mind ran back, unwillingly, to Stevie's warning about the 'clerk class'.

She wished now that she hadn't listened. She crept into bed and blew out her candle, but lay wakeful, open-eyed. She heard the couple moving about between their sitting-room and kitchen, and soon one of them paused on the landing—Mr Barber, yawning again. She watched the shrinking away of the light from under her door as he turned down the gas.

3

Her sense of disquiet passed with the night. When the couple rose in the morning they sounded ordinary, even cheerful. Mr Barber was humming as he shaved at the sink. Before he left for his half-Saturday at the office he said something in a low tone to his wife, and she answered him with laughter.

An hour or so later, Frances left the house herself: she went to the florist's to fetch the wreath for her father's grave. And as soon as she and her mother had had their lunch, they set off for the cemetery.

The weather had dulled overnight, and they had dressed for it, and for the occasion, in their soberest coats and hats. But it was May, after all: they grew warm on the journey to West Norwood, and warmer still as they made the long uphill walk to her father's plot. By the time they arrived at it, Frances was sweating. She took off her gloves, considered removing her hat—had got as far as drawing out its pin before she caught her mother's disapproving eye.

'Father wouldn't mind, would he? He hated being too warm himself, remember?'

'Father always knew when to keep a hat on, however warm he was.'

Frances thrust the pin back in, turning away. 'I'll bet he's warm just now.'

'What was that?'

'I said, "I'll get some water now."'

'Oh.' Her mother looked wary. 'Yes, do.'

They unpacked their tools, their cemetery kit: the trowel, the rake, the brush, the bottle, the bar of Monkey Brand. Her mother got to work on the weeds and the moss while Frances went to the tap. She returned to the grave to wet the brush and draw it across the soap, and then to start scrubbing at her father's headstone.

The stone was plain, solid, handsome—*expensive*, she thought, on every visit, with resentment; for, of course, the funeral arrangements had all been made in the first bewildering days after her father's death, before she and her mother had had a chance to discover just how stupendously he had managed to mishandle the family funds. JOHN FRYER WRAY, the inscription read, BELOVED HUSBAND AND FATHER, MUCH MISSED, the letters black against a marble that had once been a gleaming quartz white, but which the sooty drizzles of suburban south London were bent on staining khaki.

Running her brush in soapy circles over the tarnished marble she thought of her brother John Arthur's grave, just north of Combles: she and her mother had visited it, along with John Arthur's fiancée, Edith, in 1919. They had made the journey in December—perhaps the worst time to do it, for in the bitter weather the raw, still-shattered landscape had looked like a scene from hell. There had been no shred of comfort to be found in it, only a new sort of agony in thinking of the months that John Arthur had been forced to spend there. Since then, Frances had heard people speak of the consolations of the cemeteries. One of her mother's friends had described the sense of peace that had descended on her as she'd stood at her son's grave. She had heard his voice, she'd said, as clearly as she had ever heard it in life: he had told her not to mourn, that mourning was wasteful, mourning would keep the world in darkness when what it needed was to progress into light. At John Arthur's grave Frances had heard nothing save the wet cough of the elderly farmer who had guided the way to the site. The plot itself had meant little to her. It had simply been beyond belief that all she had known and loved about her brother should have had its finish in that slim depression of earth at her feet. She regretted ever having made the trip. She still visited the place, sometimes, in dreams, and felt the same empty horror; she was always alone on the sticky ground, sinking.

Then again, Noel had no grave at all, and that was hard in a different way. He had been lost in the Mediterranean, in the final year of the War, when the ship on which he'd been travelling out of Egypt had been torpedoed. How exactly had he died? Had he drowned? Could he have been killed in the first blast? There had been confusion at the time, someone claiming to have seen him floating face-down in the water, someone else alleging that he had been hauled on to a raft, wounded but very much alive. But no such raft had ever been found. Might the enemy have picked him up? Certainly his body was never recovered; and so many tales had been told, in those days, of the miraculous reappearances of shell-shocked soldiers that for months after his death, well into the first year of Peace, Frances's mother had clung on to the hope of his return. There had been several dreadful moments: knocks at the door at odd hours, boys on the street who faintly resembled him . . . Frances shuddered to remember that time now. Poor, poor Noel. He had been the baby of the family. When she thought of him she saw him not as the nineteen-year-old he had been when he was killed, but as a boy in a striped pyjama suit, his pink feet smooth and rounded as pebbles. She remembered him once on the beach at Eastbourne, crying because a wave had gone over his head; she had jeered at his faint heart. She would give anything to be able to take that jeer back.

Don't think of it. Chase it away. Wet the brush again, quickly,

quickly. Here was a spot that she had missed. Look how nicely the marble scrubbed up! That was better . . . She had left the headstone now and was inching her way around the coving. A few more trips to the tap, and the job was done. Next time, she and her mother decided as they rose, they would bring a garden sieve and go through the earth properly; but they'd made it neat enough for this visit. Frances put away their tools, wiped her hands and addressed the grave.

'Well, Father, there you are, all spruce and tidy for your birthday. It's more than you deserve, I'm sure.'

'Frances,' her mother scolded.

'What? I'd say the same thing to his face if he were here right now. That, and a good many other things. I suppose he'd manage not to hear them. It was about the only thing he *could* manage.'

'Hush.'

They stood a little longer, her mother dipping her head and closing her eyes in silent prayer, while Frances surreptitiously drew her wool collar away from her hot neck. They made the walk back to the gates through the older part of the cemetery, the part she by far preferred, with its vulgar last-century monuments, its weeping angels, its extinguished torches, its stone ships in full sail. She read aloud the Dickensian surnames. 'Bode . . . Epps . . . Tooley . . . Weatherwax! Queer how the names belong to the period. Can surnames change, like fashions?'

'Perhaps nobody cared to marry poor Mr Weatherwax.'

'That's what you think. "Sorely missed by his five surviving sons"! There ought to be Weatherwaxes all over the place at that rate.'

Out on the street, they gazed doubtfully upward. Frances's father had always admired the flower gardens in Dulwich Park, and they had planned to take a bus there, have their tea in the café, make a subdued Saturday afternoon of it. But the sky was darker and lower than ever—'Thundery,' said Mrs Wray, who since the

War was bothered by storms. They decided to give the day up and go straight home. They took a bus directly to Champion Hill, and had just stepped from its platform when the first great drops of rain came plashing down. They ran the last few yards to the house—Frances going quickest, to have the door open and ready. They tumbled into the hall, gasping and laughing and pulling off their wet things.

Almost as soon as the door was closed behind them they became aware of a stir of voices and movement in the rooms upstairs. There were thumps, and bursts of laughter, followed by quick, light footsteps. Mrs Wray, taking off her hat, raised apprehensive eyes: 'Good gracious!'

Frances's heart sank. 'The Barbers,' she murmured, 'must be entertaining.'

As she spoke, the footsteps crossed to the stairs, and the banisters of the upper flight were grasped and set creaking by small, sticky-looking hands. And then a couple of children appeared at the turn, a girl of seven or eight and a younger boy. The boy came first, frowning, determined, but troubled by the trickiness of the descent. Catching sight of Frances and her mother he gave a wobble, mid-step; then, blind with terror, he turned and groped his way past the girl's legs to scramble back upward. The girl stayed where she was, holding Frances's gaze, sucking in her lower lip and laughing.

'He's a baby,' she said.

Frances's mother, her hat in her hand, had moved forward to peer anxiously after him.

'He's certainly too much of a baby to be allowed on these stairs. If he should fall—Go back, child!'

The boy, safe now on the landing, and attracted by the tremor of alarm in her voice, had put his head through the spindles of the section of banister directly above her. She grew pale. 'Get away!' She made shooing motions at him. 'Go back, little boy! Oh, if the banisters should break! Frances—'

'Yes, all right,' said Frances, going ahead of her, beginning to climb.

At her approach the girl sped off with a giggle, and the boy hastily withdrew his head. He must have caught his ear against one of the spindles as he did it, because after he'd gone scampering away in terror again—into the Barbers' sitting-room this time, with the girl charging behind him—Frances heard him begin to wail. The wail was answered by a woman's voice, brisk and satisfied: 'Well, *now* what have you done!' At the same moment another woman put her face around the sitting-room door. Neither the voice nor the face belonged to Mrs Barber. This woman was older, perhaps Frances's age. Her waved hair was glossy with oil, her mouth liberally lipsticked, her features rather sharp. She saw Frances and her mother advancing warily up the stairs and said, 'Oh.' She emerged further. 'Did you want Lil? She's out the back.'

Frances, coming to a halt a stair or two from the top, explained about having been anxious for the children. She was afraid that she and her mother had frightened the little boy. She thought he might have hurt his ear on the banister?

Aside from the moans of the injured child, the Barbers' sitting-room, it seemed to her, had grown unnaturally still. She had the disturbing sense of its being packed with eavesdropping strangers. Unable to see anything past its partly open door, she said, 'Is Mr Barber here, perhaps?'

The woman snorted. 'Lenny? Not him! He's keeping out of our way. Lil won't be a minute, though, if it's her you're after.'

'No, it isn't that,' repeated Frances. 'We just wanted to be sure about the little boy.' She added, a touch crisply, 'I'm Miss Wray. This is Mrs Wray, my mother. We're the owners of the house.'

At that, from the silent sitting-room, there burst yet another woman's voice—a jolly, throaty, hop-picker's one. 'Is that Mrs Wray? Is that Mrs Wray, Vera?'

The sharp-faced woman tilted her head, and with her gaze

moving coolly between Frances and her mother she called back into the room: 'Yes, and Miss Wray too!'

'Well, for goodness sake, bring the ladies in! Don't leave the poor things standing out there on the landing, in their own house.'

The woman shrugged, and half smiled—as if to say to Frances, not unkindly, *Now you're for it.* She moved back into the sitting-room, opening the door wider so that the Wrays might follow. Frances glanced at her mother; she was madly re-pinning her hat. The two of them climbed the last few stairs and crossed the landing.

Entering a fug of scent and cigarette smoke they found—not a crowd, after all, but three women, sitting in chairs drawn together around the unlighted hearth. Frances noticed the chairs first, in fact, because one of them, a black oak armchair, looking surprisingly at home among the Barbers' rococo trimmings, was not actually the Barbers' at all; it was one of her father's Jacobean monstrosities and had been brought up from the kitchen passage downstairs. Seated on it now was a short, stout woman of fifty or so, with brown button eyes, dreadfully swollen ankles, and hair so artificially frizzed and hennaed it resembled the lustreless wig of a waxwork. It was she, obviously, who had called out to the landing, for as Frances and her mother made their awkward entrance she said, in the same game Cockney tones, 'Oh, Mrs Wray, Miss Wray, how very nice to meet you! How nice indeed! And Lil said we shouldn't see you—that you'd be out all afternoon. Oh, what luck! I'm Mrs Viney. I hope you'll excuse my not rising to shake your hands. You may see the state of things with me.' She indicated her appalling ankles. 'Once I'm down, I have to stay down. Min'—she leaned to tap at the arm of a sandy-faced girl on the sofa—'give Mrs Wray your place, my darling. You can make do with the puff, a slip like you.—This is Min, my youngest,' she told Frances, as if that explained everything. 'Miss Lynch, I suppose I ought to call her, in a well-to-do house like this! And here's Mrs Rawlins and

Mrs Grice. My Lord, don't that make me feel old! Mrs Grice you've just met, of course.'

Frances could do nothing but move forward across a floor littered with bags and scarves and elaborate hats to shake hands with each of the visitors in turn. Her mother, protesting feebly that they oughtn't to trouble, that she wouldn't stay, was somehow steered to the vacant place on the sofa, beside the sharp-faced Mrs Grice— Vera. The girl called Min sat down on a red leather pouffe. Frances took the remaining empty chair, beside the woman who had been introduced as Mrs Rawlins.

Mrs Rawlins was sitting in a pink plush easy chair of the Barbers'; she occupied it with an air of entitlement, like a slightly smug Madonna. The little boy had his face in her lap, his long-lashed eyes still wet with tears, but the tears themselves apparently forgotten; he seemed to be idly biting her thigh. He gazed up at Frances as he did it, and she repeated her anxiety about his having put his head between the banisters and possibly hurt his ear. Mrs Rawlins smiled—smiled in that pitying, knowing way in which married women often smiled, Frances had found, at the fears of spinsters, saying, Oh, they had ears of India-rubber at that age. And, to prove it, she reached for one of the boy's already scarlet ears and drew the top and bottom tips of it together, then let them spring back against his scalp. The visitors laughed—the little girl laughing loudest, on a forced, hard, jarring note. The boy clapped his hands to his head, looking torn between triumph at having made a comedian of himself and mortification at the way he had done it. Mrs Viney, still tittering, said, 'Poor Maurice. We oughtn't to laugh. But there, if little boys will go putting their heads through other people's banisters, they must expect to be laughed at.' Her tone grew indulgent as she spoke, and she held out her hands to him. 'Oh, come here to Nanny!'

Come here to Nanny . . . While she fussed with the boy, the younger women looking on, Frances began to catch the resemblances between them all. Mrs Rawlins—Netta, the others called her—was, she realised, simply a more matronly Min. Vera had Mrs Viney's button eyes, though with a drier expression in them. Even the boy and girl, she saw now, had the family look, the girl solid on sturdy legs, the boy fair but with the sort of fairness that would quickly darken, and each of them with a pink, full, elastic, unchildlike mouth—Mrs Barber's mouth, in fact. She had just, with relief and surprise, worked the mystery out, when Mrs Barber herself came breathlessly into the room.

She caught Frances's eye first. 'Miss Wray, I'm so sorry! Mrs Wray, how are you?' Her smile pulled tight, and her tone wavered. 'You've met my mother and my sisters, then?'

'Oh, we're great pals already,' said Mrs Viney comfortably. 'And there you were, Lil, saying as how the ladies would be out all day!'

'She was hoping you wouldn't meet us,' Vera told Frances. 'She's ashamed of us.'

'Don't be silly,' said Mrs Barber, blushing.

But, 'Yes, that's the truth of it!' their mother cried gaily, her old-fashioned stays giving off a volley of pops and creaks. 'Still, we make up in cheerfulness, Mrs Wray, what we lack in nice manners. And, oh, I do think this house delightful, really I do.'

Frances's mother, flushing, blinking, rapidly adjusting to the situation, said, 'Thank you. Yes, it's been a happy family home in its day. A little large, that's all, for my daughter and me to manage now.'

'Oh, no, you don't want all that trouble. No, there's nothing like a big house for trouble. There's nothing brings your spirits down, I always think, like an empty room. You shall enjoy having company here now, I expect. And don't you keep the back garden lovely!'

'Oh, you've seen the garden, then?'

'Yes, Lil took us over it.'

'Just quickly,' said Mrs Barber.

'You might be right in the country here. Why, you'd never know you had a neighbour! Gives you quite a bank holiday mood. You could bring in trippers and do them teas. Now, a pokey old place like ours—we live behind my husband's shop, on the Walworth Road, Vera, Min and me—well, that's just old-fashioned. But a charming place like this . . . '

She gazed appreciatively around the room—which seemed to have acquired even more flourishes since Frances had glimpsed it last, the hob grate with a bunch of paper poppies standing in it, the sofa covered in what looked like a chenille table-cloth, complete with bobbles on its hem, and the mantelpiece crowded now with postcards and ornaments: ebony elephants, brass monkeys, a china Buddha, a Spanish fan; the tambourine was there too, its ribbons trailing. 'I was saying to the girls before you come up,' Mrs Viney went on warmly, 'isn't it wonderful to think of all the ladies that must have lived here in days gone by, in their bonnets and fine frocks? Such skirts those frocks had, didn't they! Yards of material in them! Makes you wonder how they got on, with all the muck on the streets back then. Makes you wonder how they got up the stairs, even. As for visiting certain other little places—'

'Mum!' cried her daughters. Mrs Barber cried it loudest of all.

Mrs Viney opened wide her button eyes. 'What? Oh, Mrs Wray knows it's only my fun. So does Miss Wray, I'm sure. Besides, we're all ladies here.'

At that the little girl began to protest that they were *not* all ladies; that there were boys there too. Mrs Viney, still comfortable, said, 'Well, you know what I mean.'

But, no, the little girl *didn't* know what she meant, because *Maurice* wasn't a lady, and *Siddy* wasn't a lady. Siddy wasn't even a *boy* yet, he was too little—

'That's enough from you, madam,' said Vera sharply, while Frances, puzzled, thought, *Siddy?* The girl pushed out her grown-up mouth, but fell silent. Mrs Viney was saying again, Yes, she did

69

think the house a fine one. 'Such a bit of luck for Lil and Len. And hasn't Lil done the rooms up nice! She always was the artistic one in the family.—No, Lil, you was!' She gave Frances a wink. 'I'm making her blush, look.'

'It's her artist's temperament,' said Vera, in her dry way.

'Well, I don't know which side she gets it from. Not from mine, that's for sure! And as for her dear father, God rest him, why, he couldn't hang a picture straight on a nail, let alone paint one—'

Her words were broken into by an extraordinary noise, a snuffling, gurgling, animal sound, that made Frances and her mother give starts of alarm. The sisters, by contrast, grew hushed. Vera peered over the arm of the sofa into a large straw bag that was sitting beside it—a bag which Frances, all this time, had taken for a simple hold-all, but which she now realised was a carrying basket for an infant. There was a moment of suspense. The women spoke in whispers. Was he going off? Was he off? Had he gone? But then the snuffling started up again, and almost instantly exploded into a howl.

'Oh, dear!'

'Dear, dear!'

'Never mind!'

'*Here* he is!'

Vera had put her hands into the basket and lifted out a kicking baby in a knitted yellow suit. This was Siddy, then: she handed him across the hearth-rug to Netta, who set him on her lap with his limbs still thrashing, his big puce-coloured head rolling about on a stem-like neck.

'Won't you smile for the ladies?' she asked him. 'No? Not after Mrs Wray, and Miss Wray, have come all the way up to see you? Oh, what a face!'

'P'raps he's hungry,' suggested Mrs Viney, as the child continued to howl.

'He's always hungry, this one. He's like his dad in that department.'

'How's his napkin?'

Netta patted his bottom. 'His napkin's all right. He just wants to join in. Don't you? Hey?'

She bounced the baby on her knee, and his head rolled more wildly, though his cries began to subside.

Frances's mother, who liked babies, leaned forward for a better view. 'Quite the little emperor, isn't he?' she said, with a smile.

'He's that, all right,' said Mrs Viney, showing the gaps in her teeth. 'He can scream like a lord, anyhow. Oh, just look at him! Like a great big turnip, isn't he? We're hoping he'll grow into his head. And his big brother there was just the opposite. Do you remember, Netta? Oh, his head was that small, you could have darned your stocking on it!' She had to wipe away tears of laughter. 'Have you any other children, Mrs Wray? You won't mind my asking, I'm sure.'

'I don't mind at all,' answered Frances's mother, drawing her gaze from the wobbling infant in Netta's lap. 'I had three children altogether. My sons both gave their lives in the War.'

Mrs Viney's face became stripped of its mirth. She said, 'Oh, now ain't that a shame. Oh, I *am* sorry for you. My brother lost two of his boys the same way—and had another sent home with his eyes shrivelled right up in his head. Vera's husband, Arthur, we lost too. Didn't we, Ver? I used to pine after boys, you know, Mrs Wray, when I was a young married woman. I could never hang on to boy babies, I don't know why. I had two misses and a still, and they were all boys, the midwife told me; the last one such a dear little mite, too.'

'What's a still?' asked the girl.

The women ignored her. Min said, 'I remember that. I remember Daddy crying over it and telling me he had pepper in his eyes.'

'He was a dear man, your father,' said Mrs Viney, smiling. 'An Irishman, Mrs Wray. Sentimental, as they all are. Yes, we were both of us very cut up to lose that last one. But, now, do you know, I'm not sure I should have liked that little boy to have grown up, if he was only to have been killed like his cousins.'

She sighed and shook her head, and again her face lost its jollity, and her high colour was revealed for what it really was, a spider's web of broken veins in yellow, deflated cheeks. Her button eyes looked suddenly naked—as if life had used her so hard, thought Frances, it had had the very lashes off her.

The girl repeated, 'What's a still?'

Vera answered her at last. 'Something I wish you'd been.'

Frances's mother looked startled. Mrs Barber dipped her head as if mortified. But the visitors rocked with heartless laughter, Mrs Viney fishing a hanky from her sleeve in order to mop her freshly running eyes. The baby watched the merriment with a solemn expression—then gave a sudden chortle, as if just getting the joke. That made everyone laugh again. Netta squeezed and jiggled him to make him chortle harder. His head rolled, his mouth and chin grew wet, and he kicked her in the stomach in his excitement.

And with that, the mood of the gathering made a slight but definite shift. Vera groped about in her handbag and offered cigarettes. Frances's mother, looking startled again, shook her head; Frances reluctantly shook hers. But the younger women struck matches, reached for the stand-ashtray, and began to reclaim the conversation. There began to be mentions, Frances noticed, of 'his nibs', 'his lordship'—'Well, you can guess what *he* said!', 'I didn't pay any mind to *him*!'—at which Mrs Viney made occasional, ineffectual protests: 'Oh, now don't be nasty! Your poor step-dad don't mean no harm!' The family, like a clockwork engine, had made its way over the minor obstacle of the Wrays' entrance and was returning to what were evidently very comfortable lines. Frances, looking from sister to sister, saw clearly the role that had been won by each—or, more likely, had been foisted on them by the demands of the machine—tart Vera, capable Netta, simple-minded, sandy-faced Min.

And then, of course, there was Mrs Barber: Lilian, Lily, Lil. She had been keeping to the edge of the group all this time, leaning sometimes against the mantelpiece, sometimes against the arm of the sofa; looking, every few minutes, in a worried sort of way, at Frances and her mother. She was wearing a plum-coloured frock of soft material, with panels of crochet at its bosom and on the cuffs of its short sleeves; she had teamed it with olive-green stockings and her Turkish slippers, and around her neck was a string of red wooden beads, clicking together like an abacus with every slight movement. 'The artistic one in the family,' her mother had called her, Frances remembered, and it was certainly true that, dress-wise, she had little in common with her sisters, who were all decked out like chorus girls in faux-silk frocks, open-work stockings, high-heeled shoes, wristlets and anklets; nor did her careful accent much resemble theirs. She was moving away from the circle of chairs now. The little boy, her nephew, had approached her with some whispered request; she caught hold of his hand to lead him across the littered carpet, and began gathering titbits for him from the remains of a tea of buns and biscuits that lay scattered on the table on the other side of the room. The boy took the plate she offered and carefully held it to his chest; when its contents began to slip she tucked her skirt behind her thighs and lowered herself at his side to steady it. She did it in one smooth, supple motion, her heels rising out of her slippers, her calves showing, pale and rounded, through the sheen of her stockings. The little boy bit into a biscuit, scattering crumbs into the crochet at her bosom.

She didn't notice the crumbs. She made her plump lips plumper, to plant an idle sort of kiss on the child's fair head. Just as the kiss was finished she looked up, saw Frances watching, and dropped her gaze, self-conscious. But when Frances, smiling, continued to watch, she raised her eyes again and smiled uncertainly back.

But now the boy's cousin, the little girl, had realised that there were treats to be had. She picked her way over and asked for a biscuit of her own. That made Mrs Viney wonder if there mightn't be biscuits enough for everybody . . . Frances looked at her mother, and her mother gave the slightest of nods: they rose and began to say their farewells. Detaching themselves from the fibres of Mrs Viney's goodwill took several more minutes, but finally they made it out to the landing.

Mrs Barber made a point of going with them. And when Frances's mother had started on her way downstairs, she beckoned Frances back and spoke quietly.

'I'm so sorry about the chair, Miss Wray. I know you noticed it. Please tell your mother how sorry I am. I'd hate you to think we'd gone helping ourselves to your things. Only, my mother needs a hard armchair, because her back and her legs are bad, and Len and I haven't got one.'

'That's all right,' said Frances.

'It isn't, but you're kind to say so. It was nice of you to come in. My family's such a noisy one. They won't stay much longer. They only came for an hour, but then it started raining. And I think—' She nodded to Frances's sober costume. 'I'm afraid you must have been somewhere solemn today, you and your mother?'

Frances explained about the visit to her father's grave.

Mrs Barber looked appalled. 'Oh, and for you to have come home and found all these people here!'

She put a hand to her head, disarranging the curls of her hair. She still had crumbs in the panel of her gown: Frances felt a housewifely urge—a housespinsterly urge, she supposed it ought to be called, in her case—to brush them free. Instead, she moved towards the stairs.

'Your family must stay as long as they like, Mrs Barber. They shan't disturb us. Truly.'

Downstairs, however, it was possible to hear quite clearly the women's laughter, the drum of the children's feet. As Frances

74

closed the drawing-room door the joists above it creaked, then creaked again—even the walls seemed to creak—as if a giant had the house in his hands and was squeezing and jiggling it just as Netta had squeezed and jiggled her chortling child.

Her mother had planted herself in her chair by the French windows with an air of exhaustion.

'Well!' she said. 'What a very surprising family for Mrs Barber to have produced! Or what a surprising family to have produced Mrs Barber, is what I suppose I mean. I was under the impression that her father managed a business of some kind. Didn't she tell us that? And that she had a brother in the Navy?'

Frances leaned on the back of the sofa. 'A brother in the—? Oh, Mother, don't be so elderly. That was all my fancy, don't you remember?'

'*Is* the father a businessman?'

'The father's dead. Mrs Viney is a widow and has remarried. To a shopkeeper, whom all the girls despise. He must run that drapers by the fried fish shop.' And then, when her mother looked blankly at her: 'Can you think of another on the Walworth Road?'

Her mother took in what she was saying. 'The Walworth Road? Not really, Frances?'

'Weren't you paying attention?'

'Well, it was hard to keep one's eye from wandering. Mrs Barber's decorations—I hadn't an idea! It looks like the house of Ali Baba! Or the Moulin Rouge! Or the Taj Mahal! If only she would decide on a country and have done with it. Is that what passes for modern décor? If your dear father—You noticed his chair, I suppose?'

'Mrs Barber explained about that just now. She was most apologetic. Her mother has a "back", apparently.'

'Well, I'm amazed that's all she has! What Amazons those girls are. And Mrs Viney herself hardly more than four feet high!'

'Still,' said Frances, smiling, 'I liked her. Didn't you? A kind woman, I think.'

'I think so too,' her mother admitted. 'But the sort of kindness of which—let's be truthful, Frances—a little goes a long way. And why must people of that class always reveal so much of themselves? A few minutes more and she would have shown us her varicose veins.' She peered anxiously down the room towards the window overlooking the street. 'I wonder if the Dawsons saw her come. Oh, I know it's unchristian of me, but I do hope she doesn't think of visiting too often.'

'Well, I hope she does,' said Frances. 'She's perked me up no end. She's as good as a trip to a gin-palace.'

Her mother smiled, wanly—then flinched and looked anxious at another roar of mirth from the floor above. 'Oh, but I *do* hope they won't visit too often. I never heard such gales of laughter! And some of it in very questionable taste. No wonder Mr Barber is keeping away, poor man. Oh, they're not at all what I expected from Mrs Barber, Frances. If we had known—Oh, dear. I can't help but feel that she—well—'

'What?' asked Frances, smiling, heading for the kitchen. 'That she's sold us a pup? I think it makes her more interesting. How hard she must have worked for those green stockings!'

The children continued to charge about for another half-hour, and laughter still gusted out of the sitting-room; but then there came a spell of footsteps and creaking so intense it could mean only that the sisters were up and on the move, shifting chairs, tidying and gathering. As Frances and her mother had their tea, gas pulsed through the meter and china was rattled in the sink. There was the inevitable clip of heels on the stairs as, one after another, the women came down to visit the WC, bringing the protesting children with them. Finally there was the slow descent of Mrs Viney, and prolonged, hilarious farewells in the hall. The little girl discovered the dinner-gong, and struck it, and was smacked.

Frances's mother had taken up her work-box and sat sewing

through the hubbub as if determined not to wince. Frances herself had an open book in her lap, but, distracted, kept going over and over the same two pages. As soon as the front door was closed and Mrs Barber was on her way back upstairs she put the book aside and, unable to resist, she tiptoed across to the window and watched the visitors as they headed off in the direction of Camberwell. There they went, in their gaudy coats, their complicated hats, Netta leading the way with her baby at her shoulder, looking like the Triumph of Twentieth-Century Motherhood, while Mrs Viney, arm in arm with Vera and Min, a sham-leather bag clutched to her bosom, made her slow, good-humoured, late-Victorian progress behind. The children were twirling stems of lavender, plucked from pots in the front garden. More stems lay broken in the garden itself.

'Paul Pry,' said Frances's mother, from the rear of the long room.

Frances answered without turning. 'I don't care. I want to be certain that no one's been left behind. One, two, three, four, five, six—seven, if you include the baby. Can that be right? I'm sure there weren't so many an hour ago.'

'Perhaps they've bred another in the meantime.'

'Poor Mrs Viney. Her ankles! They look like the kind one keeps umbrellas in.'

'Perhaps one of us ought to go out to the kitchen and count the spoons.'

'Mother! As if they'd be interested in our old spoons. They're more likely to have left us a couple of shillings on the hall table. Just quietly, you know, so as not to embarrass us—'

She turned away from the glass as another thump came from the floor above.

Her mother was wincing at last. 'Oh, this really is too bad. What on earth is Mrs Barber doing now?'

The sound came again, from the landing this time, and soon the staircase began to creak, there was a bumping of wood against the banisters . . .

Frances started forward. 'She's bringing down the chair. She'll have the paper off the walls!—Everything all right, Mrs Barber?' she called, going out into the hall and closing the drawing-room door behind her.

'Yes, quite all right!' came the breathless reply. But Frances went up and found her struggling. The chair was heavy, and its legs were caught: between them they freed it, manoeuvred it around the bend of the staircase, then carried it safely down to the hall.

Frances fitted it precisely back into its spot and gave it a pat. 'There, you charlatan. A little adventure for you. I don't believe anyone's ever actually sat on it before, you know.'

Mrs Barber, still embarrassed, said, 'I really oughtn't to have taken it. My sisters talked me into it. They boss me; they always have. I'm afraid it's awfully old, too.'

'Well, my father certainly thought so. No, your sisters were quite right. I'm glad you found a use for it.'

'Well, you've been kind about it. Thank you.'

She was moving back towards the stairs already. How different she was from her husband! He would have lingered, got in the way. Frances, if anything, was sorry to see her go. She remembered how curiously appealing she had looked as she'd squatted at her nephew's side, with her green-stockinged heels rising out of her embroidered slippers. She had shaken the crumbs from her gown at last, but the curls of her hair were still disordered, and again Frances had the housewifely impulse to pat her back into shape.

Instead she said, 'You look weary, Mrs Barber.'

Mrs Barber's hand went to her cheek. 'Do I?'

'Why not sit down with me for a moment? Not on this monster, I mean, but'—she gestured over her shoulder—'out in the kitchen? Just for a minute?'

Mrs Barber looked uncertain. 'Well, I don't want to keep you.'

'You won't be keeping me from anything except perhaps thinking about my next chore. And I can do that any old time . . . Do say yes. I've meant to ask you before. Here we are, sharing a house, and we've barely spoken. It seems a pity, don't you think?'

Her tone was a sincere one, and Mrs Barber's expression changed. She said, with a smile, 'It does rather, doesn't it? Yes, all right.'

They went the short distance into the kitchen. Frances offered a chair.

'May I make you some tea?' she asked, as Mrs Barber sat.

'Oh, no. I've been drinking tea all afternoon.'

'A slice of cake, then?'

'I've been eating cake, too! You have something, though, will you?'

Frances was thinking it over. She said, 'To tell the truth, what I really want right now—' Going across to the open doorway, she put her head out into the passage, listening for sounds of activity in the drawing-room. Hearing none, she moved back, noiselessly closed the door, and reached into the pocket of the apron that was hanging on the back of it. 'My mother,' she murmured, bringing out tobacco, papers and matches, 'doesn't approve of me smoking. Watching your sisters all at it earlier I thought I'd just about burst. Now, if I'm caught, I'll blame this on you. I'm a good liar, so be prepared.' She joined Mrs Barber at the table, and offered the packet of papers. 'Want one?'

Mrs Barber gave a quick, tight shake of her head. 'I've never got the knack of rolling them.'

'Well, I could roll one for you, if you like?'

At that, she hesitated, biting her full lower lip. Then, 'Oh, why not?' she said, with an air of naughtiness. 'Yes, go on.'

The whole business seemed to amuse her. She watched in a fascinated way as Frances set out the papers and teased the tobacco from the tin, leaning in for a closer look as the first of the cigarettes took shape, resting her bare lower arms on the table. She had a bangle around one of her wrists, a red wooden thing that matched her necklace; but she wore no rings, Frances noticed, except for a slender wedding-band, with beside it, also slender, a half-hoop of tiny engagement diamonds. 'How quick you are,' she said, impressed, when Frances had raised the cigarette to her mouth to run the tip of her tongue along the line of gum. And then, when both cigarettes were finished: 'They're so neat, it seems a pity to smoke them.' But she leaned into the flame that Frances offered— placing a hand on Frances's, just for a moment, to steady herself, so that Frances had a brief but vivid sense of the warmth and the life in her fingers and palm.

And the cigarette changed her, somehow. Some of her girlishness fell away. She sat back after the first puff, picking a strand of tobacco from her lip with a casual, practised gesture, and, 'Len ought to see us now,' she said. 'He's like your mother, Miss Wray, and doesn't really want me smoking. But then, men never *do* want women to do the things they want to do themselves, have you noticed?'

She had spoken conventionally. But Frances, looking for something that would serve as an ashtray, finally pulling across a saucer, said, 'Things like voting, you mean? Standing for Parliament? No, I hadn't noticed that at all. Let's see, what else? Managing industries? Working whilst married? Suing for divorce? Stop me if I become boring.'

Mrs Barber laughed. The laughter was mixed with the smoke from her cigarette: it seemed to come visibly out of her pursed, plump mouth, and was so warm, so real, so unlike her usual automatic tittering, that Frances felt an odd thrill of triumph at having called it into life.

Once it had faded, however, they sat without speaking, in a silence broken only by soft kitchen noises, the tick of the clock, the stir of coals in the stove, the faintly musical drip of water in the scullery sink. They caught one another's eye. Frances said, 'I liked meeting your family today.'

Mrs Barber regarded her warily. 'It's nice of you to say so.'

'I'm not saying it to be nice. I don't say things I don't mean.'

'I was worried about you meeting them. You, and your mother.'

'You were? Why?'

'Well . . . Len said you'd think them common.'

Frances, remembering watching the visitors go from the drawing-room window, felt a smudge of guilt. She felt a smudge of something else, something darker, towards Mr Barber. Tapping ash into the saucer, she said firmly, 'I'm very glad they came. I specially liked your mother.—Now, why do you look like that?'

Mrs Barber had sagged slightly. 'Only that, well, people *do* like her. And the fact is, she plays up to it. She must always be a character, my mother. Some of the things she said this afternoon! I don't know what Mrs Wray must have thought. And then, she *will* go about in those cheap old things of hers, when she has plenty of money, now, to buy better.' She tapped ash from her own cigarette, looking guilty. 'I oughtn't to be so unkind, ought I? She's had such a bad time of it, one way and another. We were—We were terribly poor, you know, when I was young, after my father died and before my mother married Mr Viney. I'm ashamed to tell you how poor. My mother worked too hard. That's why her back's so bad. And you saw her legs?'

Frances grimaced. 'Can nothing be done?'

'Oh, she won't do what the doctor tells her. And then, Mr Viney will never let her rest. She must be up and down doing things for him every hour of the day and night. He looks at a woman sitting idle and sees a knife going to rust, I think.' She turned her head. The clock was chiming. 'Is that five, already? Len'll be back any minute. He's been over at his parents'. I ought to go and tidy up. His mother keeps their house like a pin.'

She spoke with a slight yawn, however, and remained in her chair, plainly enjoying her cigarette, evidently glad to be talking so freely. She had quite let slip the air she'd sometimes had with

Frances in the past, of being on her best behaviour. She put an elbow on the table and leaned with her chin on her hand, the flesh of her arm looking rounded, solid, smooth. There were no angles to her at all, thought Frances with envy. She was all warm colour and curve. How well she filled her own skin! She might have been poured generously into it, like treacle.

Now she was smiling, savouring the silence. 'Isn't it lovely and quiet here? I never knew a house be so quiet; at least, I never knew a quiet like this one. It's like velvet. When it was quiet at Cheveney Avenue—Len's parents'—it used to make me want to scream. They're not at all alike, you see, his side and mine.'

'No?'

'No! My sisters and I were all brought up Catholic like our father. Not that we ever go to mass any more or anything like that. But, well, that sort of thing sticks. Len's parents think me a heathen. They're chapel people. And his cousin was in the Black and Tans.—Len's not like that,' she added hurriedly, seeing Frances's expression. 'But his parents and his brothers—Oh, they've no sense of art, or life, or anything. If you so much as open a book in front of them you get called grand. Here, you can be calm, and the house seems to like it. And nobody needs to know what you're doing! Not like the houses I grew up in. You knew it if the neighbours stirred their tea in some of those. Oh, we lived in some awful places, Miss Wray. We lived in a house that was haunted, once.'

Frances supposed she was joking. 'Haunted? By whom, or what?'

'By an old, old man with a long white beard. He wasn't misty like a ghost in a book; he was solid, like a real person. I saw him twice, coming down the stairs. Vera and I both saw him.'

She wasn't joking at all. Frances frowned. 'Weren't you frightened?'

'Yes, but he never hurt anybody. We found out about him from the neighbours. He had lived in the house years before, and his wife had died, and he'd wasted away through missing her. They said he went up and down the stairs looking for her, night after night. Sometimes I wonder if he's still there. It's sad to think he might be, isn't it, when all he wanted was to be with her.'

Frances's cigarette had gone out. She relit it and didn't answer. She was marvelling at Mrs Barber's candour, her simplicity, her lack of self-consciousness—whatever quality it was, anyhow, that allowed her to say such a thing aloud, with such obvious sincerity. She knew that she herself would find it as hard to confess to an almost-stranger that she had seen a ghost as to admit to believing in elves and fairies.

Which was why, of course, she realised, she never would see a ghost.

She felt slightly dashed, suddenly. The feeling took her by surprise. She fiddled with the box of matches, setting it on one end and then on another. And when she raised her eyes she found that Mrs Barber was watching her, her brows drawn together in an expression of concern.

'I'm afraid I've said something to upset you, Miss Wray.'

Frances shook her head, smiled. 'No.'

'I wasn't thinking. I shouldn't have been talking about ghosts and unhappy things on a day like today.'

'A day like today?' said Frances. Then: 'You mean, because of my father? Oh, no. No, you mustn't think that. Think it about my brothers, if you like. I miss them every day of my life. But as for my father—' She tossed the matches down. 'My father, Mrs Barber, was a nuisance when he was alive, he made a nuisance of himself by dying, and he's managed to go on being a nuisance ever since.'

Mrs Barber said, 'Oh. I—I'm sorry.'

They were plunged back into silence. Frances thought of her reticent mother, just across the hall. But again the stillness was tempered by those gentle kitchen sounds, the tumble of coals, the scullery music. And Mrs Barber had spoken freely . . . She found she had an urge to meet the candour, repay it with something of her own. She took a long draw on her cigarette, and went on in a lower tone.

'It's simply that my father and I—we never got along. He had old-fashioned ideas about women, about daughters. I was a great trial to him, as perhaps you can imagine. We argued about everything, with my poor mother as referee. Most of all we argued about the War, which he saw as some sort of Great Adventure, while I—Oh, I loathed it, right from the start. My elder brother, John Arthur, the gentlest creature in the world, he more or less bullied into enlisting; I shall never forgive him for that. Noel, my other brother, went in practically as a schoolboy, and when he was killed my father's response was to have a series of "heart attacks"—to take to an armchair, in other words, while my mother and I ran about after him like a pair of fools. He died a few months before the Armistice, not of a heart attack after all, but of an apoplexy, brought on by reading something he disagreed with in *The Times*. After his death—' Her tone became rueful. 'Well, it must be obvious to you and your husband, Mrs Barber, that my mother and I aren't as well off as we might be. It turned out that my father had been putting the family money into one bad speculation after another; he'd left a pile of debts behind him that we're still paying off and—Oh.' She stubbed out her cigarette, unable to be still. 'Look, you mustn't let me talk about him! It isn't fair of me. He wasn't a bad man. He was a blusterer and a coward; but we're all cowardly sometimes. I've got into the habit of hating him, but it's a horrible habit, I know. The truth is, the most hateful thing my father ever did to me was to die. I—I'd had plans, you see, while he was alive. I'd had terrific plans—'

She paused, or faltered; then drew herself up. 'Well, my father always did say that my plans would come to nothing. He'd certainly smile if he could see me now, still here, on Champion Hill. Like your ghost!'

She smiled, herself. But Mrs Barber did not smile back. Her gaze was serious, dark, kind. 'What sort of plans did you have, Miss Wray?'

'Oh, I don't know. To change the world! To put things right! To—I've forgotten.'

'Have you?'

'It was a different time, then. A serious time. A passionate time. But an innocent time, it seems to me now. One believed in ... transformation. One looked ahead to the end of the War and felt that nothing could ever be the same. Nothing *is* the same, is it? But in such disappointing ways. And then, the fact is, I had had—There had been someone—a sort of proposal—'

But now she caught sight of those rings on Mrs Barber's finger: the wedding-band, the little diamonds. She said, 'Forgive me, Mrs Barber. I don't mean to be mysterious. I don't mean to be maudlin, either. All I'm trying to say, I suppose, is that this life, the life I have now, it isn't—' It isn't the life I was meant to have. It isn't the life I want! 'It isn't the life I thought I would have,' she finished.

She seemed to herself to have been very nearly raving. She felt as exposed and as foolish as if she had inadvertently given a glimpse of her bare backside. But Mrs Barber nodded, then dropped her gaze in her delicate way—as if, impossibly, she understood it all. And when she spoke at last, what she said was, 'It must be funny for you and your mother, having Len and me here.'

'Oh, now,' said Frances, 'I didn't mean that.'

'No, I know you didn't. But it must be funny all the same. I like this house so much. I wanted to live in it the minute I saw it. But it must be awfully strange for you to see me and Len here; as if we'd gone helping ourselves to your clothes, and were wearing them all the wrong way.'

She reached to the saucer as she spoke, tucking in her chin, self-conscious, the wooden beads of her necklace gently nudging at one another. Frances, watching the crown of her head, saw a fingertip-sized spot of scalp appear, lard-white against the glossy dark hairs that sprang from it.

'What a thoroughly nice woman you are, Mrs Barber,' she said.

That made Mrs Barber look up with a smile of surprise. But she winced, too. 'Oh, don't say that.'

'Why not?'

'Well, because some day you're sure to find out that it isn't true, and then you'll be disappointed in me.'

Frances shook her head. 'I can't imagine it. But now I like you more than ever! Shall we be friends?'

Mrs Barber laughed. 'I hope so, yes.'

And that was all it took. They smiled at each other across the table, and some sort of shift occurred between them. There was a quickening, a livening—Frances could think of nothing to compare it with save some culinary process. It was like the white of an egg growing pearly in hot water, a milk sauce thickening in the pan. It was as subtle yet as tangible as that. Did Mrs Barber feel it? She must have. Her smile grew fixed for a second, a touch of uncertainty entering her gaze. But the frown came, and was gone. She lowered her eyes, and laughed again.

And as she did it there was a sound in the hall, the rattle of the front-door latch. Her husband was back from Peckham: the two of them realised it at the same time and their poses changed. Frances drew slightly back from the table. Mrs Barber put an arm across herself, making a prop with her wrist for the elbow of her other arm, and taking a puff of her cigarette. Frances saw her sisters in the gesture, and in the new tilt of her jaw. When she spoke, it was in a whisper; but her sisters were in the whisper, too.

'Just listen to him creeping about!' He was going softly across the hall. 'He's practically on tiptoe. He's afraid my family are still here.'

Frances answered in the same low tone. 'Does he really dislike them?'

'Oh, there's no telling with him. No, he just pretends to, I think. It seems funnier to him that way.'

They sat in silence in the shadowy room, oddly intimate for a moment as they listened to Mr Barber mount the stairs. Then, with a sigh, Mrs Barber began to get to her feet. 'I'd better go up.'

Frances watched her rise. 'Had you?'

'Thank you for my cigarette.'

'You haven't quite finished it.'

'He'll only come looking for me if I stay. He'll make a joke of it, and it's been so nice, and—No, I'd better go up.'

Frances rose too. 'Of course.'

But she was sorry. She was thinking of the little alembic shift that had taken place a minute before. She was thinking of the honest way in which she had spoken—or, the almost-honest way—a way, anyhow, that was nearer honesty than any way she felt that she had spoken, to anyone, in years.

She got as far as the kitchen door, her hand extended to draw it open; then she turned back.

'Listen, Mrs Barber. Why don't you and I do something together some time? Let's—I don't know—take a walk, or something. Just locally, I mean. One afternoon next week? Tuesday?—Wait, Tuesday won't do. Wednesday, then? My mother's abandoning me that day; I'll be glad of the company. What do you say?'

The idea had come from nowhere. Was it all right? she wondered at once. Could a woman like her ask a thing like that, of a woman like Mrs Barber? Did it make her sound odd, sound lonely, sound a bit of a leech?

Mrs Barber looked slightly thrown. But it seemed she was flattered, that was all; Frances hadn't thought of that. With a blush, she said, 'That's kind of you, Miss Wray. Yes, I'd like to. Thank you.'

'You're quite sure?'

'Yes, of course. Wednesday afternoon?' She blinked, considering; then grew more decided, her chin rising, her blush fading. 'Yes, I'd like to very much.'

Again, they smiled at each other—though without the alchemy of before. Frances opened the door, and Mrs Barber nodded and was gone. There was the pat of her slippers in the hall and on the treads of the stairs, followed by the sound of her husband's voice as they greeted each other up on the landing. Frances, standing in the open doorway, listened shamelessly this time; but there was nothing to hear but murmurs.

4

And what a funny thing it was to feel excited about, she thought later. She and Mrs Barber settled on their destination—Ruskin Park, just down the hill, the most ordinary, small, unthrilling, neat and tidy place, with flower-beds and tennis courts and a stand for the band on Sundays. But she *was* excited about it, she realised; and she had the feeling, as the days passed, that Mrs Barber was excited about it too. A picnic tea, they decided, would make the event jollier, so on the Wednesday morning they spent time in their separate kitchens, putting together a few bits of food. And when she was dressing to leave the house, Frances found herself taking trouble over her outfit, rejecting a dull skirt and blouse in favour of the smart grey linen tunic she generally saved for her trips into Town, then wasting minute after minute trying out different hat-pins—amber, garnet, turquoise, pearl—in an effort to liven up her old felt hat.

Had Mrs Barber taken trouble? It was difficult to say, for she took pains over her outfit every day of the week. Frances, joining her on the landing, found her in her usual combination of warm colours and comfortable lines, a violet frock, pink stockings, grey suede shoes, lace gloves, a hat of the snug modern variety that didn't require a pin at all: she wore it pulled down nearly to her dark eyelashes. But around her wrist was the tasselled silk cord of something—Frances thought it a bag, until they moved down the stairs together; then she saw that it was a red paper parasol. And that made her think that Mrs Barber had taken trouble after all, for though the weather was sunny it wasn't so sunny as all that; the parasol was simply a flourish, to lend a gaiety to the occasion. They might have been heading for the sea-front. Suddenly, she wished they were. Hastings, Brighton—why hadn't she thought of it? She ought to have been more ambitious. Once they had left the house it took only a few minutes to reach the gates of the park. They might as well have stayed in the back garden! The sounds of trams and motor-cars barely faded once they were inside.

Still, it was nice to be among the trees, on a path of hard earth, rather than on the dusty pavement. And a stretch of long grass had bluebells in it: Mrs Barber paused to look at them, stooping, taking off a glove, running a hand across the drowsy-looking stems.

The bluebells led them to an odd sort of ruin: a pillared portico, standing alone, wound about with ivy. The park had been put together from the grounds of several large houses when Frances was a child, and she could remember very clearly the house at this end, sitting in a wilderness of bramble, grand and derelict as a mad old duchess. She had once, for a dare, led Noel into its garden, and had been punished for it later—spanked on the back of her legs with a slipper—when he had had nightmares. Now the house, like Noel himself, was gone; there were only a few stranded details to recall it and its neighbours; she thought it sad, sometimes. The park seemed self-conscious, pretending. On wintry days, in particular, the place could be depressing.

But she said some of this to Mrs Barber as they strolled, and perhaps saying it broke the spell of it—or perhaps the weather made the difference; perhaps it was something about being here with Mrs Barber herself, the parasol glowing at her shoulder—anyhow, whatever the cause, the park had a charm today that she couldn't recall it ever having had before. Its very neatness seemed appealing, everything in such perfect trim, the lawns clipped, the beds of gaudy flowers like icing piped on a cake. It was a little after four, and the passers-by were a daytime crowd of idlers, invalids, children just out of school, women with toddling infants, elderly gents with dogs on leashes—the sort of people, she thought wryly, who'd be the first to get admitted to a lifeboat. How Christina and Stevie would smile at all this! Christina and Stevie, however, seemed far away. She and Mrs Barber took paths scattered with fallen blossom. They walked the length of a terrace made dappled by hanging wisteria. When they looked for a spot on which to settle, she wished they had brought a blanket to spread out on the grass.

Instead, they found a bench, and unpacked their bags. And at once, it became apparent that they had had rather different ideas about what should constitute the picnic. Mrs Barber had made finger-rolls, pin-wheel sandwiches, miniature jam tarts: the sort of fiddly dainties written about in the women's magazines that Frances now and then read over shoulders on the bus. She herself had brought hard-boiled eggs, radishes from the garden, salt in a twist of paper, half a round of seed cake and a bottle of sugarless tea, swaddled in a dish-cloth to keep it hot. But once they had set out the food on a chequered cloth, the meal looked surprisingly complete. 'A perfect feast,' they agreed, as they touched their cups together.

The jam tarts rather fell to pieces when one picked them up, and the pin-wheel sandwiches uncurled, letting out their cheesy innards. It didn't matter. The rolls were good, the radishes were crisp, the eggs gave up their shells as if shrugging off cumbersome coats; the parasol, propped up, lent everything its winey colour. And Mrs Barber made the bench appear as comfortable as a sofa, letting herself settle sideways, resting a cheek on her fist. Once she laughed her natural laugh again, leaning forward with her wrist at her mouth; a man seated alone on a nearby bench turned his head at the sound. Frances had feared that the day might be awkward. The two of them, after all, barely knew each other. But they seemed to pick up the thread of their intimacy exactly where they had left it in the shadowy kitchen on Saturday afternoon, like retrieving a dropped stitch across a few rows of knitting.

That man, however, kept looking. She met his gaze in a frosty way; that only made him smirk. When the food was finished, she gathered the egg-shells, shook the crumbs from the cloth. 'Shall we stroll again? See the rest of the sights?'

Mrs Barber smiled. 'I'd like to.'

There was little enough to look at, really. The small formal garden had some pretty snapdragons in it. On the pond there were ducklings, and comical dirty-yellow goslings. At the tennis courts, two young women were in the middle of a match, playing well, their pleated skirts flying as they raced after the ball. Did Mrs Barber play tennis? No! She was far too lazy. Len played at the sports club at the Pearl; he'd won cups. How about Miss Wray?

'Oh,' said Frances, 'I played at school. That, and lacrosse—a beastly game. I was never much good at those team things. I did better on a bicycle. Or roller-skates. We had a skating rink right here in Camberwell for a while.'

Mrs Barber said, 'I know. I sometimes went there with my sisters.'

'You did? I used to go with my brothers—until my father decided it was vulgar, and put a stop to it. We might have been there at the same time.'

'Isn't that a funny thought?'

The idea of it seemed to impress them both. They moved on at a livelier pace—making now for the band-stand, a quaint octagonal pavilion with a red tiled roof. They crossed the gravel, climbed the steps, and the wooden floor must have made Mrs Barber think of dancing: she went across it in the slow twirls of a graceful, unpartnered waltz.

She came to a stop at the balustrade, and stood looking down at the rail. Frances, joining her there, was dismayed to discover that the glossy green paint, which had looked neat from a distance, was in fact scored with naughty drawings—a bare-breasted woman, a cat's behind—and carved with names: *Bill goes with Alice, Albert & May, Olive loves Cecil*—though the *Cecil* had been scratched through, perhaps with a hat-pin, and *Jim* carved instead.

She ran her fingers over the scorings. 'Fickle Olive,' she said.

Mrs Barber smiled, but made no reply. She seemed to have grown slightly wistful since her solitary waltz. For a minute she and Frances gazed out across the park, at the rather uninspiring view—the red-brick buildings of the local hospital. Then she turned and leaned back against the rail, catching hold of the cord of the parasol, absently running the red tassel back and forth over her lips. And since she seemed content to sit there, Frances turned and leaned beside her. It was a curious place to rest, rather a showy spot to sit in; but the parasol, raised behind them, gave an illusion of privacy.

Of course, the mood of the park would be different later, once dusk had begun to fall. Lovers would come here, clerks and shop-girls: Bill and Alice, Olive and Jim. Mrs Barber might return with her husband. Would she, though? It didn't seem very likely to Frances. She recalled the dead little conversation she had over-heard the week before; she remembered the encounter in the starlit garden that had preceded it. Looking sideways at Mrs Barber, watching her stroke the tassel in that idle way over her rounded chin and mouth, she said, 'May I ask you something, Mrs Barber?'

Mrs Barber turned, intrigued. 'Yes?'

'How did you and your husband meet?'

Frances saw her expression fix slightly. 'Me and Len? We met in the War, in my step-father's shop. I used to work in there in those days—my sisters and I, we all did. Len was going by, on one of his leaves. He looked in, and saw me through the window.'

'Just like that?'

'Just like that.'

'What happened then?'

'Oh, well, then he came inside, making out that there was something he wanted to buy. We started talking, and—I didn't think him specially handsome. He's rather a weed really, isn't he? But he had nice blue eyes. And he was fun. He made me laugh.'

She smiled as she spoke, but her gaze had turned inward, and the smile was a strange one, fond but faintly scornful. Aware of Frances waiting for more, she lifted a shoulder in a shrug. 'There isn't anything to tell about it, really. He took me to tea. We went dancing. He's a good dancer when he wants to be. And then, when he went back to France, we began to write to each other. Other boys had taken me out, but Len—I don't know. The War didn't seem to touch him in the way it touched everybody else. He never got injured—only scratches. He told me he had a charmed life, that there was something uncanny about it, that fate had picked us out for each other, and—' She let the tassel drop. 'I was awfully young. It's like you said the other day: the War made things seem more serious than they were. I don't suppose he really meant to marry me. I don't suppose I really meant to marry him.'

'And yet, you did marry each other.'

She put out a foot, began to nudge at a knot in the wooden floor. 'Yes.'

'But why, if neither of you meant to?'

'It was just one of those things, that's all.'

'One of those things?' said Frances. 'What a funny way to put it. You can't marry someone by accident, surely?'

At that, Mrs Barber looked at her with a curious expression, a mixture of embarrassment and something else, something that might almost have been pity. But, 'No, of course you can't,' she said, in an ordinary tone. She drew in her foot. 'I'm just fooling. Poor Len! His ears must be on fire, mustn't they? You oughtn't to listen to me today. He and I—we had words last night.'

'Oh,' said Frances. 'I'm sorry.'

'It doesn't matter. We're always having words about something. I thought we wouldn't, once we'd left Peckham. But it turns out we do.'

Frances found the simplicity of this statement, combined with the matter-of-fact tone in which Mrs Barber made it, rather terrible. For a few seconds she struggled to find an adequate reply. At last, in an effort to lighten the moment, she said, with a smile and an air of conclusion, 'Well, my Yorkshire grandmother used to say that marriages are like pianos: they go in and out of tune. Perhaps yours and Mr Barber's is like that.'

Mrs Barber smiled back at her; but the smile quickly faded. She lowered her gaze, and her eye was caught by something on the stretch of balustrade on which they were perched. She put her hand to it and, 'This is marriage, Miss Wray,' she murmured. 'This is marriage, exactly.'

She had found a spot on the rail where the paint was chipped, exposing several older colours, right down to the pale raw wood beneath. Running her fingers over the flaw, she said, 'You don't think about all these colours when everything's going all right; you'd go mad if you did. You just think about the colour on the top. But those colours are there, all the same. All the quarrels, and the bits of unkindness. And every so often something happens to put a chip right through; and then you can't *not* think of them.' She looked up, and grew self-conscious; her tone became ordinary again. 'No, don't ever get married, Miss Wray. Ask any wife! It isn't worth it. You don't know how lucky you are, being single, able to come and go just as you please—'

She stopped. 'Oh, I do beg your pardon. Oh, I oughtn't to have said that, about luck. Oh, that was stupid of me.'

Frances said, 'But what do you mean?'

'I wasn't thinking.'

'Thinking about what?'

'Well—'

'Yes?'

'Well, I had the impression—Maybe I misunderstood. But didn't you say, on Saturday, when we were sitting in the kitchen, that you had once been engaged to be married, and—?'

Had Frances said that? No, of course she hadn't. But she had said something, she recalled now—something careless and unguarded. Something about a proposal—was it? A disappointment? A loss?

The parasol was still raised, making that screen behind their shoulders. It was a moment for confidences, for putting things straight. But how, she thought, to explain? How to answer Mrs Barber's kind, romantic speculations, that were in one way so wildly wide of the mark and in another so horribly near? So she didn't answer at all—and, of course, her silence answered for her. It isn't a lie, she said to herself. But she knew that it was a lie, really.

The moment put a slight distance between them. They sat without speaking, side by side, their hips and shoulders close and warm, but she felt that the pleasure of the afternoon had been punctured, was beginning to leak away.

And now, yes, as if summoned up to chase off the last of their intimacy, here came someone—a man, on his own—strolling up into the band-stand, tipping his straw hat to them, then lingering stubbornly a few yards off, pretending to be admiring the view. Frances kept her face turned away from him. Mrs Barber was sitting with her own head bowed. But every so often he looked their way—Frances could see him in the corner of her vision—his eye was roving over towards them with what he must have imagined to be a 'twinkle'.

She began to feel the twinkle like the buzzing of a fly. After a minute of it she said quietly, 'Shall we find somewhere else to sit?'

Mrs Barber spoke without raising her head. 'Because of him? Oh, I don't mind.'

Their murmurs made the man draw closer. He began studying them like an artist, like a master of composition. 'Now, if only I had a camera!' he said, stooping at the side of an imaginary tripod, squeezing a bulb. He laughed at Frances's expression. 'Don't you want your picture taken? I thought all young ladies wanted that. Especially the handsome ones.'

'Shall we go?' she asked Mrs Barber again, in an ordinary tone this time.

The man protested. 'What's the hurry?'

Frances got to her feet. He saw that she meant it, and came closer, and spoke in a more insinuating way. 'Did you enjoy your picnic?'

That made her look at him. 'What?'

'I should just about say you did. I should say the picnic enjoyed it, too.' His eyes flicked to Mrs Barber, and he smirked. 'I never thought it possible for a fellow to envy a boiled egg, until I saw your friend eating hers.'

He was the man who had been watching them earlier on. He must have seen them finish their tea and been following them ever since, from the bench to the flower-beds, from the flower-beds to the pond, from the pond to the tennis courts, from the tennis courts to here. Of course, the red parasol made them rather hard to miss. That wasn't why Mrs Barber had brought it, surely? That wasn't why she'd wanted to sit here, in this oddly public spot?

No, of course it wasn't. She was doing her best to ignore the man, her head dipped, her face flaming. He ducked his own head, in an attempt to catch her eye. 'Don't want to play?'

'Look, go away, will you?' said Frances.

He looked at her with a gaze grown fishy, then spoke to Mrs Barber again, turning down the corners of his mouth. 'Your chum doesn't seem to like me much, I can't think why. How about you?'

Frances said, 'No, she doesn't like you either. Do go away.'

He held his ground for another few moments. But it was Mrs Barber he was after, and she wouldn't raise her eyes to his; at last there was nothing he could do but give up on them both. He drew in his shoulders, pretending to shudder against a chill, and, 'Brrr!' he said, still addressing Mrs Barber, but jerking his head in Frances's direction. 'Suffragette, is she?'

No one answered him. He retreated, got out a cigarette, produced a lighter, struck a flame—all in a leisurely sort of way, as if it were the only thing he'd climbed the steps for. But the twinkle had faded from his manner, and after a moment he drifted back to his previous spot at the balustrade. A moment after that, he left the band-stand.

Mrs Barber's pose loosened. She looked embarrassed, admiring, appalled. But she laughed. 'Oh, Miss Wray! What a Tartar you are!'

'Well,' said Frances, still furious, 'why should our nice day be spoiled simply because some fool of a man fancies himself a lady-killer?'

'I usually just ignore them. They always go away in the end.'

'But why should you have to waste your time ignoring them? Did you know he was following us? There he goes, look.' She was watching the man as he sauntered away across the park. 'Off to try his charms on some other poor woman, no doubt. I hope she hits him. "Suffragette". As if the word's an insult! Honestly, if I were younger I might have hit him myself.'

Mrs Barber was still laughing. 'I think you'd have beaten him, too.'

Frances said, 'I might have, at that. I was once taken in charge, you know, for throwing my shoes at an MP.'

Mrs Barber's laughter died. She said, 'You weren't. I don't believe you.'

'I was. And spent the night in a police cell with three other women. We'd caused a fuss at a political meeting. I marvel, now, at our pluck. The entire crowd was against us. I oughtn't to have thrown things, though. We were supposed to be pacifists.'

'But what happened to you?'

'Oh, the charges were dropped. The MP got wind of the fact that we were all gentlemen's daughters; he didn't want it getting into the papers. But I had to go home the next morning and explain the whole thing to my parents—they thought the white slavers had nabbed me. Still'—she got to her feet, her spirits rising at the memory—'it was worth turning up at the house in the police matron's shoes for the sake of the look on my father's face! The neighbours enjoyed it too. Shall we move on?'

She offered her arm, meaning the gesture playfully, but Mrs Barber caught hold of it and let herself be pulled upright, laughing again as she found her balance; it seemed natural, after that, to remain with their arms linked. They went down the steps and into the sunlight, wondering where to make for next. The little encounter with the man had put the polish back on the day.

But they were conscious of the time. Somehow, an hour and a half had passed. They thought of returning to the tennis courts for a final look at the match—but at last, with reluctance, decided that they ought to head home. They climbed the slope of the park, paused again to admire the bluebells; then were back on the dusty pavement.

They stayed arm in arm all the way. Only in hurrying across the busy road did they separate. But on the opposite side, as they started up the hill, Mrs Barber paused, to move the parasol from one shoulder to another, and to step around to Frances's left instead of her right. Frances was puzzled by the gesture—then realised what she was doing. She was 'taking the wall', putting Frances between herself and the traffic in just the same instinctive way that she might have done while walking with a man.

Two more minutes and they were back at the house. Frances unlatched the garden gate, led the way inside. They went up the stairs together, Mrs Barber yawning as they climbed.

'All the sun has made me dozy. What have you to do now, Miss Wray?'

'I've to start thinking about my mother's dinner.'

'And I've to start thinking about Len's. Oh, if only dinners would cook themselves! If only floors and carpets and china—if it would all just see to itself. You'd think Mr Einstein might invent a machine to help with housework, wouldn't you? Instead of saying things about time and all that, that no one can understand anyhow. I bet I know what *Mrs* Einstein thinks about it all.'

As she spoke, she hung the parasol on a peg of the coat-stand, then pulled off her lace gloves, finger by finger.

But when she had drawn both gloves free, she paused with them in her hand; and she and Frances looked at each other.

Frances said, 'I enjoyed our picnic.'

'So did I, Miss Wray.'

'We might do it again, another day.'

'I'd like that, yes.'

'In which case—well, I wonder if you'd consider calling me Frances.'

She looked pleased. 'I'd like that, too.'

'What shall I call you, though? I'll stick to Mrs Barber, if you prefer.'

'Oh, I wish you wouldn't! I hate the name; I always have. It's like a card from Happy Families, isn't it? You might call me Lil, I suppose, which is what my sisters call me, but—No, don't call me that. Len says it makes me sound like a barmaid. *He* calls me Lily.'

'Lily, Lil. Mayn't I simply call you Lilian?'

'Lilian?' She blinked, surprised. 'Hardly anybody calls me that.'

'Well, I'd like to call you a name that hardly anyone else calls you.'

'Would you? Why?'

'I don't quite know,' said Frances. 'But it's a handsome name. It suits you.'

The comment was a piece of gallantry, really. How, in the circumstances, could it have been anything else? But they stood a yard apart, in the relative gloom of the landing, and in the silence that followed her words there came another of those shifts, those alchemic little quickenings ... Once again, Mrs Barber looked uncertain for a second. Then, smiling, she dipped her head. It was just as if, Frances thought, she was unable to do anything with a compliment except receive it, absorb it; even when it came from a woman.

'How funny you are, Miss Wray,' she said quietly. 'Yes, do call me Lilian.'

And, in another moment, they parted.

Over dinner that night, when Frances's mother asked her how she had enjoyed her afternoon, she said, Yes, it had been pleasant. She and Mrs Barber had liked looking at the flowers. They had been glad to stretch their legs ... She meant to leave the matter there.

Five minutes later, however, she found herself adding, 'You know, I've begun to feel rather sorry for Mrs Barber. She spoke a bit about her marriage today, and I don't think it can be a very happy one.'

Her mother looked up from her plate. 'She didn't tell you that herself?'

'Not in so many words.'

'I should hope not, no, on so slight an acquaintance.'

'But, still, that's the impression I got.'

'Well, she and Mr Barber can't be so very unhappy. Whenever I overhear them they seem to do nothing but laugh. Probably they've had some sort of a quarrel. I dare say they'll soon be on terms again.'

'Yes, perhaps,' said Frances. 'But, I don't know. It seemed a larger thing than a quarrel, to me.'

Her mother's tone grew comfortable. 'Oh, these things often

seem larger, from the outside. Even your father and I had our occa-sional fallings-out ... But we really oughtn't to be discussing it, Frances. If Mrs Barber tries to talk to you about the matter again, do your best to discourage her, will you?' She returned to her dinner, nudging spinach on to her fork—then paused with the fork lifted. 'I hope *you* haven't been speaking frankly to her.'

Frances was sawing at a piece of mutton. 'Well, of course I haven't.'

'With relations like hers—'

'I think she's simply a little lonely. And she's a kind woman. I like her. We have to live with her, after all.' Still cutting, she spoke blandly. 'There's no reason why she and I shouldn't be friends, is there?'

Her mother hesitated, but said nothing. The bit of mutton gave at last. Frances chewed and chewed, then swallowed, then turned the conversation; and they finished the meal without mentioning the Barbers again.

And perhaps, in any case, her mother had been right. While she was out in the kitchen later, polishing the knives and forks, the Barbers' gramophone started up: she could hear it across the house, a lively modern dance tune. Whatever differences the couple had had, they must already have settled them. The music went on for half an hour, one melody giving way to another, the final record winding down in a sort of melting groan as no one ran to turn the handle; after that there was a silence, somehow more bothersome than the jazz. Frances went to bed without seeing Mrs Barber again, and when they met the following day they were both slightly shy. They made a point of calling each other by their Christian names, but the moment was awkward, contrived. Their friendship seemed to have foundered before it had barely set sail. Mrs Barber left the house in the afternoon with a shopping bag over her arm, and Frances, suddenly restless, drifted about from room to room. She hadn't planned to go into Town, but in a fit of decision she changed her clothes, went out, caught a bus to Oxford Circus and called on Christina. Christina asked how she and her mother were getting on with Len and Lil, and she answered with jokes about the crowded house, queues for the bath-tub.

But then, next morning, while Mr Barber was at work and her mother was clipping lavender bushes in the back garden, she climbed the stairs to her bedroom to fetch a bag of laundry; coming out of the room with the bag in her arms, she glanced across the stairwell—and there was Mrs Barber, seated at the table in her kitchen, shelling peas into a bowl, reading a library book as she did it. She was wearing her plum-coloured gown, and her hair was up in its red silk scarf, the ends of the scarf lying ticklingly against the nape of her neck; she was easing the peas from the pod without once looking at them. And since Frances could never see anyone absorbed in a book without itching to know its title, she called across the stairwell.

'What's that you're reading, Lilian?'

The name sounded natural at last. Lilian turned, blinked, smiled. She opened her mouth to answer, then changed her mind and lifted the book to show its spine. Frances, of course, was too far off to read it. She went around the landing and looked in from the kitchen doorway; and then she saw the library lettering. The book was *Anna Karenina*.

Exclaiming with pleasure, she moved forward. Lilian watched her come. 'Do you know it?'

'It's one of my favourites. Where are you up to?'

'Oh, it's awful. There's just been a race, and—'

'The poor horse.'

'The poor horse!'

'What's its name? Something unlikely. Mimi?'

'Frou-Frou.'

103

'Frou-Frou! That's right. Do you suppose that sounds dashing in Russian?'

'Oh, I could hardly bear to read it. And poor Vronsky—Is that how you say it?'

'I believe so. Yes, poor Vronsky. Poor Anna. Poor everyone! Even poor old dull Karenin. Oh, I haven't read it in years. You make me want to again. May I see it?'

She took the book from Lilian's hand, careful not to lose her place, and looked from one page to another. 'Princess Betsy. I'd forgotten her. Dolly, Kitty . . . Where's the bit where Anna appears at the station? Isn't it right at the start?'

'No, there are chapters and chapters first.'

'Are you sure?'

'Yes. Let me show you.'

Their fingers collided in the pages as Lilian retrieved the novel. She searched for a minute, then handed the book back—and there was the moment that Frances had remembered, nearly a hundred pages in after all, Vronsky moving aside from the door of the train to allow Anna to step down on to the Moscow platform.

She drew out a chair, and sat. She read the scene right through while Lilian shelled the peas; soon, their fingers colliding again as they reached into the bowl, they were shelling the peas together, discussing novels, poems, plays, the authors they did and didn't admire . . . The day was warm, and the window was open; from out in the garden, as they chatted, there came the snip of secateurs. And only when the secateurs fell silent and Frances's mother could be heard in the yard, making her way back to the house, did Frances get to her feet, and retrieve her laundry, and head downstairs.

After that they met more or less daily, partly to compare their thoughts on *Anna Karenina*—which Frances had begun to re-read— but mainly, simply, for the pleasure of each other's company.

Whenever they could, they shared their housework, or made their chores overlap. One Monday morning they washed blankets together in a zinc tub on the lawn, Frances feeding them through the mangle while Lilian turned the wheel; afterwards, hot, damp, their skirts hauled up over their knees, they sat on the step drinking tea and smoking cigarettes like chars. Two or three times they returned to the park, always making the same small circuit, always finishing up at the band-stand, looking for the names of new lovers in the paint. And one bright afternoon while Frances's mother was visiting a neighbour they carried cushions out to the garden and lay in the shade of the linden tree eating Turkish delight. Frances had seen the sweets on a market stall and had bought them for Lilian as a gift. 'To match your Turkish slippers,' she said, as she handed them over. They were the sham English variety, sickly pink and white cubes; she herself gave up on them after a single bite. But Lilian, delighted, prised out lump after lump, putting each piece whole into her mouth, closing her eyes in ecstasy.

Just occasionally, Frances found herself wondering what the two of them had in common. Now and then, when they were apart, she'd struggle to remember where the essence of their friendship lay. But then they would meet, exchange a smile ... and she wouldn't wonder at all. Lilian might not be amusing or clever in the way that Christina, say, was amusing and clever—But, no, she *was* amusing, and she *was* clever; she could sew, for example, like a Bond Street seamstress, thought nothing of picking apart an entire garment and restyling it, nothing of settling down at three o'clock in the afternoon with a needle and a thousand seed-pearls that had to be attached to a blouse in time for a trip to a dancing-hall that night. Frances would sit and watch her do it, and marvel at her poise—admiring again her calmness, her stillness, that capacity she had for filling her own smooth skin. It was like a cure, being with Lilian. It made one feel like a piece of wax being cradled in a soft, warm palm.

The bigger mystery, surely, was that marriage of hers. Every so often when her husband stopped in the kitchen for one of his chats Frances would study him, trying to discover some quality in him that might chime with some quality of Lilian's; more often than not, she failed to do it. She asked again about their courtship, and Lilian replied as she had before: he'd had nice blue eyes, a sense of fun ... Beyond that, she became evasive; so Frances learned to leave the subject. She had evasions of her own, after all. How little the two of them knew each other, really. They were practically strangers. She hadn't had an inkling of Lilian's existence until six weeks before. Now she'd catch herself thinking of her at all sorts of odd moments, always slightly surprised when she did so, able to follow the thought backward, stage by stage, link by link, this idea having been called to mind by that one, which in turn had been suggested by that ... But they all had their finish at Lilian, wherever they started.

But women's friendships were like that, she reflected: a giddy-up, and off they cantered. If she occasionally lapsed into gallantry—well, there was something about Lilian that inspired gallantry, that was all. And if there were more of those moments, those little licks, almost of romance, they meant nothing; she was sure they meant nothing. Lilian, at least, seemed untroubled by them. She might look doubtful for a second, but she always laughed the doubt away. She might gaze at Frances from time to time with her eyes narrowed and her head cocked, as if she could sense some enigma to her and wanted to get to the bottom of it. Or she would turn the conversation to love and marriage, in a hinting way ... And then, it was true, Frances would feel a qualm, a prick of unease, to think of the shallow foundations on which their intimacy was built. And she would resolve in future to be more cautious; but the caution unravelled, every time.

By now it was June, true summer, each day finer than the last. Mr Barber grew jauntier than ever, going off to work on Saturday mornings with his tennis racket under his arm, spending the afternoons at his sports club, coming home to boast to Frances about the points he had won, the spots he'd knocked off the opposition. And in the long, light evenings he took to wandering about the house looking for little jobs to do, things to fix and improve. He oiled hinges, re-cemented loose tiles on the hall floor, replaced the washer in the scullery tap so that it lost its plink. Frances couldn't decide if she was grateful for the help or felt piqued by it. She had been planning for ages to see to those tiles herself. Now, whenever he crossed the hall, she had to listen to him pause, test the floor with his foot, and give a murmur of satisfaction as he admired his own handiwork.

But perhaps his energy was infectious. One morning in the middle of the month she went looking for a fly-swatter, and when she opened a cupboard in the passage a pile of things tumbled out. The things were her brothers'; the house was full of them; she had got used to digging her way through layers of school caps and cricket balls and Henty novels and fossil collections whenever she searched for something in a drawer or a chest. But would she have to dig for ever? Her brothers were never coming back. She collected everything she could find, then summoned her mother. For an hour they sifted and sorted, her mother resisting at every step. The books could go to a charity, surely? Oh, but Noel had had this one as a prize; his name was inside it; it wasn't quite nice to think of another little boy looking at that. Well, all right. But, these boots? Couldn't they go? Yes, the boots could go. And the boxing-gloves, the telescope, the microscope and slides?

'Must we do it now, Frances?'

'We'll have to do it some time.'

'Mightn't we put them in a trunk, in a cellar?'

'The cellar's full of Father's things. Look, how about this stamp album? Maybe I'll take it to be valued. Some of these might bring in some money—'

'Frances, please.'

After all, it had been a bad idea. They seemed to finish up with more than they had started with. They put together one small bundle to be passed on to the vicar's wife, and Frances's mother, her cheeks sagging, carried off a few items for herself: school badges, a college scarf. Frances had found a model boat that Noel had built as a boy; he had named it after her. It made the tears stand in her eyes.

Afterwards they were both rather quiet. They ate their lunch, then settled down at the open French windows. Frances's mother put an upturned tray in her lap with paper, pens and ink on it: she had promised to write some letters, she said, for one of her charities. Frances darned stockings to the regular scratch and tap of her nib, but after fifteen minutes or so she became aware that the sound had ceased; her mother had fallen into a doze. Hastily putting down her mending and darting out of her chair, she was just able to catch the pen before it rolled out of her mother's fingers. She screwed the cap back on the ink bottle, put it safely to one side. And as she stood gazing down at her mother's slack, pale, undefended face, tears pricked at her eyes again.

Oh, but it was pointless to be gloomy. She shook the tears away. What could she do with her afternoon? The darning was all very well, but she ought really to take advantage of her mother's doze and do something grimy. The porch needed a sweep; that would be a good job done. It always made her mother twitchy to know she was out there with a broom, where any of the neighbours might stroll past and see her.

But now there were sounds overhead: Lilian was up in her bedroom. Was she dressing to go out? No, the creaks didn't suggest it. She was standing still, the boards wheezing with the shifting of her weight. What *was* she doing?

It wouldn't hurt, would it, to slip upstairs and find out?

The bedroom door was wide open. Lilian called to her from

beyond it the moment her step left the stair. 'Is that you, Frances?'

'Yes.'

'What are you doing? Come in and see me.'

Frances went in warily. It was still a shock to see her brothers' room as it was now, cluttered with Lilian's knick-knacks, hung with lace and swags of colour. The top of the chest of drawers was so crammed with scent bottles and powder-puffs and cold-creams that it looked like something from backstage at the Alhambra; over the swing-mirror a pair of newly washed pink silk stockings had been hung to dry. Lilian was standing beside the bed, gazing down at a lot of fashion papers that she had spread on the counterpane. She was making sketches, she said—trying out ideas. Her sister Netta was having a party in a couple of weeks' time, and she planned to make herself a new frock for it.

Frances looked the sketches over. They were good, she saw with surprise; at least as good, it seemed to her, as Stevie's Bloomsbury designs. She said, 'Why, you're talented, Lilian. You're an artist, in fact. Your mother said you were; I remember now. She was quite right.'

Lilian answered modestly. 'Oh, my family call you an artist if you put the clock on the left-hand side of the chimney-piece instead of in the middle.' But she added, after a second, in a shyer sort of way, 'I did want to be an artist, though, once upon a time. I used to go to picture galleries and places like that. I thought of taking classes at an art school.'

'You ought to have done. Why didn't you?'

'Oh—' She laughed. 'Well, I got married instead.'

She picked up the drawings and held them at arm's length, looking at them critically. Frances, watching her, said, 'You might go to an art school now.'

She brightened. 'I might, mightn't I?' But she spoke without much conviction. 'I don't expect I'm good enough. And I know what Len would say! He'd call it a waste of time, and a waste of his money. He's got money on the brain these days. He's not coming to Netta's party; he's going to some stupid assurance men's thing. He and Charlie are both going to it. A boys' night out.'

It was an anti-Len day, clearly. But she seemed to want to leave the subject. She studied the drawings for another moment, then made them into a bundle along with the papers on the bed. She took the bundle over to the chest of drawers and did her best to find a spot for it among the scent bottles.

Then she grew still, and raised her head, and looked at Frances through the bit of swing-glass left unobscured by the stockings. 'Why don't *you* come to Netta's with me, Frances?'

Frances was taken aback. 'To the party?'

'Yes, why not?'

'I haven't been invited.'

'Netta said I could bring who I liked. And my family would be pleased to see you. They're always asking after you. Oh, do say yes!' She had turned, was growing excited. 'It'll only be little—at Netta's house in Clapham. But it'll be fun. We'll have fun.'

'Well—' Frances was thinking it over. Would it be fun, with the Walworth sisters? 'I don't know. When is it, exactly?'

'The first of July. A Saturday night.'

'I've nothing to wear.'

'You must have something.'

'Nothing that wouldn't shame you.'

'I don't believe you. Let me take a look. Come and show me, right now!'

But, 'Oh, no,' said Frances. Her mind had gone flashing through her wardrobe. 'Half of my things are falling apart. I'd be ashamed for you to see them.'

'How can you say such a thing?'

'You'd laugh at them.'

'Oh, Frances, come on. You threw your shoes at a policeman, once.'

'Not a policeman. An MP.'

'You threw your shoes at an MP. You can bear to show me the inside of your wardrobe, can't you?'

She came across the room as she spoke, her hand extended, and when Frances still hesitated she reached and caught hold of her wrist. Her grip was surprisingly strong: Frances tugged against it for a moment, but then, protesting, complaining, she allowed herself to be drawn from the room and led around the stairwell. They went into her bedroom laughing, and had to stand, pink-faced, to let the laughter subside.

Once Lilian had recovered, she began to look around. She had never been right inside the room before: Frances saw her gazing in a polite but noticing way at the few little things on display, the candlesticks on the mantelpiece, the Friedrich landscape on the wall . . .

'This is a nice room, Frances,' she said, with a smile. 'It suits you. It isn't full of rubbish, like mine. And are those your brothers?' She had spotted the two framed photographs on the chest of drawers. 'May I see? You don't mind?' She picked them up, and her smile grew sad. 'How good-looking they were. You're awfully like them.'

Frances stood at her shoulder to look at the pictures with her, the studio shot of Noel as a handsome schoolboy, the family snap of John Arthur in the back garden, larking about, tilting his hat to the camera. He was years younger there than she was now, though she still thought of him as her elder. And how quaint he looked in his waistcoat, with the old-fashioned watch-chain across it. She had never noticed before.

All at once, she had had enough of her brothers for the day. And she could see Lilian's eyes beginning to wander again, to wander almost furtively this time, as if she were thinking that there might be another young man in a photograph somewhere, perhaps over there, on the bedside cabinet . . . ?

'Look here, this party.' Frances crossed to the wardrobe. 'You really meant it, about going through my clothes?'

Lilian returned the pictures to their places. 'Yes!'

'Well—' The wardrobe door creaked open like the door to a cemetery vault. 'Don't say I haven't warned you.'

After a moment of looking over the drooping garments on their wire shoulders she began to unhook them and pull them out. She started with her house blouses and skirts, then moved on to the things she kept for best: the grey tunic, a fawn jacket, a navy frock that she was fond of, another frock, never quite so successful, in tea-coloured silk. Lilian received each item and carefully examined it, polite and tactful for a while, finding details to praise and admire. As she warmed to the task, however, her tone grew more critical. Yes, this one was handsome enough, but it was the colour of a puddle. This skirt ought to be shortened; no one wore them so long any more. As for this—it might have belonged to Queen Victoria! What had Frances been thinking?

She piled the garments on the bed. 'Have you never wanted nice things?'

'Yes, of course,' said Frances. 'When I was young.'

'You always talk as though you're ninety.'

'I lost heart for it all. And then, there hasn't been the money. You ought to see my underclothes. They make this lot look Parisian. Some of them are held together with pins.'

'Well, what might you wear to Netta's?'

'Oh, I don't know. You've sprung it on me, rather.' She pulled a gown free from the heap on the bed. 'This, I suppose.'

It was a black moire frock, a thing she'd been wearing to suppers and parties for the last six or seven years. She shook it out, and turned it to the light of the window so that she and Lilian could look it over. But it was worse than she'd remembered. The bodice was beaded, but beads had been lost, leaving threads behind them like coarse black hairs. In one of the sleeves a line of stitches was visible where she had mended a rip. Worst of all, the armpits were pale: she had coloured them in with ink in the past, but the ink had faded, was streaked and blueish . . .

She lowered the gown, embarrassed. 'Perhaps the puddle-coloured one instead.'

'There must be something else.'

'Truly, there isn't. See for yourself.'

Side by side, they gazed into the wardrobe's bleak, plundered interior. All that hung from the rail now were things from Frances's schooldays. Serge frocks, long skirts, stiff collars, neck-ties: it was astonishing to think that only a decade ago she had been going about in cumbersome clothes like this. The very memory of the endless layers of flannel underwear made her droop.

But something had caught Lilian's eye. She put in her hand, and pulled. 'What's this?'

'Oh,' said Frances, as the garment emerged, 'I only ever had that as a fancy. Someone talked me into buying it. No, that won't do at all.'

The gown was a sage-green thing with a wide collar and a tiered skirt, laced at the bosom and cuffs with slim leather thongs. It was Christina who had persuaded her to buy it, back in that other life of theirs. It had cost three guineas—three guineas! The figure seemed astronomical now—and she had worn it only once, to a Red Cross ball. Christina's father had got hold of the tickets, and in their earnest, pacifist way she and Chrissy had debated the ethics of attending. But they had got swept up by the fun of it in the end; she remembered that ball, now, as a bright spot among shadows. Seeing the gown dangling from Lilian's fingers brought it all back: the electric intensity of the evening, the rides in the taxi through the blacked-out streets with Christina's dim Aunt Polly as chaperone, Christina herself, the sweet scent of her hair, the feel of her hands in tight kid gloves . . .

Lilian was watching her face. 'This is what you ought to wear, Frances.'

'This? Oh, no.'

'Yes. All the other things have made you frown. But this—You see? You're smiling. Put it on.'

'No, no. I'd feel a fool. And look at the state of it! It reeks of must.'

'That doesn't matter. It wants a wash and a press, that's all. Put it on and let me see. Just to please me. Will you? I'll look away until you're ready.'

She shoved the gown into Frances's hands, then turned her back to her and stood waiting. Frances, seeing no way out of it, began to undress. She did it slowly at first. But the petticoat that she was wearing was literally coming apart at the seams, and, realising that, growing afraid that Lilian would turn too soon, she worked more quickly—kicking off her slippers, wriggling free of her skirt and blouse, then shaking open the musty frock and pulling it over her head. It seemed immediately to tie itself into a knot, and she wrestled with it for several seconds, trying to work her arms along its narrow sleeves. Looking into the mirror at last she saw herself redfaced, with untidy hair, her collarbones plainly visible beneath the clinging creased material, and the dress itself, with its lacings, like something from Sherwood Forest, as if she ought be sitting in one of her father's chairs, playing a lute.

But when Lilian turned, and saw her, her expression softened.

'Oh, Frances, you look lovely. Oh, the colour suits you. You're lucky. If I wear green near my face it makes me look like a corpse. But, yes, it just suits you. All it needs is a bit of work.' Coming close, she began to tug the frock into shape with brisk, professional fingers. 'The waist wants lowering, for a start. It'll be quite a different gown then. It'll show how lovely and slim you are— oh, I'd give anything to be slender like you!—but the line will be softer. You see what I mean? You ought to wear looser stays, you know. They only need to be stiff or elastic when you've a bust like mine. And you must wear silk stockings, Frances, not these terrible cotton ones. Don't you want to make the most of your nice ankles?'

She spoke without a blush, quite unselfconscious, as if it were perfectly natural that she should have been studying and forming opinions on Frances's ankles, Frances's hips, the style of Frances's underwear. But then, of course, women like Lilian studied other women all the time. They noticed, they judged, they admired and damned, they coveted bosoms, complexions, mouths . . . She was drawing up the hem now. 'This ought to be raised. See how it's better?'

'But I don't want it raised.'

'Just an inch or two, for the party? I should have thought you'd like ladies to have shorter skirts. You don't want us to go about hobbled?'

'But—'

'Stay just like this, while I fetch my pins!'

There was no resisting her. She ran for her work-basket and returned to measure and mark, moving Frances's limbs about as if they were those of an artist's dummy. She loaded the frock with so many pins that when it was time for Frances to remove it she had to inch herself out, afraid for her skin.

And even then she hadn't finished. Once Frances was back in her harmless, laundered-to-death old blouse and skirt, she stood looking her over with a calculating expression, tapping her fingers at her plump mouth, and—'What shall we do about your hair?' she said.

Frances was aghast. 'My hair? My hair's all right, isn't it?'

'But you always wear it up. Wouldn't you like a new style, to match the frock? I could cut it for you. I could wave it! We could surprise your mother. Oh, Frances, what do you say?'

Frances didn't want a cut or a wave. She was happy with her brown, uncurly, middle-length hair, which could be trimmed when necessary at the scullery sink; which could be cheaply washed and dressed. As for surprising her mother—she knew exactly what sort of surprise that would turn out to be.

But Lilian's excitement was exciting her now. There was something seductive about the idea of putting herself into Lilian's hands, something seductive about the very passivity of the poses she had to adopt in order to do it: the bowed head, the lifted arms. She thought suddenly, I'm like one of those men one hears whispers about, who bend themselves over the knees of women in shady rooms off Piccadilly and ask to be thrashed.

But that thought was exciting, too. With only the feeblest bleat of a protest she let herself be led back out to the landing. She peered down the staircase as they passed it, thinking of her mother, dozing in the drawing-room in that unprotected way; but she didn't slow her step. And, as before, Lilian kept hold of her so that she shouldn't escape, hanging on to her cuff while awkwardly shaking out a newspaper, spreading sheets of it on the floor, lifting across a chair from beside the table. Once Frances was seated she even leaned over her with her hands on her shoulders, lightly but firmly pinning her in place.

'Now,' she said, in a warning way, 'I have to gather my things. Don't you run away from me, Frances! I am putting you on your honour.'

She left the room for two minutes and came back with a towel and combs, and swinging a leather vanity case, something like an effete doctor's bag. She closed the door with an air of conspiracy. The towel went over Frances's shoulders and was tucked into her collar. The case was set aside for now; she planned to wash the hair first. She wanted to do it all properly, and she meant to start with an egg shampoo. Oh, she knew Frances was going to say that! No, it wasn't a waste of an egg. Or, if it was, then that was the point: it was a bit of pampering. Was Frances a nun?

She spoke playfully still, but also with determination, fetching an egg from a basket and carefully breaking it, tilting the halves of

116

the shell above a saucer to separate the yolk from the white, then tipping the yolk into a cup and whisking it with vinegar. When she saw Frances begin to pull the pins from her hair she stopped her. Did ladies at the beauty parlour unpin their own hair? Of course they didn't. She stood behind the chair and drew the pins out herself, feeling for them with her fingertips and gently working them free. As the locks grew slack, then slid and tumbled, Frances's head seemed to expand, like a bud becoming a flower.

The putting on of the egg broke the spell. The sticky wet weight of it made her shiver. And then she was led to the sink and had to hang over the lip of it while Lilian filled jug after jug with water and doused her like a prison matron; she went stumbling back to the chair, her eyes stinging and her ears blocked, to have her head tugged in every direction as the tangles were combed out. There was a brief, blissful pause while the vanity case was unlatched; then she heard the unmistakable rasp and snap of a pair of scissors being opened and closed. And suddenly she was struck by the reality of what was about to happen. She turned, to see Lilian poised with the scissors in her hand, looking as though she, too, were rather daunted. The newspaper crackled under their feet. Again Frances thought of her mother, slack-mouthed and snoring. She thought of the unswept porch. How exactly had she got to this dangerous moment?

Lilian laid a hand on her shoulder. 'You aren't losing your nerve?'

She hesitated. 'Just a bit.'

'Think about that MP.'

'I'm sorry I ever told you about that wretched MP.'

'Think about that man in the park that time, how brave you were in seeing him off.'

'That wasn't bravery. It was—' Frances turned back to face the wall. 'I don't know what that was. I haven't done a real brave thing in years.'

Lilian's hand was still on her shoulder. 'I think you're brave, Frances.'

'Well, you hardly know me.'

'You do just what you want to do, and don't mind what other people make of it. I wish I was like that. And then—' Her voice dipped slightly. 'I think it's brave of you to be so cheerful when you've had—well, so many losses.'

She might have had in mind any of a number of losses: Frances's father, Frances's brothers, the vanished family fortune. But somehow it was clear that the loss she was really referring to was that of Frances's phantom fiancé.

After all the talk of bravery, the moment made Frances feel like a fraud. She didn't answer, she didn't turn. Lilian gave her shoulder a gentle, tactful pat, then drew her hand away.

And a moment after that, Frances felt the cold touch of the scissors, startlingly high up the nape of her neck; the blades closed with a scythe-like sound, and something slithered to the floor. She twisted, peered, and her heart missed a beat. There was a lock of dark hair on the newspaper, about half a yard long. Lilian took hold of her head and straightened it. 'You're not to look,' she said firmly. The cold-metal touch came again. Another snip, another slither . . . Well, it was too late now. The hair could hardly be re-attached. She stared at the varnished wallpaper while the scissors continued their chill, ravenous journey around her neck.

And perhaps the steady snipping away of her hair had something to do with it. Perhaps she was still slightly hysterical from being led across the landing. But that comment of Lilian's was on her mind. Wasn't this the moment to speak—right now, while there was no possibility of meeting Lilian's eye? Her stomach began to flutter. She waited until another lock of hair had gone slithering to the floor. Then, with a suddenly dry mouth, she said quietly, 'Listen, Lilian. I think I might have given you the idea that I was once engaged to be married. That I once had some sort of an affair.

With a man, I mean.' She hesitated, then plunged on. 'The truth is I did have a kind of love affair a few years ago. But it was—it was with a girl.'

She felt Lilian's uncertainty in the slowing of her hands. She thought Frances might be teasing. With a touch of laughter, she answered, 'A girl?'

'Another woman,' said Frances, flatly. 'I'd like to be able to say it was terribly pure and innocent, and all that. It—well, it wasn't.' There was a silence. 'You know what I mean?'

Lilian still said nothing; but she withdrew her hands. Frances gave it another few seconds, then turned to look at her. She was standing with the scissors at her side, and her colour was rising, rising even as Frances watched, spreading upward in a single tide of colour from the triangle of flesh that showed at her open-necked blouse, over her throat, her cheek, her forehead. She met Frances's gaze, then looked away.

'I—I didn't know,' she said.

'No. Well, how could you?'

'I'd supposed there was a man.'

'Yes, that was my fault. I'm sorry. I oughtn't to have misled you. But this sort of thing—one can't just drop it into conversation. I don't feel in the least ashamed about it. My friend and I, we were awfully in love.—But don't let's talk about it any more.' Lilian's colour had deepened at the word *love*. Frances turned back to the wall. 'I'm sorry I mentioned it. Don't give it another thought. It was a long time ago, and it was—it was nothing, really.'

It was not nothing. It was the crisis of her life. But she felt sick now with the knowledge that she had blundered, said too much. What on earth had she been thinking? She had let herself be seduced by the warmth and the ease of her friendship with Lilian, forgetting how unlikely their friendship actually was. Lilian was married, after all. Christ! Would she tell her husband? Tell her sisters? Tell her chatterbox mother?

119

Feeling sicker than ever, she risked another look over her shoulder. She saw Lilian wiping at the blades of the scissors, so patently struggling to digest what she had just learned that the information was almost visible, like a sharp crust going down.

But then, without meeting Frances's gaze, she moved in and began, again, to cut. Frances didn't mind the snips now. Instead, she was willing the blades forward. She'd become aware in a way she hadn't been before of the intimacy of their poses, herself a sort of captive on the chair, Lilian leaning into and over her, breathing against her neck and ear. The cutting part of it, thank God, took only another few minutes. But when Lilian had put aside the scissors she returned to the vanity case, to bring out an appalling-looking thing like a goffering-iron. Seeing her take the iron to the stove, realising what it was for, Frances said, 'You needn't do the waving as well, you know. There's no need for it. I really don't mind.' But Lilian's eyelids fluttered. No, she had promised to do the wave. She wanted to do it properly. It wouldn't take long . . . She turned the tongs in the blue gas flame, tested them on a scrap of paper, waved them about to cool them slightly—all in silence, unsmiling. Then she returned to her spot behind the chair and, with the very tips of her fingers, she straightened Frances's head. In a toneless voice, she said, 'Now, sit quite still.'

The wet hair sizzled alarmingly as the tongs took hold, and the air quickly became sour with a scent like that of burning feathers. The heat of the iron, close to Frances's scalp, was blistering, insane! Lilian, however, pressed on without a word, making her way along one length of hair and then another, regularly stepping back to survey her handiwork, every so often returning to the stove to re-heat the iron. She never once caught Frances's eye as she was doing it, and she never lost her flaming colour. Frances sat as sweating and as miserable as if she were in the dentist's chair.

At last the ordeal came to an end. Lilian spent another minute or two making adjustments with the comb. Then she fetched her husband's shaving-glass from the shelf above the sink, and put it into Frances's hands.

'Well?' she asked quietly. 'Do you like it?'

The sight of her own reflection took Frances aback. The hair was heart-stoppingly short, the waves so wonderfully well done that she struggled to recognise herself. She turned and tilted her head. 'I might be someone else completely.'

'It makes you look awfully modern and shick.'

'Shick?'

Somehow, Lilian blushed even harder. '*Chic*. It shows off the nice bones in your face.'

And, after all, perhaps it did, for the blunt bottom edge of the haircut drew attention to the line of her jaw; and Christina had always used to say that Frances's jaw was her best feature. But she couldn't enjoy it. She couldn't relax. Lilian took away the mirror and began to gather together the hair that had collected on the newspaper; it looked revolting heaped there like that, like a bit of stuffing from the inside of an armchair. Frances rose and did her best to help. They made a bulky packet of it, and stuffed the packet into the bin.

But their hands met as they did it, and they twitched away from each other; everything between them was wrong, off kilter. The hilarity of the past hour, the beauty-parlour silliness, the slipping in and out of clothes—it had all evaporated. Or, worse than that, it had all, Frances supposed, become suspect, become charged and tarnished by her confession. Lilian was tidying away the scissors and the combs now, looking almost angry. Frances had never before seen her look anything but open and kind. Was her mind running backward? Was she remembering odd incidents between Frances and herself, the Turkish delight, the chivalry, Frances chasing away her admirer from the band-stand? Was she thinking that Frances had seen him off in order to take his place?

Was that what Frances had done?

121

She watched Lilian close the vanity case, and drew a breath. 'Lilian. What I told you, just now—'

Lilian snapped the latch shut. 'It's quite all right.'

'Are you sure?'

'Yes.'

'And you won't mention it to anyone?'

'Of course not.'

'And you won't—you won't brood on it? I should hate it to come between us, now that we've become friends.'

At that, Lilian smiled and made a gesture, an airy movement with her hand. It was an attempt, perhaps, at sophistication, as if to say that women made sapphic disclosures to her—oh, every other day.

But the gesture was unconvincing, the smile rigid, confined to the mouth. And after a few more minutes of uncomfortable chat, the two of them parted. Frances went around the landing to her bedroom, to stare at her reflection in dismay. Her confidence in the haircut was gone. It seemed to have all the wrongness of the afternoon in it. She kept fingering her naked neck, feeling exposed.

And then—since it had to be done, and might as well be done right away—she screwed up her courage and went downstairs.

She opened the drawing-room door softly, in case her mother should still be dozing. But she was awake—at the bureau now, addressing an envelope. She looked at Frances over her spectacles, and it must have taken her eyes a moment to refocus. When they did, she lowered her pen, removed the glasses, and said, 'Good gracious!'

'Yes,' said Frances, with an attempt at a laugh, 'I'm afraid I allowed Lilian to twist my arm.'

'Mrs Barber did this? I hadn't an idea she was so talented. Come closer, into the light. Oh, but it's charming, Frances.'

Frances stared at her. 'You think so?'

'Very smart. Turn around, let me see. Yes, very up-to-the-minute!'

'I felt sure you wouldn't like it.'

'Why would you think that? It's a treat to see you making the best of yourself. I wish you would do it more often.'

'What do you mean?'

'Well—' Her mother flushed. 'You can sometimes look a little slipshod as you go about the house; that's all I meant. I don't mind for myself, I'm simply thinking about callers. But this—No, it's very smart.'

Her words caught Frances off guard. Coming so closely on the heels of the awkwardness with Lilian, they left her, absurdly, back on the brink of tears. She crossed to the hearth and stood at the mantel-glass, pretending to pat and tweak the new haircut. Idiot! Idiot! she said to herself, pushing the feelings down again.

When she left the room she remained in the hall for a minute, uncertain. And once she had climbed the stairs she hesitated at the top. Surely Lilian would come, if only to ask what her mother had made of her?

But though the door of the little kitchen was ajar, and there were sounds of activity beyond it, Lilian did not appear.

5

The hair held its wave for the rest of that day, but when Frances rose the next morning she looked, she thought, like someone from a mental ward, one half of the hair squashed flat where she had lain on it, the other half frizzed and bushy, impossible to comb. She didn't know what to do with it, so she ran herself a bath and ducked her head right under; after that the waves disappeared altogether and the hair dried oddly.

Her mother, looking her over, was distinctly less enthusiastic than she had been the day before.

'Why not ask Mrs Barber to put you tidy? She did such a splendid job in the first place.'

But when Frances did seek out Lilian, there was more of that wrongness between them. She showed Frances how to dress the hair so that it fell into loose waves of its own—standing behind her at her bedroom mirror, rearranging the locks with her fingertips. But her gaze, in the glass, seemed always to be in the process of sliding away, and her pose was a cautious one, as if she were reaching into a thicket, trying to avoid being snagged by thorns. Her manner made Frances feel sad. She had the sense that with her confession she had wrecked their friendship, thrown it away. And for what? For honesty. For principle. For the sake of a love-affair that in any case had already had the life pressed out of it, years before.

The hair continued to look peculiar to her in the days that followed, but she received so many compliments, from her mother's friends and from neighbours, that she supposed it must be all right. Mr Barber went about the house whistling 'A Little Bit off the Top'—which she took to be a tribute, of sorts. And Christina, when she saw her, said, in a faintly put-out tone, 'Yes, well, not bad, though it's a pity it shows up that great lantern jaw of yours,' which she took to be another. Even the boy who brought the meat looked at her in a new way. Everyone admired her, it seemed; everyone save Lilian. It was just as though, with a clash of its gears, their accelerated friendship had suddenly gone into reverse. For nearly a week they met only as landlady and lodger, on the stairs, on the landing, one of them heading out of the front door as the other crossed the hall. In *Anna Karenina*, Kitty was expecting her baby, Anna and Vronsky were wretched, disaster was on its way. But there were no more literary discussions, no more picnics in the park, no more cigarettes on the back step; and no further mentions of Netta's party.

There were also, Frances couldn't help but notice, no more anti-Len days. Quite the opposite. One night the couple went out with Mr Wismuth and his fiancée and came tiptoeing up the stairs at half-past midnight, bringing with them a sense of crowded places, lifted voices, music, drinks, laughter—or so, anyhow, it seemed to her, listening to them in the dark. Another night they blared out gramophone tunes; later, going up to bed, she found their sitting-room door open and got a glimpse of them squashed together in their pink plush easy chair. Mr Barber had hold of what appeared to be a doll or a puppet and was making it prance about in his lap; Lilian, enchanted, had worked her stockingless foot under the cuff of one of his trouser legs and seemed to be idly toeing the diamond pattern on his sock. And the sight of those questing toes had an extraordinary effect on Frances. They made her feel lonelier, suddenly, than she had ever felt before. She went creeping into her room and undressed without lighting a candle, then lay curled in bed in a ferment of misery. What was the use of her being alive? Her heart was some desiccated thing: a prune, a fossil, a piece of clinker. Her mouth might as well be filled with ashes. It was all utterly hopeless and futile . . .

Next morning, out in the WC, she discovered that her 'friend' had arrived. Why it was called a friend she could never imagine—it was more like an enemy within the gates—but, anyhow, seeing the smear of scarlet on the square of Bromo made her, perversely, feel better. One was always a bit demented, she thought, round about the time that one fell poorly. One couldn't be held accountable for one's mood then. She told her mother that she had a spot of neuralgia, and spent the rest of the day in bed with a hot water bottle.

Lying propped up on her pillows, her short hair pleasant against her neck, she was aware of the Barbers coming and going beyond her door. Now and then she heard Lilian's voice: detached from Lilian's physical presence, the elocution-class tones seemed very pronounced, and her laughter, when it came, had something grating about it. Once again, Frances struggled to understand what had ever drawn the two of them together. Had it simply been boredom, a question of empty days? She thought of the way they had spent their time. Trips to the park, Turkish delight: it all seemed so narrow, so footling. Gazing across at her wardrobe, she remembered how Lilian had gone through her frocks. *This is what you ought to wear. Not these terrible cotton stockings!* Hadn't that been rather smug of her? Hadn't there been a hint of condescension in her attitude to Frances?—as if Frances's life needed gingering up, and she was the person to ginger it?

She didn't like it, after all, when she discovered that Frances's life had already been gingered rather too liberally by someone else.

126

Well, so much the worse for her! Frances wouldn't apologise for it. Better to be me, she thought, than married. Better a spinster than a Peckham-minded wife! She rose from her bed full of new resolutions. 'We must get out and about more,' she told her startled mother. 'We must try different things. We are getting groovy.' She drew up a list of events and activities: concerts, day trips, public meetings. She went in a fit through her address book, writing letters to old friends. She borrowed novels from the library by authors who had never interested her before. She began to teach herself Esperanto, reciting phrases as she polished and swept.

La fajro brulas malbone. The fire burns badly.

Ĉu vi min komprenas? Do you understand me?

Nenie oni povis trovi mian hundon. Nowhere could they find my dog.

'You're looking awfully well, Frances,' her mother's friend Mrs Playfair told her, when she was visiting the Wrays one day in the middle of the month. 'You've shaken off that air of mopiness you sometimes have; I'm glad to see it. Now, I think you and your mother ought to come and have dinner with me. I've a wireless set now, did you hear? We can all listen in. What do you say? Shall we make it soon? Next Thursday night?'

And—oh, why not? Frances had known Mrs Playfair all her life. Her husband had been the senior broker in Frances's father's firm; Frances had gone to school with her daughters; and now she and Frances's mother sat together on the same small charity committees. She was one of those solid Edwardian women with a passion for organisation, and evenings in her company could sometimes be a little wearing. But—well, it would make for a change. And change was what Frances had been after. So, when Thursday night came round, she donned her puddle-coloured gown and carefully combed and dressed her hair, and she and her mother made the short journey across the crest of Champion Hill to Braemar, Mrs Playfair's grandish 1870s villa.

'There!' said Mrs Playfair as she greeted Frances in the drawing-room. 'How nice you look! I knew an outing would suit you. You must come and sit in the light of the window, beside Mr Crowther here. I know that you young people can stand any amount of sun. I can't, that's for sure!'

Mr Crowther, then, was the other dinner guest. Frances remembered, as she shook his hand, having heard her mother mention him. He had served in the same battalion as Mrs Playfair's son, Eric—or he had been in the bed next to Eric's when Eric had died, something like that—and Mrs Playfair had only recently tracked him down. For that was another of Mrs Playfair's passions: going over and over the details of Eric's death in Mesopotamia. She corresponded, Frances knew, with chaplains, nurses, surgeons, colonels. She had photographs of Eric's grave, and of the place where he had fallen. She had books, maps, plans—could shut her eyes, she liked to boast, and see the streets of Baghdad as vividly as she could picture those of Camberwell.

Frances wondered if Mr Crowther knew quite what he was in for. He was a nice-enough looking man of twenty-nine or thirty, dark-haired, with a trim moustache. 'You've known Mrs Playfair a good while?' he asked her as they sipped their sherry, and she explained the connection between the families.

'I was a regular here in my schooldays,' she said, 'when Kate and Delia were still at home. They're married now, and both living far away; Delia out in Ceylon.'

He gave a nod. 'I've thought of Ceylon for myself. Or perhaps South Africa. I've a cousin out there.'

'Yes? What sort of work would you look for?'

'Oh, an administrative post, if I could get it. Or engineering. I don't know.'

'You sound as though you have many talents.'

He smiled, but in a way that seemed to throw the subject off.

The dinner-gong sounded, and they went through to the

dining-room. The evening sun was just as bright in there, and again Mrs Playfair put Frances in the full of it, at Mr Crowther's side; she had to squint against the light for the whole of the meal. Still, it was a treat to eat four courses that had been prepared by someone else. Mrs Playfair, her investments undented, had managed to hang on to her servants right through the War. She had a cook, and a parlourmaid, Patty, as well as a daily woman for the roughs. Frances, cutting her buttery breast of chicken in the sunlight, was very aware of the state of her hands. She saw Mr Crowther look once at them, then politely look away.

He kept up the politeness even when the conversation turned, as it was bound to do, to Eric, talking in a stilted but obliging manner about their time in Mesopotamia, describing the heat, the grit, the marches, the rush and confusion of the skirmish in which he and Eric had been injured; Mrs Playfair nodded at his words like a collector with some new trophy, as if already seeing the spot in the display case in which it would be placed. And when the meal was finished and they returned to the drawing-room to admire the wireless set, he made himself handy with the twiddling of the switches. Frances was dubious about the wireless. She felt faintly ridiculous as she fitted on the ear-phones, and there was an anticlimactic few minutes when all that could be made out was a sort of prolonged death-rattle in the wire. But finally the crackles and the hisses resolved themselves into a voice—and then, yes, it was thrilling and uncanny to recognise a bit of Shakespeare and know that the words were coming across miles of empty space, directly into one's ear, like a whisper from God. Somehow, though, it was even more uncanny to take the ear-phones off and realise that the whisper was still going on—to think that it would go on, as passionate as ever, whether one listened in to it or not.

Patty brought the coffee, and they moved outside. It was the day after midsummer, and still fantastically balmy and light. Frances's mother and Mrs Playfair settled themselves in cane chairs on the terrace, but Frances and Mr Crowther wandered down into the garden. Mrs Playfair's Siamese cats, Ko-Ko and Yum-Yum, wandered with them, and when they sat, on a carved stone bench, the she-cat, Yum-Yum, jumped on to Mr Crowther's knee, and he stroked and fussed the little creature until she purred like an engine.

They were in full view of the terrace, but just far enough away from it so that they could talk without being overheard. Frances, watching Mr Crowther work his fingers over the cat's ecstatic face, said, 'I'm afraid you've had rather to sing for your supper tonight, Mr Crowther. Not just with the wireless, I mean. It can't be much fun.'

He answered without lifting his gaze. 'Oh, I'm not complaining. Generally when ladies learn that one was anywhere out east of Suez they rather lose interest. They want the romance of the trenches and all that.'

'You don't mind going over it?'

'No, I don't mind. It was every kind of hell, at the time. It was real, stinking hell. But the queer thing is, I sometimes find myself missing those days. There were things to do, you see, and one did them. That counts for a lot, I've discovered. Back here, now it's all over—well, there isn't a great deal for one. Lots of one's friends dead, and so on. And there are no paid posts for men like me. I ran into my second lieutenant the other day. He's shining shoes at Victoria Station! Other fellows I know are drifting about, getting into this, getting into that. None of us has any sticking power. I feel half in a daze, myself. Ceylon, South Africa—I'll never get there. Or, if I do, I'll wear my days away just as I wear them away here. I envy the ordinary working man, to be honest with you. He hasn't a job, either—but at least he has Bolshevism.'

He continued to fuss with the cat as he spoke, and Frances was struck by the absolute lack of rancour in his manner; by the absence of any sort of passion in him. She said quietly, after a pause,

'I miss the War too. You've no idea, Mr Crowther, what it costs me to admit that. But we can't succumb to the feeling, can we? We'll fade away like ghosts if we do. We have to change our expectations. The big things don't count any more. I mean the capital-letter notions that got so many of our generation killed. But that makes the small things count more than ever, doesn't it?'

'The small things?' He smiled. 'Like this little beast, you mean?'

'I mean ordinary things, to be done well. Bits of ground to till and care for. Houses to sweep.'

'Houses to sweep,' he repeated, still with that smile on his face, and she couldn't tell from his tone whether he liked the idea or was making fun of it. She didn't know, after all, whether she liked the idea herself or suddenly thought it a nonsense. The sight of him petting the cat like that had begun to get on her nerves. There seemed no life in him at all save in the tips of his restless fingers. She suspected that he had come to Mrs Playfair's tonight for the same reason she had—simply as a way of killing an evening, striking another one off the calendar. Perhaps the prospect of a free dinner had appealed to him, too.

The thought dismayed her. She turned away from him. And, in doing so, she saw that, over on the terrace, Mrs Playfair and her mother were watching her. Or, rather, they were watching her and Mr Crowther, in a sly but interested way, as if there were something significant about the fact that they were sitting quietly together in the dusky garden; as if to gauge how the two of them were 'doing'.

The predictability of it made her more dismayed than ever. She let out her breath in a puff of impatience; he heard, raised his eyes, then glanced across at the terrace himself.

'Ah, yes. I think I was meant to sing for my supper in more ways than one this evening. I can only wish, Miss Wray, that I wasn't such a poor sort of song-bird for you.'

'Not in the least,' she said tightly. 'You mustn't think that.'

'You wouldn't care to play along? We could take a turn around the garden, or—'

'No, I'd rather not.'

He looked into her face, his smile fading at last. 'I'm afraid you're upset.'

'Not upset.—Oh, I can't explain.'

He waited, in a kind enough sort of way; but he didn't wait very long. He went back to fussing with the cat, and they sat in silence for another few minutes, until the creature, suddenly bored, sprang from his knee like a pale monkey and went chasing after a moth.

Frances rose. 'Shall we join the ladies?'

Once the four of them had moved indoors she sat saying little, doing her best to return smiles; but it was no good. Her resolutions were peeling from her like bark from a tree. She could feel herself advancing steadily but helplessly into a state of dejection—as steadily and helplessly as if she were being screwed into it. Patty brought a tray of liqueurs. A game of auction bridge was proposed. 'Emily, you'll be my partner,' Mrs Playfair told Frances's mother, in her high-handed way. 'We can pit our wits against these youngsters.'

But, 'I'm afraid I shan't be up to playing,' said Frances. 'I've something of a headache. I expect it was the sun, at dinner.'

'Oh, what a pity!'

The older women were disappointed. One could hardly, after all, play auction bridge with three. So instead the gramophone was opened, and a couple of old-fashioned waltzes were aired. They discussed the day's news: loans to Germany, society divorces . . . But with Frances's rather chilling presence in it the little party quickly began to falter. In the end they were all grateful to Yum-Yum, who returned noisily to Mr Crowther's knee to butt her head against his fingers, and who at least gave them something to look at.

At twenty to ten Patty was asked to bring the hats. Mr

Crowther, obliging to the last, escorted Frances and her mother the short distance to their garden gate.

The two of them went into the house in silence, to find the hall unlighted and everything looking, as it often did after a visit to Mrs Playfair's, rather dim and small and crowded. The stairs, thought Frances in despair, might never have been polished, the floor never cleaned, though she had been down on her knees that morning, going over the skirting boards with Vim.

She took off her hat, then stood on her tiptoes to put a match to the gas.

Her mother was lingering. 'How's your head?'

'It isn't too bad.'

'Will you have an aspirin?'

'No. I'll go straight to bed, I think.'

'Oh, will you? Then it's hardly worth your doing the light.'

'The Barbers will want it, later. I suppose they're out again.'

'Oh, yes, I suppose so . . . And you're really going up right now? Won't you sit with me a minute? You could tell me what you and Mr Crowther were chatting about.'

'There's nothing to tell, Mother.'

'You seemed so deep in conversation. There must be something.'

'Nothing, I assure you!'

Her mother tutted. 'Well, you certainly seem in a very odd temper tonight. I can't think why.'

Frances put away the box of matches. 'Can't you?'

They looked at each other across the tiles, the only sound between them the slow pant of the gas. Then her mother's expression closed.

'Well, I shall let you get to your bed. I hope your head is better by the morning.'

'Thank you,' said Frances, turning away. And by the time she had seen to the stove and taken out the milk-can her mother was in her room with the door shut.

She started up the staircase, hating the sight of it. She drew together the curtains at the turn and wanted to rip them from their rings. She really did have a headache now—or, anyhow, could feel it gathering, tightening, mounting from the muscles at the top of her spine.

Then she climbed the last few stairs, and saw a light in the Barbers' sitting-room, heard the thump of feet on the boards—and realised with an extra plunge of dismay that the couple were at home after all. Her step slowed, then speeded up. But she was not quite quick enough. Mr Barber emerged on to the shadowy landing at the very moment she did.

He was slipperless and jacketless, dressed in one of his soft-collared shirts, and had two empty tumblers in his hands. 'Miss Wray! We had the notion you'd be out until late. Everything all right?'

Could he have overheard her exchange with her mother? She didn't want him to suppose that she was going to bed in a huff. So she forced a smile. 'Yes, quite all right. We've been for dinner at a neighbour's.'

'I wish we'd known you'd be back so early. We would have asked you and your mother to join us for a drink. We're celebrating tonight.'

'Oh, yes?'

'Yes, I don't like to boast, but—well, a little promotion at work, for yours truly.'

He touched his moustache as he spoke, in a mock-modest gesture. She saw then, through the gloom, that the tumblers he was carrying had a lacework of froth inside them and puddles of beer at the bottom, and that his colour was rather high. Still smiling, she began to edge past him. 'Congratulations. Good for you.'

He put out a hand. 'Well, look here, why not join us now? It isn't so late. Just a night-cap? One for the road? Lily would like it— wouldn't you, Lil?' He had moved back into the sitting-room—done it nimbly, on his shoeless feet—and now he spoke to the part of the room that was hidden from Frances by the open door. 'Miss Wray's out here, back early from her dinner. I've told her she must come in and join us.'

There was no audible answer, but Frances, hearing the creak of the sofa, simply saw no way out of it. Mr Barber beckoned to her, and she followed him into the room.

Lilian was sitting in the amber-coloured light of a single lamp, looking uncertain about whether or not to get to her feet. She was slipperless like her husband, her colour was high like his, and the cushions all around her were squashed and disarranged. Sprawled on one of them was the doll that Frances had seen the couple playing with that other time. She got a proper view of it now: a loosely-jointed thing with padded limbs and a leering expression, dressed in navy blue corduroy and a white sailor's cap.

She felt another gust of loneliness. When Lilian rose and said, in a self-conscious way, 'Hello, Frances. Isn't it nice about Len's promotion?' she found herself answering, falsely hearty, like another person altogether, 'Isn't it, though! I'll bet you're bucked.'

Mr Barber puffed out his chest, pretending smugness now. 'Yes, when the chief called me into his room this morning I thought he was going to let loose a rocket! Instead he sat me down and gave me a cigar and said, "Now, listen here, Barber. A talented fellow like you—"'

'Oh, he didn't say that,' said Lilian.

'Those were his exact words! "Now, look here, Barber m'boy. A bright spark like you oughtn't to be stuck in the sort of post that's never going to bring him in more than two-oh-five a year. Old Errington's leaving us soon. What d'you say to taking over his desk? There's a clear ten pounds extra in it for you. And just to show you how much we think of you, say we add on another fiver, make it a round two-twenty!"'

Frances's smile felt painful now. Two hundred and twenty pounds! She had just that morning received a dividend statement—

one of the doomed investments put in place by her father—for forty-five. Last year the statement had been for sixty.

'Good for you!' she said again. 'No wonder you're celebrating. But, look, I mustn't intrude—'

'Oh, don't say that.' He seemed really sorry. 'We're all friends, aren't we?'

'Of course, but—'

'And it's still broad daylight outside! It isn't even ten o'clock! I know the clock on the shelf says a quarter past, but that clock's like Lily—rather fast.' With a snigger, he dodged away from his wife's hand: she had leaned to take a swipe at him.

Frances had to move out of his path. The movement took her further into the room. She tried again. 'Please don't trouble.'

But she felt worn down. The strength had been squeezed out of her by the tangles of her own peculiar mood. Mr Barber, in a way that would brook no further protest, said, 'Now, what do you fancy? Stout? Sherry? A gin and lemonade?' And after a moment's struggle she answered, defeated, 'A gin and lemonade, then. Just a small one, Mr Barber.'

He made for the door. 'And how about Lily? Still stout, is she?'

Another swipe, another dodge, and Lilian's colour rose higher. 'I'll have the same as Frances,' she called after him, as he went off to the kitchen.

He took the life of the room with him. In his absence, she and Frances stood like strangers. After a moment, they sat, Lilian returning to her place on the dishevelled sofa, Frances taking the easy chair, perching at the front of it, not easy at all. From out in the kitchen there came the sound of a stopper being drawn from a bottle, followed by the chink of glasses.

'It seems ages since I've seen you,' said Lilian at last.

'You see me every day,' said Frances.

'You know what I mean. How are you?'

'Oh, yes, I'm tip-top. And you? What have you been up to? Did you ever finish *Anna Karenina*?'

But at that, Lilian lowered her gaze. 'I wish now that I'd never read it. It made me too sad.'

She pulled the doll on to her knee and began picking at its corduroy trousers. Frances's eye was caught by something on the mantelpiece: the Turkish delight box, tucked between the Spanish fan and the Buddha.

There was no time to comment on it. Mr Barber was back, three tumblers in his hands, one of them dark with beer, the others so full of gin and lemonade that the mixture was slopping over his fingers. He closed the door behind him with his foot, and brought the glasses across the room. Frances took hers gingerly because of the drips. He handed the other to Lilian, then stood with his hand at his mouth, sucking the spilled drink from his knuckles.

Then, 'Oh, *I* see what *you're* up to,' he said, in a tone of reproach.

Frances, just for a second, thought that he was addressing her. But he was talking to the doll.

'Sailor Sam down here,' he explained, 'has got his eye on Lil. Every time I turn my back, he manages to find his way on to her lap.' He set his glass on the floor and took hold of the doll instead. 'Up you come, my lad! You've had your fun for the evening. You can sit up here on the mantelpiece and keep your wandering hands to yourself . . . That's assuming I can find a spot for you amongst all these blessed gewgaws.' He moved aside the Buddha, the rattling tambourine. 'Did you ever see such a lot of rubbish in your life, Miss Wray? You know you should never sit too still, don't you, when Lily's around? Just in case she pins a bow on you. Not that you wouldn't look nice with a bow, I'm sure. Sailor Sam thinks so, don't you, Sailor Sam? But, what's that?' He lifted the doll's leering face to his ear. 'You aren't so sure about Lily? You think Lily looks like a—Oh, Sailor Sam, that's not a very nice word!'

Lilian put out a foot to give him a kick—a proper kick, this time—and he dodged away from it with another snigger. He fitted the doll on to the mantelpiece, making a fuss about crossing its legs, then retrieved his drink and sat down at his wife's side.

Frances, tired, uncomfortable, unenchanted by Sailor Sam, wondered if she had made a mistake. The glass was sticky in her hand. She had had sherry, wine and a crème de menthe at Mrs Playfair's, and didn't at all want another drink. Now that the door was shut, and with the pool of light from the lamp so narrow, the room seemed small and close and she was, she realised, trapped in it. She was trapped in it with Lilian, at whom she couldn't look without a gulp of dismay. She was trapped with Mr Barber, whom she did not quite trust. And, worst of all, she was trapped with their marriage, their mystifying union, which had evidently passed out of whatever affectionate phase it had recently enjoyed and was already mired in some new quarrel . . . She didn't care about the details. Lifting her glass to her lips she thought: I shan't stay longer than fifteen minutes. She took a sip—a large sip, to hurry the drink down—and instantly began to cough. The mixture had caught in her throat. It seemed all gin.

'Don't say it's too stiff for you, Miss Wray?' said Mr Barber, his blue eyes wide.

And now the innuendoes were back! Still coughing, she couldn't answer. She took a second sip to calm the first, then pointedly set the glass aside.

Almost immediately, however, he raised his own glass for a toast, and she was obliged to drink again.

'Well, here's to my two-twenty!' His narrow throat jumped as he swallowed. Wiping the froth from his moustache he said, 'I tell you what, Miss Wray. I wish my brother Dougie were here. He's been with his firm for thirteen years, and he's on less than I'll be getting.—Not that I mean to stick at two-twenty, mind,' he added, perhaps feeling that he had given too much away. 'But now, you see, I shall be right behind another fellow; and *his* is the job I want.

Still, I shan't be doing too badly. A desk to myself, a telephone, a secretary—'

'He's even had his nails done, Frances,' Lilian broke in. 'He went for a manicure on his way home from work. Aren't they fine?'

At that, his expression changed. With a frown at his fingernails he said slowly, 'I dunno. You women are allowed to spend hours beautifying yourselves, but if a chap tries to smarten himself up he gets chipped about it! I've my position to consider now. I've an example to set to the juniors.'

'I suppose it's a pretty girl that does it, is it?' Lilian asked him.

'Well, you suppose wrong, don't you? It's a pretty fellow, as it happens. Chap with a wave in his hair, and a lisp.' He gave Frances a wink. 'Likes holding my hand just a bit too much for my liking, if you get my drift, Miss Wray?'

Frances, growing hot, reached for her drink again—and saw Lilian, at the same moment, reaching for hers. *I'll stay for ten minutes,* she thought. *I'll stay for less than that—for five. He'll make a fuss about me leaving, but that doesn't matter . . .*

Already, however, after just three mouthfuls, she could feel the gin inside her, quick and warm, like a friendly flame; the friendliest thing, it seemed to her, that she had encountered in ages. And by the time she had taken a fourth sip Mr Barber had begun to seem a shade less annoying. He told her a couple of office anecdotes, but soon reverted to his theme of the night—his cool two-twenty and what he planned to do with it. There were certain bonds and investments that he had in his sights, he said. There were chaps—connections of his, stockbrokers and bankers—all poised to put first-rate deals his way.

'Of course,' he went on, with a swerve of tactic, 'it doesn't help a working fellow if he's got a certain type of wife. I mean the sort of wife'—his tone became pointed—'who likes spending her husband's money, but who doesn't understand that, in order for a chap to earn the money in the first place, he has to be made a bit of a fuss of. The sort of wife who sits at home all day in her nightie, reading books about society girls getting ravished by desert princes.'

Lilian made a face at him. 'You ought to go back to your parents', then. There aren't any books there.'

He looked at Frances and gave a shrug. 'See what I have to put up with? You know, I'm thinking of writing a book of my own one day. All about the ordinary chap and the things he's had to contend with since the War. *That*'ll be worth reading! You can have the first copy if you like.'

Frances sipped again. 'Thanks. I'll make a space on the shelf. Somewhere between Austen and Dostoevsky all right?'

'Yes, I'll sign it "To Frances, with—"' He caught himself up. 'Whoops! Miss Wray, I suppose I should say. But that sounds so awfully old-fashioned. You don't mind me calling you Frances, do you? Now that we're all getting along so well?'

His tone was so affable that it would have been impossible to protest or demur, but Frances felt taken by surprise—almost tripped up. She had no interest in calling him Leonard, she wouldn't have dreamt of calling him Len, and she had the sneaking suspicion that his slip of the tongue was less accidental than he was pretending. Worst of all, the moment somehow undid some of the specialness of her friendship with Lilian. Was this, she thought, what happened when one made friends with a married woman? One automatically got the husband too?—like a crochet pattern, coming free with a magazine?

But then, of course, the specialness of her friendship with Lilian had already melted away. Looking at her across the hearth-rug, she wasn't sure that she even liked her very much. Her figure seemed bosomy as a barmaid's tonight. She was wearing brass bangles on one of her wrists, and they kept clattering up and down her arm with a cheap sort of ring. How conventional she was, really, for all her arty pretensions! Just now, for example, she had drawn up her legs and was shifting around on the sofa. Mr Barber—Leonard,

Frances supposed she had to call him—Leonard had begun to complain that he was being kicked; that made her kick out at him in earnest, and he caught hold of her feet. They started to tussle, laughing and snorting, her skirt rising, exposing her knees. For more than a minute they kept it up, appealing to Frances for help or for judgement: 'Tell him to stop it, Frances!' 'It's her, Frances, not me!'

Even with the gin inside her this began to be tiresome. Frances had the sense that their antics were a weird kind of show, done for her but not flattering to her. She suspected that if she were to leave the room their hilarity would instantly die; that they would sit there, side by side, in silence.

Perhaps they suspected the same thing, because when she made a move to rise they grew calmer, as if really wanting her to stay. She drank more of her gin, still thinking to hurry it down; but then she was amazed, on lifting the tumbler, to find it three-quarters empty. The moment the last quarter was gone Leonard was up on his feet, whisking the glass away to be refilled along with Lilian's and his own. She protested as he took it; she protested when he brought it back. He told her it was mostly lemonade—she knew that was untrue as soon as she tried it. But the knowledge was curiously without force. And when, with a smudge of discomfort, she thought of her mother in the room below, the thought had another feeling mixed up with it, something dark and unkind. *Mother*, she told herself, sipping again, *can like it or lump it*.

What was Leonard doing now? He seemed unable to sit still. He had gone to a drawer to dig something out of it—a fancy box, with a hinged lid. He brought the box to Frances and displayed it like a waiter.

'What do you think?' The box held cigarettes, fat, black, foreign-looking. 'The real thing, these are. Given to me by a grateful client. He has them shipped in from the East. Can't you smell the Orient in them?' He waved them about under her nose.

She wasn't sure whether he was offering them or simply show-ing them off. She gave a nod. 'Very nice.'

'Well?'

'Well, what?'

'Are you up to them?'

'Oh, but I had the idea that you didn't approve of ladies smok-ing.'

He looked shocked. 'What, me? Who told you that? I'm all for ladies' rights, I am. I'm a proper Mrs Pankhurst.'

'Really.'

'Oh, yes.'

She hesitated—then heard a sound in the room below and, with another surge of dark bravado, dipped in her hand and drew out the fattest cigarette of all. Leonard gave a honk of laugher—'Oh, Frances! I always knew there was more to you than met the eye!'—and produced a book of matches from his pocket, with which he struck her a flame. There was a silver saucer near by, with one or two butts already in it, but he wouldn't let her use that. Instead he brought over the stand-ashtray, the horrid bronze-effect thing, set-ting it down with a flourish beside her chair.

Lilian watched all this from the sofa as if not quite liking what she saw. When Leonard returned to her side with the cigarettes, she reached for them and said, 'Well, if Frances is having one I'm going to have one too.'

At once he drew the box away from her. 'Oh, don't *you* have one.'

'Why not?'

'They're too good for you, these are. Besides'—he stroked his moustache—'I might want to kiss you later. It'll be like kissing a man.'

'Then you'll know what I have to put up with!'

They tussled over the box, but Lilian got hold of a cigarette at last and, grumblingly, he lit it for her. For a minute the three of them sat in silence, slightly stunned by the strength of the tobacco. The smoke unfolded from their mouths and nostrils, tangible as muslin, bluish-grey where it hung in the shadows, green where it crossed the amber lamplight.

The room quickly began to resemble Frances's notion of an opium den. Lilian and Leonard were sitting so loosely on the sofa that they were practically lolling, Lilian with her knees drawn up, Leonard low, his legs out in front of him, his feet on the red leather pouffe. Frances had been keeping near the front of the easy chair all this time, but the sight of the two of them lounging like that made the pose feel unnatural. She leaned back, giving herself over to the plush. Leonard drew her attention to a lever fitted at the side of the chair. Slightly wary, she pulled it—and with a grinding, collapsing motion the chair transformed itself into a recliner. Her head went back, her feet came up, and she felt the gin in a rush as she tilted. She might have been a hollow vessel with the liquor inside her, its surface spreading as she approached the horizontal. She said to herself, in astonishment, 'I'm a little drunk! Christ, how squalid!' Again, though, the knowledge had no bite. It seemed hardly to concern her. And the Barbers, of course, were drunker, had been at it longer than she had. She still had that advantage over them, that crucial touch of superiority. As for the chair—it was a revelation! A masterpiece of engineering! Well, that was the clerk class for you. They might be completely without culture, but they certainly knew how to make themselves comfortable . . .

In what appeared to be no time at all she lifted her glass and was once again surprised to find it empty; and once again Leonard noticed, rose, rounded up the empty tumblers and took them off to be refilled. But when he had returned and handed out the glasses he stood and gazed around the room, drawing in his lower lip, making a clicking, calculating sound against it with his mobile little tongue.

Lilian was watching him over the rim of her tumbler. 'What are you looking for?'

He spoke to Frances instead. 'How about a game of something, Frances?'

'A game?' She thought he must mean, perhaps, Charades, at which she was hopeless, painfully bad. 'Oh, no. I must get to bed. It must be late, mustn't it?'

No one answered her. Lilian was still watching Leonard. He had gone across the room again; now, from the lowest shelf of a bookcase, he pulled a battered card box. As he brought it back into the lamplight Frances caught sight of its colourful lid.

'Snakes and Ladders!'

He grinned. 'You like this game?' The grin grew sly. 'So does Lily. Don't you, Lil?'

In reply, Lilian leaned and tried to snatch the box from his hands. He held it out of her reach, however, and, once he had kicked aside the pouffe, he unfolded the board and set it down in the middle of the floor, then picked out three wooden counters—yellow for Frances, blue for Lilian, red for himself—assertively thumbing them on to the carpet like a gambler setting down coins. Frances leaned closer, for a better look. Then, since it seemed like a lark, she clambered out of the chair, kicked off her shoes, and joined him on the floor—doing it all rather unsteadily, but taking her glass of gin with her. The counters were chipped, rubbed pale at the edges. The board was furred and loose in its folds. The game looked about thirty years old, but the illustrations were still acidly colourful, and where a number was faded it had been inked back into its square. Some of the inky numerals were extravagant; they grew limbs, became flowers, hearts, musical notes. And several of the snakes had been given top hats, or spectacles and whiskers.

Lilian was still sitting on the sofa. Frances said, 'Won't you join us?'

She shook her head, her expression veiled. 'I don't want to play.'

'I'd have thought you'd like all these colours.'

Lilian looked at her, looked away. Leonard sniggered. 'She doesn't like losing.'

She frowned at him. 'That's not true!'

'She's a bad sport.'

'Is she?' asked Frances.

'No, I'm not.'

'She cheats like anything.'

'Oh, dear.'

'No, I don't! *He's* the cheater!'

'Prove it, then.'

'Yes, come on!' said her husband, reaching for her and pulling her down to the floor.

She came with a bump, spilling some of her drink on the way, and when she tried to return to the sofa he reached and pulled her back again. So she gave in—still refusing to smile, though; pulling a cushion from the sofa and shifting herself on to it, tucking her skirt around her legs, but doing it with cross, clumsy movements, then sitting with her glass raised, hiding her mouth.

Frances ran fingers across the board, tracing the curves of one of the snakes.

'What a nice old game this is.'

Leonard was straightening the spinner, a creased card hexagon on a wooden spike. He said, 'It was Dougie's, when we were boys. Don't go sucking on your yellow counter, will you? I think it might have arsenic in it.'

She heard herself titter. 'Was it your brother who added the hearts and the whiskers?'

He twirled the spinner against his palm. 'Ah. No, that was Lily and me.'

There was something behind his words. Raising her eyes, she saw him smirking. Before she knew what she was doing she had leaned and poked his knee. 'What? What is it?'

He looked at Lilian, and opened his mouth to answer. But Lilian spoke more quickly.

'It's just a thing to make the game more silly. It's just something Len and I sometimes do. If you land on a square with musical notes drawn on it, you have to sing something—a song, I mean. If you land on a flower, you have to—well, you have to pretend to be a flower, and the other person has to say what flower you are. I told you it was silly!'

Frances had tittered again. But there was more, she could see. She pointed to a square with a heart drawn on it.

'And what happens if you land on this?'

'Nothing.—Don't, Len!'

He protested. 'Frances wants to know! It's only fair to tell her the rules. It's like this, Frances. When Lily lands on a heart, she—'

Lilian put down her glass and reached across the board to hit him. She swung her hand hard, but he caught her wrist and they struggled. It wasn't quite like their tussles from before, which had been manufactured as if for Frances's benefit. They fought seriously this time, reddening with the effort of it; for several seconds they were almost still, in a sort of perfect tension, braced against each other but attempting to pull apart, like a couple of repelling magnets.

Then Lilian let out her breath in a burst of nervous laughter and Leonard, making the most of her moment of weakness, got hold of her other hand and pinned her wrists together.

'When Lily lands on that,' he told Frances, strained and breathless and beginning to laugh himself, 'she has to take off one of her things!'

Frances had been expecting something of the sort. All the same, the words came as a shock, and her first, flustered thought was: Can Mother hear? But the room, with its shut door and its cone of lamplight, had begun to feel not so much confining as insulated, snug. Lilian was rubbing at her wrists where her husband had

146

gripped them, looking flushed from the struggle, looking vexed, embarrassed, excited—Frances wasn't sure which. Leonard's smirk had broadened.

She met his gaze as if meeting a challenge. 'Just the one thing?'

'Just the one.'

'And how about when *you* land on it?'

'When I land on it,' he said, with his worst smirk yet, 'well, then Lily has to take off something else.'

'I see. And what will happen—well, if *I* land on it?'

He thought that over, or pretended to, stroking his bristly chin. 'Now, there's a poser. We've never played, you understand, with a third party . . . If you land on a heart, Frances, I should say—well, that Lilian ought to take off something else. Though you'd be welcome to take off something too, if you'd like to.'

As a piece of gallantry, she thought, that was rather belated—if an invitation to remove one's clothes over a game of Snakes and Ladders could be construed as gallantry at all. But she was at the high point of drunkenness now, excited by the gin and the tobacco—excited too, despite herself, by the atmosphere of raciness and intimacy into which the little party was plunging. And the evening had started so unpromisingly! She recalled, as if from a distance, her own bad temper, Mrs Playfair, Mr Crowther—

Oh, but Mr Crowther was a wet. Fancy sitting in a twilit garden with a girl and fussing over a Siamese cat. She could have done better than that herself!

And suddenly time had made a queer leap forward and, without her quite knowing how, the game had begun. One needed a six, Leonard told her, to start, and she spent a frustrated few minutes turning up other numbers, while first he and then Lilian sent their men hopping across the board. And when she did join the game at last, she promptly landed on one of the doctored squares, one with a treble clef drawn on it, which meant she had to sing a snatch of song. She sang the first thing that came into her head; it was 'Baa Baa Black Sheep'. She sang the first two lines only, and pitched the opening note so badly that the high 'any' came out as a tortured squeak. But Leonard applauded as if she had given an operatic solo, gripping a fresh cigarette at the side of his mouth and calling around it, as he clapped, 'Bravo!'

The next number he spun took his counter to a square with a drawing of a flower on it. He went through a writhing, complicated pantomime while Frances and Lilian attempted to guess the flower he was representing. A daisy? A rose? It turned out to be creeping ivy—which led the three of them into a noisy argument about whether ivy could be considered to be a flower at all, or was simply a plant. He ended the debate by spinning Lilian's number for her and swiftly hopping her man across the board. Whether he deliberately muddled the move or not, Frances wasn't sure, but the counter went sliding down a top-hatted snake to end on one of the inky hearts.

'No,' Lilian said quickly, 'that's not fair!'

'Yes it is. Isn't it fair, Frances?'

'Well—'

'There. Frances says it's fair; and Frances is a high-brow. I told you she cheats, Frances. She's all promises, this one.'

Lilian put out her foot and kicked him, hard; Frances heard the crack of her heel against his shin-bone. But while he howled and clutched his leg she kept still for a moment, clearly thinking the forfeit over. Then she rose to her knees, drew off her clattering bangles and slapped them down in tipsy triumph beside the board.

Leonard cried immediately: 'Cheat! She's cheating again! Bracelets don't count!'

And, 'Cheat!' echoed Frances. She cupped her hands around her mouth. 'Boo! Shame!'

Lilian made a gesture as if to swat them both away. 'Yes, they do count. They do, if creeping ivy can be a flower.'

'Rubbish!'

'They do!'

Reluctantly, they let their protests subside. But Leonard looked at Frances in disgust. 'What'll it be next time? A hair from her head?'

Lilian got hold of her drink, and the game continued. At Leonard's next turn his counter landed on a 'musical' square, and that perked him up. He sang 'Everybody's Doing It'—sang it in a boisterous Cockney manner, clipping his 'g's, hooking his thumbs into his armpits like a costermonger, finally leaning across the board to his wife and prodding her in the stomach and thighs in time to the song.

He continued to hum as the game proceeded. He drank off the last of his beer while Lilian and Frances took their turns, but Frances saw him gazing sideways down at the board as he swallowed, clearly calculating his next move. When he took hold of the spinner he gave it such a violent twist that it went cartwheeling across the floor and disappeared into the shadow of the sofa. He leapt after it, and brought it back saying, 'Five! Most definitely five!' And as he tripped his man forward it became clear that he had engineered the move in order to take the counter to another heart.

He looked glumly at Lilian. 'Oh, dear.'

Frances looked at Lilian too. She had drawn down another cushion from the sofa and was hugging it to her bosom. She shook her head. 'No.'

'Now, don't be like that,' he said reasonably. 'You know the rules. I didn't make them.'

'Yes, you did!'

'No, I didn't! It was Mr . . . Kidd.' He had picked up the lid of the box and was pretending to read the manufacturer's instructions. 'He was one of those dirty-minded Victorian so-and-sos, I expect. Yes, here it is, in black and white. "Whenever a player lands on a square marked with a heart, the lady in the room with the shadiest character must remove one of her garments." Well, I mean to say,' he appealed to his wife, 'that can't be Frances, can it?'

Lilian had been smiling at last, but at his words her smile grew fixed, and now it wavered and broke and she turned her head from him. Undeterred, he pressed on. '"If said lady refuses to remove one garment, as a forfeit she must remove *two*! *Bracelets not to be counted!*"' He punched the lid with his finger, holding it up as if to display it, then whisking it away. 'Well, we'll be kind and let the bracelet business pass. But really, Lil, rules is rules. Come along now, play the game. You're showing yourself up. Good heavens, you'd think she'd never undressed in front of a gentleman before, wouldn't you, Frances? You'd think—'

'All right,' said Lilian sharply. She got to her feet, dropping the cushion, but then for some reason stepping on to it, moving about to get her balance. The gin seemed to have caught up with her, all of it at once. She made a lurch to the side, her heel came down hard on the carpeted boards, and her barmaidy bosom gave a bounce.

Frances thought again of her mother, trying to sleep in the room below. What time was it, anyhow? She had no idea. She looked for the clock and couldn't find it.

Leonard, naturally, was as serious as ever—saying to his wife, in a warning way, 'Now, remember what I said. No *hairs*, or any tricks like that. No *earrings*. No—'

'Oh, let me alone!' she said. She stood frowning for a moment, then came to some decision and, turning, faced the chimney-breast, putting her back to him and to Frances. The back was squarest to him, however: Frances, watching from her place by the easy chair, suddenly unable to look away, saw her lift the hem of her skirt and grope beneath it for the top of her stocking; she saw the stocking grow opaque as it was eased down over her thigh, her knee, her calf and lifted foot. By the time it was free, Leonard was whistling like a workman on the street. Lilian turned back to him and dipped an ironic, inelegant curtsy. She screwed the stocking into a ball and made as if to throw it—her stance suggesting, as her hand came up, that she was wondering, just for a second, whether to throw it at him or at Frances. She chose her husband: she threw it hard, but it unrolled as it flew. He caught it and ran it across his moustache.

'Now,' he said as he did it, 'a more scrupulous fellow than me might say that, since stockings come in pairs, they ought really to count as one garment . . . But, hell, I'll be generous.'

He put the stocking around his neck and began to fuss with it, trying to tie it into a bow above his ordinary collar. Lilian sat heavily back down on her cushion and tucked her skirt around her legs. But the skirt reached only to her ankles, leaving her feet illuminated baldly by the lamp; and somehow the sight of the two plump feet together like that, one of them stockinged, one of them bare, was more unsettling, more indefinably lewd, than if both had been naked. Frances kept drawing her gaze away from them, but the gaze kept creeping back. Purely to break the spell of the thing she lifted her glass, not wanting the gin at all, but recklessly drinking it down anyhow; beginning to feel a little sick as a result.

Leonard had finished the bow at his throat. He looked like a comical cat on a picture postcard. Slapping his hands together he returned to the board. '*Allons-y!* Whose turn is it next? Well? Frances? Is it yours?'

It was his wife's turn, Frances knew. Probably he knew it himself. But Lilian kept to her cushion, saying nothing.

'Perhaps we ought to put the game away now,' Frances said.

'Put it away?' said Leonard. 'You're joking! Things are just warming up. Come on, whose turn is it? Is it yours?'

'No,' she admitted.

'I thought as much. Let's have you then, Lil! Don't keep me and Frances waiting. I want my second stocking, don't I?'

His voice jarred on Frances now. He was like a boy with a whip, trying to keep up the boisterous motion of the game. But the game seemed to be turning against him. The whole evening was turning, breaking apart on sour currents in a way she didn't quite understand.

Lilian worked the spinner in silence. The number took her to a ladder; her counter went up it to an empty square. Then it was Frances's turn, then Leonard's, then Lilian's again—the game running on without incident, though at every spin Leonard tensed, then gasped or groaned or clapped his hands to his head, like a Regency buck at the card-table watching his gold, his horse, his country estate, his entire fortune, melt away.

Then Frances's turn came round again, and, drunk as she was, she saw at once that the number she had spun carried her counter to a square with a heart drawn on it. She said quickly, 'I muddled that one. I'm going to spin again.'

Leonard, however, was quicker. 'No second spins! That's in the rules too.' He picked up her man and moved it for her: ' . . . three, four, five. Aha! Another heart! Perhaps I shall get my pair of stockings after all. What do you say, Frances?'

Lilian had drawn up her knees, and had bowed her head to meet them. Her voice was muffled by the fabric of her skirt. 'I don't want to play any more. You're ganging up on me! It's not fair!'

'Come on!' he cried. 'We're waiting. You can't welch on us now.'

'I don't want to play!' She wailed it, and when she lifted her head her face was puffed and blurry, almost ugly. She spoke like a child. 'I'm tired. I feel giddy. You've made me drink too much. You always do.'

'I like that!' he answered. 'There's you and Frances been putting it away like a right pair of sozzlers—'

Oh, shut up! thought Frances. She felt really unwell suddenly. She had changed her pose, put a hand to the floor, and found that the floor wasn't quite where it ought to have been. She said, 'It's late, isn't it? What time is it?'

'It's time for Lilian to get cracking!'

'I need my bed. I feel dreadful.'

'You need a bit more gin, that's all. Come on, Frances. I thought you were enjoying it. Don't you want to see the show?'

She gazed at him in muzzy disbelief. What on earth was she doing here? She knew that her room was close by, just on the other side of the wall, but she had a panicky feeling that she was far from home, among strangers. And was that a noise downstairs, a door opening and closing? She began to rise, saying, 'Oh, God, I need to go to bed.'

He put out his hand to her. 'Don't do that.' He actually gripped her, hotly, on the ankle. 'You're spoiling the game!'

The surprise of his touch sobered her slightly. She twisted her foot out of his grasp, then leaned unsteadily to the board. Taking hold of his wooden counter she slid it to the final square.

'There. You've won. That's what you wanted, isn't it?'

He looked sulky—or mock-sulky. She couldn't tell now.

'Well, it's no fun like that.'

'Hard luck. I'm tired. So's Lilian.'

'Oh, Lilian isn't tired. It's just a thing she likes to say.' He added quietly, turning his head, 'She'll probably say it again later. She won't mean it then, either.'

There was a silence after his words. He looked at his wife and said, 'What? Oh, Frances doesn't mind.' The sulkiness had disappeared. He leaned back on his elbows and grinned up at Frances, all his crowded teeth on display. 'Frances is a woman of the world—aren't you, Frances?'

She was trying to straighten her frock. She said, without smiling, 'I might have been once.'

He answered quickly, 'Just the once? Still, once is all it takes—unfortunately. Ask Lil.'

His tone was so unpleasant now that, gazing down at his face, Frances had the urge, shockingly powerful, to kick him in it. Instead she turned away and began to work her feet into her shoes. 'Whoops!' he said, when she swayed. But it was Lilian who rose to

153

help her. She came across the rug, her own step far from steady, her face as pinkly mottled as a plate of ham, her skirt creased like a concertina above her mismatched feet and ankles. But she offered her hand for Frances to grip; and when she spoke, her voice was kind, tired, her own.

'I'm sorry, Frances.'

Frances saw the clock at last: it was a few minutes to midnight. Holding tight on to Lilian's hand she was filled with a vision, a sad mirage, of the simple, pleasant few hours that the two of them, in a different world, a different life, might have spent together. Instead—what had they done? They had squandered those hours on Leonard. She hadn't so much as gazed honestly into Lilian's face until this moment. Instead she had cajoled and bullied her—had clapped and cheered while she took off her clothes! And she had done it, she realised now, out of some mean, malicious impulse—siding against her with her husband, in order to punish her for being his wife.

She couldn't communicate any of this to Lilian. Shaking her head she said simply, 'I'm sorry, too.' She regained her balance; and Lilian's fingers slid out of hers.

Leonard got to his feet to escort her across the room. 'At least you haven't got far to go,' he said, palely humorous, as he opened the door for her. His manner had changed again. She went to step past him and he moved closer, approaching her with such intent that she thought for a moment that he might be about to kiss her. But what he did was to touch her arm, just above the elbow.

'You've been a jolly sport, Frances. You won't give any mind, will you, to me and my big mouth?'

She found herself unable to reply. She shook her head and moved away.

She looked so dreadful in her bedroom mirror, all her features blurred and coarse, that when she had taken off her frock she tried to drape it over the glass; almost at once, it slid to the floor. She needed the lavatory rather badly, so as soon as she had changed into her night-clothes she headed purposefully downstairs. The Barbers had not yet emerged from their sitting-room—she was glad about that. The hall light was still burning, but the edges of her mother's door were dark—she was glad about that, too. In what seemed a jumble of motion she let herself into the yard, visited the WC, then returned to the kitchen to pour herself a glass of water. She wasn't aware of drinking the water, or of putting down the glass, but the next moment she was empty-handed; the next moment again she was back on the stairs with the hall light extinguished; and then she was noisily closing her bedroom door and kicking off her slippers.

She approached the bed with longing, but once she had climbed on to it and was lying flat on her back the mattress tilted like the deck of a ship; she had to push herself upright again. She sat with her head in her hands and groaned. God Almighty, what an evening! If only she had stayed at Mrs Playfair's! She felt as though she'd been fed poison. The longer she sat there, the more unnaturally aware she became of various furious currents in her body: the slosh of liquids in her stomach, the pounding of blood through the channels of her ears. Braving the tilt of the bed, she carefully lowered herself back down. But there was no ease, no relief, to be found in any position; no possibility of escape from herself. When she closed her eyes she saw a sort of futurist nightmare, snakes and ladders in acid colours, inky hearts, Leonard's grinning red face. Clearest of all, however, she saw Lilian, groping for the clasp of her suspender. She saw the silk stocking coming down, over and over again.

6

When she awoke the next morning, at just before six, the details of her evening with the Barbers seemed weirdly out of reach. On the other side of the window the sun was already blazing, but of the night that had passed she retained only a muddle of echoes and impressions, noise and laughter, a glass in her hand . . . Apart from that, she felt quite clear-headed; unnaturally well, in fact. She knew that she had drunk more than she ought to have, but she seemed for the moment so unaffected, so unharmed, that she began to grow slightly complacent. Weren't there certain people, with particularly sturdy constitutions, who could stand large amounts of alcohol without ill effect? She must be one of those.

But only a few minutes later, as the factory whistles went off, the lustre of her well-being was beginning to cloud. The light at the edge of the curtains was bothering her. She needed the lavatory again, she wanted another glass of water, she felt as hollow as though she hadn't eaten anything in days. But when she attempted to sit upright her bed, like a beast, came back to life, and her insides gave such a sour plunge that she thought for a moment that she might be sick. She hastily lay flat again, rigid and swallowing, and though the worst of the feeling soon passed, she realised that making a trip downstairs was out of the question.

Thank God for the chamber-pot! She managed to fish it from under the bed, to squat giddily over it, to scurry back between the sheets. Now her heart was thudding as if it would burst. She didn't understand it. Could she have eaten something bad at Mrs Playfair's? Queasily, she thought over the meal: the soup, the sole, the chicken, the pudding, the cheese, the crème de menthe—

The memory of the glass of green liqueur made bile leap into her mouth. But what she tasted was gin and lemonade. Gin and lemonade; and black cigarettes.

And gradually, then—gradually but relentlessly, like a series of bloated corpses surfacing in murky water—gradually the evening in the Barbers' room came back to her. She remembered reclining in the easy chair with a glass in one hand and a fag in the other. She remembered pausing with her fingers over Mr Barber's box of cigarettes, gazing girlishly up at him, practically fluttering her eyelashes: 'I had the idea you didn't approve of ladies smoking.' She recalled singing 'Baa Baa Black Sheep' at the top of her lungs. She recalled tittering, she recalled bellowing, she recalled—

No, she wouldn't admit the memory! No, no, no!

But up it came, the most bloated corpse of all . . . She remembered leering like a drunken soldier while Lilian stood on a cushion to do a wobbly strip-tease.

She hid her face under her blanket, fighting down waves of nausea and shame.

At seven o'clock the Barbers' alarm clock went, and she heard Mr Barber—Leonard, damn it, she had to call him now—she heard Leonard rise, go softly downstairs, then return and enter his kitchen. She listened in disbelief to the jaunty ordinariness of his movements as he washed, shaved, fried himself a solitary breakfast. He was even, at one point, humming through his teeth; she felt that he was quite capable of breaking into the chorus of 'Everybody's Doing It'. Once she had recalled the image of him with his thumbs hooked in his armpits it hopped about on the inside of her eyelids and made her feel queasier than ever. When she heard the splash and gurgle of tea being poured from the pot, followed by the rattle of china as he carried the cups to his bedroom, she longed so dismally for a cup of tea of her own that she nearly wept.

There came a few calmer minutes after he had left the house, but presently she heard movement downstairs: her mother, heading for the kitchen. She thought of the stove to be seen to, the milk to be brought in, the breakfast to be made, all the chores of the day ahead of her. Could she do it? She had to try. Her stomach quivering, she rose, put on her slippers, tied on her dressing-gown. So far, so good. Then she went to the glass. Her eyes were red and swollen, but her face was powder white; even her lips were white. Her hair was sticking up as though she'd been electrocuted.

She did the best she could to put herself tidy, then ventured out of the room. There was no sign of life on the landing save the smell of Leonard's rashers.

Down in the kitchen she opened her mouth to wish her mother a casual good morning, and instead began to cough. The cough had the taste of those filthy cigarettes in it; it went on and on until it almost convulsed her.

'I hope you aren't starting a cold, Frances,' her mother said at last. She was cutting herself a slice of bread.

Frances wiped her mouth and streaming eyes, and spoke hoarsely. 'I think you know very well that I'm not.'

'You enjoyed yourself with Mr and Mrs Barber?'

She nodded, swallowing something with the taste and texture of tar. 'We didn't disturb you too much, did we? We ended up playing a silly game of—' She coughed again. 'Snakes and Ladders. Things ran on later than we planned.'

'Yes, I heard them doing that.'

Now the bread was cut and on a plate. It couldn't be toasted, with the stove unlighted. Her mother was bringing over the

158

butter dish, fishing out a knife from the drawer. But, the weather being so warm, the butter was beginning to run: Frances caught the faintly rancid whiff of it as the lid of the dish came off, and had to turn sharply away. She must have grown even paler as she did it, because her mother, with a mixture of rebuke and concern, lowered the knife to say, 'Really, Frances, you look dreadfully done-up! You must remember, you aren't as young as Mr and Mrs Barber.'

Frances kept her gaze from the liquefying butter. 'Mr Barber is only a year younger than I am.'

'Mr Barber is a man, with a man's constitution.'

'What a very Victorian thing to say.'

'Yes, well, as I've often pointed out, the Victorians are much maligned. How old is Mrs Barber?'

Frances hesitated. 'I don't know. Twenty-four or -five, I think.'

She knew very well that Lilian was twenty-two. But she was counting on her mother having reached a stage in life from which it was impossible to tell the age of anyone under forty. So her mother surprised her by narrowing her eyes in a sceptical way and saying, 'Well, she has a very youthful air indeed for a woman of five-and-twenty. As for Snakes and Ladders—'

'A nice Victorian game.'

'A nice noisy one, apparently! Noisier than I remembered it. I'm amazed you were up to playing. Your head was too sore, I thought, for bridge at Mrs Playfair's.'

Frances couldn't answer. She'd had another flashing vision of Lilian's stocking coming down. If her mother knew about that! The thought went through her on a wave of heat. With a trembling hand she drew herself a glass of water. Once she had drunk it she managed to take care of the stove. But then she caught another whiff of the butter-dish.

'If it's all the same to you, Mother, I think I'll go back upstairs for an hour. Tasker's boy will be here soon, but you can take the meat from him, can't you? I'll just slip a coat on and fetch the milk—'

'The milk is in already. Mr Barber brought it in for us. And, yes, I think bed is the best place for you. Goodness knows, we don't want anyone to see you while you're in this sort of condition.'

Frances drew herself another glass of water and slunk from the room.

So Leonard had brought in the milk, had he? He had never done that before. He must have guessed that she wouldn't be up to it. The thought made her uncomfortable. She remembered how, the previous night, he had pressed the gin on her, filling up her glass the moment it was empty. He'd practically poured it down her throat! Just why, exactly, had he done that? She recalled the grip of his hand on her ankle. She remembered, again, simpering at him over the box of cigarettes. And hadn't she leaned and poked his knee? Another wave of shame ran through her. She had to pause on the stairs and put a hand across her eyes. Once she was back in her room she lay turning the scenes over in her mind until she fell into a fretful sleep.

When she awoke from that, at almost eleven, she felt much better. She made a second start to her day, taking a bath, even managing a few light chores. She and her mother spoke politely to each other. They ate their lunch in the garden, in the shadow of the linden tree.

There was still no sign of Lilian. Frances began to wonder if she mightn't have quietly left the house. In a way, she hoped she had. In another—oh, she didn't know what she wanted. Her burst of energy was already fading; bringing in the lunch things from the garden seemed to finish it off. She had planned to go out today. She had promised to visit Christina. But she thought of the jolting journey, the walking about, the four flights of stone steps up to Chrissy's flat . . . She couldn't face it. When her mother settled her-self in the drawing-room with a new book of brain-teasers, she

160

crept back upstairs to her bedroom and lay fully clothed on the bed.

She no longer felt sick; that was something. And the room was comfortingly warm and dim. She had opened the window wide but left the curtains almost closed, and now and then a breeze stirred them, making the column of light between them blur and sharpen, widen and thin. The scents were those of the garden: sweet lavender, sharp geranium. From the scullery of a house near by she could just hear the splash of water, from a kitchen the whistle of a kettle, hectically rising, rising, then falling weakly away. The sounds and the smells snagged and tussled, but struck a precarious kind of balance. She felt herself held in the balance along with them, an infinitely fragile and humble thing.

She closed her eyes. Perhaps she dozed. She was faintly aware, in time, of the opening of Lilian's bedroom door, followed by slippered footsteps on the landing. But the steps slowed, hesitating, and something about the hesitation made her wake up properly; she could feel, as it were, the direction of it. Her stomach gave an unpleasant flutter. She was just pushing herself up into a sitting position when Lilian tapped at her door.

'Are you there, Frances?'

She cleared her throat. 'Yes. Yes, come in.'

The door opened and Lilian came gingerly into the twilit room. 'You weren't asleep?'

'Not really.'

'I wanted to see how you were.'

She stood with a hand on the doorknob, her other hand raised to her face, pushing in her cheek with her knuckles. She and Frances looked at each other, neither of them knowing what to say. Then Frances let her head fall back against the iron bed-head.

'God, but I feel seedy!'

Lilian said, 'Oh, so do I! I feel like nothing on earth! I don't know what to do with myself. Can I—Can I sit with you for a bit?'

Frances's stomach fluttered again, but she nodded. 'Yes, of course.'

Lilian closed the door and moved towards the bedroom chair. But the chair was draped with clothes from the night before, all of them reeking of cigarette smoke, and Frances, seeing the uncertainty in her step, said, 'I'll have to tidy that later. I haven't the strength for it now.' She shuffled back against her pillows and drew in her legs. 'Up here, instead? Is that all right for you?'

If Lilian hesitated, it was only for a moment. She climbed on to the bed, keeping right down at the foot of it, then sinking sideways against the wall, closing her eyes. Her eyelids were heavy, Frances saw now, and her hair had lost its dark shine. She was wearing a skirt the colour of an envelope, and her plain white blouse had just a bit of violet stitching on its cuffs and at its collar—as if that was all the dash she had been able to muster.

She opened her eyes, and met Frances's gaze. 'I'm so sorry about last night.'

Frances blinked, embarrassed. 'So am I.'

'I don't know what was the matter with me. I didn't do or say a natural thing all evening. Len was even worse. What must you think of us? He feels awful about it now.'

'Does he?'

'Oh, yes. Don't you believe me?'

Frances didn't know what to think. She recalled the sound of Leonard that morning, going springily about his kitchen. But, 'It isn't that,' she said. 'It's just—Oh, Lilian, I can't make your husband out. He isn't to blame for last night. I made a fool of myself, I know that. But I can't help feeling that he enjoyed watching me do it ... And he wasn't very pleasant to you. But then, I wasn't very pleasant to you either.'

Lilian lowered her eyes. 'It's only what I deserved.'

'What do you mean?'

But she shook her head and wouldn't answer.

For a minute or two they sat sighing. Gradually Frances's sighs became groans. She rubbed her face. 'What a state to get ourselves into! I haven't been as drunk as that in the whole of my life. My stomach feels like some poor creature that's been beaten with a club. My eyes might as well have had gunpowder rubbed in them! Shall we have a smoke? Will that make us feel better, do you think, or worse?'

They didn't know, but decided to find out. Frances got out papers, tobacco and a glass ashtray, and rolled two untidy cigarettes.

When she had taken her first puff she sank back on to her pillows. 'Oh, it does help, doesn't it?'

'Does it?' asked Lilian. 'I'm not sure. It makes me feel racy.'

She meant it innocently, putting a hand to her galloping heart. But Frances, hearing the word, and seeing her hand at her bosom, had another flashing vision: the cushion on the floor and Lilian stepping tipsily about to get her balance; her heel coming down on the carpet, and the bounce of her breasts. The image brought a tangle of feelings with it: disbelief, embarrassment, and something else, a queasy remnant of the excitement of the night before.

Lilian was watching her face. 'What are you thinking, Frances?'

'Oh—' She drew on the cigarette. 'I'm thinking how frightful I was last night.'

'You weren't frightful. It was Len and me.'

'I should never have come in in the first place. Had the two of you been quarrelling?'

'No, we hadn't been quarrelling.'

'But all those awful things Leonard said to you. Is he often like that?'

'He'd just had too much to drink. Anyhow, I say awful things to him.'

'That doesn't make it any better. It makes it worse! Surely a marriage oughtn't to be so unkind?'

'We get along all right, really.'

'You never seem to, to me.'

'That's just what husbands and wives are like. You can't expect love and romance and things like that from a marriage, can you?'

'Can't you? What's the point of it, then? You and Leonard must have loved each other once, didn't you?'

'Oh, I don't know. Yes, I expect we did.'

'You don't sound at all convinced. Why did you marry, if you weren't sure?'

Lilian was rolling the tip of her cigarette against the rim of the ashtray. She frowned at it. 'You asked me that once before. Why do you mind so much?'

'I don't know. I'm simply trying to understand, I suppose.'

'Well, it isn't worth your thinking about. It was just . . . a mistake. It was all a mistake.'

'A mistake?'

'Yes, Len and I made a mistake, when we were young. We did something silly, and now we're paying for it, that's all.' Her tone had grown uneasy. But looking up, seeing the perplexity on Frances's face, she spoke almost with exasperation. 'Oh, Frances, for somebody so clever you can be awfully dull sometimes. Don't you know the sort of mistake I mean? I was going to have a baby. That's why Len and I married.' She dropped her gaze again. 'My baby died when it was born, you see.'

Frances, shocked, said, 'Lilian. I'm so sorry.'

She had begun biting her lip. 'It doesn't matter.'

'Of course it matters.'

'It seems ages ago now.'

'I had no idea. I wish I'd known.'

'You won't tell your mother, will you?'

'Well, of course I won't.'

'And it doesn't make you think badly of me? That Len and I did that?'

164

'Oh, do you really think it could?'

Lilian's expression cleared. 'No, I don't,' she said. 'But you're not like other people. Len's parents, for instance. They said one hard thing after another. That I'd fallen for the baby on purpose, as a way of getting hold of Len—as if he'd had nothing to do with it! That the baby was some other man's, not his. And then, when my baby died, they said it was a judgement on me. Oh, it was all so horrible, Frances. It made me go a bit mad, I think. It made an evil person of me. I couldn't look at other women's babies. I couldn't even be kind to Maurice, Netta's little boy. She's never forgiven me for it. Nobody understood. They said I ought to think of all the men who'd been killed in the War, and the people who'd died of the influenza, and what did one little baby boy matter, against all that . . . I suppose they were right.'

'No,' said Frances, 'they weren't. Some things are so frightful that a bit of madness is the only sane response. You know that, don't you?'

Lilian hesitated, then nodded, and answered in a murmur. 'Yes.'

'And have you never thought of—of trying for another child?'

She looked away. 'Len would like to. But what I always wonder is, what if it were to happen again? It did for my mother. I don't think I could stand it. And then, it isn't a nice world to bring babies into. But probably I will, in the end. It's against nature not to, isn't it? And if I don't—well, then it means that Len and I will have married for nothing. It isn't so bad, after all.' She spoke as if trying to convince herself. 'Len's a good husband, really. Everybody tells me he's a good husband. It's just that—well, you saw how he was last night. In the days when we were courting, he pushed and pushed me into saying yes to him. And then I did say yes to him; and it's as though he's never forgiven me.'

'He doesn't ever . . . mistreat you?'

That brought the ghost of a smile to her face. 'No! I'd like to see him try. And he knows my sisters would skin him alive.'

165

'And he never—with other women——' Frances was thinking of that moment, weeks before, in the starlit garden, Leonard's hand in the small of her back.

But, 'Oh, no,' said Lilian. 'He fancies himself as a bit of a ladies' man, but he wouldn't ever do anything about it. He learnt his lesson with me, you see.'

Her features sank as she said this, and she looked almost plain. She looked older, too, with shadows and creases around her eyes. Frances said again, 'I'm so sorry, Lilian.'

But that made her hang her head as if ashamed.

'You've always been so kind to me, Frances. Right from the start you've been kind. And you were honest with me, that time——' She faltered. 'You know the time I mean. You didn't have to be honest with me, but you were; and I wasn't kind in return. I've been thinking about it ever since.'

Frances didn't answer. From beyond the open window there came again those distant domestic noises: a barking dog, a calling woman, a spoon being tapped against a sink. The curtains rippled in the breeze, shifting on their rings with a scrape of metal, and once they had settled back into place the room seemed dimmer than before.

And perhaps the dimness made it easier for Lilian to speak. As she crushed out her cigarette she said quietly, 'What you told me that time——'

'I oughtn't to have said anything,' said Frances, adding her own cigarette stub to the ashtray, then moving the ashtray aside.

'Was it true, though, what you said? A love affair with a girl?'

'Yes.'

'There wasn't a man?'

'No, there wasn't a man. There never has been a man, for me. It seems I haven't the—the man microbe, or whatever it is one needs. My poor mother's convinced that there must be one in me somewhere. She's done everything to shake it loose save turn me upside down by my heels. But——'

'But how did it begin? How did you know?'

'I fell in love. How does anyone know that?'

'But where did you meet?'

'My friend and I? We met in Hyde Park, in the War. I had gone there with Noel, to listen to the speakers. It was just before conscription came in, and a man was speaking against it. He was being heckled and jostled by the crowd; it was shameful, horrible. But there, going calmly about, handing out pamphlets on his behalf and looking as though she wouldn't care if someone spat in her face because of it, was a small, slight, fair-haired girl in a velvet tam-o'-shanter . . . I took a pamphlet, and went to a meeting—I had to lie to my parents about it—and there she was again. She didn't remember me from Hyde Park, though I remembered her. After the meeting I walked her home, all the way from Victoria to Upper Holloway. In the perishing cold, too! I think I began to be in love with her by the time we crossed the Euston Road. We started to be friends. She stayed here, often. And then, suddenly, she loved me.'

'But weren't you shocked?'

'That someone should love me? I was astounded.'

'I didn't mean that.'

'I know you didn't. No, I wasn't shocked. The whole thing was too marvellous. There had been romances in my schooldays—but all my friends had had those; we were forever sending each other Valentines, writing sonnets on the prefect's eyes . . . This wasn't like that. It was a thing of the heart and the head and the body. A real, true thing, grown-up. Well, we thought ourselves grown-up. But the War did make young people wiser, didn't it? John Arthur had already died by then. Christina—my friend—had lost cousins. We were impatient. We had—oh, such energy! We began to want to live together. We planned it, seriously. We did everything seriously in those days. Christina took typewriting and book-keeping classes. We looked at rooms, we saved our money. Our parents thought it a nonsense, of course. Then they made it into a fight—endless, exhausting, the same quarrel over and over, how could we think of leaving home, how would it look, we were too young, people would suppose us fast, no man would ever want to marry us. But even the quarrels were thrilling, in their way. Christina and I talked as though we were part of a new society! Everything was changing. Why shouldn't we change too? We wanted to shake off tradition, caste, all that . . . '

She paused, and took a sip of water, feeling the scratch of her throat. Lilian was watching her. 'Then what happened?'

She set the glass down with a chink. 'Oh, then we got into that scrape with the police, when I threw my shoes at that MP. My father threatened to send me away. I'm afraid I laughed in his face. But my mother—' She drew a breath. 'My mother went through my things, and found a letter from Christina, and read it. I think she'd known all along that the friendship had something queer about it. She took the letter to Chrissy's parents. They turned out Chrissy's room, and found letters from me. Well, it was clear what the letters meant. I ended up with most of the blame, perhaps because I was a little older. They made me out to be some sort of vampire—'

'Vampire!'

'You know what I mean. One of those women, neurotic schoolmistresses and so on, who get written about in books. They talked of sending me to a doctor—to get my glands examined, they said.—Oh, I can't bear to think of it now.' She shuddered, remembering a scene, like something from a frightful dream, her father's stillness, his silence, the cold distaste in his expression: worse, infinitely worse and more shaming, than twenty years of bluster. 'If we'd been bolder,' she went on, 'we might have escaped. I think perhaps we ought to have tried to. We ought to have stolen away, like thieves. But we decided to face the thing out. People were saying that the War wouldn't last another year. We thought that, once it was over, everything would somehow be different . . .

And while we were waiting, Noel was lost. That was the March of 'eighteen. It had been bad when John Arthur had died, but after Noel—I don't know. My father made an invalid of himself. My mother went to pieces for a while. Our servants had left us; now we had a series of cooks and chars, one small calamity after another. It seemed easier to begin taking care of the house myself . . .

'And then, in the August, my father died too; and it all came out about our money being gone. The new society I had planned with Christina began to look rather flimsy. The Armistice came, but what could I do? I couldn't leave my mother, after everything she'd been through. She and I never discussed it, we never spoke a word about it; she knew what Chrissy was to me, but—no, I couldn't leave her. I said to myself just what your family said to you: that millions of men had been lost, that millions of women had given up lovers, brothers, sons, ambitions . . . It was one more sacrifice, that's all. I thought of it as a sort of bravery.'

Lilian was gazing at her, appalled. 'But what about your friend?'

'Oh—' Frances looked away. 'Well, it was hard when we parted. It was—It was worse than hard. But Christina did all right in the end. She got out of the suburbs, just as she meant to. You'd never know, meeting her now, that she'd grown up in a street called Hilldrop Villas.'

'Did she marry?'

'Marry? No! At any rate, not in the way you mean. She found another friend. Or, the friend found her. Someone braver than me—or harder-hearted, anyhow. She broke with her family years ago, and does just fine without them. A schoolmistress, as it happens. Well, she calls herself an artist. She has a studio in Pimlico and makes lumpy cups and saucers.' She caught Lilian's eye. 'Do I sound sour about it? I suppose I am a little sour. It isn't always easy, visiting Christina, looking at the life she has and thinking that it was meant to be mine. I would be with her today if I weren't feeling so rotten. What's the time?' She looked for the clock. 'Yes, I'd

169

be there right now.' She turned her face to the open window and called lightly: 'Sorry, Chrissy!' Turning back, she spoke with a yawn. 'At least I won't have put her to any trouble. She's the untidiest person I know.'

Lilian's face had remained colourless, all this time. Now, surprisingly, she blushed. In a flat voice, she said, 'You still care about her.'

'What? No, no. Not like that. That's all finished with, years ago.'

'But you said you were in love.'

'I was,' said Frances. 'We were. But Christina has her Stevie now, and I had the love wrung out of me. Or—what is it they do with vampires? Shove cricket stumps through their hearts? Yes, I was well and truly stumped.' She sighed, and rubbed her eyes. She felt exhausted, emptied out. 'And none of it should matter, Lilian. With the world in the state it is, it's such a small, small thing. But I think the sad fact is that I'm about as happy in my life as you are in yours. I do my best for my mother—or, I tell myself that I do. Sometimes I seem to do nothing but scold her; we cross each other like a pair of scissors. She isn't happy, either. How could she be? I think she's simply marking time. Well, perhaps we all are.'

For a while, then, they were silent, Frances sighing again, Lilian still blushing, sitting with her head lowered, frowning into her lap. She was rubbing at a wrinkle in the fabric of her skirt, going over and over the crease with her thumb in a fretful, preoccupied way.

And soon the silence had gone on so long that Frances began to be afraid that, after all, she had spoken too frankly. She said, 'You won't mention Christina's name in front of my mother, will you? She doesn't know that Chrissy and I still see each other. She'd have an absolute fit if she did. And—And you won't tell Leonard? You haven't told him already?'

That made Lilian look back at her. 'Of course I haven't told Leonard.'

'Well, I don't know how these things work. I always supposed that husbands and wives told each other everything.'

Lilian didn't answer that. She still looked preoccupied, burdened. And after another minute of silence she passed a hand across her face and said, in the same flat way as before, 'I ought to go, Frances. I've things to do, before Len gets back.'

Frances nodded. 'Yes, of course.' But she looked on in dismay as Lilian got down from the bed. Watching her straightening the seams of her skirt, she said, 'Thank you for coming in. I'm so very sorry to know about your baby. But I'm glad you told me. Thanks for talking so honestly. And thank you for listening to all that— all that vampire business.'

Again Lilian said nothing, simply stood looking back at her through the gloom. Then, with an awkward bob of her head, she turned away, towards the door.

But then she paused, as if thinking something over. And, unexpectedly, she turned back. Blushing harder than ever, she came to the head of the bed, stopping just a foot or so away from where Frances was sitting; and she put out a hand towards Frances's bosom. She didn't touch the bosom itself. Instead, while Frances watched, transfixed, bewildered, she curled her fingers as if taking hold of something that lay jutting out of Frances's breast, and, making a creaking, hissing sound with her mouth, she slowly pulled her hand back.

Only when the little charade was nearly complete did Frances understand what it was all about. The spot at which Lilian had been grasping lay just above her heart. She had been drawing an imaginary stake from it.

She did it without once meeting Frances's gaze; but she did it smoothly, deliberately—even casting the stake aside afterwards with a graceful unclosing of her hand. But then she stood as if startled by the implications of what she had done. Her own heart was thudding: Frances could see it, a drum-skin quiver at the base of her throat. They looked at each other in silence, and the moment seemed to swell, to be suspended, like a drop of water, like a tear . . .

Then the curtains billowed and rattled, and that made her start back into life. She put down her head and stepped away, left the room and closed the door behind her.

Why had she done it? What had she meant? Frances sank against her pillows, listening in wonder to the fading of her footsteps. Placing a hand on her bosom, she found that the spot through which the imaginary stake had passed was slightly tender. She pulled down the collar of her blouse, moved aside the limp camisole beneath it; she even got up and crossed the room, to look at her breast in the glass. There was nothing to see, the flesh was unbroken, unmarked. It was impossible, after all . . . But she returned to the bed, lay with her fingers over her heart, convinced that she could feel a stir of heat, a glow of blood—something, anyhow, that had been brought to the surface by Lilian's hand.

When Leonard returned from work that evening he came almost immediately downstairs again, putting his head around the kitchen door and gazing in with a guilty expression. His brow was marked, as usual, by the line of his bowler hat, but his face was pale, the whites of his eyes looking dingy as a result, and the ends of his moustache were drooping.

Could Frances spare him a minute?

She nodded, and he edged into the room, keeping one hand behind his back, awkwardly.

'I've come to beg your pardon,' he said, 'for my behaviour last night. I had a bit too much to drink and I let myself get carried away. I said lots of things I shouldn't have. It was unforgivable of me. But I hope—well, I hope you'll take these, and say no hard feelings?'

There was a dullish rattle as he brought round his arm. He had chocolates for her, the box done up with a pink satin ribbon, the lid with a picture of a ballerina on it.

She looked at it in acute embarrassment. 'You didn't have to buy me sweets, Leonard.'

'Well, I wanted to get you something, and the garden's full of flowers, so I knew roses were no good. And I bet you don't treat yourself to chocolates very often, do you?'

'It isn't me you ought to be apologising to, in any case. It's Lilian.'

To her surprise, he coloured slightly. 'I know.'

'You said some very unkind things to her.'

'I know, I know. But I didn't mean a word of it; Lily knows that. I've already told her how sorry I am. I'll find a way to make it up to her . . . I wish you'd take these chocolates, Frances. I've always thought of you and me as being good pals, and I'd hate that to change. You can give them to your mother if you don't want them yourself. I expect we annoyed her too, didn't we?'

She wiped her hands on her apron and took the box at last, doing her best to find an expression that would meet the demands of the moment, trying to admire the fancy wrapper, retain a bit of dignity—and all the time, of course, remembering that other charged moment of a few hours before, his wife's hand an inch from her bosom, easing out that imaginary stake.

He looked relieved. 'Thank you. It means a lot to me that you're prepared to do that. I hope you don't think too badly of me. We— well, we had fun last night, didn't we, before I forgot my manners?'

His moustache twitched as he spoke, and at the sight of his pink, wet mouth she again felt a ripple of the dark excitement of the night before—like finding the last slosh of gin in a near-empty bottle. That was one current too many, however. Yes, she admitted, they had had fun; but she spoke primly, turning away, putting the chocolates down unopened, and returning to the task he had interrupted—slicing shallots. For a minute or two he lingered, perhaps hoping for more from her. When nothing came he sloped off through the open back door.

He remained in the yard after he'd visited the WC. Glancing out, she saw him with his hands in his trouser pockets, scuffing his feet across cracks in the flagstones. When she looked again a minute later he had wandered on to the lawn: she watched him light himself a cigarette, throw the spent match into the bushes, begin to amble between the flower-beds, occasionally leaning to dead-head a rose. He kept his back to her as he did it; she stood still with the knife in her hand, and what she noticed most of all was the narrowness of his hips and shoulders: he seemed suddenly a lonely and vulnerable figure, drifting about like that. She thought of Lilian's lost baby; it was his lost baby, too. She recalled the hectic way in which he had whipped on the Snakes and Ladders, as if wanting something from the game, from his wife, from Frances, from the night, determined to goad and goad it until it coughed up or broke.

He's as unhappy as any of us, she realised.

Or, was he? His cigarette finished, he returned to the house, and what had clicked into place about him for her clicked out again. He looked livelier than before; his moustache had lost its droop. He'd spotted a lawn-mower, he said, tucked away at the end of the garden. The mechanism was all seized up, but he thought he might be able to get it going. He'd take a look at it later, if Frances and her mother didn't mind.

Frances said he could help himself. He went upstairs for his dinner, and when he reappeared, at just before eight, his jacket was off, his collar and tie were removed, and his sleeves were rolled nearly to his armpits.

But this time Lilian was with him: she sat on the bench beneath the linden tree, watching him spread out a square of oilskin and begin to take the mower apart. When his hands became too greasy for him to light a cigarette, she got the packet out of his pocket and lit one for him. Frances saw it all from the drawing-room window while her mother picked chocolates from the ballerina box.

'Won't you have one at all, Frances? After Mr Barber went to so much trouble? I feel quite a glutton, eating all by myself!'

But, no, she wouldn't eat a chocolate. She couldn't relax into her mending, either. She was too conscious of Lilian, there at the end of the garden, in her white blouse with the touches of violet at the collar and the cuffs.

But—could she be imagining it? She had the sense that Lilian was conscious of her. She didn't once look back at the house. She watched as Leonard worked the spanners, nodding in an encouraging way at the bits of machinery he displayed to her, the cogs and the blades and the God knew what. But even as she nodded, even as she murmured, even as she lit that cigarette and leaned to fit it between his lips, a part of her, like a long, long shadow running counter to the sun, was leaning to Frances; Frances was sure of it.

They saw very little of each other over the week-end, and when they met on the Monday they made no mention of the confidences they had exchanged in Frances's bedroom, nor of the electric but ambiguous way in which they had parted. They spoke of nothing much at all—of domestic matters, laundry bills. But for the rest of that day the rumble of the treadle sewing-machine could be heard across the house; and the following morning, while Frances was stripping the sheets from her bed, Lilian appeared at her door.

'I have your frock for you, Frances,' she said shyly.

'My frock?'

'For Saturday night. For Netta's party. Had you forgotten?'

Frances hadn't forgotten. But the trying-on of the dress, the hair-cutting—that all seemed to belong to a distant, less complicated time. She left the bed and moved to the doorway as Lilian held the frock up on its hanger; then she gaped in amazement. The gown was transformed. Lilian had made it fashionably loose and low-waisted. She had washed it and pressed it and removed all trace of must. But she'd also replaced the frock's worn leather lacings with silvery velvet ribbons, and she had faced the collar and the lowest tier of the skirt with a satiny fabric to match.

Frances lifted one of its cuffs. 'It's lovely.'

'Do you mean it?'

'I hate to think how long it must have taken you.'

'It didn't take any time at all. And I found a bag that goes with it—here.' It was an evening bag, grey plush. 'And this hat, too. What do you think?' The hat was pink with a wide brim. 'The crown's quite soft, so it won't spoil your hair. I thought I could wave you again—shall I?'

Frances turned the hat in her hands, then stood at the glass to try it. The colour suited her; the style was flattering. When she lifted it off it left a trace of Lilian's scent behind. Carefully setting it down on her chest of drawers, she said, 'I thought you must have changed your mind about the party. You haven't mentioned it in so long, and I've rather had the idea—Are you sure you'd still like me to come?'

'Don't you want to come?'

'Yes, I'd like to. But how about Leonard? Won't he mind your going with me instead of with him?'

Lilian coloured, but tilted up her chin. 'Why should he mind? He's got his assurance thing to think about. And he'll be glad to escape my family. It'll only be family—you know that, don't you? And Netta's house—it isn't very grand. Perhaps you'll hate it.'

'I won't hate it.'

'I won't a bit blame you if you do.'

'I'm sure I won't hate it, Lilian,' said Frances. *I won't hate it*, she meant, *if I'm with you.* A couple of weeks before, she might have said the words aloud. A couple of weeks before, Lilian might have dipped her head and absorbed them as another piece of funny chivalry. She couldn't have said them now, not for fifty pounds; not for five hundred.

But perhaps Lilian heard them anyhow. Her bravado seemed to

fail her. She hooked the frock on its hanger to the back of the door, and after a brief, uneasy silence she returned to her own room.

The uneasiness continued as the week wore on. With the tugging of that stake from Frances's heart some sort of potential had been released, some physical charge made possible. Catching one another's eye through an open doorway could set them both blushing. If they had to pass on the stairs they seemed to be twice their natural size, all hands and hips and bosoms. When they stopped to chat they were as awkward with each other as if they both had a touch of the jitters. No sooner had they parted, however, than they seemed to meet again. It was as if a thread were fixed between them, continually drawing them back together.

And there was another sort of thread, tugging them towards that party. The event had acquired an unlikely promise, an improbable allure. Frances could not stop thinking about it; and yet, when she spoke about it to others, she became like a hopeless liar, delivering an untruth with a yawn. To Christina, for example, she made a great joke of it. Fun and games with Lil's relations! Would there be Pin the Tail on the Donkey and Blind Man's Buff? With her mother she was casual. Well, it wasn't far to go. It had been kind of Lilian to ask her; she couldn't very well have said no. And with Leonard—

But Leonard beat her to it. He looked at her in disbelief. 'Have you any idea what you've let yourself in for? It'll be all tinkers and Sinn Féiners, you know. The O'Flanagans, the O'Hooligans . . . But I'm glad you're going, to be honest. You can keep an eye on Lily for me. Some of those hot-eyed Irish cousins of hers—I wouldn't trust them further than I could throw them!'

He was half serious, Frances realised. Mumbling a reply, she turned away before he could spot how ghastly her smile was.

That was on the Thursday evening. The Friday dawned very fair. And the Saturday, the day of the party, was warm even at five in the morning: she awoke with the light, and stole downstairs, and drank her tea in the garden. She spent the morning doing house-work—doing it extra carefully, aware of a powerful temptation not to do it at all. She cooked an elaborate lunch, with a fruit tart for dessert, and made a point of being nice to her mother, atten-tive and chatty, prolonging the meal.

But when the clearing-away was done she went upstairs, to sit again in the little kitchen while Lilian trimmed and waved her hair: the procedure was as excruciating as it had been the first time, but in a completely different way. Lilian was clumsy with the iron; one of the waves would not sit right. She had to wet it and re-do it, her face inches from Frances's. They both seemed to be holding their breath. Frances kept her gaze fixed on a spot on the wall, a sliver of bare paper that had got missed by the varnish.

Once the hair was finished, she couldn't relax. She spent time assembling her outfit, hunting down some good silk stockings, steaming the nap back into a pair of suede shoes. She scrubbed her hands with lemon juice, she cut and polished her finger-nails, she fitted a new blade into her safety-razor and carefully shaved her legs. That all took until tea-time; after that she sat in the drawing-room with an open book in her lap, too restless to read properly; too conscious of Lilian overhead, at the wardrobe, opening drawers. Half-past four ... Quarter to five ... The minutes dragged by—until she heard the clang of the gate and hollow-sounding footsteps in the front garden. Leonard was home. He let himself into the house, and with his arrival the pace of the day was suddenly accelerated: the afternoon seemed to catch its breath, to rise on to its toes and spring forward. He had his own evening to prepare for, of course, his dinner, his club-night—whatever it was. Soon Frances could hear him on the landing, calling to Lilian about shaving-soap and sock-suspenders. As she was out in the kitchen making an early Saturday supper, the gramophone blared into life, and she felt a thrill of absolute excitement. For once, the dance-tunes seemed to beckon to her rather than repel her.

The music was still playing when she went up. It buzzed in the boards at her feet while she stripped and washed. On went clean underwear. Up came the stockings, gliding with supernatural smoothness over her newly shaven legs. The frock took a bit of fiddling with. It was disconcertingly loose at the bust, alarmingly short at the hem—Lilian had raised it after all—and, gazing at her reflection, at the Burne-Jones lacing, Frances thought again of Sherwood Forest, of lutes and pageants. And did her hair look all right above the satiny collar? Her neck seemed as long as a sea-serpent's. Pointing her jaw this way and that she was reminded of those stretched wax mannequin heads and shoulders she had now and then seen on display in hairdressers' windows.

The gramophone record ended as she was dabbing her nose with a leaf of *papier poudré*. In the abruptly unnerving silence she fitted on her borrowed hat, and cautiously crossed the landing.

She found Lilian's bedroom door ajar, and could just glimpse Lilian beyond it: she was at the mirror, dressed in a frock that Frances had never seen before, the frock that she must have made for the party, a striking thing of white silk with a gauzy overskirt, and with slender shoulder straps that left her arms and upper back bare. She was pushing a gold snake bangle over her wrist when she caught sight of Frances; she paused with it part-way up her arm as their gazes met through the glass. But at once she looked away, lowering her kohl-darkened eyelids, sliding the bangle higher. And what she said was, 'Here's Frances. Doesn't she look nice?'

Leonard was in there with her; Frances hadn't realised that. But now, with the creak of a floorboard, his gingery head appeared around the door.

He pursed his lips in a silent whistle. The admiration, Frances thought, was part pretend, part genuine. 'Well, Clapham won't know what's hit it tonight! You look like the lady in the tower, in the poem—what's her name?' He came out on to the landing; he wanted the clothes brush, for his jacket. 'You're in the right colour for Lily's family, anyhow. They like anything that reminds them of the auld Emerald Oisle!'

She watched him tidying his shoulders. She had never seen him looking so dapper. He had taken as many pains over his outfit as she had over hers. His hair was severely oiled and parted; the creases in his trousers were sharp as blades. He was wearing a regimental tie, had some sort of crested ring on the smallest finger of his left hand, and his fingernails were gleaming: he'd been to see 'Thidney, my manicuritht', he told her, with a chorus-girl flop to his wrist.

But his manner had a hint of restraint to it. He had been cautious with her since the night of Snakes and Ladders. She said, 'You're looking forward to your evening?' and he nodded: 'Oh, yes.'

'What is it, exactly? A supper?'

'Yep. A slap-up one, by all accounts. Then we head off to a private room, and it's there that the real business happens. Or so I'm told.'

'Rolling up your trouser legs, learning the handshake—something like that, is it?'

He was straightening his cuffs now, and smiled at his sleeve. 'No! Just a few chaps together, all in the same line of work. "You scratch my back and I'll scratch yours." You know the sort of thing, Frances.'

'Not really, no.'

He didn't answer that. His gaze had slid over her shoulder. Lilian had come to the bedroom doorway, one of her snug cloche hats on her head, a silk shawl over her arm; he looked her up and down as if taking her in for the first time. And when he spoke again, it was with an air of grievance. 'I dunno. It doesn't seem right to me, a fellow going one way on a Saturday night and his wife going another. I must want my head read, letting you loose among those cousins of yours!'

Lilian began to step past him. 'You should have thought of that before you agreed to go to your stupid supper.'

'Stupid supper? I like that! Don't you want your man to get on? You're quick enough to spend his money.—Just a sec.' He reached for her wrist. 'What time will you be home?'

She pulled against him. 'I don't know. Earlier than you, most probably.'

'Well, mind you behave yourself. And don't I get a farewell kiss?'

He still had hold of her arm. She let herself be drawn back, and gave him a dry peck on the cheek. 'That's more like it,' he said, releasing her, and then his blue eyes twinkled at last. 'Your turn next, Frances!' He offered his face. 'How about it? Lily's warmed it up for you.'

Lilian spoke with a tut, before Frances could reply. 'Frances isn't interested. Let her alone.' She was blushing.

Down in the hall, the two of them paused. Frances had to say goodbye to her mother, but found herself loitering at the glass. She adjusted her collar and the angle of her hat, seeing again what a terrific trouble she had gone to: the shoes, the stockings, the frock, the hair. She felt half disguised by the outfit; half exposed by it.

But when she made her tentative entry into the drawing-room, her mother was as delighted as she had been that other time.

'Oh, now, *don't* you look stylish! So handsome, I shouldn't have known you!'

'Yes, thanks.'

'I don't recognise that hat. Is it one of Mrs Barber's? And the gown?'

'No, the gown's my own. It's the one—I've had it for years.'

'You ought to wear it more often. The colour becomes you. Oh, what a pity that Mrs Playfair isn't here to see you! You wouldn't think of calling in there before you go to the station?'

'No, Mother.'

'It wouldn't take you a moment.'

'No, Mother. Please!'

'Well, it was only an idea . . . And is that Mrs Barber out there? Come in from the hall, Mrs Barber, let me see you too!' Her smile grew slightly forced at the sight of Lilian's lipstick and kohl. But, 'Yes,' she said gamely, 'you both look very fine.'

Now Frances was itching to be gone. She felt more exposed than ever with Lilian standing there beside her. She edged her way towards the door. 'I don't expect we'll be late. Leonard's still here, but he'll be leaving soon. His friend Mr Wismuth's coming for him; you needn't answer the knock. You'll be quite all right, now?'

'Yes, I shall be fine. Oh, but I did have some letters for the post. You couldn't take them for me, could you? Now, have I put stamps on them yet? No, I haven't. Just a moment. Oh, and this one lacks an address. I need my letter-case. Can you see it . . . ?'

When she and Lilian escaped from the house at last, Frances felt as she imagined a fly might feel when, by some miracle, it had managed to prise its limbs free from a strip of sticky paper. It was only a little after seven, and the sun was still high in the sky. The pavement threw up heat like a griddle; they kept to the shade as much as they could as they made their way down the hill, but it was warm even on the platform of the station, in the bluish dusk of the railway cut. The crowd was a Saturday-night one. People were heading to theatres, picture-houses, dancing-halls. The men had an oiled-and-varnished look. The women were like heavy-crested birds: crimson, gold, green, violet. But none of them was as handsome as Lilian, she thought. Against the white silk and gauze of her dress the flesh of her arms and shoulders had a solid, creamy texture—as if one could dip into it with a spoon, or with a finger.

Mothers called to children to keep away from the edge of the platform, and their train arrived. Frances tugged open a compartment door and was met by a gust of warm stale air; she followed Lilian in and they sat side by side. Two boys and a man had the seat opposite, the boys about thirteen, looking at them with shy interest, the man staring at them both—staring at Lilian in particular, in that unabashed, amazing way that men, Frances had found, did stare at Lilian, even lowering his newspaper to do it, so that she felt like leaning to him to say, Put your feet up, why don't you? Make yourself comfortable. Have you a pipe? Why not light it? Go on . . . But the feeling was partly envy, she suspected. When the man got out at East Brixton, she thought of slipping into his place. She was beaten to it by a woman who came in laden with bulging string bags.

And the next halt was Clapham. They went out and down the steps and a minute later were on the High Street, picking their way along the crowded pavement. The doors of the shops stood open. The air was soupy with smells: meat, fish, ripe fruit, perspiring bodies. A gramophone-seller's was blasting out the hit of the moment, 'The Laughing Policeman'.

> *'He said "I must arrest you!"*
> *He didn't know what for.*
> *And then he started laughing*
> *Until he cracked his jaw!*
> *Oh—'*

The *ha-ha-ha*s pursued them as Lilian led the way into a residential street. The houses here were terraced, red-brick, neat, narrow, identical, each with a tiny front garden, flower-bedded or crazy-paved. In one of the gardens a boy was repairing a bicycle. In another a man in his shirt-sleeves was watering geraniums. There was the tinkle of a pianola from an open window, accompanied by the wobbly parps of a trumpet as someone tried to keep up with the tune.

Frances grew conscious all over again of the medieval flourishes on her frock. 'Are we almost there?' she asked as they made another turn, and when Lilian gestured—yes, the house was just at the end of this row—the sudden looming reality of the evening made her slow her step. When she got a glimpse of Netta's front window, its Nottingham lace curtains lighted up from within and showing the heads and shoulders of people sitting or standing inside, she faltered completely.

Lilian stopped, and looked curiously at her. 'What's the matter? You're not nervous?'

'I am, a bit.'

'Why?'

'I don't know. It's just, we've gone to so much trouble, come all this way. But now that we're actually here . . . '

Lilian glanced ahead at the house, biting her lip. 'I feel that too, a bit. Aren't we silly?'

'Are we?'

'Well, we can't not go in. The party's why we've come, after all.'

Was it, though? All at once Frances wondered what would happen if she were to catch hold of Lilian's hand and pull her in the opposite direction. *Let's go*, she wanted to say, right there on the Clapham street. *Let's go! Now! Quickly! Just you and me!*

But she didn't do it, she didn't say it; and in any case, it was too late. Someone had seen them from the window. The Nottingham lace was raised. Netta's door opened and Vera's little girl emerged, bumping a creaking doll's pram over the step. 'Auntie Lily! Come and see!'

After the houses of Champion Hill this one seemed built to a miniature scale, the narrow hall widening only slightly at the foot of the stairs, so that when Netta appeared, bringing with her her husband, Lloyd, they all had to reach around each other in order to embrace or shake hands.

'Many happy returns,' Frances remembered to say. She had brought along a gift, a jar of bath-crystals. Lilian's gift was scent.

184

There was a minute or two of unwrapping, unstoppering and sniffing, children coming to sniff too, the boys making faces, rushing away with their noses pinched. There seemed to be children everywhere. A small back room was like a school playground. Ahead was a tiny kitchen, and a few men stood drinking at the garden door, but most of the grown-ups were gathered in the front room, the room that Frances had glimpsed from the street. Seen here, from the hall, it looked even more alarming. There might have been two dozen people in there, sitting on every sort of chair, the younger ones sharing places or cross-legged on the floor. It was bright, hot, crowded, yet intimate and challenging too; the open patch of carpet in the middle recalled a space for fighting cocks. When Lilian led her in at last, she spoke only to say 'Good evening' and 'How do you do?', but she could at once sense the impact of her accent. People sat straighter in their seats. She felt herself looked over in an interested way. 'That's the lady that keeps the house that Lil and Len have,' she heard someone murmur, as if they knew all about her and had been curious to meet her. The horrible idea came into her head that perhaps the only reason Lilian had brought her here—had dressed and curled her—was to show her off.

It was a relief to recognise Vera and Min. And to spot Mrs Viney, lavishly hung about with jet, her dress rising very nearly to her knees, her swollen ankles on full display, was like seeing a dear old friend.

'Oh, Miss Wray, don't you look handsome! And ain't your hair done lovely! I bet it was Lil done that, wasn't it?'

She put out her hand as she spoke. Frances moved forward to take it, and was drawn down and given a smacking kiss on the cheek.

Places were rearranged, cushions moved, chairs passed. Frances and Lilian squeezed themselves in next to two elderly women. They proved to be Lilian's Irish aunties, a Mrs Daley and a Mrs Lynch. Other aunties sat near by, Mrs Someone, Miss

Someone Else: Frances forgot the names at once, but was glad to tuck herself in amongst them, grateful to be less on show. She was complimented on her frock. She was given a drink, a glass of claret-cup with chunks of tinned fruit bobbing about in it. The aunties offered her a piece of birthday cake, a glossy sausage roll. And how did she like Clapham? It wasn't quite what she was used to!

'And has Lenny not come, then?'

She explained about his supper.

'Oh, what a pity! He's a real comedian, that Lenny. Keeps you in stitches, that one.'

'Yes, doesn't he?'

She didn't really want the claret-cup; it brought back memories of Snakes and Ladders. But she sipped it, smiling, self-conscious, gazing about. The room was blandly showy: Toby jugs on a high shelf, tankards and salvers in factory brass. The furniture seemed all brand-new, the varnish on the side-board was gleaming. But, of course, furniture, she remembered having been told once, was Lloyd's 'line'. He managed a warehouse, somewhere in Battersea. The man over there, as round as a turnip, she guessed to be Mrs Viney's brother. The younger man beside him, scarred and sight-less, was clearly the son who had been blinded in the War. The boys in the corner must be Lilian's famous hot-eyed Irish cousins. Two of them had ordinary brown good looks; the third was handsome as a film star. The girls were like Vera, sharp-faced, but with thin unlipsticked mouths. They were calling to Lilian now: they wanted to see her Theda Bara bangle. She eased it free and passed it over, and one after another they tried it on.

It was disconcerting, Frances found, to see Lilian so at home among so many strangers, to think of her as having this world, this life, quite separate from her daily life in the house on Champion Hill. She thought, These people all have their claim on her. What's mine, exactly?

But as she began to feel almost glum about it, Lilian turned to her to ask in a murmur, 'Are you all right?'

'Yes, I'm fine.'

'It isn't too much, all these people?'

'No, it isn't too much.'

And, with that, it wasn't. They smiled at each other, and the blushes and the jitters of the past few days fell away. Instead, a knowledge seemed to leap between them, to leap all the more thrillingly for doing it there in that hot, bright, overcrowded room. And, of course, *that's* why they had come. Frances realised it all at once. They could never have looked at each other so nakedly in the dangerous privacy of Champion Hill. But here, among so many people . . . They turned from one another's eyes, but the knowledge remained. They were sitting tight together, more or less sharing a chair, Lilian so close that Frances could catch the separate scents of her, the scents of her powder, her lipstick, her hair. She called something to one of her cousins. She leaned to move an auntie's glass, and then to straighten the beads of her mother's necklace. Frances took all this in, even while angled away from her, gazing at her— how, exactly? *Perhaps with the pores of my skin,* she thought.

More guests arrived. There was a commotion in the hall: a barking dog, a crying baby. The dog came into the room with the newcomers, rushing about with a dripping tongue. The baby was handed from lap to lap, a scrap of a thing in a frilled frock, bawling its head off. The aunties rearranged themselves, and the chair to Frances's left became free. It was taken by a pleasant-looking man of about her own age, who introduced himself as Ewart and shook her hand with hot rough fingers. Was he one of the cousins? No! He didn't know the family well. He worked as a driver for Lloyd. He'd come to the party on his own. Seeing that Frances's and Lilian's glasses were empty, he took them away and refilled them. It was to Frances that he spoke, however, when he had returned.

'How do you like this weather, then?' He was wiping his neck with his handkerchief.

'Not quite so good for a party, is it?'

'Not so good in the city, full stop. I want to get out of it, I do.' He tucked the handkerchief away. 'I have it in mind to take a run down to Hampton Court one of these Sundays.'

He seemed self-conscious about the word *run*. Frances said, as she lifted her glass, 'You've a motor-car, then?'

'Near enough. I've a pal with one, and he lets me take it out when I fancy. I put him in the way of some work one time, you see, so he owes me the favour. Yes, I'm thinking of Hampton Court. Perhaps take a little row-boat on the Thames.'

'Or, why not Henley?' she suggested, struck with the image of the little row-boat; imagining herself and Lilian in it.

'Henley,' he said, rubbing his pleasant-looking chin. 'Now, I hadn't thought of Henley.'

'Or Windsor, of course.'

'No, Henley's the place. You could make a day of it at Henley. A stroll by the river, a bit of fun on the water.'

'Feed the ducks.'

'Feed the ducks. And finish up with a nice tea.'

They exchanged a smile. His eyes were the blue of Cornish china, his fairish hair sat close to his scalp in tight little lamb-like curls. He was the type of man who, twenty or even ten years before, would never have dreamed of sitting down and chatting so freely with a woman of Frances's class. Now he took a gulp of his beer, neatly wiped his mouth, and felt in his jacket pocket. 'Like a cigarette?'

The chat about Henley had perked him up. He left off huffing against the heat and told her all about a Saturday-to-Monday he had recently spent down in Brighton. He'd gone there with a pal—not the pal with the motor-car, another pal entirely. They'd had an evening on the pier, at a Wild West show. The stunts those fellows could pull with a lasso and a tomahawk had to be seen to be believed . . .

Frances listened with half an ear, nodding, smiling; still conscious of Lilian; feeling the evening ticking forward, second by second, beat by beat.

By half-past nine the sky outside was beginning to darken, and the lace at the window acquired a yellow electric sheen. Some of the children had come to their parents and started to pull at their hands: they wanted to go home, they were tired, it wasn't fair, they wanted to go. One little boy climbed on to his mother's lap and tried to press her lips shut: 'Stop talking!' Mildly, she pushed his hands away and went on chatting with her neighbour. But by ten, people were rising and gathering their things. A group was heading back to Walworth, taking the kids and the aunties home. Mrs Viney was going with them, if she could ever get out of her chair. It took all four of her daughters to raise her to her feet, the rest of the room calling encouragement, the boys making the popping noises of a cork coming out of a bottle.

When she was up and wiping her eyes at the hilarity of it all, Lilian spoke quietly to Frances.

'I'll just see Mum and Vera off at the gate. And then we needn't stay much longer. Just a little while?'

'Yes, if you'd like to.'

'Are you sure?'

'Yes, of course.'

She put a hand on Frances's shoulder, smiling down into her face, her lipstick blurred by the kisses she'd given to aunties, nephews, nieces. When she moved away she went slowly, her hand remaining in contact with Frances until the very last moment, and Frances felt drawn by her fingers, pulled along in the wake of her touch.

Once she had left it, the room became very ordinary. Ewart was still at Frances's side. He was describing the runs he'd made in his van, to Maidstone, to Guildford; he'd been as far as Gloucester and back in a single day. When he paused to light another cigarette, she got to her feet.

'I must just go and comb my hair.'

'I'll mind your drink for you, then,' he said, as if they were quite old friends.

A child in the hall directed the way to the WC. Frances went up the stairs to a half-landing and found two other women waiting; she leaned against the wall and waited with them, happy to let the minutes pass. The women were flushed and friendly with drink, making jokes about the weakness of their bladders. There was a lavatory in the yard, they said, but the men were using that. It wouldn't do to venture out there; oh, no, the men were filthy beasts . . . By the time it was Frances's turn, no one else had come, no one was waiting; she sat on the lavatory with her elbows on her stockinged knees, listening to the stew of jolly voices rising up from the rooms below. Above her, a frosted window was ajar, and in the artificial light the evening sky looked cool and moist: she wished she could wet her hands and face with it.

As she was putting herself tidy, a gramophone blared into life. She started down the stairs and found Ewart in the hall. She had forgotten all about him. He still had her drink in his hand.

'I was wondering where you'd got to!' He sounded almost aggrieved. 'This'll be warm as anything.'

She smiled, but gazed past him. 'Have you seen my friend?'

'The girl you were sitting with before? They've started dancing in the back room, you've been missing all the fun.'

'Is my friend dancing too?'

'I think so. Want to join her?'

He didn't wait for her to reply, but led the way into the room, which had been cleared of its children and had its bright lights dimmed. The gramophone was playing at high volume. The carpet had been rolled and propped in the corner, and four or five couples were already on the floor. Lilian's partner was the cousin with the film-star looks. When she saw Frances coming in from the hall she leaned out of his arms to call to her, in smiling apology, 'They won't let me go until I've danced!'

'Yes, let's have a dance,' said Ewart.

He was right at Frances's elbow. She smiled at Lilian, but shook her head. 'Oh, no, I'm a horrible dancer.'

'I bet you're not.' He put his hand to her waist, to guide her forward.

The pressure of his palm took her by surprise. She was still looking at Lilian. 'What's that? No, truly, I am.'

He moved his thumb as if to tickle her. 'Well, I am too, if you want to know the truth. How about we just sit down?'

Again, he didn't wait for a reply, but steered her towards a sofa. The sofa was small, meant for two; there was a youth and a girl already on it and only a foot of room to spare. She thought he meant her to have the space for herself, but at their approach the girl slid obligingly on to the youth's lap, and when she sat he managed to squeeze himself in beside her.

'Good job we're both little ones!'

Frances was not little at all, and neither was he; but his manner had changed now, become playful and proprietorial. He said something about the gramophone, that she didn't quite catch. He mentioned a *palais de danse* he sometimes went to, over in Catford—did she know it? She said she didn't, speaking vaguely, as if distracted by the music, and at last he gave up trying to chat, seeming happy simply to sit there, jiggling his foot. For a minute or two she made a pretence of glancing about as he did, looking from one couple to another in a benign, wallflowerish way. Gradually, however—like a compass needle swinging to the pole—gradually her gaze settled, and she surrendered herself to the pleasure of watching Lilian dance.

She danced well, of course; Frances might have predicted that.

Her cousin did too, and with the shift in music to a popular song they began paying more attention to their steps. Keeping to the few square feet that was all that the small crowded room allowed them, they managed to work in turns and flourishes; at one point the cousin took hold of Lilian and whirled her round on the spot. She came down laughing, looking for Frances as soon as her feet were on the floor, so that Frances had the feeling that the laughter was really meant for her.

Ewart spoke into her ear. 'She's a lively one, your pal.'

Frances nodded. 'Isn't she?'

'She's had a drop too much to drink. She'll be sorry in the morning.'

But Frances knew it wasn't that.

Lilian saw them discussing her. She leaned away from her partner. 'What are you saying about me?'

'Nothing!'

'I don't believe you!'

She kept looking at Frances then, across her cousin's shoulder—seeking out Frances's eye even while pretending to be bothered by it, once stretching out her hand to wave her away, claiming she was putting her off her dancing. The two men—the cousin and Ewart—began to shrug at each other. 'You're too daft tonight,' Frances heard the cousin tell Lilian, at the next change of music. 'You're like a big daft girl, I can't dance with you.' But she gripped him, protesting, and wouldn't let him go—laughing again as she did it. And again she looked at Frances, again the laughter seemed meant for her.

At last Ewart leaned closer to Frances to say, 'You and your friend are up to something. Does she think it funny that you're sitting here with me?'

'I don't think so,' said Frances, not following him.

'I think she's pulling your leg about something. She's a married girl, isn't she?'

'Yes.'

'I thought she was. You'd never know it. If I was her husband, I'd smack her behind . . . How about you?'

'Yes, I'd smack it too.'

He drew in his lower lip in a silent guffaw. 'No, I mean, have you got a chap? Is that what she's smiling at? He's not going to come and black my eye for me, is he?'

His face was such a nice one; she couldn't think what to say. She turned away from him, perhaps rather primly. But she did not feel prim, she realised. What she felt, when she thought about it, was an odd temptation to settle back against his shoulder, to give herself over to the squash of his thigh against hers. And he must have sensed a yielding in her, or at least the possibility of one, because as the frying-pan hiss of the next record gave way to a burst of music she heard him chuckle.

Lilian, she saw, had finally changed her partner. The new boy was slim, fair-haired, one of a knot of youngsters on the other side of the room. He had danced Lilian over to them and was larking about with her there. Other couples had surrounded them, and Frances's view was obscured; she caught broken glimpses, that was all, of Lilian's white dress and stockings, her glossy dark head, her blurred red mouth. Taking another sip of claret-cup, she felt Ewart shift about until the side of his knee was pressing against the side of hers. There was a flutter of breath at her ear, and she understood that he had turned, had lifted his arm and laid it along the back of the sofa. When he spoke, his voice tickled her ear like the buzz of a wasp. He said, 'How about this trip to Henley, then?'

She kept the glass at her mouth. 'Henley?'

'Yes, how about it? I told you, I can get my pal's motor-car any time I want. It's a lovely little motor—a red one. What do you say?'

Lilian and her fair-haired partner had moved away from the boy's friends at last. They were dancing a tipsy Argentine tango, their cheeks pressed together, Lilian every now and then breaking off to complain that the boy's chin was too rough against hers, or his steps too clumsy; but always letting herself be pulled back into the clinch.

'What do you say?' Ewart asked again.

'Oh, I don't know.' Frances spoke without looking at him, still with the glass at her lips. 'I'm so busy.' And then, ludicrously, groping for an excuse and catching at a well-tried one from her youth: 'My mother's awfully old-fashioned about that sort of thing.'

He laughed, and nudged her. 'You don't need your mum's permission, do you?'

She began to laugh too. 'No, not really.'

'Anyhow, I could call for you, do it properly, let your mum see what a steady chap I am. I bet she'd like me.'

Frances nodded, still smiling, still not quite looking at him. 'Well, she would and she wouldn't.'

'Go on! She'll like me all right.'

He spoke as if everything were settled. His jacket had opened with the lifting of his arm and she was conscious of his blazing torso, of the hot hard buttons of his waistcoat. As before, something about the scorching length and bulk of him was oddly persuasive: she knew that if she turned her face to his he would kiss her. Watching Lilian moving in her supple, muscular way in the grip of her fair-haired partner, she was almost ready to do it. She could simply think of no reason in the world why she should not. She took another warm sip from her glass, and closed her eyes. Ewart's breath came against her ear again, beery, but beyond the beer sweet as a boy's.

She felt a foot knocking at hers. Opening her eyes, she saw Lilian. The music was changing and she had left her partner: she wanted Frances to dance with her instead. Frances lifted a hand to say, Oh, no. Lilian caught hold of it and tried to pull her to her feet.

'No,' said Frances aloud, her drink spilling. She hastily put the glass down.

'Yes,' said Lilian, still tugging. 'Come on.'

She set her jaw in that stubborn way she had, only pulling the harder the more Frances resisted—using two hands now, and hauling almost painfully at the flesh of Frances's wrist. So Frances rose and, reluctantly, let herself be drawn into a dancer's embrace, while Ewart, shifting into her empty seat, and grinning like a good sport, looked on.

The music started up: another tango. Their arms collided.

'Who's leading?'

'I don't know!'

They tried a few steps and nearly stumbled, tried a few more and stumbled again, and finally hit on something like a slow two-step, going sedately back and forth while the other couples lunged and dipped around them. But even then they danced badly, their feet tangling, their hands sweaty. Sometimes, in avoiding a more bois- terous couple, they were pushed more closely together: their thighs or bosoms would meet, and, instantly, with a grimace, they'd attempt to move apart. Frances's smile grew fixed and painful. Lilian laughed as if she couldn't stop, saying, 'Oops!' 'Oh, dear!' 'My fault.'

'No, mine.'

The record was endless. They danced on, without rhythm, with- out a trace of delight. And yet, when the music died they stood among the other couples in their dancers' pose, with their hands still joined. And when they finally separated, it seemed to Frances that the space between them was alive and elastic, as if wanting to draw itself closed.

Still with fixed, forced smiles on their faces they moved to stand with the boys and girls who had gathered around the gramophone and were noisily debating which record ought to be played next. But they took no part in the discussion. Lilian glanced over her shoulder and spoke in the shadow of the other voices.

'He's waiting for you, that chap. What's his name?' Her tone was bright, with a quiver to it. 'You've made a conquest there, haven't you? He's taken a real shine to you.'

Frances hesitated. Then, 'It's your shine,' she said.

Lilian looked at her. 'What do you mean?'

'He's only taken a shine to me because I've taken a shine to you. It's your shine, Lilian.'

Lilian's expression changed. She dropped her gaze, parted her lips. Her heart beat harder, jumping in the hollow at the base of her throat in that percussive way that Frances had seen once before. And when it had jumped six times, seven times, eight, nine, she looked up into Frances's eyes and said, 'Take me home, will you?'

There was something to the way she said it: a complicity, an assent. Frances felt for her fingers, pressed them, then released them and moved off. Seeing Ewart just beginning to rise from the sofa, she stepped past him without a word. She went out to the hall and quickly began to search among the chaos of hats and bags for her and Lilian's things.

Looking up after a moment, she found that Ewart had followed her. He was gazing at her in astonishment.

'You're not leaving?'

She answered with a try at apology. 'I'm afraid I must. My friend—My friend isn't feeling very well.'

He said, 'I don't wonder, the way she's been carrying on! Isn't there somebody else who could see to her?'

'It isn't that, it's—oh, it's the heat, I expect. And we have to catch a train. We've a long journey home.'

'You're only going to Camberwell, aren't you?'

'Yes, but—'

'Well, I go that way. I'll see you to the station.'

'No,' she said quickly, 'don't do that. My friend—she's embarrassed. No, really. Please.'

He had dug out his hat, but now stood with it in his hands, uncertain.

'But we were getting on so nicely.'

'Yes, it's been awfully nice to meet you.'

'And what about our trip?'

'Oh—'

Netta came out of the front room, a couple of empty glasses in her hands. Frances turned to her in relief. 'Good night, Mrs Rawlins. It's been so nice. Lilian and I are leaving now.'

'Oh, you're off, are you? Is Ewart seeing you to the station?'

'No, I've told him he mustn't trouble.'

Ewart said, 'She says her pal doesn't want it. She's isn't feeling too bright.'

'Which pal?' asked Netta, as Lilian appeared.

'This lady here.'

'That's my sister. What's the matter with you, Lilian?'

Lilian was blinking at the light and at the faces, putting back a strand of hair from her cheek. She said, 'Nothing's the matter with me.' She spoke without meeting Frances's eye. 'I'm just tired, that's all.'

'Well, if you're tired, why won't you let Ewart go along with you? Or, Lloyd—' Her husband had appeared in the kitchen doorway. 'Lloyd, you could walk Lilian and Miss Wray to the station, couldn't you?'

He slowed for a fraction of a second, then came gallantly on. Of course he could, he said. He'd consider it an honour.

Lilian protested. They mustn't be silly, it would spoil the party, it wasn't fair. But she spoke weakly, and Frances could feel the tight little charm of intimacy and expectation that had wound its way around the two of them begin to unravel. She put on her hat. Ewart put on his. Lloyd took out his pocket watch and tried to recall the times of the trains. Frances looked from face to face and wanted to hit someone—really wanted it, feeling a rush of despair and frustration at the idiocy of it all. At last, with a burst of false laughter, and in what, she realised, were her worst schoolmistressy tones, she said, 'We're two grown women, good heavens! I think we can be trusted to walk to the station on our own!'

In the awkward pause that followed, Netta drew in her chin. She tapped her husband with her knuckles. 'There you are, Lloyd, the girls don't need you. They're too modern.' She spoke partly in support of Frances; partly, Frances thought, in mockery of her. 'Ewart, take your hat off and come back inside.'

Ewart took the hat off, but did not move. Frances held out her hand to him, saying, 'I do hope we'll meet again.'

He looked sulky now, as if she had played him a dirty trick. Perhaps she had. But she couldn't be sorry. She couldn't be guilty. She couldn't, couldn't! The door was open, and she and Lilian were inching towards it. More smiles, more handshakes, more apologies ... And then they were free, going out of the house like swimmers. Or so, anyhow, it seemed to Frances, for directly the door was closed again and the clamour of the party was behind them she lifted her arms, put back her head, feeling unmoored, suspended, lapped about by the liquid blue night.

Lilian watched her for a moment with an unreadable expression. She moved to the gate, released it, and the two of them went through. Without a word, and with unlinked arms, they started along the pavement. But at every step, Frances's sense of expectation mounted. When she felt the slowing of Lilian's pace her heart gave a lurch. She said to herself, Here it comes! Here it is! She slowed her own pace, and turned, almost put up her arms again, to meet it.

Then she realised that Lilian had slowed simply to catch at her shawl, which was slipping from her wrist; in another second she'd moved on again, at the same pace as before. Frances faltered, then caught up with her. Still neither of them spoke. And soon the silence between them had lasted too long. She felt unable to break it. It had become something like the awkwardness with which they had danced together, something tangible and jangling.

And after all, she thought, as they headed towards the High Street, what *could* happen, here? There had been no declaration— only a glance, a pressing of fingers. If they were a man and a girl, it would be different. There would be less confusion and blur. She would seize Lilian's hand and Lilian would know what it meant. She herself would know what it meant! Lilian would or would not allow herself to be led to a patch of shadow; she might or might not put up her mouth for a kiss. But they were not a man and a girl, they were two women, with clipping heels, and one of them was in a white dress which the moon set glowing like a beacon.

And all too soon they were on the High Street, still busy and full of life. They were in the bright, unintimate station. They were up on the crowded platform. Their train steamed in, and Frances looked in vain for an empty compartment. They got swept on board by a gang of people who had run for the train from down on the street and were full of the excitement of having caught it. They rolled in their seats, groaning and laughing. They had never moved so fast in their lives! The women had sprinted like champions! Oh, but they were paying for it now. They clambered about as the engine started, exchanging places. 'Move over!' 'Budge up!'

Frances hated every single one of them. If she could, she would have unlatched the door and kicked them on to the track. Instead she sat smiling in a rigid way, uncomplaining when they trod on her toes. Lilian, squashed beside her, smiling too, didn't catch her eye once.

At least the journey was a short one. The people called bright farewells when the two of them left the train. The engine was noisy as it puffed away, shoes were loud on the station steps, motor-cars were idling up at the entrance to the station; the final tram of the evening rattled hellishly by just as Frances and Lilian started up the hill for home. But after that, for minutes at a time, there was no sound at all save the peck of their heels on the pavement. They went in and out of lamplight, their shadows fluid under their feet. Lilian was walking as if to meet an appointment, as if fearing she might be late. Only once the house came into view did her step begin to slow. At the garden gate, Frances saw her looking at the upstairs windows, the curtains of which stood open, the rooms behind them clearly dark.

'Len's not home yet, then,' she murmured.

They looked at each other, saying nothing; and that knowledge was back. They went on tiptoe across the front garden, and by the time they were standing in the porch Frances's heart was thumping so badly she could feel it in every part of her body; she feared it would somehow announce their presence, give them both away. She got out her key, and groped for the lock. Lilian was beside her, her arm brushing hers. Again she had the helpless, electric sense that the space between them was alive and wanted to ease itself closed.

And then, inexplicably, the key sprang away from her hand. It took her a second to realise that the door had simply been pulled open from the other side. Wincing away from the sudden flood of weak light, she found herself face to face with her mother. She was in her dressing-gown and bedroom slippers, and her hair was drooping from its pins. Seeing Frances and Lilian in the porch, she clutched at the door in relief.

'Oh, Frances, thank goodness you're home! Mrs Barber, thank heavens!'

Frances's heart, that had been pounding so madly in one direction, seemed to shudder to a standstill and then begin pounding in another. She said, 'What is it? What's the matter?'

'Now, don't be alarmed.'

'What's going on?'

'It's Mr Barber—'

'Len?' said Lilian. She had shrunk back from the opening door, but now came forward. 'Where is he? What's wrong?'

'He's out in the kitchen, a little hurt. There's been a—a sort of accident.'

They found him sitting at the table in the brightly lit room, his head tilted back, a bunched tea-towel clamped to his nose. His face was streaked with blood and with dirt, there was blood and dirt on his shirt-front, his tie; a pocket on his jacket had been ripped half off, and his oiled hair had gravel in it.

When he saw Lilian in the doorway he gazed across the tea-towel at her with a mixture of sheepishness and fuming resentment. 'I thought you'd never be home!' He closed his eyes, as if in pain. 'Don't have hysterics. I'm OK.'

She and Frances moved forward. 'What on earth's happened to you?'

His eyes opened. 'What's happened to me? Some bloke's had a go at me, that's what! Some swine's come at me and knocked me down!'

'Knocked you down? What do you mean? At your dinner?'

'No, of course not at the dinner! Just here, just down the hill. Someone came at me on the street.'

'Just a few hundred yards away!' said Frances's mother. She had followed them into the kitchen.

Frances looked from her white, shocked face back to Leonard's bloody one. She couldn't take it in. She'd barely given him a thought all evening. A minute before, she and his wife had been together in the darkness, the space between them drawing itself shut. Now—

'But who was it?' she said. 'Who hit you?'

He scowled at her. 'I wish I knew. He came out of nowhere. I didn't even have a chance to put up my fists.'

'But when did you leave your supper? I thought—'

'What's the supper got to do with it? The supper—' He lowered his gaze. 'Oh, the supper was a wash-out. A load of snobs. Charlie and I were out of there by half-past ten. I very nearly went on to Netta's. I wish I had, now!'

Frances stared at him, still unnerved, still trying to make sense of it all. Just where, she asked, had the assault taken place? Not right outside? He scowled again. No, further down the hill. Near the park? Yes, near the park. He'd only just got off his tram, he said. He had been walking along, minding his own business, when he'd heard running footsteps behind him: he had turned, and in the moment of turning he had caught a blow to the face that had sent him flying. Perhaps he'd passed out for a second or two, he wasn't quite sure. But when he'd clambered to his feet his attacker was nowhere in sight. Dazed and bleeding, he'd got himself up the rest of the hill to the house—frightening the life out of Frances's mother, of course, who was just on her way to bed. She'd brought him out to the kitchen, given him brandy, tried to clean his wounds. His hands had grazes on them, but they were all right. The worst thing was his nose, which wouldn't stop bleeding.

He risked lifting the tea-towel. The nose, and the moustache beneath it, were gummy with drying blood. Even as Frances and Lilian watched, fresh blood appeared at one of his nostrils, expanded into a bubble, and popped.

'Oh, Lenny,' said Lilian.

He hastily replaced the towel and tilted back his head. 'Well, don't say it like that! It hurts like hell.'

'Look at all this blood.'

'It isn't my fault. I can't make it stop.'

'It's got all over you. It's everywhere!' She was gazing at the floor. There was a trail of grisly splashes stretching right across the kitchen.

Frances picked her way around the splashes in her suede shoes, to stand with her back to one of the counters. The room felt horribly crowded and wrong to her: too small for all the alarm and confusion. She was still wearing her hat; she still had her evening bag dangling from her wrist. Putting them both on the counter, she said, 'But I don't understand. Who was the man, and why did he do this?'

Leonard was dabbing at his nostrils, squinting at his fingertips in distaste. 'I've told you, haven't I? I don't know who he was.'

'Well, what kind of man was he?'

'I hardly saw him! He was one of these wasters you see hanging about, I suppose. Wanting money, and all that.'

'An ex-service man?'

'I don't know. Yes.'

'Did he want *your* money?'

'I don't know! He didn't give me a chance to find out—just came at me, then flew off again. He must have lost his nerve, or seen somebody coming. Not that anyone *did* come. I had to get myself home on my own. I thought he'd broken my nose! Perhaps he has. It damn well feels like it.'

Frances's mother drew out a chair with a scrape of its legs. 'Isn't it frightful, Frances? I wanted to send for a policeman. I thought of running across to Mr Dawson—'

'No, I don't want a policeman,' Leonard said, as she sat. He sounded moody again. 'What's the point?'

'But say he attacks someone else, Mr Barber? And it might be a lady next time. Or an elderly person. Frances, an ex-service man accosted you. Do you remember, a few weeks ago? He spoke most uncivilly to you. Do you think it could be the same man?'

But, 'No, no,' said Leonard irritably, before Frances could respond. 'It could have been one of ten thousand. London's full of them. I knew blokes like them in the army. They can't stand to think that someone else is doing all right for himself. He saw me in my smart clothes and thought he'd have some fun with me, that's all. A nice bit of sport on a Saturday night! Kicking fellows into the gutter on Champion Hill.' He touched the bridge of his nose. 'God, this hurts.' He looked up at his wife. 'Do you think it's supposed to hurt this much? It feels like there's a red-hot poker shoved up it.'

Lilian went gingerly across to him and he raised the tea-towel again. But when the sight of the blood made her draw back, he gave a tut of impatience and appealed, instead, to Frances.

'Have a look at it for me, will you? Tell me what you think?'

So Frances approached him and made him tilt his head to the light. His nose was still bleeding pretty freely. Could it be broken? She had no idea. She had been to a few Home Nursing classes at the start of the War, but she'd forgotten most of that now. The pupils of his eyes seemed their ordinary sizes . . . She supposed they ought to go for the doctor. When she suggested it, however, he was as perversely reluctant to bring in a medical man as he was to involve the police. 'No, I don't need someone poking me about and then sending me a bill for it afterwards. I went through worse than this in France, for God's sake. Just stop the damn thing up, can't you? Jam something into it?'

And what choice did she have? What else could she do? Drawing the silvery ribbons from the cuffs of her gown was like a final undoing of the promise of the night; but she folded back her sleeves, tied on an apron, fetched dressings from the medicine cabinet, and did her best to staunch the bleeding. He leapt like a hare when the first bit of gauze went in, clutching at the edge of the kitchen table. But after that he sat grimly, with folded arms, clearly resenting his own helplessness. When Lilian leaned to pick grit from his collar, he said, 'Are you all there? Doing that, in a white frock, with all this blood?'

Frances had never seen him so ill at ease, so out of temper with the world and himself. By the time both nostrils had been packed he looked like a schoolboy smarting at having been beaten in a fight. He felt at the bridge of his nose again, then gazed down at his spoiled clothes. Twitching the flap of his jacket pocket, looking at the dirt beneath his fingernails, surveying the wreck of his evening, he said nasally, 'God, what a night!'

And, yes, thought Frances, as she washed her hands and began to set the kitchen straight, what a night. Or, rather, what an ending to it. Her mother was white in the face. Her own heart was still fluttering. She felt faintly queasy from the sight of the blood. And Lilian—Lilian, whose hand she had held, who had stood beside her in Netta's back room, saying, *Take me home*—Lilian was lost to her, Lilian was gone, sucked back into her marriage.

For while Frances had been working at Leonard's nose, Lilian had been standing by dumbly, looking sick, looking worried. Had her mind returned to that moment in Netta's room, too? Did it seem inexplicable to her, now? Was she seeing her husband's wounds as some sort of sign, some sort of reminder? He rose from the chair, swaying, and she quickly moved forward to catch hold of his elbow. She made sure he was steady on his feet before picking up his hat and gathering her own things. She didn't look at Frances once. Frances asked, 'Will you be all right?' and it was Leonard who answered, in his bunged-up voice.

'Yes, I'll be all right. I'll take some aspirin or something, try to sleep the worst of it off. I expect I'll feel charming in the morning! But, thank you, Frances.' He sounded simply weary now. 'Thank you, Mrs Wray. I'm afraid I gave you an awful fright. You've got my hat, have you, Lily? That's ruined too, I suppose. Hell!'

He peered resentfully at the damage, then tilted up his chin, felt for his wife's hand and let her guide him from the room. She looked back at the Wrays as she went, to add her thanks to his. But her gaze when it met Frances's was as blank as marble.

'Poor Mr Barber!' said Frances's mother, as their steps on the staircase faded. 'Can you believe it? Oh, the sight of his face at the door! I thought my heart would fail me. I do wish he had let us send for the doctor.'

Frances was clearing the kitchen table. She picked up the blood-stained tea-towel, stood uncertainly with it for a moment, then poked it into the embers in the stove.

'I suppose he's embarrassed,' she said.

'Embarrassed?'

'At being—I don't know—bested by a stranger on the street. Men have odd ideas about that sort of thing, don't they?'

'He certainly wasn't at all himself. But what a thing for him to go through!'

'Well, I dare say he'll get over it. It might have been worse, after all. If the man had had some sort of weapon—'

'Oh, don't!'

'Say, a knife—'

'Don't, Frances! Oh, it's too horrible. Is it the War that's done this? Made brutes of our young men? I don't understand it.'

'Well, try not to think about it. Mr Barber will have two nasty black eyes tomorrow, but apart from that he'll be all right. And by Monday he'll be boasting. You wait and see.'

Perhaps it was the shock of it all, but she couldn't seem to summon up any real upset on Leonard's behalf. She felt vaguely impatient even with her mother. It was well past midnight now, but there was no possibility of either of them going to bed yet. The house had the dazed wide-awakeness she remembered from the after-hours of other emergencies: her father's apoplexy, Zeppelin raids. And a part of her was still with Lilian. She could hear her in the kitchen upstairs, running water. There was the clang of a bowl or a bucket being set on the floor, that must have been the sound of her putting Leonard's clothes to soak.

The stove had just enough heat left in it to warm two cups of cocoa. Frances added generous sloshes of brandy; they drank it in her mother's bedroom. And gradually, finally, the night lost some of its spin.

As she was settling back against her pillows her mother even thought to say, 'I haven't asked after your evening, Frances. Did you enjoy yourselves, you and Mrs Barber?'

'Oh,' said Frances. 'Yes, it was jolly.'

'I expect you were much admired. But what a business for you to come home to! And if you'd been half an hour earlier, while that man was on the street—It doesn't bear thinking about.'

No, it didn't bear thinking about. And yet, when Frances did think about it, she found herself oddly unable to believe in the danger. She pictured the shadowy street, with herself and Lilian on it. She let her mind run further backward, to the train, the walk through Clapham. *It's your shine, Lilian.*

The moment seemed lost, the merest glimmer of a slender lure on a cast-out line that could never be reeled in.

Out in the kitchen the light was still blazing. She stood in it with staring eyes. The clock showed ten to one, but the thought of going upstairs, alone, to lie sleepless in her hot room—No, she couldn't face it. She washed the cups from which she and her mother had drunk their cocoa. She washed the enamel pan in which she had heated the milk. Then she looked at the floor, with those grisly splashes on it; and she thought that she might just as well wash that. She took off her shoes and stockings, and fetched a bucket.

The blood, which was dark on the flagstones, regained its colour as she scrubbed at it. By the time she had finished the water was tinted like rose-hip tea. She carried it out to the yard and tipped it down the drain—standing awkwardly, pouring low, so as not to splash her skirt. Overhead, the sky had the same deep, inky look as before.

She returned to the kitchen; and found Lilian there.

She was standing just inside the doorway that led to the passage. Her hair was forward across her smudged, dark eyes. She was dressed in her nightgown and wrapper, and, like Frances's, her feet were bare.

She watched Frances set down the bucket and said, in a murmur, 'You're here, then.'

'Yes,' said Frances.

207

'I didn't hear you come upstairs, and thought you must be with your mother.'

'I knew I wouldn't sleep if I went up.'

'I don't think I shall sleep either.'

'How's Leonard?'

She raised a hand to her mouth, to pull at her lip. 'He's all right. He's got into bed. His nose has stopped bleeding now that he's lying down.'

'It's awful, what happened to him. I'm sorry.'

She didn't answer that. She simply stood, gazing at Frances across the width of the too-bright room, still pulling at her lip in that distracted way. What did she want? Frances couldn't tell. She wasn't sure that she cared any more. There had been too much dancing back and forth. The night had been over-stretched: it had lost its tension. She went into the scullery to wash her hands, and when she returned to the kitchen, and saw that Lilian was moving away, she was almost relieved.

Then she realised that Lilian was not moving away; she was simply looking out into the passage to be sure that no one else was near. Now, in fact, she was turning back, she was drawing a breath, she was stepping forward—pushing off from the doorpost as if gently but bravely launching herself into a stretch of chill water.

And with no more effort than that, no more fuss, no more surprise, she came across the room to Frances and touched her lips to hers.

The kiss was perfectly lifeless, for a second or two. It was cool and dry and chaste, the sort of kiss one might give to a child—so that the thought flashed across Frances's mind that perhaps, after everything, this was all that Lilian wanted, perhaps even all that she herself wanted; that they could separate, and nothing really would have changed. But they did not separate. They held the kiss, chaste as it was, until, by their very holding of it, it became unchaste; and in another moment again, still kissing, they had moved into an embrace, fitted themselves tightly together. With only the night-dress and wrapper on her Lilian might almost have been naked, and the push and press of her breasts and hips, combined with the yield and wetness of her mouth, gave the embrace a sway, a per-suasion . . . It was like nothing Frances had ever known. She seemed to have lost a layer of skin, to be kissing not simply with her lips but with her nerves, her muscles, her blood. It was nearly too much. They pulled apart, breathing hard, their hearts thumping. Lilian looked anxiously over her own shoulder and spoke in a whisper.

'We mustn't, Frances!'

Frances caught hold of her. 'Don't you want to?'

'Somebody might come, or—'

'You don't think Leonard would come, do you?'

'I don't think he will. But, your mother—'

'I don't think she would. And we'll hear, if she does. Let me kiss you again.'

'Wait. I don't—It isn't—It's making me giddy.'

'Please.'

'But if Len, or your mother—'

'Come outside, then. Out to the garden!'

She almost smiled. 'What? You're mad!'

'Come somewhere,' said Frances. 'Look, in here.' She had hold of Lilian's hand, had begun to draw her into the scullery. 'No one will find us. I'll lock the door.'

Lilian tugged against her. She said again, 'You're mad!'

'I can't let you go.' It was like being parched, and touching water; like being famished, and holding food. 'Please. Please. Just a little while longer. Just to kiss. I promise.'

And after another moment of uncertainty, Lilian let herself be drawn. They went silently over the threshold on their bare feet. Frances quietly closed the door, eased across the squeaky bolt.

The scullery was dark as blindness after the gaslit kitchen, and the darkness was abashing; Frances hadn't expected that. She felt suddenly apprehensive. Lilian was right. Her mother might come. Leonard was upstairs with a bleeding nose! What on earth were they doing? How would they ever, if challenged, explain away the shot bolt?

But already the darkness was lessening. Lilian was beside her, a shimmer, a blur. She put out her hands, and they found her face, they found her lips: they were smooth, cool, wet. She kissed them again, even as she touched them, kissing around and across her own fingers. She drew her hands, damply, to Lilian's throat, to the silky skin at the opening of her nightgown.

The gown had three small pearl buttons on it, hard and round. She undid the first, and then the second.

'May I do this?'

She felt Lilian hesitate. But the third button was undone now; now she had parted the cloth, had dipped her head, was stroking and kissing. And after another few seconds of it Lilian moved forward with a sigh to meet the touch of her fingers and mouth. Her breasts were warm, fantastically heavy, fantastically hard at the tips. Beyond was the thud, thud of her heart—Frances kissed every beat of it.

She forgot about her mother. She forgot about Leonard in the room upstairs. The embrace took hold of them as it had before, became hectic and skinless again, drew them on, on, on, past caution, past care. She hauled up the hem of Lilian's nightdress and touched her naked hips and buttocks. She ran her fingers over and over the hot, smooth, astounding flesh.

Then she brought a hand around Lilian's thigh to the crisp curls between her legs. But at that, Lilian stiffened, and wriggled her hips away. Reaching to feel with her own hand, she said, as if she couldn't believe it, 'I'm all over wet!'

'Move back a little,' urged Frances.

'I think we ought to stop. It's too much.'

'I can't. I want to so badly. Don't you?'

'It's too much, though.'

'I can't. I can't.'

And, even as they were whispering, Lilian was allowing herself to be guided back towards the sink; and then she was braced against the rim of it, had parted her legs and opened herself to the delicate slide of Frances's fingers. Almost at once her hips began to move to match the rhythm of the touch. Soon she was working herself against Frances's hand with a slick, quickening motion. One of her thighs came in between Frances's as she did it; Frances shifted, ungainly, to straddle it, to nudge at it, to rub and strain. The skirt of her dress was lifted and bunched, the satin panels creasing and spoiling—the thought made her nudge her hips all the harder. When Lilian began to tense, the tension communicated itself to her, a muscular charge passing between them. And when Lilian cried out, their mouths were tight together; Frances took in the cry like a breath, and it became her own.

Aside from that they made no sound, did nothing to unsettle the silence of the house; Frances was certain of it. They jolted against each other for another few moments, their rigid poses loosening. Finally they eased themselves apart, Lilian going weakly to the bath-tub, sitting down on the edge of it, pulling up the satin wrapper that had slipped from her shoulders.

'Oh, Frances,' she said, as Frances joined her. Her hair was across her eyes like a veil. She put it back, then kept her hands at her head. She was trembling. 'What have we done? We must be mad. We must be drunk. Are we drunk?'

'We aren't drunk,' said Frances. She was trembling too.

'What have we done?'

'You know what we've done. You know what it is. Don't you?'

She saw the little curving gleams of wetness at Lilian's eyes and mouth. She saw her nod, heard her whisper. 'Yes.'

'I'm in love with you. I've fallen in love with you.'

211

'Yes.'

That was all they said. Lilian reached for Frances's hand with both of hers and held it tight. She let her head sink to Frances's shoulder; Frances raised an arm and pulled her closer. She kissed the crown of Lilian's head. She lifted the hands that were joined around hers and kissed the wrists of them, kissed the thumbs of them. Lilian let her do it all, without a word, without a murmur. Only when Frances's lips began to travel to her knuckles did she draw one of the hands free—the left hand, the one with the rings on it. She set it down to steady herself against Frances's embrace, and there was the muted tap of her wedding-band, a small, chill sound in the darkness.

Part Two

7

Next morning, just for a moment, it might have all been some feverish dream. Opening her eyes in the half-light, Frances saw an unsmoked cigarette on the marble top of her bedside cabinet, stared at it in stupefaction—then felt her insides leap with excitement and alarm. She had rolled the cigarette the night before, but had been too agitated to smoke it. That had been—what time? She and Lilian had returned to the kitchen at just before two. She had helped Lilian to straighten her nightdress, to smooth and tidy her hair. They had stood in a final close embrace, and then—'Oh, Frances,' Lilian had said again, her head at Frances's shoulder, and she had pressed Frances's fingers and broken away from her, slipped from the room. Frances had remained in the kitchen, unable to sit, be still, do anything: she had seemed to be quivering, to be ringing, like a wine glass that had just been struck. By the time she had climbed the stairs to her bedroom, Lilian and Leonard's door was closed and no light showed beneath it. She had lain awake for what felt like hours, trying to take in the wonder of it all.

Now, at ten to seven, touching her fingers to her lips, she could still feel Lilian's mouth there, Lilian's impossibly full, wet mouth. She could still feel Lilian's breasts and hips pressed hard against her own.

Her stomach gave another leap. She drew up her knees and rolled on to her side. Outside, church bells were noisy, but the house itself was still. She was almost afraid to rise, to set the day in motion.

When she finally went downstairs, she found her mother already in the kitchen. And at the sight of her pale face and fretful expression, her heart seemed to hold its breath.

'What's the matter, Mother?'

Her mother frowned. 'Well, I barely slept. Did you? After last night?'

'Last night?'

'I wonder how poor Mr Barber is.'

'Oh—' Frances's heart beat naturally again. She remembered that, of course, as far as her mother was concerned—as far as Leonard was concerned, too—the assault was the thing that had happened to set the world on its head. It was only for herself and for Lilian that this other more astonishing event had taken place.

Her mother had gone to the kitchen passage and was listening for sounds of movement upstairs.

'Ought we to go up there, do you think? I should so like to know that Mr Barber is all right. One can never be too careful with blows to the head. Why don't you go, Frances, and just tap at their door?'

'Their bedroom door? No, no. Let's not disturb them. If they want our help, they'll ask for it. Sit down, and I'll see to breakfast. You don't want to be late for church.'

'Oh, I don't think I've the strength for church today. Mr Garnish will understand. Perhaps I'll run myself a bath.' She began to make for the scullery.

Nimbly, Frances got there ahead of her. 'I'll have the water when you've finished with it. I'll run it for both of us.'

She couldn't believe that she and Lilian hadn't left some mark or trace behind them. But the room seemed quite unchanged. Holding a match to the geyser, she looked over at the sink, where she had pushed with a slippery hand between Lilian's legs; and at the bath-tub, where she had said, *I've fallen in love with you.*

With a pop, the flame found the gas, and she snatched back her scorched fingers.

The next hour or so passed in a stew of frustration. She saw to the stove, made breakfast, every moment expecting to hear Lilian's step on the stairs. She took the bath after her mother but couldn't relax in the cooling water for fear that Lilian would come down while she was in there. But Lilian did not come. Her bedroom door remained closed, and Frances simply had no idea what was going on behind it. Was Lilian longing for her, as she was longing for Lilian? Had she lain in bed, as Frances had, unable to sleep for excitement?

At last there were definite sounds of movement in the rooms above, and her mother rose from her chair. 'There's Mr Barber's voice, isn't it? I think I'll go up, just for a moment. Just to put my mind at rest.'

'I'll come too, then,' said Frances, unable to stand the suspense.

They found Leonard on the sitting-room sofa in his pyjamas and dressing-gown, his nostrils crusty, his nose swollen and both of his eyes with dark shadows beneath. But the injury, Frances thought, looked rather mild for something that had produced such gallons of blood, and perhaps he was thinking the same, for he greeted her and her mother in a hang-dog, rueful way, and seemed to want to make light, now, of the entire affair. He'd slept like a dead man, he said, and had woken with the whopper of a headache, but aside from that he was perfectly all right. He'd enjoy spending the day with his feet up. No, Mrs Wray needn't worry. He was only sorry that he'd given her such a time of it last night! He was afraid he hadn't been very gentlemanly. He'd been thinking over some of the things he'd said, and wondered if he hadn't had a touch of concussion. Yes, he'd certainly speak to the police. He'd do it on his way home from work tomorrow.

'Oh, but you surely won't think of going to your office tomorrow, Mr Barber?'

'What, and miss the chance to parade these shiners!'

He caught Frances's eye as he said this; she was just about able to return his smile. For Lilian was there, right there, sitting next to him, rigid with embarrassment, her eyelids fluttering, her expression so unnatural that it might have meant anything. Frances thought back to the way they had parted the night before: *Oh, Frances.* In the over-bright kitchen she had taken the words for an exclamation of tenderness, of wonder. Now she wasn't so sure. She looked at the flushed exposed flesh of Lilian's throat, and remembered kissing it. She remembered undoing those three pearl buttons, the give of the cloth as they pushed through.

As if Lilian knew what she was thinking, she raised a hand to the lapels of her blouse and, blushing harder, pulled them closed.

Frances touched her mother's arm. 'We oughtn't to tire Leonard, Mother.'

'No, indeed not.' They rose and said their goodbyes.

And after that, unbelievably, the week-end began to be like any other, as Sunday, that dull, dull tyrant, stamped its foot. There was beef to be put in the oven, potatoes to be peeled, carrots and green beans to be washed and trimmed, pastry to be rolled, apples to be sliced, eggs, sugar and milk to be whisked into a custard . . . Frances saw to it all with an eye on the clock, over-conscious of the minutes ticking by. Surely now, she thought, her mother would settle down with a book or a paper. Surely Leonard, up on the sofa, would yawn and start to doze. Surely there'd be a way for her and Lilian to meet.

But her mother didn't settle. If anything, she grew more restless, coming out to the kitchen, getting in the way. She regretted now, she said, having missed morning service. It would have given her the chance to share the news of Mr Barber's assault. She'd begun to think that she and Frances ought to caution the neighbours. Could the food be left to itself for an hour? If the two of them set off right away, they could catch people in the lull before luncheon.

Frances looked at her in dismay. 'You don't really need me to tag along, do you?'

'Well, yes, I think I should like you to come, when it's such a serious matter as this.'

And seeing how pinched she looked, Frances resigned herself to it. She moved the pans from the stove and did her best to put herself tidy. They called on their immediate neighbours first, the Goldings on one side, the elderly Desborough sisters on the other. They crossed the road to the Dawsons, then went down to the Lambs, then climbed the hill by the cinder lane and finished up at Mrs Playfair's. Everyone, of course, responded in the same way. To think of such a thing happening in the neighbourhood! On their very door-steps, practically! Yes, the police must certainly be informed. Mr Lamb would talk to them himself. No, nothing had been the same since the War. Civilised behaviour had gone out of the window. It was all very well to blame lack of employment, but the plain fact was there were jobs aplenty; it was the men who put themselves out of work by insisting on unrealistic wages. They had had to be conscripted into defending their country while the sons of the gentry had willingly laid down their lives. And now respectable people feared to walk down their own street!

Frances couldn't bear it. At Braemar she left the drawing-room while Mrs Playfair was in full flow, and wandered through the open French windows to the garden. She felt so hollowed out by tiredness and uncertainty that she seemed to be floating. The Siamese cats trotted beside her along the gravel paths; she passed the bench where she had once sat with limp Mr Crowther, and arrived at last at the garden pond. A few stout orange fish were just visible in the murk, and a leaf was travelling across the surface of the water as if propelled by tiny oars. That made her think, with a pang, of Ewart, of the 'little row-boat'. She remembered being squashed beside him on Netta's sofa. It felt like a century ago. Then, clear across the garden, she heard the midday *ting, ting, ting* of one of Mrs Playfair's clocks, and—What in God's name was she doing there? She ought to be back with Lilian. Why had she left her, without a word, without even any kind of note? She began almost to panic about it. She had the idea that the two of them had whipped something into life the night before, something like a humming top that, unless she were at home to keep up its whirl, would falter, would tilt, would clip the ground and skitter away to a standstill.

But perhaps the faltering, the skittering, had already occurred. For when, in a fizz of impatience, she got her mother back to the house; when she had climbed the stairs and heard Leonard giving one of his leisurely yodelling yawns; when she had passed the sitting-room doorway and glimpsed Lilian herself, blandly shaking a Sunday table-cloth out of its folds, it seemed for an unbalancing moment as if she might have slipped back in time, or else as if the embrace in the scullery, her hand between Lilian's legs—as if it had all been some sort of hallucination.

She went into her bedroom, began numbly to take off her outdoor things; and she was just easing a foot from its shoe when she saw that on the cabinet beside her bed someone had placed a sprig of silk flowers in a red-and-gold jar. The flowers were blue forget-me-nots, and might have come from the trimming on a hat. The jar could only have belonged to Lilian. She went across to it, lifted the flowers to her face, touched her lips to the dainty silk petals. The thought that some time in the past hour, and all, presumably, without Leonard's knowledge, Lilian had found the flowers, had perhaps cut them from their setting, had put them into the jar, had slipped in here with them—the thought set off a quick, sharp movement inside her, a wriggling sensation, like a fish on a hook. She gazed at the wall of her room. How far was Lilian from her now? Fifteen feet? Twenty, at most? She heard

Leonard yawning again. *Oh, go away*, she begged him silently as the yawn extended itself into another yodel. *Go away! Go anywhere! For ten minutes! For five!* She felt no trace of guilt at thinking it, just as she had felt none the night before while making love to his wife. She saw him simply as some tiresome negligible thing that was keeping her from Lilian, like the bricks in the wall, the mortar, the paper, the air.

But he did not go away. And the roast was over-browning. So she gave up and went downstairs, counting on his coming to visit the WC; planning to dart up to Lilian the moment he did. Perversely, he didn't appear. In mounting frustration, she drained the vegetables, stirred the gravy . . . But it wasn't until hours later, when the lunch had been eaten and the dishes washed and dried, and she had almost given up on the day as utterly wasted, wasted, that she finally heard him on the stair. She left it a moment to be sure, then made an excuse to her mother and went softly and swiftly upstairs.

Lilian must have known that she would come: she was hovering in the sitting-room doorway, looking not at all how she'd looked that morning; looking flushed in a different way; looking open-eyed, open-faced. They stood on the landing, close together but too nervous to embrace.

'You left me flowers,' whispered Frances.

'You don't mind that I went into your room?'

'I've been longing to see you all day.'

'I've been longing for it, too. I didn't dare—'

'Have you? I thought, when I saw you this morning—'

'Oh, my heart was beating like mad! I thought it would beat right out of me! Didn't you see? I thought Len and your mother would be sure to notice.'

'I thought you didn't want to look at me. I thought you were regretting the whole thing.'

Lilian bit her lip, closed her eyes, shook her head in a sort of shiver—That was all there was time for. The back door banged and they sprang apart.

But Leonard went off to work the next morning, just as he had promised; and a little later, it being a Monday, Mrs Wray also left the house, to spend her customary three or four hours with the vicar. Frances was in the kitchen, putting chops in the meat-safe, when her mother said goodbye. The instant she heard the front door close she washed her hands, took off her apron, went cautiously out to the hall. And again she found Lilian waiting for her at the top of the stairs. She was barefoot, and dressed, as she had been on Saturday night, in her nightgown and wrapper; her hair, however, was tidier, as if she had taken trouble with it.

The detail plucked at Frances's heart. She climbed the final few steps, then slowed. They had the house to themselves at last, and were suddenly shy with each other. They stood a yard apart. Lilian said, 'I dreamt about you, Frances.'

'What did you dream?'

'We were in a motor-car, going fast. A man was driving. I was afraid, but you held my hands.'

Frances said, after a moment, 'Let me hold them now. Come into the bedroom. Let me hold them there.'

She had left the curtains drawn against the bright July morning, and once she had closed the door the plunge into twilight made them shyer than ever. They stepped towards each other with nervousness, and the embrace, when it came, felt stiff, even awkward. But then they kissed; and the kiss unfurled, unfolded like a bolt of rippling silk. After a minute of it, Lilian drew free to put her hands to Frances's face.

'What have you done to me?' she whispered, gazing into Frances's eyes.

'Come to the bed,' said Frances. 'Lie down with me.'

This time, Lilian did not pull away to say *Stop* or *Wait*. They climbed on to the bed together, and kissed again; she let Frances untie the belt of her wrapper and ease her arms from its satin sleeves. But as Frances was tugging at those pearl buttons on her nightdress, she caught at her hand. With a mixture of shyness and boldness, she said, 'Take some of your things off, too.'

So Frances slid from the bed, unhooked her skirt and wriggled out of it. She took off her corset, her stockings, her drawers, and laid herself down at Lilian's side dressed only in her shift-like cotton camisole.

Lilian ran a hand over her bare shoulder and freckled upper arm. 'You're beautiful, Frances.'

'Oh, no.'

'You are. You are. I can't stop touching you.' She stroked the line of Frances's collarbone as if fascinated by it. She touched Frances's throat, her jaw, the lobe of her ear. She said, 'It's like a dream, isn't it? It's like I'm dreaming. It's like a spell.'

Frances, shivering with pleasure at the creep of her fingers, said, 'No. It's just the opposite. I've woken up after—I don't know what. A hundred-year sleep. You woke me, Lilian.'

Lilian's eyes shone. 'I woke you.'

'That's why you came to Champion Hill. I should have guessed it, straight off. Perhaps I did. When I followed the heels of your stockings across the floor—do you remember? When I followed your heels that day, I thought it was only so that I could point out the towers of the Crystal Palace through the window. When all the time—Did you ever kiss a woman before?'

Lilian laughed, looking scandalised, but moving her fingers again. 'Of course I never did! I've hardly ever kissed anyone. Only two or three boys before Len, and they meant nothing. *You* did.'

'Yes.'

'How many times?'

'Oh, dozens and dozens. Red-headed women, and fair-headed women, and dark ones too. But none like you.'

'Oh, you're just fooling. Stop fooling.'

'Did you ever hear of such a thing, before you met me?'

Lilian was blushing, still stroking, following her fingers with her gaze. 'I don't know. Yes, I suppose so. But as something indecent. Or as something a hard society woman might do; not as something real. Len used to have some picture postcards he'd got in France. One of them was of two girls—But they were awful things, meant for soldiers. I only saw them once. I made him put them on the fire.' She looked up into Frances's eyes. 'This isn't like that, is it?'

'No, this isn't like that.'

'There's been a—a sort of romance to it, all along. Hasn't there? When we went to the park all that time ago, and you chased that man away—it was such a funny bit of gallantry. If Len had ever done something like that, he'd have done it for himself. When you did it, you did it for me, didn't you? And then we stood on the landing, and you asked if you could call me Lilian. You said you wanted to call me a name that no one else did.'

'Yes.'

'And then, when I cut your hair—'

'What did you think, about what I told you? Were you shocked?'

'I was cross with you. I felt a fool.'

'A fool?'

'For not knowing. For supposing there had been a man. I felt you had tricked me into liking you as one sort of person, when all along you'd been another. But—I don't know. I kept thinking about it. I wondered why you'd told me.'

'I wondered that, too.'

'I thought it showed that you liked me—for a friend, I mean. But then I thought, Oh, but she doesn't like me as much as she liked *her*. And that made me even crosser. It made me furious!' Her fingers were back at Frances's collarbone. 'The feeling frightened me. It didn't seem right . . . I wanted you all to myself, I suppose.'

Frances said, after a pause, 'I think you like to be admired. By men, by me, by everyone. Isn't that the truth?'

Lilian shook her head, smiling. 'No.'

'I think it is. I might be anyone, anyone at all.'

Lilian shook her head again, and a lock of hair fell across her eyes. She gazed at Frances through it, her smile fading. 'No. Only you.'

Frances's heart suddenly felt too full for its socket. She caught hold of Lilian's hand and held it above the stir of feeling. Their faces were so close now that all she could see was a giddying blur of features: damp dark eyes, brows, lashes. The lashes fluttered, and she felt the movement of them against her own.

Lilian spoke softly. 'What you said the other night. About being in love. Did you mean it?'

Had she meant it? 'Yes,' she said. 'Does that frighten you, too?'

Lilian nodded. 'But it frightens me most because—' She couldn't say it. She shut her eyes. 'Oh, I don't know what I feel. I feel it's all an enchantment! All the time we were at the party, I was longing for you to kiss me. I don't think I've longed so much for anything ever in my life. It didn't seem strange, it didn't seem wrong. I didn't think of Len, not for a moment. I know it's wicked of me, but I didn't. It doesn't seem anything to do with him. It doesn't seem anything to do with anyone but us, does it?'

'No,' said Frances simply, 'it doesn't.'

She still had Lilian's hand held flat over her heart, but now, as they gazed at each other, something shifted, something changed. She moved the hand a few inches lower, so that it was cupping her breast; and a moment later she moved it lower again. Shyly, Lilian began to touch her through the thin, worn stuff of her camisole. But then she drew the hand back. 'Put yourself against me,' she said, tugging up the camisole as she spoke, then rolling on to her back and doing the same with her own nightdress.

The curls between her legs were darker and tighter than the loose brown curls between Frances's. The flesh of her stomach and her breasts was textured with silvery, irregular lines: they took

Frances aback for a moment, until she realised that, of course, they were the marks of her unhappy pregnancy. She dipped her head to kiss them, then pushed the nightdress higher and slid forward—then caught her breath, as their bodies came scaldingly together. For a minute or two they lay still, seeming to drink each other in.

But once they were kissing again there came another of those changes. They began to shift and nudge at the hips, to strain after pressure and motion. Frances moved a little to the side and, as it had on Saturday night, Lilian's thigh slid between her legs; still kissing, they fitted themselves neatly and wetly together, began to push and rock. Push by push, the pace of it quickened. Their stomachs and breasts grew slick with sweat. Their mouths parted, met again; the rhythm grew more urgent, then broke down in a confusion of movements, almost a tussle, inelegant, exciting. Lilian stiffened and gave a cry, the sound blurting out like a gush of water, and the thrill and the release of it made Frances's own crisis start to come. She ground herself against Lilian's thigh while Lilian held her and kissed her and gazed in astonishment into her face: 'My dear! Oh, my dear!'

When they finally separated and looked at the clock they were amazed to discover that it was after eleven. Frances had done none of her morning chores. Lilian had to bathe, and tidy her rooms; she had promised to pay a visit to Walworth. They stood, and drew each other close again—but with a pang of frustration this time. For what would they do? How would they manage it? It would be hours before they could see one another again. They had to be careful. Frances's mother mustn't guess. Lilian's sisters mustn't get wind of it. Len mustn't find out! No one must know.

'But I can't let you go,' said Frances, as Lilian began to move out of her arms. 'Can't you come to me later? Tonight, when Leonard's asleep?'

'I daren't. I daren't! Oh, but I'll want to.'

'I'll want it too.'

'Will you?' Lilian gazed into her face. 'I can't believe you really mean it. I can't believe it's the same for you as it is for me. Oh, what have you *done* to me!'

They tore themselves apart at last. Lilian returned to her own room; with a wobble, Frances lowered herself on to the edge of her untidy bed. She had that wine-glass feeling again. It was as if all her senses had been wiped clean of a layer of dust. Every colour seemed sharper. Straight edges were like blades. A bit of silk trimming on the bed-clothes was marvellous to her touch. Had it been like this with Christina? She recalled a night, right here, her parents in the next room; they'd made love in silence, by inches, stealthily, like thieves. But had it really been like *this*? It must have been. No, it couldn't have been! She would never, surely, have been able to give it up.

She remembered the housework. She washed, dressed, went down, took care of her mother's bedroom, saw to the drawing-room and the stairs—doing it all at maniac speed, whirling the feather-broom like a dervish. Even so, when her mother returned at lunch-time she had not quite finished the hall floor.

'Oh, dear,' said her mother, seeing her there on the kneeling mat.

She answered with appalling glibness. 'Yes, I'm running late today. One thing after another going wrong. How's Mr Garnish?'

'He's very well. Oh, dear.'

'Now, don't mind about this. I've very nearly finished.'

She took away the pail of water, then flung together a salad lunch. They ate it outside, beneath the linden tree. She kept up a lively conversation with her mother throughout the meal, all about Mr Garnish's charity, which found seaside homes for sickly boys and girls of the parish. But once their plates were cleared they sat in a companionable silence, and she gazed around at the flower-beds with that new clarity, that new wonder. The blue of the delphiniums, for example: she'd never seen such a blue in her life. The marigolds and the orange snapdragons glowed like flames. Bees clambered in and out of velvety hollows, dusty with pollen: she seemed to see every clinging yellow grain, every wing-beat of every insect. Then she happened to look back at the house just as Lilian, dressed for Walworth, went past the staircase window, and she felt a rush of muddled excitements, a physical fluster—was that love? If it wasn't, then—Christ, it was something very like it. But if it was—oh, if it was—!

'You're very thoughtful, Frances,' her mother said mildly. 'What are you thinking of?'

Beginning to gather the lunch-things, Frances answered without a pause. 'I was thinking of a man I met at Lilian's sister's party, as it happens.'

Her mother looked interested. 'Oh, yes?'

'We talked of making a day-trip to Henley some time. I dare say it won't come off, though.'

It was as easy as that, to give a fillip to her mother's mood. A few days before, she would have despised herself for doing it; now the two of them returned to the house, and once she had taken care of the washing-up they spent a pleasant afternoon together in the drawing-room, sitting in their chairs at the open window. Lilian returned from Walworth, but Frances didn't go out to her. Her blood leapt at the sound of her step. She felt that physical fluster again, in her breasts and between her legs. But she nursed the feeling, in secret—like cradling a suckling child, she thought.

Then Leonard came home. He came later than usual. She was in the kitchen, putting plates to warm, alert for the sound of his key in the lock, when, glancing out at the garden, she was startled to see him letting himself in through the door in the wall at the end of it. She barely had time to arrange her expression before he had picked his way up the path and was in the kitchen with her, wiping the dust from his feet. Yes, he'd come by the lane, he told her, rather than by his regular route, because he'd been down at Camberwell police station, telling them all about his 'little spot of fun'. A sergeant had taken down the particulars, but didn't hold out much hope of catching the fellow. He'd said what Leonard had said himself: London these days was so full of criminal types that looking for one would be like hunting for a needle in a haystack.

He yawned as he spoke, and against his tired, yellowish face the bruises beneath his eyes looked darker than ever. He stayed for ten minutes, however, describing the ribbing he had got from the chaps at the office; he made a point, too, of mentioning the dinner that had ended so disastrously on Saturday night. But he gave a slightly different account of it this time, she noticed. The assurance men he had previously described as a lot of snobs he now dismissed, scornfully, as a 'bunch of chinless Old Boys'. He and Charlie had made their escape, he said, as soon as they decently could. No, there were better ways of doing business than getting into bed with a load of wets . . .

He was plainly trying hard to forget the humiliations of the evening; and, oddly, the very hollowness of his boasts filled Frances with pity. *It isn't anything to do with him,* Lilian had said earlier, and that had seemed true, that had seemed vital, with her face an inch from Frances's, with her hand pressed hard over Frances's heart. But he was her husband after all . . . He went off at last, twirling his bowler, whistling 'Two Lovely Black Eyes', and, *We can't,* thought Frances, with a plunge into desolation. *We can't!* Surely Lilian would think the same?

But when she went up to bed that night she found that a scrap of folded paper had been pushed beneath her door. The paper had an X put on it, that was all: a kiss. One of Lilian's full, wet kisses. The sight of it brought on a return of that wine-glass quiver. For twenty minutes or more she waited for Lilian to emerge from her sitting-room; hearing her step at last she called out to the landing, pretending that she wanted her opinion on the trimming of a gown.

They stood inside the partly open door, pressed silently together—mouths, breasts, hips, thighs, even their slippered feet tangling—while, just across the stairwell, Leonard mixed up his indigestion powder and belched. It ought to have been squalid, but somehow it wasn't squalid at all. Frances no longer thought, *We can't.* She thought, *We have to!* She thought, *I'll die if we don't!* She got into bed in the darkness, wondering if Lilian would, after all, come to her once Leonard was asleep. She lay there willing her to do it—lifting her head at every creak of every cooling floorboard, imagining that the sound was Lilian's step; then sinking back again, disappointed.

Lilian came next morning, however, the moment Leonard had left for work: they had ten minutes together in Frances's bed, before Frances heard her mother moving about and felt they had to separate. But they were able to kiss later, when her mother took letters to the post; they kissed again the next day; and on the Friday afternoon, while her mother was visiting a neighbour, they lay in a patch of sunlight on Lilian's sitting-room floor, their mouths together, their skirts pushed up . . . Saturday was harder. Sunday was harder still. Worst of all was the evening early in the second week when Lilian and Leonard went out to a dancing-hall with Mr Wismuth and his fiancée, Betty. Frances sat at home, watching the fading of the light, feeling herself seem to fade with it.

But later, as she lay in bed, there was the rattle of the front door, and while Leonard was out in the yard Lilian came slipping in to see her, bringing a haze of troubling scents into the darkness: cigarettes, lipstick, stout, sweet liquor.

She put her arms around Frances, tight. 'I thought of you all evening long!'

'Oh, I thought of you too!'

'I looked at all those people and not one of them was you, it was awful! I hated them! Everybody paid me compliments. They all said how well I was looking. I didn't care, I only wanted you!'

They kissed, until the back door banged. And then, 'I love you!' she whispered, squeezing Frances's hand as she pulled away. She hadn't said it before. 'I love you!' Their fingers tore, and she was gone.

Frances lay with the back of her hand over her eyes, wondering how on earth it had all happened. How had things changed so utterly, so rapidly? She felt as alive as a piece of radium. She felt a sort of exaltation. 'I want you with every single part of me,' she told Lilian, the next time they met. 'My fingernails want you under them. The hairs on the back of my neck rise up whenever you go by. The stoppings in my teeth want you!' They kissed, and kissed again. There was no self-consciousness between them, no sort of shame or embarrassment: they had passed through all that, she thought, their eyes glowing with triumph and wonder, as easily as runners breasting the ribbon at the end of a track. Whenever they could, they lay together naked. The summer days were heavy and hot, the air like tepid water. Lilian tucked her hair behind her ear and placed her cheek to Frances's bosom to listen to her heart. She put her mouth to Frances's breasts, her fingers between Frances's legs. 'You feel like velvet, Frances,' she whispered, the first time she did it. 'You feel like wine. My hand feels drunk.'

And meanwhile, amazingly, the routines of the house went on. There were all the usual chores, as well as new ones because of the heat. If milk was to be kept from souring it had to be scalded as soon as it arrived. Jam turned sugary in the jar. Ants invaded the larder. Frances's clothes clung to her as she worked, the dust rising from her brooms and fastening itself to her perspiring arms and face. But she did it all without fuss; she seemed to have the strength of a battalion of servants. She went to the pictures with her mother on Wednesday afternoons. There were the games of backgammon after dinner, the watery cocoa at quarter to ten ... It was simply that there was now this other thing too, this thing like a bright, bright flame at the centre of

231

her days, making the cloudy lantern-glass of her life blaze with colour. Could no one see the change in her? Sometimes she would look across at her mother as they sat together in silence, remember some kiss or caress, and marvel to think that it had left no mark on her. To her the caress was still with her; it felt as livid as a branding on the cheek. And what about Leonard? Did he have no idea? It seemed incredible. But then, since his promotion he had been busier at the Pearl, working slightly longer hours, coming home tired and complaining—but coming also with a touch of smugness, clearly rather liking the figure he cut as the weary breadwinner; his flag rising again as his bruises faded.

'He doesn't care about me,' said Lilian moodily. 'He cares more about his mates at the office. He gets his fingernails polished for *them*. What does he ever do for me? He's been my husband for three years, and he doesn't notice anything about me. You care more about me than he does, Frances. You care more about me than anybody. Even my family—they love me, but they laugh at me, too. They always have. You've never laughed at me. You never would, would you?'

'No.'

'We're like Anna and Vronsky, aren't we? No, that's too sad. We're like gipsies! Like the gipsy king and queen. Oh, don't you wish we were? We could go miles and miles from Camberwell, and live in a caravan in a wood, and pick berries, and catch rabbits, and kiss, and kiss . . . Shall we do it?'

'Yes!'

'When shall we go?'

'Tomorrow. I'll pack a spotted handkerchief. I'll tie it to the end of a stick.'

'I'll bring my tambourine, and a scarf for my head. We won't need anything else, not shoes or stockings or money, or anything.'

And in the days that followed they spent an absurd amount of time debating the route they would take, and the colours of the caravan they'd have, the style of the curtains that Lilian would sew for it; even the name of the pony that would pull it.

Then, all at once, July was nearly over, and they had been lovers for almost a month. Frances had barely left Camberwell in all that time. She'd let slip the trips into Town, she had neglected Christina; she'd sent her a picture postcard, that was all—a boring view of Champion Hill, cows grazing in a meadow—to say that she was busy and would visit soon. But she hadn't visited. She was nervous about it, she realised. She felt a sort of squeamishness about revealing the affair.

But she longed to talk about it. The longing mounted, day by day. And who was there to tell, save Chrissy? She had to do it, or burst. One night there was rain, and the following morning was cooler. It seemed a sort of sign. She saw to her chores, had lunch with her mother, then took a bus to Oxford Circus.

A moment after she had made the turn on to Clipstone Street she caught sight of Christina herself, a hundred yards ahead of her, just emerging from her building and setting off in the direction of the Tottenham Court Road. She was hatless, and dressed in one of her creased paisley frocks, with a short green velvet jacket over the top; under her arm she had what looked like a brown-paper parcel. She hadn't spotted Frances, and her pace was brisk. Frances hurried after her, but the distance between them narrowed only gradually; it wasn't until Christina paused at a crossing on the Tottenham Court Road itself that she was able to tap her on the shoulder.

'You're Christina Lucas,' she said breathlessly, 'and I claim my ten shillings!'

Christina turned, startled, blinking. 'Oh, it's you, is it? I'd begun to think you must be dead. Where on earth have you been?'

'I'm sorry, Chrissy. The month has run clean away from me.'

'Well, I can't give you tea, or anything like that. I've this package to deliver.'

'I know. I've been trailing after you for the past ten minutes. What a pace you set! Where are you headed?'

'To Clerkenwell.'

'To your newspaper people? Well, I'll go along with you. May I? Look, here's our chance.'

A policeman had put up his white-gloved hand. Frances offered her elbow, and Christina caught hold of it; they crossed the road and went on, arm in arm, with matching strides. The day had the odd glamour that a grey day can have in the middle of a heat-wave. The smells were tart London ones: petrol, soot, manure, asphalt. There were still pools of rainwater in the dips of the pavement, and once or twice Christina steadied herself against Frances's arm in order to hop across them. Aside from that, her grip was light. She seemed slim, almost bird-like, in comparison with Lilian. 'How little you are,' Frances said once. 'There's nothing to you, I'd forgotten. Let me carry that parcel for you.'

'Carry my parcel? Don't be absurd.'

They zig-zagged their way through the Bloomsbury streets, crossing the garden at Russell Square, losing themselves for a while in a maze of warehouses east of the Gray's Inn Road; then Christina found a landmark and regained her sense of direction, and fifteen minutes later they made a turn into a dilapidated Georgian square. At the bottom of a set of area steps a door was propped open; the dim old kitchen beyond had been turned into an untidy office, while in the scullery to which it led a man in his shirt-sleeves could just be glimpsed, feeding paper in and out of a noisy treadle printing-press. Another man came to greet Christina and receive her package; Frances hung back, watching, while its contents were discussed. The man was youngish, with an Oxford voice, and had the haunted sort of looks that, if she hadn't known better, she would have guessed he had got in the trenches. But he had been an objector, she remembered Chrissy having told her—one of the first, when it was hardest—and his health had been broken, not in France, but in an English prison.

The small errand was soon concluded. She and Christina climbed the steps, and, 'Where shall we make for next?' she asked.

'Don't you have to hurry home?'

'Not really. Let's wander further. I—well, I'd like the chance to talk.'

So they set off again, heading south by the sun, but taking turns more or less at random. The route grew steadily more shabby, but became fascinating too, a mixture of little businesses—leather works, sanitary works, glass merchants, rag-and-bone men—and street after street of elderly houses, some that had once been grand and were now let as sad-looking rooms, others that had never been grand in the first place and were all but derelict. They paused at a patch of waste ground, possibly the result of a Zeppelin raid: it gave a view of a sprawling, weather-boarded building with a jutting upper storey that must have been there, they decided, for three hundred years, since before the Great Fire.

By the time they had hurried through the stink of Smithfield Market, crossed Newgate Street, and were peering up at the gold figure on the dome of the Old Bailey, Christina had begun to limp. She had the remains of a corn, she said, that was giving her trouble. The limp grew worse around the start of Fleet Street, so they turned into an alley, and in the shadow of some meeting-house or chapel they found a small railed yard with three or four ancient tombs in it; they sat down to rest among the blurry inscriptions. The traffic sounds were muted here. On the other side of the railings men went by: clerks, errand-boys, even a couple of barristers in wigs and gowns. But the yard was a gloomy one, and, seeing that the men paid no attention to Christina and her, Frances got out her tobacco and papers and discreetly rolled a couple of cigarettes.

Christina yawned as the match was struck. She took a single

puff, then let herself droop sideways, resting her head on Frances's shoulder.

'What tired old ladies we've become! And to think how far you used to make me walk. What a tyrant you were. Do you remember you wanted us to walk down every street in London? I still have the little atlas we kept, full of our serious notes. We didn't get very far, did we? Shall we start it again?'

'I'd like to.'

'An hour or two, one afternoon a week. We'd cover the city by about—oh, 1955.'

The words dissolved: she was yawning again. Frances spoke to the top of her head. 'Dear me, how elderly you sound.'

'I told you,' said Christina, patting her mouth. 'I'm a tired old lady.' She added, in a different tone, almost a sly one: 'What with turning five-and-twenty, and all . . . '

She twisted as she spoke, to look up into Frances's face. Frances closed her eyes. 'Oh, Chrissy. It's the end of July. I forgot your birthday.'

'You did.'

'Which day was it?'

'Tuesday.'

'Tuesday. So it was. I'm so sorry. Will you forgive me?'

Christina settled her head more comfortably. 'I suppose I must. I had a nice day, anyhow. I went to Kew Gardens with another friend. I have heaps of other friends, you know.'

'I should have liked to send a greeting.'

'Yes, I did rather expect one.'

'I've been . . . busy.'

'So you said, on your charming postcard.'

'Something's happened, you see, at home. I—'

But Christina wasn't really listening. Her cigarette had gone out, and she plucked Frances's from her fingers in order to re-light it. 'Something's happened?' she said as she did it. 'On

236

Champion Hill? What, have you found some terrific new brand of floor polish?'

'Not floor polish—'

'Moth balls?'

'—Love.'

They had both spoken at once, so it took Christina a fraction of a second to absorb the word. When she did, she straightened up, and answered, in a not-quite-natural way, 'Love! Good gracious! But, who with?' Handing back the cigarette she added, as a joke, 'Not Lil, the lodger?'

Frances watched another clerkish man appear beyond the railings. 'Yes, in fact,' she said quietly, when he had gone by.

Christina's smile faded. 'You don't mean it, Frances.'

'I do.'

'But—wait a bit. Wait a bit. I had no idea you so much as admired her.'

'Neither had I, until about six weeks ago. Or, maybe I had. I don't know. It's all been such a whirlwind.'

'But—oh, Frances, you haven't declared yourself? I'd advise against it, really I would.'

'Declared myself?' said Frances. 'Oh, but we're miles past that.'

'You don't mean the two of you have embarked on some sort of . . . intrigue?'

'Yes.'

'With her husband in the house? Does he know?'

'Of course he doesn't.'

'How long has the thing been going on?'

'Not quite a month. That sounds no time at all, I know. But it feels longer than that. Every day we slip a bit further into it. And we were in it already, I think. Even Lilian was. We were in it up to our knees, before we'd even—Well. Now it's up to our necks.'

'But how do you contrive it? When do you see each other?'

'Whenever we can. We don't take risks. We're not stupid. But in

237

some ways, nothing's changed. We'd somehow got into the habit of spending time together almost in secret. It's what we do with the time that's changed.'

She had been speaking slightly sheepishly up until now. But the suggestion of a smirk must have crept into her features, because Christina, tutting, said, 'Yes, well, I don't want the details, thanks. Honestly, I don't know what to say. I'd always supposed this Mrs Barber a perfect man's woman.'

'So had I. So had she.'

'And so, I presume, had her husband. And your mother hasn't tumbled to it? You think you can keep it from her, in that house?'

'But you forget,' said Frances, 'what an old hand I am at keeping things from my mother. I don't mean just about—about you and me. I mean things like—oh, stuffing kippers into my handbag, so as to keep up the idea that I don't carry my own parcels. I mean going about with holes in my petticoats so that hers might be less ragged. You think I'm out to punish her, don't you, by making a martyr of myself? You don't know the countless little lies I tell for keeping the worst of our situation from her. But when I'm with Lilian I feel honest. I feel like a knot that's been unpicked. Or as if all my angles have been rubbed smooth.'

Christina was gazing at her now with a look of perplexity. 'And it's really Love? Upper case?'

'Oh, Chrissy, I don't know what else to call it.'

'But what can happen? Where can it lead? Do you expect her to abandon her husband for you?'

'I don't expect anything. Neither of us does. We aren't looking ahead. The present's too thrilling.'

That made Christina's expression harden. 'You aren't looking ahead. You're like everyone else just now, then.'

'Oh, well, and what if I am?' said Frances. 'I'm keeping step with the world for a change. Will it kill me? And there's so much antagonism everywhere, so much stress and chafe. Lilian and I—we can't let this bit of love go by. We just can't.'

Her voice had thickened with an emotion that surprised even herself, and in the pause that followed she guessed that she had been too frank, or over-sentimental. But Christina turned away from her to take a final puff on her cigarette, and then to grind the cigarette out on one of the smooth old stones beneath their feet. And what she said, as she did it, was, 'Well, lucky Mrs Barber.'

It was plain what she meant, though they hadn't discussed it in years. Frances was silent for a moment, then spoke in a murmur.

'I let you down, Chrissy.'

'Yes. I've waited all this time to hear you admit it.'

'But I lost more than you did.'

'You did? How's that?'

'Well, how do you think? You got our life, but with Stevie in it.'

Christina flicked a speck of ash from her sleeve. 'Yes, well,' she said grudgingly, 'I'd prefer to have had it with you.'

The admission astonished Frances. She said, 'You don't mean that? I'd supposed you were happy with Stevie.'

Christina made a face. 'I am. You needn't grow conceited. I wouldn't swap her for you now. And, really, Frances, you're such a queer combination of things—so conservative one minute, so reckless the next—it would have driven me to tears to live with you. I think I should have finished by wanting to throttle you! It's simply that—well, I'd like to have had the chance to find out. And most of all,' she added, 'I'd have liked it if, when faced with a choice between me and a life of buns and parish bazaars and games of two-handed patience with your mother, you had chosen me. But you didn't, so there's an end of it.'

She had lowered her head. Her hands were restless in her lap, the fingers with shadows of ink at the tips, the nails nibbled at the edges. And by some association of memories too convoluted to untangle, the sight of her hands fidgeting like that brought something into Frances's mind: a moment from the very beginning of it all, opening a book in a public meeting, finding the slip of paper inside. *You chump. Don't you know by now what a horrible huge lot I like you?*

And perhaps Christina was remembering something similar. Mixed in with the muted traffic sounds of Fleet Street there suddenly rose a bit of music: some event was being advertised from the back of a motor-van. The strains of it blared, then faded, and as they died altogether she said, with a sigh, 'No one's grinding out "our" song today, then.' She got to her feet, straightening her skirt. 'I ought to be getting along. Shall we go?'

So they left the yard and rejoined Fleet Street, their pace wearier than before. Once they had entered the Strand, Frances said, 'If you don't mind, I'll turn at the bridge. How's your corn?'

'No, I don't mind. The corn's all right.'

'And you've forgiven me?'

'Forgiven you?'

'Yes, for—Oh, wait here a sec, will you?'

There was always a flower-seller on the pavement at St Clement Dane's, an elderly, tobacco-coloured woman who, as a girl, she'd once told Frances, had sold carnations to Charles Dickens. Frances dodged across the busy road to her now and bought a bunch of white lilac. She carried it back through the hooting traffic, and Christina looked sour.

'For Mrs Barber, I suppose.'

But Frances held it out. 'For you. For your birthday. I'm sorry I forgot.'

Christina coloured. She took the flowers and raised them to her nose. 'Well, thank you. I'm glad to have seen you. Don't let it go another month.'

'I won't. And Chrissy, what I've told you—You won't go talking all about it? Not even to Stevie? Lilian has a morbid fear of it getting back to her sisters.'

'Well, I don't blame her! Do you?'

'Oh, how maddening you are. I thought you'd think it all terribly progressive and Gordon Square.'

'But Mrs Barber isn't Bloomsbury.'

'I do wish you'd call her Lilian. Is there one rule for Bloomsbury, then, and another for the suburbs?'

'What if her husband discovers it? What will happen then?'

'I don't know. We haven't thought that far. I told you, that's the joy of it.'

Christina's gaze flicked to the passers-by. She lowered her voice. 'Well, just be careful. A married woman, Frances! Properly married, not just like Stevie and me. It can't end well, can it?'

But the end, Frances wanted to say, was impossible to imagine. It was like the idea that one would grow old, when one was thrumming with youth; like the knowledge that one would die, when one felt full to one's fingertips with life.

Instead she nodded, and kissed Christina's cheek, and promised: 'I'll be careful.' And then they parted, Christina limping off in the direction of Covent Garden, Frances heading south across the bridge—pausing for a minute in the middle, to look at the toffee-coloured river below.

And on the other side, she paused again. A display in a fancy-goods shop had caught her eye. The display was of cheap china ornaments: windmills, cottages, Scottie dogs. Nestled in amongst them was a caravan and pony, a gaudy, gimcrack thing, meant for children or doting old ladies; but it made her think of that fantasy of Lilian's, about the gipsy king and queen. The price was a shilling and sixpence. It would be money thrown away. And she had already bought that lilac . . .

Oh, what the hell, she thought. One wasn't in love every day! She went inside and bought the thing, carried it home, took it up to her room, spent ages wrapping it in a bit of coloured paper and a ribbon.

She gave it to Lilian the next morning, while her mother was in the garden. And though she laughed as she handed it over, and though Lilian laughed too once she had unwrapped it, somehow when the cheap little ornament was resting between them in her upturned palms their laughter died and they grew almost grave.

'I shall look at this when we're apart,' Lilian said, 'and it won't matter who I'm with, whether it's Len or anyone. He'll think I'm here, but I won't be here. I'll be with you, Frances.'

She raised the caravan to her mouth, closed her eyes as if wishing, and kissed it. And then she set it on the mantelpiece in place of Sailor Sam—put it right there, in Leonard's own sitting-room, where his gaze, Frances thought, would pass unwittingly over it perhaps a hundred times a day. The idea set off a mixture of feelings inside her: she didn't know which of them was uppermost, excitement or disquiet.

8

And perhaps the conversation with Christina broke some sort of spell; for, almost immediately, things began to change. At breakfast a few days later, Frances's mother received a note inviting her over to Braemar for an hour or two, so that she and Mrs Playfair might discuss some new charity venture. And though Frances had planned to devote the morning to housework, and would ordinarily have used her mother's absence to throw herself into some especially grubby chore, once her mother was safely out of the way the knowledge that Lilian was upstairs, alone, unguarded, began to mount in her like a dreadful itch. At last she gave in and went up, tapped at the sitting-room door. Lilian pulled across the curtains, and the room became the dim, warm, insulated place that it had been on the night of Snakes and Ladders. They lay kissing on the sofa for a while, then moved to the floor, gently undoing each other's clothes as they went.

But when Frances made to draw up Lilian's skirt, Lilian stopped her. 'No.'

'No?'

'Not yet. Lie back first, and let me love you.'

So Frances did as she was told, lay flat, closed her eyes, let her skirt be raised, let her legs be eased apart. She felt Lilian's hand, and then her mouth, warm and mobile, on her stockinged thigh; she felt the mouth grow wet and velvety where it met the flesh above the silk. Then her underclothes were thumbed aside and the mouth was between her legs, tight against her, hot, quite still—unbearably still, so that she started to stir against it—then becoming movement, becoming lips, tongue, breath, pressure, insistence—

Then, with painful abruptness, the mouth was withdrawn. She lifted her head. 'What—?'

'Sh!' said Lilian. She was looking over at the door, a finger raised to her wet lips. And then Frances heard it too: a creak, a footstep, leaving the stairs. Before she could react, there came a voice: 'Frances? Are you up here?'

It was her mother, out on the landing, just on the other side of the not-quite-shut sitting-room door.

They leapt to their feet as if shot through with electricity. Lilian was madly wiping her mouth and chin. Frances's skirt was up around her hips, one of her stockings come free of its suspender: she groped for the catch, got it fastened, straightened seams, smoothed her hair. Where were her slippers? She spotted the heel of one: it had got kicked under the sofa. She tried to hook it out with her toe, tilting sideways as she did it . . . Now her mother was calling again. 'Frances?' She gave up on the slippers, looked once at Lilian, and, her heart hammering, went to the door.

Her mother was just turning away as if to head downstairs again. Hearing Frances, she turned back. 'Oh, you *are* here. Good.'

'Yes,' said Frances. 'Yes, I'm here.' She moved forward, pulling the door to behind her. 'What is it? Are you all right?'

'Yes, I'm fine. But it's Patty, over at Mrs Playfair's. An upset stomach. Nothing to trouble a doctor with, but she has set her mind on arrowroot as the cure; and Mrs Playfair's kitchen is out of it. Don't we have some? I was sure we would. I've promised to take it straight back to them. But I've looked right through the larder and can't see any.'

She was still in her hat and her coat. The front door hadn't sounded; she must have come by the lane and the garden, for quickness. Stammering slightly over the words, Frances said, 'How long have you been here?'

'Just a few minutes. I did wonder where you were. I saw that you weren't in the drawing-room.'

'No. No, I've been up here, with Lilian.'

Her mother was paying more attention to her now. 'Yes? What have you been doing? You look as though you'd run a race!'

'Do I?' Frances laughed. 'Oh, Lilian's been teaching me a dance step.'

It was the first thing that sprang to mind. But she'd had to say something to account for her manner and appearance. She was acutely conscious of her uncombed hair, the colour in her cheeks, her creased clothes and shoeless feet—and also of the fading slippery commotion between her thighs. Thinking to use a small lie to deflect attention from a larger one—because that was a strategy that had sometimes worked for her in the past—she added, in a coming-clean sort of way, 'We've been smoking, too. I didn't want you to be bothered by the smell of it.'

Did that help, or make things worse? Her mother's mouth straightened, conventionally. But then she seemed to hesitate, her gaze sliding past Frances to settle with a touch of wariness on the pulled-to door.

There was nothing to do now, however, but brazen it out. Frances moved forward. Poor Patty. Yes, there was certainly arrowroot. She had used it only last week, for the shape at Sunday's lunch. If her mother would just come back to the larder . . . They went down the stairs and into the kitchen in silence. The larder door was open, the box right at the front of the shelf—right there, where anyone but her mother would have spotted it. It was rather a full box. Patty, surely, wouldn't need so much as that? She fussed for a minute, tipping the powder into a bit of brown paper, making a neat packet of it with two rubber bands.

Her heart was racing the whole time, though her voice, she thought, was steady. But her mother's manner remained stilted, and her goodbye, when it came, was rather a muted one. She headed off down the garden in a rigid way, as if she knew full well that Frances was at the window watching her go.

Once she had disappeared through the door to the lane, Frances went weakly back upstairs. The sitting-room curtains were open now. Lilian was standing on the hearth rug, her clothes made neat, her hands at her face, covering her nose and mouth. She looked at Frances over her fingertips, and for a moment it seemed possible that, appalled, relieved, the two of them might burst into nervous laughter.

But somehow the moment passed. Frances sank on to the sofa. 'God!' She gazed down at her crumpled skirt. 'I look untidy as hell, don't I? And my face is blazing. Did you hear me out there? I told her we'd been dancing. That you'd been teaching me a step. Oh, it's all too music-hall for words!'

Lilian lowered her hands. 'But your mother wouldn't guess, would she?'

'I don't know. She guesses more than you'd imagine. Then again, she's good at not seeing the things that don't suit her ... Oh, *bloody* Mrs Playfair! It's exactly like her to send my mother home for half an old box of arrowroot, when she might easily have sent one of her army of maids to buy a new one. It's exactly like my mother, too, to come!'

'But she won't think of it,' insisted Lilian. 'Nobody would. They'd think of anything but that.'

Frances answered unwillingly. 'She might, though. Because of Christina and me.'

Lilian stared at her, then abruptly turned away. She sat down on the easy chair, biting at her thumb-nail. Frances looked from her to the patch of carpet where they had lain to make love. The room felt airless to her now. At least her mother hadn't come the street way and seen the pulled-across curtains. The curtains were silk summer things of Lilian's, put up just recently. They matched some of the cushions on the sofa. There were silk flowers in the hob-grate, too; the birdcage was twirling slowly on its ribbon; and there on the mantelpiece, of course, were those toys and trinkets, the china caravan amongst them ... Frances suddenly saw the room with her mother's eyes, and it looked like something from a Piccadilly back street.

She gazed across at Lilian and, in a deflated sort of way, her shoulders sinking, she said, 'What are we doing, Lilian?'

Lilian looked back at her. 'What do you mean?'

'You know what I mean. It's half-past ten in the morning. It's no surprise my mother nearly caught us. The wonder is she never has before.'

'But didn't you want it?'

'Of course I wanted it.'

'It was you that came up to me.'

'Yes, because if I hadn't come then, when would I have been able to see you? Maybe for five minutes, later, while Leonard was down in the lav?'

'But what else can we do?' Lilian asked. And then, when Frances didn't answer: 'You don't want us to stop?' She came across to the sofa, sat, took hold of Frances's hands. 'You couldn't stop, could you? Oh, Frances, say you couldn't. I think I'd die! I love you so much.'

'And I love you. But we say it, and what does it mean?'

'You know what it means. You know. Why do you even have to ask me?'

'Sometimes I think we've a sort of delirium.'

'It's the rest of the world that has that. We'll just have to be more careful. It doesn't matter what time of the day we see each other, does it? What does the time matter? It doesn't matter that it's in secret; that just makes it more special, more ours.'

'Do you suppose my mother would think it special? Do you imagine Leonard would?'

'Oh,' Lilian answered automatically, 'I don't care what he thinks. And it isn't as though I'm going with a man, is it?'

Frances's heart dropped. 'Isn't it?'

At once, Lilian grew flustered. 'I mean, that's how he would see it.'

'How, precisely?' asked Frances. 'As a small thing, you mean. Why not tell him all about it, then, if it's as small as all that?'

Lilian sat with her gaze lowered, and spoke quietly. 'It isn't a small thing. You know it isn't.'

Frances did know it. Or, she was almost sure she did. But she felt a perverse temptation to kick out, start a fight . . . The impulse subsided. She lifted Lilian's hand to her mouth, and sighed against her fingers. 'I'm sorry. Don't let's quarrel.'

Lilian smiled at her, uncertainly. 'Come back to the floor. I'll draw the curtains again. We can—'

'No. I'd better go down.' She began to get to her feet. 'Mrs Playfair might send my mother home for something else.'

Lilian kept hold of her. 'Don't go.'

'I must, Lilian.'

'Well, just—just kiss me, first, will you?'

So, after a moment of resistance, Frances allowed herself to be pulled back to the sofa; and the kiss, as usual, went on and on.

Once her mother had returned, Frances took care to keep the conversation well away from the subject of Lilian. They discussed Patty's upset stomach, which the dose of arrowroot, it seemed, had done nothing much to calm. But after dinner that evening, as they sat sewing in the drawing-room, her mother mentioned some task she had promised to do for Mrs Playfair—numbering tickets for a forthcoming raffle. Would Frances help? It was easy work, but rather boring. They might do it at the week's end? Say, Saturday afternoon?

'Of course,' said Frances. After a second she added awkwardly, 'But it might have to be Sunday, I'm afraid. Lilian and I have talked of doing something together on Saturday.'

Her mother was silent after that, sorting through the silks in her basket. She snipped off a length, moistened the end of it, ran it through the eye of a needle. But when she had secured the first of her stitches she said, 'You've been rather in Mrs Barber's pockets lately, I've noticed. Doesn't Mr Barber miss his wife?'

She said it quietly, without looking up, and sounding so unlike her normal self that Frances's stomach gave a jump as if she were ten years old. She made a stitch or two in her own work and answered, as lightly as she could, 'They often spend their Saturdays separately. He plays tennis after work, remember?'

'I wasn't thinking only of Saturdays.'

'Well, Lilian and I have become good friends.'

'You're certainly on very familiar terms these days. She must be flattered that you're taking such an interest in her.'

Frances managed a laugh. 'Taking an interest? You make it sound as though I'm running a Girls' Club!'

'Perhaps you ought to try running a Girls' Club, or something like it. Mr Garnish asked me only yesterday how you fill your time. I didn't know what to tell him.'

'I fill my time by looking after this house.'

'Yes, well, it doesn't seem to have been especially well looked after just lately.'

Frances put down her mending. 'Oh, Mother, that's a bit rum. One minute you can't bear to see me scrubbing a floor. The next you're complaining that the floor hasn't been cleaned.'

Her mother had coloured. 'I'm not complaining, Frances. You know how I feel about you and your chores; you know how very grateful I am for all you've done. But wasn't it for the sake of the house that we brought in Mr and Mrs Barber in the first place? If the housework is to suffer because you spend your mornings with her, smoking cigarettes and dancing polkas . . . Doesn't Mrs Barber have chores of her own? Or perhaps you're doing them for her.'

'Of course I'm not doing her chores for her.'

'You seem so awfully in thrall to her. And she has always struck me as such an ordinary young woman. You mustn't let her monopolise you. Don't go running around after her. Where are all your other friends? You never seem to see Margaret these days. And Mrs Barber has friends, surely? Friends of her own background?'

Was that what this was about, then? wondered Frances. Background? She almost hoped it was. She said, 'I enjoy Lilian's company, that's all. She enjoys mine.'

'More than her sisters'?'

'You know very well that they're rather different types.'

'And her husband's?'

'I've told you before, they don't always get along.'

'Well, but don't let her take advantage of you. When she patches things up with Mr Barber——'

'Perhaps she won't patch them up,' Frances couldn't help but say.

At that, her mother looked impatient. 'But of course she will! She'll make herself thoroughly unhappy if she doesn't. No wife likes to think she hasn't made a success of her marriage. I hope you haven't been putting any odd notions on the subject into her head. If I thought—If I thought for one moment that you'd been encouraging her in turning away from her husband——'

Frances spoke without a blink. 'Why on earth would I do that?'

And her manner must have been convincing. Her mother's gaze lost some of its edge. 'Well. Just don't go making some sort of "cause" out of her. She and Mr Barber won't live here for ever. There are sure to be children at some point. They'll move back into their own sphere, and then—what? You'll see less of her, and be sorry.'

'Yes,' said Frances. 'Yes, I expect you're right.'

She said it with an air of finality, hoping to put an end to the conversation—which had drawn, she thought, perilously close to the old upset over Christina.

Or, then again, she wondered as she returned to her mending, had it? Wasn't it more like the conversations she could remember having with her mother in her teens, about the school-friends and the neighbours' daughters over whom she'd regularly grown so embarrassingly romantic? 'Gordon will think he has a rival,' she recalled her mother saying once, with an awkward laugh, here in this very room. Gordon Fowler had been engaged to Mrs Playfair's daughter Kate; Frances had rather idolised Kate when she was four-teen or so. Her mother must be imagining now that she had some sort of crush on Lilian. She was warning her—was she? Was she looking into the future, seeing disappointments, tears? She couldn't guess, then, how dizzyingly far beyond a crush Frances and Lilian had already travelled. What would she think, what would she do, if she could picture them as they had been a few hours before, Frances sprawled on the sitting-room carpet, Lilian's mouth between her legs?

The idea brought with it a rush of something startlingly like tri-umph; but the feeling immediately began to change, began to shrivel and grow dark. For what, Frances asked herself, had she and Lilian done? They had allowed this passion into the house: she saw it for the first time as something unruly, something almost with a life of its own. It might have been a fugitive that the two of them had smuggled in by night, then hidden away in the attic or in the spaces behind the walls.

Turning down the gas in the hall at bedtime, hearing the creak of Lilian's ironing board in the little kitchen, she said to herself, I won't go in to her. Just this once, I won't go in. She climbed the stairs, meaning to go straight to her room and close the door. But as she left the final step she hesitated; and then, without another thought, she went softly around the stairwell to the open kitchen doorway. She and Lilian met each other's gaze, and her heart turned over. She stole further into the room.

Lilian set the iron on its trivet and looked nervously past her to the landing. 'I thought you were never going to come! I've been here ages, pressing the same pillow-case over and over. You don't hate me, do you?'

'Hate you?'

'I thought, earlier on—Oh, I've been thinking all sorts of things.'

They touched hands across the board; then she caught up the iron again. The sitting-room door had opened and, with a whistle, here came Leonard.

He was dressed for the heat—or rather, undressed for it, with his feet bare, and his sleeves rolled high, and his collarless shirt flapping at the throat, giving a glimpse of the white vest beneath it and a suggestion of the gingery chest beneath that. The bruises around his eyes, which over the past four weeks had paled from bluish-black to khaki, had now all but faded; he seemed his old self, bouncing with health. He had a bottle of beer in his hand, and took a last swig from it as he entered the kitchen.

He greeted Frances quite cheerily, moving past her in a fox-trot. He seemed to have wandered in for no particular reason, and she hoped that he would now go wandering off again. Instead he lingered, nosing about, watching Lilian at work on the pillow-slip. 'Are you going to be much longer at that?'

She answered self-consciously. 'It has to be done.'

His tone became faintly wheedling. 'Finish it tomorrow, can't you?'

She slid the iron across the cloth and made no reply. But still he watched, still he hovered, still he mooched about. He didn't look at Frances again. There was no hostility in his manner. He wanted his wife, that was all—she realised it with a pang. He didn't know—how could he?—that she wanted her too.

The thought made her step away and go across to her own room. Opening the door, she found that Lilian had slipped one of her notes underneath: a heart, with an arrow piercing it. She stared at the scrap of paper then put it aside, face down.

By the time she had undressed, and got into bed, and smoked her cigarette, Lilian and Leonard had left the kitchen and one of them was shutting off the gas on the landing; a moment later there came the soft click of their closing bedroom door. Frances had heard that click every night for the past three months, but something about the sound, tonight, unsettled her. She shifted around, over-warm despite the open window, now and then lifting her head from her pillow, thinking that she could hear murmurs, creaks, laughter, from across the landing . . . There was nothing.

When she and Lilian saw each other the following morning they agreed that, in future, they would take more care. They would keep to Frances's room, they said, where they could hear the garden door if it sounded, as well as the front one, and for a week they were very cautious, meeting only when the house was empty, and the rest of the time wringing a terrible excitement from chance encounters on the landing, catching at each other's hands as they passed on the stairs. Frances went to her mother and said that she'd been thinking things over and, yes, she had been letting herself grow a little slack. Were there any charity tasks she could help with? What about those raffle tickets? There turned out to be five hundred of them: she spent an afternoon inking in the numbers, and then another afternoon going round the local houses, trying to cajole people into buying them. A part of her enjoyed it. Even the separation from Lilian: a part of her enjoyed that. She remembered the airless feeling she'd had in the gaudy sitting-room.

But at night, in the darkness, she'd find herself lifting her head, listening out for the sound of that closing bedroom door. And the next time she and Lilian made love there was some new quality to it. They stripped naked, but nakedness somehow wasn't enough any more: she wanted to get past Lilian's skin, possess her, with her hands, her lips, her tongue ... Afterwards they lay breathless, shaken by the thud of their hearts, pressed together so tightly that she wasn't sure which of the beats were Lilian's, which her own. When she began to ease herself free, Lilian caught hold of her. 'Don't let go of me! Never let go!'

But once the thud had calmed and Lilian's grip on her had slackened, her mood began to cloud. She thought of how she would lie here later, with only a ghost in her arms; how she would listen for that closing door. She had never asked what went on beyond it. She had never wanted to know. It had seemed something that didn't concern her, something that scarcely concerned Lilian. Now, suddenly, not knowing was impossible to bear.

She drew a breath. 'Lilian, when you're with Leonard—Is it like this, with him?'

Lilian was still for a second, then rolled away from her. 'Oh, Frances, don't ask me. I don't want to think about him when I'm with you. The things I do with him—There was love in it once, at the start. But it's never been like it is with you. With you, it's all of me. With him—'

'How often do you do it?'

'Don't *ask* me, Frances.' She put a hand across her eyes.

'I'd rather know than not know, that's all. How often?'

She answered uncomfortably. 'I don't know. Not so often any more. He knows I don't want to.'

'He knows you don't want to, yet he still makes you do it? What is he?—a brute?'

'It isn't like that.'

'You *do* want it, then.'

'No! I hate it. You don't understand. You don't know what it's like to be married. If I didn't let him, ever—It's different for men. If I stopped letting him he'd want to know why, he'd pester me, he'd make scenes. He might get suspicious. It would make things harder for you and me. He already wonders why you want to see so much of me.'

The thought made Frances feel ill. 'It seems . . . obscene,' she said. 'People like me get called obscene, but—You might as well charge him by the hour. At least that would be being honest about it.'

Lilian rolled back to her. 'Oh, please don't spoil things. It's been so lovely. It's been perfect. Hasn't it been perfect for you?'

'Yes,' Frances admitted, 'it has. But—'

'But what?'

'Well, it's been perfect in the way that something's perfect when it's under a glass dome, or trapped in amber. We do nothing but embrace. We do nothing but lie in rooms with the curtains closed, like this.'

'But how could we ever do anything else?'

'When we talk, we talk nonsense. Of flying carpets. Of gipsy queens. You mean more to me than that. I don't want a make-believe life with you. I want—I don't know what I want. I almost wish I were a man. I've never wished it before. But if I were a man I could take you dancing, take you to supper—'

'If you were a man,' said Lilian, 'you wouldn't be able to do any of that. Len would hear of it, and come and fight you. People would say all sorts of things against me. You don't want to be a man, do you? I wouldn't love you if you were. You wouldn't be you, then. Dancing and suppers—what do they matter? I've done them over and over, and they mean nothing. *This* means something.'

'What does it mean?'

'It means we're in love.'

'But tonight you'll lie with him, and I'll be here, thinking of you doing it. I mind it more and more. I didn't, at first. Or I told myself that I didn't. Don't you mind it, too?'

Lilian lowered her gaze. When she answered, it was in a queer, dead tone that Frances had never heard her use before. 'I mind it every minute.'

'Then why not . . . leave him?'

She looked up. 'What?'

'Just walk away from him.'

'Oh, Frances, how could I do that?'

'Are you in love with him?'

'You know I'm not.'

'Then make an end of it.'

'Stop it, Frances. Where would I go? How would I live?'

'You might . . . live with me.'

Neither of them had ever suggested such a thing before, and Lilian looked startled. But at once, her expression changed. 'Oh, wouldn't it be wonderful!'

'No,' said Frances, catching hold of her, 'don't say it like that. As if it's another fairy tale. Why shouldn't we live together? We could find a flat, like Christina and Stevie's. We could take a room, just one room—' She could see the room already. She could see the two of them inside it, and herself locking the door. 'We could pig it, go naked, live on bread and scrape if we had to. Why shouldn't we?'

'But Len would never let me.'

'How could he stop you?'

'And what about your mother?'

'I don't know. But there must be a way. Mustn't there? If we really wanted it?'

Their hearts had begun to thud again. They looked at each other, and for a second they seemed on the verge of some dizzying plunge or leap.

But then Lilian closed her eyes and spoke lightly and longingly.

'Oh, but wouldn't it be lovely! We could have a wedding night! My proper wedding night was awful. There seemed no point in going to a hotel or anything like that. We went straight to Cheveney Avenue; you could hear Len's parents through the walls. Len kept whistling "At Trinity Church I Met My Doom". He whistled it so much he made me cry. He said he was sorry afterwards, but—Ours wouldn't be like that, would it? Where would we have it? Paris! An artist's attic, looking over the rooftops!'

In other words, thought Frances, they were back in the realm of fantasy, and might just as well be talking about gipsy caravans. She felt a surge of relief, disappointment—she wasn't sure what the feeling was. But with an effort, she let it go. They lay together a little longer, until it was time for them to rise, and dress, and return to their chores.

And what, really, did she want? She wanted Lilian, obviously. Further than that, she had never allowed her thoughts to venture. But now the vision she had had—the room, the freedom, the dizzying leap—it was in her head, small, small as a mustard seed, but taking root. Was it possible? Could they do it? Could they make a future together? Could she walk away from her mother, from the Champion Hill life that she had built up so sedulously, one dusty bit of housework at a time? And could she seriously ask Lilian to give up a *marriage*?

No, of course she couldn't. It was madness even to consider it. She had to remember what she'd told Christina: that the affair was glorious, a gift, to be enjoyed as long as it lasted. Surely it would run its course. Probably it was simply a thing of the summer, that she and Lilian would outgrow ... But another week passed, and then another. The August days kept warm, but began to be noticeably shorter. And the affair did not cool, did not run its course. On the contrary, it became ever more tearing, ever more consuming, ever more frustrating. For there, like a brick wall in the way of it, like a briar hedge—there was Leonard. The two of them could kiss and make love as fiercely as they dared during the day, but at the end of it—at every end, of every day—Lilian would go into her bedroom with him, the door would close behind them, and—Frances still shrank from picturing what happened after that. She took comfort from the fact that the couple seemed to argue more regularly now; that they sometimes passed entire evenings in a dead or bristling silence. But what a way, she thought, to have to find one's comfort! And in any case, the arguments were always made up. The silences would give way to yawns, to murmurs, to laughter. There were still trips to dancing-halls and public-houses. There was even to be a holiday: Lilian announced it miserably. At the beginning of September she and Leonard were going to Hastings for a week with Charlie and Betty. A whole week! How would they bear it?

Worse even than the thought of it, however, worse than the laughter and the dancing-halls, worse than anything, were the routine casual intimacies of married life: Leonard waiting for Lilian at the bottom of the stairs, calling, 'Come on, woman!'; Lilian straightening the angle of his hat, doing up the buckle at the back of his waistcoat—little husband-and-wifely moments which Frances might glimpse or overhear as she made her way through the house, and which, if she came upon them unreadied, could strike at her like blows to the heart. At first she did her best to turn and walk away from them. Increasingly, as the month wore to a close, she found herself seized by a pointless impulse to interrupt them. She'd invent trivial domestic dramas, find any sort of excuse—reels of thread, needles, books, that must be urgently borrowed or returned—anything, anything at all to get hold of Lilian, get her by herself, away from Leonard, even for a minute.

'What is it?' Lilian would ask, following her into her bedroom.

'I just wanted to see you, that's all.'

'Oh, Frances, you mustn't.'

For now Leonard might come too, peering in from the landing—'What are you women whispering about? You're forever whispering, you two. A man isn't safe. What are you plotting?'—making a joke of it, Frances thought; but peering all the same.

It became hard to keep from hating him. The idea of him bothering Lilian in bed, the thought of him clambering on top of her—She went out of her way to avoid him, and whenever the two of them did meet she was so cool and so unwelcoming that he would retreat, looking puzzled. He gave up stopping in the kitchen for an evening chat with her and instead mooched about the garden, pushing the mower, watering plants. But, of course, he'd always go back to Lilian at the end of it; and sometimes she would find herself creeping after him, imagining the two of them up there in that dangerous room. She'd stand at the bottom of the stairs—or on the first stair, or the second—her head cocked, listening.

Once her mother caught her at it. 'What are you doing, Frances?'

She gave a start. 'I thought I heard Lilian and Leonard calling to me, that's all.'

Her mother looked troubled. 'They're in their sitting-room, aren't they? Why should they want you?'

'I don't know.'

'Well, don't go bothering them. Mr Barber will be glad to go on holiday, I should think—glad to have some time alone with his wife.'

And yes, reflected Frances, he probably would. She thought of the days and days he'd have with Lilian, and the nights and nights . . . And suddenly she was an inch from going up there and throwing the whole thing in his face. *You think she's yours*, she imagined herself saying. *You haven't a clue! She's mine, you moron!* For wouldn't it solve everything, to do that? Or, if not solve it, then break it, change it—

Then she pictured the horror that she would see in Lilian's expression; and did nothing.

And then it was September, and the holiday was upon them. Lilian spent the day before it packing a suitcase for the trip. Frances kept her company for a while, sitting on the edge of her bed, but the sight of the things being folded into the case's striped interior—the bathing costumes, the towels for the beach, vests and underpants of Leonard's—made her heart wither. When Lilian reached past her to the bedside table for a tub of studs and cufflinks, she got up.

'I'm in the way, I fear.'

'Don't go,' said Lilian, catching hold of her.

'You'll do better without me, I think.'

'No, wait. Please, Frances. We'll be apart all next week, and—' She stood with a hand at her eyes for a moment, looking suddenly shockingly weary, all her features dulled and sinking; then she seemed to shake the tiredness away. With a smile, she tossed the tub of rattling links into the half-filled suitcase. 'I can finish the packing later. Len can help me, for once. I don't want to be indoors any more. Come out with me, will you?'

Frances was thrown by the change in her. 'Out with you? What do you mean?'

'There's somewhere I want to take you. As a treat. To make things up to you. To make up for—for everything. For going on this stupid holiday. For being married. For being a nuisance and making you love me! I don't know. You always say you're sick of stopping indoors with the curtains closed, don't you? Come out with me, then.'

'But where to?'

'I shan't tell you. It would spoil the surprise! Don't you like surprises?'

No, Frances didn't like surprises. She hated the thought of people plotting and planning on her behalf. She loathed the burden of being delighted once the surprise was disclosed. So, almost reluctantly, she got herself ready, and when, twenty minutes later, she and Lilian left the house, she immediately began to attempt to guess where they were heading. Lilian had brought no bag with her save a small velvet handbag, so she couldn't be intending a picnic; and though they approached the park they soon veered away from it, taking the long road south-west towards Herne Hill. Perhaps they were going to Herne Hill station for an outing by train. Yes, it must be that, she decided. A ramble in the country, followed by tea at a café or an inn. She thought of where they could comfortably get to in two or three hours. Somewhere in Kent, obviously. Well, that was all right. She'd enjoy a trip into Kent. She began to put a good mood in place, to fit it together, determinedly.

But they reached the turning for the station and went marching past it. Lilian had her parasol over her shoulder, and twirled it as they walked, looking mischievous, excited; looking rather like a cat. They were heading for Brixton now. The road was rather noisy. 'It isn't much further,' she said, in her enigmatic way; and Frances couldn't imagine what, on this dusty suburban street, could possibly merit all this mystery, all this fuss. She could only suppose, with a sinking heart, that their destination would prove to be something whimsical, a gipsy fortune-teller in a room above a shop, a romantic-looking tree around which she'd be invited to tie a ribbon . . .

They made a turn, and, 'You mustn't look, for this last bit,' Lilian said. 'Keep your eyes on the ground, and I'll lead you.'

Feeling foolish, but saying nothing, Frances went on with her gaze lowered, letting herself be steered around lamp-posts and over kerbs. They went through a break in the traffic across a busy road; and then they came to a halt.

'May I look now?'

'Yes,' said Lilian. Then, quickly: 'No.' Her confidence was failing. 'Perhaps you won't like it after all.'

Frances was afraid to raise her eyes. She waited another moment, as a bus went noisily by; then lifted her head.

She found herself at the colourful entrance to the Brixton Roller Skating Rink.

She looked at Lilian. 'You've brought me rinking.'

Lilian was anxiously watching her face. 'You said you used to like it. Do you remember? The first time we went to the park?'

Frances nodded. 'Yes, I remember.'

'May I take you in?'

'Yes.'

It was like being plucked from one life and hurled bang into another. They could already, as they approached the doors, hear the muddle of sounds from within. They entered the building and were met by music, by laughter, and by the low rumbling note of wheels on the rink. They saw the crowd making its circuit, its unnatural stiff-legged glide, and by the time they had queued for their tickets, then queued again for their skates, Frances was desperate to join in. The toes of her shoes went snugly into the little metal brackets; the worn leather straps pulled tight across her ankles. Straightening up, she felt ten feet tall but horribly ungainly: she'd forgotten the wild insecurity of it. She pushed forward, grabbing at nothing. 'This is mad! It's terrifying!'

Lilian rose, then shrieked and caught hold of her. Laughing, they clattered their way across the floor to the break in the barrier.

And then they were on the rink itself, on the treacherous chalked surface. Lilian pulled at her arm: 'Slow down!' She was clinging to the rail.

'Let go of it,' urged Frances.

'I daren't! I'll fall!'

'You won't fall. Or if you do, then we'll both go down together. Come on.'

She took hold of Lilian's hand and drew her away from the

barrier. Lilian shrieked again, but let herself be led; they found a place in the flow of skaters.

The building was huge, modern, charmless, like a giant church hall. The bunting that hung from the rafters was in faded Armistice colours, and the songs were mild old things from thirty or forty years before, 'Funiculì Funiculà' and 'The Merry Widow Waltz'. The crowd was thinner than the crowds that Frances could recall from her rinking youth; it might have been made up solely of people who hadn't yet twigged that thrills, these days, were to be had elsewhere—in jazz clubs, say, or cocaine houses. But the off-season air lent a camaraderie to the proceedings, and there were quite enough skaters to bump into or tumble over. It was still the school holidays, and children were darting like minnows, but there were courting couples too, and girls in pairs and groups, even the occasional game old lady. Boys raced and swooped in an inner circuit of their own, and in the rink's underpopulated middle a few grave youngsters showed off their talents. Every so often someone flailed like a windmill and went down, to cheers and hoots and sympathetic laughter; they'd pick themselves up, sheepish, hitting the chalk from their knees and behinds. A man on the staff was going about to see that nobody got hurt, and to blow a whistle if ever the boys became too rowdy.

And in amongst them all glided Frances and Lilian, getting the hang of it, picking up speed. Now and then men looked at Lilian, because men always did look at her, but no one troubled them except to smile at them, or to make way for them, politely. What a genius Lilian was! Nowhere else in the world, thought Frances, could they have been together so publicly, holding on to each other like this. It wasn't at all like making love. It was a lark, pure, childish. And yet it *was* like making love: the thrill and intimacy of it, the never letting go of each other, the clutching of fingers and the bumping of thighs, the racing and matching of heartbeats and breaths. After they'd been at it for half an hour the signal was given for the skaters to change direction; in the hilarity that ensued they made their clumsy way off the rink and, still in their skates, sat at one of the tables on the other side of the barrier, drinking tea and eating ginger nuts and watching the crowd. When they returned to the rink after that they were more confident; they put their arms around each other's waists, or held each other as if for a country dance, Lilian with her right hand raised and Frances holding it from behind, their other hands joined tight down at Frances's hip. Frances felt graceful and easy now; she wanted to stay on the rink for ever. She looked at the best of the skaters and thought, Lilian and I could do that! They could buy skates of their own, come to the rink every day. They could practise and practise . . .

She detached herself from Lilian's waist and held her hands instead, going ahead of her, skating backward, daring. They laughed into each other's faces.

'You'll go over!'

'No. Never.'

She did not fall, and neither did Lilian. They pushed on with the crowd for another twenty minutes or so. They narrowly avoided a collison with one of the sporting old ladies. But then they began to be tired; their leg muscles were aching. It was hard work, after all. Hand in hand, they made a final, regretful circuit of the rink; and then, like birds leaving a pond, they were back on the ordinary floor, waddling and ungainly. Removing the skates was, briefly, blissful. But it was sad, Frances thought, to return them to the counter, sad to exchange motion, speed, glamour for safety and unstrained arches.

And it was something worse than sad to push back out through the doors and find themselves in Brixton again, to rejoin the commonplace, unwheeled afternoon and head home to Champion Hill. They weren't so aware of it at first. They had the glow of the rink about them. Lilian put up her parasol and they walked with joined arms, humming the harmless tunes they had skated to—

still feeling as though, with a push of the foot, they could launch themselves forward into effortless arabesques. But the climb up through Herne Hill pulled at their aching muscles, and the road seemed longer and dustier than it had before. And then, all at once, they were close to home. It was almost five; Leonard would be back in an hour and a half... Frances's steps began to lag as though she were heading for the gallows. They drew level with one of the entrances to the park, and—'I can't go back just yet,' she said, coming to a halt. 'I can't.'

Lilian said nothing. Without a word they went in through the gate.

They finished up at the band-stand. The small, railed space recalled the rink, and for a minute again they were lively: Lilian glided across to the balustrade, then stood smiling as Frances joined her, the tassel of the parasol raised to her mouth. She had waltzed like that, and stood like that, Frances recalled, the very first time that they had come here. How impossibly far off that day seemed! How long ago was it? A little over three months. If she put her mind to it she could just summon up the particular quality of being here with Lilian then, the two of them still more or less strangers, Mrs Barber, Miss Wray, but their intimacy, surely, already taking root, already growing, somewhere deep, deep below the skin of their friendship ... The feeling receded and was gone. She could only see Lilian as she was now, her smile fading as they faced each other and her gaze, as it sometimes did, becoming so level, so stripped, so grave and ungirlish, that Frances felt an answering pressure around her heart, something dark and almost frightening, like the intimation of agony.

She looked away. An elderly man was passing by on one of the paths—a Mr Hawtrey, one of the residents at the local hotel. He raised his cane and called a pleasantry when he recognised Frances, and she answered with a laugh: 'Yes, we do rather, don't we? No, we've left our trombones at home today ...'

He moved on, and her laughter died. She watched him go, then dropped her gaze and ran her fingers over the scored green paint of the balustrade rail. *Bill goes with Alice. Albert & May.*

She said, 'It's real, isn't it?'

Lilian answered after a pause, with a bowed head, in a murmur. 'Yes, it's real. It's the only real thing.'

'Then, what are we to do?'

'I don't know.'

'What we talked about, living together—'

Lilian turned away from her. 'Don't, Frances.'

'Why not?'

'You know why. It's too much. You don't mean it, not really. It's just a dream.'

'I think I do mean it.'

'I couldn't. I never could.'

'You'd rather stay in an empty marriage? For the rest of your life?'

'It isn't just that. Don't ask me. If you loved me, you wouldn't ask. We'll just make ourselves unhappy if we keep thinking about it.'

'I can't love you and *not* ask you. You must see that.'

'Please don't.'

'I can't be without you.'

That sag came back into Lilian's face. 'Don't, Frances! I love you so badly. But we're different. You know we are. You don't care what people think of you. It's one of the things that made me love you, a thing I liked about you from the beginning, right from the moment I saw you cleaning the floor with that stupid duster on your head. But I'm not like that. I'm not like you. I'd have to give everything up. I shan't ever love another girl, but you—you'd grow tired of me. I've expected you to grow tired of me every day since Netta's party.'

'But I haven't. I couldn't.'

'You will, though. You might. Len's tired of me, but that doesn't matter. That's just what happens between husbands and wives. But if you were to tire of me, and leave me, after I'd left him—what would I do?'

Frances shook her head. 'How could I ever leave you, Lilian?'

Lilian looked back at her, unhappily. 'But you left your other friend.'

The words caught Frances off guard, and she found herself unable to answer.

They stood in silence for a minute. Frances stared at the park without seeing it. 'Can't we just,' said Lilian at last, 'go on the way we've been doing? Something might change, or—'

'What will change, if we don't change it ourselves?'

'I—I don't know.'

'And meanwhile, what? I must keep sharing you with Leonard?'

'It isn't like that.'

'It feels like that. It feels worse than that! He doesn't even know he's sharing you.'

'But it means nothing, my being with him. That's the stupidest thing. He might as well be dead. Sometimes I wish he was. I know it's an awful thing to say, but sometimes I wish some nice fat bus would just run him over. I wish—Oh, it isn't fair! If we could only close our eyes, and open them and have everything be different!'

She did close her eyes as she spoke, as if she were wishing. But just what, wondered Frances, was she wishing for? She had lost sight of where the heart of the difficulty lay. Was it in the fact that they were both women? Or that Lilian was married? The two things seemed hopelessly entangled. She could get one of them smooth in her mind, but the other remained twisted. That came free and the first was in knots again. There had to be something, she thought—a word, a phrase, a key to it all—but she couldn't find it, she couldn't see it.

And before they could speak again there were sounds of giggling on the other side of the band-stand: two small boys were down on the gravel, peering in. They must have sensed the sad intensity of Frances and Lilian's conversation, or perhaps seen something in their poses, for, 'Spoony!' one of them called. They raced off, screaming with laughter.

The word made Lilian jump. She pushed away from the rail. 'God! Let's go down, can we? The whole world can see us up here.'

'No one's looking. They were only schoolboys.'

'I don't like it. Let's just go down.'

So they went back down the steps and picked their way along one of the paths. Nothing had changed, Frances thought. Nothing had been resolved or decided. She wanted to say again: What are we to do? But how many times could she keep asking it? Even to her own ears, the words were beginning to sound like a whine. So she said nothing. They moved on, with unlinked arms. There was nowhere to go save back to the house.

And there was no opportunity, after that, to be alone together. Leonard came home early for once, and seemed to spend the evening on the landing: every time Frances ventured upstairs she came face to face with him, fiddling about with his tennis racket, dabbing blanco on his shoes. She saw Lilian only in glimpses, over his shoulder. They didn't kiss, they didn't embrace; next morning they didn't even say a proper goodbye. Mr Wismuth and Betty arrived at the same time as the butcher's boy, and by the time Frances had taken the meat and sorted out some quibble with the order, Lilian and Leonard's bags and cases, and then Lilian and Leonard themselves, had been squeezed into Charlie's narrow motor-car and driven away.

9

And in some ways—oh, it was a relief to be rid of them. The whole furtive business of being with Lilian, of finding and securing and making the most of scraps of time with her—those juicy but elusive morsels of time, that had to be eased like winkles out of their shells, then gobbled down with an eye on the door, an ear to the stair, never comfortably savoured—it had all, Frances realised, been crushing the life out of her. She spent the two or three hours of that Saturday morning going between the kitchen and the drawing-room in a sort of trance. After lunch she lay on the sofa with the paper, shut her eyes against the latest bit of bad news, and actually slept.

She was still yawning at bedtime. With no closing door to listen for she passed an unfidgety night, and the next day, the Sunday, while her mother was at church, she ran herself a bath, then wandered about the house barefoot, smoking a cigarette. She was ashamed, as she did it, to discover how badly she had let things slip: all she could see were grubby corners, dusty plasterwork, finger-marks, smears. She fetched a pencil and a piece of paper and drew up a list of tasks.

She started to work her way through them early the following morning, tackling the landing first, dusting and sweeping, beating the rugs. She ended up with a cloudy panful of fluff and tangled hairs: dark hairs from Lilian's head, reddish ones from Leonard's, brown from her own; the sight of them all muddled up like that made her feel queasy. She didn't want them in the house, she decided, not even burning in the stove; instead she carried them all the way down the garden to the ash-heap. The ten o'clock post arrived while she was doing it: she returned to the hall to find two or three letters on the mat. And her heart did just flutter slightly as she stooped to pick them up—for mightn't one of them be from Lilian? Wouldn't she send at least a note to say that she had arrived safely?

The letters, however, were all from tradesmen. She tucked them away in her book of accounts.

There was no post at all the next day, nor the day after that. Thursday simply brought more bills . . . But it was humiliating to watch and wait for the postman. She went into Town, and called on Christina. And when Christina asked archly, 'So? How's Love, upper case?' she blew a raspberry at her.

'Love's packed its upper case and gone to Hastings with its husband. Love's eating ices on the front, having a donkey-ride—I don't know. I don't care.'

Christina didn't ask for any of the details. She made tea, produced cigarettes, then rooted about for something to eat; she turned up a bag of monkey-nuts, and the two of them sat breaking open the shells. But when the last of the nuts was finished she moved forward in her chair and said, 'Here's an idea. How long do you have? Let's go to the music hall! We can make the second half of the matinée at the Holborn if we leg it. My treat. What do you say?'

It was the sort of thing they might have done together years before. Frances brushed the crumbs from her lap; they left the tea-table just as it was, and, still buttoning their jackets, hurried down the stone staircase to the street. They picked up a bus at once, and were at the Holborn Empire five minutes later; five minutes later again they were sitting in the hot bright darkness of the balcony, watching a couple of comedians pedalling around the stage on a tandem. The elderly, peppermint-sucking audience made Frances remember how young she was. Gazing sideways at Chrissy, catching her eye and smiling, seeing her face and fair hair lighted up by the glow of the stage, she felt a swell of affection for her—something stronger than affection, perhaps; a shiver of the heart, as if the ghost of their lost passion were gliding through it.

But later, when she got home, she looked again for a letter from Lilian, and, as before, found nothing; and it suddenly dawned on her that Lilian's silence must be a message of its own. She thought back to how they had parted, with none of their difficulties resolved. She remembered their conversation in the park, the weariness on Lilian's face. *I couldn't. I never could. Don't keep asking me, Frances.*

And she had to push down a sudden wave of fear, like fighting off nausea.

The next day, she and her mother had a visitor. She heard the knock at the front door, and something about the rather tentative nature of the sound made her think that the caller might be Margaret Lamb, from down the hill. On pulling the door open, however, she saw, not Margaret's rather dumpy figure, but a good-looking, well-dressed woman holding a bouquet of bronze chrysanthemums. She blinked—then recognised Edith, John Arthur's fiancée.

'Edith! How lovely to see you! And what glorious flowers! Not for us? Oh, you shouldn't have. I shudder to think what they must have cost you.'

'I'm not disturbing you?'

'Not in the least. You're just in time for tea. Mother will be delighted.—Mother, look who's here! Come in, come in. We didn't look for you for another month.'

Edith generally called in October, for the anniversary of John Arthur's death, so this visit was out of season. As she stepped into the hall, Frances's mother emerged from the drawing-room and came to greet her, beaming.

'Well, what a treat. And such handsome flowers! But you didn't travel all the way from Wimbledon on our account, Edith?'

Edith coloured slightly. 'I ought to have given you warning, I know.'

'I didn't mean that.'

'But I had a day to myself, and thought how I should like to see you.'

'Well, I call it very kind that you did. I shall get out the albums. And how well you're looking. You're looking wonderfully well!'

Edith *was* looking well. Her auburn hair was shining. She was wearing a cream-coloured frock and coat, and pale suede shoes; her gloves were spotless, as if fresh from the box; her hat had an exotic Bond Street feather in it, the sort of feather that Frances, in her youth, had signed letters of petition against. Had Edith always been so fashionable, so glossy? Surely not. Her background was unremarkable; her father was a banker, in a modest sort of way. But perhaps, Frances thought, her family had simply kept to its level, while she and her mother had started slipping down the scale. The idea was disconcerting. She felt ashamed of her tired indoor clothes, of her mother's drab old frock. And she was embarrassed by the house, unchanged since Edith's last visit and all the visits before that, except that it was all slightly shabbier, every surface a little more dull. As the three of them entered the drawing-room she saw Edith looking from one thing to another with a touch of wonder, and, 'Yes, everything's just exactly the same, you see!' she found herself saying, with a laugh.

At once, she wished she'd said nothing, or had kept the wryness out of her tone, because Edith blushed again, as if caught out.

Perhaps it made a bad start to the visit. She took the chrysanthemums to the scullery and put them into a vase, and when she carried them back to the drawing-room along with the tea-tray she found her mother settled in an armchair but Edith sitting at the front of the sofa, chatting brightly enough, but still wearing her gloves and her feathered hat. She kept the hat and the gloves on while Frances poured the tea. She shared her pieces of news, showed a photograph of her sister's children; she took her cup, and a plate with a slice of sticky cake on it; and still, bafflingly, she sat there in her outdoor things. Finally Frances said, 'Don't you mean to stay long, Edith? Aren't you hot, in all that get-up? You mustn't stand on ceremony here.'

Edith looked less comfortable than ever. 'Yes, I am a little warm.' She rose, to unpin the hat at the mantel-glass and to tidy her hair, then returned to the sofa and drew off her gloves. Frances noticed nothing. But almost at once her mother said, 'Edith,' in a new sort of way.

Edith's hands moved oddly, and she dipped her head. 'Yes.'

'Well, we must congratulate you.'

'Thank you.'

Then Frances saw, and understood. In all these years since John Arthur's death Edith had continued to wear her engagement ring, not on the ring finger of her left hand but on the corresponding finger of her right. Now, on the 'real' finger, another ring had appeared, a sizeable diamond in a square claw setting, rather putting John Arthur's filigree band to shame. Frances looked from the wink of the diamond to Edith's face and said, surprised and pleased, 'You're to be married.'

Edith nodded. 'At the end of the month. And then a honeymoon. Six weeks. America!'

'But, how marvellous for you. I'm so glad. And such a handsome ring! Look, Mother. Isn't it terrific?'

'Yes, I see it.'

'Will you tell us about him, Edith?'

This, of course, was why she had come. Her colour now was the flush of relief. She said, 'His name is Mr Pacey. He owns a business. Glassware—jars and bottles. Not very exciting! But he has built the business up over many years and made a great success of it. He's rather older than I am. His first wife died, just a year ago. He has children, three boys and a girl, quite grown up already.'

'So you shall be a mother right away.'

'Yes.' She put her hand to her heart. 'That part makes me nervous, I must admit. But the children are very kind. The youngest boy is at school still. The girl, Cora, is nineteen. I hope to do my best by them. It isn't at all what I expected. Two months ago I had no more idea of marrying than of flying to the moon! I met him only then, you see. Can you imagine?'

Frances answered with real feeling. 'You'll make him happy, Edith, I know it.'

'I do hope so.'

'Of course you will. Won't she, Mother?'

'Yes, indeed. And the children too! What an adventure. Your mother's pleased, Edith, I dare say. How she'll miss you though.'

'Yes, it's a great change for Mother. She means to write to you about it. I wanted to speak to you myself, before she did.'

'I'm glad that you did. Thank you.'

'Mother was so fond of Jack.'

'Yes, I know.'

'Jack' was what Edith had always called John Arthur. The name had never sounded right to Frances; it was such a roguish sort of name, and John Arthur hadn't been at all roguish, and neither was Edith herself. Had there been other marriage proposals, in the years since his death? If there had, Frances and her mother had not got wind of them. They had grown used to thinking of Edith as John Arthur's widow; and Frances knew that widowhood meant something to the women of her mother's generation that it did not mean to women now. 'I'm delighted for you, Edith,' she heard her mother say, but she could see, from the subtle working of her face, that she was not, at heart, delighted—or rather, that her delight was choked about by too many other feelings, too many griefs and disappointments on her own and John Arthur's behalf. She asked to hear more about Mr Pacey, and Edith, still blushing, told them about his factory, his motor-cars, the suppers and tennis-parties he liked to host, his large house, with the garage attached, on the outskirts of Tunbridge Wells. He sounded as unlike mild John Arthur as it was possible to imagine. He seemed almost, Frances thought, to sit in the room along with them, overbearing, slightly bored, now and then checking his watch. She saw her mother's smile become increasingly artificial, heard her responses to Edith's remarks grow briefer and more forced. From the cupboard at her side she had brought the family photograph albums, along with the muddy pencilled letters that John Arthur had sent from the Front: it was their habit to go through them, on Edith's visits. Edith noticed them now, and remembered; they rearranged the chairs so as to be closer to each other. But the turning of the pages and the reading aloud of the letters felt dry, this time—like picking through dead leaves. And once the final letter had been returned to its envelope their voices died away, and they sat in a painful silence.

Frances suggested that they look at the garden. They went out and on to the lawn, made a tour of the asters and the dahlias, and that perked the party up a little. Edith described the grounds of Mr Pacey's house, the Italianate terrace, the ponds, the fountain. The Wrays, she said, must be sure to visit her in her new home, and they promised that they would, adding that she must bring her husband to meet them, here at Champion Hill; perhaps the daughter too. She nodded at that, but her smile was rather fixed, and Frances guessed that neither visit would ever come off. It had been one thing for Edith to call as John Arthur's fiancée; it would be quite another for her to arrive as the wife of Mr Pacey. And within a few months, of course—probably before she returned from her honeymoon—she would in all likelihood be expecting a child of her own.

Out in the hall, before she left, Frances saw her looking around in the same noticing way as before. This time the wistfulness in her expression was plain: she was gazing from thing to thing as if to imprint it on her memory. The thought made Frances feel sorry. It seemed to her that, all these years, she had been short-changing Edith slightly. On impulse, she said, 'You're going down to the station, I suppose? Let me walk with you.'

'Oh, Frances, you needn't.'

But, 'Yes, do walk Edith to the station,' said Frances's mother; and from the manner in which she said it Frances guessed that she would be grateful for some time to herself. So she ran upstairs to change her shoes and to pull on a hat, and she and Edith started down the hill together.

As they passed the gate to the Lambs', Edith smiled in a troubled way. 'I remember making this walk with Jack,' she said, 'so many times. It doesn't seem six years, does it, Frances? But then in other ways—I don't know. They've been long years, too. It's always funny to see these houses, all so unchanged. You're still friends with the Playfairs, I hope?'

'Yes, we see Mrs Playfair often. Mr Playfair died, of course. The year before last.'

'Of course he did. How stupid of me! You told me, and I'd forgotten. A kind man.'

'Yes, we all liked Mr Playfair.'

'And how's your friend? I've never asked you.'

'My friend?'

'You remember? Carrie, was it?'

Frances, surprised, said, 'Chrissy, you mean?'

'The clever girl with all the masses of fair hair. I remember meeting her with you—oh, three or four times. Once just here, on the hill. You don't remember?'

276

'No, I don't remember that.'

'But you still see her? You were such great friends. You used to frighten me, the two of you. You had an opinion on everything! I've always been so muddle-headed. Mr Pacey calls me his goose. What's become of her? Did she marry?'

'She's living in Town, in a flat, with another girl. Working. She wears her hair very short now.'

'Oh, what a pity! I used to envy her her hair. Yes, I must have seen her with you three or four times, at least.'

There was nothing behind the comment, Frances decided. The scandal over Christina had happened long after John Arthur's death, and would never have been allowed to reach Edith. She was simply pulling out these memories in the same wistful way in which, a few minutes before, she had been gazing around the Wrays' hall at the black oak furniture. She must be thinking still how strange it was that here was a life, a world, of which she might have been a part, a life she had had some claim on all this time, but from the clinging fibres of which she was finally being eased away.

As they drew near to the station entrance they heard the approach of a west-bound train. But there was no question of Edith's running for it: she let the train go by, and they stood in the shade at the top of the platform steps, waiting for the next one.

Frances said, 'It was good of you to come to us today, Edith. It was good of you to tell us about Mr Pacey—rather than writing it, I mean. I'm really happy for you.'

'Are you? I wish I thought your mother was.'

'Mother is happy for you, too. She will be, anyhow, once she's had time to take it in.'

'She was always so kind to me. She thinks I've let Jack down. You don't think that, do you?'

'Of course not.'

'You know what he was to me. I shan't ever forget him. I shall always wear his ring. Mr Pacey is very understanding about that.'

She brought her gloved hands together, as if to reassure herself of the solidity of the metal under the kid—though it was the new ring that her fingers strayed to, Frances noticed, rather than the old.

And she was blushing again—blushing with excitement, with delight, for her unlikely-sounding sweetheart. For, now that they were away from the repressions of the drawing-room, Frances saw the delight for the physical thing it was; she saw it, she recognised it, because it was like her own delight for Lilian. She felt fonder of Edith suddenly than she ever had before—an artificial fondness probably, produced by the currents of the moment, but she thought that Edith also felt the leap of intimacy between them, because she gazed into Frances's face in a franker way and said, 'It's good to see you, Frances! I wish now that I'd kept up with you more. You, and your mother. Are you both all right? Your mother's quite well? She's aged, I think, since last year. And you—'

'What?' asked Frances, smiling. 'I don't look older too, I hope?'

'Not older, exactly. But—perhaps as though you're settling into your role?'

Frances was startled. 'My role?'

'I don't mean it badly! But in the past—well, you've sometimes seemed not quite happy. Your mother, too. But you must be such a comfort to each other. I'm so glad.—Oh, but I must go!' Another train was coming. 'I've arranged to meet Herbert—Mr Pacey, I mean—and he fusses if I'm late. Thank you for being so nice to me!'

They shook hands, hurriedly, though she made a point of pressing Frances's fingers. Then she turned and made her quick, smart way down the steps.

She boarded the train without looking back. Probably it didn't occur to her that Frances would stand and watch. But Frances remained there while the train moved off, and stayed even for a minute or two afterwards, thinking, *Settling into my role!* The words had filled her with horror. She had taken on the role herself; she had given up Christina to do it. But that was an age, a lifetime, ago, and since then—She stared at the shining railway line and thought of the night of Netta's party, when she and Lilian had sat squashed together in the train. She remembered their silent climb up these steps, and all that had come after. There had been no roles to follow, then. The two of them had been reborn in each other's kisses—hadn't they?

She didn't know. She'd lost her confidence in it. It all felt oddly insubstantial, as though Edith's visit had chased it away, like a cockerel crowing away a ghost. She left the station and headed home, but the thought of the house, the tired house, the empty rooms, her grieving mother, made her falter. Instead of pressing on up the hill she crossed the road and went into the park.

She was suddenly desperate to conjure up Lilian's presence, the substance and reality of her. But the fine weather had brought people out: the band-stand had a courting couple on it, the boy tickling the girl's nose with a blade of grass; Frances didn't even think of climbing the steps. She went on instead to the tennis courts, where she and Lilian had once stood to watch the young women play. A few games were in progress, but the nets were sagging, the courts worn to dust by the demands of the long summer. She approached the pond, and found the water dark, with scummy banks; she left it quickly. But everywhere was the same. It was all small, suburban, unspecial. The exposed western slope was like a desert plain. What struck her most were those remnants of the grand houses and gardens from which the park had been patched together years before: the stranded portico; a sundial, still telling the time for a lost age; a mournful avenue of trees, leading nowhere.

Frustrated, she kept moving. She thought she had come in here to find Lilian, but she realised as she made the turn from one path to another that she was not so much in search of something as in flight: she was trying to outrun the implications of Edith's visit. She kept seeing Edith's ring. She kept recalling the wink of the diamond. 'Here I am, Miss Wray,' that diamond seemed to say to her. 'The real thing. You can't compete with the likes of me, so don't try. Be content with your "role", that you are settling so nicely into, like an oyster digging its dumb way into the sea-bed.' She had resisted thinking like this for the whole of her adult life. She would as soon have worn a ring like Edith's as worn a saddle on her back! But she felt drained of strength and spirit; she felt bruised, she felt alone. Was this what the affair with Lilian had done to her? Made her a stranger to herself? With dragging feet, she left the last stretch of arid grass and started for home.

And as she approached the house, she spotted the postman just ahead of her. She arrived at the garden gate as he did; he offered her a letter, and when she took it, and saw her own name, written in Lilian's curling hand, she felt not grateful, not relieved—she felt unnerved, as if she had called the letter into life by some dark magic. The envelope was almost weightless. She didn't want to open it. She held it in her fingers, watching the retreating figure of the postman, and had the urge to run after him and stuff it back into his bag.

Instead she folded it into her pocket and went indoors. She found her mother just emerging from her bedroom, her face with a newly powdered look; and since her mother wore powder so rarely, she guessed that she had been weeping. The thought was like a final blow to her spirits. She wanted to sit at the foot of the staircase with her head in her hands. 'Oh, Mother,' she wanted to say, 'our hearts are breaking. What on earth are we to do?'

But she hadn't spoken candidly like that to her mother in about twenty years. Even after her brothers' deaths, the two of them had done their crying in private. So, with the points of the folded letter digging into her through her pocket, she stood at the looking-glass to take off her hat. And when she spoke, she made her tone breezy.

'Well! Edith marrying a jam-jar millionaire! Who ever would have thought it?'—which allowed her mother to answer, in a gently chiding way, 'Really, Frances.'

'Oh, I'm thrilled for her. I just can't help but feel that Mr Pacey is somehow getting the better half of the bargain. He must be ancient, too. And what a whopper of a ring! Perhaps there was a chip left over at the glass-works, what do you think?'

The little bit of shared snobbery was just sufficient. She caught her mother's eye in the glass and they exchanged a tremulous smile.

But once her mother had returned to the drawing-room she watched her own smile fade. She turned away from it, climbed the stairs, went into her bedroom, closed the door. The letter looked more insubstantial than ever now that it had got creased from her pocket; more sinister, too. It still seemed to have been conjured into life as an answer to the failings of the day. The trudge around the park had brought it, the loss of confidence. She had finally admitted her own unhappiness, and that had allowed Lilian to admit hers. And between them they had made this thing, this flimsy, horrible thing, that—she knew, knew, *knew* it—was about to finish what the holiday had started, was going to separate them absolutely, like a contract of law.

With a burst of bravado, she thought: Well, perhaps it's for the best.

She got the envelope open and drew out the paper. She readied herself, unfolded it, and saw the first dark line of ink.

My darling, my darling, my own true love—

Her heart, that had shrivelled, seemed rapidly to inflate. She went to her bed and leaned against the footrail, putting the back of her hand to her face, closing her eyes against her own knuckles. Then she lowered the paper and read on.

My darling, my darling, my own true love—

I am writing this by candle light in the dreariest place, the bathroom, I wonder can you picture it? The tap is running & wont be turned off, the lace at the window is dirty, there is a womans red hair in the basin. I ought to hate it oughtnt I, but I dont mind any of it, I can stand any amount of dreariness my darling while I think of you.

O my dear, my love, I wish you were here to tell me what to do. I feel so awfully trapped & lonely, I feel youre the only person in the world who cares about me even a bit. The others all say theres no fun in me. Last night they went to a show without me & I sat at my window & a man blew kisses at me & I thought of the look you would have given him & it made me laugh out loud, but it was such sad laughter it turned to tears, it just seemed too hard & unfair that there isnt a way for us to be together when any man may blow a kiss at any girl at any window & people will smile at him for a good sport. I keep thinking of how it was when we were skating, wasnt it glorious? I felt I could just fly then, with your arms about me, I felt I didnt need skates to do it.

O why arent you here! I am afraid I will come home & you will have forgotten me, or you will have found some other girl to love. You said something to me once, I have never forgotten it, you said I like to be admired, do you remember? You said I would love anybody who admired me. Dont hate this hard thing I am about to say my darling but sometimes I think its <u>you</u> that would love anybody. Sometimes it seems so astonishing that you should love me that I think you must only want me because you lost so many other things. It isnt just that, is it?

If it isnt then tell me & make me believe it because I feel right now that I am ready to do any desperate thing to be with you Frances—there I have put your name havent I & half of me, the proud half wishes that <u>you know who</u> would see this letter, but the other half, the coward half is afraid. I wish I was brave like you!

I am looking at our caravan, did you know I brought it with me? I am sending you kisses my darling, one thousand kisses by marconi all the way to C. Hill, I wonder can you feel them?

x x x x x x x x x x x x x x x x x x x x x x x x x x x x x x x x x x x x x x x x x x

Never in her life had Frances received such a letter. Never in her life would she have believed that something so artless, so entirely without guile or finish, could have stirred and moved her to such a degree. She read it over again; she read it a third time, and a fourth. Her weariness had disappeared. She held the paper to her lips, and it was exactly as Lilian had promised: she could feel her kisses, she could feel her mouth, alive and urgent against her own.

And the next day Lilian was home, back in her arms, clinging to her on the landing while Leonard was still bringing in the bags. She came again a little later, while he was running himself a bath. And on Monday morning, with the house to themselves, they lay half-dressed on Frances's bed, she put her face against Frances's shoulder, and she wept.

'I hated it, Frances! I hated it so much! I wanted to come home every day. I kept on smiling and playing the fool, but it was like being in a prison. Whenever Len kissed me, I thought of you. That was the only way I could stand it. Whenever he touched me, whenever he looked at me, I thought of you, I thought of you!'

The tears shook her like a storm. Frances held her while she shuddered and moaned, amazed at the passion in her; afterwards she stroked her wet, stained cheeks and swollen eyelids, ran fingers over her lips. 'How I love you. How I love you.'

But the words made Lilian's eyes fill again. Frances drew back to look at her properly. 'What is it? What's the matter?'

She shook her head, so that the tears spilled. 'I just wish,' she said unevenly, 'that things were different. I wish it so much.'

'No, it's more than that. Did something happen while you were away?'

She wiped her cheeks. 'I just missed you. I felt so alone.'

'And what you wrote in your letter, about wanting to be brave—did you mean it?'

'You know I did.'

Frances took hold of her hands. 'Then listen. I've been thinking, all night long. We can't go on like this. Look at you! It's killing you! And I—I can't do it any longer, not the way we've been doing it till now. I can't share you with Leonard any more. I can't share you with something that passes itself off as a marriage, but is really habit and pride and . . . empty embraces, or worse. If I loved you less, I might be able to, but—I can't. I won't. I want you to leave him, Lilian. I want you to leave him and live with me.'

She had expected Lilian's face to close against her. But Lilian looked back at her, damply, gravely. 'You really mean it,' she said.

'I do. Why not? We've been talking all this time as if it's something impossible. But women leave their husbands every day. The papers are full of them.'

'But they're society women. Things are different for women like that. They can arrange about divorces. And when they leave their husbands, they do it for other men. If it ever came out about you and me—There's too much against it, Frances.'

'Against a divorce—yes, all right. But a separation? Just walking away? No one minds about that sort of thing since the War. And once you were free, we could do as we liked.'

Lilian was wiping her face again. 'But we'd have to have money. I've no money at all. All my money comes from Len.'

'We'd find work,' said Frances. 'Wouldn't you like that? Earning your own wages, decently? God, I would. Or, listen to this. I thought of it last night. You could go to an art school.—Don't look like that.'

Lilian had turned away, disappointed. 'You're just romancing, after all.'

'No, I'm not. I've been working it out. I think we could do it, just. I've a little money of my own still, that didn't get swallowed up by my father's debts. It isn't much—about thirty pounds. But there are things I can sell, a few bits of furniture in the house that belong to me, some old pieces of jewellery that came to me from my grandmothers—'

284

'You can't go selling your grandmothers' jewellery, Frances!'

'Why not? A load of dreary old emeralds and garnets. What use are they to me?'

'But I couldn't live on your money.'

'You live on Leonard's.'

'That's different.'

'Yes, it is. He pays you to be his cook, his char and his mistress. I should be sharing my money with you until you could earn money of your own. And once I'd found work—'

'There isn't any work.'

'There's always cleaning, cooking, waitressing. I'm good at those things. I might as well be paid for them. And while I'm doing them, I can enrol on some sort of correspondence course. Book-keeping, or typewriting. Christina did it; why shouldn't I? And meanwhile, you'll take your classes. Haven't you always wanted to? Stevie can help us find you an art school.'

'But even supposing—Where would we live? I'd be a married girl, separated. People would think the worst of me. We couldn't stay here with your mother. She wouldn't want me in the house. You know she wouldn't.'

'Then we'd look for rooms right away. My mother could take in more lodgers. I've been thinking about that too. She can't live on dwindling dividends for ever. With more lodgers there'd be an income—enough for a maid, to replace me.'

'But you couldn't leave her like that, could you?'

Frances hesitated. Could she? But what was the alternative? Settle ever more neatly, ever more dumbly, ever more dishonestly, into her *role*?

She caught hold of Lilian's hands again. 'I would do it,' she said, 'for you.'

The tears came back into Lilian's eyes. She pulled away. 'Oh, Frances.'

'Don't cry. Why are you crying?'

'Because it's all too much. There are too many people in it. I don't care about Len any more, but he'd hate it. He'd come after me. I know he would.'

'Would he really, though? Isn't he as unhappy as you are?'

'But it isn't about what he wants. It's about how the thing would look. It's always been about that. He'd think of his family, his friends, the Pearl. He wants to get on; it would ruin things for him. And then, what would *my* family say?'

'They might say they wanted you to be happy.'

'*Your* mother wouldn't say that. Why should mine?—because she's from Walworth, and cares less? You know what people would think of us.'

'Not everyone thinks that way.'

'Oh, the whole world does. You know it does. Everybody's so narrow and mean and—'

'No. Only a few people are. But the rest of us—don't you see? The rest of us become narrow and mean when we live falsely. I'm sick to death of living falsely. I've been doing it for years. I had that chance with Christina to give myself over to someone I loved; I let it go by. It seemed at the time like a brave thing to do. But it wasn't bravery. I was a coward. I won't be a coward with you. I won't let you be a coward, either. But you're braver than you think. If you weren't, you would never have crossed the kitchen and kissed me, after Netta's party. You would never have said, "Take me home." You would never have pulled the stake from my heart. You remember that moment?'

Lilian looked at her, but didn't answer.

'You remember?' Frances persisted. 'You drew out that stake, and everything changed. You've been acting since then as though you can somehow tuck that change into your ordinary life. Lilian, you can't. It's too big a thing.'

'You keep saying that,' said Lilian. 'But don't you understand? It's *because* it's so big. It's everything I've ever known. What you want

286

me to do, it's everything I've ever thought, and everything everyone else thinks about me—it's all of it, changing.'

'I know it is. But isn't it marvellous, to think of changing like that? And what's the use of anything, otherwise? What's the good of having gone through the War, all that, if two people who love each other the way we do can't be together? But you have to promise me, about Leonard. You must say no to him from now on.'

Lilian turned away. 'Oh, it's all so stupid! It's all such a mess! I don't even *want* Len! I wish he'd just—just die! I wish it more than ever!'

'Then it'll be easy,' said Frances. 'Won't it? Look, here's how easy it will be.' And she reached for Lilian's left hand, took hold of her wedding and engagement rings, and, gently but firmly, began to draw them from their finger. Lilian gave the slightest of automatic twitches as the rings started to move, but after that she made no resistance, instead looking on in unhappy fascination as they caught on her knuckle and then came free.

'You see how simple it is?' said Frances, when she had tucked the rings out of sight and was running her thumb over the smooth white band of flesh exposed by their removal. 'Your hand in mine, with nothing in between. It's the simplest thing in the world. Isn't it?'

Lilian didn't answer for a moment. Instead she sank back against the pillow, closing her eyes. And when she spoke, she spoke flatly, as if surrendering at last.

But what she said was: 'It isn't simple at all.'

Frances stared at her shut, tired face. 'What do you mean?'

She opened her eyes. 'Please don't be angry with me, Frances.'

'You're—You're choosing him?'

'No, it isn't that.'

'What, then?'

She grew oddly guilty-looking. 'I don't know how to tell you.

Something's happened. It needn't make a difference, if everything you've said is true. It just makes things harder, that's all.'

'But what are you talking about? What is it?'

'Please don't blame me. It wasn't my fault. But, oh, Frances, I think—I'm almost sure—that I've started a baby.'

10

The words were so unlike any of the ones that Frances had been expecting to hear that for a moment she could hardly make sense of them. Outside, the day had darkened. She was aware of rain, in a sudden shower, producing a sound like rapid drumming on the flat lead scullery roof below her window. As the shower eased, and the drumming slowed, she put a hand across her eyes.

Lilian said, 'I'm so sorry.'

'How sure are you?'

'I'm sure, Frances. It's nearly a month over its time.'

'You couldn't simply be late?'

'I'm never late. You know I'm not. And I feel . . . different.'

'Different, how?'

'I don't know. Tired. Just different.'

Frances lowered her hand and gazed into Lilian's face. She *did* look different, she realised. She had looked different ever since she had returned from her holiday; perhaps even since before that. She was changed, in some indefinable physical way . . .

'Oh, God. I can't believe it!'

'I'm so sorry,' said Lilian again.

'When did it happen? *How* did it happen? I've always supposed that you and Leonard—' She had never wanted to know the details. 'I've always imagined that you have some way of—of—'

'We do. We did. But there was a night—He forgot to be careful.'

'Careful?'

'You know what I mean. He always . . . comes out before he's finished, and I finish him off. We've always done it like that, and it's always worked, more or less. But this time he stayed inside me. He said it was an accident. I don't know if it was or not. But I *knew*. I knew that night. That I had caught, I mean. That it had taken. I just knew.'

'Why on earth didn't you tell me?'

Lilian looked utterly miserable. 'I wanted to be sure. I didn't want to worry you for nothing. I've been hoping it would fix itself. It's done that sometimes, in the past. And then, a part of me didn't want to think about it at all . . . Are you angry with me?'

Frances covered her eyes again. 'I'm not angry. I can't think how I feel.'

'I've been worried to death.'

'I just wish I'd known.'

'It doesn't make you want to take back all those things you said?'

'Take them back? Of course it doesn't. But what's the use of them now?' She was working it out as she spoke. The disappointment of it was dreadful. 'It's no good our planning anything, is it? This keeps you stuck with him for ever.'

'What? No, don't say that.'

'Well, doesn't it?'

'No!' Lilian pushed herself up and caught hold of Frances's arm. 'It doesn't change anything about you and me. Don't think that. That's not why I'm telling you. It just makes things more difficult for us.'

'Difficult? That's putting it mildly! You think we can manage, with a child? You think he'll let us? He'll have the law on his side. He'll have everything on his side!'

'But I don't want to have Len's baby. I don't want any baby at all. If it won't sort itself out, then—then I'll sort it out myself.'

Again Frances was aware of the drumming of the raindrops. Drawing back from Lilian slightly, she said, in a hushed, shocked voice, 'Get rid of it? Is that what you're saying?'

'*Yes*. It isn't so bad, Frances. When it's only just started there are pills you can take to put yourself right—'

'Oh, Lilian, no. You can't be serious. It's too squalid.'

'I don't care, so long as they work.'

'I can't believe they ever do. And God knows what goes into them.'

'They do work, if you get the right ones, and you take them at just the right time.' Her tone was certain, knowing. She coloured. 'Don't look at me like that. It's only what lots of women do.'

Frances was staring at her. 'You've taken them before?'

'Only once. Frances, I had to. It was the year after we got married, a few months after I'd lost my baby. I—I couldn't face it. It felt all wrong. I got it into my head, you see, that it would happen again. Vera has a friend who's a nurse, and she got the pills for me. They made me feel dreadful. I thought I was dying! I tried to do it on my own, but in the end I had to tell Len. He nearly had a fit. He thought his parents would find out. We had to do it all in secret, all in their tiny little house. But it won't be so bad if I do it again, because this time I'll know what to expect. I just can't do it alone, that's all. I thought of doing it and not telling you, but—It's just too hard, when you're on your own. I can get the pills. I can go to a shop—'

'A shop? What shop? What shop are you talking about?'

'There's a place in Town, on the Edgware Road. Vera's friend told me about it. I can get them. I know what to ask for. But I'll need you to help me when the worst bit happens.'

She had clearly thought it all through. Frances was struggling to keep up with her. To be casually discussing this, there in her bedroom, on Champion Hill, on a rainy Monday morning—

'Surely there's another way?'

'There isn't, Frances.'

'You might make yourself ill!'

'I don't care about that.'

'Well, I do. One hears such stories. It isn't safe.'

'No, no, it only isn't safe when it's become a real baby, when you leave it too long and have to put something in there to get the baby out. But that's different. That's unnatural. That's a sin, and against the law. I'd never do that.'

'But what you're talking about is just the same.'

'No, Frances. It isn't.'

She spoke with certainty again—with impatience, even. Frances couldn't tell if she had genuinely misunderstood the process, or had simply decided on a convenient course of belief and was sticking to it. Either way—God, how monstrous it was! How different from the pure, true thing she'd had in mind!

She felt exposed, suddenly. She felt cold and under-dressed. She rose and crossed the room to her armchair, sat at the front of it, her limbs drawn in.

Lilian watched her. 'What are you thinking?'

'I'm trying to realise it,' she said. 'I feel . . . caught out. Tripped up. I'm sorry.'

'You mustn't feel that. It's isn't so bad. It's—'

'When did it happen, exactly?'

The abruptness of the question made Lilian blink. 'What? I've told you.'

'Yes, but which night? That's what I mean. Which particular night?'

'Oh, what does it matter? It's happened, that's all.'

'Was it that night when you were ironing? The night I came into the kitchen?'

'The kitchen?' Lilian frowned. 'No. No, it must have been after that. I don't know when it was, Frances.'

Just some ordinary night, then. Just one of those nights when Frances had lain there listening for the sound of the door . . .

Lilian was still watching her. 'Don't you want us to be together? You did, a minute ago. You said you would help me to be brave.'

'I didn't know this would be a part of it.'

'You said you'd give things up for me. Why won't you let me give this up, for you?'

And at that, Frances felt a touch of horror. Was this, after all, what she had persuaded Lilian into? She rubbed her bare shoulders, a shiver pimpling her skin. She knew that she ought to go back to the bed, take Lilian in her arms. But she couldn't do it; she felt paralysed. She kept thinking of herself lying here, while just across the landing—

Didn't they say that a woman had to enjoy it, in order for a pregnancy to take?

She shook the idea off. Lilian was about to become hers. That was the point to remember. That was the destination of it all. It had happened, it was dreadful, but they couldn't be kept apart, could they, by such a little, little thing?

She rose, returned to the bed, and they held each other tightly.

'I'm sorry,' Lilian said again. 'I'm so sorry. Don't hate me, Frances. I love you so much. But it isn't as bad as you think. It's just a nuisance. It's just . . . nothing. It's like a bad tooth that has to come out. Once I've done it, we can forget it. We can be together, just like you said.'

When Frances's mother returned to the house at lunch-time, fresh from her morning with the vicar, Frances could hardly bring herself to meet her gaze. She could hardly meet Leonard's gaze, either, when he came home from work. Her excitement about the future that she and Lilian were planning—it was lost, overwhelmed, a single pale thread in a dark, dark tangle. Lying in bed that night, she tried to pull the thing apart. Suppose the baby were to be born.

Could the two of them manage? It would be hard, but not impossible, not impossible at all. Other women managed it, with less money than they would have. There were thousands of fatherless families, since the War . . . But in her heart, she didn't want it. Apart from anything else, it would be a permanent link with Leonard, even assuming that he would let them keep the child. It might draw Lilian back to him. It might somehow repair their marriage. And what would Frances do then? Would she return to her old life, her loveless, Lilianless life, like a snake having to fit itself back into a desiccated skin?

The idea made her panic, and the panic itself dismayed her. For was that all, she thought bleakly, that love ever was? Something that saved one from loneliness? A sort of insurance policy against not counting? How real was the passion she had with Lilian, after all? She remembered how flimsy it had appeared after Edith's visit. Right there, in the darkness, it seemed suddenly to be founded on nothing. They had never spent a night together. They had never eaten a meal together—only foolish picnics in the park. And they were making all these plans, contemplating all these sacrifices, and forcing sacrifices on to other people, on to her mother, on to Leonard . . .

She lay sleepless for two or three hours, and rose the next day feeling wretched.

But Lilian, by contrast, looked better than she had looked in weeks. As soon as the two of them were alone she took hold of Frances's hands; her rings, of course, were back on their finger. She had been thinking, she said, about when they ought to 'do it'.

'It has to be soon,' she whispered. 'The sooner you do it, the better it works. And if you take the pills around the time you should be falling poorly, then that works best of all. That would be this coming Sunday, for me. Well, that's no good, because Len'll be home. Saturday's the same. But on Friday night he's going out, straight from work; he's seeing Charlie. And didn't you say that your mother's going out then, too? Round to her friend's?'

Yes, Frances remembered, there was to be a bridge party that night at Mrs Playfair's. She herself had been invited, a fortnight before. She had said no—wanting to remain at home, in earshot of Lilian and Leonard. And all the time—

'You're not changing your mind?' Lilian asked her, seeing the shift in her expression.

She answered with a frown. 'No, I—It's just all moving so quickly. I still can't believe in it all. I can't believe there won't be some difficulty, some disaster. If my mother should find out—'

'She won't.'

'We can't be sure.'

'We can. We *must* be sure, because being sure will help the pills work. I'm going to get them today.'

'Today? But can't we take a little more time? I feel I've talked you into something, and—'

'It isn't like that.'

'Well, then, you've talked *me* into something. And I know I've let you do it, against my sense of what's right, because I love you and it's the way to having you all to myself, and—I don't know if that's brave or cowardly, or what it is.'

Lilian laid a hand on her cheek. 'Oh, Frances. It's nothing so serious as that.'

'Are you certain about this? Lilian, are you absolutely certain?'

'I've made up my mind to it. Whether you help me or not, I'm going to do it.'

'But in another day or two—'

'No. It has to be today. Now that I've decided, I—I just want to be rid of it.' She moved her hand to her belly, placed it there with a look of distaste. 'I can't stand to think of it inside me, getting bigger every minute.'

Frances watched her, uneasily. She said at last, 'Well, you can't

295

go alone. I won't let you go alone. Suppose something should happen to you?'

'Nothing's going to happen. Women do this all the time. Married women, I mean, as well as other sorts of women. But I don't want you to have to go into a horrible chemist's shop with me. It'll make you stop loving me. It'll make you hate me! It's my problem, and I'm going to fix it.' She squeezed Frances's hand again. 'Please trust me, Frances.'

Reluctantly, Frances returned the pressure of her fingers.

But, still, she wouldn't let her go off entirely on her own. In a sheepish sort of way, she told her mother that she and Lilian had decided to visit a gallery, and after lunch they took a tram into Town; Lilian said that a tram would be better than a bus, because it would jolt her about more and 'might help things along'. The thought was a ghastly one to Frances. She made the journey as tensely as if she were carrying a child herself. But Lilian's spirits seemed high. When they parted at Oxford Circus, Frances stood for a minute watching her make her way westward through the crowd of shoppers, and her step didn't slow once.

It was half-past two, and they'd arranged to meet again at four, in Cavendish Square. The day was another damp one, but Frances had brought along an umbrella; she raised it and began to walk, taking random turns. With every step, she felt her disquiet mounting by another notch. She oughtn't to have let Lilian go off alone. They oughtn't to have come. What on earth were they doing? Everywhere she looked she saw prams, she saw babies with pink, alive faces.

At last, realising how close she was to Clipstone Street, she crossed a road and went the few hundred yards to call on Christina.

But the visit was a mistake—she could tell that at once. It had come too soon after the last one, and Christina was busy; she invited Frances in, but her gaze kept wandering over to the papers on her desk. When Frances began to tell her about Lilian, she listened long enough only to hear that the two of them had reconciled their differences and said, 'Oh, Frances, I can't keep pace with you! I thought the whole thing had come to nothing.'

'I was frightened that it had,' said Frances.

'Well, you don't sound very happy that it hasn't.'

'No. I—'

But what could she say? She was ashamed, she realised. She longed to speak, to unburden herself; she remembered the bond she had felt with Christina at the music hall. She could find no trace of it now. There was merely the old scratchiness—that bit of cinder in the soap. So they talked of stupid, pointless things. She stayed for less than twenty minutes, and wished she hadn't come at all.

But before she left she looked around the room, that was so full of Christina and Stevie. She and Lilian would have a room like it, once this horrible thing was done.

And when, half an hour later, seated on a bench in Cavendish Square, she spotted Lilian herself, hurrying across the garden towards her, she felt a jolt of uncomplicated love in her heart, simply at seeing her, there, among strangers. She looked flushed, damp, pleased. She joined Frances beneath the umbrella and spoke breathlessly.

'I thought I'd never get here in time! The shop turned out not to be right after all. The man sent me to another, on the Charing Cross Road. He was awful about it. He acted as though I was on the streets or something. I kept my gloves off, to show my ring; he made me feel it had come off a curtain! But it doesn't matter. The second man was all right. And I got them. Look.'

She began to unclasp her bag. Frances glanced around in alarm. But the light was poor, people were hurrying because of the rain, vehicles were loud on the wet roads: it felt oddly intimate under the silk of the umbrella. Lilian opened the bag just enough to reveal the buff-coloured packet inside it. Frances saw a poorly printed label: *Dr Ridley's Pills, for the Treatment of Female Irregularities.*

She could hardly believe that such a thing was for sale in a West-End chemist's, in 1922. It looked like something that belonged in a museum of medical curiosities alongside a two-headed baby and a leech jar. The pills themselves, she discovered when Lilian discreetly exposed them, were hard and fibrous, and smelt pungent, like a bad sort of mint. 'But they have to make them nasty,' reasoned Lilian, 'don't they? Otherwise nobody'd believe that they do any good.'

All in the cover of her open handbag, she tipped one of the pills into her gloved palm and gazed at it with distaste. Then she made to lift it to her lips.

Frances, aghast, caught hold of her wrist. 'You aren't going to take one right now?'

She said, 'I have to. You have to take some for three days, then all the rest on the fourth.'

'No, don't do it here. Not here, not yet.'

It was altogether too real, there, with a tooting taxi-cab going by, and ordinary red and white motor-buses snorting their way up and down Oxford Street.

But Lilian still had the pill in her palm. 'I have to, Frances,' she said again. And while Frances watched, she tightened her lips and sucked in her cheeks, working up the saliva in her mouth; then she popped the evil-looking pill on to her tongue and, with a grimace, quickly swallowed.

Frances kept her eyes on her face. 'How do you feel?'

She took a breath. 'I feel better for having started. But nothing will happen for ages yet.' She folded the buff packet and tucked it deep down in her bag. 'I'll take another one before I go to bed tonight, and another when I get up; and if we're lucky, maybe something will happen tomorrow.'

She said the same thing the next morning, and all through the whole of that day. She remained confident, calm; it was Frances

298

who was anxious, scrutinising her face whenever the two of them were together, looking for signs of illness in it, and, when they had to be apart, hovering at the foot of the stairs, listening out for anything odd. 'How funny you are,' Lilian said. 'You're worse than a man. If you were a wife, you'd know it was nothing. How do you think other women do it?'

'I don't care about other women. I care only about you. Suppose you should faint, or—'

'I won't faint. I didn't last time. Just be patient.'

That was on the Wednesday evening, before Leonard returned from work. And the following morning she came to Frances looking pale but excited. Something was happening, she said. She had an ache, low down in her hips. Her bowels were looser than they ought to be, and, in wiping herself in the lavatory, she'd discovered a 'show'. The only worry now was that it might come out too soon, in which case Leonard might be home when it happened, and she'd have to explain it to him as either a heavy kind of ordinary monthly, or an actual miss . . . Frances held her hands and kissed her; at the same time, she was shrinking away. She couldn't believe that in the space of a day or two her life had taken such a swerve, undergone such a narrowing, become this morbid stalking of Lilian's insides, this monitoring of blood and bowels.

But by late afternoon, Lilian's manner was less sure. The 'show' had dried up, the ache had diminished, and she had begun to feel queasy. In the middle of chopping meat for Len's dinner she'd had to rush to the sink and retch; she couldn't remember that from last time. She wanted to try a hot bath. But the bath would have to be almost scalding, she said, to do any good, and Frances's mother was at home; they dared not risk being seen heating up kettles of water. They sat together in her sitting-room and she fidgeted, her hand at her stomach.

'Isn't it awful to think of that little egg inside me, doing its best to stay in there while I'm doing everything I can to get it out?

Come on, little egg.' She was willing it out of her womb. 'You don't want to stay in me. I'd be a bad, bad mother. Fly away to someone else. Fly away to some poor woman who wants a baby and can't have one. Fly away! Now!'

She raised her arm on the final word, making a fist of her hand; and then she thumped herself, hard, in the belly.

Frances flinched. 'God! Don't.'

She did it again, harder than before.

'Don't!' said Frances. 'Please! I can't bear it!'

'Well, I've got to do something! I can't just sit here. Oh, why won't your mother go out? I'm sure a bath would do it, if it was only hot enough. Isn't there somewhere you can take her?'

'I don't want you to bathe like that on your own. You might pass out. You might drown!'

'There must be something I can do.' She thought it over, then got to her feet. 'I'm going to take more of the pills.'

'No,' said Frances, rising too. 'I won't let you. They've made you ill enough already.'

'They've got to make me a lot iller than this.'

'Please don't. Lilian, please!'

But Lilian was already on her way to her bedroom, and by the time Frances had joined her she had retrieved the buff-coloured packet from a drawer and was tipping out its contents. Frances saw two or three or possibly even more of the filthy-looking pills go tumbling into her hand and get shovelled into her mouth. She saw Lilian screw up her face as the pills went down.

She looked pale again as she made her way to bed that night, and when Frances saw her on the Friday morning, just after Leonard had left for work, it was immediately obvious that something had changed. Her face now was the colour of dough, and her hair was sticking to her forehead; she came shuffling out of her bedroom like a weak old lady. She had been woken in the night, she said, by awful pains. She felt as though someone had given her

300

a kick in the stomach. She'd been lying there for hours, not wanting to tell Len. But there was still no bleeding, and that was bothering her.

Frances didn't care about the bleeding. She was too alarmed by the ghastliness of Lilian's appearance. She hurried her back into the bedroom, lit a fire in the grate. She filled a kettle in the little kitchen, made tea and a hot water bottle.

'I'll go down in a moment,' she whispered, as she handed the bottle over. Already there were sounds of movement downstairs. 'But once I've seen to the stove I'll come back. I'll tell my mother that you're ill, that you need someone to sit with you—'

But, 'No,' said Lilian, hugging the bottle to her belly. 'No, you mustn't do that. I don't want your mother to think I'm ill. She might want to come and see me, and I'd be so guilty and ashamed. And she'd be bound to say something to Len.'

'But I can't leave you!'

'Yes, you can. Just come up now and then.'

'Well, drink your tea, at least. I'll bring you a breakfast.'

She screwed up her face at the thought. 'No, I don't want any breakfast, I'll be sick. I've had some aspirin, and that'll help. Just let me be, Frances.'

'I'll come up as often as I can, then. But if you start to feel really bad—'

'I won't.'

'But if you do, you'll call me, won't you? Never mind about my mother.'

Lilian nodded, her eyes closed. Frances kissed her, and, feeling the coolness of her cheek, she unhooked Leonard's dressing-gown from the back of the door; she left her sitting on the side of the bed with the gown draped round her like a cloak. But even before she had reached the bottom of the stairs, she heard the creak of the ceiling. Lilian was up on her feet and walking about, going now from the door to the window, now

301

from the window back to the door, like a prisoner in a cell, desperately pacing.

After that, the day seemed to stretch and grow endless, to become taut as a jangling nerve. Frances slipped upstairs as often as she dared, to find Lilian still white in the face, and still pacing. She wouldn't stop moving, she said, until the bleeding had started; late in the morning she began shifting furniture about, picking up chairs, setting them down, lifting the treadle sewing-machine. The creaks and the bumps seemed to sound right through the house; at last even Frances's mother commented on them. Frances, her heart fluttering, told her that Lilian was doing some out-of-season spring cleaning.

In the middle of the afternoon, however, all sounds of movement ceased. Apprehensively, Frances climbed the stairs, to find Lilian on the sitting-room sofa, lying propped against cushions with a blanket over her knees, and looking so like an ordinary invalid that the sight of her, just for a moment, was reassuring. Then she went closer, and saw her face. It was more doughy than ever—colourless, faintly swollen beneath a tight upper layer of skin, and with a sheen of unhealthy-looking moisture across it. She didn't protest against Frances's having come up to see her. Instead she put out her hand, saying, 'Oh, Frances, it's awful!' She gripped Frances's fingers and shut her eyes tight, evidently bracing herself against cramping pain.

Frances was horrified. 'This can't be right! I've got to get you a doctor.'

But at that, Lilian's eyes flew open. 'No, a doctor mustn't see me! He'll know what I've done! Just keep hold of my hand. Don't let go. The bleeding's started, that's all. It's bad, but—*Oh!*' She grew rigid as the pain mounted, and held the stiffened pose for what seemed an impossibly long time; Frances saw tiny beads of sweat appear on her brow and top lip. When at last her limbs began to loosen, she sank back against the sofa cushions, wiping her face, and panting. 'It's all right. I'm all right.'

Frances had grown rigid, and then slack, along with her. 'Surely it oughtn't to be so bad? You look dreadful, Lilian.'

That made her weakly turn her face away. 'Don't look at me.'

'I didn't mean that. But you're as pale as death.'

'It's worse some times than others. That was a bad one, that's all.' She stirred uncomfortably, raising one of her hips, sliding a hand beneath the seat of her skirt. 'The blood keeps coming. I'm afraid of it getting on the couch. There's nothing there, is there?'

Frances looked. 'No, there's nothing.'

'I've got through three napkins already. I've been putting them on the fire. But it's still only blood, not the proper thing. You can tell when that comes out. It's hasn't come yet. It's no good till it does.'

Her voice had a new, fretful note to it, and her eyes seemed glazed. It crossed Frances's mind that she might be feverish. She rested a hand on her damp forehead; but the forehead was chill, if anything. Was that a good sign, or a bad? She didn't know. She didn't know! Her own uselessness appalled her. How could she have allowed this to happen? What on earth had she been thinking? How could she possibly have let Lilian do this reckless, reckless thing—

Already Lilian was stiffening against another wave of pain, moving her feet beneath the blanket. 'Oh, it's starting again.'

'What can I do?'

'Just hold my hand.'

'Isn't there something I can get you, to help you bear it?'

But Lilian wasn't listening. Her eyes were closed, her features contorted. 'Oh, it's worse than ever this time! Oh, Frances! *Oh!*' She was doubled up with the pain, nearly twisting Frances's fingers from their sockets.

Frances couldn't bear to do nothing. She pulled herself free, ran to her bedroom, looked in her bedside cabinet for more aspirin. All she found was a bottle of kaolin and morphine: she held the brown bottle up to the light. There was a solid chalky block at the base of it, with an inch or two of fluid above; the fluid, she thought, was more or less pure morphine. It was better than nothing, surely? She hurried to the kitchen for a spoon, then ran back to the sitting-room. Lilian was still doubled up, and her cheeks were wet with tears. She didn't ask what the medicine was. She took three spoonfuls, like an obedient child, then lay back against the cushions with tightly closed eyes.

And the morphine must have eased the pain a little, for after a few minutes her face grew less clenched. She parted her lips and let out her breath in a long, uneven sigh.

Frances thought of her mother, calmly writing letters downstairs. If she knew what was happening here, if she knew what Lilian had done—

Lilian was watching her. 'This is too awful, Frances. You must go back down.'

'I can't.'

'I want you to, though. And your mother will wonder where you are. She'll want her tea.'

She was right, Frances realised. It was well after four. But the thought of having to go and set cups on saucers, arrange bread and butter on a plate, was horrible—grotesque!

'I can't leave you,' she said.

'It isn't so bad. Honestly. And soon—soon you'll never have to leave me again. When we're together, I mean. We can do as we like then, can't we? But I don't want your mother to know something's wrong, and tell Len, and get him thinking. Please, Frances. It's just a few more hours.'

Her voice had that fretful note to it again, but her gaze seemed clearer. In an agony of indecision, Frances kissed her, and left her, and returned downstairs. She made the tea, and sat in the drawing-room, managing to chat with her mother, about the weather, about the garden—about God only knew what.

An instant after she'd made a comment she'd forgotten what it was.

At six she even started work on a pie for her own dinner. She could hear her mother getting ready to go out as she was doing it, and longed for her to move more quickly; she looked at the clock, and willed its hands forward. The sunless day had given way to a chill, moonless dusk, and her mother, she suspected, would be glad to be walked the short distance to Mrs Playfair's house; she had grown a little nervous since the attack on Leonard. But Frances had escorted her to Mrs Playfair's one evening last week, and had been drawn inside and kept talking for half an hour; she was afraid to leave Lilian alone so long. So when her mother appeared in the kitchen, she kept her hands in the mixing bowl.

Her mother hovered, watching her work. 'You won't change your mind about coming?'

Frances showed her floury fingers. 'Well, I've started this now. And I'll only upset the card tables if I turn up at the last minute.'

'Oh—yes, I suppose so.'

She was plainly disappointed. But it couldn't be helped. Not this once. Not tonight. She lingered for another minute, then buttoned her coat and said goodbye. There was the sound of her crossing the hall, followed by the thud of the closing front door.

And then it was weirdly like the early, urgent days of the affair. Frances shook the moment off along with the flour on her hands. She untied her apron, ran to the stairs, started up them—then jumped with fright. Lilian was at the top, leaning over the banisters, clutching at the rail.

'Is that your mother just gone? I need the lavatory!'

Frances hurried towards her. 'It's cold out. Use the pot.'

But she came down. 'I need it badly, Frances! I need it now!'

She moved with a combination of speed and caution that, at any other moment, might have been funny, the sort of agonised closed-kneed hobble with which a low comedian would signify a pressing case of the trots. To Frances the pose seemed horrifying: she took hold of her hand with shaking fingers, helped her negotiate the staircase, supported her as she made her way along the passage and through the kitchen. She paused to light a lantern, but Lilian wouldn't wait for that: she went scuttling across the twilit yard and into the WC.

She left the door to swing open behind her, and by the time Frances had caught up with her she was sitting on the lavatory with her legs exposed, leaning forward as if convulsed, a blood-stained napkin in her hand. When she saw Frances, however, she made a weak shooing gesture, saying, 'Oh, Frances, don't come near me! I don't want you to see! Put the lantern down and leave me! Oh! *Oh, Christ!*' And though the curse was shocking, because Frances had never heard Lilian swear before, not once, it was also queerly reassuring, a burst of anger rather than despair, the final snapping of tolerance; the breaking-point of the day. She did as she was told, set down the light and stepped away. She heard the rustle of the Bromo, followed by the gushing of the cistern. A minute of silence, then more Bromo—endless amounts of Bromo, it seemed—then the gushing of the cistern again.

And then Lilian emerged. She had the lantern in her hand, and her face looked ghastly with the light striking it from underneath. There was blood in the lavatory, she said; she couldn't get it to go away. But apart from that she was all right. It was finished, all over.

Her teeth were chattering, though. Frances got her into the house, made sure that she was capable of climbing the stairs. Then she returned to the WC and peered gingerly into the pan. The china rim was spotted with red, but the stuff at the bottom was dark as black treacle. She stirred the whole thing up with the lavatory brush, added paper, pulled the chain. And when she had done that two more times, the water settled clear.

Upstairs, Lilian was back on the sofa, shivering, her hair sticking to her cheeks: Frances couldn't tell if that was with sweat, or simply

306

from the dampness of the night. She tucked the blanket more tightly around her, drew the slippers from her feet, tried to warm her toes and fingers—they felt like stiff white roots. The hot water bottle was cooling. She went to the kitchen, filled the kettle for a fresh one. There was no food about anywhere—Lilian had had nothing all day—but she found a jar of beef essence, made a spoonful of it into a broth, and took it back to the sitting-room along with a slice of dry bread. Lilian grimaced and turned away at the sight of the little meal, but gave in to it at last; and after that her shivering subsided and a trace of colour began to appear in her cheeks. She looked, unmistakably, less burdened and fretful.

And soon she sighed and grew still. Frances put an arm around her; they leaned into each other, exhausted. The fire leapt and crackled in the grate, and the room became improbably cosy. The clock on the shelf showed twenty to eight. What a day it had been! Frances felt as wrung-out as a dish-swab. And yet, the fantastic thing was that it had worked out just as Lilian had promised, even down to the timing of it all. Her mother wouldn't be back from Mrs Playfair's until half-past ten or so. Leonard might well not return until after eleven. They had a good three hours now to collect themselves, to regain their calm.

She kissed the crown of Lilian's head, and spoke softly. 'How is it?'

Lilian felt for her hand, and answered on a sigh. 'It's not so bad. Just an ordinary pain now. Not like it was this afternoon.'

'I was frightened to death when I saw you! I thought I would lose you.'

Lilian shifted back to look up at her. 'Did you?' She was almost smiling.

'But I think it's worse than you're making out. I wish I could take the pain myself.'

'I'd never let you do that.'

'Half the pain, then. Half each.'

She shook her head. 'No. It's my pain, and I can bear it. It's my old life coming out of me; my life with Len. That's why it was bad. But it's better now.'

They leaned into each other again and sat with closed eyes, hand in hand.

But she was still worried about her napkin, about blood getting on the sofa. Once or twice, as she had before, she ran her hand under her thighs to be sure that none was escaping; and presently she got to her feet. Turning away, touchingly prim, she drew up the hem of her skirt, and Frances heard her groan. The blood was slowing at last, she said, but it had made an awful mess of her legs, her stockings and slip. She ought to wash herself, and change the napkin, before she grew any sleepier.

So Frances hauled herself up and went back to the little kitchen for a bowl of water, soap and a towel. She returned to find Lilian with her legs bare, unfastening the soiled napkin from a narrow linen belt around her hips. 'Oh, don't look!' she cried, as she'd been crying all day; but she moved so wearily, and fumbled the pins so badly, that Frances set down the bowl and stepped to assist her.

The napkin, heavy with blood, resembled a piece of raw meat. Frances did her best to fold it, and then, for want of anywhere else to put it, she placed it among the cinders on the hearthstone. Lilian lowered herself with a wobble over the bowl, and soaped and rinsed between her legs. The water grew pink, then distinctly crimson: her pose had brought on another gush. Frances, alarmed, could see it falling from her; it was like a glistening dark thread. She helped her to rise and dab at her thighs with the towel. They quickly put the new napkin in place and attached it to the belt. Lilian stepped back into her skirt, then sat heavily down again, blowing out her breath with the effort of it all, letting herself sag sideways until her cheek met the arm of the sofa.

She watched from under heavy eyelids as Frances collected her cast-off clothes, the blood-smeared petticoat and stockings. And when Frances had lifted the bowl of grisly water and was carrying it across to the door, she said, 'I'm so sorry, Frances. It's all been so horrible, and you've been so good. I'd have died to have anybody but you see me like this.'

Frances answered after a hesitation. 'You said you weren't brave.'

Lilian looked back at her, not understanding.

'You said you weren't brave. Look how brave you've been today.'

Lilian's eyes filled with tears. She shook her head and couldn't answer. Her dark hair fell lankly. Her face was still doughy, and her lips were dry. But Frances, gazing across at her, felt that she had never in her life loved anyone so much, nor so purely.

She adjusted her grip on the bowl of water and got hold of the knob of the door. Hooking the door open with her foot, moving awkwardly around it, she stepped out to the landing.

There, at the turn of the stairs, just coming up them—just undoing the buttons of his overcoat—was Leonard.

She gave such a start at the sight of him that the bowl jumped in her hands and the water almost slopped. But after that she stood still, in a paralysis of confusion and fear. He came on towards her in an ordinary evening way, perhaps not quite thrilled to see her, but raising his hand in tired greeting. Then he began to take in the strangeness of her manner. Once he'd mounted the last of the steps and could see what she was holding—the blood-stained clothing, and the bowl, which there was absolutely no way of concealing—his gaze sharpened.

'What's going on?' ·

She answered absurdly, 'It's nothing.'

'Is it Lily?'

He stuck his hat on the newel post and pushed past her into the sitting-room. 'Lily?' she heard him say. 'What the hell's the matter?'

All she could think of was to get rid of the blood. She went hastily into the kitchen and tipped the bowl into the sink, running the tap until the water lost its rustiness, then roughly wiping down the spattered porcelain. The petticoat and stockings she tried to rinse—but that simply made more rust, more spatters. At last she threw them into the empty bowl and carried them over to her own room, dumping them on the floor and closing the door on them.

Then, with a racing heart, wiping her wet hands on her skirt as she went, she returned to the sitting-room.

Leonard was seated at the front of the sofa with his back to her, still in his overcoat. He had one of Lilian's hands in his and she was trying to pull it away. 'I'm all right,' she was saying. She had pushed herself up, and was smiling. The smile looked terrible on her strained white face. The flesh around her eyes suddenly seemed dark as a bruise. When she caught sight of Frances she gazed up at her, helpless, frightened.

Leonard twisted around to Frances too. 'How long has she been like this?'

Lilian spoke before she could answer. She said, as Frances had before, 'It's nothing, Len.'

He twisted back to her. 'Nothing? Jesus Christ, you look awful! I just saw Frances carrying off about a bucketful of blood. And— God Almighty, what's that?' He had spotted the bunched-up napkin on the hearthstone.

Lilian's smile grew more terrible still. 'I've been bleeding, that's all. It's been a bad one, I can't think why. Frances has been helping. What are you looking at? Oh, don't look at that! It's just a napkin. Don't look at it! It isn't a thing for husbands to see!' She put up her hand, drew his face back to hers. 'Why are you home? Why are you here? Why aren't you with Charlie?'

He said, 'Charlie had to leave early. We only had time for a couple of beers.'

'We didn't hear you come in.'

'No, I got the bus to Camberwell, so I came the garden way. You look shocking, Lily. It isn't usually like this, is it?'

310

'No, it's a bad one this time.'

'When I saw that bowl—'

'It was just water.'

'It didn't look like water to me.' He twisted round to Frances again. She was standing just inside the room with her hand on the doorknob; her legs would simply not carry her any further forward. 'Has she been like this all day?' he asked her.

She gazed at him and couldn't speak.

Lilian answered instead. 'You mustn't worry. It's nothing.'

He turned back to her. 'Why do you keep saying that? What's the matter?'

'Nothing's the matter. I—'

But Frances could see that she hadn't the strength for it. Her voice had begun to waver, and the smile was tugging ever more unnaturally at her face. As Leonard stared at her, bewildered, she sank back against the cushions with a hand across her eyes. And when she let the hand drop she said, in a defeated way, 'I didn't want to tell you, Len. I—I think it's a miss. That's why it's been so bad.'

He looked quickly over his shoulder at Frances, his sandy eyelashes fluttering. Turning to Lilian again, he dropped his voice. 'Why on earth didn't you tell me?'

'I don't know. It was only a few weeks along, and—'

'Did you get a doctor? Today, I mean. Have you seen a doctor?'

'I haven't needed a doctor. Frances has looked after me.—What are you doing?'

He was getting to his feet. 'What's the time?' It was quarter to nine. 'It isn't too late for me to run for a doctor now, is it? Where's the nearest man?'

Panicked, Lilian put out her hand to pull him back. 'Please, Len. I don't want a doctor. There's no point. It's all finished.'

'Just someone to look you over.'

'There's nothing for a doctor to do. It'll be a waste of money.

And Mrs Wray will come home when he's here, and it'll all be a big fuss, and I'll be embarrassed. Please, Len.'

'But you look like death! Frances, you must agree with me, don't you? Just tell me where the nearest man is.'

Again Frances found herself unable to answer. She felt too ashamed, too exposed. The success of the thing, the cosy room, the romance: it had vanished. Lilian had scrambled to her knees now, the blanket slithering from her, the hot water bottle falling plumply to the floor. Their gazes met over Leonard's shoulder and she gave Frances a small, urgent, warning shake of her head.

And Leonard turned back to her just as she did it. Caught out, she blinked, then lowered her eyes. He stood and watched her, his expression shifting. 'Just what the hell is going on here?' He waited. 'Frances? What's going on?' Then his face cleared, as he worked it out. He turned to his wife again. 'You've never—?'

Lilian spoke in a guilty rush. 'It just happened by itself. I just woke up and it had come on. I swear it, Len.'

He gazed at her, saying nothing. His silence made her bluster all the more. She appealed to Frances. 'Tell him, Frances. You saw me this morning, didn't you? Didn't I tell you that it had come on? Didn't I—Oh!' She sat back, clamping her hands across her belly. 'Oh, I feel so ill!'

The sight of her made Frances able to move forward at last. Leonard, however, remained where he was. 'If you're as ill as all that,' he said coldly, 'why won't you let me fetch you a doctor? Are you afraid of what he'll find?'

'Please don't, Len.'

'I don't believe this.—No, Frances, let her alone.' Frances had been drawing up the blanket around Lilian's shoulders, but he'd caught hold of her arm and was pulling her away. 'You let my dear wife alone until you hear what she's done.'

'Stop it, Len,' said Lilian weakly.

'Why? Don't you want Frances to know? Are you ashamed of

yourself? No? Tell Frances, then. Go on. Or shall I tell her for you? I know, let's call for Mrs Wray and tell her too, shall we?'

He still had hold of Frances's arm. She tried to tug herself free. 'Please, Leonard,' she said at last.

'No, no. I'm waiting for Lily to tell you.'

'Leonard, for God's sake!' Her tone made him turn and look into her face. She blinked away from his gaze. 'Please. It's been a dreadful day.'

And her manner, her guilty pose, must have been as good as a confession. He released her arm. 'You were in on it too? Jesus Christ! I don't believe it!'

Lilian said, 'Frances has been looking after me.'

'Oh, she's been looking after you, all right.' He put his hand to his greased hair. 'God! Is this what you women get up to? And then you complain when men call you devious! How many other times have you done it?—No, look at me. Listen to me. I don't care how ill you are.' He stood over Lilian. 'How many times, since that first one?'

She groaned. 'Oh, don't be stupid.'

'I suppose this is your idea of—what? Paying me out? Having a go at me, are you?'

'It's got nothing to do with you.'

'Nothing to do with me? Christ!' His face twisted. 'Oh, I can't look at you. It's making me sick. What the hell's the matter with you, girl? I just don't know what you want. You couldn't stand it at Cheveney Avenue; all right, so I moved you here. I don't keep you short of money. You do whatever the hell you want with the rooms; you've got them decked out like a bloody bordello! A kid would—what? Spoil the decorations? There's more to life than silk ribbons, you know.'

Lilian was hugging her aching belly. 'I don't care about the ribbons. I don't care about the rooms. Don't you understand? I don't care about *you*.'

313

'Oh, don't you? Well, I've got some news for you. I'm not all that crazy about you, either. But we're stuck with each other, aren't we?'

'No, we're not.'

He put a hand to his moustache, to wipe his mouth. 'Oh, talk sense.'

'It is sense. I—I mean it, Lenny. Frances knows I mean it, too. We make each other too unhappy. I can't stand it any more. I want us to live apart.'

His hand was still at his moustache. He stared at her across it. 'What?'

'I want a separation! Why do you think I've done all this?'

It was the first truthful thing she had said since he'd got home, and the honesty of it was unmistakable. He kept his eyes on her face in silence, then dipped his head, turned away, drew his hand down from his mouth. Catching sight of his expression from the side, seeing the twist of his features, Frances was appalled to think that he was about to cry. Then she was even more appalled to realise that he was laughing.

But the laughter disappeared, just like that, like a mask coming off. He straightened up. And what he said, with eerie blandness, was: 'Who is he?'

Lilian's shoulders sank. 'Oh, I knew you'd think that. I knew it!'

'Who is he?'

'It isn't all about men, you know! Can't I just want to get away from you? Can't I just have a life of my own? I'm going to get a job. I'm going to go to college.'

His lip rose on his crowded teeth. 'A job?'

'Well, why shouldn't I? I had a job when I met you.'

'Selling knickers for your step-dad! I'd like to see how long you'd last in a real job. And college! You expect me to believe that?'

'I don't care what you believe.'

'Oh, don't mess me about. There's only one reason you'd want to leave me, and that's to let some other poor sap make you his tart.' He turned to Frances. 'You knew all about this already, didn't you? God, I *knew* something was going on with you two! All that whispering and darting about every time my back was turned. Does she bring him here, when your mother's out? Keep watch at the door for them, do you? Deliver his little letters? And I thought you and I were pals.'

'It isn't like that!' cried Lilian, before Frances could respond.

He ignored her. 'Where did she meet him?' His blue gaze had loosened slightly; Frances could almost see the grinding of his thoughts as he tried to work it out. 'Was it at that party, in the summer? That party of her sister's? Is it some Walworth Road swine? Some Irish tinker waster? Or—that little shitpot with the bicycle clips! What's his name? Ernie?'

'There isn't any man!' cried Lilian.

The words came out as a sort of shriek, making Frances jump. But they had no effect at all on Leonard. He kept on with his rant: Who was the man? Where did he live? When had she met him? When had it started? Just how long had the two of them been carrying on? He was working himself up, slowly but steadily letting go of reason and caution. His lips and moustache grew wet with spittle; he wiped them with a finger and thumb, then made a wide sweep of his arm that took in Lilian on the sofa, the blanket, the napkin in the hearth. Was that, he asked with horrible triumph, what this was all about? Her getting rid of another man's child? Jesus, and to think that for a minute he'd felt sorry for her!

Frances began to grow frightened. She looked at Lilian and saw that she was frightened too. The atmosphere in the room, which so far had simply been tense and unhappy, now felt charged with actual danger. She thought with horror of her mother coming home. 'Leonard, please stop it,' she kept saying, making ineffectual movements towards him. 'This is pointless. For God's sake, calm down!' But he ignored her completely, and when he fell silent at

315

last he stood with his eyes darting, clearly searching for something. His gaze fastened on Lilian's handbag. He strode to it and picked it up, undid its clasp and overturned it. 'No, no!' cried Lilian, beginning to dash towards him. But she was too late. The bag's contents fell to the floor, to make a chaos of papers and coins, postage stamps, combs, lipsticks. He went roughly through them—he was looking for evidence, Frances supposed, appalled, of Lilian's affair. Not finding anything there, he gazed around the room again, and spotted her work-basket: he seized that and tipped it up, too. The result was a shower of balls of wool, needle cases, paper patterns, cotton reels, scraps of material. A little tub hit the rug and burst open, and out flew a hundred pearl-headed pins.

As if the pins were the very last straw, Lilian began to weep. 'Go away!' she cried. 'I hate you!' She flung a cushion at him.

The cushion, a yellow one, bounced from his shoulder to add to the chaos on the floor. He stepped through it all, caught hold of her by her upper arms, and shook her.

'Who is he? Who's the man?'

'There isn't a man!'

'Oh, don't insult me. Tell me who he is. I'll bloody well kill him!'

He shook her again as he spoke, and she moved in his hands like something lifeless—like a rug or a table-cloth having the crumbs jounced from it. Frances ran to the two of them and tried to prise off his fingers. When that had no effect she caught hold of the back of his collar and pulled. In response he shoved into her with his shoulder and she went stumbling back, and still he kept on shaking Lilian and hissing into her face. 'Who's the man? Tell me his name. Where does he live? *Tell* me!'

At last Frances couldn't bear it; something inside her gave or snapped.

'*I'm* the man, Leonard!' she cried. '*I'm* the man. Do you understand me? Lilian and I are lovers. We have been for months.'

It was the sort of thing she had imagined herself saying to him, countless times. She had longed and longed for the opportunity to do it. All those nights when she'd lain in bed, desolate or furious, thinking of him at Lilian's side . . . But this was nothing like her fantasies. Her voice was shrill, unsteady, and the moment had no triumph in it, no triumph at all. Leonard looked at her, at first, in pure irritation, as if ready to shoulder her away again and get a better grip on his wife. Then he saw her expression, and the meaning of the words must have got through to him. He held his pose, but opened his hands; Lilian slumped back on to the sofa. Her face was streaked and wet with weeping. She kept her head tilted forward, but gazed up at him, plainly guilty. He said to her, 'Is it true? What Frances said?'

After a little hesitation, she nodded.

He looked at Frances again, then; and in the bareness of his gaze she saw how thoroughly she had betrayed him. His face twitched. He closed his mouth in a firm straight line, drew a few noisy breaths through his nose, then turned his back on both of them, took two or three steps away from the sofa.

But then, in a rush, he turned back. Frances moved too, thinking that he was going after Lilian again. But he came straight at her. Hooking an arm around her neck he started to haul her towards the door.

'Get out!' he said, as he did it. 'Get away from my wife, you unnatural bitch!'

The shock of it made her stumble, and that almost pulled him over. They went staggering together across the rug, through the chaos of wools, papers, knitting needles, pins: she could feel it all slithering about under the soles of her slippers. She heard Lilian crying, sobbing, pleading with him to let her go. But his grip was an intent and terrifying one, his arm still tight around her neck, the roughness of his sleeve like a burn on her throat. She twisted about in an effort to push him away with her shoulder; her hand slid into the open folds of his coat and for a second they were embracing more closely than lovers, their arms and legs entwined, their faces grinding together; she felt the heat and the rasp of his blazing unshaved cheek. Then she twisted again and managed to get her back to him, bracing her feet against the floor. He loosened his grip around her throat and his hand groped for a hold lower down, catching painfully at one of her breasts, finally settling, more painfully still, in the crook of her armpit.

His mouth was close to her ear now, his breath a series of gusts and grunts. Through them came Lilian's voice, still pleading with him to release her; a scuffle and a pressure at her shoulder must have been Lilian's hands trying to prise the two of them apart. Then came the thud of small blows, travelling hollowly through his body to hers, that she understood dimly were Lilian's fists on his back.

Then he kicked out at her ankles and they both lurched forward; and as they righted themselves there came another sort of blow, with a different sound to it—a smack, but an oddly liquid one, like a cricket bat meeting a wet ball. It knocked the breath from Leonard in a noisy, groaning rush; he caught hold of Frances's shoulders as if trying to press her to her knees. Then she thought that he must have lost his footing on the slippery carpet, because his grip on her loosened and he slid heavily down her to the floor. And even when she turned and saw Lilian, a few feet behind him, something grasped in her hands like a club—what was it? The ashtray! The stand-ashtray!—even then, it didn't occur to her that Lilian or the ashtray had had anything to do with his fall. She thought only of getting away from him before he could rise and grab her again.

But then she took in Lilian's expression, and, following her gaze with her own, she realised that, far from trying to rise, Leonard was lying quite still. He had fallen on to his front with his arms pinned beneath him and his face squashed against the carpet. His breathing was shallow and laboured; he looked and sounded like a helpless drunk. The lapels of his overcoat were up around his ears, putting his head into shadow.

Frances stood panting, bent forward, her hands on her knees, her heart racing.

'What happened? Lilian? What's happened? Did you hit him? What did you do?'

Lilian blinked at her. 'I just wanted him to let go of you. I just wanted—' She looked at the ashtray as if she couldn't imagine how it had got into her hands. She set it down with a shrinking gesture, then went warily over to Leonard. 'Len?' she said. 'Len? Lenny?' Still he did not stir. She squatted at his side, put her hand to his shoulder, then drew back his turned-up collar. And then she screamed, starting away from what she had exposed.

The side of his head was running with blood.

Frances's heart stumbled, then began to race faster. She looked wildly around for something with which to staunch the bleeding; she got hold of the yellow cushion and placed it against the wound. Holding it there as firmly as she dared, she carefully turned his head so that she could look into his face. But his face—oh, his face was frightful, his eyelids parted but the eyes unseeing, his mouth open, made slack and misshapen by the position of his head on the floor. Worst of all, his tongue was showing, shockingly pink and uncontrolled, with a string of spittle running from the tip of it to the gaudy carpet. His breaths were more laboured than ever—wet and stertorous, like snores. Blood had cascaded down his cheek and had already drenched his white collar.

Still keeping the cushion in place, she patted him. 'Leonard. Leonard!' She wanted to get some response from him, something ordinary and undreadful.

'Oh, make him wake up!' wailed Lilian. She'd begun, in fear, to weep again.

Frances shook his shoulder. 'Leonard. Len. Can you hear me?'

But she couldn't rouse him. When she shook him more

roughly, it simply jolted a thicker sort of spittle from his mouth. The horrible breaths went on and on. She looked at Lilian. 'What on earth were you thinking?'

Lilian was shaking like a hare. 'I wasn't thinking anything! I was just trying to get him to stop. He was throttling you, wasn't he? I tried hitting him with my hands and it didn't do any good.'

'But why did you pick up the ashtray?'

'I don't know! There was nothing else.'

'But to hit him on the head, Lilian!'

'I didn't mean to. I swear. I just swung it. I didn't mean—' She gazed down at her quivering hands, then pulled at her sleeve, showing Frances. 'Look!' The sleeve had a long streak of ash on it. 'I knew I oughtn't to hit him with the ashy end, you see, in case it dirtied his coat. That shows I didn't mean to hurt him, doesn't it? Doesn't that show it?' Her gaze returned to Leonard. 'Oh, God, there's so much blood! How can there be so much blood? And why won't he wake up?'

'He's unconscious,' said Frances. She still had the cushion pressed in place. She was frightened to lift it. She was frightened to move.

'There's so much blood,' repeated Lilian. 'It's all over his clothes. It's going to get everywhere. Oh, why does he sound like that? Why won't he—'

She stopped. Something had changed. Something new had happened to him. He had taken one of those atrocious breaths, but this time the air, as it came out of him, sounded different, was noisier, wetter. 'Len?' she said, leaning over him. Frances peered again into his face. The breath came on and on, bubbling around the point of his tongue. They saw his back and shoulders sinking, and watched for them to rise again. But they did not rise. The bubbling ceased, and gave way to a terrible silence.

'Len?' repeated Lilian, less certainly than before.

Frances pushed her out of the way. Leaving the cushion sitting in place, she drew back the bunched-up collar of his coat and felt at his neck for a pulse. His flesh was hot and sweaty and seemed full of life, but she could find no beat of blood in it. She laid her ear against his overcoated back, moving about from one spot to another; again, the heat was streaming from him, but she heard no heartbeat save her own terrified one. She caught sight of Lilian's powder-compact in the mess of things on the floor. She ran and got it, and unclasped it, and held its mirror to his misshapen mouth. She held it for ten seconds, fifteen, twenty; it remained unmisted.

She couldn't believe it. Still keeping the cushion clamped to his head, she heaved him over on to his back. A single, breathy groan came out of him, that made Lilian scuttle close to him and call his name again. But the groan was oddly inanimate, like the gust of air that might rise from the neck of a thrown-down bag, and his limbs lay where they had landed, as if not quite connected to the rest of him. Frances got hold of his arms and lifted them, and let them fall again. She tried pushing at his chest, at his stomach—anything to get air into his lungs. But even in the short space of time that she had spent attempting to rouse him it seemed to her that the surface of his partly open eyes, and of his lips and pink tongue, had lost some of their wetness. He'd become not a man, but something resembling a man, something bulky and empty and wrong.

She sat back on her heels. The room still seemed to be ringing with his voice. She could still feel the grip of his hand in her armpit, the weight of his body against hers. But, 'Lily,' she said, in a whisper, 'I think he's dead. I think you've killed him.'

Lilian stared as if not understanding. Then her face crumpled. 'No! He can't be! He just can't! He's fooling, to tease us!' She went back to him, took hold of him. 'Lenny! Wake up! Come on! It isn't funny! Stop it, Lenny! You're frightening me. You're frightening Frances. We didn't mean it, what we said before. It wasn't true. We didn't mean it. Please! Oh, please wake up!'

But even as she begged, the urgency began to fade from her voice. She must have been struck, as Frances had been, by the transformation, the wrongness of him. 'Please, oh, please,' she kept saying; but the word became mechanical, meaningless. At last she fell silent, and took her hand from him, and looked at him in horror.

Then she looked at Frances. 'What are we going to do?'

Frances was still catching her breath. There was blood on her fingers, sticky. 'I don't know.'

'But he can't—I didn't—Oh, what will his mum and dad say!' The thought sent her back to him in terror. 'Oh, what have I done? I can't believe it. He *can't* be dead. He *can't* be! You can't die from something like that! Lenny, *wake up*! Oh, look at all the blood on his clothes! It can't be true. He can't be dead. He went through the War, Frances! Oh, why did he have to come home? And why did you have to tell him, about you and me? Oh, God, it's like an awful dream!'

Her voice was sliding from disbelief into something like hysteria. Frances went over to her and took her in her arms. They embraced as best they could, one of them squatting, the other kneeling, a yard or so from Leonard's stuck-up, splayed-out feet. Lilian pressed her face to Frances's shoulder and moaned and moaned. But the embrace was as wrong, somehow, as Leonard's lifeless body. Their fingers clutched, but their fear was between them, dark, electric. Their hearts were pounding, but pounding separately, each to its own horrified rhythm.

Frances couldn't bear it. She broke free, turned away. Lilian was right: it couldn't be true. She went back to Leonard's body and tried again to revive him. There must be a way. There must be! He had lost all that blood, the yellow cushion was sodden with it; there were splashes of it all over the clutter of things on the carpet. But, even so, you couldn't just die, not like that, not like this. And the wound itself, she saw, had ceased bleeding now. That could only be good—couldn't it? A shock to his system might bring him round. A blow, a jolt. She saw a glass of water on the mantelpiece, and tried dashing a handful of it into his face. It mixed with the blood, that was all. She poured the rest of it into his mouth, moving aside his tongue to do it. But the water sat in there like water in a vase—horrible, horrible.

Setting the glass down with a shaking hand, she looked at the clock: ten past nine. She tried to pull her thoughts together. She closed her eyes for what felt like a moment, then looked at the clock again and found that two whole minutes had gone by.

She said, 'We have to do something. I'll have to get a doctor.'

Lilian trembled. 'A doctor?'

'I think it's too late for one, but—What else can we do?'

'But what will we tell him?'

'I don't know. The truth, I suppose.'

'That I hit him?'

'What else can we say?'

'But we can't tell him that! He'll send for the police, won't he?'

'I think—I think he'll have to.'

'No, Frances. No. Oh, it can't be true! He *can't* be dead! There has to be something we can do.' And again she took hold of him—caught at his hand, this time. 'Len! Lenny!' She squeezed and patted it. 'Stop it, Lenny! Please! Help me, Frances. There has to be a way.'

She had hold of his other hand now. Now she was patting his thighs, his knees. The clock ticked on, unhurried but relentless. Frances tried to draw her back. 'It's no good. It's no use.'

She continued to pat him. Her eyes and cheeks were wet with tears. 'It isn't true.'

'It is. You know it is, Lilian. Stop it. We have to do something real. The longer we leave it, the odder it'll look. The odder, I mean, it'll look to the police—'

That made Lilian grow still. Gazing up at Frances, she spoke in a voice as small as a child's.

'You won't say I hit him, will you?'

Frances swallowed. 'They'll have my word as well as yours that you didn't mean it.'

'They'll say it was murder. They'll hang me, Frances!'

'They won't do that. They couldn't. They wouldn't!' But Frances's voice had begun to tremble. Her heart seemed to be squirming in her breast. It was almost twenty past nine now. Another ten minutes gone! She drew a couple of shaky breaths. 'We just have to be clear about what happened. So long as we're clear, it'll be all right. Leonard was attacking me, after all. I must have bruises—do I?' She pulled down her collar. 'Am I marked, here?'

Lilian looked at her throat without seeing it. 'But they'll want to know why we were fighting. They'll find out about you and me. They'll find out about the baby. I can't go through with it, Frances. I can't! There must be something we can do. Oh, I feel so ill, I think I'll die!—No, Frances, wait!' Frances had begun to move away. Lilian caught hold of her—her hand, her cuff. She was still on her knees. 'There must be something, some other way. We've done so much to be together. They'll keep us apart, I know they will. It isn't fair! We've done so much!'

Her grip had all her fear in it. Her face was greeny-white. 'Please, Frances. Please. Can't we say something—anything? Can't we say that—that he fell?' She seized on the idea, her grip growing tighter. 'Can't we say he just fell and hit his head? If we were to move him on to his side, put something underneath him—'

'But, put what?' Frances gazed around in frustration. 'There's no fender. There's nothing hard in the room at all. There's only a thousand fancy cushions! Look at the wound, at all that blood! The doctor would know we were lying. It would need a step or a stone to make a wound like that.'

'Well, then, suppose he'd fallen outside? We could say he came in, that we tried to help him. You remember that time, when someone hit him? He got himself back to the house that time, didn't he? He was bleeding, then. We could say he did that—that he came in, and told us he'd fallen, and then just—just died—'

'Oh, Lilian, be rational. He couldn't have got anywhere with a wound like this. They'd never believe it.'

Lilian was wringing her fingers. 'Well, say he'd never come home at all? Couldn't we take him, lay him down somewhere?'

'Take him out to the street? With people going by? How could we do that?'

'But he didn't come the street way. He came the garden way. Couldn't we carry him out to the garden?'

'You aren't serious?'

'I don't know. Yes, I am. I'm just so afraid! If we could only get him outside. They'd have to say it was an accident then, even if they weren't sure. Couldn't we take him right out of the garden? Right out to the back lane? Someone will find him. It won't be like hiding him. It won't be like that. Please, Frances. *Please.*'

Christ, what a nightmare it was! What a worse-than-nightmare! Frances tugged her fingers free and put her hands to her face. What she could see were two paths, both of them dark, both of them terrible. To start down one of the paths she would have to run for the doctor, right now. He would look at Leonard's body with its broken head, and then he would look at Lilian—Lilian like this, helpless and ill. There would be questions, tears, lies. Her mother would come home to a house in turmoil, to a policeman at the door—

It was the thought of that, bizarrely, rather than anything to do with Lilian, that made her begin to waver towards the other path. She gazed down at Leonard's body. She went over to peer at that sickening wound. Could it be passed off as an accident? If they were to lie him in a certain way, place something beneath his head? Could they do it? *Could* they?

She said slowly, 'We'd both have to carry him. I'd never manage it alone. You'd have to help me. Oh, this is madness! Even supposing—You haven't the strength.'

325

Lilian was wiping her eyes with the heels of her hands. 'I can do it.'

'You're too ill! God, I don't know. I can't think straight! And time's going by.' The minute hand had snuck forward again.

'Can't we just try?' pleaded Lilian.

Frances looked at her. 'Do you really mean it?'

But Lilian was already scrambling to her feet. 'What will we need? Our shoes? What else? Tell me, Frances!'

Frances didn't know what to do. She put her ear to Leonard's chest again, just in case, by some miracle, there was some sign, some beat or flutter that had escaped her before ... There was nothing. Even the heat seemed to be leaving him now. And his face, with its lustreless slits of eyes and pink, protruding tongue, looked more inhuman than ever.

She tried to think it all through. 'We'll have to keep the cushion against him. We'll get blood everywhere, otherwise. We'll have to bind it. Will that work? Oh, Christ, I don't know! What can we use? One of his scarves? And I'll need something to cover my clothes, an apron, or a towel, or—'

Her hands at her belly, Lilian darted away.

She seemed to return almost instantly, with her arms full of things. She dropped them on the floor at Frances's feet: a gingham apron from the kitchen, a blue knitted scarf from the rack, a pair of dark shoes of her own, another pair, of Frances's, that she had got from Frances's bedroom. Frances stared at the tangle of it all in disbelief. Lilian picked up the apron and held it out to her.

'Please, Frances. Let's just try.'

So, with a feeling of unreality, Frances tied the apron on, rolled back her sleeves, stepped into the shoes; then, shuddering, she squatted and took hold of Leonard's head. It lolled in her hands, as heavy and uncontrolled as a cabbage in a string bag, and as she tilted it to fasten the cushion in place, the water that she had poured into his mouth came spilling out.

At the same time, once his face was obscured by the scarf it was harder to believe that he was really dead. She got herself behind his shoulders and tried to ease him up from the floor, nervously certain that he was about to wriggle about, protest. But as soon as she'd worked her hands under his armpits and had heaved him a little way towards the door, she had to let him drop: he was as unwieldy as a sodden roll of carpet. She thought, *That's it. We can't do it.* The words came with a gush of relief. Then she saw the fright and the helplessness on Lilian's greenish face ... She gripped again, and this time, by getting her arms hooked further under his, so that his padded head rested bulkily against her chin and shoulder, she was able to lift him and begin to drag. When his feet pulled at the carpet Lilian caught hold of his ankles. They slipped from her fingers after two steps, and she caught instead at his trouser-cuffs.

By the time they had staggered the few yards out to the landing and across to the top of the stairs, Frances was exhausted. And Leonard's coat was dragging; she set him down and did up its buttons. Then her eye was caught by something dark on the newel post. His hat! They'd forgotten all about it! God, what else might they have forgotten? She reached across and picked it up: his City bowler, stained on the inside, sour and fragrant from the rub of his hair. But how could they carry it, as well as carrying him? The only way was to wear it herself. She began to raise the hat to her head, then looked at Lilian, and couldn't do it. She couldn't! It was all too much. It was madness!

But they had moved Leonard this far. And it must be almost quarter to ten by now. If they moved him back, and unbound him, and she ran for the doctor, how would they explain the delay? How would they explain the fact that they had moved him at all? They should never have begun. They had made a mistake! *Let's just try,* Lilian had said. But this wasn't a thing, Frances realised now, that could be tried and then un-started. The panic rose in her again, that black, electric fear . . . And suddenly the only possible way to beat the fear off was to keep going. She put the hat on her head, and, gesturing for Lilian to be silent, she leaned over the banister, listening. Suppose her mother had come home, unnoticed, some time in the past half-hour? And mightn't neighbours or passers-by have heard the sounds of argument? But the windows were closed, and the street, so far as she could judge it, was still. She could hear nothing but the pulse of the gaslight, the tick of clocks.

She nodded to Lilian, caught hold of Leonard again, and began to back her way down the stairs.

It was terrifyingly different from crossing the level floor. She had to grope blindly with her foot for each step, taking more and more of the weight of the tilting body as she descended. Lilian, above her, struggling for footholds of her own, held on to Leonard's trouser-cuffs for as long as she was able, but soon one and then the other slipped from her fingers; the force of his collapsing limbs sent Frances swaying backward and she cried out, imagining herself going tumbling down with the body coming heavily after her. Sweating, straining, she at last found her balance, and managed the rest of the descent without Lilian's help, simply hauling Leonard down like a sack of potatoes, so that his feet bumped and bounced about on the stairs and against the banisters.

At the bottom she let him sag completely to the floor and stood doubled over, panting after her breath. But she felt more exposed and anxious here, more impressed by the horrifying reality of it all. If her mother should walk in now—! The thought made her reach for Leonard again. Her arms, however, felt as though they'd been half torn from her shoulders, and her hands, for the moment, had lost their power to close. She plucked uselessly at his body, another wave of panic running through her. They couldn't get him back up the stairs now, even if they wanted to!

She hooked her wrists under his armpits and nodded to Lilian. 'Help me!'

But Lilian, after following her down, had sunk on to the lowest step. She was shivering. 'I need to rest, just for a minute.'

'There isn't time. Come on!'

'I can't, Frances.'

Frances's voice burst free by itself. 'You made us do this! You have to! You have to!'

And as the cry faded there were footsteps in the street, followed by a man's voice, and laughter: the sounds seemed to pass hideously close on the other side of the shut front door, and made them both leap back into life. Frances caught up the body properly and, again, began simply to drag it. 'Go on ahead of me,' she panted to Lilian, and Lilian, with a sob, scurried past her to get the back door open. The heels of Leonard's shoes were leaving long scuff lines on the floor of the passage; now his foot caught the leg of a table and pulled it inches out of place. But Frances kept on without a pause, staggering backward into the kitchen and across to the open door, then practically falling down the two worn steps that led to the yard. And then she was out in the damp, coal-scented night. Lilian, following, was silhouetted for a moment in the bright oblong of the doorway, but once the door was closed the yard was lighted only by the glow of the curtained kitchen window, and seemed full of shadow.

Frances, in sheer relief to be out of the house, let go Leonard's body so that it slumped forward like a Guy Fawkes over its own splayed legs. She went to the wall of the WC to lean against the bricks. Her arms were trembling, the strength in them gone. It was as much as she could do to raise a hand to her sweating face. She lifted the hat from her forehead and it felt like something made of lead.

Even now, though, they mustn't rest. They must keep going. The yard was not so dark, after all. She could see very clearly Lilian's ash-pale, tear-wet features. She could make out Leonard's lolling hands, the white of his cuffs and his collar, the yellow cushion bound so grotesquely to his head. But she was conscious, too, that what they had to do next—get him down the garden and into the lane—was the most dangerous part of the whole business. She had to gather her thoughts, hang on to her nerve. She beckoned to Lilian, felt for her hand, and spoke in an urgent whisper.

'We're nearly there. It isn't far now. Say, fifty steps. You can take fifty steps, I know it. But, listen. This is important. Once we've started down the garden we mustn't let Leonard drop. We mustn't let his feet drag, even. There mustn't be any marks on his clothes or his shoes to show that he's been carried. You understand? Lilian? You've got to keep tight hold of his ankles. We've got to go quickly, too, but silently. As silently as we possibly can. Now, wait here. I'm going to go a little way down, to be sure that no one's about. Keep him like this, with his shoulders high—'

'Don't leave me with him!'

'Just for a moment! Keep him like this, away from the wet ground.'

Lilian's fingers clutched at hers, but she broke free and stole across to the start of the lawn. She picked her way along the path and then she paused, turning her head. The darkness here was much deeper than the darkness of the yard, and there was mist and chimney-smoke in it, making the air feel flannelly. Even so, the sensation of openness and exposure was terrifying. She could hear no voices or movements from any of the gardens close by, but beyond the wall, through the leaves of the trees, she could see lights at the Goldings', lights at the Desboroughs': that meant that any of her neighbours, should they chance to be looking out, could also see her. Or, could they? How concealing was the darkness? She wasn't sure. She ought to have tested it. She ought to have made Lilian come and stand here while she herself remained indoors, peering out from her bedroom window. There wasn't time for it now. Lilian's strength was failing. Her own was failing, too. And in

330

any case, she thought again, what else could they do? Having brought Leonard down here, they had to get rid of him somehow.

Making her way back to the yard, looking again at the rosily lighted windows of her own and her neighbours' houses, she had the stifling sensation that she was putting herself beyond the reach of those warm, ordinary rooms, cutting herself off for ever from all that was decent and calm.

Lilian put out her hands to her the moment she stepped down from the lawn. Leonard lay slumped where they had left him, looking more than ever like some sort of horrible dummy. Frances braced herself to catch hold of him.

'Are you ready?' she whispered. 'And remember what I said, about not letting go. We must keep to the path, too. The grass is wet. We don't want to leave footprints on it. Now, quickly, but quietly. Fifty steps, that's all. Fifty steps, and then it's finished.'

With a tearing of muscles she heaved Leonard up, fought for and found a better grip on him, and then, feeling Lilian raise his ankles, she stepped backward and they were off. The soles of their shoes seemed loud on the path, and their breaths instantly grew laboured and noisy, but they went more swiftly than Frances had hoped for—impelled in part by the weight of their burden, but more by the prick of their own fear. Only once did Lilian seem to be about to lose her hold: Frances felt the tug and jolt of her groping hands, heard the sobbing catch of her breath. But her pace didn't fail, even then; they forced themselves onward, and were soon at the far garden wall. Here they had to set Leonard down again. Frances stood listening at the door to the lane. When she was sure that all beyond was still, she carefully lifted the bar of its latch and, inch by inch, she drew the door open. The darkness that met her was so complete, her gaze seemed to slide about on its surface. The temptation rose in her, shamefully strong, simply to bundle Leonard into it, to close the door on him, to run away. But they mustn't do that! There was still so much to do, still so much care to be taken.

She waited, listening again, then groped her way back to Lilian, and they took up Leonard's body for the final time. She had hoped to carry him far along the lane, but their strength gave out almost at once: he slid from their fingers as if weary of the journey himself, and she knew that they simply had to let him lie where he had fallen. In the absolute darkness he had become invisible. She squatted beside him and went over him with her hands, straightening his coat, neatening his trouser-cuffs—thinking of how his clothing must have got tugged and twisted on its passage through the house. If only she could see what she was doing! If only she had light, and time! But she'd already lost track of how long they had spent on him, and now, alarmed by sounds from a street near by, the creaking open of a car door, the starting of an engine, she gave up on his clothes and felt her way to his head. She carefully unwound the scarf; that came easily enough. But the cushion was more resistant: it had stuck to his scalp and had to be coaxed free. God knew what sort of a mess that was making of the wound. God knew what the cushion might have left behind it in the way of threads or dye. She ought to have thought of that. Why hadn't she thought of that?

It was too late now. Quickly, she groped across the surface of the lane, and in a patch of grass and bramble she found a stone with a smooth, round edge—an edge, as near as she could judge it, resembling the base of the stand-ashtray. She went back to Leonard, lifted his head and put the stone underneath it. At once, the head and the stone wobbled. As a deception it felt hopeless, clownish. But it was the best that she could contrive. And after that there was nothing to do but leave him.

But, now that the moment had come, she was unable to tear herself away. It seemed such a terrible thing, to leave him, with his broken head and only a stone for a pillow. To leave him there, in the choking darkness! It seemed worse than killing him. She put out her hands, and they met his face. She passed her fingertips over his stubbly cheek, his chin, his mouth. Beneath the bristles of his moustache his lips were soft as a woman's.

The touch of a hand on her arm made her cry out: it was Lilian, reaching for her. They clung together for a second, then hurried back to the doorway in the wall, going through it with a stumble, clipping each other in their haste. Frances closed and latched the door, and they started down the garden; only when they were halfway along it did she remember the wretched bowler hat, still sitting sweatily on her head. Leaving Lilian to hobble to the house with the scarf and the cushion, she returned to the lane and got the door open again.

But here, at the last, her courage failed her. She couldn't bring herself to grope her way through the darkness to Leonard's body. Instead she tore the hat from her head and simply flung it into the void. An instant later she caught the thud of it, striking the surface of the cinder lane and bouncing jauntily away.

Back indoors, a frantic series of tasks awaited her. She saw to the first of them at once, scrubbing the blood and the dirt from her hands at the scullery sink, then wetting a cloth and going hastily over the floor of the kitchen and the hall, mopping up the trail of mud and blades of grass that Lilian's shoes had left behind them, and wiping away the marks of Leonard's dragging heels.

Lilian herself was up in her sitting-room, collapsed on the sofa. She raised her head when she saw Frances and said weakly, 'I started to tidy, but I couldn't. I'm sorry—'

'It's all right.' Frances covered her over with the blanket. 'It's all right. I can do it.'

The room was just as they had left it, with its grisly chaotic floor. She stood and looked at it all, and for a moment her thoughts faltered. What ought she to do next? Her mind was a terrifying blank. Then her brain lurched back into life. She must get rid of anything with blood on it, of course. Thank God for the fire, still blazing in the grate! She added another shovelful of coal, then ran to her bedroom for the bowl containing Lilian's cast-off clothing and went about flinging things into it, the cushion and the scarf, but also the balls of wool and the paper patterns that had lain on the floor around Leonard's head. The patterns had caught the worst of it. Only a scattering of coin-sized spots of crimson seemed to have got on to the carpet itself.

She burned the scarf first. It gave a twitch, like a snake, the moment she dropped it on to the heat, then burst into yellow flame and steadily shrivelled up into nothing. And the sight of it disappearing into the heart of the fire like that laid the first calming touch upon her panic: she began to think more coherently, to act more decisively. She took up the cushion next. It was a ghastly thing to handle, weighty with blood—and far too big, she realised, to burn in one piece. She had to fetch a pair of scissors and slice open its cover, then pull out its wet woolly innards, clump by clump. Only the fact that she had already had to deal with so much gore today enabled her to do it; even so, the revolting savoury sizzle with which the clumps went on to the fire brought her stomach into her mouth. But she was thankful, at least, that the cushion wasn't feather: the stink of burning feathers would have been impossible to hide.

By now her hands were brown with blood again, the fingers adhering together, and her gingham apron looked like something from a butcher's shop. Closing her mind to the horror of it, she tipped the remaining contents of the bowl on to the coals; she added the soiled napkin, then looked at the clock. It was gone ten—gone ten, and there was still so much to do! But the fire had given her confidence. She took the bowl and the scissors across to Lilian's kitchen and carefully washed them; she fetched Lilian's chamber-pot and emptied and washed that; and then she made a mixture of salt and water, returned with it to the sitting-room, and got to work on the stains on the carpet. The carpet would never come properly clean; there wasn't the time for it. She ought to use starch, or peroxide—It couldn't be helped. After five whole minutes of frantic soaking and dabbing, the spots had spread but lightened, become ghosts of themselves, haunting the gaudy pattern; she had to be satisfied with that. The cleaning-cloths went on to the fire, to steam and sizzle with everything else. The ashtray, the hideous ashtray, made her stomach heave again: there was a scrap of something pale, with hairs attached, clinging to its base. She plunged it into the coals, turning it to scorch and cleanse it; then, with a shudder, she wiped it and stuck it behind the sofa. What else? There must be more. *Think, Frances. Concentrate.* She remembered the packet that had held the pills: she ran and got it, and threw it on the flames. She examined her clothes, examined Lilian's, and found smears of blood on their sleeves and skirts: she mixed more salt water and did what she could to sponge the smears away. She even thought of the uncooked pastry, sitting in the bowl on her kitchen table. She dashed down, covered it with a plate, and hid it in the pantry.

By the time she was back in the sitting-room, on her hands and knees again, picking up a hundred pearl-headed pins, she felt like a character in a fairy tale who had been set some impossible task and yet, by a miracle, had managed to complete it. Lilian lay helpless on the sofa, watching with dazed, wet eyes. 'I'm sorry, I'm sorry,' she kept saying. 'I'm so sorry, Frances.'

But then she pushed herself up, and spoke in a terrified whisper. 'What's that?'

Frances grew still. There were footsteps, out in the porch. Now a key was being put into the lock of the front door. She raised a finger to her lips. 'It must be my mother.'

'But there's someone else, isn't there? A man?'

She listened. Yes, there was definitely a man's voice, answering some question of her mother's. Not the police, already? She rose and tiptoed to the door.

335

But, 'It's all right,' she said after a moment. 'It's Mr Lamb.'

'Mr Lamb?'

'From down the hill. He's walked Mother home. He must have been there tonight, too. What shall I do? Shall I go down?'

'Yes, go! Go quickly, in case they come looking for you!'

The panic in Lilian's voice made her tear off the apron and hurry out to the landing; but she paused, catching sight of her face in the oval mirror of the coat-stand. There was a crust of blood on her forehead, where she must have raised gory fingers to put back a lock of hair. Appalled, she rubbed it away. Was there anything else? Something in her expression? Some mark, some change? She held her own gaze, willing her features to be smooth, to be calm. For if she couldn't manage this, she thought, then they were done for. If she couldn't manage this, then what was the use of the horror and the fever of the past ninety minutes?

She heard her mother's voice. 'That might be Frances now. Let me see—'

She mustn't come up! Frances moved forward and they met at the turn of the stairs.

'There you are.' Her mother was smiling, but sounded not quite happy. Frances followed her down to the hall. 'Here's Mr Lamb, look. He's been so kind in seeing me home, I thought we might offer him a glass of your father's whisky. But the drawing-room fire is dead in the grate!'

Frances said, with what sounded to her like unnatural smoothness, 'I've been in my room, reading. How are you, Mr Lamb? Were you lucky at cards tonight?'

Mr Lamb smiled. 'The ladies trounced us gentlemen, I'm afraid. They always do. Your mother's far too clever; I don't like it one little bit. But, how are you? It must have been a good book—was it?'

'Book? Oh—' Her mind, for a moment, was another terrifying blank. Then it clicked into gear again. She said, 'To tell the truth, I was dozing. I'm sorry about the fire. I can soon lay a new one.'

But at that, her mother gave an awkward laugh. 'We can't expect Mr Lamb to sit and watch you do that!'

'No, I wouldn't dream of putting you to the trouble,' Mr Lamb said, laughing too.

He was as embarrassed as her mother, embarrassed at having caught them out in their economies over coal and servants; and the smallness of it all, the aching drab simplicity of it, after the violence of what she had been through, nearly pushed her off balance. They chatted for another minute or two, but she grew ever more wooden and unnatural. The strain in her muscles was like a howl. There was a wet patch in the folds of her cuff, where she had soaked away a bloodstain. She could feel the perspiration rising on her lip, and was afraid to draw attention to it by wiping it away.

Anyhow, they could hardly all stand there in the hall. Her mother, moving towards the front door, said, 'I'm afraid you shall have to have your whisky some other time, Mr Lamb. Thank you so much for seeing me home. Do give our love to Margaret.'

When the door was closed behind him she began twitching off her gloves. 'Really, Frances. You might make a little more effort. What on earth's the matter with you?'

'Nothing's the matter,' said Frances, wiping her mouth at last. 'What do you mean?'

'Well, poor Mr Lamb—' But now her mother's fingers had slowed and she was looking at Frances oddly. '*Is* something the matter?'

Frances smiled, or attempted to. 'I was on my way to bed. I wasn't expecting visitors. I might have been in my dressing-gown!'

'Well, he was kind enough to walk with me. I felt I had to ask him in. It isn't half-past ten yet, is it?'

'I don't know what the time is.—No, leave the locks.' Her mother had gone back to the door, to fasten the chain and draw the bolt. 'I haven't put out the milk-can. And besides—' Her heart fluttered; she could hear the flutter in her voice. 'Leonard isn't home yet.'

Her mother let the chain fall. 'Oh, isn't he?' She spoke with dismay.

But then she grew still, and looked at Frances in a sharper way. 'Mr Barber has been out all evening? But Mrs Barber's been at home?'

Frances stumbled over the little word. 'Yes.'

Her mother said nothing. But it was plain what she was thinking. It was plain what she was supposing, about how Frances had spent her time. And the gap between even the worst of her suspicions and the hideous nightmare reality was again almost too much. Frances felt an urge to step towards her, catch hold of her hand. 'Oh, Mother,' she wanted to say, 'it's frightful! Oh, Mother, make it better!'

She forced herself to turn away, and went, with bowed head, to the kitchen.

For there were still the bedtime chores to see to, even tonight: the stove to be riddled, the breakfast things to be put out. Her eyes were darting the whole time, looking for marks, for splashes of blood. When her mother followed her along the passage and headed out to the WC she thought of the lavatory pan, remembering how hastily she had cleaned it. That was Lilian's blood, of course, incriminating in a different way. God, there'd been nothing but blood, all day! The house felt as though it were swimming in it! If her mother should see some trace of it—

But, no, it was too dark for that. Her mother returned from the yard in silence. She poured herself a glass of water and said a chill good night.

Once Frances had shut off the gas in the hall she went softly back up to the sitting-room and leaned weak-kneed against the arm of the sofa. Lilian, seeing her pose and expression, whispered, 'What? What is it?'

She shook her head. 'It's nothing.'

'What did they say? They haven't guessed?'

She answered in a hiss. 'No, of course they haven't guessed! How could my mother ever guess such a thing? It was only foul, to have to stand there and pretend that nothing was wrong, when all the time—'

She didn't finish. Lilian's eyes filled with tears. 'Please don't start to hate me now.'

'I don't hate you,' said Frances with an effort. 'I just—'

'You don't wish we hadn't done it?'

'Yes, I wish we hadn't done it! I wish you hadn't hit him, Lilian! But what does it matter what I wish? We've done it, and that's that. We've done it, and can't undo it, and—' She saw the gingham apron, still lying in a heap on the floor. She bundled it up and threw it on the fire. 'If only we might have more time! I can't believe there isn't something to give us away. But we can't keep looking. My mother will hear us moving about, and start to wonder. We must go to bed—'

Lilian looked terrified. 'You won't make me go to bed on my own?'

Frances sagged. 'Lily, you must. We must do just what we would do on an ordinary night. It'll look odd, otherwise. We mustn't do anything to raise suspicion. The police will want to know, when they come—' A fresh wave of panic rose in her. 'But we haven't talked about this at all! We have to be sure to say the same thing. There mightn't be time to discuss it in the morning.'

'Let me come into bed with you, then. We can talk about it there. Please don't make me sleep on my own tonight. I can't do it. Please, Frances.'

Please, Frances. Please, Frances. Frances had heard those words all evening. But the tears were running from Lilian's eyes now; she was trembling again; and it was impossible to do anything but go over to her and embrace her.

And in clutching at each other, they both grew a little calmer.

'All right,' murmured Frances, as she helped her to her feet. 'All right. Put on your night-clothes. Can you do that? Don't get cold.'

While Lilian went weakly off to undress, she herself remained in the sitting-room, looking again at the stains on the carpet, and searching for anything she might have missed before, any evidence of Leonard's having been there ... She found only more pearl-headed pins.

Out on the landing they called good night to each other, and Lilian closed her bedroom door. That was for Frances's mother's benefit; a minute later she came creeping across the landing and Frances hurried her into bed. They left a candle burning. Her face was grey in the light of it. She lay under the blankets with chattering teeth, her arms and legs twitching with cold, her hands at her still-aching belly. Frances spread herself against her, pulling her close, trying to warm her.

Once her shivering had begun to subside they talked for a while, in strained whispers, about what might happen in the days to come. They settled on the stories they would tell, as to how they had spent their evening. But Lilian by now was exhausted, and began to frighten herself by growing muddled; so Frances kissed her, and let her be, and soon she lay still and heavy in the bed, marble-cold, like a toppled statue. She stirred only twice more before sinking completely into sleep. The first time was to squeeze Frances's hand, to look into her eyes and murmur, 'We used to want to do this, didn't we?' She might have been mournfully recalling the habits of a long-ago love affair. But the second time was to raise her head with a start, and peer over at the curtained window.

'What was that?'

'There's nothing,' said Frances.

'Are you sure? I thought I heard——' She met Frances's gaze. 'Suppose we made a mistake? Suppose he wakes up? Suppose——?'

'He won't wake up,' said Frances. 'There's nothing we can do. It's too late. Don't think about him.'

But she was thinking about him herself. She was recalling the weight of his body in her arms, the bulk of his padded head against her shoulder. She kept remembering the moment in the sitting-room when she had had that vision of the two dark paths. What had made her choose one over the other? She could recall the urgency of her feelings, but the feelings themselves eluded her. The only urgency she felt now was the urgency of fear. She was afraid of what she had done, and of what she might have neglected to do. Those twists and tugs in Leonard's clothing, for example: she ought to have taken more care over putting them right. And then, the position of his limbs. She hadn't thought of that at all, but surely there was a way that a man fell, when he'd slipped or stumbled, and a way that he didn't fall ... ?

Most of all, however, she thought of his wound, that had had the cushion pressed against it. She couldn't believe that the yellow fabric hadn't left threads and tufts behind. Could she go back? For a moment she considered it. She actually began to ease herself out of Lilian's statue-like grip, thinking that she could steal downstairs and out across the garden with a lantern in her hand.

But then she heard a noise, a rustling or creaking on the other side of the window; after a few suffocating heartbeats she realised that the noise was the patter of rain. It came gently at first, then fell more persistently, until she could picture it making its blameless, cleansing assault on Leonard's clothes, Leonard's body, his smashed head, his soft, soft mouth. She lay there listening to the drum of it, sick to her bones with relief and shame.

Part Three

11

The rain fell steadily all night long. The candle died, the fire burned lower in the grate; the room grew dark, then less dark, and still the tumble of water went on, until Frances began to think that she had heard every separate drop of it. She didn't sleep. She barely closed her eyes. Somewhere around six she managed to prise herself from Lilian's grip, to slide from the bed, creep to the window and part the curtains. She could just make out a line of roofs and chimneys through the downpour, but of the far garden wall she could see nothing: only a black mass of shadow.

She was aching in every limb, and the room seemed piercingly cold. She struck a match, tiptoed to the hearth, did her best to light a new fire in the ashes of the old. Once the flames had begun to crackle, she heard a murmur: 'Frances.' Lilian was awake, looking at her. She went back to the bed and they held each other tightly. 'I thought it was a dream,' Lilian whispered. 'I thought it was a dream; and then I remembered.' A shudder ran right through her, just like the shudder that came with love.

But she didn't cry. The tears seemed all wrung out of her. A change had come over them both: they were calm, perhaps dazed. Frances looked at the clock. 'You ought to go back to your own room. Now that it's light, someone will find him; a workman, or someone. Someone might come to the house.'

Lilian rose without complaint, only wincing a little with pain. She was still bleeding into the napkin, though not so heavily as before. She fitted her arms into her dressing-gown with her shoulders drooping. She and Frances stood together in a last, wordless embrace. Then Frances eased open the door and she stole across the landing, pale and silent as a ghost.

The knock came at five to eight, as Frances was pulling on a skirt, and just as she'd begun to wonder whether it was ever going to come at all. There could be no mistaking it for the postman's brisk double rap. It was heavy, ominous: the sound of bad news. With her heart like lead in her chest, and her torn muscles seeming to tear again at every step, she made her way downstairs.

She found her mother in the hall, just emerging from her own room.

'Are you expecting any sort of delivery, Frances?'

She shook her head.

The small gesture felt false. Her leaden heart stirred unpleasantly. Then she opened the door, and the sight of the policeman, tall and bulky in his mackintosh cape, nearly took the strength right out of her.

But the man was one they knew slightly from having seen him make his rounds: a Constable Hardy, rather young, and new to the job. She saw his Adam's apple moving in a boyish way as he swallowed. He said, 'Miss Wray, I think?'

She nodded. 'Is something the matter?'

'Well, I'm afraid to say something is.'

Her mother came forward. 'What is it, Frances?'

He addressed himself to her then, swallowing again before he spoke. 'I understand that a Mr Leonard Barber normally resides in the house. Is that correct?'

'Yes. Yes, it is. He has rooms upstairs with his wife. But he'll have left for work by now. At least—*Did* he leave today, Frances? I don't know that I heard him. Has something happened, Constable? Come in, will you, out of the porch.'

He came forward, taking trouble over wiping his feet. When the door was closed behind him he said, 'I'm afraid there's reason to believe that Mr Barber has been injured.'

Frances's mother put a hand to her throat. 'Injured? On his way to work, you mean?'

He hesitated, then looked over at the staircase. 'Is Mrs Barber at home?'

Frances touched her mother's arm. 'I'll fetch her. Wait here.'

Her heart had calmed, but her manner still felt strained and artificial, and her aching legs, as she began to climb, seemed not quite under control. She meant to go right to the top and call to Lilian from there; but Lilian, of course, had heard the knock, had heard the constable's voice. She was out of her room already, still in her nightdress and dressing-gown but with a shawl over her shoulders, and looking so pale, so hunched, so worn—so *ill*—that Frances's knees almost buckled completely. She spoke from the turn of the stairs, horribly conscious that Constable Hardy and her mother were watching as she did it.

'Don't be frightened, Lilian. But a policeman's here. He's saying that something'—her mouth felt tacky—'that something has happened to Leonard. I don't understand. Has Leonard left for work already?'

Lilian stared at her. She had heard the oddness in her voice, and it had made her afraid. She mustn't be afraid! Frances swallowed, and spoke less stickily. 'Is Leonard here?'

Finally, Lilian came forward. 'No. No, he isn't here.'

'Has he gone to work?'

'He hasn't come home. I—I don't know where he is.'

She followed Frances down the staircase, and when she caught

347

sight of the policeman she faltered, just as Frances had, and reached for the banister. But that was all right, Frances thought; that was natural. Wasn't it? She took hold of her hand to help her down the last few stairs, trying to will strength and confidence into her grip. The constable said again that he was sorry, but he had something very grave to say, and perhaps Mrs Barber would like to sit down? So they all went into the drawing-room, Frances going quickly to the windows to open the curtains. Lilian sat at the end of the sofa; Frances's mother took the place beside her, put a hand on her arm. Constable Hardy removed his helmet and came gingerly forward, doing his best to avoid the carpet; he was concerned about the rainwater dripping from his cape.

With his Adam's apple jerking more wildly than ever, he told them that a man's body had been discovered in the lane at the back of the garden, and that he had reason to believe, from items in the man's possession, that the body was that of Mr Leonard Barber. Could Mrs Barber confirm that her husband was absent from the house?

Lilian said nothing for a moment. It was Frances's mother who cried out. Constable Hardy looked more awkward than ever.

'If Mrs Barber could just confirm—'

'Yes,' said Lilian at last. Then: 'No. I don't know. I don't know where Len is. He didn't come home last night. Oh, but it can't be him! Can it?'

There was fear in her voice. Was it the right sort of fear, or the wrong? Frances couldn't tell. She went swiftly around the sofa and put a hand on her shoulder. *Be calm. Be brave. I'm here. I love you.*

Constable Hardy had got out his notebook and now began to take down the details of the case. Could Mrs Barber tell him when she had last seen her husband? What had his movements been yesterday? He had gone to work? Where was that? And afterwards? When had she first missed him?

In a wavering tone Lilian gave him the address of the Pearl headquarters, then told him about Leonard's plans to meet up with

348

Charlie Wismuth. He made a careful note of the name in a laborious, schoolboy hand, his helmet tucked awkwardly under his elbow as he wrote. Then he turned to Frances and her mother. They hadn't seen Mr Barber?

They shook their heads. And, 'No,' said Frances. 'No. Out in the lane! You're quite sure? It seems incredible.' She stared over at the window, her hand still on Lilian's shoulder, trying desperately to shrug off the artificiality of her manner—trying, too, to work out what questions she ought to be asking, which bits of knowledge she should and shouldn't have. 'I know,' she said, in the same inauthentic way, 'that Mr Barber sometimes uses the lane as a short-cut. Do you think he might have done that late last night? But that means—How long do you suppose he's been out there?'

'Well, his clothes are soaked right through.'

'But how on earth did it happen? How did he—?'

'We think, from an injury to his head.'

The words made Lilian twitch: Frances felt the jump of her shoulder. She tightened her grip on it. *Be brave!*

But now her mother looked up at her. 'Oh, this is dreadful. Dreadful! It's just like that other time, Frances!'

Constable Hardy blinked at them. 'Other time?'

On slightly safer ground now, her manner more natural, Frances told him about Leonard's having been assaulted by a stranger back in July. He took down the details, in his arduous way; she had the impression, however, that he was doing it mainly for form's sake. For it was too early, he said, to determine cause of death. The police surgeon would be able to tell them more, once he'd made his examination. There had been no robbery from Mr Barber's person, so far as they'd been able to ascertain. His pocket-book still had money in it, and his wristwatch and wedding-band were still in place. That made it very possible that he had simply lost his footing on the wet ground and struck his head. The surface of the lane was covered with stones—

Frances felt Lilian twitch again; again she tightened her grip on her shoulder. She said, to make it be true, 'A fall, you mean?' And Constable Hardy answered, 'Well—yes, that was certainly how it looked.'

Her mother had risen from the sofa and gone over to the French windows. Her face was grey. 'It doesn't seem possible! To think of poor Mr Barber out there! And the rain still falling! Mrs Barber, we must bring him inside, surely? Frances—'

Frances felt a wave of nausea at the thought of going anywhere near him. If she had to touch him, if she had to lift him again—! But Constable Hardy said, 'I'm afraid it would do no good. I've already sent a man for an ambulance.'

'But to think of him out there! Who's with him now?'

'PC Edwards is with the body. One of your neighbours at the back gave us a piece of mackintosh for it. It was the man who discovered him, while walking his dog. He supposed him a tramp at first, because he had no hat on him; the hat had gone rolling off, you see. But then he saw that he was respectable, and after he'd had a closer look he thought he knew him for a clerk from one of the houses on Grove Lane. I've been over there for half an hour, knocking on doors. We got a doctor in the meantime, to come and confirm that life was extinguished, and it was only then that we found a paper in Mr Barber's pocket, with this address on it . . . That looks like the ambulance now,' he added, as a grey, featureless van went up the street, past the front garden. He turned to Lilian, and drew himself together. 'Mrs Barber, I'm afraid it's my duty to have to ask you, as next of kin, to follow us on to the mortuary to make a formal identification.'

Lilian paled further. 'What do you mean? To look at Len, do you mean?'

'I'm afraid so. We'll have a taxi drive you there and bring you back. It won't take long. The coroner's officer will want to take a statement from you too, but I expect he'll call here later for that.'

Lilian had begun to breathe more quickly. She said, 'I don't know if I can.' She raised her hand to Frances's, looked up into her face. 'I don't think I can.'

Her gaze was panicked, unguarded. Alarmed, Frances squeezed her fingers. She didn't want to look at him, either. She remembered his pink, protruding tongue. But, 'It's all right,' she made herself say. 'I'll do it with you. Will that make it easier? I'll go with you. You won't be alone.' She turned to her mother. 'You'll manage here, Mother, if I go with Lilian?'

'Yes, of course,' answered her mother. 'No, Mrs Barber mustn't go alone.' But she spoke distractedly. She was still peering down the garden. 'I simply can't believe it. The idea of us being in our beds while—'

Lilian gazed across at her. 'I'm so sorry, Mrs Wray.'

She turned from the glass, shocked. 'What are you sorry for?'

'I don't know.'

Lilian's voice broke on the words, and she started to cry. She dried her eyes with her handkerchief, but cried again when Constable Hardy asked if there were any persons she would like to be notified—relations of her husband's, or of her own?

She nodded. 'Len's mum and dad. Oh, this'll kill them, I know it will!' And in a voice broken up by upset and fear she gave him the Peckham address, along with her own mother's address on the Walworth Road.

He put his notebook away, then fitted on his helmet, fiddling with the strap under his chin. He would talk to his colleagues at the police station, he said, and call for a taxi at the same time. Did the house have the telephone, by any chance? No? Then he would use the police box down the hill.

Once he had left, the three of them stood absolutely helpless for a moment; then they started into jittery life. 'You must eat something, Frances,' her mother told her. 'You, and Mrs Barber. You mustn't go with nothing inside you. Mrs Barber, this is awful for you. May I come and help you to dress, or——?' Lilian shook her head. 'Are you sure? You've a horrible thing ahead of you.'

Frances said, 'I'll see to Lilian, just as soon as I've done the stove.—No, there isn't time for the stove. I'll make the tea upstairs, on the gas.'

She raced about, fetching the things. Lilian weakly climbed the stairs. She was in her bedroom, a hand at her forehead, when Frances went up. She let Frances pull her close, then trembled in her arms. 'I don't know what I'm doing, Frances. I feel giddy. It's all too much.'

Frances spoke in a whisper. 'But you've done a part of it. You heard what he said about the stones. That's one part done already.'

Lilian drew back to look into her face. 'Do you think so?'

'Yes. Yes.'

She closed her eyes, and nodded. Frances pulled her close again, and kissed her, then ran to see to the tea.

And while the water was boiling, she went into the sitting-room. She wanted to take another look at the blood-stains on the floor. She quietly drew back the curtains, and—God, there they were, four, five, six, seven of them, plain as anything if one knew what to look for. When she stooped and put her hand to them she found them damp, still, to her touch. And the fireplace was black with smuts, the grate a mess of greasy-looking clinker and scraps of unburned apron: there was no way to get rid of that just yet. She shovelled the worst of it into the ash-pail and hastily laid a new fire; she got it burning, and heaped on the coal. So long as the room was kept warm, the carpet would dry, and the stains fade into the pattern—wouldn't they?

She set the guard across the grate and hurried out to the boiling kettle.

Downstairs, her mother was back at the French windows. 'I can't take it in, Frances,' she said. 'I can't be still. It doesn't seem true.' She took the tea from Frances's hand, and the cup rattled on the saucer. Her face was still without colour; would she be all right, left here alone? Was there time to run and fetch Mrs Playfair and Patty? But, no, Frances remembered, Mrs Playfair wouldn't be at home; she was leaving early this morning for a week at her sister's in Sussex. Was there no one else? One of the neighbours? She thought of the Dawsons opposite . . . So, just as she was, hatless and coatless, she headed out into the rain, ran across the road and gave the family a quick, breathless account of what had happened. Yes, it was frightful. A dreadful shock. No, not at all like that other time. An accident, the policeman thought. But could Mrs Dawson come and sit with her mother for the hour or so that it would take her to accompany Mrs Barber to the mortuary and back? Could one of the maids come too, to lay the fires and make a breakfast?

Of course, of course, they said, with startled faces. They would come at once; they would follow her over. And she left them darting about, looking for coats and umbrellas.

Stepping from their garden path, she noticed a tradesman up at the turn of the road: he was standing on the pavement in a fixed, interested pose, his attention caught by something further along the crest of the hill. As she reached the kerb, she saw what it was. The ambulance had emerged from the lane. It came nosing around the corner, slow and careful, like a snuffling beast; when it passed her, it drew so close that she could almost have put out her hand and touched it. She watched its blank rump receding as it lumbered down towards Camberwell. Could Leonard really be inside it? Queasily, she pictured his smashed head, jolting about.

But she felt a little better for having spoken to the Dawsons. She had shaken off some of her falseness; she could feel herself responding to the crisis as if she had come to it innocently. Back at the house, she found her mother and Lilian together in the drawing-room, Lilian dressed, but dressed badly, in clashing colours—a navy skirt, her crimson jersey, a brown coat—as if she had pulled on the garments at random; there were swipes of powder and lipstick on her face, which only emphasised her pallor. She was shivering as if very cold, and Frances's mother must have been trying to get her to drink her tea; the cup, still almost full, sat on the table beside the sofa, the mark of her red mouth on it. At the sound of Mrs Dawson and her maid following Frances to the house, she started; and when she saw them coming in she bowed her head. Mrs Dawson said, 'Oh, Mrs Barber, I'm so very sorry for you. Mrs Wray, what a sad thing this is!'

The taxi arrived while Frances was upstairs fetching her coat and hat. She took Lilian's arm in hers for the journey across the front garden, conscious of the stares of passers-by. Perhaps news of the upset had already spread; or perhaps there was simply something odd about her and Lilian's poses, their combination of fragility and haste. The driver also looked curiously at them. How much, she wondered, had the police told him? There was no debate about the destination, at any rate. He simply helped them into the vehicle, then returned to his cabin, and with a great and ghastly creaking of its chassis the taxi started down the hill.

Neither she nor Lilian spoke. The man was separated from them by the glass, the noise of the engine, the hiss of the wheels on the road, but they were too anxious and wary to risk speech. Instead they held hands, low down, out of sight. Now and then Lilian closed her eyes, her lips moving as if in prayer.

They drove through the rain-lashed Saturday-morning streets, past the park, past the hospital, the picture-theatre, the shops, past every ordinary, friendly landmark. A short way beyond Camberwell Green they made a turn to the right, and entered a dreary warren of low terraced houses; a few minutes later they came to a halt at a small, chapel-like building at the back of what Frances realised must be the coroner's court. She opened the taxi door, uncertain of what to do next—then saw Constable Hardy, who, by some disconcerting police magic, had got here ahead of them. He came forward to greet them, and to hurry them through the wet. They went into the building and were put to wait on a couple of hard chairs in a grim little lobby.

A ribbed glass window let in a weak light. Muffled male voices could be heard; a telephone rang and was answered, just as it might have been in an office or in the back room of a shop. Was this the mortuary itself, or simply some stop on their journey to it? Frances wasn't sure. The place was so ordinary, so anonymous. It was even more difficult to believe that Leonard's body was here, close by, than it had been to watch that ambulance and understand that he was inside.

But then she caught the scent of disinfectant, like a creeping, jaundiced colour in the air. She looked at Lilian and saw that she had noticed it too. She'd started to shift about on the chair. Suddenly she grabbed at Frances's arm. 'I don't think I can do it, Frances.'

Frances felt for her fingers. 'It'll only take a moment, he said.'

'I'm afraid, of what he'll look like.'

'You just have to look, then look away.'

'I'm afraid. I can't—Oh, God!'

Constable Hardy had returned, and wanted them to go with him.

Lilian closed her eyes, drawing a long, uneven breath. She let Frances help her to her feet, then stood with her hand on her heart, hesitating for so long that Frances felt the whole thing begin to slide away, to crumble, like salt, like sand. She spoke with quiet desperation. 'It's only a moment. The worst has happened. You're through the worst. A small, small moment, that's all it is.'

Lilian drew another steadying breath; and then she nodded. With an awkward gesture, Constable Hardy led them away from the lobby.

And only now that they were actually following him did Frances begin to take in what they were here for. A part of her still didn't believe it. That telephone was ringing again. She was still half-imagining that they would pass from this place to another building, a more impressive, convincing one. But even if they did, would they really find Leonard there? He was at his office, surely. He was playing tennis. He was at his parents'. He was back at Champion Hill, pushing the mower across the lawn . . . But they turned abruptly into a passage, Constable Hardy opened a door, stepped aside for them to pass him—and suddenly she found herself in a scrubbed, electric-lighted room, in the centre of which was a queer sort of altar with a sheeted, man-shaped lump on the top. An aproned attendant stood beside it. The door was closed, and he asked if they were ready. She looked at him blankly; she had no idea what he meant. Lilian, however, must have nodded or made some sign, for, with the discreet, practised, impersonal gesture of a waiter moving forward to place a napkin on a lady's lap, he reached to take hold of the top of the sheet. And as he began to raise it Frances's scattered thoughts flew back together in a rush of understanding and terror.

But after all, once the sheet was lifted, her fear dissolved again. It was all so unintimate, so unmenacing, compared with the sweaty horrors of the night before. Leonard's face, it seemed to her, might have been a bad plasticine model, one side grey, the other almost purple, with no care taken over the join. His eyes were part-way open, but his mouth was closed and tidy. The attendant had tucked a white towel around his head, and the wimple-like effect, against the piebald skin and the gingerish moustache, was too uncanny to be true. This was not a Leonard who would wake, raise his arms, grab and denounce one. This was not Leonard at all. Even Lilian must have felt that. She stood staring at his features with a trace of bewilderment, and when she said, at a prompting from Constable Hardy, 'Yes. Yes, it's him,' she sounded not quite certain. She was far more upset, on turning away, to see the things that had been removed from his body: his clothes and hat, which sat together in a sodden pile on a steel tray; his unlaced shoes, misshapen from their night in the rain; and lastly the items that had come from his pockets, and which had been set, with appalling neatness, on a sheet of greaseproof paper: keys, cigarettes, handkerchiefs, a Boys' Brigade penknife, odd coins, notes, letters, his wristwatch and wedding-ring.

By the time they had returned to the lobby she was sobbing. Frances helped her back into a chair, then sat beside her with an arm across her heaving shoulders. Constable Hardy stood by, self-conscious; he had a document, it seemed, that required her signature. She wiped her eyes and nose at last, and looked vaguely at the paper. But then there was some trouble with his pen, the ink having run out or dried up. He fiddled with the nib, blushing from his throat to the tips of his ears.

That jaundiced odour seemed stronger than ever. Frances was longing to get away from it. Through the ribbed window she could just discern the suddenly reassuring shape of their taxi-cab, sitting out there with its engine running, waiting to take them home.

Even as she gazed at the glass, however, a misshapen dark figure passed across it; a second later the door opened, letting in another mackintoshed policeman. This one was older and more senior than Constable Hardy. He seemed to know all about the case already; he came forward to shake their hands. His name was Police Sergeant Heath, he said, and he was acting for the coroner. Mrs Barber had made the identification, had she? They were grateful to her for that. And Miss Wray, he understood, was the landlady of the house? Very good. There were just a few facts that he needed to establish, in order for the investigation to proceed—if they didn't mind?

He didn't wait for their permission, but pulled over a chair and sat. Lilian looked at him with swollen eyes. Frances watched uneasily as he got out his notebook, groped in his pocket for a pencil, gave the lead a lick. Now, could they confirm their address for him? Could they tell him when exactly they had last seen Mr Barber alive? Could they say how Mr Barber had intended to spend the previous evening?

They were all the questions that Constable Hardy had already asked, and which had already been answered, Frances thought, back at Champion Hill. She shut her eyes in simple weariness. She hadn't slept. She hadn't eaten. The day had begun to feel tinny: a pretend day, a dream day, that for some unaccountable reason she had to go on and on with as if it were real. But soon, surely, it would come to a close. Soon they would all be allowed back into their ordinary lives . . . The sergeant's list of questions seemed endless. He took so long to note down their responses, and did it so impassively, that he might have been some sort of machine. She began to answer automatically: No. Yes. No, she didn't think so. No, she'd heard nothing, nothing at all . . . At last he read their words back to them, then had them sign their names to the statements. He added a note of his own, snapped the elastic around the book and returned it to his pocket with an air of finality. In relief, she watched him stand, and prepared her over-strained muscles for the rise from the chair.

But what he said, to her amazement, was, 'Well, we can go into all this in a bit more detail at the Camberwell police station. If Mrs Barber could come with me?'

He held out his hand, to help Lilian to her feet. Lilian looked up at him, blinking, then looked at Frances. Frances said, 'Just a minute. I don't understand. Surely you've finished with Mrs Barber for now? This has been a dreadful shock for her. Constable Hardy gave us the impression that we could go home directly.'

'Well,' he said, with a glance at the younger man, 'Mrs Barber's under no obligation. But it would help speed the inquiry along, you see.'

There was something to his tone, Frances realised now: a hard edge, a rigidity, like a busk beneath the padding of his manner. Her

358

weariness fled. The blood hissed in her ears. She rose from the chair, saying, 'Is everything all right?' and he nodded grimly.

'Yes, everything's in order. Except that a man has died, of course. We have to ascertain how that happened.'

'But I thought you knew that already. Constable Hardy said that Mr Barber must have slipped and hit his head.'

'Yes, he might very well have slipped. But we have to consider every possibility. Our surgeon has had a quick look at the deceased and—well, I'll be honest with you, he isn't quite satisfied with what he's found. Nothing to be alarmed about just yet. Once he's made a thorough examination we shall know more. In the meantime, we just have a few more questions for Mrs Barber. You yourself might go home, Miss Wray. We can have a woman sit with Mrs Barber until her family arrive.'

Lilian caught hold of Frances's arm. 'No, don't leave me!'

'No, of course I won't,' said Frances, frightened by the unguardedness that had reappeared in her face. 'I wouldn't dream of leaving you. I may stay with her, I suppose?' she asked the sergeant.

'Oh, certainly,' he answered, his manner padded again.

So they went back out into the rain, leaving kind young Constable Hardy behind; and this time, when Frances and Lilian climbed into the taxi, Sergeant Heath produced a bicycle and prepared to follow. He was a stoutish man, made stouter by his oilskin cape. There ought to have been something comical about the sight of him, in that weather, fitting on the cycle clips. But as the taxi moved off Frances turned and looked back, to see him, apparently unbothered by the rain, stepping on to the pedal and pushing forward. She turned again a few minutes later, and again a few minutes after that, and each time there he was, doggedly keeping pace with them, his eyes hidden by the peak of his helmet; not looking comical at all.

The journey at least was a short one, and took them back in the direction of home. Frances had been to the police station before—

once, she remembered, to report a cabman she had seen mistreating a horse, another time with her mother, on some charity business. This visit felt very different. They went in by a back entrance, pulling up in a cobbled yard, waiting for a minute while Sergeant Heath put his bicycle under cover, then letting him usher them into the soot-stained building through an unmarked door. After that they climbed a flight of stairs, made a turn or two, and she lost her bearings. Again the windows were of thick ribbed glass. Some had actual bars across them. The floors were stone, the walls were tiled: the surfaces threw back steps and voices in hard, institutional echoes.

But the room they were shown into—the matron's room—was unexpectedly comfortable. A fire was burning in the grate, and the floor had a square of carpet on it. The matron herself brought them a pot of tea and a plate of biscuits.

'Poor thing,' she said, of Lilian, as she put her to sit beside the fire. And then, to Frances, less familiarly, having heard her speak and caught her accent: 'You're looking after her, are you, madam? That's kind of you.' She poured them cups of sugary tea and left them alone.

Again, however, they were too frightened to risk speech. Footsteps went smartly past the door, and after that the corridor was still. But might someone be out there, listening? Could there be grilles in the wall, secret tubes and devices? Frances's heart was pounding; it had been pounding ever since Sergeant Heath had held out his hand at the mortuary.

They oughtn't to behave unnaturally, though. She offered Lilian her cup. 'You must drink this, Lilian. And you should eat these biscuits. You've had nothing, for hours and hours.'

But Lilian shook her head, looking queasy. 'I can't. I feel so dreadful. Almost worse than—' Startled by new footsteps, she looked over at the door; then went on in a whisper: 'Almost worse than I did last night. My insides feel like they're falling out of me! I just—I just want to go home.'

'Well, they won't need you for long, surely? They said you were under no obligation. Isn't that what the sergeant said? That you were under no obligation?'

'What are they going to ask me?'

'I don't know. Just try to stay calm.'

'He said they'd found something. Didn't he? He said they weren't satisfied. Why would he say that? Suppose—'

More footsteps in the corridor. Abruptly, they moved apart. And after that they didn't dare speak again.

Soon, anyhow, there was a knock at the door, and Sergeant Heath was back, bringing with him another man. This man was neat, un-uniformed, clean-shaven, slightly tubby, with the watch-chain and round steel spectacles of a senior bank clerk: seeing him come forward, Frances could only think, confusingly, that he was some colleague of Leonard's from the Pearl. Then he offered his hand, and introduced himself as Divisional Detective Inspector Kemp, and said that he was here to go over Mrs Barber's statement. And at that word 'detective', together with the realisation that he was a plain-clothes man, her confidence toppled and her heart seemed to pound right into her throat.

He said he would try not to keep Mrs Barber too long. Perhaps Miss Wray—she was the landlady, yes?—perhaps she would like to just step outside?

But Lilian caught hold of Frances again, in that terrified, terri-fying way. 'Mayn't Frances stay with me?'

'Well—' He thought about it. 'I don't see why not. If you've no objection, Miss Wray?'

Frances gave an awkward shake of her head and joined Lilian at the matron's table. The two of them sat on one side; the men sat on the other. Inspector Kemp looked through a sheaf of notes. How on earth had he got so many notes already?

To begin with, however, his questions were familiar ones; famil-iar, too, was that disconcerting delay while he made his careful, unemotional record of the answers. When had Mrs Barber last seen her husband? What had his movements been the day before? He had spent his evening, so far as she knew, with his friend Charles Wismuth? Could she confirm the spelling of Mr Wismuth's name? Could she confirm Mr Wismuth's address, and the address of his employer?

And what about Mrs Barber herself? How had she spent her evening?

There was the small, distinct sound of Lilian parting her dry lips. Well, she said, she had done nothing; a bit of reading, a bit of sewing. She'd gone to bed early, just after ten.

Did she often go to bed early?—No, she wouldn't say often. Just when she was tired.

She had been tired last night?—Yes. No, she couldn't think why.

And at what time had she been expecting her husband? Hadn't she missed him when he didn't appear?—Well, he was sometimes late. She'd fallen asleep, that was all. When she'd woken this morning and realised that he hadn't come home she'd supposed that he'd missed his tram and gone to Charlie's, or—She didn't know what she'd thought. She hadn't had time to think anything before the policeman came to the door.

She spoke earnestly; perhaps too earnestly. Her manner struck Frances as not at all convincing. But she had no idea what sort of an impression was being made on the men. They were not like Constable Hardy. Their faces were grave and unrevealing, and when they smiled, the smiles were professional, insincere, cold-eyed. Now and then she saw the inspector's gaze flick over Lilian as she spoke, and she thought she could see him taking in her pallor, and the touches of powder and lipstick. She thought she saw him gazing in a speculative way at the curves revealed by her crimson jersey.

And then, in an apparent change of direction, he asked about the events of that night in the summer when Leonard had been assaulted. When, exactly, had that been?

Frances felt Lilian hesitate. She knew the date; they both did. It was the night of their first embrace, and had had a talismanic significance for them ever since. At last she parted her dry lips again and said, 'The first of July.'

He tilted his head. 'You remember it well? A Saturday night, wasn't it? Were you with your husband when the assault took place?'

'No. I—I saw him just after. I'd been at my sister's birthday party. That's how I know the date.'

'Your husband hadn't gone to the party with you?'

'No.'

'How about Mr—' He consulted his notes. 'Wismuth? Was he there?'

She frowned. 'Charlie? No. He was with Len.'

'They were together that night, too?'

'There was a dinner. An assurance dinner. Charlie was there.'

'And what did your husband tell you about the assault, at the time?'

'He just said that somebody had hit him.'

'Did he know who the person was?'

'Just a man on the street, he said.'

'Do *you* have any idea who assaulted him?'

She looked at him. 'Me? No.'

'And did he describe the man to you?'

But Lilian had begun to tremble. She put her hand to her throat, looking ill, closing her eyes. 'I—I'm sorry.'

Frances touched her arm and spoke quietly to her. 'Take your time.'

'Yes, take your time, Mrs Barber.'

'It's just—I feel so giddy.'

'Perhaps you'd like a glass of water?'

She nodded. The sergeant fetched a jug and tumbler from the matron's desk. Frances kept her hand on Lilian's arm as she sipped, and spoke across the table.

'I don't think Mr Barber saw the man who hit him, Inspector. An ex-service man, he said; someone perhaps wanting money. He came here and reported the incident, a day or two later.'

The inspector regarded her levelly, then turned back to Lilian. 'Is that your understanding, Mrs Barber?' And then, when again she didn't answer: 'I am interested, you see, because I believe there might be a link between that other assault and this one.'

He left a pause after the words. Frances felt the muscle of Lilian's arm tighten under her hand. Her own heart began to rise again. She said, with an effort, 'You think, then, that this was an assault? Constable Hardy told us—'

'Constable Hardy hadn't had the benefit of our surgeon's preliminary report. I've just spoken to the mortuary by telephone, and I'm afraid there are one or two features that make the wound a suspicious one. In fact'—he put his hands together on the table and looked squarely at Lilian—'well, I'm sorry to have to tell you this, Mrs Barber, but it seems there's a very real possibility that your husband was murdered.'

Frances was horrified at the bluntness of the word, then horrified all over again to realise that he had said it in just that manner— deliberately, brutally—as a way of gauging Lilian's response to it.

Did Lilian realise it too? She gazed at the inspector, and her face crumpled.

'It wasn't like that!' she said—making Frances, in fright, grab at her hand. 'It can't have been! Don't say it! Oh!' She bent forward, her arms across her belly. 'I need the lavatory. Frances—!'

She got up, staggering a little. Frances supported her on one side, and Sergeant Heath came nimbly around the table to support her on the other. Inspector Kemp went to the door, put out his head and called for the matron; she appeared at once. 'I have her now,' she told Frances stoutly, once the two of them had got Lilian out into the passage. And, 'Yes, Miss Wray,' called the inspector, 'Matron Wrigley will look after Mrs Barber now.'

He gestured for Frances to return to the table. She hesitated, watching Lilian being led away. It was terrible, sickening, to see her being taken out of reach like that.

But the men's eyes were on her. She moved back into the room. The door was closed again by Sergeant Heath, and the inspector held out her chair.

'A nasty shock for Mrs Barber, all this,' he said, as she sat. 'And for you and your neighbours too, of course . . . A nice couple, were they?'

She was listening out for sounds from the corridor. 'Mr and Mrs Barber? Yes.'

'Good tenants, would you call them? They've lived in your house for—let's see, six months or so?'

'About that, yes.'

'You weren't acquainted with them before that?'

'No.'

'And what were relations between them like, in your opinion?'

She looked at him properly then. He was still on his feet, standing in a casual sort of way, a hip against the table, his arms folded high across his chest.

She said, 'All right, I think.'

'No disagreements? Quarrels? Things like that?'

'Well, I really couldn't say.'

'Did they often spend their evenings separately, as they did last night? I ask, you see, because in a case like this, where a respectable man is assaulted and killed—'

'You don't know that for sure, do you?'

'No, we don't know it for sure. I'm simply trying to get a sense of Mr Barber's character, his habits. It seems to me, Miss Wray, that you're in a position to help us a good deal. You must have seen more of the couple's comings and goings than most people. You haven't noticed anything? No one hanging about outside? No curious letters arriving at the house?'

She willed herself to speak coolly. 'I'm not in the habit of examining my lodgers' post.'

He gave one of his professional smiles. 'I'm sure you're not. But, still, there might have been things you saw, or heard . . . Yesterday, for example: was Mrs Barber at home all day?'

Frances pretended to consider. But she was losing touch with what she ought to know and not know. And her heart was still beating so horribly hard! She was afraid that he would see it—that he would hear it, even. Finally she nodded. 'Yes, all day and all evening.'

'And how did she pass the time, do you know?'

She remembered what she had told her mother. 'I think she was . . . spring cleaning.'

'Spring cleaning? Turning things out, drawers and boxes?'

Why had he seized on that? 'I don't know. Yes, I suppose so.'

'And the husband? He seemed quite himself to you, the last time you saw him?'

'Yes.'

'Would you say he was the type of man to make enemies?'

'Enemies? No, I wouldn't say that.'

'You remember the assault, back in July?'

'Yes, very well.'

'You were at home that night, while Mrs Barber was at her party?'

She couldn't bring herself to admit that she had been at the party too. She answered vaguely. 'I saw the injury directly it had happened.'

'You saw the actual injury? Bad, was it? Was a doctor called?'

'No, it wasn't as bad as all that. A bleeding nose, black eyes. A lot of blood on the kitchen floor, but—No, it wasn't so very bad. My mother and I sorted it out. Mr Barber came here, a day or two later, to report it.'

'He told you that, did he?'

'Yes, he told me on the Monday or the Tuesday. He said he'd spoken to a—a sergeant, I believe he said.'

The inspector grew thoughtful and confiding. 'Now, I wonder why he did that. No report was ever filed, you see, Miss Wray. We had complaints from one or two of your neighbours, but from Mr Barber himself—not a peep. Can you imagine why that might have been?'

Genuinely bewildered now, Frances gazed into his smooth, bank-manager's face; and couldn't answer.

And then she jumped, at the sounds of a commotion out in the corridor: it took her a moment to separate the noise from its own echoes and realise that it was made up mainly of women's voices, Lilian's among them. Sick with fear, she got to her feet; Sergeant Heath rose at the same time. She followed him out into the passage—and saw Lilian, a few yards along it, sagging almost to the floor, being supported by her mother and her sister Vera. They had just arrived at the police station, Matron Wrigley came to explain. Lilian had seen them, gone running to them, and fainted in their arms.

They got her back into the warm room, put her in the chair beside the fire. The matron stirred sal volatile into a glass of water and held it to her lips. She turned her head from the tumbler with a moan, then opened her eyes and looked in terror at the faces ringed around her. Then she burst into tears.

'There, there,' said Mrs Viney shakily. 'There, now.'

She had one of Lilian's hands in hers and was madly patting it. Her face had its stripped, lashless look. She stared around the room as if stupefied herself; then she recognised Frances, and the corners of her mouth and button eyes turned down like those of a tragedy mask.

'Oh, Miss Wray! Can you believe it?'

The matron began to try to move her back. 'Stand off, please. Right off. We must give Mrs Barber some air.'

Lilian gripped her mother's hand. 'Don't leave me, Mummy!'

'Leave you?' cried Mrs Viney. 'No, indeed I shan't!'

But her protests were cut across by a brisk knock at the door. A man entered the room—evidently the police doctor. He set his bag on the table and drew out a stethoscope. 'A little privacy, please?' he said, meeting no one's eye as he spoke. And then, a moment later, in a tired bark of impatience: 'Really, I can't be expected to make any sort of examination with the place full of women like this.'

The matron succeeded in chivvying Mrs Viney, Vera and Frances from the room. 'I shall be just out here, my darling!' Mrs Viney called to Lilian, as the door was closed. But they were not allowed to wait in the corridor, no matter how much fuss she raised. They were shown down a flight of stairs to a public waiting-area noisy with voices and footsteps—another grim lobby, with a dozen poor-looking people in it, who lifted their heads at their approach, broke off their conversations, to stare at them in open curiosity.

Mrs Viney, in response, seemed to expand into the stares. A youth in a torn jacket gave up his chair so that she might sit, and she sank on to it in a grateful, unembarrassed way, saying, 'Thank you, love. Thank you, son.' She took out her handkerchief and wiped her lips. 'Oh, my Lord. I can't hardly believe it. I can't *credit* it, Miss Wray! When the policeman stepped into the shop and I saw his face—well, it gave me such a turn. I made sure it was one of the grandchildren, burned in a fire or drowned. Then he said it was poor Lenny killed in an accident, and that we was to come here for Lil! Thank heavens you've been with her, anyhow. Oh, but don't she look shocking, though! I should hardly have known her, she looks that dragged! What's happened? Do *you* know? The police haven't told us nothing. Only a blow to the head, they said. Was it a motor-car done it, or what?'

Frances was conscious of the other people in the lobby. She had not said the words yet, to anyone. When she spoke, her mouth felt rubbery.

'They're saying that someone might have killed him.'

'*What?*'

And, 'What?' echoed Vera, her gaze sharpening. 'Killed him? Len?'

'Why would they say such a thing as that?'

'I don't know,' said Frances.

'But who are they saying done it, and why?'

'I don't know.'

Mrs Viney looked stricken. She wiped her mouth, wiped it again, then made a ball of her handkerchief and held it at her breast. Vera asked Frances what she knew. Where had Len been found? When had it happened? What time had the police come to the house?

'Oh, what a thing,' Mrs Viney said once, 'for you and your mother, Miss Wray!'

All the time that they were talking, they kept peering over at the stairs leading back to the matron's room. Policemen passed and re-passed, but no summons came. The muddle of echoing steps and voices went on without a pause. Frances grew increasingly uneasy—a dreadful, animal unease it was, at being separated from Lilian. She pictured her up there, frightened to death. What might she be doing? What might she be saying?

At last the matron reappeared. She darted forward to greet her—but it was Mrs Viney, of course, who was wanted. She stumped back upstairs as fast as her monstrous legs would carry her; when she returned to the lobby a few minutes later, her face was a tragedy mask again. Frances's heart gave another leap of fear at the sight of her—but she had already started on a noisy account of what had happened. Oh, wasn't it atrocious bad luck? Didn't it beggar belief? Poor Lil had been in the family way for the first time in years and the doctor was saying that the shock of Len's death had brought on a miss.

*

369

At least now, Frances thought, Lilian could admit to being ill. When they returned to the matron's room they found her looking pale but tearless, sipping another cup of tea. She met Frances's gaze just once, and after that kept her eyes lowered, but Frances could see that some of the panic had gone from her expression, and that made her own anxiety die down. Even Mrs Viney grew calmer. For here, of course, was something she could understand, a homely female crisis over which policemen and doctors, with all their non-sense, could have no sway. She held her hand to Lilian's forehead as she drank; she put back the hair from her white face. As soon as her teacup was empty she took it and handed it to the matron.

'Thank you for that, nurse. But I shall take my daughter home now. Vera, pass us Lil's hat and coat. Here you are, my darling, you just put your arms through here.'

The matron, alarmed, went off to fetch the inspector; he returned in time to find Mrs Viney doing up the buttons of Lilian's coat. With his face as smooth as ever, he said he was sorry to hear that Mrs Barber had fallen ill. Had they known about her condition, they of course would never have asked her to identify her husband's body.

'I shall speak to Constable Hardy about it, you may be sure,' he said. To which Mrs Viney answered hotly, 'Yes, I should think you will! A disgrace, I call it, asking a wife to do that! Police or no police, we'd be quite within our rights to bring an action against you!'

Lilian put a hand on her mother's arm. 'It's all right. It doesn't matter.'

'Doesn't matter?'

'I just want to go home.'

And, yes, said Inspector Kemp, Mrs Barber should certainly go home now and do all she could to recover her strength. Sergeant Heath would report to the coroner, and would advise him to hold over opening the inquest until Monday, by which point it was to be hoped that she would be well enough to give her evidence.

'As a matter of fact,' he told her, 'I shall be glad of the extra days. It'll give us more time to gather information. We'll keep you posted as to our progress, of course. You'll remain at home now?'

'Oh, she's coming back with us,' said Mrs Viney, before Lilian could respond. 'Don't you think that's the best thing, Ver? We'll take her to ours. She can go in with you and Violet, and—'

Lilian took in what her mother was saying. 'No,' she said. 'No, I don't want to go to the shop. I want to go back to Champion Hill.'

'Back there? It'll give you the horrors! You ain't in a fit state. Look at you!'

'I don't care. I just—' She glanced at Frances. 'I just want to go home, and have all my own things around me.'

And again the inspector agreed. Yes, it might be best if Mrs Barber stayed at her own address for now, in case he and his men 'should need to get hold of her in a hurry'.

Had the situation been different they could have walked up the hill in twenty minutes. As it was, Sergeant Heath led them back to the cobbled yard and the four of them piled into another taxi, Mrs Viney and Vera sitting with Lilian between them, each holding one of her hands, Frances looking on uselessly from the small seat opposite. The rain was falling as heavily as ever; it came down the gutters in a torrent. Champion Hill had one or two pedestrians on it, hurrying beneath umbrellas, but apart from that the street was quiet; Frances was glad of that, at any rate. As they pulled up before the house her mother's pinched face swam into view at the drawing-room window, and by the time they'd got across the front garden she had opened the door for them.

For an aimless few moments they all stood about in the hall. No, nobody could believe it. It was too horrible for words.

'It just ain't sunk in,' said Mrs Viney. 'Poor Lenny, as never harmed no one! I tell you this much, Mrs Wray, I hope they catch the devil that done it, and I hope to God they hang him! I hope

371

they hang him twice over! Once for what he did to Lenny, and a second time for what he's done to Lil!'

'All right, Mum,' said Vera. She had seen Lilian's expression.

'No, I *will* have my say!'

'Yes, I know. But you can have it upstairs, can't you?'

So, puffing, exclaiming, Mrs Viney made her slow way up, with Vera following, supporting Lilian for the climb. Frances helped as far as the turn; after that, Lilian's arm slid out of her hand like the rope of a boat tugged away on a current of water, and she could only stand and watch the three of them disappear across the landing.

'Frances?' Her mother was looking up at her with frightened eyes.

She went back down the stairs, trying to disguise the stiffness of her movements. She said quietly, 'Yes, the police are saying now that it might be murder.'

'Murder!'

'And Lilian—' She dropped her voice further. 'It seems she was pregnant. But in the shock of all this—'

'Oh, no.'

They went together into the drawing-room. She looked around. 'Where's Mrs Dawson?'

Her mother lowered herself like an invalid on to the sofa. 'Oh, I sent her home an hour ago. Another policeman came—'

'Another policeman?'

'Wanting to ask more questions. It was too dreadful, somehow, to have to answer in front of her. The men have been up and down the street, and all over the lane. One of them has been in the garden. I think he might be there still. Frances, it can't be murder—can it?'

Frances didn't reply. Instead she went quickly to the French windows, to see another mackintoshed constable, dark, bulky, anonymous: they were becoming objects of horror to her. This one had a measure in his hand and was making notes, as best he could in the rain, using his arm to shield his notebook. The door in the wall stood wide open. He must have been sketching a plan of the lane and how it related to the house. Had he spotted anything? Had she and Lilian left any traces of their journey with Leonard's body? But even if they had, wouldn't the endless rain have washed it all away?

She heard movement in the kitchen overhead, and thought of the stains on the sitting-room carpet, the greasy clinker in the pail.

But her mother was waiting. 'Frances? Come and sit down, will you? You've told me nothing. You've been gone for hours. Why were you away so long?'

Reluctantly, she left the window. She went to the chair beside the hearth. Again she had to disguise the soreness of her legs and arms as she sat. She kept at the front of the chair with her hands held out to the flames; she felt unnaturally cold, she realised. 'We've been at the police station.'

'The police station?'

'They drove us there from the mortuary. They wanted to go through Lilian's statement.'

'They took a statement from me. They said there'll have to be an inquest, that we might have to give evidence at it!'

'Yes, I know. What—What did you tell them?'

'Well, just exactly what I told Constable Hardy.'

'They didn't go upstairs?'

'No, they didn't go upstairs. But they asked some very odd things. All about Mr and Mrs Barber, whether there were ever arguments between them, or strange callers at the house. They seemed almost to be suggesting—Oh, it's too horrible.' She put her fingers to her temples. 'It was bad enough to think of poor Mr Barber falling over, hitting his head, then lying there helplessly in the dark. But the idea of someone setting on him, deliberately— Surely it *can't* be murder. It *can't* be. Do you believe it?'

373

Frances looked away. 'I don't know. Yes, perhaps.'

'But why? Who could have done it? And so close to the house! Just yards from our garden door! When you were in bed last night did you hear nothing?'

'No, nothing.'

'No cries, no——?'

'The rain. I heard the rain, that's all.'

Self-conscious, she moved forward, to scrape up a shovelful of coal from the scuttle and tip it on to the grate. But moving back, dusting her hands, she felt her mother's eyes still on her; and when she met her mother's gaze she was unnerved to see in it a touch of that oddness, that wariness, that had been there the night before.

With a jerk, she got to her feet. 'I think I'm too on edge to sit. We're all at our wits' end, aren't we? Have you eaten?'

It took her mother a moment to answer. 'No. No, I've no appetite.'

'Neither have I. But we must eat. What time is it?'

She looked at the clock, and saw with astonishment that it was nearly one. The morning had passed with the weird pacing—hectic, yet clogged with repetition and reversal—of a bad dream.

Going over to the sofa, she offered her hand.

'Come out to the kitchen with me, and keep me company. I'll make some sort of a lunch. Come on. You oughtn't to sit here fretting.'

Her heart was squirming as she spoke, but her voice was strong again. Her mother looked up at her, hesitating, still with a touch of that oddness about her; then she lowered her eyes, nodded, and let herself be helped from the sofa.

While they were in the kitchen, Vera came down in her hat and coat. Lilian, she said, had been put to bed with a hot water bottle. She had had a mouthful of bread and butter, more tea, and some Chlorodyne, and they hoped now that she would sleep; her mother was sitting in the bedroom with her. She herself was heading off to the post office to telephone to the rest of the family. No, there was nothing else they needed, though it was kind of Miss Wray to offer. She wasn't to trouble any more. They could look after Lil now.

She must have taken Lilian's key with her, because as Frances was clearing away the lunch things she heard her letting herself back in. And when, a half-hour later, there was a knock at the front door, she came clattering down again to answer, beating Frances to the hall. Netta and Lloyd had arrived. They'd brought along the baby, Siddy, and the youngest sister, Min. The women went straight upstairs without attempting to speak to the Wrays, but Lloyd came out to the kitchen to say how shocked they all were, and to ask if he could go down the garden: he wanted to take a look at the lane. Frances supposed she ought to go with him. She ought really to have gone already, to be sure that nothing was amiss. But the thought of doing it brought on a flicker of the terror she had felt at the mortuary. She got as far as the back step, then stood and watched, transfixed, as he picked his way along the wet garden path and peered from the doorway at the end of it. He came back shaking his wet head. It was just like something from on the films! The police had put ropes at the end of the lane to keep people from coming through. They had marked the place where Len's body had fallen, and set a constable to guard it.

He took the black oak armchair with him when he went upstairs; and after that the house became a stew of anxiety and unfamiliar voices, of impossibly creaking ceilings and frayed nerves. Frances's mother sat by the drawing-room fire; Frances fetched her a shawl, a book, a newspaper, a parish magazine. But the papers lay in her lap, unopened. Instead she gazed bleakly into the hearth, or closed her eyes with a troubled expression—or flinched, at some extra-heavy footstep overhead. Some time after four, Mr Lamb and Margaret called. A little later, Mrs Dawson returned; she was followed by Mrs Golding, from the house next door. Had Frances seen that policemen were still in the lane? Did she know that they'd been going up and down the street, poking about in gutters and gardens? Was it true what people were beginning to say? Could Mr Barber's death really be *murder*?

Frances told them all that, so far as she knew, the police were still undecided. They were waiting for the surgeon to examine the body. 'You didn't hear anything, last night?' she forced herself to ask Mrs Golding. But the woman shook her head. No, no one had heard a thing. That's what made it all the more strange and frightening . . .

By the time she had left, the endless twilight of the wet day was beginning to thicken, and Frances's mother looked ill with tiredness and strain. Frances, exhausted herself, drew the curtains at the front window and put a match to the gas, keeping the hall light low to discourage further visitors. When, at half-past five or so, the door-knocker sounded again, she groaned. 'I don't think I can face any more questions. Shall I leave it?'

Her mother had twitched at the sound. 'I don't know. It might be someone for the Barbers—' She corrected herself, unhappily. 'For Mrs Barber, I mean. Or it might be a policeman, Frances.'

A policeman! Yes, thought Frances with a sick sensation, it very well might be. She'd remembered what Inspector Kemp had said, about wanting Lilian to remain at home, in case he should need— that sinister phrase—to get hold of her in a hurry . . . The knock came again, and this time she went to answer it. She fought down her fear, saying to herself, Be calm, be ready.

But on opening the door she found not a policeman after all, but a drab middle-aged couple and a boy of about fourteen, their expressions a baffling combination of apology and anguish. As she stared at them, the husband took off his hat. She saw the gingerish cast to his hair, and the blood rushed to her cheeks.

They were Leonard's parents and his younger brother.

She would almost rather have faced the inspector. With an awkward gesture she moved back to let them in. They had heard the news, they told her, just an hour ago. They'd been away from home—over in Croydon, visiting Len's uncle and aunt. A policeman had come to them there and had brought them back in a car. They hadn't believed him at first. They'd supposed there'd been some sort of a mix-up. Then he'd told them that Lilian had identified the body. It was true, then, what he'd said? They were out of their minds with worry. They'd come to see Lilian herself. Was she here?

Frances led them upstairs, unable to think of a thing to say to them, and once she had handed them over to Netta and Lloyd she got away from them as quickly as she could. She re-joined her mother, and the two of them sat without speaking, uncomfortably conscious of the creaks overhead that meant that the visitors were being taken into Lilian's bedroom; a moment later there were murmurs, rising and breaking, perhaps dissolving into tears. Soon the sounds began to feel to Frances like pressure on a bruise. She stirred the fire. She got to her feet. If only her muscles would stop hurting! She went nervously back to the French windows to peer down the garden again. The door in the wall still stood open. Upstairs, the murmurs went on and on.

But when, forty minutes later, she heard the couple leave Lilian's room and join the boy on the landing, it suddenly seemed indecent to let them go away so soon. She nerved herself up, and as they came down she went out and invited them to spend a minute in the drawing-room. They sat on the sofa in a stunned sort of way, the husband with his hat in his lap, the wife hanging on to her handbag, as if they were desperate not to put the house to any more trouble. The boy, Hugh, embarrassed by his own grief, smiled and smiled.

Frances said, 'You've spoken to Lilian, then.'

Mr Barber nodded. 'Yes. You know, do you—?'

'It's very sad.'

'It's terrible. Terrible. We could hardly believe it, could we?' He appealed to his wife, who didn't reply. 'On top of the other thing— No, it's knocked us for six. It just doesn't make any sense to us. To have had him come safe through the War . . . And then, he's been getting on so well at the Pearl. We just wish we knew what happened. They're all up there talking about it as if it were a murder. But I said, Well, how can it be a murder? Len's always been so popular. The police didn't give much away, you see.'

'They didn't?' Guiltily, Frances found herself encouraging him to say more. But he clearly knew very little—hadn't yet heard, for example, that no robbery had taken place; it seemed to hearten him slightly when she told him that. Then he learned that she had accompanied Lilian to identify Leonard's body, and he looked at her with a bright, sad gleam of envy.

'You saw him too, did you? We wanted to see him, but the police said not to. The surgeon had only just finished his examination and they hadn't quite made him tidy. How was he looking, when you saw him?'

Frances thought back to that plasticine face. She said, 'Quite peaceful. Quite—Quite calm.'

'Was he? That's good. Yes, we wanted to see him, but they said best not to, today. They said we can have him at home, though, while the funeral's being arranged. We've spoken to Lilian about it, and we're going to take him. You and your mother won't have any of the bother of it, that way. We shan't take him tomorrow, it being a Sunday; we'll take him on Monday, and keep him at home. They've been very decent about it, the police. Yes, very decent. Of course—'

Here the boy gave a sort of squeal, making all of them jump: the grief had burst out of him; he hid his face in his sleeve. His father patted his twitching shoulder, but his mother spoke scoldingly. 'A great boy like you! What must the ladies be thinking?' He lifted his

378

head at last, and Frances was horrified to see that his smile was still in place, rigid and agonised, even as his face ran with tears.

Once she had closed the front door on them, she returned to the sofa and sat down with a thump. 'God, that was awful.'

Her mother was fishing for her handkerchief, looking iller than ever. 'I wish this day would be over, Frances. Those poor parents! To have lost their son—and in such a way!'

'Yes, I know.'

'And to have lost their grandchild, too.'

'Yes. It—It's too cruel.'

Her mother had the handkerchief at her mouth. Her head was bowed, her eyes were tearless but tightly closed, and Frances, recognising the posture, knew that she was thinking now not so much of Leonard but of her own lost sons and grandsons—was slipping away into some bleak interior place peopled only by ghosts, by absences.

The thought brought with it a wave of absolute loneliness, and she longed and longed for Lilian. Could she venture upstairs, just for five or ten minutes? Just to be sure that she was all right? But there was fresh activity up there now. The baby was crying. Water was running. The drawing-room lights gave a dip, as a kettle was put to heat on the stove. A barrier of fuss and motion still lay between the two of them—so that it dawned on her that, of course, this was how life was to be now, not just for a few chaotic hours but for days and days. The single emergency of Leonard's death, with which, last night, they had dealt together, had simply bred other emergencies, that were now certain to keep them apart.

The realisation made her shake. In an effort to calm herself, and to keep up some semblance of routine, she went out to the kitchen to put together some kind of supper; after staring blankly at the larder shelves she keyed open a tin of corned beef, put a couple of eggs on to boil. She and her mother queasily forced the small meal down. And then there was nothing to do but return to their chairs beside the fire to sit out the tatters of the day.

At nine o'clock there were footsteps on the stairs, followed by a tap at the drawing-room door. It was Netta and Lloyd, with Siddy asleep in his father's arms. They were heading home, they told Frances. They were taking Mrs Viney and Min back to Walworth on their way. Vera was staying to look after Lilian, who couldn't be persuaded to leave the house.

'We thought it best not to cross her,' Mrs Viney confided as she came down behind them. 'She's had a little sleep, and a little feed; she still looks like death, mind. But Vera'll keep an eye on her, and we'll see how she feels about it tomorrow. I should be easier with her near me, I do know that. And it ain't fair on you and your mother, all this upset in the house!'

'Please, please don't think that,' said Frances.

'No, Miss Wray, you've done enough! We wouldn't dream of asking any more of you. We shall get her to Walworth, don't you fear, by hook or by crook; and until we do, me or one of her sisters'll stop here with her.'

Frances couldn't answer. With a sense almost of despair she saw the family from the house, then made a start on the bedtime chores. Her mother was anxious that the windows be properly fastened; she had to go from one to another, making a display of checking the bolts. When she climbed the stairs at last, and found Lilian's bedroom door still shut, she paused, and considered tapping on it; only the thought of having to speak before Vera made her move on. But the sound of her step must have carried. As she crossed the landing she heard Lilian's voice, strained but clear—'There's Frances, isn't it? Go on!'—and a moment later the door was opened and Vera's sharp face appeared around it. Did Miss Wray mind? She wanted the lavatory. She ought to have gone while the others were here. She wouldn't be a minute, but didn't like to leave Lil on her own . . .

She took a lamp with her, and the room was left lighted only by a single shaded candle. Lilian was in the bed: she pushed herself up when she saw Frances, and they went into each other's arms, clinging breathily together until the steps had faded from the stairs.

'Oh, Frances, it's been so dreadful!'

Frances drew free, to look at her properly, to take her white face in her hands. 'Are you all right? I've been out of my mind! You aren't still bleeding?'

'Only a bit. It isn't that. It's just, they won't leave me, not for a minute. I just want you! They keep on at me to go to the shop. You don't want me to go, do you?'

'Of course I don't.'

'They said you'd rather it.'

'How could you think that?'

'I don't know. I don't know what to think. They gave me something to make me sleep, but it—it's left me muddled.'

They had given her Chlorodyne, Frances remembered. She turned her face to the candlelight and saw the glassiness of her gaze. The fear in her eyes, though, was as sharp as ever. She caught at Frances's hands and spoke in an urgent whisper. 'What do you think is happening, Frances? What they said—the police, I mean—They know, don't they? That Len didn't fall? That somebody hit him?'

Frances squeezed her fingers. 'They don't know that for certain. And they don't know *who* hit him.'

'But they're bound to work it out! They must be talking to other people. They must have spoken to Charlie by now. They'll know that Len wasn't with him last night. They'll start to put it all together. That Inspector—he'll figure it out, I know he will.'

'No. Why would he? They're just—just trying out ideas. *We* know what happened. We're the only people who do. Remember that. It makes us strong. But you've got to be careful, when you talk to them again. You've got to take care. We both have. Lilian? Do you understand me?'

Lilian's gaze had loosened. She was like Frances's mother now, looking not at Frances but into the depths of her own misery. But she blinked, and nodded. 'Yes. Yes, I'll be careful.'

'At least you got the doctor on your side.'

She started. 'The doctor? No, there mustn't be a doctor!'

'At the police station, Lily.'

Her gaze refocused properly. 'Oh, it feels like a lifetime ago! The matron saw that I was bleeding, so I had to say something about it. I pretended it had all come out in a rush, right there. I thought for a while they wouldn't believe me. The doctor kept saying how pale I was. But he must have believed me, mustn't he? Or they wouldn't have let me come home?'

'Yes, he must have believed you,' said Frances. 'Yes, I'm sure he did.'

She wasn't sure. How could she be? And the uncertainty had crept into her voice. Lilian's grip on her hands grew tighter, and for a moment that electric panic was back—or, anyhow, the possibility of it—Frances could feel it like a threat, ready to race between them.

But they were too worn out to sustain it. Lilian closed her swollen eyes, and her shoulders slumped. When she spoke again, her voice was small.

'It was so awful seeing Len's parents. They wanted to talk about the baby. They wanted to know why Len hadn't said anything. I had to pretend we were keeping it quiet, because of what happened last time. The way his mother looked at me, though. She hates me worse than ever now. She blames me for this. I knew she would. Oh, I wish I could sleep for a hundred years!'

She looked so ill that Frances almost feared to take hold of her again. But they couldn't be apart: they moved back into an embrace, their arms tight around each other—as if, she thought, by love, by passion, they could make everything all right.

'You won't leave me?' Lilian whispered.

'No! How could I?'

'I've been so afraid. If I could just have you with me, none of it would be so bad. If I could just——' But clear across her words there came the sound of the closing back door, and, 'There's Len!' she said, in alarm and excitement, twitching free in the old way.

For a second, Frances, aghast, could see that she believed it. Then she looked into Frances's face, realised what she had said, and her own face pulled tight. She covered her eyes. By the time Vera returned, she was crying.

Once Frances was in her own room, she didn't believe that she would sleep. There was so much to think about still. She was reluctant even to undress. Suppose Lilian should give something away? And then, there were the stains on the carpet, the ashtray tucked behind the sofa: oughtn't she to have another look at it all? Finally, wincing with pain and stiffness, she put on her nightgown, climbed into bed, and rolled herself a cigarette. She'd give it half an hour, she thought, and then go creeping into the sitting-room, just to be sure that everything was all right.

But even before she'd got the cigarette lit, she closed her eyes, leaned back into her pillow—and suddenly she found herself in an unfamiliar house with crumbling walls. How had she got there? She had no idea. She knew only that she had to keep the place from collapsing. But the task was like torture. The moment she got one wall upright, the next would start to tilt; soon she was rushing from room to room, propping up sagging ceilings, hauling back the slithering treads of tumbling staircases. On and on she went, through all the hours of the night; on and on, without pause, staving off one impossible catastrophe after another.

12

She awoke to more darkness. The rain had stopped—that was something—but a mist hung just beyond the window, like a dirty veil on the world. The Sunday bells rang as usual, but her mother, who had slept badly, didn't attempt to go to church, and since neither of them could face breakfast they simply sat at the kitchen table with a cooling pot of tea between them, too dazed for conversation, paralysed by the wrongness of things.

Presently they rose to go over to the drawing-room, and as they were crossing the hall Lilian came down to take a bath. She came a step at a time, leaning heavily on her sister's arm.

Frances darted forward to help. Her mother, hanging back, said, 'How are you feeling, Mrs Barber?'

She was still ghastly pale, though her gaze, to Frances's relief, was clearer. 'I feel so weak,' she answered.

'I'm sure you do. I'm glad you have someone here to look after you'—with the ghost of a smile for Vera. 'I meant to go to morning service. I should so like to have said a prayer for you there. But I couldn't quite manage it today. I shall say my prayers for you here instead.'

Lilian dipped her head. 'Thank you, Mrs Wray. I'm sorry everything's been so—so awful.'

'You mustn't think that. You must keep up your strength. And if there's anything at all that Frances or I can do to help you, you must tell us—will you?'

Lilian nodded, grateful, her eyes filming with tears.

But there was something, Frances thought, slightly strained about the encounter, an odd lack of warmth on her mother's part, despite the kindness of her words. And when the two of them had gone through to the drawing-room, her mother sat down and said in an almost querulous way, 'Mrs Barber looks dreadful! Surely it would make more sense for her to be with her family? Why on earth didn't her mother take her home with her last night?'

'She tried to take her,' said Frances, as she laid kindling in the grate. 'Lilian doesn't want to go.'

'Why not?'

'She wants to stay here.'

'But, why?'

She looked up. 'Well, why do you think? It's her home.'

Her mother didn't answer that. She sat with her hands in her lap, her papery fingers fidgeting.

The morning wore on in its off-kilter way. Frances waited for another chance to see Lilian alone, and found none. Outside, the mist thickened until it might have been pressing at the house. Indoors, she seemed to feel the drawing-room steadily filling with her mother's sighs. When, at around midday, she answered a knock at the front door and saw that Mrs Viney was back, with Netta, Min, baby Siddy and Vera's little girl, Violet, she felt genuinely pleased to see them. Violet had her doll's pram with her, and she helped her manoeuvre it into the hall.

But Mrs Viney came in puffing, her colour higher than ever. Had Miss Wray and her mother seen the *News of the World*? No? With a sort of grim pride she fished the paper out of a balding carpet bag on her arm, to show Frances a smudged half-column entitled MURDER AT CHAMPION HILL: CLERK'S MYSTERIOUS DEATH.

A frightful discovery was made early yesterday morning at Champion-hill, Camberwell. The body of Mr Leonard Barber, a resident of the good-class street, was found in a secluded spot where it had apparently been lying for many hours. Mr Barber, an insurance-clerk, had plainly received a most ghastly blow to the head. Policemen and a doctor were summoned at once, but life being found to be extinct the body was conveyed to the Camberwell mortuary. Mr Barber's widow, on being informed of her husband's death, is said to have plunged into a collapsed condition, with very pitiful results.

Frances felt sick. To see the case reported like that—unequivocally like that, as murder; to see the reference to Lilian; to see it all there, between another lurid headline, BOY'S ESCAPE, and cheap advertisements for winter woollies and a constipation cure—!

'"Insurance-clerk",' she said. 'How do they know so much already? And "pitiful results"! Where did they get that from?'

'Well, not from anyone in our family,' said Mrs Viney, 'that's for sure! There was a chap at the shop yesterday asking questions, my husband told me. He sent him off with a flea in his ear—and I shall do the same, if I see him! But word gets about, that's the trouble. People will talk; well, it's human nature. One thing I *am* pleased about: they mention the class of the street. As soon as I saw that I said to Min, "Well, thank heavens for that, if only for Miss Wray's and her mother's sake!"—didn't I, Min? Still,' she added, in a lower tone, 'I shan't show this to Lil. It wouldn't do her no good, would it? Have you seen her this morning, Miss Wray? Is she any better in herself? It's a terrible thing to lose your husband. I remember when her poor father died, I didn't know whether I was on my heels or on my head. I ran out into the street in my petticoat; a man crying brooms had to dash water in my face!'

As she spoke, she tucked the newspaper back into her bag, and Frances saw, in the bag's interior, open packets of black material, along with a jumble of black silk flowers, black threads, ribbons and dye. Yes, said Mrs Viney, noticing the direction of her gaze, they planned to make Lil some mourning costumes this afternoon. They'd gone right through her wardrobe yesterday and, would you believe it, with all those colours of hers she'd barely got a bit of black to her name.

Hearing movement overhead, she stumped forward. 'Are you there, my darling? It's only me and your sisters, love!' She began to haul herself up the stairs.

And so, once again, the house became a muddle of footsteps, creaking floorboards and raised voices. Drawers were opened in Lilian's bedroom. There were arguments in the little kitchen. Frances heard pans and kettles being filled, then set to heat on the stove; soon lids were rattling above simmering water, and the sour-ish, briny smell of the black dye began to creep downstairs. She recognised it with a shiver, for it was one of those scents, like the smell of khaki and of certain French cigarettes, forever to be associated with the worst days of the War.

But she couldn't bear to let all the activity keep her from Lilian; not again. She and her mother ate an unhappy, un-Sunday lunch, and her mother returned to the chair by the fire. But she herself went up and tapped shyly at the sitting-room door—just wanting to know, she said, if the family needed any help.

They had begun sewing already: they all had pools of black silk in their laps. The curtains at the windows were part-way shut—out of respect for Leonard, she supposed—but the lamps were lighted, coals were piled high in the grate, and the stains on the carpet were lost in the general clutter; the room retained its cosiness, in spite of everything that had happened. Vera was at one end of the sofa, a saucer of cigarette stubs by her arm. Min was beside her, sitting with her legs drawn up. Lilian was at the other end, closest to the fire. She was sewing like her sisters, but she let the work fall, and dropped her head against a cushion, to look over at Frances while Netta fetched a kitchen chair.

On Friday evening, Frances thought, she herself had sat where Min was now, holding on to Lilian's hand. Their future had felt real, close, palpable, just an inch or two beyond their outstretched fingers. Now, returning Lilian's gaze, she saw her tired dark eyes begin to brim with tears, as if exactly the same vision had occurred to her. They exchanged a tiny shake of the head, a shrug of hopeless regret. If only, if only, if only . . .

The little girl was at one of the windows, tracing patterns on the steamy glass. She turned to the room. 'There's a policeman coming!'

Frances looked at her. 'Coming to the house?'

She answered as if to a half-wit. '*No*, coming to the *moon*.' And while Vera got up, to smack her, Frances pushed past her and, wiping a pane, saw two men down on the pavement, just lifting the latch of the garden gate. She recognised Sergeant Heath at once. The other man wore an ordinary brown ulster, with a Homburg hiding his face. But as they crossed the front garden he tilted back his head—and then she saw his pink bank-manager's lips and chin, his steel glasses. It was Inspector Kemp. He spotted her at the window, and raised his hand.

She couldn't tell anything from their expressions when she let them in. And their tones, when they spoke, were as bland as ever. They apologised for disturbing her. They wanted a word with Mrs Barber, that was all. They were assuming she was at home?

She gestured them up the staircase, looked in on her mother, then followed them up to the sitting-room.

The bits of black sewing had been hastily tidied away. Lilian had shifted to the front of the sofa and was nervously smoothing down her hair. 'I hope you're feeling better?' the inspector asked her, once a few subdued greetings had been exchanged. 'I don't mean to keep you too long today. But if you can spare me a few minutes, I'd be grateful. I'd like to tell you about the progress we're making with the case.'

He sounded amiable enough. Again, however, Frances had the impression that his friendliness was all surface—or, worse than that, was somehow strategic, designed to put Lilian at her ease, the better, later, to trip her up. In the minute or two that it took to bring in another chair she saw him gazing around the room, clearly taking it all in. When Siddy awoke and began crying, and had to be bounced on Netta's knee, he stood in a patient way on the hearth-rug, looking politely at the objects on the mantelpiece: the elephants, the Buddha, the tambourine, the china caravan . . .

Siddy's howls subsided and the room settled down. Frances remained over by the door, on one of the kitchen chairs; Sergeant Heath had the other, between Netta and Mrs Viney. The inspector took the easy chair, across the hearth from Lilian. He sat at the front of it, still in his overcoat, his elbows on his parted knees, his hat dangling from his pudgy fingers.

'Well,' he said, addressing Lilian, 'I dare say you've seen the morning papers. I should like to have spoken to you before we made our statement to the press, but they caught us on the hop a bit last night; I must apologise for that. I'm afraid what they're saying is true. We've had our suspicions from the start, as you know. But there's no doubt whatever now that this is a case of murder.'

Frances's heart seemed to lose its footing. All this time, in spite of everything, she'd had a small, persistent hope that there would be too much uncertainty for the police to be able to commit themselves to the idea of the crime, to the *word*. Lilian must have felt the same: she closed her eyes, held herself tensely, as if unable to answer. Min, sitting beside her, gave her an awkward comforting pat. Netta drew Siddy closer. The little girl, cross-legged on the pouffe now, pinning scraps of black material together, sensed the stir and lifted her head.

Only the men were still—still and watchful, Frances thought. And partly to draw their attention from Lilian, who remained in that fixed, incapable pose, she cleared her throat and said, 'How can you be sure?'

The inspector looked across at her. 'Our medical examiner, Mr Palmer, has confirmed it.'

'Yes, but how?'

'Well, there are certain details. The nature of the injury, and so on . . . I don't wish to distress Mrs Barber by saying too much.'

But they had to hear, thought Frances. They had to know what the police had discovered. And, again, Lilian must have been thinking the same thing. She said, 'You might as well tell me. I'll have to hear it some time, won't I?'

So now he looked over at the little girl, in a meaningful sort of way. Vera said smoothly, 'Vi, take Siddy next door and show him Auntie Lily's perfume bottles, there's a good girl.'

Violet pulled a face. 'I don't want to.'

'You take him right now, or there'll be trouble! The sergeant's got his eye on you, look.'

With a glance at Sergeant Heath, half doubtful, half fearful, Violet slid from the pouffe, took Siddy from Netta's arms, and carried him gracelessly from the room.

'Well,' began the inspector, when the door had banged shut behind her, 'it's a matter of the different effect of different sorts of blows to the human head. A man taking a tumble, you see, and striking his head: that produces one quite distinct sort of wound. But a man being hit—let's say, by a hammer—well, that produces quite another. Mr Palmer was alerted right away by the appearance of the fracture, and by the direction in which the blood had run into Mr Barber's clothes. Once he'd made a full examination he found, from the bruising on Mr Barber's brain, that—Well, it put the matter quite beyond question.'

He kept his gaze on Lilian as he spoke. She had lowered her eyes, but her breast had begun to rise and fall. *She wants to look at me*, thought Frances, able to feel the tug of her fear, and growing fearful in response. She pleaded with her, silently, *Don't! Don't!* The look would give everything away!

But now Mrs Viney leaned forward. Fixing the inspector with a lashless eye, a touch of challenge in the creak of her stays, she said, '*How* it was done is one thing. Can you say *who* done it?'

After a second, he sat back. 'We can't, just yet. But we're confident that the killer will be found. You'll have seen our men, going up and down the street. We're putting things together, one piece at a time. There's not much evidence, unfortunately, from the actual scene of the crime. One or two interesting details on Mr Barber's overcoat, but aside from them, and a fingerprint—'

'A fingerprint?' echoed Frances.

He said, 'A print was discovered in among the blood on Mr Barber's shirt-front. It's more or less useless, I'm sorry to say. It was too long in the rain. It might have come from Mr Barber himself, or might have got there in some sort of a struggle. His clothes were pulled about, you see, and his hat was off before the blow came, suggesting to us that he grappled with his attacker before he died.'

Frances had been right about the clothes, then. But the fingerprint—that was almost as bad as the stuff about the brain. It must have got on to Leonard's shirt as she was tidying him in the dark. She felt suddenly conscious of her hands, had to fight down the urge to clench them, hide them away. Had she made any other blunders? What the hell were those 'interesting details' on Leonard's coat?

Again she felt the pull of Lilian's fear, and this time her own fear seemed to extend across the room to meet it. Risking a look at the sofa, she saw her with her head bowed and a hand in front of her face, her lips parted; Inspector Kemp had begun to talk about the interviews that he and Sergeant Heath had conducted the day before. They had spoken to several people at Pearl Assurance, he said, who had confirmed that Leonard had left work on Friday at the usual time. And they'd talked at length with Mr Wismuth—'who, naturally, was of particular interest to us, as being able to help us put together a sense of Mr Barber's movements just before his death.'

At the mention of Charlie's name, Lilian briefly closed her eyes. Frances knew that she was readying herself for what would come next. Chafing at her forehead with her fingertips, she looked up at the inspector and said in a thin, brave voice, 'What did Charlie tell you?'

He fished in a pocket. 'Oh, he was very useful to us—gave us a good sense of the various timings of the night. He last saw your husband—Let me see.' He brought out a notebook, located a page; and Frances, too, prepared herself for the revelation. 'Yes, he last saw Mr Barber at just after ten. They'd been drinking in the City together, going from one public house to another. He can't recall which one they ended up in—that's a pity, of course; we're sending officers to all the likely ones, to ask for witnesses—but he remembers very clearly saying good night to Mr Barber at the Blackfriars tram-stop just after closing-time. Now, assuming that Mr Barber had no trouble in catching his tram, and taking into account the length of the journey from Blackfriars to Camberwell, we calculate that he arrived back here at around a quarter to eleven. That would have been when you yourself, Mrs Barber, were already asleep in bed. That's what you told us yesterday?'

Lilian's head was still bowed, her hand was still in front of her face; she'd been staring at him through her fingers. Now she lowered the hand. 'Yes.'

'And Miss Wray and her mother,' he went on, with a nod to Frances, 'were also in bed at that time. Which is perhaps why Mr Barber went to the trouble of walking all the way round to the back lane? To avoid disturbing the house too much? Can you think of any other reason?'

Unable to answer, Lilian shook her head. 'Well,' he said, after a second, 'it's a great shame that he did, for he must have been killed more or less straight off. Mr Palmer says his body was lying in the lane for above eight hours. It's possible that he disturbed a burglar; that was one of our first ideas. But given that his pocket-book remained untouched we're ruling robbery out for the moment. Instead, we're working on the theory that he was pursued or lured into the lane by a person or persons unknown, who either set on him with the intention of killing him, or hit out at him as the result of some altercation. The blow was a vicious one, we do know that, and struck from behind, by a right-handed assailant, someone not over-tall. Death must have been almost instant: the bleeding seems to have stopped very nearly before he hit the ground. The instrument was blunt—a pipe or a mallet, I'd say. We've been looking in gardens and storm-drains for it, without success so far. But we'll turn it up, you mark my words; and it'll lead us straight to our man.'

He said all this to Lilian, with occasional glances around the room to draw in and impress the rest of them, and Lilian returned his gaze as he spoke, as if mesmerised. But once he was silent she changed her pose, looking over at Frances as she shifted, and there was a flash of something between them—part apprehension, part bafflement. For why on earth, thought Frances, would Charlie Wismuth have said that he had been with Leonard until past ten? At ten o'clock Leonard was already dead, already out in the lane. At ten o'clock she was cutting up the grisly yellow cushion. Leonard had told Lilian—

393

hadn't he?—that Charlie had had to leave early; that they'd only had time for a couple of beers. But why would Charlie lie?

Again it was Mrs Viney who spoke first. 'Poor Lenny! He didn't deserve that, did he? Not to be hit from behind like that. No, nobody deserves that. And he wasn't a quarrelling man! That's what I don't understand. Why would he have *gone* into the lane with a blackguard like that?'

'He didn't go in there with him,' said Vera, in a brittle, patient way. 'The inspector says that somebody must have followed him.'

'Followed him?'

'Gone in after him, quietly.'

Mrs Viney looked outraged. 'Oh, now that's a dirty trick!'

Inspector Kemp said again that that was one of their theories, at any rate. And he repeated his claim about the pipe or the mallet: that they were sure to turn it up, and then the case would be halfway solved.

'A professional killer, you see,' he said, 'or a man used to violence: he knows how to dispose of a weapon. He has pals he can pass it on to. But we're not looking for a professional killer. We think our fellow's more steady than that. Someone with regular habits—'

'Regular habits?' cried Mrs Viney. 'When he goes about murdering people in the dark? I thought it was some old soldier you was after. Wasn't it some old soldier who set on Lenny that other time?'

'Well, of course,' said the inspector, 'there was only Mr Barber's own word about that. He might well have been mistaken. The fact that no robbery took place, either that time or this—'

'The man might have meant to do a robbery,' said Vera, 'and got the wind up.'

'Or he might,' put in Netta, 'have heard a noise—seen someone coming—'

'Yes, it's possible,' the inspector answered, in the polite, patient tone he must, thought Frances, keep in reserve for thriller-

394

enthusiasts. 'But——' He tapped his fingers on the brim of his hat. 'I don't know. There's just something about this case. When you've been in the police force for as long as Sergeant Heath and I have, you develop a "nose". And just now my nose is telling me that this wasn't a cold-blooded act; that it was the work of a person with a grudge, or a score to settle, or some reason for wanting to get Mr Barber out of his way. And a person like that, with a used weapon in hand—his first thought is to get rid of it. His second thought is to get home as quick as he can. That works to our advantage, too. He has nowhere to hide, you see. He has neighbours, he has family, people seeing him come and go. Some of them might protect him for a time. He might have a wife, a girl, a lady-friend, someone who thinks it her romantic duty to keep quiet about what she knows. But she won't think that for long, if she's got any sense about her. She'll come forward sooner or later—the sooner the better, of course, from the point of view of her own safety.'

Again he made gestures to Mrs Viney, to the sisters and to Frances as he spoke. But it was unmistakably Lilian to whom he was addressing himself, and now, leaning forward, he fixed his gaze on hers.

'I'm afraid your thoughts weren't quite in order yesterday, Mrs Barber. Nobody could have expected otherwise, in the circumstances. But you've had time, since then, to turn things over in your mind, and I have to ask you what I asked you once before, in case some new piece of information should have occurred to you. Do you have any idea who might have killed your husband?'

Lilian stared at him in that mesmerised way, but shook her head: 'No.'

He pressed her. 'No idea at all?'

She turned away. 'No! None of it makes any sense to me. It's like a horrible dream, that's all.'

He sat back, it seemed to Frances, as if not quite satisfied with what he'd heard, but with an air of patience, of calculation, of being prepared to accept it for now . . . Or perhaps she was imagining things. How much could he know? How far could he guess? He had being speaking confidently, even complacently; but his account of the case had been a muddle of fact and fantasy, sometimes approaching the heart of the matter, more often veering wildly away from it. As for all his talk about the man, the grudge, the score to settle—

She suddenly absorbed the implication of his words, and for the first time in days she felt a lifting of anxiety, like a drop in the pressure in her brain. She and Lilian had failed to pass off Leonard's death as an accident: all right. But wasn't this the next best thing? The inspector could search for his man for ever. He couldn't catch someone who didn't exist . . .

She came out of her own thoughts, to find him talking about the inquest. It was to be opened tomorrow morning at the coroner's court, but would be a relatively brief affair, he said, with the case having turned into a murder inquiry; he would request an adjournment from the coroner, Mr Samson. But they would still appreciate it if Mrs Barber would attend—'and you and your mother, too, Miss Wray, I'm afraid'—in case Mr Samson wished to interview them. He was sorry to say that they must be prepared for a certain amount of newspaper interest in Mr Barber's death, and he hoped that that wouldn't prove troublesome. Mrs Barber must be sure to let him or Sergeant Heath or one of his constables know if any reporters made a nuisance of themselves.

'Now that you're feeling a little better,' he said to her, rising from the easy chair, 'I'd just like to run over your statement with you, and clear up a few other points we're still unsure about. I'd also like your permission to look through your husband's things—the pockets of his clothes, for example; any personal papers or boxes.'

He waited. Lilian looked up at him. 'You want to do all that now?'

'We'd be very grateful. Perhaps there's another room we might go to, to save troubling your family? Oh, and there's one other matter,' he added as, uncertainly, she got to her feet. 'Rather an intimate one; I'm sorry. But I think I might have mentioned Mr Barber's overcoat? It's been with the analysts at Scotland Yard, and they've found a number of hairs on it, not all of them from Mr Barber's own head. I dare say the strays became attached just in the general way of things, but since there seems to have been a tussle before your husband died it's possible that one or two of them came from the head of his attacker. It would help our inquiry if we could rule out the ones that must have got on to the coat while it was here in the house. Could I ask you to provide me with a sample of hairs from your own head? Just half a dozen from a comb or a hairbrush will do.' Then, unexpectedly, he looked across at Frances. 'Could I ask the same thing of you, Miss Wray? The hairs in question are all brown or black, so we needn't trouble your mother, I think.'

She couldn't answer for a moment. The question had called up a shock of memories in her muscles and her skin: the digging of Leonard's fingers into her armpit, the push and weight of his body as the two of them staggered across the carpet—this carpet, right here, with the stains of his blood still on it. She blushed, and felt her face blaze where his cheek had rasped against hers. 'Yes, of course,' she said. She put down her head and left the room. But then she stood at her chest of drawers with the hairbrush trembling in her hand. She didn't want to do it. They couldn't make her, could they? She had to force herself to tug free the hairs from the tangle caught in the bristles. And when, out on the landing, she handed the hairs to Sergeant Heath, he had an envelope waiting for them, with her name already on it; and that made her tremble again.

Back in the sitting-room, the women looked at her, impressed.

'Scotland Yard!' said Mrs Viney. 'Would you ever have believed it, Miss Wray! Isn't it wonderful how they can put it all together?

397

But just fancy them going through Lenny's bits and pieces like that. Murder or no murder, I shouldn't want them poking about in my husband's things—should you, Netta?' She cocked her head. Lilian had taken the men into her bedroom and was murmuring with them there. 'Still, they've got to do it, I suppose, if it helps their investigations. Oh, but didn't it turn you right over, hearing all that talk about poor Lenny's brains!'

The little girl had returned, in a cloud of eau-de-Cologne. Dumping a wriggling Siddy into his mother's lap, she said, 'What did they say about Uncle Lenny's brains?'

Mrs Viney pulled a sad face. 'They said there was a great big bruise on them.'

'How do they know?'

'The doctors saw it.'

'How did they see it?'

'Well—'

Vera was reaching for her cigarettes. 'They cut his head open, didn't they?'

Min squealed. Netta protested. The little girl looked appalled and delighted. 'Did they, Mum? Did they, Nanny?'

'Of course they never did!' said Mrs Viney.

'How did they do it, then?'

'Oh, well . . . The doctor's got a special light, I expect, and he shone it in Uncle Lenny's ear.'

Hearing that, Violet got hold of a crayon lipstick from her mother's bag and, calling it the doctor's light, she started to go from person to person saying she had to put it in their ears so that she could look at their brains. Frances obliged, tilting her head, tucking back her hair. But she did it distractedly, her eye on Vera. For, having offered her cigarettes, Vera had risen from the sofa to carry the saucer of stubs to the hearth and throw its contents on to the coals; but instead of returning to her place she had set the saucer on the mantelpiece and was looking around, in search of something. Frances, her heart beginning to thud, watched her go to the easy chair and glance over the back of it; she watched her wander across the room, to look in the shadows beneath the table. After that, there was only one more place for her to try. She went to the sofa, peered behind it, and—oh, Christ, here it came. She reached a muscular braceleted arm into the gap between the sofa and the wall, brought out the stand-ashtray and, with a grunt of satisfaction, set it squarely down on the rug.

Frances stared at the thing with eyes that, for a moment, seemed unable to close. There was a scorch-mark on the base of it, from where she had held it to the coals. And just an inch from where it stood on the carpet she could see, now, one of the stains. Again she felt the grip of Leonard's fingers, the burn of his cheek. The violence, the horror—it was all still here, in this cosy room. Couldn't anyone else feel it?

But Netta, Min and Mrs Viney were fussing with the baby, Vera was thumbing a flame from a ladies' lighter, and no one gave the ashtray a glance—no one save the little girl, who capered around it, the lipstick held between her fingers in a flapperish way. She hadn't got a doctor's light now, she announced, she'd got a cigarette; no she hadn't, she'd got a cigar. And for the next few minutes she made elaborate play of puffing on the end of the crayon, then tapping it into the bronze-effect bowl.

When Lilian and the men emerged from the bedroom, Lilian stood in the doorway, saw the ashtray, and the last remaining bit of blood in her face seemed to drain out of it. She looked so dreadful that her mother gave a cry at the sight of her, and Inspector Kemp said, Yes, he was sorry to have kept Mrs Barber so long. 'But,' with a lift of his eyebrows at Sergeant Heath, 'we've everything we need for now, I think?'

Frances saw the sergeant nod. He was tucking a bundle of things into his pocket: letters and papers, perhaps a railway ticket . . . She was too far off to be sure. The inspector stepped forward to retrieve his hat. Passing Violet at the ashtray, he gave her a genial tap on the head. 'Having a smoke like the ladies, are you? What have you got there, a Player's?'

'It's a De Reszke,' she answered, in her withering way.

'Oh! It is, is it?'

Chuckling, he and the sergeant made their way out to the landing. When Frances rose to escort them, they waved her back. They could see themselves out, they assured her. They had put her to too much trouble already . . .

As their steps faded on the staircase, she looked at Lilian. 'Are you all right?'

Lilian nodded, her head lowered. 'Yes. Yes, I'm all right. They just asked the same things, all over again. I—I need the WC, though. I've been needing it all this time. Where are my shoes?'

Her mother found them, and held them out. 'But don't go down there on your own! Not with murderers all over the place! Have someone go with you. Ver—'

'I'm all right,' said Lilian. She sounded fretful. 'Just let me be.'

'Let you be?'

Frances moved forward. 'I'll go down with Lilian, Mrs Viney.'

'Oh, Miss Wray, are you sure? You've been so good.'

And, 'Yes,' said Lilian, 'let Frances take me down. She's the only one who doesn't fuss me. I can't stand it! Let Frances take me.'

The sharpness of her tone set Siddy off crying. She put a hand to her forehead, then caught hold of Frances's arm; they left the sisters seeing to the baby, and went in silence down the stairs.

Once they were in the kitchen with the door shut she sank into a chair, making a pillow of her arms on the table and letting her head fall forward.

Frances, alarmed, sat beside her. 'What's happened? What is it?'

She shook her head without raising it, and answered in a murmur. 'Nothing.'

'What did the inspector ask you, really?'

'He asked all sorts of things. All about me and Len. Where we go, what we do, who our friends are—things like that. But something's not right, Frances. He kept asking me about *Charlie*. You heard what he said Charlie told him, about Friday night?'

Frances nodded. 'Why would Charlie say that?'

She hid her face again. 'I don't know.'

'To lie like that. It doesn't make sense, unless—well, unless he has something to hide. Something he's keeping from Betty? Do you think he's been seeing another girl? It must be that, mustn't it?' And then, when Lilian didn't answer: 'God! It's more of a muddle than ever. And what did the sergeant take away?'

'I'm not sure. It was all Len's stuff. Oh, it was dreadful, having to go through his things like that. And what they said about his— his brain. It was almost worse, wasn't it, than seeing it?' She looked over at the door. Her pose, with the twist in it, added an extra layer of strain and urgency to her voice. 'What did they say about the wound? That it was vicious? How could they say that? They don't know. They weren't there! They're turning it into something else!'

Frances caught hold of her hand. 'But that's what we want, isn't it? It doesn't matter what they turn it into, so long as they don't think of us. It doesn't matter about Charlie. It might even help us, because of the timing. If they think he died at eleven—well, my mother was here then. She knows that you and I were in bed.'

'But they've taken those hairs.'

'The hairs don't prove a thing.'

'And they must have seen the ashtray! Oh, Frances!'

Frances squeezed her fingers. 'But they're not looking for an ashtray. They're looking for a pipe, or a mallet. They're looking for a *man*. Don't you see what it means? *It means we've done it.* The whole horrible business—it means it was worth it. It means it worked.'

Lilian was gazing bleakly at her, but began to take in what she was saying.

'Do you think so? Truly?'

'I think so, for now. We still have to be careful, but—I think so, for now.'

Some of the strain left Lilian's expression. But when she spoke again, it was with dreadful weariness. 'I almost don't care any more. I care for your sake, but not for mine. I care for our sake, I mean. For the sake of everything we planned. But—'

'That's all still there.'

'Last night I kept dreaming about Len. I kept waking, and putting out my hand, and Vera was there, and I thought it was him, and—' She gave a shudder, and couldn't finish.

After a long moment of silence, she pushed herself to her feet. 'I'd better not take too long or they'll think I've fainted or something. I really do need the lavatory. There's still blood. It's still sore. Will you—Will you come outside with me?'

She asked it as if embarrassed. And once the door was opened she hesitated on the step. She must have been thinking, as Frances was, of the trips they'd made out here on Friday: the agonised hobble to the WC and then, a few hours later, the darkness, the haste, the strain and terror . . . She went quickly across the yard, then let Frances hurry her back out of the cold. In the kitchen they hugged each other, and Frances felt her quiver like a string.

But soon she eased herself away. 'I'll go back up on my own. It might look funny if they see us together too much.'

Frances kept hold of her hands. She felt, weirdly, almost elated. 'I don't want to let you go!'

'I don't want it either. But sometimes it's worse being with you in front of them than not seeing you at all. Don't you feel that?'

'No. I can't bear to be apart from you.'

'It puts me on edge. They're still on at me to go to the shop with them. Maybe I should, Frances.'

'What? No, you mustn't!'

'They don't understand why I want to stay here. I can't say it's because of you . . . Oh, if only we could just be together, alone! I feel like we never will be again. There's the inquest, and then the funeral; and how will it be after that?'

'Don't think about all that yet. I love you. I love you! Think about that.'

She came back into Frances's arms. 'Oh, I love you too.'

But her features were doughy with tiredness again, and she didn't cling to Frances as she had clung to her the night before. Even that quiver had gone out of her now. Once more she eased herself free, to spend a moment putting herself tidy. She let Frances support her to the bottom of the stairs, then dragged herself up them alone.

This time it was Mrs Viney who stayed the night, while the sisters and the children went home. She was less noticing than Vera, but more of a presence in the house, clattering about, sweeping and tidying, letting out bursts of sentimental song in a music-hall quaver. When Frances went up at half-past nine she found her in the little kitchen, already undressed for bed, her hennaed hair loose about her shoulders, an inch-wide strip of grey at the parting; from beneath the hem of her nightdress her stockingless ankles stuck out like two great pegs. She was happy to linger and chat, however, as she heated the water for Lilian's hot bottle, regaling Frances with stories of other family catastrophes. Hard confinements there'd been plenty of, sudden deaths, maulings, scaldings. A Midlands cousin had got her scalp torn off by a loom . . . But they'd never had a murder, she concluded with a sigh, screwing in the rubber stopper. No, there'd never been a murder in the family; never till now.

Frances was almost sorry to say good night to her. Her own mood was still unnaturally buoyant. She lay in bed open-eyed, going over and over the inspector's visit, her mind running like an engine in too high a gear.

Even next morning the feeling persisted. She was up at half-past six, had washed and dressed by seven, determined to be ready for anything the day might spring on her. To the goggling boys who brought the bread and the meat she spoke in a terse, unencouraging way. When *The Times* arrived she went through it looking for a mention of the case, and found only a brief, brief report; Leonard's name was misspelled as 'Bamber'. The paper was full of events in Turkey and Greece. There was an account of a massacre at Smyrna. It was the sort of bad news from which, ordinarily, she turned in despair. Now she seized on it as real, important—nothing like the patchwork of blunder and police supposition that had become this phantom thing, this imaginary murder, on Champion Hill.

But at nine Vera returned, to help prepare Lilian for the inquest. The five of them set off an hour later; and after that her spirits lost some of their buoyancy. The day was gusty and chill. Their journey was the one that she and Lilian had taken to view Leonard's body, but this time they were travelling on foot: they must have made an odd-looking group, processing down the road at Mrs Viney's clumping pace. Shoppers paused to stare at them; they were stared at again in the mean little residential streets beyond the Green. And as they approached the coroner's court they discovered that a crowd had gathered, people who had heard about the case and, attracted by the horror and glamour of murder, had come simply to gawp. Unnerved, they pushed their way through them. But then there was the confusion of arrival at the building itself; there were newspaper men, starting forward with questions, all calling Lilian's name. When Frances caught sight of Inspector Kemp, she felt a rush of pure relief; he was bizarrely like an ally here. He took them along a corridor into a crowded panelled chamber. She saw faces that she recognised: Constable Hardy, Leonard's father, Charlie Wismuth and Betty. There was more uncertainty for a minute or two—over where to sit, this time. Finally a clerk led Lilian to a lonely place beside the coroner's chair while Frances and her mother remained with Mrs Viney and Vera, beside a man who introduced himself as Leonard's superior at the Pearl.

The whole thing, she decided, was like a nightmarish wedding, with Lilian the unhappy bride, Leonard the eternally jilting bridegroom, and none of the guests wanting to be there or quite knowing what to do. Even the coroner, Mr Samson, looked a little vicar-like, in a chinless, wet-lipped sort of way. He settled himself fussily in his special chair, and the jurymen were brought in. Inspector Kemp rose to give a statement of events, the police surgeon spoke briefly about the suspicious nature of the injury, but the only other witness called was Lilian. It was agonising to have to watch from a distance as she got to her feet, her face as pale as ivory, her figure made small by the trumpery panelling of the room. She was asked to state her name and her relationship with the deceased, and to confirm that she had made the identification of the body. She spoke almost inaudibly, her gloved hand put out to a table at her side to steady herself. Her dark velvet hat had been borrowed from Vera. The open collar of her coat gave a glimpse of sooty-looking crochet: her frock was the plum-coloured one, Frances realised, dyed black.

The coroner declared the inquest adjourned, pending the results of the police inquiry, and they found themselves dismissed. Again it was oddly like a wedding: the abrupt release from ceremony, the confusion about what was coming next. But this time they were all thrown together in the narrow corridor. The man from the Pearl approached Lilian to tell her how stunned they all were at the office. Leonard's father came to exchange a few words with Frances and her mother. 'To think of people like us being mixed up in something like this!' he said, mopping his forehead.

And there too, of course, was Charlie. He gave Lilian a clumsy hug. 'How are you bearing up?' Frances heard him ask her.

Lilian shook her head. 'I can't think how I am, Charlie. It doesn't feel real, any of it. When I saw you sitting in there, before, I couldn't believe that Len wasn't going to walk in and join you.'

'I thought the same,' he said, 'when I saw you. It just—It just beggars belief.'

Betty took hold of his arm. 'The police won't leave him alone, you know. They saw him on Saturday, and yesterday too.'

He blushed. 'I just wish I had something to tell them! They say this fellow might have followed Len all the way home from Blackfriars. That he'd been watching him all evening. But if that's true—well, I didn't see him. Honest to God, I wish I had! When I think of Len going off like that—when I think of us shaking hands at the tram-stop, saying, Good night, see you next week—'

His voice thickened, with real emotion. But Frances, who knew that he was lying, though she still had no idea why, could see the falseness of his manner; she could see it in the tug in the muscles of his face. And it struck her that, of course, they needed his lie now. They needed it almost as much as their own. The same thought must have occurred to Lilian: Frances saw her pose slip as his did, her expression grow forced.

But then someone produced newspapers, the *Daily Express* and the *Daily Mirror*. The crush in the corridor grew more awkward as people drew together to look. The papers were not like *The Times*, Frances saw with a chill. They'd both made room on their front pages for the CHAMPION HILL MURDER, and while the *Express* offered only a blurry artist's impression of 'The Lonely Spot At Which The Body Was Found', the *Mirror* included two good-quality photographs. One showed policemen on the street, picking their way through the gutters: 'The Search for the Weapon'. The other, more startling, was of Leonard himself—a younger Leonard, uniformed, some studio portrait from the War.

When Lilian caught sight of this she gave a cry, and Frances and Vera moved close to her, to read the paper over her shoulder. The report had a quote from the man who had found Leonard's body, and another from Inspector Kemp. It mentioned Lilian by name: she was said to be still in that 'collapsed condition'. But it was the photograph of Leonard that seemed to bother her the most. She didn't understand. Who had let the paper have it?

Leonard's father looked slightly shifty. Well, he said, a man from the *Mirror* had been round at Cheveney Avenue yesterday. 'We didn't see any harm in it, Lilian.'

'*You* gave it?'

'Len's Uncle Ted did. We didn't feel easy about letting a picture go. But Ted ran home and fetched his album, and we picked out the best. It might help the investigation, the *Mirror* fellow said. It might prick a conscience or two, to show what a fine boy Len was.'

Lilian wouldn't answer him. She stared at the photograph for another few seconds, then pushed it away from her as though the sight of it made her sick.

Outside, the crowd seemed bigger than before, and a man with a camera was darting about. There was no chance to say an ordinary goodbye to Leonard's father, to Charlie or Betty; Frances and her mother became separated from them as soon as they left the steps. The gusty weather made everything worse. Hats and coats were flapping. Then two reporters approached Frances, having discovered—how? she wondered—her connection with the case. Could she and her mother say what their feelings had been, on learning of Mr Barber's murder? Could they spare a few moments for the readers of the *News of the World*?

'No, we can't,' she said, turning her back on them.

Her mother's hand had tightened on her arm. 'This is frightful, Frances. Let's get home, can we? As quickly as we can.'

'Yes, of course. I'm just looking for Lilian. Wasn't she behind us when we came out?'

'I don't know. Does it matter? We've done enough for her, surely?'

'We can't go without her.'

'Her family can see to her now.'

But there she was, just emerging from the building with her mother and sister, seeing the man with the camera and nervously putting down her head. She moved forward into the crowd, then lifted her gaze and looked around. 'Where's Frances?' she asked Vera; Frances saw the words rather than heard them. She raised her hand, and after another moment or two of blind searching, Lilian's gaze caught on hers. They picked their way to each other through the stares and the jostles.

'All these people!' said Lilian. 'What do they want?'

Frances took hold of her arm. 'Come quickly. This way.'

But she pulled back. 'Frances, wait.'

Her mother and sister had caught up with her. Mrs Viney, brick-red, was glaring furiously at the faces turned their way.

'A lot of vultures, I call 'em! Ain't they got no sense of decency? Ain't they got no notion of shame? You and your mother get going, Miss Wray, or they'll have the skin off your backs! We'll go by the quiet way back to the shop. Lil's coming with us. We managed to talk her round at last.'

Frances looked at Lilian. 'You're—You're going, then?'

Lilian's expression was wretched. 'It seems the best thing, after all. Vera and my mum can't keep coming to the house. It isn't fair on them. It isn't fair on your mother, either. I'll stay just for a few days. Till after the funeral.' She saw Frances's face. 'It isn't so long, Frances.'

'You don't have any of your things.'

'Vera says she'll fetch them tomorrow. I can borrow hers till then.'

'I could bring them to you. Say we need to talk, or—?'

'I don't know. But Vera will get them. I won't need much.'

There seemed a thousand things to be said, but no chance to say anything with so many people about—with Mrs Viney and Vera right there, and Frances's mother looking on tensely from the crowded pavement. Even Inspector Kemp had appeared and was

408

watching them now. So Frances nodded, that was all. They reached and patted at each other—patted, she thought, so clumsily, that they might have had paws rather than hands, or been wearing boxing-gloves. And then they parted. Lilian turned, to catch hold of her sister's arm. Frances re-joined her mother; they headed back to Camberwell.

13

For the remainder of that day, and for the two or three days that followed, though Frances and her mother were regularly bothered by reporters, there was no further sign of police activity on the streets around Champion Hill—no more going through the gutters, no more knocking on residents' doors. The cinder lane was re-opened: Frances screwed up her courage and went down the garden to look at it. But there was nothing to be seen. She couldn't even with any certainty pick out the spot where she and Lilian had dropped Leonard's body. That part of the affair had been so densely dark, so urgent and improbable, that it had begun to seem like something from a dream—just like one of those violent acts she'd sometimes committed in her dreams, then marvelled at on waking.

On Tuesday morning Vera came, to put together a suitcase of Lilian's things. Frances went up to the bedroom with her, desperate to make the most of the link with Walworth; wanting to know, or to gauge, how Lilian was coping. Vera said that she was feeling stronger, was eating and sleeping better. Inspector Kemp had called to see her again the previous night—

'He saw her again?' asked Frances. 'What did he want?'

Vera didn't know. Just more questions like the others. Anyhow, he hadn't stayed long. But some press men had called too, and they had been more of a nuisance. Had Miss Wray read today's papers? They were full of the murder; it was awful. Lil had taken one look at them and burst into tears.

Frances had seen only that morning's *Times*—which, she'd thought, was unsettling enough, the original inaccurate mention expanded now into an account of the opening and adjourning of the inquest and Lilian's 'trembling' attendance at it. So when Vera left she went with her as far as the news-stand on the hill; she bought every paper she could afford, the *Mirror*, the *Mail*, the *Sketch*, the *Express*, the local papers too. Lilian's image, she saw, unnerved, was on all the pictorials—she tucked the bundle under her arm, feeling squeamish about looking at them there on the street. She didn't want her mother to see them, either. Once she was back at the house she took them straight up to her bedroom and spread them out on the floor.

She recalled the man with the camera. The pictures showed Lilian leaving the inquest, leaning on her sister's arm, nervously lowering her head. They were grainy and unsubtle—mere approximations, really—but, all the same, they had captured something of Lilian, they had got the life and solidity of her, and it was incredible, dizzying, mad! to think of the masses of people who, just that morning, must have studied her face over their breakfast eggs and on their trains and buses; who must be gazing at it right now. The *Daily Mirror* carried a second picture. Perhaps it had been lent, along with that portrait of Leonard, by helpful Uncle Ted. It showed Lilian and Leonard in what might have been someone's back garden. Leonard had an arm around Lilian's waist, her hip was tight against his; they looked like any young couple of the clerk class, smiling into their future in Hammersmith or Forest Hill. The caption read, 'Mr and Mrs Barber, before the tragedy'.

The tone was the same in the other papers. There was no suggestion anywhere that the marriage had been anything other than happy. There was nothing but sympathy for Lilian, the 'pitiful young widow', the 'pathetic wife'. The accounts of the inquest stressed her bravery, her emotion and her looks; there were careful, approving descriptions of her costume. The murder was condemned as the work of a brute who would soon be apprehended, and the police were said to be 'pursuing several lines of inquiry', one of which was that theory, already reported by Charlie, that Leonard's killer might have marked him out in the City and followed him home. Inspector Kemp was inviting members of the public to come forward if they'd noticed any suspicious behaviour on the streets of Blackfriars or Champion Hill on the fatal night.

Going from article to article, from picture to picture, Frances felt as if something that had, until now, been secure in her hand had dropped, had shattered, had burst into a thousand flying pieces. Then again—well, wasn't it all just what she and Lilian could have hoped for? Charlie's lie, whatever was behind it, had been enough to give the police their pointer; it didn't matter which direction they went in now, so long as it took them away from the house. And for how long would the case attract this sort of interest? Another day or two? A week, at most? Soon, surely, it would become clear that the lines of inquiry were so many dead-ends— that Inspector Kemp, for all his confidence, had failed to deliver his man—and the newspapers would look elsewhere. Some more sensational story would be bound to come along. It's just a question, she told herself, of doggedly sitting it out . . . But she looked again at those grainy front-page phantoms, more unsettled than ever to think of all the strangers' gazes to which they had been exposed. Finally she tore the pictures free, screwed them into a ball, took them down to the kitchen, and stuffed them into the stove.

Then neighbours began to call. They had bought the papers too—or had been shown them, they claimed, by their cooks and parlourmaids—and wanted to discuss the latest developments. Mrs Dawson had heard that Mrs Barber had suffered some sort of seizure at the inquest—was that true? The elder Miss Desborough, from the house next door, understood that a *second* murder had now been committed, but that the police were keeping the matter quiet for some reason of their own. Mr Lamb and Margaret, on the other hand, had been told on good authority that the police were poised to make an arrest. No, there was absolutely no doubt about it. The man was local—a shop-keeper or trader. He had taken against Mr Barber because of an unpaid bill.

And next came Mrs Playfair. She had just that moment returned from Sussex, having cut short her holiday on the Wrays' behalf.

'I simply can't believe it!' she said, as Frances let her into the house.

Frances answered thinly. 'Yes, everyone's saying that.'

'I opened *The Times* and actually yelled. You look ill, Frances.'

'I'm worn out, that's all. The last few days have seemed endless.'

'Oh, why wasn't I here! I could have done so much. But, tell me, how's your mother?'

For answer, Frances led the way into the drawing-room. Her mother had heard Mrs Playfair's voice; now, at the sight of her, she seemed close to tears. Mrs Playfair stepped quickly to her and took hold of her hands.

'What an ordeal, Emily! You look worse even than Frances. I don't wonder at it. We thought all our horrors were behind us, didn't we?'

Frances's mother nodded, unable to speak. But as she wiped her eyes and put away her handkerchief some of the tension went out of her.

'It's such a great relief to see you, Jane.'

'You ought to have telegraphed to me at once.'

'I've hardly known what I've been doing. Frances has taken care of most of it, but—I don't know. It isn't like an ordinary death or an illness at all.'

413

Mrs Playfair sat down and began to tug off her gloves. 'Well, I want to hear everything that's happened, every little last thing.'

Frances sat down too. The prospect of going through it all over again made her feel boneless with exhaustion. At the same time, she realised that here was an opportunity to tell the story of the murder as the police had begun to construct it—to fix it more firmly in her mind. So, with her mother now and then putting in some detail of her own, she gave a careful, thorough account of the events of the past few days, beginning with Constable Hardy's arrival at the house on Saturday morning, and finishing with the inquest. Mrs Playfair looked shocked, appalled—but also, unmistakably, excited. As soon as she'd heard Frances out she narrowed her eyes.

'Now, who's the coroner at the moment? Is it still Edward Samson? I know him a little. He used to be friendly with George. I might pay him a call, do some digging. What do you think?'

'Oh, I wish you would,' said Frances's mother. 'If he knows anything at all that the police aren't saying, I'd so like to hear it. It's the senselessness of the thing that I find so horrible. The blindness, the waste. Poor, *poor* Mr Barber. He was such a cheerful young man, so very full of life. Can you really believe, as Inspector Kemp seems to think, that someone set out, purposely, to kill him? Someone with some sort of grudge against him?'

'Well, no,' Mrs Playfair answered, 'I'm not sure I do believe it. There seems no evidence, for one thing. The attacker was clearly one of these louts one sees hanging about on the street corners! I wonder the inspector doesn't simply round them all up and question them one by one. That's what I would do.'

She went on like this, laying down certainty after certainty—and sounding oddly, in her confidence, like the inspector himself, so that Frances, listening to her, began to feel a return of the mild elation she had felt on Sunday while listening to him. For, the street-corner lout, the man with the grudge: whoever the culprit was meant to be, what did it matter? So long, she thought again, as no one was thinking of Lilian and her. So long as no one was imagining that they had ever made that journey down the stairs and over the garden with Leonard's body . . . She remembered leaving him in the darkness. She remembered closing the door on him. And then another thought came—came like a whisper behind the hand. *He's gone.* Lilian was free now. If they could just hang on to their courage, just until everything died down . . .

She chased the thought away. But the touch of elation remained. She put back her head, and closed her eyes, while Mrs Playfair laid her plans.

After tea that day, however, Mrs Playfair returned; and this time she looked uncharacteristically subdued. Yes, she said, she had spoken to Mr Samson. He had been quite willing to talk in confidence about the case. She had also had two or three conversations with her parlourmaid, Patty.

'With Patty?' repeated Frances.

'Patty's sister's girl, over at Brixton, is engaged to be married. The boy's a constable in the police, and he's let one or two things slip.'

Frances couldn't believe it. 'You sound like Mr Lamb! According to him, Leonard was killed by a disgruntled local grocer. Mother and I will be next on the list, at that rate.'

'Frances,' protested her mother tiredly.

'Well,' Mrs Playfair went on, 'this boy's meant to be the horse's mouth. Patty speaks very highly of him. And the fact is, both he and Mr Samson—' She paused, strangely awkward. 'It caught me quite by surprise, I can tell you. But they both gave me more or less the same impression. They both hinted pretty plainly that—well, that there's something not quite right about the case.'

Frances looked at her. 'What do you mean, "not quite right"?'

Mrs Playfair paused again. She seemed to be carefully choosing her words. 'Well, for one thing, Mr Barber is supposed to have spent Friday evening with his friend, Mr—What's his name?'

'Wismuth.'

'Mr Wismuth, yes. They're supposed to have gone from one public house to another, getting drunk as lords on the way. But the police have been to every public house in the City, showing photographs of the two men, and no publican or barmaid has any recollection of them. What's more, the police surgeon, Mr Palmer, tested Mr Barber's body for alcohol when he carried out his postmortem. He found very little trace of it, apparently—less than the equivalent of half a glass of beer. Looks odd, don't you think?'

It took Frances a moment to answer. 'Well, it sounds to me as though Mr Wismuth was the drunker, that's all.'

'Yes, perhaps,' said Mrs Playfair. 'But here's the queerest part. It seems now that a man and a girl have come forward to say that they heard some sort of disturbance in the lane on Friday night, and—'

Frances felt the words as an almost physical shock. She began to blush—a horrible feeling, nothing at all like simple embarrassment, more a scalding of her cheeks, as if she'd had boiling water flung at them. Mrs Playfair, seeing her reaction and misunderstanding it, said, 'Yes, isn't it a ghastly thought? The girl's in service at one of the houses further down the hill. She'd slipped out without the family's knowledge—a naughty girl, obviously—but still, it's enough to give one nightmares. She didn't *see* anything, I believe; evidently it was too dark for that, and she was too far off—down where the Hillyards' wall juts out. But she and the man both say they heard footsteps and sighs. The man made light of it at the time, said it must be another pair of sweethearts. Then, of course, when they heard about the murder . . . It took them until last night to make up their minds to talk to the police. The girl was frightened for her place; the man didn't want to come forward on his own for fear of making himself a suspect. But the point is, you see—the point *is*, it was quite early in the evening when they were out in the lane—not later than half-past nine. Well, according to Mr Wismuth, he and Mr Barber were still in the City then.'

The blood was roaring through Frances's ears. To think that when she and Lilian had gone staggering out into the darkness— that when she was going over Leonard's body, trying to pull his clothes straight—to think that all that time, less than fifty yards away, there had been this couple, this sinister spooning couple—

'They must be mistaken,' she said, trying to will the heat and colour from her face. 'Whatever they heard—probably it *was* another couple. I've seen couples in the lane myself, countless times. Or else they imagined the whole thing—or are telling stories, for the thrill of it.'

'It's certainly possible,' said Mrs Playfair, with a doubtful air. 'But the police seem to be taking them seriously all the same. They've kept the detail out of the papers for now. And they're—well, they're keeping a close eye on Mr Wismuth, I can tell you that.'

Now Frances couldn't answer. Miss Desborough had spoken yesterday of things being kept out of the papers, and she hadn't believed it. But if the police really were doing devious things like that, if they were plotting and watchful like that—And if they really suspected Charlie—!

Her mother had begun to fidget about in her chair. 'Oh, but this is awful. Surely no one's imagining that Mr Wismuth had anything to do with Mr Barber's death? Mr Wismuth, who's always so pleasant? The two of them were such great friends. Didn't they go through the War together? No, I can't believe it.'

'Well,' said Mrs Playfair, '*someone* killed Mr Barber. And you have to allow, it does look very much as though Mr Wismuth has something to conceal.'

'But why would he do such a thing?'

'What did the inspector tell Frances? That the murderer might have wanted to get Mr Barber out of his way?'

'Yes, but why?'

'Well, I hate to play drawing-room detective, but—' Again Mrs Playfair seemed to be carefully choosing her words. 'Just think about it for a moment. On the one hand you have Mr Wismuth, spending a great deal of his time with Mr Barber and his wife. On the other—well, there's the wife herself. My dear, she's an awfully attractive woman, of a very particular sort. Haven't you told me, more than once, that the couple didn't get along?'

Frances felt rather than saw her mother's horrified gaze. She couldn't bring herself to return it. Was this what the police were thinking? Had they been thinking it all along? She began to recall moments from her interviews with Inspector Kemp, odd questions that he had asked, about Lilian, about Charlie . . .

She turned to Mrs Playfair. 'Did you mention that to Mr Samson or to Patty? About Lilian and Leonard not getting along?'

Her tone made Mrs Playfair blink. 'I—I don't recall.'

She sat still for a second, then got to her feet. 'Oh, this is nonsense. This is rubbish! What is it exactly that Lilian's supposed to have done? She was here all Friday night with me.'

Mrs Playfair gazed up at her, startled. 'No one's accusing Mrs Barber of anything. I dare say she's innocent of the whole affair.'

'Oh, you dare say?'

'Yes—yes, I do. But isn't it possible that Mr Wismuth has been harbouring some passion—? I know that Mrs Barber is a sort of friend of yours, Frances. But, well, let's not be unworldly. Men don't kill each other for no reason.'

'Don't they? It seems to me that men do that all the time. We've just come out of a war in which they did nothing else! Eric and Noel and John Arthur—what were they killed for, but for nonsense, for lies! And who protested against that? Not you and my mother! And now a single man has lost his life and everyone's leaping to these ludicrous conclusions—'

Mrs Playfair looked amazed. 'Good heavens, Frances!'

'This isn't an Edgar Wallace story. If we've to listen to police-men's swank, to servants' gossip—!'

She was shaking, and couldn't go on. Her mother said, 'Frances, please, sit down.' But she felt that if she sat she would only have to spring back up again. She stepped closer to the hearth, put out a steadying hand to the mantelpiece.

After an uncomfortable silence Mrs Playfair gave a bird-like twitch of her chin and shoulder.

'Well, naturally I understand that you're upset. This is a des-perate thing for everyone concerned. But, as you say, a man's life has been lost; that didn't happen by itself. I don't see what the War has to do with it at all.—No, that isn't true.' Her tone had sharp-ened. 'I see exactly what the War has to do with it, and so, I imagine, does your mother. The War took all our best men. It isn't consid-ered correct to say so, but I shall say it anyhow. The War took all our best men, and with them went everything that's decent and lawful and—' She leaned forward in her chair. 'A *murder*, Frances! *On Champion Hill!* Would that have happened ten years ago?'

Again, Frances couldn't answer. She stood with her hand at the mantelpiece still, not wanting to surrender the feel of the cool hard marble shelf. Looking into the mirror above it she met her own reflection and thought, Calm down! For God's sake! You're giving too much away!

Then her gaze shifted and refocused and, through the glass, she caught her mother's eye. Her mother was watching her with a look of unhappy embarrassment, but there was something else in her face—Frances was almost certain—that oddness, that doubt, that fear—

Abruptly, she turned away from it, saying, 'Forgive me, Mrs Playfair.' She left the fireplace, crossed to the window, stood gazing out at the street.

But they were all rattled now. After a minute or two of subdued chat between Mrs Playfair and her mother she heard sounds of movement, and, turning back to the room, found them both on their feet. Mrs Playfair was shrugging on her coat, fastening the chain of her fox collar. But, 'Don't trouble,' she said quietly, when Frances moved forward to walk her to the door. 'I shall see myself out. Really, I'm sorry I came, if it was only to upset you.'

Once she had gone, Frances returned to the sofa. Her mother remained standing, looking down at her as if she hardly recognised her.

'How could you talk to Mrs Playfair like that about the War?'

'Mrs Playfair knows what I think about the War. She called me a traitor to my country once, don't you remember?'

'I don't know what's the matter with you. I don't know what's the matter with anything any more. If your father could have foreseen—'

'Oh,' said Frances, in her automatic way, 'Father foresaw nothing. That was his great talent.'

'Yes,' said her mother, with surprising bitterness, 'and yours is—' She struggled, and didn't finish.

Frances looked at her. 'Mine is what?'

But her mother turned her head and wouldn't answer.

Frances waited, then gave it up. She tapped her thumb against her lips. 'The idea of the police being out there thinking all this, "keeping their eye on" Charlie. The idea of people saying these things about Lilian! It's grotesque!' She got to her feet. 'I'll have to go and see her. I'll have to warn her.'

Her mother's head jerked back. 'No, Frances. Let it alone.'

'Let it alone? How can I do that?'

'Aren't we involved enough? The police must know their own business.'

'The police don't know anything.'

'What do you mean?'

Frances took a step away from the sofa. 'I don't mean anything. I just—'

There was a *rat-tat-tat* at the front door, that made her jump as if she'd been hit. 'Christ!' she said, incautiously. 'What now?' She hesitated, her heart thumping. But it was less suspenseful, she had discovered, simply to go out and answer than to stand there dithering. If it was a newspaper man she would close the door in his face.

It wasn't a newspaper man, it was a trim little military figure— a messenger boy, who handed over a telegram, addressed to her.

Her first idea was that something must have happened to Lilian. Lilian had broken down, told everything. Lilian was ill. Lilian was dead. She held the envelope without opening it, thinking, in a bleak, braced way, Is this it, then? Is this the moment when everything falls apart?

Finally she ungummed the flap, drew out and unfolded the salmon-coloured sheet.

> SAW NEWS AGHAST
> PLEASE CONFIRM ALL WELL
> WAITING C.

The words made no sense, until she saw the Clipstone Street stamp.

She became aware that her mother had followed her out to the hall and was anxiously watching. 'What is it? Who's written? Not more bad news?' She came and took the paper from Frances's hand, and frowned. 'But who's the sender? I don't understand. Is it your cousin, Caroline?'

Frances opened her mouth to answer, groping for one of the old untruths. But the lie seemed such a weary one suddenly. Weary, and trifling; almost quaint. She said, instead, 'It's from Christina.'

Her mother actually looked blank for a moment. Then her features tightened. '*Her.*' She handed the telegram back. 'Why on earth is she writing to you?'

'She saw the case in the papers, she says.'

'But how did she connect it with you? Have our names appeared now?'

'She must have recognised the Barbers'.'

'But—'

'I've spoken about them to her.'

Frances saw her mother absorbing that, felt the further rapid chilling of her manner.

'You've seen each other, then.'

'A few times, this year, on my trips into Town. She lives near Oxford Street with a friend . . . I thought you might have guessed it.'

Her mother's face twisted. 'No, of course I didn't! Why should I ever have thought of it?'

'I don't know. I wasn't thinking, I suppose.'

'It never occurred to me that you would be so untruthful. After giving me your word that you wouldn't see her!'

Frances was astonished. 'I never gave you my word.'

'As good as, then.'

'No, not even so much as that. We never spoke about it. You never wanted to know. And it's down to me, isn't it, whether I see my friends or not? Oh, what does it matter, after all!'

'Well, evidently it does matter, since you've been going about it in this sneaking sort of way.'

'Because I knew you'd react like this!'

Her mother's tone grew even tighter. 'I don't wish to discuss it any further. You know my opinion of that young woman. Go ahead and see her, if you must. I don't like your friendship with her, I don't understand it, I don't respect it; I never shall. But what I like and respect even less is your deceit. On top of everything that's happened! I don't know what to expect next! I feel I hardly know you at the moment. What else have you lied to me about?'

There was nothing sinister to the question, Frances was almost sure. But it caught her off guard, and again she felt herself colour, in that scalding, incriminating way . . . And suddenly it might have been Friday night again, she might have just come down the stairs with Leonard's body in her arms. She felt it all, more vivid than in ordinary memory or even in dream: the tearing weight of him, the bulk of his padded head against her shoulder, even the clownish pressure of his bowler hat. Her heart had begun racing like an engine with no connection to the rest of her. She went to one of her father's chairs, leaned heavily against the back of it. And when, a moment later, she looked up, her mother was staring at her— and there it was, that fear, that suspicion, showing again in her expression.

She returned the telegram to its envelope, doing it badly, stuffing it in. 'Please don't let's quarrel,' she said, with an effort. 'Whatever you're thinking about Christina, about—about anything, it isn't like that. It isn't worth it. Come back into the warm, will you?' And she made to step past her mother to the drawing-room.

But with an odd, darting movement her mother caught hold of her arm. 'Frances.' She had the air of someone who must speak quickly or not at all. 'Frances, the night that Mr Barber died, I came home with Mr Lamb, and you—you didn't seem yourself. Tell me truthfully, had something happened?'

Frances tried to draw her arm away. 'No.'

Her mother kept hold of her. 'With Mrs Barber, I mean. There hadn't been some sort of a quarrel between her and Mr Barber?'

'No. How could there have been? Leonard wasn't even here. We never saw him.'

'She hasn't confided anything to you? Nothing about Mr Wismuth, or any other man? There's nothing you're keeping from the police?'

'No.'

'I want to believe you, Frances. But all your life you've had these—these queer enthusiasms. If I were to think, even for an instant, that that woman had involved you—'

'There's nothing, Mother.'

'Do you promise me? Do you swear it? On your honour?'

Frances wouldn't answer that. For a moment they pulled against each other, both of them frightened as much by the oddness and tension of their pose as by anything that had or hadn't been admitted.

Then Frances gave a twist to her wrist and her arm came free; and in the process her mother was tugged off balance and nearly stumbled. With Frances's help she righted herself, but then she quickly moved away. They stood breathless, face to face on the black-and-white tiles.

Frances said again, in a steadying way, 'There's nothing. All right? Look, come back to the drawing-room.' She held out her hand.

But her mother wouldn't come. Her manner had changed, grown guarded. Still breathless, she answered, 'No. I—I shan't. My head is hurting. I think I'll lie down for an hour or so.'

And without meeting Frances's gaze, but keeping a wary eye on her, almost as if she were afraid of her, she crossed the hall to her bedroom and softly closed its door.

Suddenly weak at the knees, Frances tottered back to the stiff black chair. The thoughts, as she sat, came in a panicky rush. What ought she to do? Her mother knew. Her mother had guessed! Or at any rate, she had guessed a part of it. But how long before she worked out more? How long before the whole thing knitted itself together, like one of her wretched acrostics? And if *she* could see the design of it, then how soon would Inspector Kemp and Sergeant Heath, and Patty's niece's boy, and Mr Samson the coroner—how soon would they—how soon—

She couldn't frame the words to herself. She pressed her hands to her eyes. More than anything else, she wanted to see Lilian. But how would it look to her mother if she went dashing off to Walworth? And suppose something should happen while she was away from the house? Suppose Sergeant Heath should arrive, wanting to put together another of his mysterious bundles? Suppose he should speak to her mother while her mother was like this? She simply couldn't risk it. She felt an uneasiness—a terror—at the prospect of leaving things so unguarded.

She could write to Lilian, of course! That thought made her twitch into life. She went upstairs to her bedroom, got out paper, pen, ink, started to put down, in a hasty, intimate way, everything that Mrs Playfair had told her. And she had actually filled three-quarters of a page before she was struck by the recklessness of what she was doing. *You need to be extra careful, Lily. Don't for God's sake do or say anything that might give the police the impression*—What was she thinking? In horror she screwed the letter up, took it over to the empty grate and held the flame of a match to it. The bare idea that she had come so close to doing something so incriminating made her begin to doubt everything she had done so far. She'd supposed herself in control of the whole affair. She didn't have a clue! Her own mother suspected her of having some part in a murder! All the confidence of the previous day was shattered. She rolled a cigarette, doing it so ineptly that half the tobacco fell to the floor. She smoked it at the window, peering out at the garden, the door in the wall—wondering how on earth she'd ever thought any of it could work.

But she resolved, at least, to answer Christina's telegram. When the cigarette was finished, and as quickly as she could, she put on her outdoor things and, saying nothing to her mother, she went down the hill to the post office at Camberwell Green. OH CHRISSY SO GRIM BUT JUST COPING SEE SOON PROMISE LOVE. The girl at the counter looked at her as though she thought her slightly mad. Perhaps I *have* gone mad, she said to herself. Leaving the building she stood gazing towards Walworth, utterly unable to decide whether or not to press on to Mr Viney's shop. The desire to see

425

Lilian was like a craving, like the craving she imagined came after the taking of a drug. But she thought of the reception she'd be bound to get, the surprise and commotion of it. Would there even be anywhere for the two of them to be alone together? And what did she have to tell Lilian, in any case? It was Charlie who was most in danger. Lilian might say that they ought to warn him; but they couldn't do that without giving themselves away. Wouldn't she simply make Lilian more frightened, more likely to let something slip?

And even in the twenty or so minutes that she had been away from the house she had started to worry about what might be happening there in her absence. She turned her back on Walworth and hurried up the hill, with every step growing more convinced that she would find the place swarming with policemen.

The house was just as she had left it. Her mother was still in her room: she didn't emerge until after seven, when Frances tapped meekly at her door to say that dinner was ready. They passed a strained evening together, Mrs Wray keeping to her chair with a blanket over her knees, and answering any remark of Frances's with a vagueness, a doubt, a delay . . . Frances lay wide awake in bed that night, knowing that her mother was downstairs lying wide awake too; thinking of the tick, tick of her mother's mind as it pieced things together.

But nothing was said the following morning. Her mother was pale, calm, distant. Frances went out as soon as she could for the early papers, fully expecting to see some change in the reporting of the case; there was no mention anywhere, however, of the spooning couple. The police were pressing on with their manhunt and had evidently widened their search: they were said to be interviewing people as far away as Dulwich. But Charlie's name did not appear in any of the columns, and, realising that, she began to recover some of her confidence. How strong, after all, was the case against him? It was all speculation, surely? There was no evidence to support it. And even if the police were to go so far as to arrest him—well, she thought determinedly, arresting someone wasn't the same as charging them. He'd simply have to come clean, then, about what he'd been up to on Friday night. If he was at some brothel or drug-den, or whatever the hell he'd been doing, he'd surely sooner admit that than be charged with his best friend's murder. As for the timings of it all—it couldn't matter what time Leonard was killed. There was still absolutely nothing to suggest that he had been killed in the house; nothing to link his death with Lilian or with her.

After a silent lunch, her mother announced quietly that she was going out for an hour or two. Frances looked at her, and felt herself whiten: she imagined that she had made up her mind to speak to the police. But it was some charity business, her mother said as she put on her coat; a set of minutes that had to be delivered to one of her committees. No, Frances was kind to offer, but she was happy to take them herself. She wanted to call in to church—her eyelids fluttered as she spoke—she wanted to call in to church on her way home.

Perhaps, then, she planned to confide not in the police but in the vicar. Frances watched her go with a feeling of doom. Suppose Mr Garnish were to talk? She had to think it through, be ready.

But she had the house to herself: that was an unexpected gift. This was the first time since Leonard's death that she had been alone in it. She had to make the most of the next two hours. She ought to look for signs, for evidence.

She felt better as soon as she'd started. Upstairs in the sitting-room, the blood-stains were as visible as ever, but the carpet, she saw now, had other marks on it, streaks of dirt and spots of ink, something that might have been a splash of tea: there was no reason for the eye to travel to one stain over another. It was the same with the ashtray. The scorch on the base meant nothing. And though she could hide it away, get it out of the house—wouldn't that simply draw attention to it? It was less incriminating to leave it right where it was . . . The hearth was brimming over with a new mess, from Sunday's fires—that was good—but the ash-pail was still there, with those scraps of gingham and lumps of clinker in it, the latter looking like the sort of greasy black nuggets one might find at the bottom of a roasting-dish. But those, at least, she could take care of. She carefully carried the pail downstairs, put on an apron and galoshes, then picked her way down the muddy garden to the ash-heap. She didn't rush the job. She took her time as she stirred the clinker into the slurry, not caring if a neighbour should chance to look out and see her—for, after all, emptying ash-pails was the sort of chore she did every day. Even when she spotted an unburned scrap of yellow fabric in the grey her nerve remained strong. She fetched a spade, made a cut in the earth at the side of a rosemary bush, pushed the yellow fragment into it, and sealed up the ground.

Next she got a dustpan and brush, and then a bucket of soapy water, and went over the treads of the stairs, the floor of the hall, the passage, the kitchen—the route that she and Lilian had taken with Leonard's body. Again she worked slowly and methodically, doing far more than she needed to, moving the pieces of hall furniture out of their places, even hauling the oak coat-stand away from the wall in order to get behind and beneath it. Near the threshold of the kitchen she found a single rusty splash that she thought had probably come from Lilian rather than from Leonard, and in the shadowiest corner of the passage she discovered the neat half of a black button that might, just possibly, have got tugged from one of Leonard's cuffs as she had dragged him down the stairs. But the splash was easily wiped away, and the button she carried out to the kitchen stove along with the rest of the contents of the dustpan. She hesitated about throwing it in, though. If the police should ever take it into their heads to go through the ashes . . . In the end, remembering how she had buried the scrap of material, she pushed the button into the earth of the potted aspidistra that, for as long as she could remember, had sat on the largest of the hall tables beside the brass dinner-gong. The police would never look there, surely?

And she had just moved away from it, was just, almost complacently, picking the earth from beneath her fingernail, when she heard the clang of the garden gate, followed by unhurried footsteps across the front garden. The footsteps made their way, grittily, into the porch. There was a charged little silence, and then the knocker was lifted and dropped.

Don't answer it! she told herself. She held her breath, and did nothing.

The knock came again. She couldn't leave it. It might be news of Lilian. She went across, opened the door—and found herself face to face with Inspector Kemp.

He lifted his hat. 'Good afternoon, Miss Wray.'

'Good afternoon, Inspector.'

Her voice had no scrap of welcome in it. He took in her apron, her bare lower arms, the bits of furniture standing about behind her at random angles on the floor, and said, 'Ah. I'm afraid I'm disturbing you.'

She tried to speak with more life. 'It doesn't matter. But have you come to see Mrs Barber? She isn't here. I thought you knew that.'

'Yes, I do. No, it isn't Mrs Barber I'd like to speak to.' He paused, fractionally. 'It's you. Do you have a few minutes?'

She would rather have done almost anything than let him into the house. But in silence, she moved back. He stepped gingerly on to the still-wet tiles, giving a grimace of apology for the dirt on his shoes. Pulling off her apron, tugging down her cuffs a little, she led him into the drawing-room.

He unbuttoned his overcoat as he sat, then drew out his notebook from an inside pocket. Eyeing the book warily, she said, 'Have you brought news? Is that why you're here?'

'Well,' he said, thumbing his way through the small pages, 'yes and no. We're no closer to an arrest, I'm sorry to say. But we expect to be, very soon. There's been a development, you see, that we think significant.'

She swallowed. 'Oh, yes?'

'Yes, we've been keeping the matter quiet for the sake of the inquiry, but the newspapers have just got wind of it, so it won't be secret for long.' He looked up. 'Two possible witnesses from the night of the murder . . . '

And he proceeded to tell her everything she'd heard already from Mrs Playfair, about the man and the girl and the scuffling in the lane. She struggled at first to arrange her features, wanting to hit just the right balance between surprise and concern. But the longer he went on, the calmer she grew. If this was all he'd come for . . .

'Naturally,' he finished, 'the biggest puzzle for us now is Mr Wismuth's statement. He's quite adamant that he last saw Mr Barber at Blackfriars at ten. But—'

'Yes,' she said helpfully, 'I see how that places you.'

'And, to tell you the truth, there are one or two other things about his story that make us not quite satisfied with it.'

She paused at that, as if just getting the point. 'But you surely don't suspect Mr Wismuth of having anything to do with the murder?'

'Well, we're keeping an open mind.'

'But Mr Wismuth—No, it couldn't possibly have been him.'

He looked interested. 'You don't think so? I'll remember that you said that. However—' He returned to his book. 'It's really Mr and Mrs Barber that I'd like to talk about today. You won't mind if I make a few notes?'

Again she eyed the little book. 'No, I don't mind. What is it you'd like to know?'

He brought out a pencil. 'Oh, just general things about the couple and their routines. How well, would you say, did you and your mother know them?'

She pretended to think it over. 'Not very well, I suppose.'

'You didn't tend to spend time with them?'

'Our habits were rather different. My mother sometimes chatted with Mr Barber.'

'Your mother got along all right with him?'

'Yes.'

'How about you? Did you get along with him?'

'Yes, I suppose so.'

'Ever see him much on his own?'

'No, never.'

'Not even casually, about the house?'

'Well, of course, on the stairs and places like that . . . '

'And Mrs Barber? You saw more of her, I suppose?'

She nodded. 'A little more.'

'At parties and so on?'

That took her by surprise. When she didn't answer he went on, 'I understand you accompanied Mrs Barber to the party given by her sister in July—the night, of course, that Mr Barber was first assaulted. You didn't mention that, Miss Wray, when we talked about it at the police station.'

She made her voice very level. 'I didn't? It was rather hard to concentrate that day.'

'And yet the party seems, by all accounts, to have been a memorable one. I've spoken to several of the other guests. They tell me that Mrs Barber was—let's say, making the most of her husband's absence. Taking rather a lot to drink, and so on? Dancing with a number of men?'

Now she knew what he was getting at, why he had come. Quite steadily, she said, 'Mrs Barber danced with her cousins, as far as I recall.'

He consulted his book. 'James Daley, Patrick Daley, Thomas Lynch—'

'I'm afraid I don't know their names.'

'But Mrs Barber was dancing pretty freely with them?'

'It was a family party. Mrs Barber danced with several people. She danced with me, as it happens.'

'She did?'

He said it in that bland way of his, that was somehow like the lenses of his spectacles, making his gaze more penetrating even while appearing to screen it. She went on, after a second, 'All I mean is, the dancing was harmless.'

'You don't recall there being anyone—a cousin, or some other man—with whom Mrs Barber seemed on particularly friendly terms?'

'No, I don't.'

'No one who seemed specially to admire her? Just cast your mind back for me, would you?'

But her mind had gone back already. She was remembering watching Lilian from the sofa. She was remembering standing with her at the gramophone, the space between them tugging itself closed.

She shook her head. 'No.'

'And you were with her all evening? You left the party together? No one else travelled with you? You weren't aware, before you left, of Mrs Barber making any sort of arrangement with any other guest? I ask because the people I've spoken to, they all say there was something about Mrs Barber that night. Nobody can quite put a finger on it, but—just something. She had taken a great deal of trouble over her costume, apparently. You didn't notice anything?'

'No.'

'Could you describe Mrs Barber's temperament?'

'Her temperament?'

'Her likes and dislikes, and so on. I've been given the impression

432

that she's rather a romancer—rather dreamy, rather discontented. It seems to have been well known among her friends and family that she wasn't quite happy in her married life.'

'Well, that's true of half the wives in England, isn't it?'

He gave a faint smile. 'Is it? I shall have to ask mine. You knew yourself that she was unhappy, then?'

She hesitated. 'What do you mean?'

'It doesn't surprise you, to hear of it.'

'I—I never thought much about it.'

'She never confided in you? She seemed rather to cling to you, I thought, on Saturday, at the police station.'

'Well, she'd just had to view her husband's body. She'd have clung to anyone sympathetic, I imagine.'

'There haven't been callers to the house? No notes? No letters?'

'You asked me that once before.'

'Yes, but as you've said, it was hard to concentrate then. Nothing's sprung to mind since we last spoke? The day of the murder, for example. You and your mother both mention in your statements that you heard the sounds of Mrs Barber doing some spring cleaning—moving boxes, emptying drawers. I keep thinking about that, Miss Wray. It seems to me an odd thing for Mrs Barber to have been doing, given what we now know about her condition at the time. She couldn't have been . . . packing things up? Putting clothes and so on together for some sort of trip?'

Frances looked at him. 'Some sort of trip?'

'A hasty departure? A flight of some kind?'

She was appalled. 'No. Not at all.'

'You seem very certain.'

'I am certain.'

'Did you know that Mr Barber's life was insured, with his wife as sole beneficiary?'

The question was like a wire drawn tight at ankle level: it brought her down with a bump. Leonard's life insured? Such a thing had never occurred to her. She desperately tried to think through the implications of it. But she couldn't think anything at all with the inspector watching her. She moistened her dry lips. 'No, I didn't know that.'

He nodded. 'Sergeant Heath came across the paperwork when he was going through Mr Barber's things. The company has confirmed it. The policy was opened when Mr Barber was first married, but it was extended in July this year—not long after the night of that party, as a matter of fact. Altogether, Mr Barber's life was insured for five hundred pounds.'

Five hundred pounds! The figure took her aback. After another awkward pause, she said, 'Well, insurance was Mr Barber's business.'

'That's true.'

'It sounds to me as though you're going about picking on any detail that suits you, jumping to all sorts of wild conclusions—'

But she mustn't lose her head, as she'd lost it yesterday! The inspector watched her, waiting for more, but when she didn't go on he closed his book and said, in a comfortable tone, 'Well, I dare say you're right. As I think I've said before, I have to consider every eventuality; it wouldn't be just to the murdered man if I didn't. You'll keep my questions in mind, I hope? And let me know if anything occurs to you? It isn't pleasant, I know—especially for respectable people like you and your mother. But unfortunately even the most respectable of people sometimes find themselves drawn into unpleasant situations.' He got to his feet. 'I'd be obliged, of course, if you didn't mention our conversation to Mrs Barber. I imagine you're in contact with her?'

Was this another trip-wire? She said, as she rose, 'I haven't seen Mrs Barber since the inquest.'

'You haven't? I mean to call in on her later today. I want to let her know, amongst other things, that we've heard back from the police laboratory. We were quite right about those hairs on Mr Barber's overcoat. Some are very clearly Mrs Barber's. Some—' He

434

paused, to tuck away the notebook, his eyes on hers. 'Some are a good match with yours. One is definitely Mr Wismuth's. As for the others—they're unaccounted for. They may take us nowhere—but, you never know. They might come in useful later on.'

He was almost chummy now. He buttoned up his overcoat with a remark about the unseasonal chillness of the day. She took him back out to the hall and, seeing the trail of muddy splodges his shoes had left on the drying floor, he gave another grimace of apology. 'I'm afraid I've made more housework for you.'

She crossed the tiles. 'It doesn't matter. There's always housework here.'

'And always done at odd hours, it seems . . . You take care of it all yourself? I noticed that you keep no servant.'

'Yes, I do it all. We lost our servants in the War. I'm used to it now.'

She wanted simply to get rid of him. She had her hand on the latch of the door. But, turning, she saw that his step had slowed. He was gazing around, at the stairs, at the bits of furniture; he seemed struck by the heavy-looking coat-stand that she had pulled out of its place. His eyes travelled from that to Frances herself, to her heel-less shoes, her hips and shoulders, her lifted arm, her bare strong wrists.

At last he looked into her face with a funny half-smile. 'You're an interesting young woman, Miss Wray, if you don't mind my saying so. You've a colourful past, I gather.'

She left the latch unturned. 'What do you mean?'

'Oh, all sorts of things come up in our inquiries, odd details from old police files. We like to know if any of our witnesses has any sort of a criminal record. I must admit, when I ordered a check on your name I did it as a mere formality. But it seems my colleagues over at A Division had some dealings with you, a few years ago.'

She realised that he was referring to that ridiculous occasion during the War: the thrown shoes, the night in the police cell. She felt herself blush. 'Oh, that. I did that, you know, mainly to annoy my father.'

'And did it work?'

'Yes, very well.'

He was smiling broadly now. Her own expression felt as though it had been nailed to her face. She drew open the door and, still in that friendly way, his spectacles flashing as the watery sunlight caught them, he fitted on his hat and moved past her. She waited until he had stepped from the porch, then quietly closed the door behind him.

And then she leaned against it, in a sickening combination of relief at being rid of him and alarm at what he had revealed to her. It was all so much worse than she'd been supposing! He didn't simply suspect Charlie; that much was obvious. Perhaps he didn't even really suspect Charlie at all. But he'd worked out that there was a lover involved. All those questions about the party, dancing, other men . . . How long before that 'nose' of his led him away from them, to her?

But maybe he was on her trail already. She kept thinking back to the way in which he had told her about that insurance policy. He had done it in the same deliberate manner in which he'd first mentioned murder to Lilian—as if to get a reaction from her, as if to observe her response. He knew she was hiding something, then. But just what did he suspect her of concealing? Why had he mentioned those hairs that had been found on Leonard's coat? And why bring up her 'colourful past', in that apparently casual way?

She didn't know what to think. The whole conversation seemed to her to have been a series of tests. She had no idea whether she had passed or failed them.

She had to see Lilian. She had to see Lilian! She had put off going to her after Mrs Playfair's visit, but she had to go to her now; she had to do it before *he* did. She went quickly around the hall, shoving the furniture back into place; then she dashed up to her bedroom for her shoes, coat and hat. Thank God her mother wasn't here. She came racing back out of the room, the carpet slithering under her feet. She nearly slipped on her way down the stairs—and after that she slowed her pace, standing at the mirror in the hall to put herself tidy, calm herself down.

As she let herself out of the house she grew cautious again, suddenly fearful that Inspector Kemp might still be somewhere on the street. Suppose he had lingered to take more notes? To peer at the gutters or the gardens? But she looked keenly all around as she started down the hill, and there was no sign of him. A nursemaid was pushing a baby-carriage. A delivery boy was going by on a bicycle, whistling. A man in a buckled grey mackintosh was at the bend of the road, lighting a cigarette—turning away, out of the breeze, to strike his match and cup the flame, as Frances went past him. None of them paid any attention to her. She put up the collar of her coat and quickened her pace.

But it was Wednesday—early closing day. At the bottom of the hill the road was noisy with traffic streaming in and out of Town, but the pavement had a thinned-out, Sundayish feel, and she felt conspicuous hurrying along it, especially once the shops had become slightly humbler, as they did almost as soon as she'd broken away from Camberwell. It occurred to her to take a bus or a tram, but whenever she paused at a stop she managed to time it badly: she waited in vain at the stop itself, then saw buses and trams go sailing past her the moment she'd moved on. It seemed simpler to keep walking. It wasn't so far, in any case. A little over half an hour after she'd left home she reached the start of the Walworth Road.

Mr Viney's shop was a few hundred yards along it: a modest Victorian front still with its mirrored 'seventies lettering, one half of its display given over to collars, to masculine vests and pants, the other festooned with stockings and elastic corsets. The blind on the door was down and there was no sign of life behind it, but to the left of the window was another door, an ordinary street-door, painted in matching chocolate gloss: this led, Frances supposed, to the rooms above. She put her finger to the bell-push, and waited. When nothing happened she pressed again.

The door was yanked open at last by a stout, freckled girl of about fifteen. Was she one of Lilian's cousins? She coolly looked Frances up and down. 'Yes, what is it?'

Frances explained why she had come—that she hoped to speak to Mrs Barber. But at that the girl's manner cooled even further.

'She's not seeing nobody from the papers.'

'No, I'm not from the papers. I'm Miss Wray, her friend, from Champion Hill.'

'Well, I don't know nothing about that.'

'I'm sure Mrs Barber will be glad to see me.'

'Well—'

'It's rather urgent.'

The girl spoke grudgingly. 'Well, all right. But if you ain't who you say you are, mind, there'll be trouble!' Still hostile, she moved back, opening the door fully, doing her best to flatten her bulky figure against the wall.

Stepping forward, Frances found herself in a long brown passage leading to a set of narrow stairs. Somewhere up above a small dog was madly barking, and there seemed nowhere to go save closer to the sound. Once the door was closed, however, the passage was dark, lighted only by a dusty transom. She paused, and the girl pushed past her, to go ahead of her up the staircase. As they reached the minuscule half-landing an inner door was opened and a Jack Russell came scrabbling out. It was followed by a pink-faced Mrs Viney, peering button-eyed into the gloom. When she recognised Frances her eyes grew even rounder.

'Oh, Miss Wray, is it you? What must you think of us, keeping you out on the street like that! Here, Monty! Oh, isn't he a villain!' The dog was jumping up and barking. 'Catch hold of him, Lydia, before he knocks poor Miss Wray down the stairs!—This is Lydia, Miss Wray, who lives next door to us, and who's been helping us out while Lil's been here. We've had that many callers, you see, we are sick to death of them, but Lydia—well, she don't take no non-sense from no one! But, oh, to think of it's being you! And me in my pinny! Come in off them draughty old stairs.—Monty! Be quiet, do!'

Frances moved forward as best she could around the demented dog, and, following Mrs Viney, emerged in a stuffy kitchen. She took in the immense black range in the chimney-breast, the laun-dry dangling from the rack above it, the coconut mat on the floor, the dresser shelves crammed with blue china—all of it meaner and more old-fashioned than she had been expecting, so that for a moment, disconcerted, she bent to the leaping dog, trying to pat and calm it; it kept twisting its jaws to her hands.

When she straightened up, Lilian was there, just coming in through a second doorway. She was dressed in what must have been some outfit of Vera's, an artificial silk frock in a muted floral pattern, with her hair pulled up in a pair of combs; she looked even less like herself than she had at the inquest. Her face had lost its horrible doughiness, however, and had more colour to it—though when she met Frances's gaze some of the colour drained away. She must have seen in her expression that something had happened.

She came forward to catch hold of the dog, lifting it up and sit-ting it in her arms. Drawing her chin away from its muzzle, she said, 'Is everything all right?'

No, answered Frances, with her eyes, her breath, her skin. 'Yes,' she said aloud. 'I happened to be passing, and—well, I thought I'd call in. You wouldn't rather be left alone?'

Lilian looked around, troubled. 'No, I—No, it's nice to see you. But there isn't anywhere to take you. Vera and Violet are upstairs. Violet's off school, she's been sick all morning—'

And, 'No,' cried her mother, 'you don't want to take Miss Wray up there! She's come all this way; she wants a proper chair to sit in. Take her through to the parlour. Your step-dad won't mind. He'll be glad to meet her, he's heard that much about her. You take her through—go on—and me and Lydia'll make some tea.'

There was clearly nothing else for it. Gazing at Frances in a sort of forlorn frustration, Lilian led her out of the kitchen into a dingy little parlour, over-furnished and over-hot, where they found a lean, balding figure with a toothbrush moustache—Mr Viney. He had heard them coming and was already up on his feet. He greeted Frances with the flustered, faintly resentful air of a man who'd hastily pulled on his jacket or shoved in his teeth.

'You're here about this business of Lilian's, I suppose?' he asked sourly. 'Have the newspapers been pestering you? They've been plaguing the life out of us. Parasites, I call 'em! Suck your blood, the whole lot of 'em!'

He grumbled on in a practised way until Mrs Viney and Lydia brought in the tea; he had his in a special cup, slightly larger than the others. There was a bit of fussing with the dog, who was made to 'shake hands' before being allowed a biscuit. Mrs Viney asked after Frances's mother; they discussed the preparations for the funeral, the inspector's recent visit, the fact that no more progress seemed to have been made with the case . . . The talk went on and on, Frances sitting tensely the whole time, gazing across the room at Lilian, seeing the tension in her pose, too. It wasn't until Vera had appeared, shuffling down from some upstairs room to say that Violet had left off being sick and was asking for a bit of bread and butter, but wanted her nan to take it up—it wasn't until then, in the upheaval that followed, with the dog barking again, wriggling away like a greased pig every time someone tried to catch hold of it, that she and Lilian could snatch a few minutes together, alone. 'I just need to talk to Frances for a bit about some things at the house,' Lilian told her mother, once Frances had risen and said her goodbyes; and before Mrs Viney could throw in some kind word to prevent it they had headed down the narrow stairs to the badly lighted passage. Behind them, the dog was still yapping its head off. On the other side of the street-door the whole of the Walworth Road seemed to be thundering by. Frances thought of all they had to say—all they had to discuss and to plan, with only ever hurried, harried moments like this in which to do it—and felt a touch of despair.

Lilian said, 'What is it? Something's happened, hasn't it?'

She nodded. 'But I don't know how bad it is. I just don't know what to think.'

And quickly, quietly, she told Lilian everything: the conversation with Mrs Playfair, the scene with her mother to which it had led, the visit from the inspector . . . Lilian grew pale again as she listened. By the time Frances had finished she had reached for the newel-post at the bottom of the stairs, leaning against it as if she might faint.

'Oh, Frances, it's the end! If your mother's guessed—'

'She hasn't guessed all of it.'

'And those people in the lane!'

'They didn't *see* anything. Even the inspector admitted that.'

'But why did he tell you about them at all? Why would he tell you so much?'

'Yes, that's the frightening part. He was trying to startle me into confessing something. Something about you and Charlie? Or about you and other men?'

'Not—Not about you and me?'

'I don't know. No, I don't believe it. But he knows I was at Netta's party with you, and that I pretended I wasn't. I wish to God I'd never done that! And I wish I'd never thought to say you were spring-cleaning on the day Leonard died. There's no going back from that now. It's in all our statements. Everything he's turning up looks so damaging! That—That insurance policy.'

She must have sounded odd as she said it. Lilian looked at her in a new way. 'But that's nothing. All the married men at the Pearl have them. They get them as part of their job.'

'Five hundred pounds. It seems such a lot.'

'But I'd forgotten all about it.'

'Had you?'

'Yes! Or——' She shook her head, confused. 'I don't know. Len used to make jokes about it, I suppose. You're not thinking——?'

'No,' said Frances quickly, 'of course not.' She wouldn't allow the thought at all. 'I'm just trying to look at it as *he'll* look at it.'

At the mention of the inspector, Lilian sank on to the lowest step of the staircase. 'Oh, he frightens me to death! I knew he was thinking things about Charlie and me. I guessed it, from all the questions he asked me on Monday night. If only Charlie would tell the truth! He'll have to now, won't he? If that couple were really in the lane? But then, if he does—Oh, Frances, I don't know what's going to happen next. Every time the doorbell goes I think it's the police. But if it's Charlie they're watching . . . Betty was here yesterday. I could hardly look her in the eye. I can't look anyone in the eye, except you. They won't arrest him or anything, will they?'

Frances squatted down beside her. 'I don't know. I think they might.'

She looked terrified. 'Oh, don't say that! It's getting worse and worse! First you're caught up in it; now him. And all from that stupid, stupid moment——'

It was clear what she was remembering: the swing of the ashtray, the cricket-bat crack, Leonard's heavy collapse to the floor. Upstairs there were voices in the kitchen, the scrabble of the dog's claws on the lino; she seemed not to hear them. Instead she hung her head, and spoke levelly and wretchedly.

'You wanted to go for a doctor, didn't you? I should have let you, I know it now. Whatever might have happened, it couldn't have been worse than all this. I've started to think——' She couldn't say it.

Frances stared at her. 'What?'

442

'I've started to wonder whether I shouldn't just tell the police everything.'

'*What?*'

'I'd say I did it all by myself. That you didn't know anything about it.'

'Oh, Lilian, you mustn't! We've left it too long. They'd never believe you.'

'But it's the truth. They'd have to believe me.'

'Believe that you carried him? Down the stairs? Up the garden to the lane? And all without my knowing?'

Lilian's mouth had begun to tremble. 'Well, I can't think what else to do! I've got you into all this—'

'Don't think about me.'

'You've done so much. You've done it all!'

'You've been brave too. You just have to be brave for a little longer.'

'I don't know if I can be. It's more like a nightmare than ever.'

'I know it feels that way,' said Frances, 'but there's no evidence against anyone. They can't arrest people with no evidence. They can't—'

But her voice was wavering now. Her last bit of confidence seemed to be melting away. Lilian looked at her, then caught hold of her hands. 'Oh, don't be frightened too! You mustn't be frightened too! If I know you're frightened, I'll die!'

She was wringing Frances's fingers. That panic was back, that dark electricity. They hung on to one another, but might have been gripping each other's hands over some great gulf, so horribly fused yet separated were they by their terror.

As it had once or twice before, the panic ran through them, then burned itself out. Lilian drew free and put her head in her hands. 'I wish I could make it be different,' she said. 'I wish I could take it all back. I wish, I wish—' She stopped, exhausted. 'But wishing's no good. It never was, was it?'

Frances put an arm around her, kissed the side of her pale face. 'Just be careful, when the inspector comes. Don't let him catch you out. We've come so far; we can keep going, I know we can . . . But you won't think again about—about what you said? Telling the truth? You won't think of it?'

Lilian hesitated, then shook her head. 'Not if you don't think I ought to.'

They hauled themselves upright, stood close for a minute, and kissed with dry, clumsy mouths before they parted.

Out on the pavement, Frances blinked against the daylight. A man was standing at the window of the shop, looking over the display, and in the blindness of the moment she just avoided colliding with him. She caught his eye in the dusty glass, mumbled an apology and moved on.

But after a second or two she looked back, to see him stepping rapidly away in the opposite direction. He was dressed in a buckled grey mackintosh, she realised now. Was he the man she had passed earlier, on her way down the hill? She wasn't sure; but the thought set her panicking again. It hadn't occurred to her before, but wasn't it possible that Inspector Kemp had put men to watch the house? Men to follow her when she left it? Perhaps they'd been doing it all week. How else, after all, would he have known to find her on her own today? And she had done just what he'd wanted her to do! Gone rushing off to Lilian! Gone to Lilian, to get to her first, because he had taken care to let her know that he would be coming here later himself . . .

She headed home feeling sick, feeling trapped and exposed— now and then, as she crossed a road, furtively turning her head to glance back over her shoulder. But there was no further sign of the man in the mackintosh.

14

Two days later, the funeral took place. Frances had planned to attend it with her mother. But her mother rose in the morning looking more burdened and fretful than ever, and complaining of a sore throat; so she went alone, walking gloomily to Peckham through the sunless, shadowless streets, then taking a bus to the cemetery gates. She found a crowd of black-clad figures there, waiting for the cortège to arrive. She recognised aunties and cousins from Netta's party; she shook one or two hands. When the motor-hearse and cars appeared she strained for a sight of Lilian, catching only the merest glimpse of her as the vehicles crept by. The last of the cars entered the cemetery, and she and the other mourners moved silently to follow. It took about ten minutes, then, on a winding road through the graves, to reach the dour little chapel where the service was to be held.

The atmosphere, in the circumstances, could not have been anything other than grim. The coffin was set on trestles in the aisle; gingery with brass and varnish, it was disconcertingly reminiscent of Leonard himself, and the floral wreaths that were placed on it— one marked BROTHER, the other SON—recalled the awful untimeliness of his death. People wept into their handkerchiefs as the minister gave his address. Frances, afraid of where grief would lead her, feeling their tears as a sort of contagion, sat as rigidly among them as if she were holding her breath.

But there was something else to the occasion, she began to realise, some extra current in the general distress: she saw it in the closed, set faces of Leonard's family; she saw it in the oddly challenging way in which, when it was time to leave the chapel, the Barber men rose to shoulder the coffin. On the slow walk to the grave, the mourners, like vinegar and oil, somehow divided themselves into two distinct streams. And at the grave itself the streams pooled, with the Peckham crowd gathering on one side and the Walworth crowd gathering on the other, and only a few individuals—men who might have been colleagues of Leonard's from the insurance business or, perhaps, had fought alongside him in the War—looking bewildered about where their loyalties lay. Frances didn't care whom she stood with. She simply wanted the thing to be over. She kept trying for more glimpses of Lilian; she could see only her bowed head and shoulders, shaking with sobs as the coffin went down. As soon as the minister had uttered the closing blessing and the mourners began to disperse, she tried to pick her way through the grim-faced crowd towards her.

But, as if the tension that had been simmering just below the surface of the whole affair had at last been allowed its release, she had barely taken a dozen steps before she became aware of a small commotion at the head of the grave. Those family wreaths, SON and BROTHER, had been placed prominently among the flowers, but Vera and Netta, it seemed, were attempting to move them in favour of a large sheaf of lilies. Leonard's mother, and another woman who must have been a sister or sister-in-law, had hold of the stems of the lilies and, with white, determined expressions, were trying to tug them from Netta's hands.

It was all done in silence, but the dumb-show hostility was as shocking as a shout. People had turned to watch, open-mouthed; no one seemed to know what to do. Mrs Viney, scarlet and furious,

446

was heading back to the grave as though she intended to join in the fight. Lilian was pulling on one of her arms: 'Leave it, Mum. Oh, it isn't worth it!'

A couple of the cousins stood near by, along with Min and Min's young man. Frances joined them. 'What on earth's going on?'

At the sight of her, Min's hand flew to her mouth and she let out a burst of nervous laughter. 'Oh, Miss Wray, isn't it awful! Lenny's mum won't let Lil's flowers be put at the top of the grave!'

'But why not?'

'It's all on account of what's been in the paper. Haven't you seen? A man and a woman are saying they heard things on the night of the murder, and—'

Frances looked at her in sick dismay. 'That's in the papers now?'

'It was in the *Express* this morning. But we knew already, from the police, and Lenny's family have been ever so funny with Charlie over it; they say they don't know who to believe. He was meant to have helped carry the coffin, but they only told him last night that they didn't want him to do it. They got one of Lenny's cousins to do it instead—the Black and Tan one, too! Lil thinks they did that to get at her. They've been saying such awful things about her.'

'What sort of things?'

'That she wasn't a proper wife. That she and Charlie have been too friendly. And things about her money. That it's too much, or—?'

'Her money?'

'The money she's meant to get because of Lenny's having died.'

That damn insurance policy! If the five hundred pounds had become public knowledge, how long before the papers got hold of it? What would *that* do to the case?

'Lil's been in such a state about it,' Min was saying now. 'The Barbers won't say anything to her face, but none of them will look her in the eye. They wouldn't let our car go first after the hearse. And now they've moved her flowers—'

She was interrupted by Vera and Netta, who had come striding over from the grave. They were furiously brushing yellow pollen from their black silk gloves.

'Well, Miss Wray,' said Vera, 'isn't this charming? Len would laugh his head off, wouldn't he? We're all meant to be going back to Cheveney Avenue now for tea and biscuits. I'm surprised they asked us, aren't you? You'd think they'd be afraid of Lil putting arsenic in the drinks! I wouldn't set foot in their house after this, not if they paid me. We're going home.' She looked around. 'Where did Mum go?'

One of the cousins said, 'She and Auntie Cathy've taken Lil to the gate. Lloyd's gone on with Pat and Jimmy to fetch the cars.'

'Right.'

The three sisters put down their heads and started off along the narrowish path, with Min's young man and the cousins following. Frances stood still for a second, then hurried after them—hoping to see Lilian, if only for a moment, before she was whisked away.

But even in the fifty or so minutes that had elapsed since they'd all arrived, news of the funeral must have spread. Back at the cemetery entrance, the scene was chaotic. There were reporters and photographers, and more of the sort of gawpers who had been at the inquest, people who'd materialised on the pavement to watch the mourners emerge. Boys were sticking their heads through the railings; a few were even balanced on top. Two of them caught Frances's eye and called to her—called in the urgent yet amiable way in which they might have appealed for directions in the street.

'Hi! Lady! Which is the chap?'

They meant Charlie, she realised. And an instant later she saw him, talking to one of the undertakers; Betty was beside him, holding on to his arm. They both had mortified expressions. Charlie's face was so peaked it looked waxy. Perhaps he was asking if the cemetery had any other exits to it: the undertaker was nodding, gesturing back towards the graves.

A motor-car blasting its horn made her jump with fright. But she turned her head to it, recognised the car as Lloyd's—and at last saw Lilian, sitting in the back of it with her mother and her aunt. The car was trying to leave the cemetery, but was being prevented from doing so by another car, which had stopped to open its doors to a harassed-looking Barber party. Lloyd and the Barbers' driver had let down their windows in order to remonstrate with each other, and a red-haired man, whom Frances had never met before but had seen in the chapel and identified at once as Leonard's older brother Douglas, had got involved in the argument. He had Leonard's voice exactly, she noticed with a chill.

Finally the Barbers' vehicle closed its doors and shuddered into life; Lloyd's car began to inch forward; and then there was nothing she could do but stand and watch it leave. Its windows reflected the grey and black of the scene: when, at the very last moment, Lilian turned, caught her eye, put up a gloved hand to the glass, she might have been gazing hopelessly out at her, Frances thought, through flowing water; she might have been drowning.

Her expression haunted Frances on the journey back to Champion Hill. She kept remembering what she had said, the last time they had met—that she'd been thinking of going to the police and telling them everything. Suppose she had made up her mind to do it? If only they could have spoken! Was it worth pressing on to Walworth, trying to see her again? But what was the point, if all they could do was stand and murmur in that narrow passage?

By the time she arrived home, to find her mother still unwell, she felt ill herself, her throat gritty, her eyes sore. She went to bed straight after dinner that night, but lay fretful and restless for hours; she felt ill again the next morning, but made herself go down to the news-stand for the papers. Every one of them, now, had picked up the story of the couple in the lane. There were quotes, and pictures, along with descriptions of the funeral. And for the first time, too, there were photographs of Charlie. The *Daily Sketch* had even got hold of an old snapshot of him and Lilian. It showed them dressed for a party, Lilian with a band across her forehead and drop jewels at her ears; the picture, clearly, was a group one that had been cropped, but cropped in such a way as to make them look almost like sweethearts. The caption identified them as 'The widow, Mrs Barber, and her friend Mr Wismuth, who is continuing to assist the police with their inquiries.'

The horror of it stayed with Frances all day. It followed her like a shadow to bed, and found its way into her dreams. In the early hours of Monday morning she awoke with a dreadful start, convinced that she'd heard the sound of someone furiously knocking at the front door. Could it be the police? Could it even be Lilian? The hallucination was so vivid that at last, quaking with apprehension, she lit her candle, tiptoed downstairs, and quietly drew the door open on its chain. She found the porch quite empty, the street beyond it dark and still, with only a few mouse-like movements here and there as the breeze got hold of fallen leaves and made them scuttle.

Later that day, worn out by the lonely churning of her thoughts, she took a tram into Town and went to Clipstone Street. And the moment the door to the flat was opened and she saw Christina's familiar face—the childish blue eyes, the terrible haircut—she appalled herself by bursting into tears.

'Oh, Chrissy.'

Christina came forward and took her in her arms. Frances wept against her shoulder, then fished for a handkerchief, holding the back of her hand to her running nose, embarrassed. 'Stevie isn't here, is she?'

'No, Stevie's at school, of course. Come in off the landing.'

'I'm disturbing you.'

'Don't be an idiot. Come in. I've been longing to see you.'

450

She led Frances into the flat, put her to sit in the velveteen arm-chair. She drew the hat from her head and the gloves from her fingers; she set a kettle of water to heat on the gas-ring, then opened a drawer and produced a bottle of brandy and two tum-blers. Frances's tears had begun to subside. She was wiping her face. But when Christina put the tumbler into her hand the gesture set her off again, worse than before. She took a single unsteady sip, the glass rattling against her teeth. Then she set it down and cried into her handkerchief—cried until her head was throbbing.

'I'm sorry,' she managed at last.

'Don't say that,' said Christina, 'for God's sake. Drink your brandy. Will you have a blanket? You're freezing! Why are you so cold?'

Frances tried another sip, then put the tumbler aside. 'I don't think I've been warm, not for a moment, since—' She couldn't finish.

Christina fetched a tartan rug, brought out the electric fire. Sitting down in the opposite chair, she said, 'What on earth's been happening to you?'

Frances shuddered. 'The first couple of days after he died—I don't know, now, how we all got through them. We did it inch by inch, I think, like climbing a cliff. Then it seemed to be all right. But now—I don't know what's going on. The police have got some idea in their heads. It's terrifying.'

'Terrifying, how?'

'Have you been following the case in the papers? You know there's this man, Leonard's friend? Charlie Wismuth? He's supposed to have spent the evening with Leonard before he died. But the police don't believe him. And the worst of it is, they think that Lilian—they think that Lilian might have—Christ!' Her lips were twitching. 'I can't even say it. I haven't seen her since the funeral. And even then I couldn't get near her. It was unbelievable. No one on Leonard's side will talk to her. The two families were practically tearing up tombstones and hurling them at each other! At home

451

I do nothing but worry. My mother's as bad as the police. I just don't know what to do. Lilian's at Walworth. We can't talk, we can't see each other—'

'It can't last for ever, surely?'

'I feel so utterly alone.'

'But it can't go on and on, can it?'

'Something dreadful's going to happen, I know it is.'

'But I still don't understand. You say the police suspect Lilian? But of what, exactly? And why?'

'It all turns on Charlie's statement. He isn't telling the truth about where he was on the night Leonard died.'

'They think he had something to do with the murder?'

'Yes. But he didn't.'

'How do you know?'

'I just—I just know he didn't. But they're imagining that there's been some sort of love affair between him and Lilian. That she . . . put him up to it. I don't know.'

'Do they have any evidence?'

'Of course they don't.'

'You're sure?'

'Well, of course I'm sure! What are you suggesting?'

'Nothing, I suppose. It's just, to see you dragged into all this . . . '

'The police are simply fastening things together. Ridiculous things. Lilian's behaviour at her sister's party. The fact that she and Leonard weren't happy. The fact that his life was insured—' But Frances didn't want to talk about that. She shook her head. 'It's all nonsense. But they believe it! They're twisting things about.'

Christina said, after a pause, 'I wish you had come to me sooner. I've been worried to death about you. I very nearly came to Camberwell.'

Frances was rubbing her stinging eyes. 'You might as well have done. My mother saw your telegram. The whole thing's out in the open now.'

'Oh, Frances, I'm sorry. I didn't know what else to do.'

'It doesn't matter. It was cowardly of me to keep it from her. And anyhow, it's the last thing on her mind. She thinks—I don't know what she thinks. She's taken against Lilian along with everyone else.'

'And how is Lilian herself?'

'Oh, dreadful. Frightened. More frightened than I am; that's the trouble. And she's been ill. Did you know that? No, of course you didn't.' She put a hand to her forehead. 'I'm losing all sense of who knows what. It turned out—' She hesitated. 'It turned out she'd started a baby.'

Christina's mouth fell open. 'A baby?'

'Yes.'

'But—'

'It was lost. In all the upset. It was lost.'

She couldn't say any more. In any case, the kettle was whistling. Christina watched her for another moment, then hurried over to the stove.

With the rug tucked around her, she had finally stopped shivering. But the bout of sobbing had left her feeling bruised, wrung out, swollen and dirty in the face. She twisted sideways in the armchair, kicking off her shoes, drawing up her legs. Wiping her eyes and nose again, she said, 'God, I feel like hell. You're quite sure Stevie isn't going to pop up?'

'I told you, Stevie's at school. And she's going from there to her studio. She'll be hours yet.'

'What does she make of all this?'

'Well, what do you think? She's been horrified, of course. We both have. It doesn't seem real.'

Frances gave her weight over to the chair, resting her cheek against the napless velveteen. 'It didn't feel real to me, for the first day or two. Now it's everything else that feels unreal. What day is it, even? Monday, is it? Only just over a week, then, since it happened!

It feels like a lifetime. As if I've had all the fear and horror of a lifetime crammed into ten days.'

Christina brought over the tray of tea-things. Filling Frances's cup, she said, 'You look ill, you know. You look ill and . . . I don't know. Not yourself.'

Frances took the tea and sipped it gratefully. 'I don't think I'll ever be myself again. Not with the police sniffing about. Not with Inspector Kemp and his wretched nose.'

'An inspector?' said Christina. 'Just like in the books?'

Her tone had brightened slightly. Frances, looking across the tray at her, thought, Yes, you're just like everyone else, excited by the loathsome glamour of it all. And yet you call yourself a pacifist. And so, for that matter, do I . . . She gave brief, tired answers to the questions Christina began to ask, about the events of the previous Saturday, the finding of Leonard's body in the lane. She had gone over it all so many times, with the police and with neighbours, that it felt stale and lifeless, someone else's story.

But Chrissy, of course, knew more than the police and the neighbours did; she knew about Frances and Lilian. And that meant that Frances had to be careful. There was so much that couldn't be said; she felt weighed down by it. Every so often, as they spoke, they hit a sort of dead wall. 'I'm so desperately worried about Lilian,' she kept saying, and Christina looked baffled.

'But what can the police possibly do?'

'It's what they're thinking.'

'But, surely, if they're working this hard on the case—Isn't it only a matter of time before they track the murderer down? And then—'

'They won't track anyone down.'

'Why do you say that? Why shouldn't they?'

'They think they've solved the case already. They're going to act, I know they are. Lilian knows it too. I'm worried she'll do something rash. I know how her mind works. She's thinking that if things have got this bad, that if people have already taken against Charlie, and against her—She's thinking—'

'Thinking what? You're not making any sense. Drink some more of that brandy, will you?'

Frances shook her head. 'I daren't. I can't risk getting muddled. If you only knew how much planning and thinking and fretting I've had to do!'

'But what do you mean?' cried Christina. 'What sort of fretting? Why has it all fallen on you?'

Frances gazed into her face, and suddenly the urge to tell her everything—about Dr Ridley's Pills, about the blood, about Leonard, about the horrible journey down the stairs and over the garden—the urge was overwhelming. Could she do it? Dare she do it? She'd been brooding so narrowly over the memory of that evening that she had lost all sense of perspective on it. How bad, in fact, was the thing that she and Lilian had done? It wasn't a crime, after all. They had made it feel like a crime by being so frightened, by acting so guilty. But all it was, in reality, was a catastrophic blunder. Perhaps she could tell it to Chrissy, and Chrissy would stare, would look scandalised, would—

But she looked at the crumpled frock and the mud-coloured cardigan that Christina was wearing; she glanced around the untidy flat, at the sham Bohemianism of it. The lies that were being told here were such harmless ones. It was all so uncorrupted, so safe . . . And she knew that she couldn't tell Chrissy anything. More than that, she knew that the not-telling would make a breach between them; that it had made the breach already. She thought bleakly, *This is what I saw in the garden that night.* She had put herself beyond the ordinary. Or, rather, Lilian had put her there. She would never blame Lilian for it. She would never do that. But, oh, why had she picked up that ashtray? How bloody unfair it was! They'd been about to start their new life. Frances had already been cheated out of one life—this life, here with Christina. Was she really to be cheated out of another?

She shed a few more tears—self-pitying ones, this time. 'Forgive me, Chrissy,' she said.

'What can I do to help you?'

She wiped her face, blew her nose. 'I'm just so horribly tired! It makes everything so black. I feel as though I could sleep and sleep. Then at night I can't sleep at all.'

'Sleep now, then. You can have the bed.'

'No, I can't do that. I ought to be at home, keeping an eye on my mother. But—' Her tone grew humble. 'May I just sit here for a little while? What were you doing when I arrived? Were you typing? Won't you carry on?'

'Well, but won't the racket disturb you?'

'No, I'd like it. Really, I would.'

So, looking doubtful, Christina returned to her desk, uncovered her typewriter, started work; and Frances curled up in the armchair and closed her eyes. The crackety-crack of the machine seemed loud at first. Then her mind began to detach itself from her surroundings and glide over the sound. She was aware as if distantly of the crampedness of the chair; her ear grew hot and painful where it was pressed against the back of it, but she seemed to lack the will or the energy to change her pose. She slept deeply for a time, awoke with a start, then slept deeply again. When she roused herself properly, she saw the furious orange bars of the electric fire, she saw the illuminated green shade of Chrissy's desk lamp; and then she saw the clock. It was twenty past five. She oughtn't to have stayed here so long. Anything might be happening at home.

But as she began the painful business of uncurling herself from the chair she heard a sound over the intermittent crack of the typewriter—a raised voice, out on the street. She had heard the voice two or three times already, she realised, along with the grumble of the Clipstone Street traffic; but only now, as it broke through to the front of her mind, did she take in what it was. A newsboy was calling the evening edition of one of the London papers. What was the headline he was shouting?

She looked over at Christina. 'Chrissy, stop typing, will you?'

Christina jumped. 'You're awake! I thought—What's the matter?'

'Don't you hear that?'

'Hear what?'

Frances was sitting tensely. 'There!' The cry had come again. 'What's that he's saying?' But she knew. 'He's saying "Champion Hill", isn't he? Open the window!'

'Stop it, Frances. You're frightening me.'

'Can't you hear it?'

'No, I—'

But, yes, now Christina caught it. The boy was drawing nearer. '*Champion Hill Murder!*' he was calling; Frances had been right. But there was another word—what was it? Was it '*Latest*'? She wasn't sure. She listened harder. The call was repeated. '*Champion Hill Murder!*'—that was distinct. But the word that followed—*was* it '*latest*'? Again, she knew in her heart that it wasn't. She knew! She struggled to get out of the chair, but Christina had already risen and gone across to the window. Frances watched her turn the catch. And once the sash was lifted the call came clear as anything: '*Champion Hill Murder! Arrest!*'

She and Christina stared at each other. Then Christina started into life—looking around for her purse, then giving up on that idea and tipping out a couple of coins from a china money-box on her desk. Then she hurried out of the flat, leaving the door open behind her.

Frances remained in the chair, too frightened to get to her feet, listening to the fading slap of the soles of Christina's slippers on the stairs. This was it, she realised. This was the moment she'd been dreading and expecting since the beginning of it all. The police had arrested Charlie, or Lilian, or the two of them together. They had been patiently gathering their misinformation and now they had swooped. She closed her eyes. Oh, let it be Charlie, let it be Charlie—But that was no good! It couldn't be Charlie! It couldn't be anyone! Oh, Christ, let it be no one! Let it be no one! All a mistake!

Minute after minute seemed to go by before she heard the rapid return of slippered footsteps. She watched the open doorway, and finally Christina came racing through it with the paper in her hand and her short hair flying. She looked excited but relieved. 'I think it's all right,' she said breathlessly. 'They say a man's been arrested, but—'

It was Charlie, then! 'Charles Wismuth?'

She shook her head, still panting after her breath. 'No, that isn't the name.'

Frances almost snatched the paper from her. But the words jumped about in front of her eyes; she had to hand it back. Christina began to read aloud to her, in a hasty, telegraphic way.

'"Sensational developments in the Champion Hill case ... A young man has today appeared before the Lambeth magistrate, charged with the murder of Leonard Arthur Barber ... The apprehended man"'—her voice rose—'"has been named as Spencer Ward, a motor-mechanic, of Bermondsey."'

Frances gaped at her. 'What?'

'"Police were led to Mr Ward after the sudden receipt of new information from an important witness in the case, Mr Charles Wismuth. Mr Ward, who has put in a plea of Not Guilty, is suspected of having committed the assault after taking exception to an intimacy between the married Mr Barber and his own fiancée, Miss Billie Grey—"'

Frances snatched the paper back again and read the report for herself. But it still didn't make any sense. All she could see were the unfamiliar names: Spencer Ward, Billie Grey. What on earth did it mean? *New information ... taking exception ... intimacy ... the married Mr Barber ...*

Intimacy ... the married Mr Barber ...

At last, as if the words were so many things—coins, say—that had been sent spinning up into the air and now, one by one, dropped and settled, the whole thing fell into place.

All this time, Leonard must have been having an affair of his own. He'd been seeing some girl, some girl named Billie. It was the girl's boy-friend who'd been accused of killing him.

Her first, astonishing feeling was something like betrayal, a spasm of outrage at the thought that Leonard could have done this thing, maintained this lie, while she knew nothing. Then she took in the implications of the boy-friend's arrest; and she grew sick.

'No,' she said. 'No. No. It isn't possible.'

'But—'

'It's too dreadful, Chrissy!'

'What? I thought—Well, if the police have got the killer, doesn't it solve everything?'

'No! Don't you see?'

But how could Christina see? How could she possibly understand the utter mess and horror of it? The police had arrested an innocent man! Frances looked into her face. *Can I tell you?* she thought again. *Can I? Dare I?*

Then she remembered Lilian. She threw down the paper and picked up her hat. 'I have to go.'

Christina blinked. 'What? Where to?'

'To Lilian. She'll have seen the papers too.'

'Well, but don't go like this. You look demented!'

'I feel demented,' said Frances. 'But I'll feel worse if I don't see her.' She pulled on her gloves. 'I'll take a cab.' Then she thought of her purse, and gave a wail of despair. 'I haven't the money!'

'I can give you the money. But—'

'Will you? Oh, Chrissy, will you, please?'

So Christina fetched the money-box and emptied its contents into Frances's hands. But as Frances began to move off she caught hold of her arm. 'Wait, Frances.'

Frances was pulling away, impatient. 'I have to go. There isn't time.'

'Frances, please. Be careful, will you?'

Frances looked at her properly then, and they moved back together. They embraced, their two hearts thudding like fists on the opposite sides of a bolted door.

Down on the street she picked up a cab almost immediately. The driver made good time to the river, then got caught in a snarl of traffic on Waterloo Bridge. She sat watching the dial as the three-pences mounted up, fidgeting about with anxiety, seeing people all around her with ordinary expressions on their faces and unable to believe that they weren't sharing her panic. But then with the sudden give of liquid coming out of a blocked pipe the traffic ran smoothly again. Another little jam at the Elephant and Castle, and she was on the Walworth Road.

The street was busy with shoppers. Mr Viney's window was bright this time, and the blind on the door was lifted: she could see him behind the counter, with Min beside him, serving a customer. But again she went to the other door and put her finger to the bell; again it was freckled, unfriendly Lydia who came down to let her in; again the dog was madly yapping as she climbed the narrow staircase. The door at the top was shut, but she could hear women's voices beyond. She didn't pause, she didn't knock. She turned the doorknob and went through.

Gathered around the kitchen table she found Mrs Viney, Vera, Lilian and the little girl, Violet. They looked at her in amazement. Vera had a cigarette halfway to her mouth, her lips parted to receive it. Mrs Viney, clambering to her feet, said, 'Miss Wray, well I never! We thought it was Lydia's big sister, come to fetch her home!'

Lilian's eyes were red with weeping. Frances spoke directly to her. 'I just saw the paper. I just saw the news.'

She looked frightened. 'Is it in the papers already? What are they saying?'

'They're saying a man's been charged. They're saying something about Leonard and a girl—?'

Her expression of fear turned to one of simple misery. She dipped her head and wouldn't answer.

The dog barked again. Violet caught hold of it by its stub of a tail. Mrs Viney began to recover herself.

'Oh, Miss Wray, aren't you kind? To think of you coming all this way!' She found Frances a chair. 'We had it all from Sergeant Heath first thing this morning. Well, you could have knocked me down with a feather! Poor Lil's quite floored. Who'd have believed it of Lenny? He'd been seeing this girl quite regular, by all accounts, for months and months. And Charlie doing the same with the girl's married sister! It all come out last night, the sergeant said. They had Charlie in for more questions, and he broke right down and told them the lot. They went straight off, then, and caught the boy—picked him up just like that. He had the weapon on him and everything.'

'He had the weapon?' repeated Frances. She looked at Lilian again. 'But—'

'He's one of these rough types,' Mrs Viney went on. 'Been in all sorts of trouble before. Well, it was him that had a go at Lenny back in the summer, it turns out. Do you remember? When we was all so worried? And Lenny told us it was a soldier? Well, it was this boy all along! He'd found out about Lenny and his girl and went after him to scare him off. Yes, it's all come out now. Nineteen, that's all he is! It's his poor mother I feel sorry for.'

Vera was finally lighting her cigarette. 'It's Len's mother *I* feel sorry for.'

'Oh, now don't,' said Mrs Viney.

'I should like to see her face, that's all.'

The little girl, as usual, was taking everything in. 'Why should you like to see it?'

'Because she's a mean old woman,' said Vera, 'who thought that the sun shone out of Uncle Lenny's you-know-what. And now'—she drew savagely on her fag, her features sharp as a hatchet—'now she'll know that it didn't. That's why.'

Again Mrs Viney protested. It wasn't fair to speak ill of the dead. And the funeral flowers barely drooping! Still, she did think Lenny had played Lil a very shabby trick . . .

There was a teapot on the table in a knitted cosy; someone tipped it over a cup as the conversation ran on, and when a bit of brown sludge came out someone else filled the kettle, fetched extra milk for the jug . . . Frances knew what was going to happen now. She and Lilian would sit here in this overcrowded room, gazing in agony at each other while the dog did tricks for a biscuit; and then they would have to stand in some dark corner to talk the thing furtively through, in whispers.

She wouldn't do it; not this time. The cup was put on a saucer and set in front of her, but she spoke across it, directly to Lilian again.

'May I see you somewhere, alone?'

The room fell silent at her words. After a pause, blushing, uncertain, Lilian got to her feet. 'Yes, of course, if you want. I'll—I'll take you upstairs.'

The women were watching. Even Violet was watching. For once, Mrs Viney seemed doubtful. 'You're taking Miss Wray up to the bedroom, are you? None of the fires are lit up there.'

'It doesn't matter,' said Lilian, her head lowered.

'Well, why don't you go through to the parlour?'

'No, we just need to talk for a minute about—Oh, we just need to talk!'

She was blushing worse than ever. Clumsily, she led Frances

from the room. They went out to the half-landing, then climbed another narrow flight of stairs.

The house grew gloomier the higher they went. The staircase window had lace across it; a skylight was dingy with smuts. The bedroom they entered was small and cluttered, almost filled by its few bits of furniture, a high iron bedstead, a chest of drawers, a dressing-table with a blue satin skirt; a puppet hung on tangled strings from a crucifix on the wall. Here and there in the lino were odd little shining commas and stars: Frances peered at them in confusion, then heard the scrape of a chair, a murmur, and realised that they were chinks of light. The room below was the bright kitchen. She had a vivid sense of the women down there, still sitting at the table, perhaps gazing wonderingly up.

Lilian had gone around the bed to open the curtains wider, in order to let in the last of the fading grey daylight. When she had done it she turned back, then stood there, hunched and wretched. They looked at each other across the flowery eiderdown.

'What are we going to do?' whispered Frances. And then, when Lilian didn't answer: 'You know what it means? An innocent boy! We never thought of that, did we? We thought of Charlie. That was bad enough.'

'It's like a judgement on me,' said Lilian.

'What?'

'It's like a judgement on me, for everything I've done.'

Frances was thrown by her expression, and by the bitterness of her tone. She said, 'It isn't a judgement on anyone. It's just—oh, I don't know what the hell it is. What exactly did Sergeant Heath say?'

'Just what my mother's told you.'

'You don't know anything about this boy? How can they possibly have *charged* him? It doesn't make any sense. What was your mother saying about a weapon?'

Lilian had lifted her hand to her mouth. 'He had something on him—a cosh or something. Something, anyhow, that they think could have done it. And they're talking about those hairs on Len's coat again. They think some of them might be his.'

'But that's impossible. Isn't it?'

Now she was gnawing at her lip. 'I don't know. I've been thinking about it. Some of them might have got there from the girl. From this—this *Billie*. If one of the boy's hairs was on her shoulder, and then if she and Len—if they—'

'That couldn't happen, could it?'

'I don't know.'

'How *could* that happen?'

'I don't know! I don't know anything, do I? Len might have been seeing her every other evening for all I know! He might have been taking her to hotels—'

'Hotels! Do you think he was?'

'I don't know! Yes, probably. Every time he said he was kept at work or had to go to some dinner—probably he was seeing her then. Anything could have got passed between them.'

Frances put her hands to her forehead, trying to take it all in. 'God!' She couldn't draw her thoughts together; they felt as though they'd been hammered apart. 'How could he have kept up the secret like that? For months and months, did your mother say? But, look.' She lowered her hands, in a steadying sort of way. 'It doesn't matter now what he did or didn't do. It doesn't matter how long it went on for. What matters is this thing with the boy. What matters is that someone's been arrested for a crime he didn't commit. What on earth can we do about it? What did the sergeant tell you about what's going to happen next?'

Lilian was chewing her lip again. She answered unwillingly. 'He said the boy will have to appear at the police court on Thursday morning, for the prosecution to start making their case. If it looks strong enough to the magistrate, it'll go to trial at the Old Bailey.'

'The Old Bailey! Oh, this is dreadful. But, then, he isn't on trial just yet? It could all still come to nothing?'

'I—I don't know. Yes, I think so. The police have to put their side of it together. And the inquest's got to be re-opened. But that won't happen straight away. The whole thing might take weeks, the sergeant said.'

'Weeks! And meanwhile the boy will be—what? Kept in a prison cell?'

'I think so.'

'Oh, Lilian. It's unbelievable! After everything we've been through. You know what we ought to do, don't you? We ought to go straight to the police. We ought to walk into Camberwell police station and tell them everything. Suppose it does go to a trial? There wouldn't be the evidence to convict him; a few stupid hairs won't hang anyone. But we oughtn't to let it go on for even another hour. We ought to speak to Inspector Kemp. But, then, if we were to do that—Oh, God!' Her mind was leaping ahead, just as it had on the night of Leonard's death: she was seeing the newspapers, the neighbours, her mother's stricken face. She had to lean against the bed. 'What would happen? They'd keep us at the police station. We'd have to think about lawyers; Mrs Playfair might help with that. But where on earth would the money come from?'

They paused, taking in the enormity of it all. Lilian blinked her red-rimmed eyes. She said, 'You—You don't really want us to go?'

Frances wiped her mouth. 'No, of course I don't want to. I'm just thinking of this boy. Aren't you thinking of him?'

'It's just, I'm frightened.'

'I know, Lily. I'm frightened, too.'

'I'm frightened for you. I'm frightened for him. But most of all—I can't help it—I'm frightened for myself. If we were to tell them the truth now, I don't know what they'd do to me. Everybody hates me as it is. This would make it all a hundred times worse. They'd say I murdered him—'

Frances leaned across the bed towards her. 'They wouldn't say that. I promise you, I swear to you! I'd never let them say that.'

'Then they'd just say that you helped me do it. How could we ever prove that you didn't? They'd put us on trial for it, Frances. If we could just—just wait a bit. Until we know what's going to happen next. I know it's dreadful of me. But when Sergeant Heath came today, I thought he'd come to arrest me; and then, when he told me they'd arrested someone else, I felt sick. I felt sick with relief. It was just such a relief to think that now no one would be looking at me and hating me ... If we could just let it be like that, just for a little while. I wouldn't say it if it was any other sort of boy. But he's been in trouble with the police before. It won't be as bad for him as it would be for—for us.'

Frances was still leaning across the bed; the springs were creaking beneath her hands. She dropped her head in a sort of agony. 'I don't know, Lilian. I don't know what we ought to do. It's been clear up till now, but—Won't it go against us, if it ever comes out? If they find out, I mean, that we waited? It was one thing when it was just the two of us, but if someone else has been dragged in ... Won't it look better if we go forward at once? Last week you were talking about going to the police yourself. Maybe you were right. I don't know any more.'

'But it's different now,' said Lilian. 'They might have believed it was an accident if I'd told them about it then. Now they'll think I did it on purpose, won't they, because of Len and this girl?'

'But you didn't know anything about Len and the girl.'

'I think—I think she might say that I did.'

Her hand was back at her mouth; she had spoken indistinctly. And perhaps because of that, or because of something in her pose or expression, Frances suddenly grew wary. She said, 'Well, why would she say that?' And then, when Lilian didn't answer: '*Did* you know about them?'

Lilian was silent for a moment. Then she dropped her hand. 'Yes.'

Frances straightened up. 'What?'

'At least—A few weeks ago I found something in one of Len's pockets. The tickets from a show. They were from a night he said he'd been at his parents'; I knew he must have taken some girl. We had an awful row about it. In the end he told me the people at his office had set it all up, as a joke. I didn't know whether or not to believe him. I never thought it was like this! I never thought there was just the one girl he was seeing over and over!'

Frances's heart had grown oddly heavy. 'But why didn't you tell me?'

Lilian wouldn't meet her eye. 'I don't know. I didn't want to think about it.'

'But I wish you'd told me. I thought—I thought that was the point. That we were honest with each other, about everything, right from the start.'

'It doesn't matter, does it?'

'But these tickets. When did you find them? You said there was a row. Why didn't you *tell* me?'

Again, Lilian didn't answer. Frances waited—then, somehow, understood.

'It was when you were on holiday. That's what made you write me that letter.'

Lilian shook her head, and spoke quickly. 'It wasn't like that, Frances.'

'The letter wasn't about me at all. It was simply about hating *him*.'

'No.'

But Frances had stepped back from the bed. She was painfully piecing things together. 'When the police told us about Charlie, when we knew that Charlie was lying—you must have known what it meant. Why didn't you say something then?'

'I don't know,' Lilian answered. 'I couldn't bear to think of it, not on top of everything else. When Len and I got married—You don't

467

know what it was like for me, Frances. We had to do it in such a hurry. People laughed at me. They said it served me right, for having been grand. I couldn't bear the thought of them knowing, of them laughing at me again.'

'You were ashamed?' said Frances. 'Of *that*?'

Lilian bowed her head, put a hand across her eyes. 'Please, Frances. Don't be like this.'

But Frances's sense of dismay was giving way to anger. The anger was so pure, so complete, it amazed her. It was as if the feeling had been inside her, waiting for the signal to come out. She thought of all she had done in the past ten days, all those crumbling walls she had been frantically propping up. She thought of the breach with Christina, the suspicion in her mother's eyes.

She heard her own voice hardening. 'You knew you were pregnant when you were on that holiday. You knew you were pregnant when you found those tickets. Didn't you?'

'Don't, Frances—'

'Didn't you?'

'Please—'

'No wonder you didn't want the baby.'

Lilian lifted her head. 'What? No, that was all for you and me.'

'No wonder you swung that ashtray so hard.'

'But—But I didn't mean to swing it at all. You know I didn't. It was an accident.'

Frances held her gaze. 'Was it?'

Again, she hadn't planned to ask the question, but the moment the words were out of her mouth she realised that they had been somewhere inside her, agitating to be said. They had been there since—since when? Since Inspector Kemp had told her about that life insurance? Or, since before that? Since the very beginning of it all? Since she had first placed her ear against Leonard's overcoated back and failed to find a beat behind it?

From across the gloomy room Lilian was looking at her as if she could follow the movement of her thoughts. She stood still for a moment; then her whole frame seemed to soften. Like a lighted candle folding in on itself, she sank down at the side of the bed, putting her arms on the eiderdown, letting her head droop forward on to her wrists.

'I knew it would make you hate me,' she said.

Frances began to straighten the cuffs of her gloves. The gesture felt jerky, not quite real. 'It doesn't matter,' she heard herself say—and the words were jerky and unreal, too; the words of a prim-faced spinster. 'We can't think of ourselves now. We have to think of this boy.'

'I'd give anything to undo it, Frances.'

'We have to find Inspector Kemp.'

'I'd give anything to undo it—not for Len's sake, but for ours. I don't know what I was thinking when I hit him. I know I was hating him. Does that make it murder? But, then, what does loving make? I love you more than I ever hated him. Please, Frances—'

'Stop saying that!' said Frances sharply. 'It's all you've ever said to me! Right from the start! When we went to the park—you remember? We barely knew each other. But we went to the park. And we left, and were walking up the hill—and you took the wall. You took the wall, Lilian. I thought it charming, at the time. But you've been taking the wall ever since. You can't take it for ever. You can't take it now.'

Her tone must have carried: she was conscious of the women in the room below, grown still and attentive. Lilian, perhaps conscious of them too, remained in her crouch, but looked up, white-faced.

But then, as Frances watched, her expression changed, smoothed itself out. She got to her feet and, without another word, she moved around the bed and, slowly, pointedly, began to make herself ready. She found a fresh handkerchief to exchange for the damp one in her sleeve. She took money from a tin in a drawer, hesitating for a moment about how much to take, finally folding the coins into the notes and tucking them all into her handbag. She stood at the dressing-table mirror and powdered her face and swollen eyelids. She dabbed rouge on to her cheeks and lips. She took up a hairbrush and carefully brushed her hair.

Frances saw all this and didn't believe in any of it. She kept expecting Lilian to slow, to falter, to start to cry. But Lilian did none of those things. In the same deliberate way she drew back a curtain from across an alcove and unhooked her coat from the rail beyond. She returned with it to the mirror and shrugged it on, straightening its collar. The coat had a long line of buttons to it. She began, calmly, to fasten them.

And as Frances watched the neat upward progress of her fingers, something odd began to happen to her. First her heart started to flutter, then she felt a sort of giving way, around it: a caving in, like the slither of sand through the waist of an hour-glass. It was as if her blood, her muscles, her organs, were steadily dissolving. Lilian's buttons were all fastened now. She returned to the alcove for her hat and, still calm, still neat, she settled it on her head. Now Frances's face was tingling as if growing numb. The caved-in feeling had reached her legs: she had to support herself on the side of the creaking bed. She wanted to be sick. Her heart felt squeezed. She thought with astonishment, I'm ill. Christ, I'm really ill. I'm dying!

Then she looked up, saw that Lilian was ready, saw that she had turned and was waiting to go; and she realised that she wasn't dying, she was simply afraid. She was more afraid than she had ever been before, with a fear that was stronger than any feeling she could remember—grief, anger, passion, love, anything. For she knew that Lilian was right. The police would never believe that Leonard had been killed by accident. She knew it, because of that moment, a few minutes before, when she hadn't believed it herself. Lilian would be tried for murder, and she would be tried along with her as—what? An accessory? An accomplice? Perhaps the inspector would do some digging, turn up her old affair with Christina.

He'd make something filthy of that; something filthy of her love for Lilian.

He'd make a motive of it. They might be hanged.

Beyond the window, the day was darkening. On the lino floor the stars and commas were brighter than before. Downstairs, there were murmurs; something was dropped, someone was scolded, the little dog let out a yelp.

Lilian was still waiting. Frances met her gaze, then shook her head and, with a shiver of self-loathing, turned away.

'Take off your hat and coat,' she said. 'We'll do as you said and— and wait. We'll wait till Thursday, till the police court hearing. We'll wait to see how bad it looks.'

15

For the first time, they parted without touching, without even attempting to embrace, after making the barest of arrangements for how they would deal with what came next. Down on the half-landing, Frances couldn't bring herself to look into the kitchen to say goodbye to Mrs Viney and Vera; she left Lilian to say it for her, and to make up any excuse she liked to explain away her strange behaviour. She went down the second flight of stairs, and along the narrow passage, alone. The street seemed busier than ever when she opened the door on it. But the swell of terror that had engulfed her in the bedroom had sunk like a tide, and as she passed along the crowded pavement she didn't feel much of anything. There seemed to be a sort of oil-skin layer—tiredness; hunger, perhaps—between herself and the world.

Arriving home, she found Mrs Playfair in the drawing-room with her mother. The two of them got to their feet, looking anxious, the moment she appeared. Had she heard about the arrest? Yes, she told them dully, she had seen the evening paper; she had gone straight to Lilian's to get the story from her.

Her mother hesitated when she heard that. That fretfulness, that inwardness, had disappeared from her expression. Her manner now was tentative, awkward—troubled in a different sort of way. 'How has Mrs Barber taken the news?' she asked.

Frances answered as dully as before. 'I don't think she knows what to make of it yet.'

'No, I don't suppose she does. It's such a very distressing mixture. Could she tell you anything more about the man who's been arrested?'

'No, not much. He's young, they say. Nineteen, I think.'

'Nineteen! And, Mr Barber?' Her mother hesitated again. 'Is it really true what the newspapers claim?'

Frances nodded. 'The police say so. He'd been seeing the girl for months, apparently.'

Her mother sat down. 'Poor Mrs Barber. For this to be added to everything else. I—I feel I've been unfair to her. You used to say how unhappy she was in her marriage, Frances, and now I understand why. To think of Mr Barber behaving in such a way. All this time, under all our noses! Yes, I feel I've been very unfair to her.'

Mrs Playfair, returning to the sofa, agreed that it was a most deplorable business. She'd always said that men were the weaker sex; this sort of thing just went to prove it. But she, too, looked awkward, and seemed not quite able to meet Frances's eye. 'There,' she said at last. 'At least the thing is settled now. It must be a great comfort to Mrs Barber that this young man has been caught. It's a comfort to all of us, isn't it, to know that he's no longer on the streets.'

Frances agreed that it was. She still felt oddly lifeless. She excused herself, left the drawing-room and climbed the stairs. What she wanted more than anything, she'd realised, was a cigarette. She went straight to her bedside drawer for her papers and tobacco. Her hand was quite untrembling as she rolled the little thing up.

But almost on the first puff she began to cough. The cough grew steadily more violent until it was shaking her right through and had become something else, become nausea. At last she had to lean into the fireplace, retching drily over the grate, while tears and saliva streamed from her face to mingle with the ashes on the hearthstone.

By the time Mrs Playfair left she had calmed herself down. That oil-skin layer seemed to be back in place. She cooked a dinner, and enjoyed eating it. She drew herself a bath and lay in the water watching the steam rise from her arms into the cold scullery air like fantastic smoke. When, later, she sat with her mother by the drawing-room fire, it was quite like old times. They had their cocoa, she wound the clock, plumped the cushions, locked the door, and they both went yawning to bed. The grittiness had gone from her throat; her muscles, even, had lost their ache. For the first time since Leonard's death she slept deeply, without dreams.

Next day, the newspapers all carried something about the arrest, about the boy, Spencer Ward—Frances was growing used to the name already, and to the girl's name, Billie Grey. But there were no new photographs, and perhaps that helped to keep the whole thing not quite real. The *Mirror* had the most to report: the boy was employed at a garage at Tower Bridge; he lived with his mother, a War-widow; he was 'leanly built, with brown hair and hazel eyes'—it could have been a description of anyone. The girl was an assistant in a West End 'beauty shop', whatever the hell that was, and it was in a public house close to the shop, whilst enjoying a drink with her sister in the summer, that she had apparently 'first made the acquaintance of the murdered Mr Barber'.

Seeing Leonard's name like that made Frances begin to grow frightened again. And because she was afraid of the fear expanding, becoming the debilitating terror it had been the day before, she hurriedly put the paper aside. What did it matter, anyhow, whether she read it or not? What would it change? They had made their decision.

That afternoon, she and her mother received a visit from Sergeant Heath. He'd come to make sure they had seen the news, and to let them know that their statements were to be read at the police court on Thursday morning. There was no necessity, he said, for them to attend the hearing themselves; not unless they wished to, and he hardly imagined that they would. Oh, Miss Wray planned to go, did she? That was entirely up to her, of course . . . Yes, he and Inspector Kemp were both feeling very satisfied now that they had got their man. It was a great pity that Mr Wismuth hadn't spoken up sooner, and so spared everyone a lot of trouble and worry—but, naturally, no one was regretting that more than Mr Wismuth himself, who was now in a certain amount of trouble of his own, charged with making a false statement and wasting police time. Evidently his fiancée, Miss Nixon, had thrown him over, too! Well, that wasn't to be wondered at, in the circumstances . . .

He was cheerful, almost chatty; had quite cast off that guardedness that had made him so unnerving a figure to Frances in the past. He didn't mention Lilian. He didn't mention life insurance. He and the inspector, she recalled, had once spoken confidently of the killer's being 'a man of regular habits', but he seemed to have forgotten that too: the boy Ward, he said, with relish, was 'a real little villain. Oh, yes, a proper little tough.' She knew there were things she ought to be asking, things she ought to find out; she didn't seem to have the ingenuity for it. In any case, he stayed only ten minutes. He had people to interview over in Bermondsey, neighbours of the boy and his mother. She let him out of the house, then watched him from the drawing-room window, stepping on to his bicycle and pushing away from the kerb. And, in shame, she knew she was feeling what Lilian had felt the day before: simple relief, like a letting go of weight, a giving up of resistance, at seeing him heading so purposefully out of her life and into someone else's.

*

But she did not sleep quite so soundly that night. And by Thursday morning she was beginning to recover the sense of urgency that had gripped her at the start of it all, an itch to put herself at the very worst point of things in order to know just how bad they were. The police court was two or three miles away, close to the Elephant and Castle; she left the house in good time, determined to get there ahead of any crowd. But the papers had advertised the hearing. She could sense an excitement in the streets as she made her way through Kennington, and on turning the final corner she was taken aback to see a jostling swarm of people at the modest court-house entrance, all apparently hell-bent on getting places inside. She couldn't imagine herself joining in with them, pushing her way through that press of bodies. But she had to be there, she had to know. If the boy were committed for trial, how would she prevent it? What might Lilian, without her, do or say?

She was just starting to panic about it when she saw Constable Hardy on his way into the building. He recognised her from the morning he had brought the bad news, and led her away from the public doors to the witnesses' entrance.

He had to leave her as soon as he had got her inside, and then there was more of that uncertainty about what to do and where to go that she remembered from the inquest; this time, she felt very much alone in it. Even when she spotted Netta's husband, Lloyd, on the far side of the small but crowded lobby—even when she saw Lilian, standing just beyond him with her mother and Vera, talking to a man who might have been a lawyer, nodding gravely and anxiously at what the man was saying—even then, she felt uncertain of her role. Vera caught her eye with a frown—as if she were thinking, in disbelief, *What, here too?* At any rate, though she raised her chin in greeting she didn't beckon for Frances to join them. Lilian didn't beckon, either. She met Frances's gaze, still talking to the lawyer, still gravely nodding at what he was telling her; and a shadow of apprehension passed across her pale face. But then

476

another man came, to lead her away, and the family turned and went with her. By the time Frances had made her own way into the courtroom the four of them were established in there, sitting in a pew-like bench close to the front. When again they made no invitation to her she took herself to the end of another pew, off to the side.

The pew was faintly sticky beneath her skirt and gloves. The room was a grubbier version of the chamber in which they'd gathered for the inquest, with the same trumped-up, blustering feel to its heavy panelling, its thrones and coronets. The only difference was the square enclosure—something like a horse's stall—set facing the magistrate's bench: Frances's gaze passed over it several times before she realised that, of course, it was the dock for the accused. She felt another faint stirring of panic at that—then saw how far she was from any exit. Suppose that terror should overtake her again? Suppose she should faint, or be sick?

It was too late. The pews were filling up, with reporters, with officials—she noticed Inspector Kemp, looking more than ever as if he belonged behind the desk of a bank as he added notes with a fountain pen to a folder of type-written papers. A moment later the doors were opened to the public and in came two or three dozen people, all with the same look on their faces: the repellent triumph of shoppers bagging the best of the bargains in the January sales. A woman of fifty-five or so plonked herself down next to Frances. She blew out her cheeks, rolled her eyes, undid the top two buttons of her tartan coat and flapped the lapel back and forth. It was always a squeeze when it was a murder, wasn't it! Had Frances come far? She herself had come all the way from Paddington. She generally came to the courts with a friend—that made it easier to keep places—but today her friend had the neuralgia, so she had come along on her own. It was worth it, though. She hadn't wanted to miss this one; she'd been following it in the papers. Oh, her friend *would* be sick when she heard how well she'd got on!

Her gaze was darting about the courtroom as she spoke; now, leech-like, it fastened on Lilian. 'There's the widow, of course. Doesn't look quite so handsome as she does in her pictures, does she? No, she's quite a disappointment. The ladies beside her—that's the mother, I believe, and a sister. I don't know who the gentleman is . . . Oh, now, who's this?' She had turned her head as the court-room doors swung open to admit three newcomers.

They were Leonard's father and Uncle Ted, with the older brother, Douglas. They came in with a self-conscious air, and were shown to a place by a court official. 'Here, do you mean?' Frances heard Douglas ask, through a lull in the general hubbub; and at the sound of his voice, once again, a chill came over her: it was so very like Leonard's.

Automatically, she looked at Lilian. She too was watching the Barbers find their seats. This must have been the first time since the funeral that the two families had met. For a minute Frances saw them all eyeing each other across the room, Vera with a face like thunder, Mrs Viney and Lloyd with their colour high, but Lilian simply looking embarrassed and unhappy. Then the three Barber men spoke quietly together, and Leonard's father got to his feet and made his way around the crowded pews, baring his sandy head as he went. He and Lilian murmured and nodded; finally she put out her gloved hand to him. He took it and held it, and they murmured again.

On his way back to his seat he had to pause for a moment to let Constable Hardy lead in a new arrival. This was a sad little wisp of a woman in a limp brown coat and hat. She looked around with a bewildered air as she headed to the place pointed out to her, then lifted her face to Mr Barber in dazed apology as he went by. A change had come over him, however: his cheeks were suddenly blazing. He returned to his brother and his son, appeared to mutter something to them; they turned to study the woman, in a con-spicuous sort of way. People all around the room were also gazing

478

keenly at her. Frances's neighbour in tartan was staring at her as she might have stared at a monkey in a cage. Finally, noticing Frances's blank expression, she said, 'But you know who that is, don't you? That's Mrs Ward, the mother of the boy who's up for the murder!'

Frances looked again at the cowed little woman; then dropped her eyes in shame.

And then the magistrate came in, and they all had to clamber to their feet. People settled down again with the throat-clearings, the rustles and readjustments, of an expectant theatre crowd. His own manner, as he ran through the preliminaries, was unexcited—for, of course, thought Frances in wonder, this was simply the beginning of a long day of business for him. He would see case after case, crime after crime, between now and tea-time . . . Still, murder was murder, and even he looked interested as the usher summoned the accused. As for the crowd—the room grew stiller. There was a sudden extra hush, like a drop in temperature. A door at the side of the court was opened. Sergeant Heath brought in the boy, Spencer Ward, and escorted him to the dock.

Frances's immediate feeling was one of plunging disappointment. What exactly had she been expecting? The boy was slight and quite unmemorable, at least as far as appearances went. He had ordinary darkish hair, parted and flattened with ordinary pomade. He wore an ordinary ready-made blue suit, with a young man's tie, ordinarily garish. His face was lean, with prominent cheekbones; his jaw was narrow and overcrowded—a little like Leonard's jaw, in fact, though, unlike Leonard's, his chin was weak, and overall he had none of Leonard's bounce, Leonard's gingery vitality. Instead he slouched his way across the room at Sergeant Heath's elbow, then climbed the two or three steps to the dock with an air—she could hardly believe it—of smirking nonchalance. He seemed to be chewing gum. Did he look for his mother at all? Frances didn't think so. Rather, recognising some friends on the public benches, he leaned over the rail of the enclosure to call a question to them, and then to query the answer with a curled upper lip, displaying a mouthful of awful teeth.

Sergeant Heath caught hold of his elbow and yanked him upright—that set him off smirking again. He kept the smirk in place while the clerk asked him to confirm that he was William Spencer Ward, of Victory Buildings, Tower Bridge Road; and when he answered, he did it with a snigger. The naming of the crime with which he was charged produced no response from him at all. Frances had expected him to protest his innocence; all he did was change his pose, shifting his weight from one foot to another and putting his hands in his trouser pockets, chewing more vigorously on his gum. His neck was a child's neck, she saw then, thin, white, unmuscular. Beneath the padding in the shoulders of his jacket she could make out the lines of his shoulder-blades, sharp as two narrow plates of metal.

She was struggling to find something about him that she could pity, that she could like. At the same time, it seemed impossible to her that anyone could seriously believe that he had committed a murder: he was so puny, so youthful, so sham. All around the room, though, she saw people looking at him in fascinated horror. The three Barber men were bristling, Leonard's brother leaning forward, his eyes fixed on the boy in a sort of malevolent challenge.

The magistrate called for the prosecution to make their case, and Inspector Kemp got to his feet. With his folder of papers under his arm he stepped smartly up to the witness stand, to take a Bible from the clerk and swear his oath on it. He was Detective Inspector Ronald Kemp, he said, of Metropolitan Division P, and he had been leading the inquiry into the murder of Leonard Arthur Barber. He proposed to read to the magistrate a number of witness statements that, in his opinion, would justify the committal to trial of the prisoner Spencer Ward.

He began with those documents relating to Leonard's final hours, and to the finding of his body. He read the reports of Constables Hardy and Evans, the first policemen to arrive at the scene. He read the statements given by Lilian, by Frances's mother and by Frances herself; Frances listened to the last with her gaze lowered, feeling herself grow hot. What a thing to blush about, she thought, with so much else to be ashamed of! But it was odd and uncomfortable to have her words, her lies, read back to her so publicly. It was odd, too, to realise how phlegmatic the inspector's tone was, and to note how quickly he passed on from her statement, and even from Lilian's, to those of the spooning couple who'd heard the scuffling in the lane; and then how briskly he moved on again, to what he plainly considered to be the meat of the case. For, once he'd gone through the principal points of the police surgeon's report, he cleared his throat, took a sip of water, and uncovered the next document in his folder. The statement he was turning to now, he announced, was that of Charles Price Wismuth. It was the second statement that Mr Wismuth had made to the police, replacing an earlier, false statement which Mr Wismuth had since withdrawn.

Another rustle of anticipation went around the court. People had begun to look slightly glazed at the continuous reading. They had been here for twenty minutes, and the room was growing stuffy; the inspector had told them nothing that they hadn't seen already in the *News of the World*. But now they all became more alert. Leonard's brother drew his challenging gaze away from the boy in the dock, and his father and uncle grew braced. And it was only as she looked from their faces to those of the men seated around them that Frances realised that Charlie himself was not here. He must have been too ashamed to come. Or did the police have him locked up somewhere?

Christ, what a mess it all was!

Then Inspector Kemp began to read, and she understood why Charlie had kept away.

The statement described how, back in the summer, he and Leonard had become acquainted with two women in a Holborn public house. The women were Miss Mabel Grey, commonly known as Billie, and her elder sister Mrs King. "'I knew that Mrs King was married,'" the inspector read out, in his bland, unvarnished way. "'She said that she and her husband did not get along; that they had an understanding, that he went his way and she went hers. I did not tell her that I was myself engaged to be married. I did not consider it important. I did hear Mr Barber telling Miss Grey that he was married. I heard him telling her that he and his wife had a similar arrangement to that of Mrs King and her husband. I heard him profess the belief that such an arrangement was a good idea.'"

Unable to help herself, Frances glanced again at Lilian. She was sitting with her head lowered, blushing slightly, but apart from that her expression was a dead one.

"'Mr Barber and I,'" the statement ran on, "'continued to meet Miss Grey and Mrs King over a period of four months, between June and September this year. We would meet them once or twice a week, generally at public houses or for walks in the Green Park. We several times made them gifts of jewellery, or of items of female clothing.

"'On Saturday the first of July this year Mr Barber and I spent an evening with Miss Grey and Mrs King at the Honey Bee night-club at Peter Street, Soho. Here we were approached in a threatening manner by two men. The men identified themselves as Alfred King, Mrs King's husband, and Spencer Ward, who claimed to be the fiancé of Miss Grey. I had never heard Miss Grey mention a fiancé previously, but I had the impression that she and Mr Ward were well acquainted. The two men spoke in angry terms to Mr Barber and myself, and an argument ensued, during which Mr Barber and I thought it wisest to leave the Honey Bee. We travelled together to Camberwell Green, where I left Mr Barber to return to his home at Champion Hill, while I continued on to Peckham to visit my fiancée Miss Elizabeth Nixon. I did not see Spencer Ward again that night, but the next time I saw Mr Barber he had an injury to the face, and he informed me that Mr Ward had pursued him to Champion Hill and had there assaulted him. During the assault Mr Ward had warned Mr Barber to keep clear of Miss Grey, or he would be sorry. Mr Ward's words, as reported to me by Mr Barber, were something like, 'If you do not stay away from Billie I will do something to make you sorry. In fact, I will knock your bloody head off.' He may have said bloody, or he may have used a coarser word—"' Here the inspector paused for a second, as the boy in the dock let out a snort of laughter, '"—but he definitely, as Mr Barber related it, threatened to knock his head off.

'"Following this incident I continued to see Mrs King, but less frequently than before. Mr Barber, however, continued to see Miss Grey regularly. On several occasions I was aware that he had represented to his wife that he had made an arrangement to spend an evening with me, when in fact he had arranged to meet Miss Grey, and I know for a fact that the two of them remained on intimate terms. By 'intimate terms' I mean that those relations were taking place between them which normally occur between a husband and a wife. I know it because Mr Barber sometimes met Miss Grey privately at my rooms at Tulse Hill, where he left particular traces behind him. I remained uneasy about this, because of the warning given to Mr Barber by Mr Ward. I considered Mr Ward to be a dangerous man."'

Another sip of water and a clearing of the throat, another page turned; and the tortuous mincing language ran on.

'"Friday the fifteenth of September this year was one of those evenings which Mr Barber had arranged to spend in the company of Miss Grey, having previously told Mrs Barber that he would be spending it with me. I myself did not see Mr Barber at all that evening, but passed it with Mrs King at the Empress Picture

483

Theatre, Islington. The following day I received a visit at my home from Police Sergeant Heath of P Division, informing me of Mr Barber's death, and enquiring as to my whereabouts the previous night. I immediately suspected that Mr Barber had been killed by Mr Ward. I did not mention my suspicions to the police because I feared that my own activities with Mrs King would be brought to light, and that her husband would hear of it. I also feared the effect that such a disclosure would have on my fiancée Miss Nixon, on Mr Barber's wife and on Miss Grey. I knowingly made a false statement to the police in which I said that Mr Barber and I had spent the evening together at public houses in the City, and that I had last seen him at the Blackfriars tram-stop at ten p.m. In the days which followed I had several opportunities to retract my statement, and I did not do so. This decision is one which I now heartily regret."'

Here the inspector had to pause again, in order to rearrange his folder. For a minute there were murmurs, along with the furious whisper of pens on paper as the court recorder made his notes and the newspaper men made theirs.

Frances sat staring at nothing, trying to weave the grubby threads of Charlie's statement around her own recollections of the past few months. She thought of all those summer evenings when Leonard had been kept late at work. She remembered occasions when he'd come home yawning in that showy way of his; or other nights when he'd come whistling, then gone springing up the stairs. All those times, when she and Lilian had leapt apart at the sound of his key in the door, he must have just come from his girl, come straight from kissing her to—She bent her head, put a hand to her mouth, seeing clearly, for the first time, the tawdry chain of lies and infidelity that had been in place without her knowledge, a chain with Leonard at its centre, and herself at one end, and—who, precisely, at the other? This boy, this boy in the dock! This boy with his slouch and his smirk and his Dickensian teeth. She gazed across at Lilian's profile, and for a moment, just a moment, she felt a burst of resentment towards her so violent that it could only be called hatred. How could you do it? she wanted to cry at her. How could you involve me in all this? How could you have brought me to this place, this horrible room, with its beastly people and its revolting peelings-back?

But the inspector's voice had started up again; she had to haul her attention back to it. He had begun on his next document—the statement of the girl, Billie Grey, confirming the essentials of Charlie's account. Yes, she had seen Mr Barber on many occasions in the summer, and, yes, her friend Spencer Ward had sometimes objected to it; they had once had a 'falling out' because of it, in which he had knocked out one of her teeth. On the night of the first of July, after the incident at the Honey Bee night-club, Mr Ward had come to her rooms at half-past midnight and shown her bruises on his knuckles that he said he had got from having 'smashed Mr Barber's face in'. But on the night of Mr Barber's murder she did not know where he had been. She herself had had an arrangement to spend that evening with Mr Barber, but had been 'suffering from an indisposition': she'd had tea and bread and butter with him at the Corner House on the Tottenham Court Road, but had been obliged to part from him at half-past seven. She had known nothing about his death until she had seen it reported in the Sunday newspapers, and she had been thoroughly shocked and upset. She had immediately found Spencer Ward and challenged him over it, and the news of the murder had not seemed to surprise him. He had said that Mr Barber had been 'owed a wallop like that for a very long time'.

There were hisses from Leonard's father and brother at that— though the boy, Frances saw, was smirking again. He still had his hands in his trouser pockets, he was still chewing away at his gum. His gaze was fixed on the floor of the dock; he seemed to be worrying at a splinter in the boards with the toe of one of his shoes.

He lifted his head, however, for the series of statements that were read next. They were from men, youths, boys—associates of his from Bermondsey; pals or, perhaps, enemies—anyhow, four or five people who said he had boasted 'pretty freely' of having attacked his fiancée's boy-friend in July, threatening to 'do worse to him next time'. None of them could say what he had been doing on the night of Leonard's death. But all of them confirmed that he was in the habit of carrying a cosh.

Here the inspector looked up from his papers to ask a uniformed policeman to bring him the weapon that had been removed from the accused at the time of his arrest. He was handed a brown-paper parcel, from which he produced a stubby dark-leather object with a bulbous head and tapering handle. The court officials regarded the horrible thing without excitement, but Frances's neighbour in tartan craned for a better view, the newspaper men stopped scribbling to watch, and even the boy, finally, paid proper attention as, sure of his audience, the inspector held the cosh higher, then brought it down with a loud smack on the sill of the witness stand. The head, he explained to the magistrate, was loaded with shot. He and his men had found traces on it of what they believed to be blood. The traces were currently being analysed at the Home Office laboratory.

The cosh was returned to its paper wrapper and handed back to the constable. Leonard's father, Frances saw, was fishing for his handkerchief; as soon as he got it, he covered his face.

After that, the reading aloud of the final statement—that of Spencer Ward himself—seemed a mere formality. It was the one testimony, Frances thought, that quite possibly contained no lies; the one document to which they should all have given their fullest attention. But the parading of the cosh had blurred the focus of the chamber. People in the pews behind her were openly chatting: she turned around to glare at them; they met the glare and chatted on. And even the inspector's tone was perfunctory now. Yes, the boy admitted to having assaulted Leonard Barber on the first of July. He

486

might have threatened to knock his head off; he couldn't recall. But he strenuously denied the other charge. He'd acquired a cosh for killing rats and black-beetles in the building in which he lived. He carried it about for self-protection; he'd never used it in a fight. He'd certainly never used it on Mr Barber on the fifteenth of September. He could remember that evening very clearly, because he'd been suffering from a headache. He had been at home with his mother and had gone early to bed.

And that, incredibly, was it. There was no calling of witnesses, no one to speak for the defence. The inspector closed his folder. The clerk and the newspaper men wrote on for a few seconds more; the magistrate turned to Spencer to inform him that since he was currently without a counsel he was at liberty to cross-examine Inspector Kemp on his own behalf. Did he wish to do so?

It took the boy a moment to understand that he was being addressed. He looked blankly back at the magistrate, who spoke again, with impatience.

'You are charged with the gravest possible crime, Mr Ward. Do you have anything to say to the court in support of yourself against it?'

Finding all eyes turned his way, the boy began to smirk again. 'Yeah,' he said. 'I never done it. But I'd like to shake hands with the bloke that did!'

His friends in the crowd laughed out loud. Leonard's father, uncle and brother let out more hisses of outrage. Frances's heart sank.

The magistrate, unimpressed, turned back to Inspector Kemp. 'Well, I am satisfied that there is enough evidence against the suspect to justify keeping him on remand for seven days. You'll have the laboratory findings by the end of that period, I take it? And Mr Ward, I trust, will have secured a counsel by then. For now, you may remove him to Brixton Prison. Mr Wells—'

He called forward some court official. Sergeant Heath led the boy from the dock. People rose to leave the chamber; others shuffled in to take their places. 'Quickly, please!' cried the usher, with a shooing gesture. He had to keep the police-court day grinding on, after all.

Frances got to her feet, and made her way across the courtroom, feeling almost dazed. She had expected some sort of resolution. She had supposed that everything would be decided, for better or for worse. She reached the doors to the lobby at the same moment as the Walworth party, and this time they turned to include her; they went out as a single group.

Mrs Viney and Vera were flushed. Lloyd was incandescent.

'What a bloody little waster. Excuse my language, Miss Wray, but, really. A good flogging's what he needs. They should take a horse-whip to him! When I think of the mates I lost in France, and all so as little swines like him can—I was just saying, Mr Barber—' Leonard's father had appeared, with Douglas and Uncle Ted behind him; they all moved away from the doors, to allow other people to come and go. 'I was just saying, that boy needs a bloody horse-whip taking to him! Standing there with his hands in his pockets, chewing gum and grinning like that. I could see Sergeant Heath itching to have a go at him, couldn't you? I wanted to have a go at him myself.'

Mr Barber couldn't speak; he was still mopping his eyes with his handkerchief. It was Leonard's brother who answered, in that unnerving voice of his.

'Oh, he's not worth bruising your hand on. He's filth. He's trash! I'm just glad my mother wasn't here to see him. You saw *his* mother, I suppose? A nice job she's done of bringing him up, hasn't she? Here she comes, look.' The poor little woman, apparently more bewildered than ever, had just pushed her way through the swing doors. Seeing the eyes of the family on her, she hesitated; then, realising who they were—or, perhaps, simply recognising their hostility—she ducked her head, turned away, and headed off, all alone.

'Oh, God love her,' said Mrs Viney, in her feeling way.

Douglas almost spat. 'God love her? She'll get what she deserves from Him, all right. And so will that little thug. But he'll get what he deserves down here, first. Or he will if I've got anything to do with it.'

'I'm with you there,' said Lloyd grimly.

Uncle Ted said, 'At least they're keeping him in prison for the week. Not that that will bother him, mind.'

'Bother him?' answered Douglas. 'He'll probably have the time of his life in there! You know he was in the waiting-room this morning, bragging to all the other men about how his crime was the finest on the charge-sheet? Constable Evans told us, earlier. No, there's no morality in him. You only have to look at his face to see that.'

'I did wonder,' said Mrs Viney, 'whether he's quite all there.'

'Oh, he's all there, all right.'

Frances gazed at them in frustration. Couldn't they see that the boy's manner was all bravado, all pose? She said, 'I don't think he's taken it in yet. I don't think he understands his situation.'

Douglas snorted. 'He understood his situation when he went after my brother in July, Miss Wray. He hasn't denied that, has he? Yes, he understood his way from Soho to Champion Hill!'

'Didn't he just,' said Vera, as the others nodded. 'Mind, he wouldn't have had to understand it, if Len hadn't been in Soho in the first place.'

That shut Douglas up. There was an uncomfortable silence. People lowered their heads and looked furtively at Lilian, who all this time had been standing just behind Frances's shoulder, staring at the floor.

Finally Mr Barber, tucking away his handkerchief, said, 'I hope Lilian knows how sorry I am that she had to hear those things read out from Charlie's statement like that. If I hadn't heard them myself, I should never have believed them. To think of Leonard carrying on in such a way—well, it's upset me almost more than anything.'

And, 'Yes,' said Douglas stiffly. 'Yes, that was very shabby. I can't think what Len thought he was playing at.'

Mrs Viney said, 'Well, neither can I! It didn't even sound like Lenny, did it? It didn't sound like Charlie, either. I said to Lil, "Do you think it's all true?" I wonder if the inspector hasn't made it out to be worse than what it was—put words in Charlie's mouth, I mean. The police can be very artful, you know. And those two girls—'

'*Them!*' said Douglas, suddenly back on surer ground. 'I'd like to get my hands on them! That Billie, or Mabel, or whatever the hell she calls herself. I've a few choice names for her! Her, and that sister of hers. If they know nothing about the murder, then I'm a Dutchman!'

Mrs Viney looked shocked. 'You don't say so!'

'I do. You just wait. It'll all come out. You notice they didn't turn up today? Didn't want to look us in the eye, I suppose. No, I bet they damn well didn't . . . '

And he was off again, railing against the two girls now, his colour higher than ever, his brother's infidelities forgotten.

Frances felt Lilian change her pose. She turned, and found her with her head raised, her eyes on Douglas and the men. As Lloyd repeated his call for a horse-whip, she spoke to Frances softly.

'They've all got someone else to hate now, haven't they?'

But then that shadow of apprehension came across her face again; and Frances grew sick. For this, of course, was the moment—the moment they had put off confronting on Monday. Here they were, face to face. They had to talk, they had to plan, come to some sort of a decision . . . While Douglas ranted on they moved away from the others. There was no privacy to be had; the lobby was filled with men and women wanting admission to the cases still to be heard in the courtroom. In the midst of so many individual emergencies, however, it was possible to stand and murmur. They found a spot near a ragged woman with a grotesquely beaten face, who kept starting forward every time the doors to the street were opened, only to fall back, dashed, when the wrong person appeared.

Lilian spoke with an effort. 'What do you want us to do, Frances?'

Frances answered after a pause. 'Nothing's changed, has it? I thought everything would be different. I had no idea that the hearing would be so one-sided. I thought it would all have become clear. But nothing's clear. I feel badly for the boy's mother. I feel very badly for her. As for him—'

'He isn't at all how I thought he'd be.'

'No.'

'He seemed almost to—to like it.'

Their gazes met, then slid apart. Frances said, 'Seven more days in prison, though . . . But then, he'll get himself a solicitor. His alibi will be proved. There's nothing against him save hearsay and boasts.'

She could feel Lilian looking at her, wanting it to be true. 'Do you think so?'

'I just can't believe it'll go all the way to a trial.'

'Do you really think so?'

'Don't you?'

Lilian said miserably, 'I don't know what I think any more. I don't trust myself. This morning I was all ready for it to be the worst it could be. I was really, truly ready. But now that I've seen him . . . I know it isn't fair. But he did hurt Len that other time. And the girl said he'd knocked her teeth out, didn't she? Nobody's mentioned that.' Here the doors to the street were pushed open and she fell silent, watching the beaten woman dart forward then slink back in fresh disappointment.

And when she spoke again, her tone had changed, become shy. 'What—What do you think she can be like?'

491

Frances frowned. 'The girl? Billie?'

'I keep trying to imagine her. I thought she would be here. I wish I could just see her and get it over with. I still can't believe it of him. A girl like that! I just can't believe that he was meeting her for all those months. I keep thinking of things, little things, things he said, things he did. She must have been doing his nails for him, Frances.'

'His nails?'

'You remember? His manicures? We used to laugh at him, didn't we? But she must have been doing it. I'm sure she was. I thought of it when the inspector was reading, and I felt such a fool. *Such* a fool. If you could die from feeling a fool, I'd have died right then . . . '

Her voice had begun to waver, and her mouth to twitch. But perhaps now she was remembering that moment in Vera's bedroom when Frances had spoken so sharply to her about taking the wall. She drew in her breath, and her features steadied.

'I don't want to go to the police,' she said. 'Not if you really think it'll all come to nothing. I wouldn't say it if the boy was different, but we've waited three days and he's all right. We might as well wait another seven. I want us to wait another seven. It must become clear then, mustn't it?'

Frances hadn't realised that her heart was clenched, but at Lilian's words she felt it slacken like an uncurling fist. Another seven days of freedom! The sudden release of it made her giddy. She nodded, saying nothing. She couldn't look at Lilian again. She couldn't speak warmly or kindly to her. She didn't know if that was from shame, or squeamishness, or what it was. They hadn't so much as touched hands since before Leonard's funeral, and there were only inches between them now. If they could somehow close the space—But how could they do that, there? And Lilian had made no mention of coming home to Champion Hill.

So they stood in an awkward silence, then moved back to join the others.

As they did it, Inspector Kemp and Sergeant Heath appeared in the lobby. They came across to discuss the hearing, seeming well pleased with how it had gone. The sergeant had just seen the boy put into the police van for his journey to Brixton Prison. 'They'll look after him there, don't you worry,' he assured Leonard's father, in an ominous way. Frances caught the inspector's eye over Mrs Viney's shoulder. He gave her a nod—and then, as if unable to resist it, he came around the group to her. He was smirking, just as Spencer had smirked in the dock.

'So, Miss Wray, you were sharper than me.'

She didn't understand. 'What do you mean?'

'You seemed to take a dim view of husbands when I spoke to you last week. You were right to be doubtful, you see. You were right about Mr Wismuth's innocence, too. I hope you feel that we are up to the mark at last.'

He spoke lightly, of course. She answered in earnest. 'No, I don't.'

His smirk faltered. 'You don't?'

'The boy's all swagger. Can't you see it?'

'He's an out-and-out villain! They've had their eye on him for years, up at Bermondsey.'

'He didn't murder Leonard Barber. He just likes the idea that he did.'

Now he was shaking his head. 'Oh, Miss Wray, what an extraordinary woman you are.'

'He didn't do it,' she repeated. 'You're making a mistake.'

There must have been something to her tone, something out of place, excessive. His smile returned, but less naturally than before. He was impatient with her, perhaps even slightly disappointed; she could see him putting her down, finally, as a simple crank. He made some humouring remark about keeping her words in mind, but even as he did it he was gesturing to Sergeant Heath. They were busy men, of course—busy in a way that didn't include her now;

busy in a way that barely included Lilian. When he said his good-byes to the others, he spoke mainly to Douglas and to Lloyd. He would 'keep the families informed', he promised, as he and the sergeant moved off.

Frances watched them go, thinking, *I could call you back and astound you. I could do it right now* . . .

She didn't do it. She saw them disappear into some other part of the court-house. They passed the woman with the beaten face, who was still starting forward in her hopeful way, still falling back.

And then it was time to leave the building. They steeled themselves to face the spectators gathered outside. Vera took Lloyd's arm, Frances offered hers to Mrs Viney; they put Lilian between the four of them, to shield her from the worst of it. But when they went out through the doors, though people strained to look at them, something else happened to the crowd: there was a tremor at one of its edges, and then, before their eyes, the tremor spread. People were turning, moving away. It took Frances a moment to understand why. The police van was just emerging from some side gate, and everyone was desperate for a glimpse of the boy inside it. A couple of youths were jumping up, trying to see through its louvred windows. Others were hammering on its panels as it passed—she couldn't tell if they were doing it in malice or in glee. She didn't care why they were doing it, she realised, so long as they weren't doing it to her.

16

She had the same uneasy mixture of feelings as the week wore on. Every morning she lay in bed, giddy again with sheer relief at the thought of the hours of liberty ahead of her; but every morning she made herself rise and dress and go down the hill to the news-stand, convinced that if she once let a day go by without thinking of Spencer Ward, without giving him her anxious attention, he would be lost. It was as if he were caught in a piece of machinery and only she could see it; as if all that was keeping him from the grinding cogs was her hand, hauling at his collar.

But every morning he seemed to have been tugged away from her by another half-inch.

'DO WORSE TO HIM NEXT TIME' appeared as a headline in two or three of the papers, the day after the police court hearing, along with SMILES IN DOCK and 'OWED A WALLOP'. There were pictures of the boy being led to the prison van, one of him grinning full at the camera with his deplorable teeth, another of him attempting to shield his face in a spread-fingered style he could only, Frances thought, have got from American crook dramas he had seen at the cinema. On the Sunday there were dismal quotes from some of his Bermondsey neighbours: he'd been in and out of trouble since he was a lad, and during the War he had 'run quite wild'. He had stolen a motor-car and overturned it on Streatham Common; he'd been involved in a ration-book racket; he'd gone on numerous pilfering sprees. His uncle, a railway porter, gave an interview to the *News of the World* asking for understanding. 'There is no real harm in Spencer,' he said. 'He is the victim of circumstances. He was a sweet-tempered child, but has been a different character ever since the death of his father at Neuve Chapelle. A year ago we were in hopes that he was settling down, but then he met Miss Billie Grey and lost his head to her completely. She led him to believe that the two of them were engaged, and as far as I know she accepted his ring. But once she got to know Mr Leonard Barber it was a different story.' He finished by saying: 'I cannot believe that my nephew was capable of this despicable crime, and I cannot help but ask myself why Miss Grey is so keen to pin the blame for the murder upon him. I have stated my concerns in a letter to Scotland Yard, and am awaiting their reply.'

That sent Frances's anxiety hurtling in a brand new direction. She recalled what Douglas had said about the girl and her sister having had some part in Leonard's death. If they were to be blamed now, too—! When photographs of Billie began to appear in the press, she found herself poring over them in just the same tense way that, a week before, she had pored over those pictures of Lilian. They showed an ordinary face made cheaply pretty by bottle-blonded hair, by a darkened mouth and lashes, by eyebrows plucked into two thin arcs. 'The Bermondsey *femme fatale*,' was how the *Express* snidely described her; in a similar vein there were frequent mentions in all the papers of her 'Tulse Hill trysts' with Leonard—as if the south London settings somehow made the whole thing worse. But, oh, thought Frances, how squalid it was! What on earth had Leonard been thinking? Looking into the girl's face, she recalled that moment in the starlit garden . . . And again she felt an odd sting of betrayal, at the thought that he had had such a secret; at the knowledge that he had been, at heart, a greater liar than she.

'Oh, put them away!' her mother pleaded, when she found her at the kitchen table with the newspapers spread out before her. 'I can't think why you persist in reading them. What good is all this brooding? Give yourself a rest from it, can't you?'

'How on earth can I rest?' Frances answered—and she knew she was speaking all the more indignantly because resting was secretly what she longed and longed to do. 'How can I rest while that boy's in prison with all this hanging over his head?'

'But surely it's out of our hands now? Do you plan to follow the case all the way to the Old Bailey?'

She began to fold up the newspapers, and spoke stubbornly. 'It won't go as far as that.'

'What do you mean? Why do you say that? We must hope that it does, mustn't we? For the sake of Mr Barber's family.'

'It can't go anywhere on no evidence.'

'Oh, Frances, how contrary you are! The boy's to be pitied, of course, but—' Her mother's tone grew delicate. 'Well, from everything I've seen and read, he sounds a thoroughly nasty type.'

'He's a thug,' said Frances bluntly. 'But who turned him into one? The rest of us did. The War. Poverty. The papers themselves. The pictures! He comes from a world where killing a man is something to boast about. Can you blame him? A few years ago they were doling out medals for the same thing. And in any case, he could be the biggest thug in London—that doesn't mean he killed Leonard.'

'But if he didn't do it,' said her mother in perplexity, 'then who did?'

And that, of course, was the one question that Frances could not answer—or, rather, the one question that she *could* answer, and, in answering, utterly resolve. That terror stirred in her again. She put the papers out of sight.

If only she could talk it through with Lilian. If only Lilian would come home . . . As the days passed, and there was no word from her, she began to want to see her, in the old, pure craving way. At last she gave in, and trudged back to Walworth. But she regretted it almost at once. Her visit had coincided with some break in Mr Viney's working day: he was in the kitchen in his shirt-sleeves, eating fried bread and bacon. The little girl had just arrived home from school, and was full of the hardness of the playground. 'Why do you keep coming here?' she asked Frances loudly; and Frances could tell from the violence with which she was scolded that the others were wondering the same thing. She was wondering it herself. The craving for Lilian seemed to have disappeared at the first sight of her. She took Frances through to the parlour; the door was closed, they were left alone. But it was just as it had been at the police court: now that they had made their decision there seemed nothing more to say. The little over-furnished room was drab and oppressive. Lilian was again dressed in some gown of Vera's, with her hair put up in combs.

'You've been following the papers?' Frances asked her.

She shook her head. 'I can't bear to do it.'

Frances drew back from her. 'You'd rather do nothing? You'd rather do that?'

She spoke with scorn—again, because she longed so hard to do nothing herself. And Lilian looked at her, for a moment, in a way she never had before: a level, wounded, let-down way. Ashamed, Frances put out her hand. 'Lily—'

Then the door burst open and the little girl ran in, bringing the hysterical Jack Russell.

The next day the *Daily Mirror* reported that when Spencer Ward was sixteen he had been one of a gang of youths who had assaulted another boy by tying him up and setting fire to his trousers. *The Times* ran an article on juvenile delinquents; the *Express* lamented the 'great tide of youthful lawlessness' that had swept the country since the War. The case was still in its earliest stages. The boy hadn't even been given a chance, yet, to speak in his own defence. But everything Frances read, every neighbour she spoke to, seemed to take it for granted that he had murdered Leonard. She could see the guilty verdict being steadily built up against him—it was like the word game, Gallows, that she had used to play with her brothers, where each false guess resulted in another stroke of the chalk on the slate, and before one's eyes there appeared the beams of the scaffold, the round head, the body, the stick-like limbs . . .

She couldn't believe it. She wouldn't believe it. She kept telling herself, The plain fact is, he isn't a murderer. He's done nothing. It was like arithmetic, she thought: a sum could only come out one way. He couldn't be found guilty of a crime he hadn't committed. And she fixed all her hopes on the second police court hearing.

But when the hearing took place, it was worse than the first one. Spencer was paler, less cocky, but no more likeable this time than he had been the week before, and though he had got himself a counsel—a Mr Strickland, a Bermondsey solicitor who, Frances gathered, had taken on the case under some sort of legal assistance scheme—the man did not inspire confidence. He had wispy hair, and lopsided spectacles, and nicotine stains on his fingers; he looked, she thought, like a harassed Latin master from a third-rate school.

The prosecuting counsel was altogether more impressive. He went smoothly over the facts as put together by Inspector Kemp, then summoned a series of witnesses to the stand. The first was one of the boys who claimed to have heard Spencer making threats against Leonard's life. He kept looking at Spencer as he spoke, in a sly, gloating way: it was so patent that he had come to settle some sort of score that Frances's spirits rose slightly. No one could possibly consider him a credible witness, she thought. But after him came the Camberwell servant who had been in the lane with her sweetheart on the night of Leonard's death; and as she began to answer the prosecutor's questions, Frances's confidence shrivelled.

Now that the girl was in front of her, real, solid, fattish-faced, it was more horrible than ever to think that she had been there in that stretch of impenetrable darkness with Lilian and herself, breathing the same flannelly air. The prosecutor wanted to know what precisely she had heard. She repeated what she'd stated to the papers: there had been footsteps and sighs, along with a cry of 'No!' or 'Don't!'—that could only, thought Frances, unnerved, have been the cry that she herself had given when Lilian had touched her arm. Could the girl describe the voice? It had been 'high', she said, so high that just at first she'd mistook it for a woman's. Frances began to sweat. 'Then I saw about the murder, and—'

'You decided, on reflection, that the voice was a man's? Perhaps made high or light by fear?'

'Oh, yes, it was awful fearful. I should hate to have to hear it again. Oh, it made your blood run cold!'

It was obvious that she believed every word she was saying, and the simplicity and sincerity of her manner impressed the room. Leonard's father was hunched up with his hand across his eyes; Douglas was patting his shoulder—and Frances could see that their distress was impressing people, too.

Then the prosecutor called on the police surgeon, Mr Palmer, to report on the findings of the Home Office laboratory. He spoke first about those hairs that had been taken from Leonard's coat: they were a 'fair' match with the head of the accused, he said; but no more than fair. He wouldn't care to stake his reputation on them. The traces of blood that had been found on the cosh, however, were 'almost certainly human'. The laboratory couldn't be more precise than that, but he had seen the slides himself and, in his opinion as well as theirs—yes, almost certainly. The shape of the weapon was also a reasonable fit with the shape of the wound on Mr Barber's head.

Could he say with what degree of violence the blow to the head had been delivered?—Oh, a great degree of violence.

It wasn't a casual blow? A glancing blow? It couldn't have been delivered accidentally? It couldn't have been made in self-defence?

Mr Palmer almost smiled. 'Oh, no. I shouldn't think that likely, given that the wound was slightly to the rear of Mr Barber's head. As for the intention—If I might have the instrument for a moment, please?' A constable took it to him, and he held it up as Inspector Kemp had held it up at the first hearing. 'A short weapon like this, you see,' he went on, pushing his cuff back from his wrist, 'can have no momentum of its own. The momentum comes all from the arm.' He swung his own arm, two or three times, to demonstrate the action. 'With a longer object—a mallet, a poker, something like that—then, yes, I would certainly suggest that the force of the blow might be greater than the assailant had anticipated. An inexperienced assailant, that is. But with this sort of thing—no. The person who made that injury to Mr Barber's head, with this particular weapon, would have known precisely what he was doing.'

'He would have intended his blow to be fatal?'

'He must have expected that result.'

Frances couldn't believe what she was hearing. The thing had taken on a life of its own. The surgeon, the lawyers, the police— they were all working backwards from their own idea of what had happened to Leonard and tailoring everything else to fit. There was no logic to it. Why couldn't anyone else see? If she and Lilian were to stand up now and say what had really happened, the trial would fall to bits. If they could only bring themselves to do it! Wouldn't it be easier than sitting here, listening to the facts being mangled? If they could only tell the truth, calmly—if they could just lead Inspector Kemp back to Champion Hill; if they just could show him the ashtray—he might be brought to believe, now, that it was all an accident. The surgeon had as good as said so, hadn't he?

But even as she raised her hands to the back of the pew in front of her, all the power in her muscles seemed to begin to drain away. She had to lean forward for a moment, close her eyes, fight off her own fear . . . And in that moment the trial moved on, and she did nothing. Mr Strickland requested more time in which to pursue his client's defence. With every respect to Mr Palmer, he wished to consult another surgeon. He hoped that the medical evidence might be put at his disposal.

The magistrate ordered that the hearing be adjourned. Spencer Ward was to be returned to Brixton for another seven days.

And that was how it went on—exactly like that, not just for one week but for two, with, incredibly, no advance, no resolution; with Frances every time preparing herself for the worst, then receiving that sickening reprieve; with the boy being dispatched back to prison—until she began to feel as though they'd all slipped into some nightmarish other life, some hell or purgatory from which they would never get free.

The complications of it all were beyond unpicking. Leonard's father, for example: he seemed to be ageing before her eyes. Could she and Lilian really allow him to sit through another hearing, keep seeing that cosh displayed, imagine his son being pursued and beaten and left to die in a lane? Spencer's mother was the same: she looked more faded by the week. But then, Frances's own mother was looking older, too. What would a confession do to her? What would she think of the fact that Frances and Lilian had waited so long to make it? They ought to have spoken out at once; Frances saw that now. It was the two dark paths all over again and, just like last time, she had chosen the wrong one. It was too late to turn back. September gave way to October; the fourth hearing came and went. Already the boy had been in prison nearly a month. It was terrible, it was horrible. But at what precise moment should she and Lilian present themselves to the police? At what point did his safety start to outweigh theirs? While there was still a chance that the case would come to nothing, they had to keep on with it— didn't they?

Yes, said Lilian, they had to keep on with it.

'But suppose it goes to the Old Bailey?' said Frances. 'He'll be on trial for his life, then. *His life.*'

Lilian paled. 'But you said it wouldn't.'

'I thought it wouldn't. Now—I don't know.'

'You were *sure* it wouldn't. You said—'

'Well, how could I possibly have been sure? It was you that wanted to wait!'

They'd begun to go on like this when they met—arguing in whispers, in the Vineys' parlour, or Vera's bedroom, or down in the badly lighted passage behind the Walworth Road door. Or else they sat in a dead silence, struggling and failing to break it. Their plans for the future, the art classes, the bread and scrape: where had it gone? Frances thought of that room they'd used to dream about. She'd seen herself closing the door of it, turning a key against the world. They were in a room now, certainly: the room of their poisonous secret. It might be a prison cell already! Sometimes she raged. Sometimes she could have wept. Sometimes they clung together before they parted, and it was almost all right. But, 'Do you love me?' Lilian asked once, with a note of yearning in her voice, and the question was as jarring as if it had been asked by Vera or Min. Frances drew her close and kissed her; but she did it mainly to hide her own face.

She went home that day so dejected, she wondered if their passion had ever been real. The house when she went into it clamoured drably for her attention. Rent-days had come and gone; she and her mother were slipping back towards debt. She made herself go into Lilian's sitting-room. The stains on the carpet seemed vivid again. But the stains didn't matter now, of course, she had to remind herself. Even the ashtray didn't matter. Her eyes went instead to the birdcage, the tambourine. She could see nothing but a lot of old junk. The china caravan was still on the mantelpiece: she picked it up and was amazed by how light it was.

Turning it over she saw that it was hollow, with a hole in the bottom; somehow she hadn't realised that. She held it in her hand, and remembered Lilian dipping her mouth to it, and, for a second, desire stirred in her, like a flame brought to life by a breath on a cinder. Then she thought of Leonard in his coffin, Spencer in his prison cell, and felt a rush of shame and embarrassment so acute she was almost sick.

That night she dreamt she was pushing Leonard's body through crowded streets in a thing like Violet's doll's pram, with only a little doll's blanket to cover it. She kept pulling the blanket over his head, only to put his sprawled legs on display; kept twitching the blanket down again, exposing his bloated purplish face. She awoke in a sweat in the dark early morning, but what remained with her was not the horror of Leonard's body in the pram so much as the loneliness of the dream—for she had been utterly on her own in it, the burden of the crime entirely hers. Where was Lilian? Lilian had left her! She felt like a child, abandoned. She had given her heart to Lilian and Lilian had given her nothing in return save half-truths, evasions, prevarications, lies.

Then, from nowhere, there came a whisper: *Five hundred pounds . . .* The fact was, the swing of that ashtray had made Lilian a wealthy woman. The fact was, Lilian had done rather nicely out of the whole affair. She had rid herself of an unwanted child. She had rid herself of an unwanted husband. She had pinned the blame on an innocent boy—

And I helped her with every stage of it, thought Frances in a panic. I even carted Leonard's body down the stairs for her!

She lay there in the darkness, turning it over in her mind. She could recollect times—she was sure she could—when Lilian had wished Leonard dead. *Oh, why can't some nice fat bus just run him over! Oh, if only he would just die!* She forgot that there were times when she had wished him dead herself.

Then, with a dreadful jolt, she thought of the letter that Lilian had once written her. Didn't that letter have something in it? Some desire, some plea?

She lit a candle, got out of bed, went shivering across to her chest of drawers to fish out the box in which, sentimentally, she kept the tokens of their love affair. There they all were, the silk forget-me-nots, the slips of paper with the kisses and the hearts: they looked childish, grotesque. Right at the bottom was the letter. She took it out of its envelope. What a scrap it was, after all! Mawkish and badly written. She found the lines she had remembered. *If it isnt then tell me & make me believe it because I feel right now that I am ready to do any desperate thing to be with you*—Her heart leapt into her throat. *I am ready to do any desperate thing* ... Lilian had written those words after finding those tickets in Leonard's pocket, in the knowledge that she had started a baby by him. Had she written them in spite? Had she written them in calculation? Had she planned the whole thing, even then?

But then, Frances asked herself, how do I know for sure that the baby was even Leonard's? Leonard had doubted it, hadn't he? Maybe he'd been right! Lilian was unfaithful to him; why shouldn't she also have been unfaithful to me? She looked again at the letter— and this time a different line caught her eye. *You said I like to be admired ... You said I would love anybody who admired me ...* Now her mind ran over those admirers of Lilian's, the lady-killer in the park, the men in trains lowering their newspapers for a better look at her. She remembered the cousins she had danced with so freely at Netta's party. She remembered curly-haired Ewart. 'If she was my wife, I'd smack her behind.' So, even he had seen it! There must be something about Lilian—mustn't there? There must be something instinctual, something almost morbid, something like an unhealthy perfume, that drew those men, those boys? Drew Frances herself?

In a sort of fever now, she took the letter and the box over to the hearth, tipped it all into the grate and put a match to it. She couldn't

505

have things like that in the house! Suppose the police should find them! She watched the papers being eaten by the flame and, for a moment, grew calmer. Then her mind began racing again. What else was there to incriminate her? The china caravan, next door? She thought seriously of fetching it and smashing it up. Then she remembered the half-button that she had found in the kitchen passage, that might or might not have been pulled from Leonard's cuff. She had pushed it into the earth of the aspidistra plant. That was a crazy thing to have done! She ought to have taken the button away from the house—right away somewhere. She ought to have dropped it into the Thames! If the police should come—!

The police wouldn't come, so long as Spencer Ward was in prison. But she had got to a point almost of madness now. It seemed to her quite possible that Lilian might go to Inspector Kemp and tell him some sort of tale against her. She might have gone to him already. He might be on his way to the house. Didn't they come in the early morning? Wasn't that how they did it?

It was ten to six, and pitch dark. She was shivering right through. But she put on her dressing-gown and slippers, picked up her candle, stole downstairs, and—quietly, quietly, thinking of her mother, asleep near by—she lifted the aspidistra from its spot beside the dinner-gong and carried it out to the kitchen table. It was trickier than she'd expected to get hold of the button. She couldn't reach it with the blade of a knife; she had to tip the pot, scrabble in the earth with her fingers. The dusty leaves got into her face, sharp and hard against her eyes. The earth began to spill, but she kept on digging, growing more and more anxious, feeling more and more desperate—until the pot fell noisily sideways and the plant came free, a mass of dirt and writhing white roots. The button came tumbling out along with everything else: just a black half-button it was, like a thousand others in the house, probably not from Leonard at all. The sight of it broke the spell of her insanity; she covered her face and started to cry.

When she looked up a few minutes later, her mother was there, gazing at her from the kitchen doorway. 'Frances, good heavens! What on earth's the matter?'

Frances shook her head. 'Nothing,' she said, as she sobbed and sobbed into her dirty fingers. 'Nothing.'

She spent that day in bed. Her mother brought her tea and aspirin, along with ill-cooked little meals: rubbery buttered eggs, collapsed potatoes. After lunch there was a tap at the bedroom door and in came the family physician, an elderly man named Dr Lawrence. Her mother must have sent one of the tradesmen's boys to him with a note. He took her blood-pressure, and listened to her heart, and felt beneath her jaw with his warm, dry fingers. 'Any giddiness?' he asked her. 'Fainting spells? Shortness of breath?' She shook her head at every question, embarrassed about her tattered night-gown, worried about how much his visit was costing. But his manner was so mild, so unsuspecting, that her eyes filled with tears. He patted her hand, then spoke quietly to her mother out on the landing. 'Nerve strain' was his conclusion, perhaps a delayed response to the War, and to the deaths in the family, all aggravated by recent upsets. Frances must rest, avoid excitements . . . He left her a jar of tabloids to be taken at bedtime.

She lay and thought of her father, of her father's 'heart attacks'. She thought of the terrors that must have seized him over his failing fortune, his lost sons, his cross-grained, unmarriageable daughter; and she wept again.

For two or three days after that she gave herself over to the idea of invalidism. She didn't dare venture out for the morning papers. Spencer Ward, for once, had to go un-thought-about, un-imagined; she couldn't help it if the machinery sucked him in and crushed him. She kept to the sofa with worn old books from her child-hood, *Treasure Island* and *The Swiss Family Robinson*. She took her tabloid at nine o'clock each night, and dropped straight into a dreamless sleep.

And then, on a Sunday morning, when she was least expecting it—when she had given up hoping for it, and was no longer sure that she even wanted it to happen—Lilian returned.

She had just cleared the breakfast table and was out in the scullery, washing up. When she heard the sound of a key going into the lock of the front door, she thought it was her mother, come back early from church. Puzzled, she called across the kitchen: 'Is everything all right?' There was no answer: only the tap, oddly uncertain, of heels on the floor.

Her heart made an unpleasant movement in her chest. Shaking the suds from her fingers she went out into the passage—and there was Lilian, in her widow's coat and hat, with a suitcase in her hand, looking nothing at all like the sinister scheming creature that madness had made of her; looking sheepish, like a visitor who had stayed out too long; looking thin, looking pale, but, apart from that, looking achingly familiar and dear . . . Frances's step faltered. She was horribly conscious of her own appearance, her face still puffy from her drugged, unnatural sleep, her hair unwashed, her clothes at their drabbest. She blotted her hands on her apron. 'You ought to have let me know you were coming. I could have got myself ready for you.'

Lilian's face fell slightly. 'You don't have to get yourself ready for me, do you?'

'Got the house ready, then.'

'Oh, but—No, it's all right.' Frances had come forward to take the suitcase from her. She swung and raised it, awkwardly; it struck Frances's elbow with a hollow sound, and Frances realised that it was empty. She looked at Lilian, not understanding. But Lilian was blushing now. 'I can't keep borrowing Vera's things,' she said. 'I—I've come to get some more clothes to take back to Walworth.'

So she hadn't come back to stay . . . Frances felt a rush of the abandonment that had overwhelmed her a few nights before. The feeling was like a wailing infant suddenly thrust into her arms: she didn't want it, couldn't calm it, had nowhere to set it down. Without a word, she turned away, went out to the kitchen to remove her apron and wash her hands.

She took her time over it, doing all she could to press her mood into some more manageable shape. She supposed that Lilian would go on upstairs without her. But when she returned to the hall Lilian was still standing there, gazing upward but hesitating about starting the climb. 'I just need to get my courage up,' she said. 'I've been dreading coming back. Will you—Will you go up ahead of me?'

Again Frances said nothing, but climbed the stairs at an ordinary pace, then stood in silence on the landing while Lilian cautiously followed.

They went into the sitting-room first. Lilian set down the case but made no move to take off her hat and coat. Instead she stood looking around like a wondering stranger.

'It feels so long since I was here. It's only a month. But everything seems different. Everything looks wrong. All these things. So many things . . . And everything with dust on it already.' She had gone to the cold fireplace and was gazing at the clutter on the mantelpiece, the elephants, the tambourine, the caravan, all of it dulled, the bright surfaces clouded as if by gusts of sour breath.

Then she noticed the substantial pile of letters that had accumulated in her absence. She picked them up, and Frances said awkwardly, 'I didn't know what to do with them, whether to take them to you at your mother's, or—I didn't know when you'd be coming back.'

Lilian was going through the bundle with a look of dismay. 'Most of them are for Len.'

'Yes.'

'I never thought of ordinary things like post still coming for him. But these others—I've had letters like these at Walworth. They're from people who've read about me in the papers; they say all sorts of things. Unkind things, sometimes. I don't open them any more.'

'Leave them, then,' said Frances. 'I'll burn them.'

She had been speaking flatly all this time, but Lilian didn't appear to notice. She put the letters down, then stood like a stranger again. She seemed not to know what to do with herself. Frances offered to make her tea, but, no, she didn't want that . . . Finally she closed her eyes tight and gave a shake of her head. 'Oh, I knew if I came back I'd start to feel like this! While I'm at my mother's it doesn't seem real. About Len, I mean. But here, I'm still wondering where he is.' She looked at Frances. 'Aren't you? I'm still expecting him to walk through the door. Then I have to remember that even if he did come—well, he'd have come from *her*, wouldn't he? He'd been with her that night, the night it all happened. And, do you remember? When he thought I was seeing another man, he—he laughed. Just for a second, before he got angry. As if it was funny. I couldn't think why he laughed like that. I know now. I—'

'Are you here,' said Frances, 'simply to grouse about your husband? What with one thing and another, I'm not sure I'm quite in the mood for it today.'

She didn't know where the comment had come from. It seemed to have said itself. She couldn't remember ever before having used the word grouse like that; it was much more the sort of thing that Leonard would have said. Startled, she and Lilian looked at each other; but the moment for apology came, then went. Lilian put down her head, stepped past Frances for her suitcase, and carried it out of the sitting-room and into the room next door.

It was the first time that they had been properly alone together, and they were wasting it, Frances thought in despair; it was all grating, discordant. She followed Lilian as far as the landing, looked in at her through the bedroom doorway. She had put the suitcase on the bed and removed her hat and coat at last, but removed them only so that she could go more freely to the wardrobe and the chest of drawers and pull out the things she needed.

Frances thought back to that day in the summer when she had watched her packing this same suitcase for her trip to Hastings. They had gone rinking that day. Rinking! It seemed too quaint and wholesome to be true. She remembered the speed, the laughter, the holding of hands. Afterwards, they had gone to the park. *It's the only real thing*, Lilian had said.

She was working quickly now, seeming to be taking clothes at random, and the small case was already almost full. Frances watched her fit in another nightdress, another pair of shoes. 'You surely don't mean to carry all that to Walworth?' she said, as Lilian drew over the case's lid and tried to press it shut.

Lilian answered tightly, without looking up. 'I'll take a tram. I'm all right, now. I'm not ill like I was before.'

'And you really have to take quite so much?'

'It's easier to just take everything. We don't know what's going to happen, do we? I don't know what I'll need.'

Frances didn't answer that. But after another moment of watching the struggle with the suitcase she moved forward to help, leaning her weight on the springy lid so that the latches could be clicked home. Lilian drew the case from the bed and, caught out by the weight of it, set it down with a thump. But, 'I can manage,' she insisted, still without meeting Frances's eye, as Frances automatically reached to take it. 'I told you, I'm all right now.' She added, after a second, in a different, more hesitant tone, 'I've something for you, though.'

She picked up her handbag and drew out an envelope. She put it into Frances's hand, and Frances heard the chink of coins. 'What's this?'

She answered self-consciously. 'It's my rent. Did you think I had forgotten? There's nearly twelve pounds there, enough for two months. Is that all right?'

And once again the moment had another moment inside it: that time, back in April, when they were still strangers to each other and Lilian had shyly held out her first paper packet of rent. It was as though their life, thought Frances, were being mercilessly spooled back on to a reel; or as if, one by one, the stitches that had fastened them together were being unpicked.

The thought upset her. She tried to give the envelope back. 'I can't take this, Lilian. You can't pay rent for rooms you aren't living in.'

'Please take it. It's yours. Yours and your mother's.'

'I'd far rather you kept it.'

'Don't you need the money?'

'Well, yes. But so do you, don't you?'

Lilian looked more self-conscious than ever. She said, 'I saw a solicitor yesterday. He wrote to me about Len's money. The money from his insurance, I mean. He gave me a cheque.—Oh, please don't do that.' Frances had gone close to her, to stuff the envelope back into her bag. She got it out again and attempted to return it to Frances's hand.

Frances made fists, lifted her arms. 'I don't want it.' They dodged and scuffled, absurdly.

'Just take it, Frances.'

'I don't want it.'

'Please.'

'No! I hate that money!'

'Well, I hate it too!' said Lilian. She had flung the envelope on to the bed; her face was patched with colour. 'How do you think it makes me feel? Have you thought about that? You know when Len took the policy out. It was right after that night in July, that night when the boy hit him. He must have thought it all through. He must have thought that the boy really meant it—that he might go after him again. He must have really thought he might die! But

512

even then, even thinking that—well, that didn't keep him from seeing *her*, did it? He thought enough of me to get me that five hundred pounds. But he thought more of *her*.'

'God!' said Frances, unable to bear it. 'Why do you care?'

'I don't know! But I do. I do.'

'You used to say that you didn't even love him. You were planning to leave him, weren't you?'

'Yes, but—'

'Weren't you?'

'Yes! Don't bully me, Frances. You always bully me. I can't explain it. I *hate* him for wanting her. I know he was only doing with her what I was doing with you, but I hate him for it. And I hate her, too. I never wanted his money. You say you don't want it either, but—' With a bruised, stubborn expression she retrieved the envelope and set it on the chest of drawers. 'I'll leave it here, and you can take it or forget about it as you like.'

And then she picked up her coat. Watching her slide an arm into its sleeve, Frances said, 'You're going right now then, are you?' She loathed the sound of her own voice. 'We haven't even talked about the case.'

Lilian let the coat fall slightly. 'There's nothing to say, is there? We're just going to wait, we said. You haven't changed your mind?'

'No, I haven't changed my mind.'

'You wouldn't change it and not tell me?'

'Well, of course I wouldn't.'

'Well, don't say it like that! I don't know what's in your head any more. You feel so far away from me.'

'All the way between here and Walworth.'

'Oh, now you're not being fair! You know why it is I'm staying there. It makes the other things easier. We've still got men from the newspapers coming. Some of them wait outside, with cameras. We've still got policemen coming, too. You wouldn't rather they all came here?'

Frances was silent for a moment. Then, 'No,' she admitted. 'No, I wouldn't rather that.'

Lilian's tone softened. 'Being apart for a while—it's just something we have to bear. It's hard, now. Everything's hard. But it'll seem small afterwards. Won't it? If everything comes right?'

Frances was silent again, but nodded. In a deliberate sort of way, Lilian put down the coat and came to her, and they embraced.

But there was no match between them, Frances thought. There was no fit, no comfort. She stood rigid, hating it, then began to move out of Lilian's arms.

But, as she edged away, Lilian caught hold of her. 'Frances—' Her heart had quickened its pace: Frances could feel the thud of it. She bowed her head to Frances's shoulder, and when she spoke, the race of her heart was in her voice. 'Frances, tell me it'll be all right between us when all this is finished. Tell me it'll be how it used to be. I know you hate me for what I did, and I know you think I'm weak. I'm trying hard not to be weak any more. But let me be weak for just one minute, now. Tell me nothing will have changed, that I haven't ruined it. I get so frightened. I don't mean just about the boy. That's bad enough. But I think I could bear it better if I knew, if I thought—It was all so clear, everything we planned to do. It was all so wonderful. Now it's like there's a curtain across it. I don't know what's going to be there when the curtain's pulled back. I don't know what you're thinking.'

She drew back her head on the last words, and looked into Frances's eyes. Their faces were inches apart; Frances caught the scent of her lipstick and powder, felt the heat and stir of her lips. It was as impossible not to kiss her as not to blink, not to breathe. But when their mouths came together they did so drily and uneasily, like the meeting mouths of strangers, so that it seemed to Frances for a moment that the kiss would be worse than no kiss at all—would be like an unkiss, an undoing.

But then she felt the shy, tentative pressure of Lilian's tongue against hers: just the tip of a tongue, warm and familiar against hers. She met it with a pressure of her own, put up a hand to Lilian's face; and all at once the kiss had changed, was wet, open, intimate. The sudden flooding relief of it made them both grow weak. They broke the kiss to clutch at each other, to pull each other closer. 'Oh, I love you! I love you!' said Lilian, her words coming in a hot rush against Frances's ear, on the breath that was being squeezed out of her.

They kissed again, more hectically than before. Where their breasts and hips met it was like the pushing of something through skin, a bursting back into life, almost painful. But there were too many bulky layers of fabric between them. Still kissing, they began to fret and tug at each other's clothing. Frances worked her hands under Lilian's blouse, got hold of the waistband of her skirt. She fumbled for a moment with hooks and a button, then gave up and reached lower, catching at the skirt itself, hauling it high, handful by handful, plucking at it and bunching it, until her fingers met the silk beneath, then found the flesh beneath that.

They were still on their feet, swaying and ungainly. She put out a foot to kick closed the door and they almost stumbled. Lilian's arms were around her, her hands chill on a strip of bare skin; only when she had brought her own hand around Lilian's thigh and her fingers were slipping and rubbing between Lilian's legs did Lilian pull away from her slightly, to catch her breath, to dip her head, and to reach, blindly, behind her—wanting the wall or the bedstead, something to get hold of to give her balance. Finding nothing, she gradually surrendered herself to the instability of the pose, letting her arms fall, letting Frances brace and support her. She lifted her head, that was all; as Frances's hand moved faster, as the muscles of her face began to tense, she lifted her head and held Frances's gaze—as if wanting Frances to see, as if determined for her to see, that there was nothing in the way of the two of them, nothing between them but skin.

But then—what happened? Something happened, something like the change that had come before; but a wrong thing, this time, a dimming, a draining away. Lilian closed her eyes after all. She held her breath, the lines of her face pulled tighter, the colour mounted in her cheeks; but the tension led nowhere, and with the loss of urgency their pose began to feel awkward, odd. Frances's arms and legs were aching now, the strain building like a burn in her muscles. She altered her stance, shifted her weight, trying to keep up the rhythm of her hand. Now Lilian's face was clenched. Dismayed, Frances could see that she was having to will the thing to its crisis. Her own fingers felt blind, suddenly. She quickened the slide of them and, 'What shall I do?' she asked. 'Lilian? How shall I do it?' But the question, the admission, only made her more self-conscious. The ease and familiarity were gone. She became aware that she was chafing at cooling, sticky, unenchanted flesh; abashed, she let her hand slow.

And after another few seconds of it, Lilian reached to still her fingers. They stood like that, with bowed heads, drooping shoulders, while their breathing steadied and the race of their hearts subsided.

Even then it might have been all right. 'Come and lie down with me,' Lilian said softly. She led Frances to the bed; they lay with their heads on a single pillow, drew the counterpane over each other so that they shouldn't get cold, just as they'd done when they were lovers. The pillow smelled faintly of Leonard's hair-oil. On the dusty bedside cabinet were his box of links and studs, his handkerchief, his public-library thriller racking up a fine; on the back of the bedroom door his dressing-gown still clung to Lilian's kimono. But if one closed one's eyes, thought Frances. If one forgot the fumble and failure of a few minutes before. If one forgot the blood, the electric panic, the police, the newspapers. If one made one's mind a blank. Then couldn't it be how it used to be, the two of them together, warm and true? *It's the only real thing.* Couldn't they let it be real again? Just for a moment?

But, then, that boy, trapped in the machine ... Already, her mind was lurching back into horrible life. She turned her head. She opened her eyes. And what she saw, over on the chest of drawers, was the envelope with twelve pounds in it.

Don't look at it, she told herself. Don't think it. Say nothing. For God's sake! But she couldn't help it. The madness was rising in her again. She let out a horrid little sneering laugh, and in a voice that didn't even sound like her own, she said, 'I'm afraid you didn't quite get your money's worth today.'

Lilian lifted her head from the pillow, her face creasing into a frown. 'Money's worth?'

'Or have I misunderstood? Is the payment for something else entirely? Don't worry, I won't go to the police, if that's what's troubling you. The boy will stay nicely tucked up at Brixton.'

Lilian held herself quite still for a moment. Then she jerked away, threw off the counterpane, got down from the bed. She turned her back to Frances as she straightened her skirt and blouse. Her hair was untidy, but she didn't pause to comb it; in a series of rigid, furious movements she found her hat, stepped into her shoes, pulled on her coat, stuffed her gloves into her handbag. Only when the strap of the bag was looped over her arm and she had leaned to pick up the suitcase did she turn back to Frances, who, all this time, had been watching from the bed.

And what she said, coldly and levelly, was: 'I'm sorry you aren't as brave as you thought you were, Frances.'

Frances stared at her. 'What?'

'But don't punish me because of it, and make out you're doing it because of that boy. If I want punishing I'll go to Inspector Kemp and get it for something I deserve.'

She covered her eyes, and spoke less steadily. 'Now you've made me be sharp with you, when all I came for, all I came for was—'

She dropped her hand. 'I gave things up for you, Frances. I gave my baby up for you. I never asked for what we had. If I'd asked for something like that, don't you think I'd have asked for it to be easier? Instead—No, get off me. Get away from me.' Frances had jumped down from the bed and was reaching for her. She pushed her back. 'Let me alone.'

But Frances was panicking now. The madness had vanished, as completely as if pricked by a pin and exploded. 'Lily, forgive me. Please. I don't know what's the matter with me. I—'

'Get off!'

'I think—I think I'm losing my mind. The other night, I— Please, Lily.' Lilian was at the door, had got it open. 'Don't go. Don't leave me again. I don't know why I said what I did. I didn't mean it. I—'

'Let me alone!'

She had struck out properly this time. The blow caught Frances on the bone of the cheek and made her start back. She put a hand to the sting of it, and for a second the two of them faced each other, horrified at what they were doing, horrified at what the moment recalled; but part of their horror, Frances knew, was at their own helplessness, their own inability to do anything to the tangle they were in but make it pull tighter. 'Don't go,' she said again. But it was too late. It was all too late. Lilian had already turned, was fleeing. In the silent house, her heels were noisy as gunshots as she went down.

The Tuesday of that week was the anniversary of John Arthur's death; Frances looked at his picture, dry-eyed. On the same day, the inquest was re-opened at Camberwell, and the jury, instructed by the coroner, brought back a verdict of wilful murder. When, two days later, it was time to make her way to the next police court hearing, she hadn't the energy for it. She stayed at home, curled up on the sofa with a copy of *Kidnapped*. The news came at lunch-time, brought down by Mrs Playfair, who had had it from Patty, whose niece was engaged to that boy in the police. There was no surprise about it. The hearing had been over in a matter of minutes. The prosecutor had concluded his case, and the magistrate had declared himself satisfied. To applause from Leonard's family, and cheers from the crowded public benches, Spencer Ward was committed to trial at the Old Bailey in just over a fortnight's time.

17

And, well, if nothing else, she thought bleakly, there would soon be an end to it now: an end to madness, to secrecy, to skulking about in corners. November the sixth, and the trial would open. It was a relief to have the date to fix one's mind on; a relief to know that the affair would be decided at last. Once, she never would have thought it possible for a person to be bored by fear. She recalled all the various terrors that had seized and shaken her since the thing had begun: the black panics, the dreads and uncertainties, the physical cavings-in. There hadn't been a dull moment! But she *was* almost bored now, she realised. Bored to tears. Bored to the bone. Bored to death by those exacting lodgers, her own fright and cowardice.

Lilian she saw only once as the fortnight passed, early in the second week. They didn't mention the appalling way in which they had last parted. They didn't mention that meeting at all. Lilian's expression was a closed one, her manner quite dead; they came together at the request of one of the solicitors, sitting with him in an upstairs office while he ran for a final time through their recollections of the night of Leonard's death. Frances was afraid, at first, that he meant to ask her to be a witness: she imagined having to stand and give evidence for the prosecution, gazing across at the

520

boy as she did it. But it was only Lilian he wanted for that. He was sorry to request it, he told her, but they wouldn't keep her in the box for long. Mr Ives, the counsel to whom the case had been handed, simply needed her to confirm a few details about her husband's final day, and would perhaps just touch on her recollections of that night in July when he had been injured . . . They might have heard of Humphrey Ives, KC? His name was often in the papers. He was a most experienced advocate, a very able chap indeed, and with his involvement the trial shouldn't take longer than three days; it 'might just squeak to a fourth' if the defending barrister, Mr Tresillian, proved tricky. He was rather an untried man—a junior, who had accepted the brief at a nominal fee, and one never knew with fellows like that. Sometimes they were in a tearing hurry, other times they liked to make a bit of a splash by 'going down kicking'. But Mrs Barber must keep her mind on the certain outcome. Mr Ives had let it be known that he'd rarely seen so straightforward a case.

He meant, of course, to be reassuring. But once the two of them had left his building they paused on the pavement, speechless.

'Three or four days!' managed Frances at last. 'Will you be all right, having to give evidence?' And then, when Lilian didn't answer: 'You needn't stay there once you've done it. I can see to it all, when the time comes. If it comes, I mean. The moment the verdict's returned, if it's the wrong one, I can go to this Mr Tresillian and—'

'You think I'd let you do that for me, too?' said Lilian, coldly. 'No, I want to be there for the whole of it. I want to be ready. I've told my family I want to be there, and that's that. And—' A touch of colour crept into her face, and into her tone. 'I've told them I want you beside me in the court. Is that all right? I've said I want you, and no one else.'

Frances looked at her. 'You told them that? They—They didn't think it odd?'

The life left her again. 'I don't know. It doesn't matter now, does it?'

And, no, thought Frances, it didn't matter now, not if they could stand here like this, with a sort of sheet of ice between them. Not if Lilian could look back at her with such wounded, lightless eyes, as if they'd never kissed, lain naked together, lost themselves in each other's gazes . . . She searched for words, and couldn't find them. They made their final arrangements, and parted.

November the first, November the second: the days slithered by. She went to the cinema with her mother; she forgot the film the moment it ended. She paid a visit to Christina, but sat there with nothing to say. At home she gave herself over to chores, wanting to put the house in order before the trial began; but the chores, she realised, were a losing battle. The house had begun to fall apart. The geyser shrieked as it burned. Paint was peeling from window frames and revealing them to be rotten. The scullery roof had sprung a leak: she put down a bowl to catch the drips, but the rain-water spread and darkened, to make treasure maps and Whistler nocturnes of the walls and ceiling. It was just as if the house were suddenly as weary as she was. Or as if it could sense that the jig was up: that their little contract was about to expire. Perhaps, all this time, it had only ever been humouring her, politely.

She worried most about her mother. What would become of her? How would she cope? Would there even be time to explain it, on the day, if the worst happened? Once she and Lilian had stepped forward, wouldn't the police want to take them into custody right away? Her mother might hear of it from a newspaper! No, that wasn't to be borne. Night after night she fretted about it. She wondered if her brothers had used to feel like this, on leave from the War. Noel, she remembered, had given her a letter to be handed to her mother in the case of his death; her mother had taken the letter, tucked it away, never referred to it again. It crossed her mind to leave a similar sort of note, 'To be opened in the event of my not returning from the Old Bailey'—Oh, but that was too sensational, surely.

Then she thought of Mrs Playfair. The thought came like an answer to a prayer. For Mrs Playfair, of course, could be reached by telephone from the court, and she would see to everything, get Frances's mother to the police station, handle any newspaper men. And if, at the end of it all, Frances were put into prison or—or worse, then she could be relied upon to take charge of her mother's finances, help her find new lodgers for the house. She might even put the house up for sale and have her mother to live with her over at Braemar. Yes, the more Frances thought about it, the more likely that seemed. The vision was not quite a happy one. She saw her mother dwindling into some sort of unpaid companion, reading aloud from parish newsletters, winding balls of wool. But better that than being left alone, to brood on her daughter's disgrace. God! How incredible it was, to think of them being on the brink of such ruin! Two months before, she had been ready to turn her back on her mother, to walk away from the house. But that had been for something, hadn't it? That had been for Lilian, for love; not for this chaos of bad luck and blunder.

It was that that made her cry, sometimes: the sheer waste and futility of it. She would turn her face to her pillow, her arms drawn in, holding nothing.

And then it was the eve of the trial, Guy Fawkes Day. It fell on a Sunday this year, so there were no bonfires—that seemed to her a pity—but early in the evening a few rockets went up in defiance of the sabbath; she stood at the window in her darkened bedroom and watched the colours burst and die. She gathered her things for the morning, and when, later, she climbed into bed, she prepared herself for a sleepless night. But perhaps she really had reached the limits of her own fear now: she slept quite dreamlessly, awoke feeling no more than mildly apprehensive, and she washed and dressed, and ate a breakfast, with only the sick, fluttery feeling she could remember from the mornings of examination days at school. It proved difficult, when it came to it, to part from her mother with a bright goodbye—though, after all, not that difficult, because this was only the beginning, and there were still two or three more goodbyes to come. For the same reason, as she made the walk down to Camberwell and along the Walworth Road, though she tried to gaze at everything in the knowledge that she might soon be taken away from it, she couldn't keep it up, she felt mannered and inauthentic—like an actress, she thought, playing a character to whom the doctor had just delivered the fatal diagnosis.

At Mrs Viney's, Lydia was guarding the door and the dog was barking, exactly as usual. Lilian was ready in a smart hat and coat—but so were her sisters and her mother. They didn't want her to go without them. It wasn't right. What was she thinking? Say she was to be taken ill? Suppose she was to fall in a faint again? It wasn't fair on poor Miss Wray! Or, why not telephone to Lloyd? There was still the time for it. He'd bring her home the moment she'd got through the nasty business in the court. And later on Lydia would run for the evening papers and—

'No,' said Lilian. 'No.' Her hat had a veil to it; she drew it down. 'This is how I want to do it. He was my husband, wasn't he? This is how it's going to be.' And her tone was so final, so forbidding, that her sisters fell silent; even her mother was abashed.

They insisted on seeing her down to the street, however, once the taxi had arrived. A couple of reporters and photographers were down there too, and some of the passers-by paused; customers came out of Mr Viney's shop to watch her leave and to wish her well. 'It's like when I got married,' she murmured, gazing out from the taxi window at the waves of the small, forlorn crowd. But she spoke to the glass rather than to Frances, and once the vehicle had started forward she didn't speak again. Her coat was a new one, stiff and black with a greenish beetly sheen to it. Behind her widow's veil, her face looked blurry and remote. Frances was dressed in her soberest costume, the grey tunic, a darker grey coat. She had cleaned and polished her worn black boots—as if polished boots, she thought, gazing down at the toes of them, could make a difference.

The first shock came when they'd crossed the river and were taking the turn off Ludgate Hill. They found a queue stretching down the street from the public entrance of the Old Bailey, not the scrum of people they'd grown used to but a solid line of ordinary men and women with bags and scarves and neatly furled umbrellas. 'They can't all be here for us,' said Frances, 'surely?' But even as she said it the faces began to turn, and she saw a shudder of excitement run the length of the queue as Lilian was recognised. By the time the taxi had pulled up at the kerb people were straining for a proper look at her, and policemen were gesturing them back. She fumbled with coins for the driver, and they got themselves into the building as quickly as they could.

But here was the next shock: the scale and grandeur of it all. A flight of stairs took them up to an impressive lobby; a second staircase led to a domed marble hall that was hectic with decoration and as dwarfing as the nave of a cathedral. They stood in it at an absolute loss, until an official took charge of them. Mrs Barber was to give evidence? She was to come with him, please. There was a waiting-place for witnesses; she would have to remain there until she was called. The other lady could go straight to the courtroom. The policeman at the door would let her through.

So they were separated at once, and Frances went into the court alone. And though for a minute it was all right—the room, she thought, was simply another of the brown panelled chambers in which she had spent so much time for the inquest and the police court hearings, and the bench to which she was led, beneath the jut of the public gallery, had Leonard's father, and brother Douglas, and Uncle Ted already on it, rising gravely to shake her hand—though at first it seemed all right, once she was seated, and could look around, she saw that it wasn't all right at all. There was no grubbiness here, no bluster: it was the real thing, at last. The clerks and barristers, in their wigs and gowns, were like crafty jackdaws. The chair for the judge had a sword above it. The dock for the prisoner—But that was the worst. Men had been sent to their deaths from there. Hadn't Crippen stood there? And Seddon? And George Smith?

A stir overhead, out of sight, made her flinch. The doors to the gallery must have been thrown open. There came a rush of footsteps and excited voices as people piled in from the street; they settled down with the protests and shufflings-along of a phantom music-hall audience. Or perhaps it was she herself who was the phantom. How little her thumping heart mattered to any of this, after all! For soon, without warning, without any sort of signal appearing to be have been made, the room, which so far had had a sort of looseness to it, began to knit itself together. Men moved in different directions, taking places at benches and desks; overhead, the invisible audience became hushed and poised. The order was given for the court to rise, and she scrambled to her feet. A gowned official stepped smoothly to a small door beside the judge's dais. There was some sort of proclamation, there were the raps of a staff or a gavel: they sounded to her like the measured, unnatural raps of the dead on a seance table. And then the judge was admitted, a frightful figure, his robe a bright, bright scarlet; he carried, bafflingly, grotesquely, a posy of flowers. Three other robed men came with him, one in a gold chain of office. They mounted the dais, took their places, and—Where was Lilian? She wanted Lilian!—the thing had begun.

For a time, then, her fear was so sharp that it all came to her as if from a distance. She saw Spencer appear in the dock, rising like a conjurer's assistant from the floor of the pen as a warder brought him up from some underground passage. She watched them read the charge to him and ask him how he pleaded, and heard his answer—'I plead not guilty'—his voice splintering on the words like a schoolboy's. Then came the swearing-in of the jury, eleven men and a single woman: with the monotony of the process her panic receded a little, and she searched their faces for signs of kindness as they took their oaths. But they looked ordinary, inexpert, the woman in a fussy hat, the men with the slightly silly expressions that came from knowing they were being stared at, or else straight-backed, with lifted chins, enjoying their own importance. That one at the end, she thought, would make himself foreman. He was a man like a clever shopkeeper: already she could see him gazing at the boy as he might have turned in his experienced hand some bit of cheap merchandise that had come to him soiled from the supplier.

Now a middle-aged barrister with a pouchy face had risen and begun to address the court. She understood that he was Mr Ives, of whom the solicitor had spoken, and that this was the opening speech for the prosecution. She forced herself to pay attention, leaning forward, sitting tensely; beside her, Douglas was doing the same. But the boy's threats, the first assault, the cosh, the blood, the hairs on the coat: it was all crushingly familiar from the police court hearings, right down to the horrid thrill that coursed around the room when, after twenty minutes or so, Mr Ives paused to have the weapon displayed to the jury. Once he had begun to call in his witnesses Frances could have stood in the box for them, for they were all men whom she had seen give evidence before: a policeman to show a plan of the lane, Constables Hardy and Evans to describe the finding of the body, the doctor who had pronounced Leonard dead at the scene . . . He was followed on to the stand by the police surgeon, Mr Palmer, and then came all the grisly details about the bruising to Leonard's brain. But this time he had brought along an exhibit to give an idea of the nature of the bleeding: he drew the lid from a small box and produced a curled, earth-coloured thing that was, apparently, Leonard's collar. His collar! Frances gazed at it in disbelief. It didn't resemble anything she could remember from the night; it might have been the withered skin of a snake. When it was taken and shown to the jury, some of them leaned for a better view; some of them looked once, then looked away. The woman made a show of turning her face from it, queasily. But they all looked queasy at what came next: photographs of Leonard's broken head, which were handed to the clever shopkeeper and passed on by him. Up in the public gallery there were tuts of frustration as people tried, and failed, to see.

Here, for the first time, Mr Tresillian rose to ask questions for the defence. He wanted to know more about the bleeding. Wasn't it likely that, with such an injury, splashes of blood would have found their way on to the clothing of Mr Barber's attacker?

Mr Palmer nodded, in a generous way. 'Yes, there might very well have been splashes.'

'Then what do you have to say about the fact that no such splashes were ever discovered on the clothes of the accused?'

'I have nothing to say—except, of course, that clothes are easily washed or discarded. Blood was certainly discovered on the cosh.'

'Blood that has not been proved to be human?'

'Blood that is almost sure to be human.'

'Blood, however, that cannot be proved to have belonged to the human named Leonard Barber, any more than the hairs that were taken from Mr Barber's overcoat can be matched, to your own satisfaction, with the hair of the accused?'

The surgeon inclined his head, less generously than before. 'No.'

With that, Mr Tresillian returned to his place at the counsels' bench. Frances watched him sit, thinking, What are you doing? Don't leave it there! Keep going! But he was adding notes to a piece of paper now, in the most leisurely way imaginable: a plain young man in horn-rimmed spectacles, only a year or two older than herself, with a lean face and long, pale hands that brought to mind those of John Arthur. He might have a sister like her, a mother like hers at home. He had risen this morning from an ordinary bed, and eaten a breakfast just as she had, perhaps with a flutter in the pit of his stomach . . . Her heart shrivelled at the uselessness of it all. He'd never manage it. He was too young. She wanted the other man, Mr Ives. He was like a barrister in a book, like a barrister in a film—just now, for example, he was discussing some detail with the judge, and that was what she wanted, someone who would debate a point of law like that, with one hand nonchalantly clasping the lapel of his gown. She and Lilian would never be saved by a man who might as well be her own brother, who went about the house in his socks, who lay on the sofa with his long legs raised and crossed at the bony ankle.

She listened tensely again to the two or three witnesses who came next. One of them was Inspector Kemp, looking pink and pleased with himself, describing the stages of the inquiry, making it sound like a game of hopscotch, one square leading neatly to another with only a few small sideways jumps. She became aware that her head was aching. The court had a white glazed ceiling; the clear, cold light was hard on the eyes. And then, sounds were travelling oddly. There were regular scrapings of chairs, and coughs and rustles up in the gallery; clerks and policemen came and went, in creaking shoes, with slips of paper. What must the boy be making of it all? He had seemed to listen keenly at the start, but his expression had grown blanker as the witnesses had come and gone, and now he was leaning forward with his elbows on the high ledge in front of him, his chin in his hand. She remembered his chewing-gum, his sniggers. His suit today was the same cheap blue one that he had worn at the police court, but someone had found him a soberer neck-tie, and his hair was improbably neat. His face was pale but slightly fuller, less ratty, than she recalled. He must have been eating better in prison, she thought, than in his own home.

As she watched him, he changed his pose, turned his head, and caught her eye. The blush rose in her like sickness, sour and unstoppable.

And then suddenly the inspector had stepped down from the stand; she was amazed to discover that half a day had passed, and the trial was adjourned for lunch. Lunch! It seemed too commonplace and casual a thing to think about, but once the jury had filed away and the robed men had left the dais, and Spencer had disappeared back down through the floor of the dock, the room became loose and unfocused again. Uncertain of what else to do, she followed the Barber men out to the marble hall, to a waiting-area with padded benches; Uncle Ted opened a briefcase, produced a wax-paper parcel and a thermos flask, and there appeared before her an unlikely spread of fish-paste sandwiches and tea. She had no appetite whatsoever, and it was surely the worst possible insult to them to take their food, but she accepted a sandwich at last, since they pressed her to. They discussed the progress of the trial, in grim, subdued voices. Douglas, fuming as usual, wanted to know what that fairy Tresillian thought he was playing at. He supposed there were men who'd defend anyone if there was a fee in it for them . . .

Frances's headache had expanded into a settled dull throb. The dry little triangle of bread and paste stuck to the roof of her mouth. She wondered what the boy was being given for lunch, and whether he had any more heart for it than she had. She wished she knew where Lilian was; she thought of going in search of her. But what would she say to her if she found her? Half a day gone already; all this grandeur, all these clever men; and it was all as hopeless as ever. After a while she made an excuse, and rose, and wandered down the overdecorated hall. But the walk took her to another set of padded benches, with a lot of unhappy-looking people on them, also nibbling at sandwiches. She realised that the people had come from another court, with another trial going on in it, with its own judge, its own jury, its own clerks and barristers; and that there was another court beyond that. And she had a vision of the building with its veined marble walls as a sort of stone monster into which crimes, guilts, griefs were continually being fed, in which they were even now being digested, and from which all too soon they would be revoltingly expelled.

She looked back to see Leonard's father signalling to her. It was time to return to the courtroom for the afternoon session. She followed him in; they settled themselves, and the remorseless digestion continued. Again, for a while, the witnesses were ones that she had seen before: the boys who'd heard Spencer making threats against Leonard, the couple from the lane. Then Charlie Wismuth's name was called, and to her bewilderment he came in limping, with his arm in a sling and bruises on his face. Douglas saw her staring, and leaned to whisper to her, his lip curled in a horrible mixture of disgust and relish. Hadn't she heard? Charlie'd got a pasting from the husband of that woman he'd been carrying on with! The man was heading for prison himself; he'd been up before the magistrate the week before . . . The thought of that, and the sight of the injuries, made Frances's spirits droop further. And, of course, the details that came now were all the miserable ones about Leonard's affair, the walks with the girls in the Green Park, the gifts, the spat at the Honey Bee night-club, the Tulse Hill meetings, the 'particular traces'—

'We need not go further than that, I think,' interrupted the judge, 'since there are women present.'

And the next name called was Lilian's. There had been whispers up in the gallery as Charlie had given his evidence, but the room fell silent for her: she was one of the star turns, after all. Frances grew nervous as soon as she saw her, recalling the trembling figure she had cut at the inquest. But she climbed calmly into the witness-box, and stood with her veiled head high, and took her oath, and answered the counsels' questions, in a voice that was low but quite steady ... And that was worse than anything. It made Frances hardly able to look at her. For she knew that her calm came partly from courage, but more from a devastating indifference to what might happen to her now; that she had withstood so many horrors since the night of Leonard's death that she had become stripped and smooth and colourless, like a tree in a hurricane, like a stone in a pounding sea.

She was asked about her husband's final day. No, he had not seemed nervous when he had left for work that morning. No, he had never done or said anything to make her think he feared for his safety. She had known nothing of his friendship with Miss Grey. She had known nothing of Spencer Ward. Yes, she remembered the evening of the first of July, when her husband had been assaulted.

Would she mind just describing that first injury?

He had been hit in the face, and his nose had bled.

It had bled badly?

Yes, she supposed so.

Had they discussed sending for a doctor?

That was the only time she hesitated and let her gaze fall. Yes, they had discussed sending for a doctor, she said, but had decided against it.

She didn't once look in Frances's direction as she spoke. But when she stepped down from the stand she murmured for a moment with the usher, and instead of leaving the courtroom as most of the other witnesses had done she came across it, to join the Barber men and Frances on their bench. She had to pass in front of the dock to do it, and Spencer stared dully at her as she went by, but there was an almost audible stretching of necks in the gallery as the spectators up there tried to follow her with their gazes; even the stolid court officials, the clerks and policemen, watched her go. She seated herself beside Leonard's father, who put up a hand to pat her shoulder. Frances saw a small shudder pass through her at his touch.

And already something else had grabbed the attention of the room. A name had been called, and Frances had missed it. She heard the door to the court creak open, and then a slim female figure appeared. Only when the figure had entered the box, and she saw a curl of bottle-blonded hair, a pair of thinned eyebrows, did she recognise Billie Grey.

Because she had come so soon after Lilian, all that was apparent for the first few minutes was what a contrast the two of them made. She had dressed, it seemed, with no thought for the solemnity of the occasion, but might have been on her way to a tea-dance, in a coat of powder blue, and a close-fitting hat of pink velvet with an ostrich feather curling at the side; her cream suede gloves had scarlet beads on them that rivalled the robes of the judge. She blinked up at the gallery, and all around the court, with what Frances guessed to be a touch of short-sightedness. She didn't seem to notice Lilian—but she saw Spencer all right; she drew her gaze back from his as if frightened. She stumbled slightly over the oath, then tittered at herself. She continued to titter as she gave her evidence, though Mr Ives guided her as patiently as he might have done a child: 'Now, is that *quite* your recollection?' 'Just think about that remark for me, would you?' But all he wanted was for her to confirm the statements she had made to the police regarding her relationship with Leonard, and the incident at the night-club, and Spencer's rages and threats. Yes, she recalled very clearly that remark he had made about Mr Barber having been 'owed a wallop'.

And what about that 'falling out' she'd had with him earlier in the summer. Could she remind the jury how that altercation had ended?

With another apprehensive glance at the dock, she said it had ended with Spencer striking her face and knocking out one of her back teeth. And when the boy huffed or muttered at the comment she spoke across the court to him directly—and Frances was startled

533

to find that her tone was not fearful after all, but was chiding and faintly exasperated. 'Well, you did do it, Spence.'

At once, she was rebuked by the judge. 'You must not engage in conversation with the prisoner.'

'Well, he did do it,' she said again—with stubbornness, this time.

And whether the stubbornness was responsible, or—Frances wasn't sure what it was. But for all that the girl, at first, had appeared so bewilderingly different from Lilian, the longer she stood there, gaining in confidence, the less unlike her she seemed to grow. She had the same wide, guileless face. Her eyes were dark and alive. Her mouth was full, though she had tried to make it fashionably smaller. Even the beads on her gloves and the feather on her hat recalled Lilian. She might just, Frances thought, have been Lilian at eighteen, Lilian unmarked by the hurried marriage, the still-born baby, the disappointments; Lilian, perhaps, as Leonard had first glimpsed her through the Walworth Road window.

Could Lilian herself see it? It was impossible to say. She was watching the girl in the level, lifeless way in which she did everything now. It was Billie who was growing flustered—for Mr Ives had finished with her and Mr Tresillian had begun his cross-examination, and he was not kind and patient, as the other man had been; he was not like John Arthur; he was sarcastic and rather savage. He had every respect, he said, for Miss Grey's lost tooth, and a gentleman could never be forgiven for lifting his hand against a lady. But there were surely people present who could sympathise with the dismay a young man might feel on discovering that his fiancée had been going about on intimate terms with another woman's husband. Wasn't it true that Miss Grey and Mr Ward had been engaged to be married?

Billie widened her guileless eyes. Oh, no. That was just an idea that Spencer had got into his head.

Wasn't it true that she had accepted a ring from him?

But he was always giving her presents; she couldn't keep count

534

of them. She wished he wouldn't waste his money on her. They had been boy-and-girl friends, and she liked him well enough, but not in the way she'd liked Lenny—She blushed. 'Mr Barber, I mean.'

Mr Barber had made her presents, too, had he not?

Well, he'd given her a few little things, 'just to show his love by'.

And she had known that Mr Barber was married, when she had accepted those 'little things'?

Yes, she'd known he was married. He had never been anything but straight with her about it. But his marriage wasn't a proper one. There was no heart in it. It was all kept up for the look of the thing.—Lilian's expression remained level at that, though once again people right across the court craned for a glimpse of her. No, Billie had never felt ashamed of herself. Lenny—Mr Barber—had said that life was too short for shame.

Too short for shame, echoed Mr Tresillian, heavily. Well, Mr Barber's life had certainly proved to be a short one. As for shame—it was up to the jury to decide where precisely the shame lay, in this case. He wanted to remind them, however, that they were in a court of law; they might just, in the past few minutes, have been forgiven for supposing that they had strayed into a picture-theatre and had been watching the antics of characters in a so-called *romance*. Miss Grey had spoken of love, but wasn't it true that her friendship with Mr Barber had in fact been of the most squalid kind imaginable? A thing of furtive meetings in parks and rented rooms?

The girl stared at him. No, it hadn't been like that. That was making it out to be something common, but she and Lenny—They had been in love. They had used to talk and talk to each other. He'd told her all about when he was a boy and things like that. It hadn't been their fault that the world was against them. They had been like Adam and Eve.

And here, horribly, there was a snort of laughter in the public gallery; and the girl blinked up at the faces again, and her mouth gave a twitch, and she began to cry. That produced a boo from someone. Frances didn't know if the boo was aimed at Billie herself or at the person who had laughed at her, but she cried harder at the sound, and the tears—real, grown-up, painful—quickly transformed her face into a swollen mask of grief. The usher handed her a glass of water, doing it in the neutral, professional way in which he might have retrieved a sheet of paper that had glided to the floor. Mr Tresillian waited, unmoved and unimpressed. The only figure visibly agitated by her upset was the boy in the dock: he was leaning forward, urgently trying to pass something to the nearest clerk. Frances, seeing the small square whiteness of it, thought at first that it was a note. Then she realised that it was a handkerchief that he had fished from his pocket; he wanted it carried to the witness-box for the girl to wipe her eyes with. The clerk took it, looking uncertain, but the judge saw, and waved him back.

'No, no. There must be no communications from the prisoner. Mr Tresillian, I don't see that this sort of display is assisting matters at all. Do you mean it to continue?'

Mr Tresillian said, while the girl wept on, 'It's a question of reliability, my lord. Miss Grey has made some damaging allegations against my client. I have been trying to establish her character for the jury.'

The judge spoke with distaste. 'Yes, well, it seems to me that you have established it all too plainly. If there are no further questions from you or from Mr Ives, you might ask the wretched young woman to step down, I think.'

The two men consulted for a moment, and Billie was gestured from the stand. The usher had to catch hold of her arm in order to help her out of the courtroom; she was sobbing worse than ever.

From his place beside Frances, Douglas watched her go with another curl of his lip. 'Go on, clear off, you little tart,' he muttered.

Soon after that, the court was adjourned for the day. Frances and Lilian made the journey back to Walworth in silence.

The second morning was easier only in the sense that they knew now what to expect from it. Again Frances presented herself like a hapless suitor at Mrs Viney's; again Lilian received her in her veil and beetly coat. They even had the same taxi-driver that they had had the day before. For all Frances knew, the crowd outside the Old Bailey might have been the same crowd, too. But, anyhow, they went through it less flinchingly this time, entered the building without a blink, found 'their' bench in the courtroom: she felt quite like an old hand. By the time the robed men were back on the dais and Spencer had done his conjuring trick in the dock, there might never have been a pause in the proceedings at all. The only difference was in the weather, which was wet and very grey: the rain came drumming on to the glazed roof to blunt the harsh light of the room, but make it harder than ever to hear.

But was it even worth straining one's ears to listen? The damaging evidence continued. A clerk from the Pearl, for example, was called to confirm that Leonard had extended his life assurance policy in July. And wasn't that, mused Mr Ives, rather a curious thing for him to have done? A man in the very pink of health, perhaps in hopes of starting a family, who might have been expected, not to increase his premiums, but to save his money? Could the clerk think of any reason why Mr Barber would have done that, unless he'd had in mind the wife he had wronged, and her future as his widow? Unless, in other words, he had been in real and serious fear of his life?

It was the point, Frances remembered, that Lilian herself had made: she saw the jurymen whispering together; she saw that shrewd shopkeeper making notes, as if totting up a bill. If only they could be brought to appreciate the tangle of it all! But no one was interested in tangles here. And though Mr Tresillian rose to protest

537

to the judge against Mr Ives's question—they had not gathered, he said, to hear the speculations of witnesses—the discussion that followed was like an elaborate sport between the three well-bred men, with little to do with the boy who sat gazing blankly on at it from the dock.

By the time the case for the defence had been opened, and Spencer himself had been called as a witness, and Frances had watched him cross the court, and enter the stand, and make his first, stumbling responses to Mr Tresillian's easy, leading questions, she had begun to be frightened again. All this time, she had imagined herself to be entirely without hope, but she *had* had hope, she realised: it had all been pinned on this moment, when at last, after so many weeks, the boy would have the chance to put his own case, clear up every scrap of confusion. But how could he possibly do it? How could anyone have done it, in that crushing, unnatural place, with so many greedy eyes on them, and with everyone present save herself and Lilian convinced of their guilt? He repeated the statement he had made at the start, that on the evening of Leonard's death he had gone home from work with a headache and spent the evening with his mother. The tale sounded stilted— but of course it did. He must have told it a thousand times. He couldn't remember having said that Mr Barber had been owed a wallop, but he supposed he must have said it, if Billie said he had. But there was a difference between saying a thing and doing it, wasn't there? It was like going about with that cosh in his pocket. There was a difference between carrying something and using it. If there was blood on the cosh, that had come from rats and black-beetles. He'd never used it on Leonard Barber. Yes, he had given him a smack in the face that time in the summer, but that had only been to scare him off from messing about with Billie.

'I think you rather enjoy giving people smacks, don't you, Mr Ward?' said Mr Ives, when he rose to begin his cross-examination. 'Did you enjoy knocking out Miss Grey's tooth, back in June?'

The boy's narrow shoulders sank. 'For God's sake, I only tapped her to try and get some sense into her! Half the teeth in her head have fell out by themselves. She said I done her a favour, after it. She's been putting money by for a set of uppers. She didn't tell you that, did she?'

'Did you enjoy going after Leonard Barber on the fifteenth of September?'

'How could I have enjoyed it? I've already said, I never went near him!'

'Did you enjoy pursuing him into that dark lane and striking him down, from behind, with your cosh?'

The boy appealed to the judge, to Mr Tresillian, to the clerks, to anyone who would listen. 'This is mad, all of this is. I never done it. I never done it! Some bloke's going about right now laughing himself sick over all of this . . . '

On and on it went, while Frances and Lilian sat and watched. It was like looking on at torture, Frances thought, knowing that with a word they could stop it; feeling the word wanting to come out, feeling it rise in her gullet, but swallowing and swallowing to choke it back down. For, of course, in saying the word they would simply have to take the boy's place . . . By the time he had been released, they were limp and sweating. The court broke for lunch, and they let the Barbers go. 'God! God!' said Lilian softly. Her face shone white as a bone through the mesh of her veil.

Then it all started up again. The boy's railway-porter uncle offered a feeble character reference. A man who ran a Bermondsey boxing club said that Spencer had been 'willing to learn' and 'quick to get the hang of the punching'—there were more snorts of laughter up in the gallery at that. And then the mother, Mrs Ward, was called to the court. She went creeping into the stand, to answer the counsels' questions in a voice so faint and uncertain it was like the cobwebby voice of a ghost; the judge had to lean forward out of his chair in order to catch it. She confirmed that the cosh on display was one she had seen in her son's possession. He had killed any amount of vermin with it at home. But as for carrying it about the streets with him, it was her belief that he did that—well, as he might have carried a boy's pistol. In fun, she meant.

In fun, said Mr Ives. And on the night of the murder? Had Mr Ward been out having fun, then?

Oh, no. It was all just how he'd told the police. He had come home from work that day with his head hurting; he had spent the evening indoors with her. No, they hadn't had no visitors, but—well, she had seen him there with her own two eyes.

Did he often suffer from headaches?

Oh, yes, he had them quite regular. He'd had them since he was little.

Could she refer the court to a doctor who might vouch for that?

She looked thrown. 'Well, he never saw the doctor, sir.'

'He never did. That's a pity. And how did he pass the evening, precisely?'

'He was on his bed, sir.'

'In his bedroom?'

'He has his bed in the parlour, sir.'

'I see. And what was he doing?'

'He was reading his *British Boy*, sir.'

Here Mr Ives paused, and the judge leaned further out of his chair, his hand cupping his ear. 'What does the witness say?'

'The witness was telling us, my lord, that on the night in question her son was reading a copy of the *British Boy*. I believe it's a—'

'Yes, I know what it is. My grandson reads it. Mrs Ward—' Screwing up his face, the judge addressed the woman directly. 'You are asking the court to believe that your son, a young man of nineteen years, used, as we have heard, to going about the town to night-clubs and dance-palaces, spent his Friday evening at home with you, reading a boy's picture-paper?'

540

She looked at him doubtfully, clearly sensing that there was a catch in his question; but just unable, Frances thought, to put her finger on what it was.

'Yes, sir,' she said.

He sat back without comment. In the dock, Spencer hung his head. The jurymen whispered again, and Frances covered her eyes.

And when she uncovered them, and saw the next witness, and understood that he was some Bermondsey neighbour, here perhaps to offer another lacklustre character reference, the futility of it all nearly overwhelmed her. The man had a yellowish, underfed cast to his features, and shiny patches on his ill-fitting suit. He looked like the sort of ex-service man who asked for money on the streets—as though he might swear to anything for the price of a meal. And, yes, Mr Tresillian's first questions were all to establish his War record, the campaigns he had fought in, the wounds he had received. He had been demobilised in February 'nineteen, he said, and had had various addresses after that. But since March of this year he had been living in the same building as the accused and his mother. He had a single room there, that he rented from another family.

'Now,' said Mr Tresillian briskly, 'to get one unpleasant detail out of the way first: have you ever seen rats and black-beetles in the building?'

The man nodded. 'You might say that. The place is crawling with them. The rats come up the drain-pipes. The beetles come out from behind the wallpapers at night.'

'And what is the best way of dealing with them, in your experience?'

'If you can catch them, you can give them a thump—say, with the heel of your shoe. Or with a heavy book, if you have one.' He added, after the slightest of pauses, 'A book like a Bible will do it.'

The deliberate way in which he said this made Frances pay more attention to him. He wasn't like a beggar on the street, after all. He was too truculent for that, or had been too ill-used, perhaps; he gave the impression of no longer caring whether he got the coin or not. Mr Tresillian asked what he was employed at. He said he'd had a number of situations since the Army had 'dispensed with his services': he had put the bristles on brooms in a factory, he had sold boot-laces door to door. Until very recently—here, inexplicably, he became almost sour—he had been a traveller for an electric light-bulb company.

'A good position?' suggested Mr Tresillian. 'One you were keen to hold on to? And an occupation which, naturally, took you away from home now and then; but not to the extent of making you a stranger to your neighbours, nor of making them strangers to you . . . By which we come to the heart of the matter. Your room, I understand, faces, across a small courtyard, the rooms in which Mr Ward resides with his mother. You're used to seeing them at their windows, going back and forth and so on?'

Frances grew still. The man was nodding. 'Yes, I see them more than I care to; especially the boy. In the summer just gone he used to think it a great sport to shoot things across at me—stones, and dried peas and what have you.'

Mr Tresillian spoke rather hastily. 'At any rate, you know him well?'

'I do.'

'And you remember the evening of the fifteenth of September? How did you spend that evening?'

'I spent it at home.'

'With your window-curtains open or closed?'

'Not quite closed.'

'Why was that? On a chill autumn evening?'

'I find I want air, since the War. I'd rather be cold than stifled. I keep the window ajar, and the curtains parted, all year round.'

'And did you look out of the window, that night?'

'As I passed it, I did.'

'You looked out of the window, as it might be, as a diversion, whilst stretching your legs? And what did you see?'

He jerked his head at the dock. 'I saw that boy over there, lying on his bed with his picture-paper.'

Frances's heart contracted so sharply that it might have been touched by the point of a blade. Beside her, Lilian drew a breath. There were murmurs across the court. Mr Tresillian waited for the murmurs to subside.

'You're quite sure it was Mr Ward you saw?'

'Well, I wouldn't call him mister, myself—but, yes, it was him all right.'

'There could be no mistake about it? No other curtain was in the way?'

'No, there was no mistake. His mother has nothing but a scrap of lace up; you can see clean through it when the lamps are lit. He was lying there giving out the orders to her as he usually does. She was fetching him cups of tea and the like all evening long. And when she took herself off to bed at a quarter to eleven he was still there; and he called her out of her bed a half-hour later to fetch him a glass of water. I heard his voice, that time, clear across the courtyard.'

Now the blade seemed to be pushing its way right into Frances's heart. There were more murmurs, from the benches in front of her and from the spectators overhead. She couldn't tell, however, if the murmurs were sceptical or impressed. She looked at Mr Ives, at the boy in the dock, at the jury, at the judge. The latter was sitting forward making notes, his face impassive.

As before, Mr Tresillian paused to let the disturbance subside— and also, she thought, to choose his next words carefully. When he addressed the man again, his tone had grown delicate.

'I am going to put a question to you now,' he said, 'because I know that if I do not, my learned friend Mr Ives will, quite correctly, put it to you himself. That boy over there has been in prison for many weeks. I imagine you read the newspapers. I imagine you talk to your neighbours. I imagine there have been police about, asking questions, all over your building. You must have known the bearing your evidence would have on this case. Why did you delay so long in volunteering it?'

And, for the first time, the man looked uncomfortable. A touch of shiftiness entered his gaze. 'Yes, I knew all about it,' he said. 'I was in two minds about going to the police, for reasons of my own.'

'And those reasons were? Remember now, it is Mr Ward who is on trial here, not you. Remember, too, will you, that he is on trial for his life.'

The man changed his pose, moved his weight from one foot to another; and answered grudgingly at last. 'I was in fear for my position. My employers had supposed me in Leeds on the night of the fifteenth. It wasn't in my interest to enlighten them.'

'You had misrepresented your movements to them?'

'I had claimed expenses that weren't due me . . . It sounds shabby to admit it, here.'

'It does sound shabby,' said Mr Tresillian. 'But, then, there can't be a man in this room—saving, of course, his lordship on the bench—who hasn't given way to a shabby impulse at one time or another. When was it that you approached the police with your statement?'

'Last week, when I heard how black things had got for the boy. I'd had a month of looking out my window, seeing his poor mother—I couldn't live with myself.'

'And the police, I imagine, spoke with your employers?'

'That's correct.'

'With what result?'

'I was given my marching orders.'

'Your position lost, your good name tarnished. Just what you had anticipated, in fact. And yet, you still felt it your duty to come forward?'

The man looked sour again. 'I did. I don't like the boy. No one in our building does. I can't speak for anything else he might have done or not done. He might want hanging ten times over for all I know about it. But as far as the murder of this Mr Barber goes, he doesn't want hanging for that, for he was at home with his mother all that evening long, and nothing could make me tell you he wasn't, though I should be hanged for it my—'

Myself, Frances knew he was going to finish. But from the corner of her eye she had seen Douglas rise and lean forward, and now he shouted at the man in a fury: 'Liar!'

There were exclamations, protests. His father and uncle attempted to restrain him; he shook off their hands and shouted again, more hoarsely. 'Liar!' He spoke to the jury: 'He's been put up to this! He's been paid to do it! Can't you see?'

The judge called sternly for him to be silent. Faces peered over the balcony, a woolly scarf dangled. Spencer looked on openmouthed, showing all his dreadful teeth. A policeman came across the well of the court, and at his approach Douglas gave a snort of disgust but grew calmer and, with a flick of the tails of his overcoat, sat back down. And by the time the room had settled, Frances understood that the force of the man's evidence had been dispelled. Mr Ives rose to cross-examine him, and he grew truculent again, and looked seedy and dishonest; his little moment of nobility, she realised, had come and gone. But they had to believe him, didn't they? He had been brave. He had been brave where she and Lilian had been cowards. They had to believe him! She gazed from face to face, desperate to see some change in people's expressions. But the faces remained closed to her. The mechanism of the trial had stuttered and jammed for a moment, but was already running smooth again.

She couldn't listen to the final few witnesses. When it was time to leave the court, she found that she was trembling. Lilian's face was whiter than ever. The mix of feelings was too much, the slim new chance almost unwelcome; it had been easier to remain in despair. They got down to the street and hailed a taxi, but she didn't want to be still, not even for the brief ride to Walworth. She didn't want to have to speak, in case all that came out of her were tears. She saw Lilian into the cab, then shook her head and drew back. She closed the door, and if Lilian called to her to wait, the words were lost. She began to walk. The rain had turned to a fine drizzle, and the pavements were slimy. Her boots began to let in the filthy water at once. But as she made the long journey home to Champion Hill she felt what she had tried and failed to feel the day before: she looked at the city and was sick with love for it, sick with yearning to remain a part of it, to remain alive and young and unconfined and bursting with sensation. Her tired muscles began to ache, but even the ache was dear to her, even the blisters on her heels. She'd be a thing of aches and blisters for the rest of her days, she thought; she'd ask for nothing, trouble no one; if only they'd let her keep her freedom, if only they'd let her keep her life.

By the time she arrived at the house the fizz of her feelings had begun to subside. Her mother exclaimed at the sight of her, hurried her out of her wet things. She warmed herself at the kitchen stove, washed the dirt from her feet, stuffed newspaper into her boots, put her coat and hat to dry. But when she went up to her bedroom, the spell of the walk was still on her. She lit a lamp, drew on clean clothes, then stood and gazed around the neat, plain room with passionate eyes. Who would love these things when she was gone? What would they mean to anyone else? The candlesticks, the photographs of her brothers, the prints on the wall, the books—

Her eye was caught by *Anna Karenina*. She drew it free, and opened it up at the page at which she'd left a marker: the scene at the Moscow station, Anna stepping down from the train.

She took the lamp, and crossed the landing, and went into the sitting-room.

She thought she had gone in there looking for Lilian. But this time the things she noticed all belonged to Leonard, his leather writing-case on the shelf, the battered box of Snakes and Ladders, his tennis racket, still in its frame, ready for the next tournament. Had they been real, those matches of his? Or had he spent the days with Billie? Had he loved her, as she'd loved Lilian?

Gipsy caravans. Adam and Eve.

Oh, Leonard, she thought, what a mess we made of things! She remembered the intent and frightening way in which he had grabbed her, that night. She remembered the look of betrayal and rage that had come into his face. But he couldn't have fore-seen all this; he couldn't have wanted any of this . . . If only she could talk to him! It seemed absurd, all at once, that she couldn't. She had carted his body down the stairs, she had seen him laid out on a mortuary slab, she had watched his coffin being lowered into the ground; but somehow she hadn't until this moment absorbed the simple, staggering fact that he had once been here and now was gone. His whistling, his boasting, his yodelling yawns, his innuendoes: it was all of it gone. Where on earth was he? She moved forward, lifting the lamp, almost as if she were searching for him and the light would reveal him. But even the stains of his blood were invisible, in the gloom. He might have been spirited away by a wizard: it was as confounding and as pointless as that.

She heard a creaking on the landing, and turned to find that her mother had come up the stairs. She was peering cautiously in from the open doorway.

'Is everything all right, Frances? I wondered what you were doing.'

She answered, after a hesitation, 'I was thinking of Leonard.'

Her mother must have heard the catch of emotion in her voice. She came forward into the room. 'I think of him too. I think of him often. It wasn't kind, it wasn't right, the way he behaved to

Mrs Barber; but one can't help but miss him. I still have nightmares when I picture him lying alone out there, don't you?'

'Yes,' said Frances, truthfully.

'And all his things, still here . . . ' She sighed, and tutted. 'Dear, dear.' The words and the gesture were mild, but had an infinite weight of grief behind them. 'What an unlucky house this has been for men, hasn't it? Or unlucky for women, I suppose I ought to say. I know your brothers are at peace now.'

Frances said, 'Do you really know it?'

'I haven't a single doubt about it. Them, and your dear father. And Mr Barber, too—though it's hard to imagine him at rest, he was so lively. There are his tennis shoes, look, with the heels trodden down. I remember after your father died finding his pipe with tobacco in it—fresh tobacco, waiting for the match. It was almost more distressing than seeing him in his coffin. Mrs Barber will find it hard, when she comes to take her things. Has she spoken to you about that? She'll be able to think more clearly, of course, once this dreadful trial is behind her. But has she given you any sense of her plans? She'll remain at her mother's, I suppose.'

'I—I'm not sure. Yes, I suppose so.'

'Well, be certain to tell her to take just as long as she needs. And then, once she has gone—' She paused. 'Well, we must do it all over again, must we? Find new people for these rooms?'

The thought was terrible. But Frances nodded. 'What else can we do, if we mean to stay? But, then, the house—I don't know. So many things are going wrong.'

'Yes.'

'I thought I could hold it all together, but—'

'Well, don't think about it now. We'll sort it out, between us. It's only a lot of bricks and mortar. Its heart stopped, Frances, years ago . . . You look tired again. This frightful business at the court! I wish you'd keep away from it. You really think it will end tomorrow?'

Frances lowered her gaze. 'Yes, tomorrow will end it.'

'Though not, I suppose, for that boy and his family. What a nightmare we've all been caught in! If you had told me, in the summer—No, I should never have believed you. Oh, won't it be a weight off our minds when it's all over and done with!'

She turned away as she spoke, rubbing her arms against the chill. Frances noticed the stoop of her shoulders, the elderly way she reached for the doorpost as she headed out to the landing.

She felt her mouth grow dry. 'Mother—'

Her mother turned back to her, her dark brows lifted. 'Yes?'

'If anything were ever to happen to me—'

'Happen to you? What do you mean? Oh, we've let ourselves grow morbid! Come back down out of the gloom.'

'No, wait. If something were to happen—I know I haven't always been kind to you. I know I wasn't kind to Father. I've always tried to do what I thought to be right. But sometimes—'

Her mother's joined hands made their papery sound. 'You mustn't grow upset, Frances. Remember what Dr Lawrence said.'

'It's just—You wouldn't ever despise me, would you, Mother?'

'Despise you! Good gracious! Why would I ever do that?'

'Sometimes things become a muddle. They become such a muddle, Mother, that they turn into a sort of quicksand. You take a step, and can't get free, and—'

She couldn't continue. Her mother waited, looking troubled—but looking weary, too. Finally she sighed. 'What a fight you've always made of everything, Frances. And all I ever wanted for you were such ordinary things: a husband, a home, a family of your own. Such ordinary, ordinary things. You mustn't worry about the house. The house has become too great a burden. It isn't a house for guests, after all. Mrs Barber came here as an unhappy woman, and I'm afraid she took advantage of your—your kindness. But, despise you! I could never despise you, any more than I could despise my own hand. Now, come down with me, will you? Back to the warm.'

Frances hesitated, still struggling—though she didn't know now if she was struggling to speak or to stay silent. But at last she nodded, and moved forward, and followed her mother from the room. She wanted to be comforted, that was all. She wanted it so much. It didn't matter, she told herself, as they started down the stairs, it didn't really matter that the two of them had been talking about different things.

And once the final day had arrived, and she and Lilian were back in their taxi, back at the Old Bailey, back on their bench, she found it hard to remember that they had ever had a life beyond the courtroom. It seemed an absolute eternity since, three mornings before, she had crossed the floor, alone and uncertain; an eternity since she had looked at the clerks and the barristers and seen only a flock of jackdaws. She knew them now as individuals, almost as friends: the man who breathed with a whistle, the one who liked to crack his knuckles, the one who sucked white peppermints, that sometimes appeared, startlingly, from between his thin, dry lips. The court was much fuller than it had been at the start. The trial had gathered spectators as the days had passed, and witnesses had stayed or returned, to be fitted in as best they could—so that, if she peered past the heads and shoulders in front of her, she could see Spencer's mother and uncle elbow to elbow with the police surgeon, while Inspector Kemp and Sergeant Heath sat squashed beside Leonard's boss from the Pearl. How extraordinary it was to realise that all this fuss had been set in motion by that little collision in her mother's old bedroom on Champion Hill. How astonishing that all these people had been hoicked together in this bright place because of that single intimate encounter between Lilian, Leonard and her.

The morning was given over to the counsels' closing speeches. Mr Ives went first, and there it was, laid out again, every incriminating detail, the threats, the boasts, the weapon, the blood. The boy's distress over the behaviour of his fiancée, he told the jury, was of no account at all. He had shown himself in his treatment of her to be a most degenerate character. As for his alibi, well—Here his tone grew withering. Mrs Ward's devotion to her son was so complete, it might almost be said to be blind. Her neighbour claimed to have seen the boy at home on the critical night, but he had admitted his own dishonesty in other matters, and it was for the jury to decide how far that dishonesty extended. Perhaps the best that could be said about a man like that was that he would take on just about any sort of employment for a fee ...

He spoke for an hour and three-quarters. When Mr Tresillian rose to begin his own long speech for the defence, the room had begun to feel airless; he had to raise his voice over coughs and shuffles. He had every respect, he said, for his learned colleague Mr Ives, but the Crown in this case had failed in its first duty: that of establishing the guilt, beyond any particle of doubt, of the accused, Spencer Ward. What, after all, did the evidence against the boy really amount to? Miss Grey, a key witness, had morals that would shame a shop-girl. The hairs and the blood were as good as worthless. The rest was circumstance and supposition. There were two points only on which the jury could be certain, and one was that Leonard Arthur Barber had been killed by a blow to the head; the other was that the person or persons who had struck that blow had so far evaded capture. The accused himself had speculated that they were 'laughing themselves sick'. Mr Tresillian did not know about that, but they must certainly be looking on at these proceedings with very mixed feelings indeed ...

By the time the lunch hour had passed, and it was the judge's turn to speak, and Frances understood that he meant to take them in close, dry detail through the crime, the police inquiry, through every single scrap of evidence that had been submitted to the court, a great weariness overtook her—not just the accumulated weariness of the past few days, but a vaster fatigue, a thing like a heavy, heavy cloak suddenly laid across her shoulders. She did her best to listen, but his voice was nasal and elderly and retained its peevish note, and it was shockingly easy, she found, simply to think of other things. He reminded the jury that the accused, by his own confession, was a violent young man, who had never attempted to deny the grudge that he had borne against the victim . . . Here she found herself gazing at a man on the bench in front of her: he was holding his head at such an angle that she could see right into his ear, see the hairs in the little tunnel and the crumbs of wax that clung to them. She blinked, and returned her attention to the judge. He was talking now about the traces of blood that had been found on the cosh. Mr Palmer, he said, a police surgeon of many years' standing, had given it as his opinion that the blood was human. Another surgeon, of lesser experience, but nonetheless a man to whom the jury might feel inclined to give credence, had stated by contrast that . . .

But she'd begun looking around the court again, at the people gathered in it. A uniformed policeman was blank-eyed with boredom: he was fingering his chin, worrying away at a pimple or shaving-cut. Mr Ives and Mr Tresillian were both making notes. Inspector Kemp and Sergeant Heath were murmuring together, the inspector polishing his spectacles as he did it: without the discs of glass before them his eyes looked naked as unshelled molluscs. Spencer's face was slightly puffy. Perhaps he had passed a sleepless night.

She thought of that little chalk gallows: the stick figure was almost complete. She heard the ticking of the courtroom clock, casually chipping away at the future. If only Lilian would turn to her—if only Lilian would look, just once, in the old way—it would all be a shade, just a shade, more bearable.

But Lilian sat rigid, in that beetly coat, that horrible veil, and looked at nothing.

And presently the nasal voice paused, then changed its note. 'Members of the jury,' it was saying, 'you have had the evidence laid before you. I am going to ask you now to retire and begin your deliberations. Have you any questions or requests?'

Frances's heart lost a beat. They had got to this point already! All eyes went to the jury; but it seemed they had everything they needed. They rose and filed away, she noticed, without a glance at the boy, without once looking at his mother or his uncle.

And then there was nothing to do but wait, and nowhere to do it but there in the courtroom or just outside, in the cathedral-like hall. They had been sitting for hours, and the room was stuffier than ever. The Barber men went off at once, and after a few indecisive minutes she and Lilian followed, to stand blinking at the riot of marble and fresco. Why on earth, she wondered, couldn't the place have been made restful? Why couldn't it have plain white monastery walls? The swirls of colour set her stomach quivering. The polished hard floor made her think of falling over with a smack. Leonard's father and Uncle Ted and Douglas had claimed one of the padded benches. A neighbouring bench came free; she and Lilian took it, in silence. Presently Spencer's mother and uncle appeared, and settled down a few yards off, avoiding the Barbers' eyes as they did it. Douglas watched them, but addressed his father in a pointed, unmuted way.

'All right, Dad? We won't be here long. The jury's got nothing to debate, has it?'

His confidence, however, went for nothing. Thirty minutes became forty, became fifty, became an hour. Lilian remained shut in a realm of her own. The padding on the bench seemed to lose its spring. Voices and footsteps swelled and faded. A bit of heat struggled inadequately from a metal grating. If one closed one's eyes, Frances found, the sensation was that of sitting in some bleak but unavoidable municipal place—a bus station, say.

But she was used to that by now, used to this kind of waiting, that was slack as worn elastic yet had the tautness of wire. She thought of all the lobbies, corridors and ante-rooms in which she and Lilian had had to sit and wait since Leonard's death, all the institutional spaces, not quite public, not quite private. They were like places outside time, outside life—a kind of limbo. Was that where Leonard was, after all? She tried to imagine the people who might staff it. Wingless angels, perhaps. And every one of them with the same expression that she had seen on the faces of the policemen, porters, matrons, warders, clerks and officials who had guided the way through the nightmare of the past two months, the obliging but impersonal look of men and women who saw other people's catastrophes every working day and could shrug them off for a tea-break and a stretch of the legs.

Oh, for a cup of tea now! But, of course, they dared not stray too far, for fear that the verdict would come. Spencer's uncle wandered the length of the hall like a man on a station platform. 'Gets on your nerves, don't it?' he announced grimly, on his return. The Barber men bristled and ignored him, but Frances met his gaze and nodded, though without a smile. How could she smile at him? When had she smiled last, in fact? When had she laughed? She couldn't remember. A sudden dreadful idea took hold of her. Suppose she were never to laugh again? Suppose she were never to sing or dance or kiss or do anything careless again? Suppose she were never to walk in a garden, never walk anywhere save grey prison spaces, never see a child, a cat, a dog, a river, a mountain, an open sky—

The bubble of panic was punctured by one of Douglas's snorts of disgust. Footsteps were approaching from the staircase. She turned her head to follow his gaze and saw that the girl, Billie, was back.

She must have come to hear the verdict. She was, apparently, quite alone. She went to the door of the courtroom first, and spoke to the policeman there. He explained the situation, and gestured to the waiting-area; she looked over, saw the Barbers, saw the Wards, saw Lilian, but came bravely, in her tapping heels, to perch herself at the end of a bench—she put herself almost directly opposite to Lilian and Frances. Her coat was the powder-blue one that she had worn on Monday. Her hat was different, a thing of mauve velour with a silk rose on the brim: it was pulled down low, nearly meeting her collar, so that, from the side, all that was visible of her face was the tip of her nose and her childish chin. She nodded awkwardly to Spencer's mother, and the little woman nodded awkwardly back. The uncle, however, glared at her—her arrival, bizarrely, having put him, just for the moment, on the same side as the Barbers. As for Lilian, she watched the girl come, she watched her sit, she watched her take out a powder-compact and tidy her face, she watched her put the compact away—the stare going on for so long, yet remaining so blank and unbroken, that Frances began to be unnerved by it; it was like the stare of a corpse.

Then, abruptly, without warning, without a word to Frances or anyone, Lilian got to her feet and began to make her way across the marble floor. There could be no mistake about where she was headed. Spencer's mother and uncle and the Barber men all turned at the sound of her steps. The girl turned too at her approach— then gave a start, her courage failing; she even shrank back when Lilian came to a halt in front of her, as if expecting to be struck. When Lilian simply spoke to her in a murmur, she looked up at her with her lips parted and her eyes wide. 'Yes,' Frances heard her say in surprise. Then: 'No. Yes.' And then: 'Thank you.'

And that was it. The whole exchange took perhaps twenty seconds. She ducked her head again as Lilian moved off, her face flaming through its powder.

Lilian looked at no one. She didn't re-join Frances on the bench. Instead she left the hall, disappearing into the passage that led to the ladies' cloak-room.

When five minutes went by and she did not return, Frances went after her.

She was alone in the small room. The lavatory doors stood open. A frosted window was ajar on to a light-well; she was leaning against the sill, smoking the last of a cigarette. When she saw Frances she was still for a moment, then turned away, stubbed the cigarette out, and flicked it from the window. Then she went to one of the basins, to examine her face in the mirror above it.

Frances addressed her almost shyly. 'I wondered if you were all right.'

She had opened her handbag and was fishing in it. 'Yes, I'm all right.'

'What—What did you say to her?'

She brought out a little pot of rouge. As Frances watched, she drew off her glove and tapped a fingertip into the colour, tapped the colour on to her lower lip, her upper lip, her cheeks—the gesture accentuating that odd resemblance between her and the girl herself. 'I told her I was sorry for her,' she said, as she returned the rouge to her handbag. 'I said she ought to be in my clothes. That she's more Len's widow than I am. It's true, isn't it? She ought to have that horrible money. Maybe I'll leave it to her in my will. She'll get it soon enough, that way.'

Her voice shook on the last few words. She snapped the handbag closed, then leaned forward over the basin, holding on to the straight white sides of it as though to keep herself from sinking to the floor. But when Frances went towards her, she moved away.

'Don't, Frances. It's no good, you know it isn't.'

'Please, Lilian. I can't bear it. I—'

'No. Don't you see? If you try, if you touch me, you'll only remind me, you'll make it worse . . . Oh, why can't it all be over with! We know what the jury's going to say. I wish they'd just say it about me. Say it here and now, today! They could give me the rope and I'd do it myself.'

'It won't come to that. There's still a chance.'

She drooped, exhausted. 'Oh, Frances, you know there isn't. You know it, deep down. All this time we've been pretending. We've been pretending from the start. The start of everything, I mean.'

'The start of everything,' repeated Frances. Then, 'I never pretended for a moment, Lilian,' she said simply, 'when I was with you. It was everyone else I pretended with.—No, don't answer, listen to me, because there isn't any time any more, and I want to tell you, I have to tell you—Nothing's changed, in how I feel about you. I went mad for a while, that's all. I let what happened—I let it spoil things. It's broken my heart that I did that. I burned your letter. You remember? The most wonderful letter anyone ever wrote me, and I burned it. I burned it! I did it to save my own skin. I barely knew I had a skin until I met you. Tell me you believe it. This is a place for truth, isn't it? We've heard nothing in it but lies, but tell me, please tell me, that you know I love you, that you know it's true.'

Breathless, she came to a halt. They faced each other in a silence broken by the trickle of a faulty cistern, by the flutter of pigeons in the light-well. The room smelt of bleach and of sour wet mops. But Lilian looked back at her with eyes grown silvery with tears, and for a moment the room, the trial, Leonard, the summer, their whole affair—it was as if none of it had yet happened. As if their love were all to be done again, but done properly, done honestly. As if they were back in Frances's bedroom the day after Snakes and Ladders, that imaginary stake just drawn from her heart.

But across the moment there came, from out in the hall, the clanging of a bell, followed almost instantly by footsteps in the passage; and at that, Lilian's gaze slid fearfully past Frances to the door. Frances turned to see the shadow of a figure against its ground-glass panel. It was one of the Old Bailey officials, come to tap, and to call discreetly. Was Mrs Barber inside? Did she wish to hear the verdict? Word had just come that the jury were on their way back to the court.

They faced each other again. Lilian had wiped her tears away. Frances could barely get the words out.

'Here it is, then.'

And now, after the torpor of the wait, there was suddenly a horrible speed to it all—or, not a speed exactly, not a haste, but a remorseless forward movement, like the drop of a china cup towards a stone floor. With a shaking hand, Lilian lowered her veil. They returned to the hall and found it deserted. They had to hurry into the courtroom like tardy theatre-goers, had to push their way to their places—for the room was crowded to bursting-point now. Men must have come from other courts—come, as it were, for the finale—clerks and officials, reporters, policemen: they were standing against the walls, had fitted themselves into every corner. Up in the gallery, people were squashed together and seemed still to be piling in. She and Lilian sat—then almost at once had to stand again, as the door beside the dais was opened to admit the judge.

And as he came forward into the sudden electric hush, Frances saw that he had something in his hand—not the absurd little posy this time, but a dreadful limp black thing—a thing, she thought with a burst of horror, that oughtn't to be allowed to exist—it was the cap that he would place over his wig if he had to pass sentence. He carried it without a qualm. He moved in an ordinary way, took his seat at an ordinary pace; unflustered, too, were the robed and gold-chained men who came with him, whose identity and function she had never been able to fathom. Then the jury filed in, still avoiding the boy's eye—he had been kept on his feet in the dock, was passing his cuff across his sweating top lip. Frances watched them settle themselves. She watched the chief clerk approach them. This couldn't be the moment, could it? It was all too smooth and unconsidered. A life was at stake. It couldn't be now. It was all too quick!

But the foreman was making himself known, was rising—it was not the shopkeeper after all, but a slim, colourless man to whom she had paid no attention. She felt a movement against her wrist, and looked down to see Lilian's hand feeling for hers. She caught hold of it; their fingers met, and slid into a clasp. There was a moment of dreadful suspense while some last detail was taken care of. Then:

'Members of the jury, have you agreed upon your verdict?'

The colourless man nodded, and answered in a colourless voice. 'We have.'

'Do you find the prisoner, William Spencer Ward, guilty or not guilty of the murder of Leonard Arthur Barber?'

'We find him not guilty.'

Christ! Had Frances cried out? She might as well have. Other people had cried out too, in disbelief and excitement, though somewhere in the gallery a strange, lone cheer had gone up, to be almost instantly stifled. Lilian was leaning forward, her face hidden, her shoulders heaving; she had burst into tears. Douglas was up on his feet. The boy in the dock was looking about as if uncertain of what he'd heard. Reporters were rushing from the room and a voice was calling for order.

Not guilty! What was happening now? Frances couldn't take it in. The judge spoke; she didn't hear him. He must have been discharging the prisoner, for the next time she looked at Spencer all she saw was his dipped, youthful head disappearing down the stairs in the dock. Not guilty! It couldn't be real! That blade was back in her heart. Lilian was still crying. The jurymen had been dismissed and now the judge was leaving the chamber; the courtroom was coming apart at the seams, everyone moving from their places, chairs scraping, a hubbub of voices. She rose, and felt herself sway. Lilian got to her feet beside her; she had put back her veil, was wiping her face. Ought they to go? Ought they to stay? They had no plan, suddenly. The Barber men were elbowing their way down into the well of the court. She and Lilian stumbled after them, but the whole thing was like a dream, it seemed to rush at her and then to break into fragments, Spencer's mother and uncle being hustled from the room, Billie smiling, revealing dimples, as she spoke with

559

a reporter, the barristers shaking hands with each other like club-men after a wager, the solicitor coming to apologise, misinterpreting Lilian's tears: 'A bad conclusion, Mrs Barber. These slips do happen, I'm afraid.' Inspector Kemp and Sergeant Heath had faces lumpy with disgust. 'Oh, he was our lad all right,' the inspector was telling Leonard's father. 'We lost him to the squeamishness of the jury. But we'll get him for something else before too long, don't you worry.' And there was Douglas, darting about—Douglas seeming to be everywhere at once—grabbing at people, calling in Leonard's voice, with Leonard's furious face and wet, red lips: 'This is a joke! How is this justice? What the hell were the jury thinking? This won't stop here! Bring those men back! I want the judge!'

And somehow, somehow, though she and Lilian had been together when they had left their bench, by the time Frances had fought her way across the courtroom she was alone. She stood close to the door and peered back into the crowd. She spotted the widow's hat, the coat: Lilian had been stopped by Mr Ives, who had her hands in his; he was like the solicitor, grave and apologetic. Now Douglas had joined them. He had got hold of a newspaper man . . . Frances tucked herself, as best she could, out of the flow of people. She watched the crowd leaving the gallery. She watched a clerk going from desk to desk on the dais, gathering papers.

And it was only then, seeing him make his tidy bundle of ink-stained documents, that she began to believe it. The burden had gone, and had left her light. She felt that, without any trouble at all—a flex of the toes, a jolt from an elbow—she might start float-ing from the floor. But the feeling had something wrong about it. The lightness was the lightness of ash. She was scorched, dried out. She couldn't even kneel and thank God. For God, she was sure, had had nothing to do with it. There was nothing and no one to thank, here at the very end of it all, just as there'd been nothing and no one to blame for the accident at the very beginning. Or—

no, there was that man, that Bermondsey neighbour. What was his name? She'd forgotten it already. But he was the one who had saved them—saved the boy, and Lilian, and her. The jury had persuaded themselves that he was decent, because they had wanted to think that in his shoes they would have been decent too. They had no idea how decency, loyalty, courage, how it all shrivelled away when one was frightened.

She remembered Lilian reaching for her hand as the foreman got to his feet. In the seconds before the verdict, her own grip had tightened like a vice. Had she been about to urge Lilian forward, or to hold her back?

She didn't know. She would never know. And the not knowing wasn't like the absence of something, it was like another burden, a different shape and weight from the last. The lightness left her. She wanted to get out. She looked for Lilian again. But when their gazes finally met it was only for an instant; and then it seemed to her that she saw Lilian turn away.

She saw it almost without surprise. The thing was finished now, wasn't it?

She turned, and pushed free of the courtroom. The hall was thick with people, but no one watched her as she made her way across to the staircase and down. Even out on the street, though a crowd had gathered to hear the verdict and see the boy, she got through it easily enough: faces lit up when she appeared, like misers' at the gleam of gold, then dimmed and turned away from her when they saw what a dud she was. The light was a flat grey twilight. It must be some time after four. She left the massive building behind and followed the downward slope of the streets towards the river.

She said to herself, as she plodded: You are safe, you are safe. They were all safe now, she supposed: she, Lilian, the boy. For, having once been cleared of the murder he couldn't be re-arrested for it, and if the police truly believed him guilty then the case,

561

perhaps, would languish . . . Or perhaps it wouldn't. She had no idea. She could still see Spencer in the dock, wiping the sweat from his top lip. You are safe, you are safe . . . But, no, she thought, this wasn't safety—or, if it was, then it was the kind of safety that came after a war, the kind of safety she had always despised, because it was got by doing harm. So much harm! She felt sick to think of it. Leonard, Leonard's parents, Spencer, his mother, Billie, Charlie: the list of casualties seemed endless. They seemed to be trudging along with her. There was the miscarried baby, too . . .

She had got on to Blackfriars Bridge now. She had been walking like a blind woman all this time, moving by every sense save sight. But then, which way could she go, except this way? And what was her future but a dark one? She pictured the house on Champion Hill. She pictured herself stepping into the porch, opening the door, passing through it. She saw the door closing behind her and sealing her in.

At that, like a clockwork figure running down, she slowed to a standstill. She was on the high mid-point of the bridge, had barely travelled half a mile; glancing back over her shoulder, she could still see the black dome of the Old Bailey, the golden figure on the top. One or two people looked curiously at her as she stood there in the middle of the pavement, so she moved to the parapet, put her back to the traffic and the passers-by. Ahead of her were the sooty criss-crossed girders of the neighbouring railway bridge. Below, the river was swollen, sullen; it had the lustreless colour of clay. Why not pitch herself into it? The parapet was low enough. Why not just chuck herself right over? Add one more casualty to the list? She leaned forward, feeling the tilt of her own weight, startlingly persuasive.

But now she was being like a bad actress again. She straightened up and looked around. At regular points across the bridge the parapet became a sort of alcove, with a shallow stone seat inside it; she went gratefully into the nearest of these, and sat.

At once, she felt that she would never be able to get up again. There seemed nothing to get up for. She was out of the breeze here, out of the chill, tucked away in the deepening twilight. A bus went by, a score of faces staring blankly into hers: she simply closed her eyes against them. The roar of the motor gave way to another, and to another after that. Minute by minute, layer upon layer, the sounds came and were withdrawn: hooves, voices, hurrying steps, the clash and grind of iron wheels. She could feel it all in the stone on which she was resting. It felt like the tired turn of the world.

And when she opened her eyes again, Lilian was there.

How long had she been standing there? Not long at all perhaps, because she was breathless, as if she'd been running. Her head was bare, her hair untidy; she had her widow's hat in her hand, the veil of it fluttering. She said, in a disbelieving way, 'I saw you from the taxi. I came looking for you, and I found you. Why didn't you wait for me? Why did you go?'

Frances was staring at her as if she might be a figure in a dream. 'I thought you wouldn't want to look at me.'

'How could you think that?'

'Because—' She lowered her head. 'Because I'm not sure that I can bear to look at myself.'

Lilian stood still for a moment, then came into the alcove and sat down at her side.

After a silence, she spoke wearily. 'I wish there was something I could say to you, Frances, to make it all right.' She passed a gloved hand over her face. Her hands were slim as a mannequin's now, and her cheeks had hollows in them; all her treacly loveliness had faded. She sighed, and let the hand drop. 'But he will always be dead. He will always, always be dead. And I will always have killed him. And all the time I've been at Walworth I've gone over and over it in my mind, trying to see what I could have done differently—where I could have stopped it, where I could have kept it from becoming what it became. But every time, it seemed to me that the only thing I could have done differently was never to have kissed you, that night, after the party ... And even now, after everything, I can't wish that. You made me want to, for a while, but—I can't. I can't.'

I can't. They were a queer two words by which to be reunited: a statement of failure, Frances thought, as much as of love. But they were like the two words that the jury had brought back: the moment she heard them she began to shake, to imagine if they had not been said.

Lilian saw, and put a hand over hers; and presently the tremble passed away. They didn't try to speak again. They leaned together by an inch—that was all it took, after all, to close the space between them. Would it be all right, wondered Frances, if they were to allow themselves to be happy? Wouldn't it be a sort of insult to all those others who had been harmed? Or oughtn't they to do all they could—didn't they almost have a duty—to make one small brave thing happen at last?

She didn't know. She couldn't think of it. Her mind wouldn't reach that far. It wouldn't reach further than Lilian's hand and shoulder and hip, warm against hers. They'd have to rise soon, she supposed. A boy was calling the evening edition. At home, her mother would be waiting. Lilian's family were waiting too. But for now there was this, and it was enough, it was more than they could have hoped for: the two of them in their stone corner, their dark clothes bleeding into the dusk, lights being kindled across the city, and a few pale stars in the sky.

Author's Note

Many books helped to inform and inspire this one. I am particularly indebted to the following: Nicola Humble's *The Feminine Middlebrow Novel, 1920s to 1950s: Class, Domesticity, and Bohemianism* (Oxford, 2001), Billie Melman's *Women and the Popular Imagination in the Twenties: Flappers and Nymphs* (Basingstoke, 1988), Vera Brittain's *Testament of Youth: An Autobiographical Study of the Years 1900–1925* (London, 1933) and *Chronicle of Youth: War Diary 1913–1917* (London, 1981), Carol Acton's *Grief in Wartime: Private Pain, Public Discourse* (Basingstoke, 2007), Patricia Jalland's *Death in War and Peace: A History of Loss and Grief in England, 1914–1970* (Oxford, 2010), Lucy Bland's *Modern Women on Trial: Sexual Transgression in the Age of the Flapper* (Manchester, 2013), Winifred Duke's *Trial of Harold Greenwood* (Edinburgh and London, 1930), F. Tennyson Jesse's *Trial of Alma Victoria Rattenbury and George Percy Stoner* (London and Edinburgh, 1935) and *A Pin to See the Peepshow* (London, 1934), David Napley's *Murder at the Villa Madeira: The Rattenbury Case* (London, 1988), Filson Young's *Trial of Frederick Bywaters and Edith Thompson* (Edinburgh and London, 1923) and René Weis's *Criminal Justice: The True Story of Edith Thompson* (London, 1988). As these titles perhaps reveal, this novel had as its starting-point my interest in some of the high-profile British murder cases of the twenties and thirties. *The Paying Guests*, however, is a work of fiction.

Acknowledgements

Thanks to my wonderful editors in the UK, the US and Canada: Lennie Goodings, Megan Lynch and Lara Hinchberger. Thanks to everyone at Greene & Heaton, and to Jean Naggar, Jennifer Weltz and Dean Cooke. Thanks to the staff at the Southwark Local History Library, the Lambeth Archives, the London Library, the Cinema Museum and the London Jamyang Buddhist Centre (formerly the Lambeth Police Court); to my insightful early readers Susan de Soissons, Antony Topping, Christie Hickman, Ursula Doyle and Kendra Ward; and to the following people for expertise and/or moral support: Laura Doan, James Tayler, Alison Oram, Jackie Malton, Val McDermid, Professor Sue Black, Zoë Gullen, Fiona Leach, Julia Parry and Kate Taylor. Special thanks to Sally O-J, whose enthusiasm for this novel helped keep it afloat in choppy waters. Above all: thank you Lucy, for your wisdom, your patience and your love.

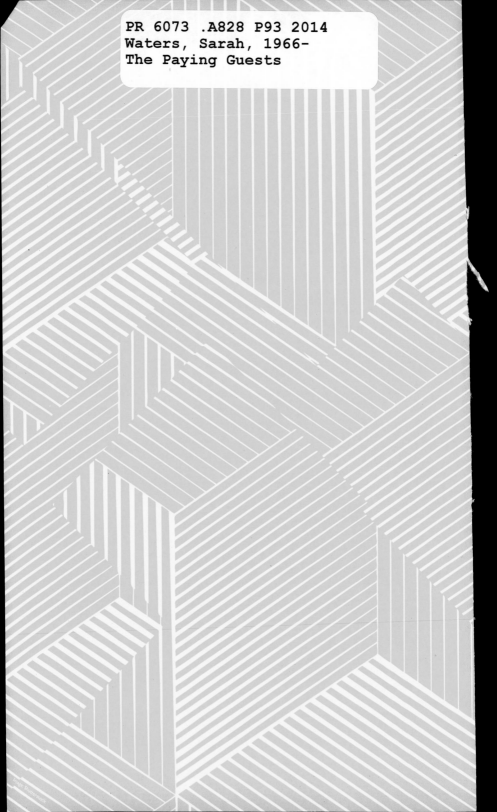